THE KROZAIR CYCLE

The Dray Prescot Series

THE KROZAIR CYCLE

Kenneth Bulmer

writing as
Alan Burt Akers

Published by
Bladud Books

First published in paperback in 2007 by Bladud Books
(not including "Wizard of Scorpio")

eBook edition published in 2010 by Mushroom eBooks

Originally published separately by Daw Books, Inc., as:
"Wizard of Scorpio" in *The DAW Science Fiction Reader*,
ed. Donald A. Wollheim (1976)
The Tides of Kregen (1976)
Renegade of Kregen (1976)
Krozair of Kregen (1977)

This new edition (including "Wizard of Scorpio")
published in 2011 by
Bladud Books, an imprint of Mushroom Publishing,
Bath, BA1 4EB, United Kingdom

www.bladudbooks.com

ISBN 978-1-84319-132-2

Contents

"Wizard of Scorpio"

Wizard of Scorpio is the first story written about Dray Prescot that is not of novel length. It was written especially for the 200th DAW book, The DAW Science Fiction Reader, *edited by Donald A. Wollheim, and in the epic of Prescot's adventures it falls between the Havilfar Cycle and the Krozair Cycle.*

Delia is the most perfect woman in two worlds. Had she not been so perfect on that particular day of mellow sunshine in Foke Lyrsmin's garden as we waited to witness his wedding with the lady Merle, then the subsequent harebrained adventures and headlong action that hurled me furiously through the sweet-scented air beneath the moons of Kregen would not have occurred. But, had I not gone through those ordeals and fought those fights, then I would have been the poorer, as you will hear.

A merry group of nobles nearby on the lawn laughed and chattered and so the screams and shouts from the little marble pavilion where the airboat had just touched down reached me attenuated, distant and without menace. This was a cheerful wedding day and everyone was determined to enjoy the occasion to the utmost. The bride had been surrounded by an excited flutter of her friends, envious of her good fortune in marrying a kov, for to marry a noble of higher rank she must needs wed a prince or king, and I put the commotion down to high spirits.

The airboat lifted away, going fast over the trees. Her side flamed brilliantly as the polished brasswork caught the mingled streaming lights of the suns of Scorpio. Then she was gone from my view over the garden, for I stood talking to Foke Lyrsmin in his study, with the tall Windows thrown wide.

Foke had been showing me his latest rapier, an acquisition of which he was proud and which he intended to wear at the ceremony. Now he turned back from the window.

"These young people," he said, spreading his hands. He was a cheerful little fellow, a trifle on the small side, wiry, and I had found him not unreasonable company on this first meeting. "Your father-in-law does me great honor, prince," he went on. "But—"

"The emperor will arrive in his own time, Kov."

That old devil, the Emperor of Vallia, father of my Delia, had not turned up yet and we were all waiting for him. Well, it may be the privilege of an emperor to be late; but I've always taught the emperor's grandchildren that politeness demands punctuality on parade.

This Foke Lyrsmin was the Kov of Vyborg, and Vyborg is a Kovnate province on the western edge of Vallia. By this marriage with the lady Merle, daughter of Trylon Jefan Werden, he reinforced the links with his northern borders. That puissant man, the Emperor of Vallia, approved, and as Merle was a girlhood friend of Delia's, we had left our children back home in Valka, away to the east, and come to the wedding in the hopes of relaxation and enjoyment.

The door at our backs burst open and Jefan Werden came hobbling in, his lined and dyspeptic face exhibiting all the agony of a man with gout having his foot run over by a tram.

"My daughter!" he shouted. He was genuinely angry and alarmed, his face sagging with shock. "Merle! Merle! She's gone!"

"Merle! Gone?" Kov Foke put out a hand. He looked not so much shattered as bewildered. "What do you mean?"

"What I say! Merle—she's been taken—kid-napped!"

They glared at each other, oblivious of my presence. That suited me. If someone had kidnapped the lady Merle and he was captured his head would roll. That was for sure. I would do what I could to help. That, also, was sure.

The noise outside increased. People were running aimlessly amid a screaming and a shrieking. The facts must be established at once. But Merle's father burst out:

"Four men, all dressed in black—the cramphs! They took my daughter—and they—"

"Who? Who?" yelped Kov Foke, interrupting, his face now as crimson as a moment before it had been green.

"They wore metal masks. But I know who hired them! I know who it was who paid them, the rast! Vangar Riurik! He's been sniffing around after my daughter for the last five seasons. I gave him his marching orders—and this is what he does! What the emperor will say—"

I stepped forward. This was suddenly more serious.

2

"You say it was Vangar Riurik. How can you be sure? He is the Strom of Quivir."

"I know, prince, I know!" Even as Merle's father shouted so the yelling outside went on and on. "And Quivir is a stromnate of the island of Zamra, and you, Prince Majister, are the Kov of Zamra. Riurik owes allegiance to you." He stared at me, and I saw the abrupt, crafty light in his eyes.

If he was going to suggest I'd had anything to do with this lover's argument, this romantic kidnapping of the bride just before the ceremony, then he'd picked the wrong man. He knew enough of me to still the tongue in his head. This was an affair of mine only in so far as I must discipline an unruly follower, who held the stromnate of Quivir at my hands. I knew young Vangar Riurik, a right tearaway and a fine fighting man, and I knew also that this was a thing perfectly possible for him.

"He will no doubt fly back to Zamra with Merle," I said, putting Foke's rapier down on his desk and knocking over an inkwell. The bright red ink splattered the carpet—luckily the carpet was not of Walfarg Weave. "We shall follow at once. I will replace your carpet, Kov."

I made for the door.

A mass of people spilled from the corridor, creating a tremendous noise. The whole household had been overturned like an ant's nest with boiling water. I saw young Oby trying to force his way through. His face was contorted with the effort of wedging his lithe young body between a fat dowager stromni and an equally plump kotera whose violet dress caught about Oby's ears. He pulled it with an anger that seemed to me to be quite out of proportion. A scamp, an imp of Satan, Oby; but his actions made me curious.

The Trylon Jefan Werden hobbled up at my back. He was still panting with exertion and anger and I half-turned to see what he wanted.

"Prince," he began.

I have heard that tone of voice before.

"Prince, my daughter was talking to her friends—they were laughing and joking, and—"

"Well? Spit it out!"

"The Princess Majestrix—"

He had no need to go on. He licked his lips. He saw my face and he seemed to shrivel.

The crowd of people milling and pushing in the corridor, creating a babel of confusion, flowed around me as butter flows around a hot knife. I do not think I knocked anyone down. I do remember running outside onto the grass into that glorious mingled radiance from the twin suns Zim and Genodras. Oby ran at my side, yelling. I heard something of what he said. An airboat rested on a paved court by the ornamental fishponds. The neat petal shape of fabric-covered wooded frames, the windshield glittering in the light, told me the craft was a small four-place runabout. It would do. I leaped in and thrust savagely at the controls.

The flier leaped forward, rose perhaps four feet into the air, almost knocked Oby sprawling, nosed down and went with an almighty splash into the fishpond. Water smashed my face and lily-pads wrapped around my neck.

I did not curse.

Oby sprinted up, shouting, pulled the access panels out to get at the silver boxes that controlled the airboat. He looked back up. "Finished, my prince! Exhausted!" Since he had disavowed his ambitions to fight in the arena, Oby had taken up the study of the fliers, and was a useful hand. If he said the silver boxes were finished, they were. After a life of varying length the boxes would turn a leaden color, and then one must buy new.

"Another flier, Oby! As you love the Princess!"

"Aye, my prince!" And Oby was off, a limber young lad, full of fire and energy and deviltry.

Do not wonder that I let Oby fetch the flier. We had flown here from Valka in a small air boat with just a few people and I had talked Vangar ti Valkanium, my chief of fliers, into allowing Oby to pilot us. He would know where every flier was parked and to whom every voller belonged. Being an imp, he would fetch the fastest voller, no matter whose.

So for a few moments in which I forced myself—Zair knows how!—to remain calm, I had time to understand what had happened.

As I said, my Delia is the most perfect woman in two worlds. She is also the most beautiful. I say this in all humility. In addition she possesses a superb courage that matches the courage of a mother zhantil who will fight to the death anyone or anything that molests her cubs. So I had no difficulty in imagining that scene in which the kidnappers had leaped from their voller to seize Merle and just as they were bundling her aboard smothered in a cloak Delia had leaped forward. Yes! The sight of my Delia rushing into the fray with that thin slender dagger glittering is enough to make the stoutest of assassins blanch. So they had taken her as well. It had all been a scramble, a confusion, and the airboat had lifted off with my Delia aboard.

My Delia! My Delia of Delphond, my Delia of the Blue Mountains, flew through the bright skies of Kregen in the grip of kidnappers who did not want her along. What might happen made my heart a stone, made my fist grip onto my rapier, made me even more of a devil than I already am.

Here came Oby with the voller, swirling down directly to land before me without a wasted moment. He stepped out and handed me my scabbarded longsword and a glossy black flying fur made up from foburf skins. I leaped in.

He yelled at me, skipping around to the other side. "My prince!" he bellowed, and I knew what he was saying before he shouted. "I'm coming too!"

"No, you're not, young Oby. You will raise all Valka, all Zamra, all Delphond, all of the Blue Mountains! Tell the emperor! Riurik will probably fly seaward of Rahartdrin. I'm relying on you, Oby!"

"Aye, my prince." But he looked mighty chapfallen, all the same.

By the time I was airborne a number of other vollers were being crammed with men and were taking off. But Oby had chosen well. I did not know whose this voller was; she was a fleet craft and flew like a dream. If Vangar Riurik chose to return to Zamra by flying between the mainland and the island of Rahartdrin I would miss him. But I suspected he would attempt to avoid pursuit by going out to sea. I smashed the voller's controls hard over and the little craft soared into the mingled lights of the Suns of Scorpio.

The blue, blue sea of Kregen flashed past below.

Rahartdrin was a brown smudge on the southern horizon. I saw the dots of fliers there. If Riurik had gone that way the pursuit would bay on his heels. I kept my ugly old face turned seawards. Oxkalin the Blind Spirit must guide me now.

Onwards through the thin air with the slipstream blattering about my ears, on and on! Ahead two black dots... Vollers! Two—had Riurik chosen to meet Merle and her abductors here, pay them off and carry the girl in triumph back to Quivir? It was a plan.

One flier ahead span away, turning end over end, dropped to the sea. I stared. I felt the pains gripping my chest, eating at my guts. Dots with tiny arms and legs spread-eagled fell away from the voller. Uselessly I forced the levers over, urging the voller to the limit. Now the second flier was speeding away—speeding directly away, straight out to sea. That was a strange course to steer for a man wanting to fly east, to Quivir. Maybe he had seen me. If Delia had fallen—and I did not believe she had—then the cramph would see nothing else after I caught up with him.

I could not believe that of Vangar Riurik. Rather, I would believe that the moment he saw the ghastly mistake his hired men had made he would turn and in all humility bring Delia, the Princess Majestrix of the Empire of Vallia, straight away back to her ugly great leem-slayer of a husband. At once!

Those two glorious suns of Scorpio, the red and the green of Antares, sank into the ocean and those constellations so strange and yet so familiar to me burned overhead. Soon Kregen's first moon appeared, the Maiden with the Many Smiles, casting down her fuzzy pink and golden light, and I could make out the distant glitter of light that was the voller I pursued.

There was no gaining on the distance; the two fliers were matched for speed. I cursed and raved, was deathly quiet, fingered my rapier and left-hand dagger, smashed at the control levers, and cursed again. We bore on through the moon-drenched night over Kregen, the wind in my face.

The time passed away and still no impression could be made on the gap and Kregen's fourth moon, She of the Veils, rose and added to the light so that I could see that damned flier ahead with all the tantalizing clarity of the untouchable. My Delia must be aboard, alive, vibrant, and I would reach her! I would!

If we persisted in this course long enough we would reach the Hoboling Islands that fringe the northern tip of the continent of Loh. Viridia the Render would be somewhere ahead of me, pirating away among the islands. There were other isolated islands I did not know well to the east of the Hobolings. And, long before dawn, the flier ahead began to slant down to a black mass sparsely speckled with lights upon the face of the sea.

We had flown a long way, for they were both fast vollers; I felt keyed up to fighting pitch as I gently eased the levers and sent my craft hurtling down in pursuit.

The voller did not malfunction as so many vollers still do on Kregen; it was all the fault of my own idiot self. The craft ahead plunged down towards a grouping of lights. Glimpses of stone walls and domes and towers, all pink and golden beneath the moons, rolled away beneath. Clouds banked ahead, visible by their blackness and the absence of stars. The voller plunged through them and I followed. The lights vanished. I was hurtling through darkness as pitchy as the cloak of Notor Zan. Wind tugged at me and I did not see but rather felt the embracing mass of trees ahead and sought to lift the voller and she rose, rose a fraction, rose to crash rendingly through the bristly branches of thick-trunked trees.

Then the real cloak of Notor Zan enveloped me and I span away into blackness.

"You're all right, dom. Just a crack on the head." The voice whispered to me over the shushing of an invisible sea. "By Opaz! You must have a head like a vosk skull!"

I opened my eyes. Pain clawed at my head and I put my fingers up, into my brown hair; they probed and felt no wound, they came away without blood. But my head rang with all those famous Bells of Beng Kishi.

About me the darkling forest rustled gently in the night wind. I lay on a rough pallet of branches with leaves for mattress and pillow. The little fellow peering down at me in the light of the Moons was apim, a homo sapiens like me, with bristly light brown hair and a nutcracker face and rags for clothes all liberally smeared with ash. I could guess what he was without trouble, and as I lifted myself on an arm, wincing, he helped me up, chattering away the while. Clearly, having a stranger fall on him was a novelty.

"It seems your hut has been demolished, dom."

He cackled at this, finding it amusing. The hut of withes and sods had been as neatly cracked as a loloo's egg under a spoon. Moonlight sifted down between the leaves. His snaggle teeth showed raggedly in his gash-grin, his lips wide in the pleasure he took in having his hut squashed by a voller.

"Soon build another. You are all right? Got a bottle of dopa here, somewhere..."

He rattled on. He was Nath the Ash, a charcoal burner, and the evidences of his craft stood about in clearings between the trees. Charcoal burning is a highly skilled task. The neatly cut logs, first in their tripod shape, then in the triangular interleaving up to a man's height, and then the careful stacking of thick and thin logs into the pile and the packing with clay and sods, demand concentration. The actual burning for a day and a night or so, depending on size, and the putting out of the fire, are matters of high art within the craft.

I said, "Did you see another flier?"

"Aye, dom, aye." He bustled about trying to find the dopa. I hadn't the heart to tell him I wouldn't touch the stuff. "Went across so low afore you came down." He chuckled, highly amused. He would move to another spot for wood and make another hut there, anyway, so he had suffered no real loss. "Went down over in the ruins."

"Ruins?" I licked my lips. Perhaps just a sip... "Where is this, by Vox!"

"Why, dom, this is Ogra-gemush—"

"I know it. King Wazur—he grows fat from the chemzite quarries and—"

"Aye," chuckled Nath the Ash, throwing broken sticks and mangled sods about and still not finding the dopa. "And what he makes out o' trading with the renders. I know!"

"Where away are these ruins?"

He pointed without looking, still searching for the dopa, a fiery drink calculated to make a man fighting drunk in no time. I padded off towards the flier. The thing had been punctured and splintered and stood now on its nose half leaning against the wreck of the hut. It might fly again. I took out the longsword and strapped it to my back. Then I said, "Thank you for your hospitality, Nath. Remberee."

He jerked up like a steel trap unspringing. "Hey, hey!" he called after me. "Here it is!" He was still waving the dopa bottle over his bristly head the last time I looked back in that mingled flood of pink and gold moonlight.

I knew of this King Wazur of Ogra-gemush but had never met him. We in Vallia had bought a consignment of chemzite, for the mines here produce a marvelous yellow-tawny tinged stone, much prized. Also I knew he was the provider of one of the entrepots in which the pirates disposed of their gains. He was a rich man and although his island kingdom might be small, he would have many hired mercenaries. Why had his men taken the voller with the lady Merle and my Delia aboard? I felt the longsword on my back and I plunged recklessly through the forest until the jagged columns and shattered stones of the ruins glimmered palely before me, the crumbled outlines festooned with vines, the light of the moons pallid upon this wreck of time.

Strange blossoms clustered thickly upon the vines, wax-like blooms glimmering palely under the moons like entwined ropes of severed heads. The silence hung about these ruins as though undisturbed since the sunset people passed by. I padded silent as a hunting leem along the broad broken avenues, looking past the corpse-like remnants of buildings, peering into every pink shadow, wary in case real leems should be lurking ready to pounce with their deadly wedge-shaped heads gaping vicious fangs at my back. I did not tarry overlong in any part but pressed on to where what had once been a domed and towered palace hung now in time-blasted wreckage against the face of the Maiden with the Many Smiles. She was almost gone. Soon the twin suns would rise. She of the Veils would float for a few burs in the daytime sky, a sign and an omen. I heard nothing as I passed along, and yet that intense prickly feeling of a presence, intangible, manifest, unseen, made my fingers itch.

An abrupt and unexpected noise made me swing about, the longsword scraping from the scabbard at my back. The moons light struck along the blade, turning it pink-gold. The noise chinked again, much like the sound of leathern armor striking against stone. In the shadows, I waited, fierce, predatory, more vicious than any of the wild beasts of Kregen, for I could not wait long.

I could see no movement. The sounds ceased. With a muffled Makki-Grodno oath I glided swiftly from the shadows and over the last steps across a shattered paving into the black archway. The archway led into gloom as deep as Cottmer's Caverns. I halted and turned. Now I was looking out onto the moon-drenched shadows of the paving. If anything followed me I would see. Nothing moved. There was no sign of the flier; there was nothing here for me. If I had to search until all the Ice Floes of Sicce melted into the fires I would search; I would never give up my Delia, my Delia of Delphond.

If this ancient ruin was indeed a city then I would search every smashed alley, every ruined street. I stuck the longsword back into the scabbard and put my foot out into the moonlight—and froze.

A whisper ghosted at my back.

I whirled.

Against the darkness I could see the moon reflections striking from the long slender blade of a rapier—a rapier darting directly for my heart!

Even as I swayed aside my own rapier leaped into my fist and the blades scraped and rang as I parried that treacherous blow. Instantly I was engaged with an unseen adversary, fighting for my life.

My dagger parried the next successive flurries. Whoever the attacker might be, and still I could not make him out in the gloom, he was good. Unless he wore a black mask, he must be a black man, probably from Xuntal. Now his main gauche caught my thrust and twisted, and I leaped back and flashed a feinting stroke and so cut with my own blade. I knew I had him. I have some reputation as a swordsman; now was no time for fancy work. Now was a time for speed and more speed, so that I might seek for the flier and my Delia.

The cut missed.

Without a curse to slow me down I dazzled a succession of passages, took his blade and thrust him through.

The rapier licked back, bright and clean; I felt no shock of bodily encounter. The two blades against my two continued to lick in and out and seek to spit me through the guts. I had to hop and skip with great cunning and fury. I circled on the cracked stone, working my way around. Now I would have this fellow with his uncanny swordplay silhouetted against the light of the moon. He was very good for he had avoided a cut and a thrust I had thought lethal. Perhaps, here in this moon-shot darkness on the isle of Ogra-gemush, I had at last met my match and was about to die. I would not let that happen. I would fight until they screwed me down, and then I'd as lief shove the coffin lid up for a last go at them all.

Around him I circled and so brought the bladesman fronting me with his back to the arched opening and the moon-light dappled shadows outside.

I let out a furious yell. Yes, I shouted—in anger, in fear, in panic—I shouted. "By Zim-Zair!" I bellowed. "There's only one way to deal with you!"

And, skipping back out of arm's reach, I threw down the rapier and dagger so that they rang and bounced on the stone.

For—against that silhouetting light showed only the rapier and dagger of my opponent. No living hand wielded those blades! They hung unsupported in mid air. Moving by some uncanny power they went through all the motions of swordsmanship and had rung and scraped against my blades, and yet no mortal hands grasped them, no flesh and blood urged them in cunning combat. No wonder my blade had passed so easily through nothing!

Out came the longsword, ripped from the scabbard over my back. This was not a true Krozair longsword; but it had been forged in cunning and beauty by Naghan the Gnat and me in the smithy of Esser Rarioch, and was a true blade. This was the blade with which I had led on my aerial troops to victory in the Battle of Jholaix. I did not waste time.

Using that subtle and deadly Krozair two-handed grip I flicked the brand left and right, brought it back with just the right amount of force and smashed it down squarely upon the jeweled hilt of the rapier. The rapier blade snapped across and the hilt shattered, spraying jewels. The blade dropped to clang against the floor. Over that sound I heard a gasp. Without a pause, instantly, the superb longsword slashed down in a short and wicked arc and served the main gauche in similar fashion.

The beautiful rapier and dagger lay in shards upon the stone.

I lifted my head, and I know my face must have shown all that evil and ugly malefic power that so transfixes those upon whom I gaze in that diabolical fashion. I shouted:

"Come out, you miserable cramph! Come out before I cut your heart from your body and tear your liver smoking from your guts!"

A slither, a scrape, the sound of pebbles falling, and into the shaft of moonlight stepped a young man with a face expressing the most extreme surprise. No fear, no horror, just surprise.

Decently clad in a white robe cinctured by a crimson cord, with sandals upon his feet, with golden bracelets about his arms, and a face of great handsomeness, he might pass as any noble idler in the more riotous quarters of any city of Havilfar. But I saw his hair and I knew. For his hair shone with that peculiar gleaming red-black in the pinkish light of the moons. I knew him and what he was.

"A damned Wizard of Loh!" I shouted. "By the disgusting diseased intestines of Makki-Grodno! What are you trying to do?"

His surprise increased. These famous Wizards of Loh are accustomed to receiving the most perfect respect from men, respect and fear, for, indeed, they do possess weird and uncanny skills—as, by Vox!—I had just witnessed.

"I am Khe-Hi-Bjanching," he said, in a voice like chiseled steel. "I have great powers—you had best beware and—" Here the rapier scraped evilly against the stone. "Swordomancy."

"I've heard of your damned swordomancy, or gladiomancy, call it what you will, wizard. It has not served you well."

"And I have awful powers to blast the eyes in your skull!"

"You're not skulking in these ruins for nothing!" I bellowed at him. I made the longsword tremble so the moonlight snaked down the patina. "Tell me where the voller is, cramph!"

He shook his head in amazement, and half lifted a hand.

"You are a strange man, of a kind new to me. What is your name?"

I did not hesitate.

"I am Dray Prescot, the Lord of Strombor, and if you do not answer, your head will skip about right merrily on these stones."

"Yes, I brought the fliers to earth. I caused a cloud—oh, only a small one, a mere nothing—"

10

I put my left hand on his throat and I lifted him and glared madly into his eyes. The longsword poised above his head.

"Where, wizard? Where?"

One should address a Wizard of Loh with all reverence as San, a sage or dominie, a master. He gobbled a trifle and choked and his cheeks took on a dark plum color in the moons light. I let my gripping fingers relax a trifle—not much.

"By the Copper Cylinder—" he squeaked. I let him breathe. I am a humane man in these things. "It is ruined—but the flier went down by the Copper Cylinder."

"Then we will go there now, together." I dragged him along, running through the shadows with the last of the moons light falling about my heels, with the promise of dawn and the rising of Zim and Genodras in my face. The Copper Cylinder reared ahead, sliced off diagonally some hundred feet from the ground. As we ran over those ancient stones the first brilliance broke through the eastern horizon and a single copper gleam, red-gold, burst like a star against the upflung jagged point of the Copper Cylinder.

My own rapier and main gauche were back in their scabbards; we had left this Wizard Khe-Hi-Bjanching's smashed weapons on the stones. I had no fear of him stabbing me in the back as I hauled him along.

Shadows still clung darkly about the base of the Cylinder; but now that shaft glowed, the light slowly running down the copper which gleamed red-gold with no trace of green patina. I saw the wrecked voller. I let out a yell, a furious joyful shout: "Delia! Delia of Strombor! Delia of Vallia!"

For answer a shattering roar reverberated from the mildewed stones. The very ground seemed to tremble beneath my feet. I ran on; the voller lay on her side, crumpled, and a body clad in the black leather trap-pings and metal of a flyer lay sprawled alongside, his head a mere mass of clotted blood and brains.

"Delia!"

The roar smashed out again and into the rising glory of the Suns stepped a tralk, his six legs scrabbling against the stones, his horse-sized armored body glowing brick-red in the light. His wide horny mouth, designed to crush armored monsters like himself, opened. Before his flat head his two enormous pincers opened and closed in deadly menace, their serrated edges able to rip and puncture the armor of his natural enemies. I sought no fight with him; but again that angry roar smashed out. The pincers, each as large as a kitchen table, clashed. Down went his head, the six legs bunched for a swiftly savage charge, the horny crushing mouth opened—and with a last and stone-shattering roar the tralk charged.

"Run, man, or you're done for!" screamed the Wizard.

It was nice of him to worry over my safety. I've fought worse monsters than a tralk before and, no doubt, Kregen being the marvelous and wonderful, terrible and horrific world it is, will fight many more before I take the last journey to the Ice Floes of Sicce.

The longsword snapped into my fists. The Wizard ran, screeching. I poised, ready to deal with the tralk as he deserved. The only enmity I bore him lay simply in that he delayed me in my search for Delia. The tralk, for all his fierceness, and he is a fearsome risslaca among risslacas, acted merely out of his nature; what he was doing was what he was born and intended for.

That first rush with the intention of seizing me up in one of his iron-hard pincers and so crushing me into that horny mouth was met by me in the old barbaric ways of Kregen. I skipped to the side at the last minute and that superb longsword swished and bit deeply into the joint abaft the pincer. It did not cut through. The tralk's armor was thick and horny. But I knew what a real Krozair longsword would do; now I was testing what the sword Naghan and I had made would do. Again I slashed and got an eye. The thick pus and mucus ran out. The tralk screeched; but pity him though I might, my mind hungered to press on, filled with horror for the fate of Delia. Nothing in two worlds can stand against the well-being of my Delia. I have waded through lakes of blood, as you know, and would see two worlds mere oceans of blood to preserve my Delia. This makes me a sinner. I am. But then, that is me, Dray Prescot. As for this poor dinosaur; he lasted no time at all after his second eye burst like the first.

He thrashed about, his pincers clashing open and shut with a pathetic sound. Then he screeched, as though understanding, and lumbered away, crashing into walls and stones as he went, for his two remaining eyes were both on the left side of his head.

"You are a devil!" panted the Wizard. "By Hlo-Hli! A very devil!"

"Aye!" I said, snatching up a handful of ferns to cleanse the sword. As you know, I do not like thrusting a sword fouled with blood into a scabbard given to me by Delia. "Aye, wizard. I am a very devil. You brought the voller to ground. The woman I seek is not here. If you do not go into lupu and tell me where she is—now!—I swear you will find out your ideas of a devil are a pallid nothing beside the reality I'll show you."

This was not empty boasting. Boasting is for fools. I simply told this Wizard of Loh, Khe-Hi-Bjanching, what I would do to him if he failed me. He believed me. When I wish, I can have that effect on people. As I say, I am not a nice man.

And then, after all this arrogant display of petty power, I heard the slither, and turned viciously, and the whole world of Kregen fell on me and even Notor Zan had time for only one swirl of his cloak before I fell into the deep darkness.

* * * *

12

"Dray!" said my Delia, her voice making me curse myself for the greatest onker in two worlds. "Dray!"

"Sink me!" I said. "I don't like making the acquaintance of Notor Zan so often, by Zair!"

We were chained up in a dungeon with the lady Merle and the Wizard. I have spent some interesting times in dungeons, Kregen being a world where dungeons are a way of life to some kings, and I detest them all. I looked about for the way out. The chains would not be broken had I ten times the strength I have, which is not inconsiderable. We were all naked save for our breechclouts. Delia and I wore the brave old scarlet. That cheered me, at least.

"I thought you would never—they must have hit you hard."

"I have a vosk skull for a head, as you have told me many a time. So Strom Vangar was not with the kidnappers. I'll have a word to say to that young man, by the Black Chunkrah, yes!"

Whilst we waited to find out what this King Wazur intended for us, we talked. This Wazur was exceedingly rich and wielded a despotic power on his own island. There are many absolute despots in many places upon Kregen. What he was going to do would not be opposed by any of his people. His hired mercenaries would see to that.

"So your brother is a Wizard to this maniacal king?" I said.

"I have been training in the arts in Loh." Khe-Hi-Bjanching was the very first very young Wizard of Loh I'd run across. He told me he sometimes still muffed a chance, and could produce a marvelous effect of making a person's hair stand on end when he'd really been trying to wither their nose off. He told me these things with the air of one waiting to die. He'd come from Loh to join his brother, hoping for employment, being a young Wizard, and his brother—of whom he spoke slightingly—had chased him off and he had taken refuge in the ruins, bringing down the fliers imagining them in chase of him. In any event, King Wazur's mercenaries had found us and a crossbow bolt had caressed my head and I'd awakened in the dungeon.

The lady Merle, sprightly still but with trembling lips, held up wonderfully well. "And I truly love Vangar, but my father said I was to marry the old Kov Foke. He's funny. And poor Vangar arranged this; I didn't know, and this horrible King Wazur wants to put us to the test, and look at us—"

"Test?"

Bjanching made a strangled noise. "The two doors."

"Oh, that test," I said. "Well, two doors is a fifty-fifty chance. Usually it's three doors."

So we waited to see what Wazur intended in this test. I had the shrewdest of ideas what the cramph was really up to in giving an apparently even chance. It is not new. It is still lethal.

So, as we hung there in the damp and the cold and the silence with the water dripping slimily from the roof and streaking our naked bodies, I saw the lissom form of the lady Merle droop, and the tears falling from her eyes, the soft red lips shaking.

I said, "We will sing The Bowmen of Loh. It is Seg's favorite song. Now, I rather fancy I like the idea of Seg, and Inch, and Turko, coming walking through that door, over by the torch in its iron becket. Now, that would be grand!"

"Dear Seg," said Delia. "And Inch. As for Turko—he'd tear them limb from limb."

Turko the Shield would, too. So we sang the beginning of The Bowmen of Loh, and could wish Seg Segutorio was here with his great Lohvian longbow, and Inch was here also with his Saxon axe. Together, I fancied, we could fight our way across the Ice Floes of Sicce against all the Demons of Gundarlo, especially if we had Hap Loder and Kytun Dom along also...

The singing brought our jailers, Rapas with their vulturine beaks and their smell and their vicious handling of prisoners. I still couldn't get to like many Rapas. The diffs hustled us out, still in our chains unhitched from the wall-chains, and so we went up to be introduced to King Wazur. By Vox! I felt better already with Delia at my side, swinging along with all her blazing beauty emphasized by the flaunting scarlet breechclout, and the harsh iron chains upon her body mere reminders of how much we had been through together on this barbaric yet beautiful world of Kregen.

This King Wazur's palace exhibited the wealth acquired by selling chemzite from the mines and by trading with the pirates along the Hoboling Islands. The renders needed a safe haven to sell their plunder; Wazur grew fat on the profits. He employed Rapas, Ochs, Brokelsh, Womoxes, as mercenary guards. I saw no Pachaks or Chuliks. Although they are among the costliest of guards, their hire would not be beyond Wazur. Also I noticed the way we went, like any civilized barbarian—or, rather, barbaric citizen—and I kept my eyes open. The great hall was lofty and filled with the light of the twin suns, and there were many of his people there come for the spectacle. The throne was cut from a single gigantic block of chemzite. Zhantil skins lay strewn upon the seats and arms, and the steps were inlaid with ivory from Chem. Jewels and fans blazed in the emerald and ruby light of Genodras and Zim. The old rast was crafty, too, for his guards lined out by the throne and their bows were ready spanned. As for the king himself, he looked like a toad, he spoke like a rusty hinge, he smelled like a sewer. He leaned on a skinny elbow and opened his mouth and all his courtiers hung on his words.

"You great rast of an onker!" I bellowed up at him. "You nurdling cramph! You had best release us before a doom falls upon you that will horrify the whole world!"

The magnificence that was the clustered nobles and courtiers let out a single mutual gasp of terror. The king's face turned that color a malsidge turns just before it must be thrown in the garbage.

"Rast!" he screeched. "The test for you will be—"

"Save your breath, kleesh!"

That drove him to a frenzy. Foam spittled his lips. He half-rose, and clutched his chest, and panted. Majordomos hustled forward. The guards began to hit us. Well, I cracked a few skulls before they dragged us off.

Whilst it had been interesting it had no doubt not been at all clever. I had achieved one object. My Delia had not been subjected to humiliation and torture beyond what she had already endured. The guards took us through passages which, beginning with tapestried walls and carpeted floors changed to dank stone walls and slimy cobbles. We were thrust into a large square chamber and the door at our backs thunked shut. Before us in the opposite wall stood two doors. The chains clanked about us.

One by one the two doors opened and two girls stepped out.

One was apim, a young beauty, brilliant of eye, and in mortal terror. The other was a Fristle fifi, and her catlike face with all its pretty vivaciousness was likewise set in a grimace of mortal terror. The two girls carried clumsy keys with which they unfastened our chains to the penultimate link. Then they ran back to the doors. The lenken iron-bound valves thudded shut with the clang of doom as the locks engaged.

We stripped off the rest of the chains.

A voice spoke to us from the wall.

"Rasts! Listen to what I say, for I am a merciful king and am minded to let you live, if you have the wit."

Over the door we had entered, the wall was pierced with many small holes, making a grille pattern. Shadows moved there. So the king would watch his test, and gloat over our agonies.

From this back wall and running perfectly straight to the wall with the two doors were a series of slots in the floor. They were a fist in thickness and spaced about a foot apart.

"You may choose one door," the disembodied voice went on.

"Yes, yes, you onker," I roared up. "I should tell you that you make a disastrous mistake here. Do you not know the mighty power of the Empire of Vallia? Should you not stand in mortal terror of her fliers, her galleons, the thousands of fighting men her gold can buy? Yes, onker, you should!" I could hear muffled sounds up there beyond the grille, as of a gasping and a clutching at chests. "Know, then, kleesh, that this lady is the Princess Majestrix of Vallia! Better for you to release us now, and clothe us, and give us food and wine, lest a doom—"

"Cramph!" the voice whispered down. "You do not fool me. And were she the Princess Majestrix of Vallia, who is to know? Answer me that, onker, who is to know?"

15

The lady Merle let out a shriek, and the faceless voice whispered like a rusty hinge. "And you would tell me you are the Prince Majister of Vallia! Ho! And were it so, I would rather see you take my test than ransom you a tenfold! Choose your door and see if Oxkalin smiles or frowns! Choose!"

Even as he spoke thick iron bars rose up from the wall end of the floor slots. They rose until they slotted into the ceiling and then they began to press inwards towards us. They could not be broken. If we did not open a door we would be crushed. I stared at those iron bars sliding with grating ominous creaks towards us. The noise emphasized the weird evil of this place.

I picked up a length of chain. I have fought with chains. The Wizard, Khe-Hi-Bjanching, looked at me, and he smiled very lopsidedly. "My brother has become an evil man in the employ of this mad king. I do not think it matters which door we choose."

"Of course not," I said, and Delia put her arms around Merle, whispering to her, trying to ease the fear. "This king gives us a fifty-fifty chance. I think I will make that chance a little more even." I stared at him. "Can you work?"

He spread his hands, so I did not enquire further. He was a very young Wizard of Loh. He would learn, if he lived.

Those remorseless iron bars creaked and groaned down their slots towards us. I could waste no more time. The Wizard saw my advance to the nearest door, and he said: "What think you? A leem? A chavonth? A wersting? A tralk? It is an amusing thought, and by the Seven Arcades, I never thought to end life thus." He looked sorrowful. Not frightened, just regretful. "A whole life's study and discipline and diligence wasted."

"You're not battened down yet, Bjanching. Or burned atop your pyre, if you prefer."

"That, indeed, by Hlo-Hli, is what I would have preferred."

"Stand by that door. Grasp the lock and be ready. Delia! Stand with Merle midway between the doors. Bjanching, on my signal—and instantly, mind! Open your door!"

He started to say something, saw my face, and studiously grasped the bolt of the lock in his hand. I said, "Now!"

Together we flung both doors open simultaneously.

I swear I heard a shriek from the grating above the door.

Then all sounds vanished in the beast-roars from the two doors. We four cowered midway between against the wall. I gripped my length of chain, ready to fight for Delia until I was a mere bloody pulp.

From the Wizard's door sprang a tralk on its six legs, waddling forward after that first spring, its pincers opening and closing with the clash of steel.

From my door sprang—a Manhound!

16

I saw that blasphemous human form contorted into the shape of a feral beast, running on all fours, with the jagged fangs glittering, the red tongue lolling. I saw that Manhound and I felt very sorry for the tralk.

Both vicious beasts saw each other at the same time. The animal roar and the quasi-human shriek blended as both hurled themselves into blinding feral action. I grabbed Delia and hurled her around the door edge and I shouted, "Hurry, Bjanching, Merle!"

For the door began to close of itself, groaning on its hinges. We barely slid through. In total darkness we groped along until a lenken door studded with iron yielded to my thrusts and we stumbled up into a courtyard surrounded by wild-beast pens.

So swift had been our departure that the guards did not yet know we had gone. I smashed a few foolish fellows who sought to stop us, possessed myself of a clanxer, that cutlass-like sword of the sea-faring folk, and so we ran fleetly from the courtyard slinging tunics about ourselves as we ran, sprinting for the ornately carved gate at the end of the alley. Out through the gate, with a dead Rapa, beakless in the dust, at our backs, out and along a paved road fringed by bushes with the trees beyond, out and away and—

The pain struck like a risslaca bite up my leg. I yelled. But I struggled on into the trees before I stopped to look at the cross-bow bolt through my leg. The bleeding would have to be stopped quickly; Delia very firmly stripped the bolt of its leather flight and pushed it through, then used the tunic slashed into strips and wadded to plug the wound. I'd recover; but I'd been slowed down, a burden to the others. We ran on through the forest. They ran. I hobbled, cursing foully.

The Wizard knew the way.

What with those infernal bangs on the head, and the beatings and now this Opaz-forsaken bolt through my leg, I was in vile condition. I was also, as you may imagine, in an equally vile temper.

Delia ran fleetly ahead followed by Merle and the Wizard. I thumped along after. Delia vanished. Merle screamed and tottered and fell as the Wizard crashed into her. By the time I reached the lip of the pit and looked down the disaster had struck.

"Prince!" called up Merle. She was shaking, her face distraught. "We are trapped!"

I stared down and saw my Delia lying on the packed earth of the pit with the tumbled remains of the twigs. She was unconscious. The others must have fallen on her. I saw a large part of that scarlet veil that drops over a man's eyes, then, the scarlet veil I disavow and condemn.

I remember picking her up tenderly in my arms. I do not remember climbing down. I looked up. The walls were sheer but the handholds and footholds that had brought me down would take me up, and with Delia on my back, lashed by the strips of tunic.

I climbed. My muscles cracked, my head span, I felt the hollowness of the world within me and the weight of Kregen upon me; but I climbed out and lay on the top gasping like a stranded fish. How I had done it I did not know. I heard a crash and looked down. Both Merle and Bjanching were trying to climb out, and falling. Delia opened her eyes.

"We must run for the voller, Delia. The werstings will be on our tracks soon, if they do not use Manhounds."

She made a face at that. She had broken no bones, for which I thanked Zair. "Where are Merle and the Wizard? I fell..."

She looked into the pit. She turned and looked at me.

"No," I said. I thought I spoke firmly; but my voice husked. "I think of our twins, Drak and Lela. And our new twins, Segnik and Velia. They need their mother. Merle is—"

"Merle is Merle."

"Aye. And we must go."

There was no hesitation on my part. Merle was a nice girl, a lady of Vallia, a human being. But she was not Delia.

"Dray."

"Let us go. The guards and the werstings—"

"Are you concerned over mere guards? And you have slain many a wersting—or so you said—in Havilfar."

I didn't like this. "My duty is plain. You and the children are all that concern me. You know that. There is no sin in leaving these two, no shame." I am, after all, only a man.

"Dray, you would give your life for me. I know that. And I would do the same and you know that!"

"That is beside the point."

"Dear heart, that is the point!"

"Sink me!" I burst out. "I've been hit on the head, beaten, shot through the leg, and now my own wife turns on me! By Krun! Listen! Werstings! You can tell those vicious brutes miles off."

"Then there is little time."

"Delia!" I said, as I started down into the pit again. "Delia, my Delia of Delphond, my Delia of the Blue Mountains!"

Somehow, and I still do not remember it all right, I got the two out. Merle had to be carried by Bjanching, a task he was not averse to, I saw. But my head roared and the ground surged under me like the deck of a swifter or a swordship and I hobbled and lurched along and only when we saw the voller on its keel beside the remains of Nath the Ash's hut was it borne in on me that Delia had been supporting me for the last part of our flight. Nath the Ash with a huge bundle of wood on his shoulder cackled when he saw me.

"Knew you'd be back, dom! Found the bottle—all ready—"

We tumbled into the voller. If the thing did not work now we were done for. The werstings were close. I managed to shout.

"Clear away, Nath the Ash! You have not seen us! Else they'll put you to the test!" Then, as he cackled and chuckled and started rummaging for the dopa bottle, I was rude.

"Schtump!" I brayed at him. "Schtump, Nath the Ash!"

He looked shattered; but he heard the werstings and he knew what those vicious hunting dogs could do, and he made off.

Delia took the voller into the air with a sure clean sweep of power that reassured me. We would make Vallia! By Zair! We would fly all the way home across the Sunset Sea, and then...

The island of Ogra-gemush vanished beneath us as we rose through the low clouds. We were leaving King Wazur and his test. The suns of Scorpio streamed their mingled glorious radiance about us. But I made myself a little promise...

Before that promise was carried out Delia and I, with a lightly-dropped hint from the emperor, sorted out the love-life of the lady Merle and that rapscallion, Vangar Riurik, the Strom of Quivir. Old Foke, the Kov of Vyborg, found himself another sweet little lady of Vallia to make his Kovneva. So that was settled.

But for the other settlement and the fulfillment of my promise, I took an aerial fleet from Vallia and Valka, and regiments of my Valkan Archers and blade comrades, a host of fighting men, and Seg and his Bowmen of Loh and Inch and his Black Mountain Men came along for the ride, and we flew into action. Over us fluttered that brave old yellow cross on the scarlet field, that battle-flag fighting men call Old Superb. I must tell you that when my promise was fulfilled it was solely to recover a possession.

That is the truth, as Zair is my witness.

I led that host of warriors back to pay a social call on King Wazur only so as to recover the longsword Naghan the Gnat and I had made. This is true.

I would not like you to think otherwise.

At least, my Delia, my Delia of the Blue Mountains, my Delia of Delphond, knows that was the true reason—whatever else may have happened whilst we were regaining the sword.

The Tides of Kregen

A note on the Krozair Cycle

With this volume of his saga, Dray Prescot is hurled afresh into brand-new adventures on the planet of Kregen, that grim and beautiful, marvelous and terrible world four hundred light-years away beneath the red and green fires of Antares, under the Suns of Scorpio.

Dray Prescot is a man of above medium height, with brown hair and brown eyes that are level and dominating. His shoulders are immensely wide and he carries himself with an abrasive honesty and a fearless courage. He moves like a great hunting cat, quiet and deadly. Born in 1775 and educated in the inhumanly harsh conditions of the late eighteenth century English navy, he presents a picture of himself that, the more we learn of him, grows no less enigmatic.

Through the machinations of the Savanti nal Aphrasöe, mortal but superhuman men dedicated to the aid of humanity, and of the Star Lords, the Everoinye, he has been taken to Kregen many times. On that savage and exotic world he rose to become Zorcander of the clansmen of Segesthes, and Lord of Strombor in Zenicce.

Against all odds Prescot won his highest desire and in that immortal battle at The Dragon's Bones claimed his Delia, Delia of Delphond, Delia of the Blue Mountains. And Delia claimed him in the face of her father, the dread Emperor of Vallia. Amid the rolling thunder of the acclamations of "Hai Jikai!" Prescot became Prince Majister of Vallia and wed his Delia, the Princess Majestrix. One of their favorite homes is Esser Rarioch in Valkanium, capital of the island of Valka of which Prescot is Strom.

Far to the west of Turismond, the western continent of this grouping of continents and islands called Paz, lies the inner sea, the Eye of the World. There Prescot as a swifter captain became a member of the mystic and martial Order of Krozairs of Zy. He says he values his membership of the Krzy more highly than any other of his honors.

After a series of adventures on the continent of Havilfar, during which he fought in the arena of the Jikhorkdun and became King of Djanduin, idolized by his ferocious four-armed Djangs, Prescot managed to stay alive to thwart the plans of the Empress Thyllis of Hamal. In the Battle of Jholaix, Hamal was defeated and an uneasy peace ensued. Prescot and Delia and the children returned to Esser Rarioch in Valka looking forward to a happy and contented life.

Thus ends the Havilfar cycle. This volume, *Tides of Kregen*, opens the Krozair Cycle. Kregen is a world too rich in passion and action to allow a fighting man like Dray Prescot to rest for long. Once more, then, Prescot is launched into fresh adventures, but this time there is a hiatus which, I believe, might easily break a man of lesser fire and spirit than Dray Prescot, Krozair of Zy.

Alan Burt Akers

One
The Star Lords' warning

When two wizards begin quarreling it is time for sensible men to take cover.

"You young fambly, Khe-Hi!" Evold Scavander spluttered and fumed, his bewhiskered peppery features fairly glowing with baffled fury. "You lord of mumbo jumbo!" I fancied he would explode at any moment. He sneezed, powerfully, and Khe-Hi-Bjanching took a smart step backward, waving a hand before his young and handsome face.

"Now, old man, admit you have no powers to penetrate—"

"Powers! Powers! I've had more powers than you've had loloo's eggs for breakfast!" Evold swiped away at his face with a huge square of silk, all bright orange and red and brown. "I tell you, you arrogant puffed-up wizard of Loh, I put no store by this tomfoolery of appearances—"

"I saw, Evold, you ninny! I *saw*!"

"You saw the remains of last night's dopa, you young whippersnapper." He sneezed again, a veritable gusher of effort. The handkerchief swiped fretfully. "I'm the wizard to the Prince and don't you forget it!"

"To the Prince you may be anything, old man, I do not doubt. But a wizard!" Here Khe-Hi-Bjanching, that young and superior Wizard of Loh, laughed most sardonically, cutting old San Evold to the quick. "I grant you do have a power, aye, a mighty fine power of drowning a man in your sneezes! But as a wizard you would do well sweeping out the zorcadrome."

"I'll—I'll—"

"What? Cast a spell and turn me into a toad? Well, go on. Try."

"That mumbo jumbo is for you young fools. I know what I know."

They were really going at each other now, there on the terrace of my high fortress of Esser Rarioch in Valkanium. Only by chance had I come on them, being troubled in mind and going to find old Evold Scavander. When two wizards quarrel it behooves a mere man to be circumspect about taking himself off, but I stood for a short space in the shadow of a pillar watching them, the pressure on my spirits a little relieved by their antics.

23

Khe-Hi-Bjanching waxed more vociferous, his white gown with the crimson rope around his waist a blaze of radiance in the streaming light of the suns. "And I know we have had a visitation. If you do not instantly let me pass to report to the Prince he'll have your head off and have you hanging by the heels from the highest battlements of Esser Rarioch."

"The Prince would not condone such barbarities. He'd as lief trim your height by a head."

They went on like fighting cocks. With shrill squeals my younger twins, Segnik and Velia, scampered around the corner. They could run well now and were involved in some activity that made them oblivious to the quarrel. By the time they realized what was going on, a realization matched to their understanding of funny old San Evold and clever San Khe-Hi, Turko the Shield appeared, his face grim, to seize them up with two muscular heaves, one under each arm. He did not see me and he carried the twins off with a gentle concern that pleased me, despite all their squawking for Unca Turko to let them watch the fight.

Turko the Shield, a mighty Khamorro whose superb body and muscles could break men and destroy armed and armored foemen, felt that altogether sensible desire to place as much distance as he could between himself and a couple of wizards about to do each other mischief.

This quarrel appeared to me to be the outcome of the perfectly natural friction to be expected. Evold, who was the wisest of the wise men of my island Stromnate of Valka, shared the fears of the old when confronted by the eager zest of the young. But Evold had served me well and he ought to know he would never be cast off. Khe-Hi-Bjanching had yet to prove himself.

Turko's rumble, carrying off the younger twins, faded, and I smiled. Oh, yes here in my wonderful island of Valka in my high fortress of Esser Rarioch I could smile because I was with my Delia and my children; I could smile even though I knew with a pang of misgiving just what the Wizard of Loh meant when he talked of an apparition, of an appearance. This, then, explained the trouble that lay on my spirit. Although I had not seen the apparition this time, I had felt it and its evil power, malefic and altogether horrible in that high palace of light and laughter.

The twin Suns of Scorpio flooded their jade and ruby lights onto the high terrace; the bees buzzed in the flowers; the whole scene in that clear limpid air was one to dizzy the senses with beauty. Young Yallan halted at the end of the terrace, the hefty jar of water on his shoulder shaking and slopping as he hesitated to dare to pass. Yallan worked in the kitchens—he was not a slave, for neither Delia nor I will allow slaves in our lands—and he was paid well. He was a man, an apim, for we did not consider the carrying of heavy jars of water up the flights of steps a girl's work. He saw me and he slopped more water.

The time for fun had gone.

"Sans, Sans," I said, stepping forward. I used a gentle voice, but they both switched around smartly, knowing just who it was who spoke to them, and instantly started in hurling their sides of the argument at me. I held up a hand. They fell at once to silence.

"For the sake of Sweet Merrilissa, let young Yallan past. He spills the water, and it is a heavy task to carry it up."

"Yes, my Prince," they said, together, looking at Yallan as though he had sprouted horns. Yallan swallowed, walked past and turned and said, "My thanks, my Prince. Shall I call the palace guard? When two wizards..." He looked troubled.

"They merely riddle a puzzle, good Yallan. I thank you for your thought."

"Well, my Prince," he said, looking doubtfully at the two wizards, still standing on tiptoe and glowering at each other.

San Khe-Hi half turned his head, stared at Yallan and said with very much of a snake's hiss in his voice: "Be off, or I shall turn you into one of the little insects that crawl upon the floor!"

Yallan let out a screech and fled. He spilled drops of water as he went, but he did not drop the jar.

I said, "That was unkind, San. Unkind even if funny."

"There are important affairs of state, my Prince, that you must know—"

San Evold choked and sneezed. "Important! He wakes with a sore head from dopa and sees visions!"

"Not so, Evold. I know whereof Khe-Hi speaks. I have had visitations before, apparitions."

The Wizard of Loh nodded his head, the suns-light catching that blazing red hair and sheening brilliantly. "I told you so, you old dodderer! Go back to your chemicals and your cayferm and your silver boxes!"

But San Evold Scavander was not the wisest wise man in all Valka, just to be foisted off by a youngster, even if that young man was one of the famed and feared Wizards of Loh. He looked at me closely and he no longer sneezed.

"You speak sooth, my Prince. I know that. Then I would like to know more—all there is to tell. For there must be danger here." Then, unable to resist a last dig at Bjanching, he added: "For if danger threatens in Valka, I would not like to repose much confidence in this young fambly, for all he claims to be a Wizard of Loh."

"I'll show you!" began Bjanching.

I silenced them.

"Tell me what you have seen, San. All of it. And quickly."

He knew that tone of voice. As you know I had picked up this Wizard of

Loh in the island of Ogra-gemush, when Delia and Merle and Bjanching and I had been put to the test of the two doors by that unhappy King Wazur of Ogra-gemush. He had heard me and he had seen me in very different circumstances from these wonderful surroundings of Esser Rarioch, so he answered up quickly and succinctly.

"I awoke with the sure knowledge that a Wizard of Loh in lupu had appeared here. I could sense the locus. I saw him, not a strong manifestation; but I know he was evil."

"Aye," I said. "Aye. Unless I am mistaken that is the manifestation of the Wizard of Loh called Phu-si-Yantong."

Bjanching drew in his breath with a hiss. I had spoken to him of Yantong, enough to acquaint him with that devil's evil intentions toward not only me and my family here in Valka, but also of his insane ambition to rule the whole continent of Havilfar and the island Empire of Vallia also, of which my Delia's father was Emperor.

"The malefic force was great," said Bjanching. He was a young man, the only young Wizard of Loh I had seen up to then. Sometimes his spells did not work. He was eager and willing to learn, and highly contemptuous of those who put no store by his powers. "He was in lupu at a great distance."

"The greater the distance the better," I said. Lupu is that trancelike state into which the Wizards of Loh can place themselves and so see and observe over distances. Phu-si-Yantong had given orders that I was not to be assassinated, for he planned to use me in his evil schemes. From time to time he kept an observation on me. Now that I had my own Wizard of Loh I wondered if I might use Bjanching in more practical ways.

I looked at him. He was well aware of his enormous good fortune in being still alive and, into the bargain, of having a standing at my court in Esser Rarioch.

"Tell me, San. Is it possible to counter these intrusions in some way?"

"Yes, Prince," he said quickly. Too quickly, for his face clouded and he thought, then said: "It depends on the strength of the wizard."

"He is very powerful. With no disrespect to you, I hazard the guess he is the most powerful Wizard of Loh outside Loh itself, at least as far as I can judge."

"Then I can set up a defense which will slow him down. I can fool him, for a space. After that…"

"He has purely physical ambitions. He wishes, quite insanely, to assume powers of overlordship in as many countries and nations as he can contrive. I think that weakens him."

All this time San Evold had been spluttering and sneezing away in a minor key. Now he burst out: "Well, by Vox! Why do you not take a great armada and crush him, my Prince?"

I smiled. "The question is, San, where is he? What are his powers? I

26

do not forget he is in alliance with two evil men I know: Vad Garnath of Hamal, a man who would benefit the whole of Kregen by dying, and the Kataki Strom, the personification of devilment."

"Katakis." Khe-Hi-Bjanching pursed his lips. "They are bad business, by Hlo-Hli!"

"Then begin at once, San. Call on my chamberlain Panshi for whatever you require. I would have my house cleansed of these visitations. One day Phu-si-Yantong may appear with a greater desire than mere observation." I turned to Evold. "And, San Evold, you would greatly oblige me by rendering assistance to San Khe-Hi."

Evold's old stained smock quivered. He sneezed. But he got out, "Right gladly, my Prince," well enough. I knew I could trust him, and he would provide a useful check on Bjanching until I was fully satisfied as to that young Wizard of Loh's credentials.

As they went off, to go by way of the long hall of the images to that lofty room given over to San Evold as a laboratory, I was pleased to see they had forgotten their quarrel. Already they were talking as wizard to wizard, in their two very different disciplines, anxious to hatch out a likely scheme to foil this Opaz-forsaken Wizard of Loh who was trying to play dirty tricks on their ruler.

I sighed. Truly, I had to be thankful to Zair for the quality of my friends and companions.

That made me itch for Seg—for Seg Segutorio had taken his wife Thelda and their children and gone flying off to pay a call on his homeland of Erthyrdrin. That was a visit long overdue. As for Inch, he was up in his Black Mountains of Vallia working like a beaver on a new dam that would bring prosperity to one of his valleys and its people.

There was nothing I could do about Seg and Inch, for I never forgot they had their own lives to lead, both being Kovs of Vallia, and for the moment there was nothing more I could do about foiling that rast of a Phu-si-Yantong. So, throwing off these cares that were, after all, only dreamlike in quality, I went off to find Balass the Hawk and my eldest son Drak and see how they fared. I was most interested in Drak's education. He was growing up now, he and his twin sister Lela, and while my Delia had indicated very firmly that she fully intended to take care of Lela's education herself, it was my responsibility to see about that rapscallion Drak. I had not smothered him with titles and honors, as so many powerful men of the Empire suffocated their sons. Delia and I had created the rank and title of Amak in Valka. This was, in Hamal, the lowest rank of nobility. We possessed a tiny island just off the north coast of Valka, a place no more than a dwabur across and three dwaburs long. It was called Vellendur. So with a small and deliberately low-key ceremony we had created our son Drak the Amak of Vellendur. The people there were apims, a simple fisher and weaving folk, who had sent as many stalwart sons—aye, and daughters—as they could when we had freed Valka from the evil grip of the slave-masters and the aragorn.

An ample gift had seen to many of their wants and they were grateful for what had been done for them, for they had suffered when the aragorn had ridden in, powerful and haughty, to drag away their people into slavery. So now Drak was the Amak of Vellendur. I fancied he was pleased. But I'd told him in no uncertain terms that he wasn't to begin to get puffed-up ideas of his own importance, and his allowance was kept very low. Delia handled that; I felt it was perhaps a trifle too low and so from time to time I would slip him a handful of valens, or buy him a zorca colt or a stavrer pup. When Delia found out she was angry, but I thought that Drak was learning the lessons he must learn for life not only on Kregen but on any world where men traffic together and there are lords and those who are not lords.

Balass the Hawk, that fierce hyr-kaidur, was giving Drak all the benefits of the higher arts of swordsmanship as it affected Balass. He'd been a hyr-kaidur in the arena of Hyrklana with me and was a supreme secutor. This meant he understood the ways of sword and shield. For others of the arts of war we went to others of my friends and companions.

So, going down the stairs that led to the walled-in sandy enclosure where Balass sweated away, I paused, looking out under the steaming rays of the twin suns.

I felt shock.

It was quick—far too quick, by Zim-Zair!

Against that opaline radiance floated a dark shadow. I saw the wide-spread wings, the squat head, the raked-forward talons. This bird of prey was not large enough, or shaped correctly, to be a flutduin, the superb saddle bird we in Valka were adopting slowly. This was a bird I had seen many and many a time during my life on Kregen, this planet four hundred light-years from the world of my birth, this glorious world of Kregen under Antares which held all of life I held dear.

This marvelous world of Kregen held also the Gdoinye, the messenger and spy for the Everoinye, the Star Lords.

I stared up at the silhouette of the bird and the Gdoinye flicked his wings and so dived directly for me.

My hand jerked spasmodically to the rapier scabbarded at my side. But, even then, I wondered of what use mortal steel would be against this gorgeous scarlet and gold raptor. The bird wheeled before me with a harsh and raucous cry. I knew that if anyone looked on this scene they would not see the bird, for the Star Lords, who had brought me across the interstellar gulfs, protected their servants, although they took scant heed for my hide.

"Dray Prescot! Idiot! Fool! Onker!"

28

The bird screeched again, windblown laughter or a mere bird's cry I knew not. "You are a high and mighty man, these latter days. You are a noble, a prince, a Prince Majister, no less."

"These things have come to me through no seeking of mine." I hurled the words at the Gdoinye but I know now that I spoke of my humility with pride, with foolish pride.

"Nonetheless you hold high position here in Valka, and in Vallia, no less than in Strombor or with your clansmen of Segesthes. And, Dray Prescot, are you not also the King of Djanduin?"

"You know it, you cramph of a bird."

"You are the cramph, onker, for you forget why you were brought to Kregen at all."

"I never knew, you get-onker!"

The bird screeched again, and this time, I swear, the mocking amusement at my own stupidity sounded clearly in the cry.

"You were never meant to know. And you think you may defy the Star Lords, you puny human mortal?"

I made no reply. The Star Lords, who could hurl me away from Kregen and all I loved back to Earth four hundred light-years off through space, had never bothered themselves about my welfare, only calling on me to perform tasks for them. But they had not troubled me for a very long time now. Although it would be foolish to say I had forgotten them, their eternal menace had drifted into the back of my mind. Now I was being reminded of my true position.

"Have I failed you yet?" I spoke quickly as the Gdoinye swerved, all a shimmer of scarlet and gold beneath that streaming opaline radiance from the twin suns.

"You fail at your peril! There is work to your hand!"

"And if I refuse?"

"You may not refuse, Dray Prescot. You are not a pawn nor yet are you the master of your fate. Think on it, Dray Prescot, think on these things."

The Gdoinye said *swod* and not pawn, but I knew damn well what he meant. But I did not know what he meant by saying I was not a pawn. I had struggled against the Star Lords in the past and felt I had gained some advantage over them; I fancied there was a great deal more to learn before I could banish them from my scheme of things.

"You are a great man, Dray Prescot, with your string of titles and your lands and money and power. The Star Lords exact strict obedience from those they select to serve their ends."

"You nurdling great onker!" I bellowed. "What are these ends and what are the Star Lords trying to do here on Kregen?"

This time I was certain the damned bird laughed at me in a great cackling cry and a ruffling of feathers. He bore up and his pinions beat widely and he soared up and away. As I stared up after him his departing cry wafted down, hoarse and mocking.

"The Star Lords are most considerate of you, Dray Prescot. They send me to warn you, to give you time. Think how puissant are the Star Lords, and how generous!"

Then he was a mere dot against the radiance and then he was gone.

Feeling in a foul mood I went down to the sandy arena. Drak was thwacking away at Balass, making his shield gong. Every now and then Balass would reach out and touch Drak with his wooden sword, just to remind him and make him jump about a bit.

"Father!" said Drak, leaping back most agilely and turning to me. "Father! I saw a monstrous great bird, all red and gold, in the sky, making a most terrible noise."

I just stared at him.

"There was no bird, Drak," said Balass. "I saw nothing."

"No," I said, most heavily. "No, Drak. I saw nothing."

Two
Shanks against Valka

Delia was swimming when I walked into our private walled garden high on the flank of Esser Rarioch. Below the far wall the expanse of the Bay was visible, with a small portion of the city of Valkanium and ships sailing to and from the harbor with white sails burnished by the sun's glow. I stood for a while on the flags watching as Delia lazed through the water.

Every time I look at my Delia, my Delia of the Blue Mountains, my Delia of Delphond, I feel that thump of blood at my heart, that constriction of my throat. I may be accused of many things on two worlds, and if I am accused of saying the name of Delia more often than most, then I defend my right to that—no! I do not defend! I scorn anyone cloddish enough not to understand the glory and the magic and the love her name evokes—my Delia, my Delia of Strombor, my Delia of Vallia!

Thinking these savage and chauvinistic thoughts I walked down the wide shallow steps into the garden until the flower-covered wall concealed all the vista below so that Delia and I were completely alone in our own private garden.

She saw me and waved a bare arm and dived and swam under the water to the marble edge of the pool. I waited for her and bent to lift her out while she caught me cunningly and pulled, dropping back. With a mighty splash we both went in.

I spluttered and tried to catch her, but she was eel-like, flashing, glorious, and for a while we swam and played and I forgot the cares of government and high politics and the snares and entrapments of my enemies.

That gorgeous brown hair of Delia's with those enraging chestnut highlights floated on the water as she lay on her back, kicking with her feet. She splashed me, so I splashed back, and we met, breast to breast, without struggling, and sank down into the blue water. When we came up for breath she said: "And have you seen Segnik and Velia, Dray? They both deserve a spanking for what they did to poor Aunt Katri."

"They only hid her wool, dear—"

"They must learn to behave themselves."

"Yes."

We climbed out and sat on the grass to sun ourselves dry. The glory of the suns fell on the garden and on the fairest flower within that garden— well, I will not maunder on. All this made me feel the agony of what might befall if the Star Lords called on me again. I meant to speak to Delia. But how to explain to your wife that you had never been born on the world where she was born? How to explain that you came from a speck of light in the sky four hundred light-years away, a world that possessed only one sun? Only one moon?

How tell that on that world lived men, apims, Homo sapiens, and there were none of the other races of men that made Kregen so marvelous and horrible a place? How could she be expected to believe? One sun only? A solitary moon? Only apims? She would shake her head and laugh and push me in the pool.

I said: "I may have to go away again."

It was brutal.

She turned to me.

"You mean it?"

"Yes."

"Oh, Dray! Can you tell me? Long ago I made up my mind never to ask. I remember the strangeness of our first meetings, the time I spent in the Opal Palace of Zenicce, and the time you said you had spent with our clansmen. Dray! I am frightened to know, and yet, and yet I must know..."

"I will tell you, Delia, my heart, one day. I promise."

"And how you made yourself the Strom of Valka, and yet there was no time, for we marched through the hostile territories of Turismond, with Seg and Thelda, and that awful Umgar Stro, and—"

"Hush, hush. It will not hurt you, save for the parting."

"That is like a death."

"I know."

Banal words. But then, banal words mean so much when the hearts of those saying them tremble so in agitation and unspoken apprehension.

We spoke then of the ordinary familiar things of our life, those items of consuming importance to us. Segnik and Velia must be spoken to. Lela was to visit friends in Quivir, where that rip Vangar Riurik, the Strom owing allegiance to me as the Kov of Zamra, was throwing a party. For Drak I had other plans, and as I spelled them out Delia nodded, her sweet face down-turned and her hair spreading in a glowing brown and golden flood. She knew from our experiences together that what I suggested was not only sensible, it would give Drak the best of all possible chances on this terrible world of Kregen. We spoke of the new watercourses to be sculpted into the gardens, and I slowly suggested that we change the plans to a pump to bring water up higher still, a wind-driven pump, so the kitchen staff might be relieved of one burden. Delia agreed at once.

She lay back, glanced under the suns and rubbed her bare tanned stomach. "I am hungry."

"Yes, and I have a meeting with my Elders after the meal..."

"After! Why didn't you invite them?"

"I wanted to be with you and the twins."

"Oh."

So we stood up and, our arms around each other, went slowly up out of that scented garden back into the high fortress of Esser Rarioch and, after one of the essential meals of Kregen, got to the business of running the country.

There was much to discuss but I will not weary you with a recounting of the measures we took, for although they were of consuming interest to me then—and still are, by Zair!—they were much of the stuff of government in many places and worlds, I dare say. Zamra was still giving us a little trouble over the question of slaves. I ruled—if that is not too strong a word to use—from my palace of Esser Rarioch in Valkanium, the capital of Valka, not only Valka herself, but Zamra and the other islands also. These included Can Thirda. So far no one had agreed on a new name for the island since it had been pacified after the troubles and then given to me as a gift by the Emperor. I had vetoed Prescotdrin and Dray-drin, regarding the latter as downright ugly. I thought then that I would never have a land named after me, in which I was wrong, as you shall hear. I wanted Deliadrin. My word carried much weight, of course, the chief opponent being Delia herself.

She rather fancied Can Drak, but then again perhaps Leladrin would be nice, or maybe... and she would pause and put her chin on her fist and gaze around the table, her laughing eyes sizing us up, one by one, until those solid, respectable—aye, and some ruffianly too!—men of mine would shuffle their feet and then, despite all, smile broadly in response. I think we had a good life then. I know it. I knew, very positively, that I did not wish to leave.

32

So we discussed and decided on the cares of statecraft until a messenger burst in, wild-eyed, disheveled, thrusting past the guards who had the sense to let him pass.

"My Prince!" he bellowed. Blood stained down his face, brown and cracked, oozing where the sweat ran across the bright wound. "Leem Lovers! They have razed Fossheim! The village burned—burned—" He staggered and would have fallen but a guard caught him and quickly carried him to a seat.

Delia brought wine herself. He swallowed painfully. "My Princess—"

"What of Fossana?" I said. I spoke more roughly than I intended, for the man braced up in the seat staring with wild eyes.

"The island—" He choked and swallowed and began again. "We fought. There were ten of us, ten and a Deldar—lookouts—we fought—Deldar Nath the Shiv—they were devils, devils! Fishheads! They cut us down!"

Tom Tomor ti Vulheim, an old blade comrade and a man with whom I had happily fought when we took Valka from those damned aragorn, was already running for the door, the sword on his hip banging. He was yelling. Tom, whom I had made take the name of Tomor from the battle we had fought under Tomor Peak, and who was the Elten of Avanar, was now the general of my armies of Valka. I could trust him to take what were the immediately necessary measures against these fishheads, these weirdly repellent diffs sailing around the curve of the world from the other grouping of continents and islands of Kregen to rape and plunder and burn.

The full significance of this latest assault was not lost on us. We were to the north of the equator, and the Leem Lovers sailed up generally from the south, to attack the continent of Havilfar and its associated islands down there. They had penetrated to the north of Havilfar and over to the west up the Hoboling Islands. For them to have come this far north could only mean they had stepped up their activity. Why they had done so still remained a mystery. Our immediate task was to drive them back and prevent their making a base on the sweet little island of Fossana.

Delia glanced at me and I saw that she was moved.

There was more than mere agony over the despoiling of one of the islands which looked to us for protection. For the island of Fossana, to the south and east of the island of Valka, had been marked out by me as so charming and delightful a spot that the title of Amakni of Fossana should be the proud title of our daughter Lela, to match her twin brother Drak. But Delia had put a slender finger to her lips and shaken her head and said, "Not yet, my great grizzly graint of a husband. You always rush into things headlong. Let Drak have the glory for a space, for he will…" And then she had paused and bit her lip.

So I finished for her: "One day, if we were ordinary people, he would take my place."

But, speaking thoughtlessly, she had forgotten that by virtue of a dip in the Pool of Baptism in the River Zelph of far Aphrasöe, she and I were assured of a thousand years of life.

The fuller implications of that situation must wait their rightful place in this telling of my life on Kregen.

For now Delia was indicating to me that, had we let Lela become the Amakni of Fossana, she might have been there now, when the shanks came in their swift strange craft. She might have...

I said, "We must drive them out of Fossana rapidly. I believe they seek a secure base here." I looked down on the swod and his blood-caked face. "You have done well to reach here. Your name?"

"Barlanga, my Prince. I took our patrol flier. I ran from them—I flew away—" He choked and then got it out. "My comrades were dead. I was the last. I should have—"

"No, Barlanga. You did the right thing. Now we know and may fall on these devil shanks with great force."

Then I was out of the conference chamber and yelling.

Very few burs after that the fliers took to the air, all the airboats crammed with fighting men, raging to hurl these hated shanks, these evil Leem Lovers, these fishheads, back into the sea where they belonged.

"We were slow, by Vox!" Vangar ti Valkanium, my chief of fliers, grumbled away as he gripped the rail of the high deck, peering over the head of the timoneer at the controls. Men massed forward on the main deck of the flier, armed and armored men, raging to get at the shanks. This flier was one we had acquired in the old days and so far she had failed us less often than others. Those fliers I had taken from Hamal, built for the Hamalians themselves, formed an elite squadron and they were well ahead with Tom Tomor in command.

I fretted at the delay, but I said, "We must have sure knowledge before we attack, Vangar. The onslaught on Fossana could easily be a ruse. These devil fishheads are not fools."

"You are right, Majister. I meant we were slow assembling and forming and taking to the air."

My ugly old face does not smile easily when I am not with Delia and the children. "We did well, Vangar, and you know it. Does the title of Elten then sit so heavily on you?"

"You have created me an Elten, my Prince; that is the least of my worries."

The air streamed past, whirling the banners and pennons high, blowing the bright arbora feathers in helmets into riotous color. Up there on a gilded staff my flag flew, the yellow cross on the scarlet ground, that battle flag fighting men call Old Superb. It felt good to have that war banner flying there. Ahead the sky remained clear and blue and the sea below lapped deep and calm. Ahead lay horror and battle and sudden death.

The parting with Delia had been brief, for I had kissed her and then run to don my trappings of war. She had insisted I wear armor, and not only to please her but because it was a sensible precaution I wore a breast and back. The short scarlet cape flared in the wind of our passage. The old scarlet breechclout was wrapped securely and pulled in with a broad plain lestenhide belt with a dull silver buckle. I do not, as you know, care to have straps around my chest or shoulders, and generally hang my varied collection of swords from whatever number of belts is necessary around my waist. I had a rapier and main-gauche of fine Vallian manufacture. That particular sword which Naghan the Gnat, a superb armorer, and I had made in imitation of a Krozair longsword hung scabbarded down my back under the cape. These were weapons enough, but in addition I had belted on a fine thraxter that had come into my possession after the Battle of Jholaix. As for headgear, I wore a plain steel cap with a rim of trimmed ling fur and with a rather more flaunting scarlet tuft of feathers than I would ordinarily relish. The thing had a most Tartar air about it, but Delia had insisted I wear some helmet, and the tall scarlet tufts of feathers would show my men where I was.

That made me glance at Turko, massive and muscled, where he stood with the enormous shield he would bear in action to protect me. Where Turko the Shield went, men knew, there went Dray Prescot, Prince Majister of Vallia, Strom of Valka.

As the aerial armada pressed on I had time to consider, somewhat ruefully, that Valka's own fleet of great sailing fliers could not hurtle across the wind as we were doing. I had assigned them to defense of the island. One day I must return to Havilfar and go to Hamal, that puissant Empire under its evil ruler Thyllis, who was now crowned Empress, and discover the final secrets of the silver boxes that powered, uplifted and directed the fliers.

Our fleet of airboats pressed on. Now we flew over the scattering of islands called the Nairnairsh Islands, from the huge numbers of nairnair birds that made of every rocky headland a cawing, fluttering colony of white and brown feathers. I could see a few small ships sailing, fishermen, local traders, and I looked—thankfully in vain—for a sight of the tall, wing-like banded sails of the shanks.

"Not far now, my Prince."

Balass the Hawk stood at my side, fully armored, his visor thrown up, grim and yet splendid, with his hawklike black face a great comfort to me.

The wind bluster cracked Old Superb above our heads. The suns glittered from armor and weapons. I turned and, looking ahead, said, "Not long now, Balass."

In those days I felt no admiration for the true courage of the shanks, those fishheads who sailed in their superb craft around the curve of the world, sailing from their grouping of continents and islands to sack and destroy the fair cities of our continental grouping of Paz. These shanks, these Leem Lovers, were superb seamen. Yet I knew, as an old sailor, that after their immense voyage across the open sea they would need a secure base, a good anchorage, a place to careen and refurbish their ships, a place to get their breath back after the voyage. Fossana would be such a place. They must not be allowed to make a base so close to Valka...

"We must stop them here," I said, still looking across the sea, willing the voller to fly faster and bring us to the battle quickly. "They must not be allowed a chance to fester here."

A voice spoke at my back, a voice that made me go cold from the very first syllables.

"We will fight them, Father, and we will win!"

Slowly I turned around.

Young Drak—my son—Drak—stood there in brave panoply, all scarlet and gold, staring up at me with a set and defiant expression across his face. He knew what he had done. He had no fear of the terrible shanks, but he was most uneasy about my reaction.

With him—Delia!

She smiled at me.

My heart leaped. She wore a scarlet breechclout, a breast and back, and a helmet very much like the one she had insisted I wear. She carried her rapier and main-gauche scabbarded to her slender waist, and I knew how well she could use them, the Jiktar and the Hikdar.

"Delia," I said. "You should not have allowed him."

"He is like you, Dray. A wild leem. And is this not to be his portion in life?"

"Aye."

Oby stood there also, accoutered, smiling away at me, relishing his part in the coming battle. As a young rip he had a most dubious effect on Drak. Young Oby had mended much of his wild ways when he had been my assistant in the arena; now his passion was all for vollers and the mysteries of aerial navigation, but it was clear he intended to get into the coming fight.

"And Naghan the Gnat?"

"I am here!" shouted Naghan and, in truth, there he was, loaded down with choice specimens from his own armory, smiling away like a loon. I shook my head.

"Mad, the lot of you..." I looked past Naghan. "And you, Tilly, you are here also."

"Yes, my Prince," said Tilly, her glorious golden fur glowing in the light of the Suns of Scorpio, for Tilly was a most delicious little Fristle fifi.

A mewling and harshly screeching roar told me that Melow the Supple had also come with us. I stared at Melow and the ferocious manhound stretched her neck up, then put out a fearsomely clawed hand to keep her son Kardo from beginning one of the interminable fights he was always into with Drak. Well, I welcomed Melow and Kardo, for the jiklos are terrible and ferocious, mighty in their strength. Although really human beings, they have been changed so that they run on all fours and possess the fighting ferocity of the leem.

"Melow, your son Kardo will be with Drak?"

"Yes, Dray Prescot. For that is where he wills he should be."

"And you will be with the Princess Majestrix."

Melow lolled her red tongue between those horrific jagged teeth, and I felt a little more easy. Mind you, once I had this circus home I would let them know just what my true thoughts were on this foolhardy rushing into danger. Didn't they understand the sheerly awful power of the shanks? Didn't they realize they could all be killed?

A lookout shouted from forward and I swung around to look ahead. A cloud hung in the sky athwart our passage, a cloud that must have grown with incredible swiftness, for only murs before the sky had been clear.

A dun shadow swept across the glittering sea below and in an instant we plunged into the cloud. Dank tendrils of vapor brushed us, clinging and unpleasant. Vision was reduced so that I could see only those faces near me; beyond the quarterdeck the ship vanished.

Shouts and yells arose. That cloud—how could it have formed so quickly?

The voller jerked. I knew that feeling. The flier lurched and skidded sideways. Her nose went down. We were falling.

"Those Opaz-forsaken cramphs of Hamal!" yelled Vangar, incensed that once again his duty as chief of fliers was to preside over a crash.

"Silence!" I bellowed.

In the ensuing hush we heard the wind bluster and roar as we fell. Slowly the haze cleared and we dropped free of the cloud. I looked up. The rest of our fleet was winging swiftly on, arrow-straight for Fossana. Now it would all be up to Tom Tomor, and it would be to him the responsibility would fall. I looked down. An island below showed creamy surf breaking on a beach. Massive trees crowded close, and there were at least three village clearings visible. Men were running below. Men like myself, apims, and also weird forms with grotesque fish heads, scaled and armored, running with vicious tridents flashing in the suns, weapons stained with the blood of my people.

"Shanks!"

The voller hit the sand. Ahead the wooden palisade of a village offered shelter. Everyone leaped from the stranded voller, running fleetly for the village. Heads appeared over the stockade.

A flight of arrows rose and I cursed. Then I realized the arrows curved away, falling into a body of fishheads who were trying to cut us off.

"Run!" I bellowed.

Straight for the village gate we raced. The valves were dragged open. We tumbled through the opened portal and the villagers slammed the heavy lenken logs back with a thunk. Iron bars dropped. The headman came running up, distraught, wringing his hands. Simple fisher folk these, used to landing fine fat fish in their nets, and now they faced man-sized fish-heads raging at them, armed with tridents, swords and bows, their plunder from the sea revenging itself horribly on them.

He knew me.

"Majister! Majister! Monsters—they—"

"Man the walls! Keep your heads down!" I shook his shoulder. "It will be all right, Koter, all right."

"Yes, Majister, yes—but the fishheads—"

We could hold this place until my fliers returned. We must hold this place! Nothing else would do. Nothing.

The Leem Lovers were in force, roaring in to attack, hurling spears and tridents, shooting arrows. My men replied with the cool precise shooting Seg Segutorio had drilled into them. These men were Valkan Archers, but they used the great Lohvian longbow and they could outshoot the com-pound reflex bows of the shanks. Spare supplies of shafts had been brought from the flier, for Jiktar Orlon Llodar in command of the regiment was an officer in whom I reposed confidence. He did not have his full regiment with him, for half had been embarked on another flier, packed in like fish in a barrel. With three pastangs of sixty men each we must hold off an unknown number of fishheads.

I leaped up onto the parapet around the stockade. The village pos-sessed a stockade because these islands were often the scene of raids from Pandahem, or from a dissident nation of Segesthes beyond Zenicce, or, in the old days, from the slavers and aragorn. Along the beach the voller lay stranded, and shanks were already clambering and running there. I cursed. From the trees other shanks were running. The devils must have beached their ships and marched overland. There had not been a sign of a shank ship as we crash-landed.

A circuit of the stockade brought me back to the parapet over the main gate. This faced along the beach, as I have said, and not out to sea or inland. Defensive considerations dictated that choice. A small protected harbor held a few fishing boats, little better than dories. The circuit of the walls had shown me we could hold. A stream trickled down from the forest so we would have water, if the Leem Lovers did not divert or dam the stream.

"Now, Jiktar," I said brusquely to Orion Llodar. "Now is the chance to show that the Second Regiment of Valkan Archers can do better than the First."

Before Llodar could answer, young Drak, who had followed me around most carefully, sniffed. "I would like very much to see that," he said. I glared at him. As you know, Drak is the Hyr-Jiktar—colonel in chief—of the First Regiment of Valkan Archers. Lela was Hyr-Jiktar of the Second.

Orion Llodar smacked his buff-sleeved arm across his breastplate. He wore a bob there. "We shall, my Prince, and with due respect to Prince Drak, outshoot the finest the First could offer this day."

"I believe you. These yetches of fishheads will try to fool us. They will feint an attack on one flank and then drive in on another. All faces of the stockade must be kept under observation at all times. Have a party of swordsmen handy to rush to the threatened wall. And watch out for their Opaz-forsaken tridents. They are vicious."

"My Prince!" he bellowed, in the old soldierly way.

Barbaric and savage are my warriors of Valka and they love little better than a rousing fight, but we had been knocking drill and discipline into them. They would have full need of all their courage and skill now.

But we could hold. With determined and skillful leadership we could defy the Leem Lovers. I was determined enough, Zair knows, and as to skill… well, this bore the appearance of a militarily simple defense of the fortified place. If they tried to burn us out… I bellowed for the headman, one Remush the Trident, for he was a noted fisherman, and got him to organize fire fighting parties of his people with all the buckets and containers they could find. This was the village of Panashti on the island of Lower Kairfowen. I fancied these names would be remembered henceforth, filling men's mouths.

"I wish, my Prince, that my pastangs were at full strength." Jiktar Llodar stared with venom at the shanks as they massed at the forest edge.

"All the more glory, Jiktar, for those who are here."

That was cheap enough, Zair knows, but it fitted the occasion.

The gate looked sturdy in construction, with square towers and a walkway across the gap. "Here, Planath," I said, pointing. "Raise the standard here."

Planath Pe-Na, my standard-bearer, was a Pachak and a man of exceptional virtues. He rammed the standard pole into a crevice in the wood and then lashed it upright. Dead or alive, Planath would stay by the standard. I turned to Kodar ti Vakkansmot, the chief of my corps of trumpeters. "Give a few good bracing calls, Kodar. Rouse the blood in 'em!"

"Aye, Majister."

The lilting peals of the trumpet sounded over the small stockaded village of Panashti on the island of Lower Kairfowen. I fancied the men would brace up at the sound, grip their weapons more firmly, glare the more murderously at their antagonists.

The blueness stole in quietly. It muffled the bright, brilliant sounds of the trumpet. It wrapped its baleful coils around me. I saw the blue radiance churning everywhere. The world was slipping away, I was falling, the whole world turning into the semblance of a giant Scorpion, come from the Star Lords to carry me far and far away.

Three
I defy the Star Lords

I, Dray Prescot, of Earth and of Kregen, knew what was happening to me.

This obscenity had taken me before, many times, snatched me away from pleasant home life with those I loved and hurled me into fresh adventures in Kregen under Antares. Even more balefully still, it had thrust me contemptuously back to the world of my birth four hundred light-years off through the depths of interstellar space.

"No!" I shouted.

I was falling, in actuality. For the blueness lifted, the radiance dwindled a little and I felt myself falling and in the next instant the ground smashed up iron hard. I was winded. I tried to yell again, to shout my defiance of the Star Lords and their commands.

I heard voices—Delia's voice, Drak's, others—shouting; through the misty blueness I saw forms above me; hands grasped my arms and legs and I was carried, swaying and swinging above the packed earth. A shadow blotted my sight of the forms dimly visible through the blue mist. I thought I must have been carried into one of the huts. The blueness grew again. "No! I will not leave! It is unthinkable!"

The blueness twirled about me, the Scorpion shape grew and grew and then, in very final truth, I was falling.

I was encompassed in a floating blueness. Everything turned blue, roaring and twisting in my skull.

"I will stay on Kregen!" I screamed it out, and I knew with a feeling close to despair that my scream gushed voicelessly from my mouth. I tried again. "I will not leave! More! I will not leave *here!*"

The sensations of falling persisted now with dread finality. The blueness coiled in my eyes and head; I could not speak, could scarcely breathe; a weight oppressed my chest. All manner of thoughts flitted like black bats through my mind. I felt the ground again, dust and heat, and the abrupt hammer of conflict bursting painfully through into my skull.

All the sensations I had come to expect of a transition smashed at me. I was naked. I lay in the dust. And nearby a battle took place.

The Star Lords had contemptuously ignored my feeble yells of defiance. They had not banished me to Earth, for as I opened my eyes the glorious mingled lights of Antares fell about me, but I was no longer within the stockaded village of Panashti. I was no longer near Delia and Drak and all my other friends there.

On occasions before I had attempted to defy the Everoinye and instead of being banished to Earth had been dumped down, naked and unarmed, on some unknown spot on Kregen, there to sort out a problem for the Star Lords. Always before I had obeyed. I knew that the quickest way to rid myself of the immediate obligation to the Star Lords was to obey their injunctions and to settle the problem at hand. Then, always, before, I had been able to go about my own business.

This time was different.

I sat up on the dusty ground and saw a sickeningly familiar sight.

A mass of crazed Relts ran and fell and were slaughtered as the shanks pursued them. I sat under the shadow of a voller parked beside two other vollers at the edge of a gulley in the dusty ground. I would have to stand up, all naked as I was, and run forward, into the fight, possess myself of a weapon and so defend these people against the Leem Lovers. This I could do. This was the way of it, the way of my life on Kregen. I was expected to take up arms at once and rush in to save the life of the one person—perhaps two, if a mother and child were involved—in that melee whom the Star Lords wished preserved.

What they were planning with the people whose lives I thus perpetuated I did not then know.

I didn't care, didn't give a damn.

This time I was Prince Majister. This time my wife and child were penned in a tiny rickety wooden village under savage attack from monsters from around the curve of the world.

Against the skyline beyond the struggle I saw twin peaks, forested, shaped like sugar loaves. They bulked there against the blue. I knew them. I knew where I was. This was the island of Vilasca. Vilasca, barely twenty dwaburs from the Nairnairsh Islands, and south of them the island of Lower Kairfowen. And, on that island, the village of Panashti!

I leaped up.

Barely twenty dwaburs. A mere hundred miles! A fleet voller might take less than two burs—much less—to cover that distance—a little over an hour. There are forty Earth minutes to a bur. If the flier was speedy…

Over there across the dusty earth where the Leem Lovers had swarmed ashore to catch these people all unprepared, a vicious and bloody struggle raged. This island of Vilasca did not owe allegiance to me; I was not its Strom or Kov or any other noble. I felt desperately sorry for those people, but there was no question, no hesitation in my mind. My duty lay elsewhere.

The voller controls felt warm under my hands. I thrust the levers hard over. Again I forced the speed lever all the way across, hard against the stop. The voller leaped into the air, screaming away, curving to the east and south. Twenty dwaburs to go...

As I shot over the beach and left that struggle I looked down.

What I saw shocked a fresh and awful knowledge into my brain. I saw the fighting down there, the wicked shapes of Leem Lovers as they went about their business of slaughtering the people of Vilasca. Among those shanks I saw the hideous forms of shtarkins. No one then knew the name these fishheads gave themselves; we called them by a variety of names of which shant, shank and shtarkin were only three. But the ones I called shtarkins were not fishheads. As I looked down I saw the reptilian heads, the snakelike features, the hard, unfishlike scales closely set, the wide eyes and the trap-mouths set flatly in wedge-shaped heads, a flicker of forked tongue darting through as they fought. Snakeheads!

The voller bore me up and away and I left those fearsome fighting shtarkins to slaughter the good people of Vilasca.

The shtarkins employed the tall asymmetric bow instead of the short compound reflex bow. I had no real knowledge of the asymmetric bow, but the thing shot an arrow fully as long as a great Lohvian longbow and was reputed accurate to prodigious ranges. Seg would have had his keen professional instincts immediately aroused. The arrows, cloth yard shafts, were tipped with long serrated heads. I saw one burst clean through a running woman, and as she fell my hands twisted the levers to bring me down.

But a vision arose, a vision of another woman falling beneath the arrows of the Leem Lovers. And that woman was Delia. With agony, with remorse, but decisively and with bitter determination, I smashed the levers back and shot the voller up and away.

I had selected this airboat as the fastest of the three, and my faith in my own judgment was proved as I cleaved the air, heading east and south. Somewhere far over the northwestern horizon lay the main island of Vallia, that great and puissant Empire of Vallia of which Delia's father, my children's grandfather, was Emperor. They would have to buckle to, now that they were thus cruelly beset.

As for the Star Lords—I would see them abandoned to the Ice Floes of Sicce before I would abandon Delia and Drak!

So I shot on. Looking back, I suppose the Star Lords, having always seen me operate in obedience to their commands before, held their hand. Once before I had taken a flier and left the scene of my labors to raise an army. That had been in Migladrin, when Turko and I had flown back to Valka to bring those fighting men of mine who had won the Battle of the Crimson Missals. But then I had not left a scene where immediate action had been necessary. Always before, when I had been hurled all naked into a strange part of Kregen, I had jumped up and obediently gone into action to save the lives of those the Star Lords wished preserved.

This time I had turned my back.

A bur ticked by, then a quarter of a bur.

Below me the sea clumped with the Nairnairsh Islands.

Not long to go now! My men must resist. They must hold out until I was once more back among them to lead them to victory.

So puffed up with pride are the princes of the two worlds.

A shadow fleeted across me. I looked up. The scarlet and gold messenger of the Star Lords swung up there, circling lazily, riding the air currents. He was watching me, I did not shake my fist. I ignored him.

Frail hope!

He stooped, swooping down on the voller. He screeched.

"What is this thing you do, Dray Prescot?"

I said nothing.

"Onker! You destroy yourself!"

I flared back at him. "You great nurdling onker! Do you think I can leave my wife and my child in mortal danger for you?"

"Yes."

I hurled abuse at him, shaking my fist, screaming. The voller surged on. And there, below me the village of Panashti!

I slanted the voller down headlong through the air.

The shanks had put in an attack, for bodies sprawled before the stockade. Activity in the forest edge indicated a fresh attack at any moment. I had to be there, leading my men, fighting to protect my Delia and my son!

Even as the Gdoinye swooped in fast, I saw the scaled and fishy forms leaping forward with a shower of arrows to cover them. And, among the arrows, there blazed forth fire-arrows. Pots of fire were being hurled. Wisps of smoke lifted from the huts as the fire-arrows struck, as the pots of fire burst. Men and women ran with their water buckets to douse the flames.

Almost there! I was yelling and shouting and beating my fist against the speed lever. I scarcely heard the Gdoinye.

"Onker, Dray Prescot! This is not for you! This is not the way of the Everoinye!"

"Get away, rast!" I bellowed. "I am needed below!"

Part of the stockade was burning. The shanks were making a determined attack there. They were running with ladders made from cut branches. I saw men struggling, the flash and wink of steel. Faintly through the wind's rush I could hear the bestial screams and shrieks. My fist beat the lever, I shouted and the Gdoinye swerved in and alighted on the very gunwale of the voller. I had never seen him so close before. He was truly magnificent, full of throat where the golden feathers encircled him, his scarlet feathers ruffling in the slipstream. His predatory black talons fastened on the wood and canvas of the voller. His black eyes, lit with inhuman intelligence, regarded me implacably.

"You are to be given another chance! Dray Prescot, get-onker! You are to serve the Star Lords. They grant you a boon, a boon never granted to you before."

"Keep your boons, nulsh!"

The burning corner of the stockade was down. The shanks were smashing in with axes. Men were running. My Valkan Archers were running up to reinforce this threatened corner. The swordsmen were already in violent combat inside the palisade. More and more fishheads were clambering over the ruin of the walls. I screamed in baffled fury and swung the voller to alight directly on their heads. I would smash down from the sky clean on top of them. That should give my men a chance to rally.

The moment was coming. I measured the drop and checked the speed of the flier.

In a knot of struggling men I saw the glittering armored figure of Balass the Hawk, striking fishheads down. Turko the Shield appeared from a hut, struggling—struggling with Delia! She was trying to run after Drak—and Drak was racing headlong to hurl himself into the fray!

I shrieked—I, Dray Prescot, Lord of Strombor and Krozair Of Zy—I shrieked like an insane man.

Melow the Supple and her son Kardo appeared, raging, striking down fishheads with the awful venom of the manhound. Their jagged teeth ran green with the spilled blood of the Leem Lovers. All the others were there, battling desperately to protect Delia. The voller slowed, for if I smashed headlong into the shanks I'd as likely kill myself as well as them. Any minute now. I perched up on the gunwale just abaft the windscreen, ready to leap into the fray.

Turko still held Delia and his great shield deflected two arrows that caromed away, spinning.

"Remember the great gift the Star Lords bestow on you, Dray Prescot, you onker!"

And then the scarlet and gold bird shifted and changed and flowed and the blueness of the Scorpion enfolded me.

Falling... Falling... Dropping down and down...

I felt the dusty earth at my back. I heard the shrieks and cries of battle and I knew that this battle was not the one into which I wished to plunge but that other, strange, uninteresting, unwanted battle on the island of Vilasca.

I sprang up.

Then, instantly, I realized this great gift of the Star Lords.

For the very first time on Kregen I had been transported and had not arrived naked. I wore all my battle gear, the trappings in which I had flown off to fight the shanks.

"I curse you, Star Lords! This small thing is no great gift to me! I defy you! *I defy you!*"

44

Without a thought, without a prayer, I sprang into the second voller. She went up at full lever, and I did not even bother to look back.

Again I set her toward the east and south and this time I did pray, pray that I could arrive in time to see my Delia and Drak alive, to hold my dear Delia in my arms once more.

A ripping sound brought me around, the rapier instantly in my fist. The long barbed serrated head of an arrow thrust up through the floor of the voller. I cursed the thing and thrust the rapier back.

Bending to pick up the arrow, dragging it through, I thought to assuage the pangs of agony tearing at my mind by learning what I might of the shtarkins.

The hateful voice croaked by my ear as I straightened up.

"The Star Lords are most wroth. You have sinned mightily."

The Gdoinye perched on the rim of the voller. His feathers glittered in the light of the suns, glittering golden and scarlet in that streaming opaline radiance.

I said nothing. I whipped the longsword from my back, hefted it in that cunning Krozair grip, swung it full-force horizontally.

Had the Gdoinye been a mortal bird he would have been sheared in two.

He skipped lightly away and the great blade hissed through thin air.

"You have made a mistake, Dray Prescot, and now you must pay. No man defies the Everoinye!"

"I do! I, Dray Prescot, onker of onkers, defy any man who seeks to destroy my Delia!"

"Then are you a doomed man!"

The Gdoinye vanished. The blueness swelled. The enormous form of the Scorpion swooped upon me, radiant blueness washed all around me, washed me away, washed my senses away so that as I fell I fell soundlessly and hopelessly, for the very last words of that inhuman bird were: "Back to Earth, Dray Prescot, get-onker of onkers, back to Earth—to *stay!*"

Four
Soldiering, science and secrets

Back to Earth—to stay!

What a fool! What a fool!

Yet I could not have done other than I had.

I should have helped those poor devils of Vilasca. The island owed allegiance to Trylon Werfed, a man I knew only moderately well, a man against whom I had heard no whispers of plots against the Emperor. I should have jumped in and helped them beat off those damned Leem Lovers and then I could have taken voller for Delia.

But I am me, Dray Prescot, as thick-skulled a man as ever lived on two worlds. As I made my way back to civilization I reflected that I could not have done other than I had, and to pretend otherwise was folly. Dangerous folly. I admitted that I must have grown mighty proud and aloof in all these ridiculous titles and ranks I had amassed through no fault of my own. Well, leave out that I had deliberately made myself King of Djanduin. That is true. But the reasons for that decision were rooted in Khokkak the Meddler at first, and then in a sober understanding of a duty laid upon me. No, I had grown fat and comfortable and supine, and now I must pay the price of arrogance and pride.

But to stay on Earth—to stay!

I reflected on that. The Star Lords had dumped me down all naked and miserable in Morocco, which was in a fine old state of unrest. The locals were standing up for their rights, and the French from Algeria, which they had taken in the 1830's, were trying to take over there. By virtue of my tutor Maspero and the genetically coded language pill he had given me in Aphrasöe, the Swinging City, I could understand and speak the languages of people with whom I came into contact. The Moors—although that is hardly the correct term for the Sharifs, for the Moors were a light-skinned people—would no doubt have cut up a European dumped among them naked and defenseless. But I was enraged, and I used fury as a weapon to drown my maniacal despondency. I simply treated them as I would a people among whom I found myself on Kregen.

It has to be said that if a man can survive on Kregen he can find survival much easier on this Earth. I exclude from that the refined life of cities which in its artificiality can destroy more surely than sword thrust or ax bite.

With language no barrier it was easier, of course. Even as I talked with these dark-bearded, hawk-faced warriors of the desert, after I had shown them I was not a man to be lightly killed, I could still hear the hissing shrills of the shanks as they swarmed to the attack. "Ishtish! Ishtish!" they shrieked as they charged forward. And as my men shot them down or struggled hand-to-hand with them, so my archers shouted: "Vallia! Vallia!" Or: "Valka! Valka! Prince Dray!"

Well, I was a prince no longer. I was a foolish European among the Arabs and I had to fend for myself. I made my way to Fez and from there to the sea where I took passage for Marseilles. Once there I arranged with London for funds. I do not reveal the name of the bankers who looked after me. I had saved the founder of the bank from a nasty experience on the field of Waterloo; now his sons merely took me for my own son. But they were a closed-mouth lot. I do not think a great deal can discompose a tight-fisted, crafty, elegant banker of the City of London.

46

Through canny investment by these same people I was now a wealthy man. Of course, it meant nothing.

Every day those dread words echoed in my obstinate skull: "Stay on Earth—*stay!*"

I had to take it for granted that Delia and Drak and the others were safe, that they had repelled the attack from the village, and that Tom had come sweeping back to look for his prince and so brought my fighting men down in their regiments to save the day. I had to assume that. Any other course would leave me more of a madman than I already was.

The bankers, cool, assured men though they were, looked at me askance as I did business with them. I took myself off to become a solitary. A year passed, then another. Despair clawed at me. But I did not know how long that damned bird meant by his infernal "Stay!" It could be forever.

One foggy day as I stared out from my narrow leaded windows at the hurrying people passing in the London street, the carriages burning their lamps in spectral glimmers, each a little circular glow isolated from the others, with the moisture hanging on the trees and the railings, I made up my mind. One day, I said to myself, one day I would return to Kregen. I would take up the broken threads of my life. Why, then wouldn't it be a fine thing to learn all I could, here on this Earth, against the time of my return to all that I held dear? I needed a purpose in life, here on Earth. I would make that purpose a conscious effort to learn all I could. I would return a master of statecraft, of science, of engineering, of war. I would seek the answers to the questions on Kregen that had plagued me, and I would seek what I could here.

Foolish, pathetic, ludicrous even. Oh, yes, all of those. But it gave me back a semblance of sanity, for by studying I assured myself that I did have a future on Kregen to which to return one day.

So rousing myself from my lethargy, I left London. On Magdalen Bridge in Oxford I stood and gazed up at the stars.

That upflung tail of the Scorpion was barely visible, but even if it was not, I could visualize it clearly. The red star that was Antares, the huge red star and the smaller green companion—I imagined I could see the constellation of Scorpio, and I would stand gazing up into the star-speckled night. I know the look on my face must have been one of infinite longing and infinite regret.

I am sure you can see that the idea of secrets on Kregen plaguing me was a fallacy, for I had long since felt that my life with Delia and my family far outweighed anything else on Kregen. But to bolster my resolve and to give a neat scientific and logical approach, I set down in tabular form the questions to which I would like answers.

The very first name was, of course, the Everoinye, the Star Lords.

Next the Savanti, those mortal but superhuman people of Aphrasöe.

Then the Todalpheme, the meteorologists and tide-watchers.

Then followed a list of various strange peoples, of whom I have introduced you so far to only a fraction. These included the volroks, the flying men of Havilfar.

Then the Wizards of Loh.

The secrets of the silver boxes of the fliers, of course, had to figure, for we in Valka were still only able to produce flying craft which could merely lift and must find their propulsion from the breeze like sailing ships.

As to unfinished business, well, there was indeed a formidable list of that, as you who have listened to these tapes must be aware.

Various religious cults were written down, and chief of these was the abominable practice of Lem the Silver Leem.

If I fail to mention anything in connection with the inner sea of the continent of Turismond, the Eye of the World, it was because I ached for that locale and for the Krozairs of Zy.

All the titles I had won on Kregen could be stripped from me and I would not care a jot. But I was a Krozair Brother, a Krozair of Zy, and that did mean something.

How often I had planned to revisit Zy, that magnificent island fortress of the Brotherhood, or Sanurkazz, the chief city of the Zairians of the red southern shore of the Eye of the World. Well, something or other had always cropped up to prevent me. Now, back on Earth, that something had turned out to be the biggest obstacle of all.

The list did not satisfy me. Nothing satisfied me. Oxford at this time appeared to me to be an intellectual desert, its ancient halls given over to mindless pursuits after false doctrines. The studies pursued here seemed to me to offer no help or guidance to the things a man needed to know in the real world, for all its products strutted the preeminent stages of this world here on Earth. Through my accrued wealth and the machinations of powerful friends on my bankers, doors were opened to me that would, had I remained simply Dray Prescot, lieutenant in the Royal Navy, have remained firmly closed in my face. I tried Cambridge with a similar result. The best hope of education in these times lay with the Dissenting Academies, although my knowledge of the Greek Heroes was furbished up, for although, as I have said, I have always considered Achilles to be a poor show beside Hector, the sheer rage and panache and barbarity and honor of those times bears some pale reflection of times on Kregen that go on to this present hour.

The Star Lords had dumped me down on Earth after what has since come to be called the Year of Revolutions. For a time I was too nearly a madman to bother with the world and its doings. There had been a king come and gone on the throne of England and now we had a queen. I knew about queens. The one at this time, though, bore no possible connection with any of the queens I had known, and I thought longingly of the fabled Queens of Pain of Loh. Queen Lilah, Queen Fahia and Queen Thyllis, she who was now the Empress Thyllis. By Vox! What a spectacular collection they were, and all up there on Kregen waiting, waiting...

As for the kings, because of my connection with the July days in Paris in 1830 and the dismissal of Charles X and the installation of Louis Phillipe, I sought as a change from universities and academies, and as an anodyne to my agony, some light action, as Prince Louis Napoleon, President of the French Republic for three years, overturned that Republic and obtained election as President for ten years. I did not then think that I would still be on Earth when his term came up for renewal; I saw him made Emperor, Napoleon III, and I cursed the day I still remained on Earth.

The attempt of Russia to dismember the Sick Man of Europe and the involvement of France and England are well known. As they affected me, however, I let events take their course. The Crimean War, it seemed to me, a fighting man, might give me fresh opportunities to bash a few skulls and so in my sinful way find a trifle of surcease from the despair and anguish consuming me.

My part led me to action earlier than the Light Brigade on that fateful day of October 25. As a participant in the Heavy Brigade charge I believe we did a more thorough job than the more highly publicized Charge of the Lights. Three hundred British heavy cavalrymen charging uphill against three thousand Russian cavalrymen. It sounds as maniacal as events on Kregen. The Grays were in the thick of it. General Scarlett's second line came on, piecemeal, driving through and through the thick gray ranks. The Russians, incredible though it sounds, had enough and broke and scattered and fled.

The Light Brigade fiasco—however glorious—followed later. I fancied that even on Kregen soldiers would look askance at generals who had last fought forty years ago, or who had never fought, or who were often so old and doddery, without any clear understanding of what they were about, that they were as much a menace to their own men as to the enemy.

After that came the Indian Mutiny and I went to take a part. I have said that I do not intend to dwell on those portions of my life spent on this Earth. But on this occasion the years ticked by and I grew ever more morose and savage, bitter with the bitterness that eats the spirit, and it is right that you who listen to my story should understand.

My studies progressed by fits and starts. The marvels of steam and engineering and iron ships and the industrial changes that shook and transformed England were absorbed. I followed closely all the developments of science and philosophy and the arts of war I could. Agriculture also repaid study. But through all this I was aware that I was like a man asleep, merely walking through a part on a dimly lit stage.

As for the war in America—the American Civil War or the War between the States—I was there. I shall not say now what side I fought on, although that may appear more obvious than it truly was, and I did not enjoy it. By the end of May on that last dreadful year of war I was sailing back to England. A gentleman I had met and talked with in odd circumstances, a gentleman from Virginia, struck me as a man who would go to far places and, perhaps, hunger for a life akin to mine on Kregen. I wished him well as we parted.

Whenever the opportunity had offered I had made fresh inquiries about Alex Hunter. He had been a Savapim, an agent of the Savanti, recruited from Earth. I had seen him die on a beach in Valka and had buried him and said two prayers over his grave. As a shavetail in the old U.S. Army he had been subject to influences I fancied I could duplicate during my period in the U.S., but the armies of the war were very different from the armies both before and after. There was nothing, I thought, to be gained from the trail of Alex Hunter.

The idea that the Savanti—who labored to bring dignity to Kregen, they had told me—recruited people from this Earth to work for them led me on to a consideration that perhaps they maintained agents here. I had seen the Savapim Wolfgang fight to protect apims against diffs in the *Scented Sylvie*, a notorious drinking den of the Sacred Quarter of Ruathytu, the capital of Hamal, the Empire on the continent of Havilfar, which is on Kregen, Kregen! I do not think a single day of my life on Earth passed without a longing thought of Kregen under Antares. No, I am wrong. I do not think—I *know*.

In working out a scheme whereby I might put myself in contact with a terrestrial agent of the Savanti I had to discount the Everoinye completely from the calculations. The idea began to obsess me. Where hitherto, after that first destructive fit of lethargy, I had flung myself into violent action to blot cruel thoughts from my brain, I now positively dwelt on all I knew of Kregen as it affected the Savanti, the mortal but non-human people of Aphrasöe.

If newspaper advertisements would help I would deluge the daily sheets with advertisements. This was the time I became involved with some of the more dubious aspects of Victorian science.

As a trapped rat will turn and struggle against whatever opposes it so I struggled against invisible bonds. In the process I ran across weird people, ordinary human beings, and yet people possessed of some quirk of nature that led them to gather to themselves superior powers. Most of the time they were mere quacks, charlatans, impostors. Of Doctor Quinney, I had my doubts.

A thin, snuffly individual, blessed with a quantity of lank brown hair—hair that grew, it seemed, from every part of his face except his eyes—Doctor Quinney dressed in shiny black clothes, much worn, and a stovepipe hat elegantly blocked out after whoever it was had sat on it. His snuff blew everywhere. His eyes watered and gleamed with fanaticism; he claimed to know the Secrets of the Spheres.

"And I assure you, my dear sir"—his steel-rimmed pince-nez flashed in time to the pendulum motion of his head, the dramatic gestures of his gleaming-knuckled hands—"inthe Spheres like mystic gossamer balls lie the ultimate Secrets!"

I had taken chambers in a quiet London side street and the landlady, Mrs. Benton, was slowly growing accustomed to the procession of odd characters daily pulling the doorbell. As for my own clothes, they were unremarkable, simple English town clothes of sober cut and style. Doctor Quinney regarded me as a man who, also anxious to unravel the Secrets of the Spheres, happened most fortunately to be blessed with the wherewithal to satisfy that craving.

I tolerated him for what he might bring me, rather as a ponsho might be staked out for a leem.

"Listen to me, Doctor Quinney, and mark me well. I expect results from you. It might go very ill for you else." He started back and dropped his handkerchief. I know that he had seen in my face that awful mad glare marking a clansman of Segesthes, marking me, Dray Prescot, the Lord of Strombor.

Five
Madam Ivanovna

Now began a different period of my life on Earth. More and more I mixed with the learned men, the savants, the scientists and chemists, the philosophers and engineers. To speak the truth, many of the new discoveries daily amazing this Victorian world had been spoken of in Aphrasöe. Because of this I was able to hold my own in argument and debate.

When Charles Darwin and Alfred Wallace read their paper before the Linnean Society, I had been in India charging about with a saber and uselessly trying either to blot out all thought of Kregen or to imagine myself there as we battled. Many of the ideas expressed in *The Origin of Species by Means of Natural Selection*, Darwin's book that appeared in the November of the following year, made me realize that people on Earth were capable of great things, despite their flaws, and that Aphrasöe was a place of logical human development.

One day, it seems to me, our selfish brawling Earth may turn into the paradise I still—despite all!—believe the Swinging City to be. As you must be aware, since I speak to you in the seventies of the twentieth century and much has transpired over the past one hundred years on Kregen, I know much more now than I knew then. At the time of which I speak, though, I knew practically nothing. Nothing. The Savanti had their purposes, and I had surmised these were for the good of Kregen and for the dignity of humanity. As to the purposes of the Star Lords, I held hazy ideas, nebulous theories, but all was embittered by their 'treatment of me and my resentment against them for their aloof high-handedness.

When the Savapim who called himself Wolfgang had talked in Ruathytu of the problem of evolution changing the many different races set down on Kregen I had been able to talk with him and understand. Now Darwin, of Earth, was opening terrestrial eyes to this mutable genetic structure.

My advertisements in search of a Savapim, an agent of the Savanti, here on Earth, proved fruitless.

Doctor Quinney, filled with an excitable eagerness and blowing snuff everywhere, told me he had found a "wonderful and incredible new source of psychic powers."

Arrangements were made. I canceled a trip planned to take me to Vienna, for I found I had grown inordinately fond of the music of Johann Strauss, and thus thankfully missed the Seven Weeks War in which Prussia dealt with Austria and set herself on the course of German unification. There was another new emperor on Earth now, Kaiser Wilhelm I. The agonizing thought that my son was the grandson of an emperor, you may readily conceive, touched me with renewed longing. Every day, every single day, I longed for my Delia and for Kregen.

Before this meeting with the "new source of psychic powers" discovered by Doctor Quinney, I finally parted with Victorian scientists over many questions. They were working on the right lines, in many cases, for what they required. I had worked with chemists in stinking laboratories attempting to duplicate the gas used in the paol silver box, and had got nowhere. As to the minerals in the vaol box, simple nomenclature defeated even the first stumbling attempts. I made mental notes on rare earths and scarce minerals, trace elements as known at that time—a time of great expansion and, equally, a time of ludicrous conservatism among the ignorant—and came to the conclusion that Earth science held no help at all. I went ballooning and enjoyed it enormously, but a Kregen voller was out of any balloon's league. And, into the bargain, my own experience as a sailor meant I already knew enough to sail my driveless fliers by means of the wind alone, as I have told you.

The date of the meeting was set. Doctor Quinney, canny old Quinney, kept his new protégé secret. I could not blame him, for I knew of the intense professional jealousy animating the people of the mystic circles and their adherents. And then, out of nowhere, came a situation which presented me with a problem I felt a sense of humanity compelled me to solve.

In our little group, among a Grub Street scribbler, a civil servant connected with the sewers, I believe, and a prosperous leather merchant who had recently lost his wife, a certain lordling attended our meetings. This young lord—I do not give his name—seemed to me a revolting example of that chinless pop-eyed, insufferable scion of an ancient noble family gone to seed. He owed his title to the dubious bedtime antics of an ancestor who had been rewarded for her exertions by being created a countess, in the name of her complaisant husband, the first earl. The young lord possessed wealth, a vicious temper and a good eye with a gun. I spoke only the necessary civil words to him. For his part, it was quite clear that plain Mr. Prescot was mere dirt beneath his feet, like all the others who did not overshadow him in nobility. Without breeding, without a lineage, a man could never enter his world. I did not wish to. There were far more important things to be accomplished than spending idle days, vapidly admiring oneself among cronies, a parasite upon the nation.

One day my landlady's daughter, young Mary Benton, wore a red and tear-swollen face as she tidied my chambers. I chided her and soon the whole story came out. It was sickeningly familiar. As I looked at Mary, a sweet, innocent creature who worked hard from crack of dawn until well into the night, and heard her broken words, her shame, and contrasted her life with the elegant, luxurious, feckless life of this lord and his cronies, I fancied I might assist her. Money, of course, was immediately forthcoming.

Probably I would have left it at that. Mrs. Benton was grateful; I shushed her and Mary was packed off to reappear subsequently with a new sister or brother, niece or nephew. I would have done what I could and left it, but this young lord could not leave well alone. On a night before the meeting that, however much I considered Doctor Quinney to be a fraud, yet excited me with its possibilities, the young lord was boasting and laughing, elegantly waving his hand, his blue pop-eyes very bright, his pink tongue tip licking the spittle on his lips.

My chambers were filled with Victorian shadows, the oil lamps casting their separated pools of light, the old furniture highly polished to mirror-gleams, the smell of cigar smoke and distant cooking in the air; through the curtained windows the clip-clop of passing horses and the grind of iron-rimmed wheels reminded me I was in London and not in Valkanium.

The hot words were spoken, words that might have been: "Damned impertinence! D'you forget who I am?" And: "I know what you are, and no gentleman would tolerate your presence." And: I'll horsewhip you, you guttersnipe!" And: "You are perfectly at liberty to try." And the blows and the bleeding nose and the challenge, the hostility, brittle and bitter, and the hushed-up scandal.

It would have to be in Boulogne.

"I shall meet you at the place and time you choose."

"My seconds will call."

Well, as I recall it all went as the copybook said it should.

The sobering aspect of this struck me as we waited for Doctor Quinney. Something had happened to stir the sluggish blood. I didn't give a damn if this puppy spitted me or shot me through the heart. I'd do it for him, if I could. He had brought his own downfall on his head, through his folly and his damned superior ways and his unthinking selfishness. Had he eyes in his head he could read—and see!—information on the state of the poor. There was no excuse for the rich to plead ignorance. Pure selfishness, allied to a grotesque assumption of superiority led the people of his class to act the way they did. I looked forward to Boulogne with grim and unpleasant relish, Zair forgive me. For wasn't I, Dray Prescot, acting in just such a selfish way?

Well, for those of you who have followed my story so far, perhaps you will understand what I only vaguely grasped of my character.

Of all the incidents of my stay on Earth, that evening in the oil lamps' glow, with the sounds of London muted through the windows and the circle sitting around the polished mahogany table, remains most vividly with me. Doctor Quinney arrived, his snuffbox under firm control, ushering in a tall cloaked figure. When the cloak's hood was thrown back everyone in the room sat up. We all felt the magnetic presence, the consciousness of power allied with understanding, the sheer authority of this lady.

"Madam Ivanovna!" cried Quinney, his voice near to cracking with pride and emotion.

The woman seated herself after a slight inclination of her head that embraced the company and seemed to take us all into her confidence. I saw a mass of gleaming dark hair and a face, white and unlined, of a purity of outline quite remarkable. Her eyes were brown, large, finely set, dominating. Her mouth puzzled me, being firm and yet softly full, suggesting a complex character. She wore long loose garments of somber black. This was quite usual, yet she wore the garments in a way suggesting mystery and excitement and great peril—quite alarming and yet amusing, charming, and I sat forward, ready to take part in the evening's charade.

As I moved I observed that Quinney still stood there, an idiotic grin on his face, his hand outstretched. The others of the circle sat perfectly still. Sounds stretched and became muted. The ticking of the ormolu clock sounded like lead weights dropped slowly into a bottomless pool. I stared at Madam Ivanovna, feeling the tensions, the excitements, feeling that, perhaps, my staked ponsho had brought a leem...

"Mr. Prescot," said this enigmatic Madam Ivanovna. "You will disregard the people here, even Doctor Quinney. You have been causing trouble and I am here because it seems meet to us that you should work again."

I remained mute. There was no doubt about it. The other people in the room remained silent, static, unmoving—*frozen.*

"Mr. Prescot, you do not appear surprised."

I had to speak. "I have been trying—"

"You have been successful."

I swallowed. Now that it had happened I could not believe it. I licked my lips. "Perhaps, then, I should not say, 'Good evening' to you, Madam Ivanovna. "Perhaps I should say 'Happy Swinging.'"

"You may say 'Happy Swinging' and you may say 'Lahal.' Neither would be correct."

Through the roar of blood in my head—for she had said "Lahal," which is the Kregish form for greeting new acquaintances—I wondered what on Kregen she could mean by saying neither would be correct.

"You are from the Savanti?"

"No."

"The Everoinye?"

"No."

If this was madness, a phantom conjured from my own sick longings, then I would press on. I recall every minute, every second, as we two sat and talked in a Victorian room stuffed with mummified people who saw and heard nothing.

"You know me, Madam Ivanovna. You know who I am. Why have you sought me out?"

"First, I use the name Ivanovna because it is exotic, foreign. It will soon be fashionable to have a Russian name in psychic matters. It helps belief when you found a society. But you may know my use-name. It is Zena Iztar."

I knew about use-names. My comrade Inch from Ng'groga was called Inch; his real name was different, secret, something, I then thought, he would share with no one.

"You are from Kregen?"

"Well, yes and no."

The blood in my head pained. I thumped the table. "Damn it!" I burst out. "You'll pardon my manner, Madam Ivanovna, or Madam Zena Iztar, but, by Zair! I wish you'd—"

She smiled.

That smile could have launched a million ships.

"Yes, Pur Dray."

I felt numb.

"You call me Pur Dray," I whispered. I swallowed. "You must know I hold only being a Krozair of Zy as of importance. Tell me, Madam Zena Iztar, tell me, for the sweet sake of Zair!"

She placed both white hands on the table. Her fingers were long and slender and white, as they should be, and she wore no rings. She wore no jewelry of any kind that I could see.

"Now," she said, and her voice in its hard practicality made me sit up. "The Savanti have set their hands to the work they consider proper for Kregen, for they are of that world and are a last faint remnant of a once mighty race. You have heard of them as the Sunset People or the Sunrise People. The Savanti have at heart the well-being of apims, Homo sapiens like yourself. As for the Star Lords, their plans are different, wider and more universe-embracing, and I shall tell you only that you will have to make a choice one day, and the choice will be the hardest thing you have ever done."

"Put me back on Kregen and I will choose!"

"Oh, yes, Pur Dray! You would promise anything now, just to return. I know."

"Can you—?"

Her look made me hold my foolish tongue.

"Am I not here? Do you require any other proof?"

"No, I meant only—"

"You have always been reckless, foolhardy, as that brash bird the Gdoinye says, an onker of onkers."

How it warmed my heart to hear the brave Kregish words, here in London, even if they were insults!

"Now," she went on, in that firm mellow voice. "If you will cast your mind back to your arrival in the inner sea at the Akhram, when you struggled to remain on Kregen?"

"Yes. They were going to banish me back to Earth, but I fought them and so returned—"

"That was a compromise. The Star Lords and the Savanti had different purposes, as the Gdoinye and the white dove of the Savanti showed. So you went to Magdag, along the Grodnim green northern shore. You became a Krozair of Zy, a fanatical believer in Zair, the red sun deity of Zim, and an opponent of Grodno, the green sun deity of Genodras; that was our doing."

"Your doing? Who—?"

Again she smiled and lifted one slender finger. I stopped.

"All in good time. The Star Lords have other instruments, as have the Savanti. They were not pleased. But there are checks and balances, and you lived. Mortal men may see only so far. It is a wearisome burden to see further. One day, I believe, you will be called on to see and to make your choice, and you will feel an outcast, a pariah, a traitor. Yet think back to this day and remember."

I could bottle up my screaming fears and questions no longer. This talk of the mysterious destiny of Kregen and the shadowy desires of powerful

56

superhuman beings was all very fine. But I was Dray Prescot, and there were torments tearing at me far and away more important than the fate of worlds.

I said: "You are from Kregen. You have great powers. Tell me, Madam Zena Iztar, what of—?"

Her smile would have melted the blasphemous heart of a silver statue of Lem the Silver Leem.

"Fear not, Pur Dray. Your Chuktar Tom returned in good time. Your Delia and your son, Drak, live."

"Thank Zair!" I could say no more for a while, just put a hand to my face, and so we sat in silence.

Then, quietly, she said, "Yes. Yes, you should thank Zair."

Slowly I looked up at her.

"Your son is a great man now. And your daughter has already refused five offers of marriage."

"Good God!" I said, dumbfounded.

"Time passes on Kregen as on this Earth, although not necessarily at the same rates, as you know. Reckoning in Earthly years, you left—" As she said *left* I know my fierce old lips twisted up, for the word more appropriate was "banished." She put a hand to her cloak and felt some object beneath, under the curve of her shoulder. "In Earthly years your son Drak was near fourteen and he is nigh on thirty-two now."

At this I groaned. Aye, I, Dray Prescot, groaned. Thirty-two! Incredible and impossible and yet true. What years I had missed! As for Lela, in a life span of two hundred years or so, a maiden of thirty-two had no fears of the future or of being left on the shelf. I also knew this would make Segnik and Velia both twenty-one. My Delia had been twenty-one when we had first met, although it is a curious fact that on Kregen people appear to put little store by their ages or their birthdays. As to the latter, that is easily understood, I suppose, given the forty-year cycle, the absence of definite terrestrial years and the confusing mass of temporal measurements by the different moons. I became aware of Madam Zena Iztar looking at me with a quizzical gaze, almost a look of mockery.

"And you will send me back, Madam Iztar, now?"

"I stand here in a merely consultative capacity. You have been causing trouble and there is work for you to do. When the time comes you will know what the work is. To tell you now would invalidate your integrity." I guessed she spoke in these terms to conceal a blunter meaning.

"Eighteen years!" I said. If the words came out of my mouth as a plea, I do not think I can be blamed.

"The Savanti are a mere rump of a once proud people. They may well find a use for you yet, despite your flouting of their principles. As for the Star Lords, certain events on Kregen have not turned out as they expected—"

"So they cannot see the future?"

"Oh, they can riddle a future or two, but the trick is guessing which one will eventuate. They will use you again, Pur Dray, I am quite sure."

"And can I resist them?"

"You must try, if that is your wish. Your will may then receive help from…" Here she paused and smoothed her cloak reflectively so the black material shone in the lamps' gleam. "I can say that the Star Lords are only partially to blame for some of your misfortunes; they are not omnipotent on Kregen—who is?—and intense effort of the will may deflect their hold."

"And you will tell me nothing more of their purposes?"

"There are many clues if you open your eyes." She spoke with an edge of testiness, very bracing. "But I will tell you no more. For one thing, even the Star Lords are divided among themselves. For another, to tell you what they think they plan to do will quite evidently, given their nature, cause them to do something else."

"Out of spite? The Star Lords… out of spite?"

"Not out of spite, you onker!"

Then it was my turn to smile. How familiar that was!

She looked around my room at the few belongings I had collected. "I must wake these poor famblys. Your Doctor Quinney proved a fine ponsho, Pur Dray."

I had the grace to nod my head without speaking.

"Now you have this tiresome business over the duel. After that—who knows? Even Grodno may play a part; stranger things than that have happened."

Chancing a venture that might prove disastrous, for I saw she was arranging her cloak and gown and preparing to wake up my guests, I said, "And Lem the Silver Leem? Do you…?"

She flashed those large brown eyes at me, very fierce and commanding. "If you obliterate Lem completely," and she said it with a fair old temper, I can tell you, "Then you would do well in the eyes of the people of Kregen—and of Earth."

Before I could ask what she meant by that last alarming statement Doctor Quinney was starting forward, grinning, and the others were moving about and buzzing with the arrival of this formidable Madam Ivanovna in our midst. The meeting which followed meant nothing, of course. What ideas, what concepts, what conjectures flashed through my aching head!

Eventually things were brought to a conclusion and an astral voice came from Madam Ivanovna in her part as a psychic; the voice chilled the company and satisfactorily ensured a fat check would pass from me to Doctor Quinney. Then we were saying our farewells. No one cared to partake of the refreshment Mrs. Benton had provided. I shook hands and ushered them out. As she passed me Zena Iztar smiled, a quick flash that was gone as soon as formed.

"Good night, Mr. Prescot." She was very close and she bent a little forward, her words for me alone. "Remberee, Dray Prescot, Krozair of Zy. Remberee."

I caught a flash from the black of her gown where the cloak lapped open. A tiny gem gleamed there, hidden before. I saw a jeweled representation of a cogwheel, a gearwheel, and I found myself thinking that this was a strange device, so mechanical, for one so psychic. Then she had gone and I was alone with Doctor Quinney. The check was written, dried and handed over. Quinney took it as a man accepts a flask of water in the burning deserts far south of Sanurkazz.

"A pity," he said, folding the check, "that we were not honored with our lordship tonight."

"A pity," I agreed two-facedly.

"I hear he has taken a trip to Boulogne."

"Has he? No doubt he has business there."

As Doctor Quinney took himself off I determined that no one should know of my intention to catch the packet to Boulogne the next day.

If you imagine I slept that night you could be right, for everything passed in a daze until I realized I was in Boulogne and must meet this lecherous, dandified earl the following morning at first light, when the air was cool and limpid and no curious observers would be around. My second, a courageous, empty-headed army officer with whom I had had a few skirmishes in India, was already in France. He met me on the appointed day, a polished mahogany box under his arm, with the information that all was ready, a doctor was in attendance and the carriage waited. With blinds pulled down we wheeled out along the seashore.

Well, as with all my fights, this duel could mark the end of me. The weapons were to be pistols. I account myself a fine shot. I'd had plenty of experience in America. A pair of very fine London-made dueling pistols had come into my possession and I knew how they shot. The lordling would have his own, no doubt. I well remember a remarkable man in the Royal Navy who was the finest shot I have ever known. As he used to say, in his own tarpaulin way, "If I can see it I can hit it—if I know the gun."

He had been a captain when I knew him and we had got along, for he was a man who, like myself, had come up onto the quarterdeck through the hawse hole. I would have liked him at my side on Kregen. His middle name was Abe, but only his family called him that, of course. I missed him. He was ten years older than myself, so if he still lived he'd be one hundred and two years old. With a pang I recollected myself. He lived on Earth, not Kregen.

The petty formalities of the duel wended through their paces: the apology was asked for and refused, we took up our positions, the signal was given, we walked, turned, fired. Two flat smacks of evil hatred in the cool morning air. Two puffs of smoke. He hit me in the right shoulder, high. I shot the kleesh clean through the guts.

Turmoil followed and the doctor scurried. The seconds tried to hurry me away, but I had been keyed up. I acted as I might have acted on Kregen and not on Earth. I walked over to the lordling as he lay writhing, screaming in pain, choking. I bent over him. His second tried to drag me away and I pushed him and he staggered and fell. The doctor wadded a handful of white cloth that turned red in an instant. The lecher would most likely die. I did not think Earthly medical science at that time could save him.

I bent over him and he glared up at me, choking, screaming.

"You are going to die, you bastard," I said, quite calmly. "In your agony, think. Think if your pain was worth what you did to Mary Benton."

I did not spit in his face. I remembered I was on Earth and, anyway, that would give him greater importance than the rast deserved.

My second said in his gruff army way; "My God, Prescot! You're a devil!" And then, brushing his stiff mustache, "You won't be able to go back to England now."

"There will be other things to do. Thank you for your assistance."

We parted then, and I suppose he is buried somewhere on Earth, his gravestone moldering away over a corrupting coffin. Time has no mercy.

So it happened that, waiting for the summons of the Scorpion, I was in France for the pathetic business of the Franco-Prussian War, a most unhappy affair. I admired the brisk efficiency of the German Army and felt great sorrow for the shambles that overtook the French Army. I'd fought them at Waterloo, and fought with them in the Crimea, and I'd fought with the Germans in that old war and was to fight against them unhappily in wars to come. The nonsense of national identities when they destroy happiness had been laid plainly open to me in the disputes between Vallia and Pandahem and between Vallia and Hamal. I was learning all the time.

Although I now have a much clearer idea of what must have gone on in the three years between Zena Iztar's visit and the day I found myself helping in a bloody hospital in Paris as the guns thundered about our ears, I will refrain from a guess, for that would destroy the appreciation of many of my actions. Hindsight can destroy logic and truth. I am making the attempt, painful though it is, to be as truthful as I can possibly be in this record. If that record makes me out to be the prize fool I am, then I stand guilty of being an onker.

A balloon had just been inflated and sent off and the Prussians were firing at it. I stood a little apart, my hands and arms smothered in blood, looking. I looked up. The blueness stole in, or so it seemed to me, on the clouds of gun smoke. The noise of the cannon and rifles blended away and away and I was falling—heavenly, wonderful, superb, sublime!—falling, and the Scorpion enfolded me in its arms and bore me away. Never did man more thankfully quit this Earth.

Six
Of slings and knives

Twenty-one years!

Twenty-one whole terrestrial years had now passed since I had set foot on Kregen. What might have happened in that long span of time? I admit to a tremulous feeling as I stood up and looked around, wonderfully conscious of the streaming mingled radiance of Zim and Genodras falling all about me and lighting up with glory all my new hopes for the future. I felt weak, like a newly born ponsho. I felt lightheaded. My heart wanted to burst from my breast. I stamped my naked foot on the ground, on the short tufted grass, and deeply breathed in that indescribably bracing air of Kregen, air like wine, air that no man of Earth can possibly imagine. I was home!

And yet Kregen is a large world with a greater landmass than Earth. Home, for me, was Valka or Zenicce or Djanduin. I might be anywhere. I didn't give a damn where I was. Just so that I trod once more the same earth as my Delia, that when I had cleared up whatever mischief lay to my hand I could fly or sail or ride—walk or crawl—back to my Delia, that was all I craved. I would return to my Delia, my Delia of the Blue Mountains, my Delia of Delphond.

Many and many a time have I returned to Kregen, and few times ever created in me more sheer joyful feelings of thankfulness as that occasion. I had thought myself abandoned and cast off. Now I was back.

These thoughts sped through my mind with the speed of a Lohvian longbow shaft. As I stood up the reason for my arrival and the problem confronting me revealed itself plainly and, as always, unpleasantly.

Naked as usual—for it had been a unique exception when the Star Lords had taken me back to Vilasca for the second time and given me my weapons—I would have to be the same old hasty, reckless, intemperate Dray Prescot. Maybe the Star Lords had gone down in my estimation for having provided me with weapons. I do not know.

A flung stone whistled past my ear.

The slinger, a small and agile fellow almost as naked as I was, had come springing out of the thick-leaved bushes. The sounds of combat beyond him told me where the action lay; those sounds combined in the light of Antares with the scream of frightened people and the shrill, shocking yells of vicious killers. I started toward the slinger.

He was apim. The next stone missed also, but only because I dodged sideways. This fellow might be one of the people I had been sent here to assist; he might be one of those I must fight. I did not know. This problem confronted me as of old, the difference on this occasion being that I had no guidelines at all. A second man now followed the first, swirling a sling about his head. His stone barely missed the first slinger, who turned, reloaded and swung. By the time I had reached him he had sent his missile full into his pursuer's face. The second man pitched to the ground, minus an eye and with blood flowing.

I grabbed the slinger as he swung back. I had run noiselessly and his face contorted with terror, shattered at thus being taken without warning.

"Now, dom," I said. "You can tell me all about it."

"The slavers!" he cried, wincing from my grip, trying to kick me, trying to bite, struggling to get his knife out. He wore a breechclout of decent fawn cloth, with a bag for his slingshots, a leather belt, the knife and dusty sandals.

"Slavers," I said.

"They are taking away the girls! I must save them, and yet..." Here he stopped struggling. He was very young. His voice fell. "And yet I ran away."

"Then we must run back and see what we can do."

If the Star Lords looked down on this comedy and were displeased with what they saw, I might find myself back on Earth for another twenty-one years. Even as I took a grip on the lad's arm and ran him back to the bushes, I considered that from what had happened to me on Earth it could well be that the Star Lords had had no hand in this return to Kregen. It could be the Savanti who had called on me. We ran into the bushes.

At my back the ground trended dustily away to mountains with no sign of human habitation. Beyond the bushes lay a well-trodden path. Further bushes and then a few scattered cultivated fields extended ahead. A house burned. Well, as I have said, sounds of strife and sights of burning houses are often my lot when I return to Kregen.

Along the path the girls in their fetters struggled, shrieking and wailing, terrified. The difficulty was in judging who was attempting to abduct the girls and who was trying to rescue them. At first glance there seemed very little difference between the two sides. Both wore the fawn-colored breechclouts, both used slings and knives. They were all apims, with a mixture of hair ranging from light to dark brown, so I must discard that as an identification. A stone almost took my eye out, and I moved away smartly, marking the man who had flung.

"Him," I said to my captive. "Is he friend or enemy?"

"That is Noki and he was always an onker! He couldn't hit the mark at twenty paces!"

A trifle local friction here, I decided. Noki saw what was going on and tried again, whereat my captive bellowed, "Hold, you get-onker! This man will help us!"

"I thought you were slain, Mako!" yelped this Noki. "Hurry! They are dragging the girls to their ship."

I perked up at this. So far this appeared to me to be a parody of the times I had fought for the Star Lords. The time was slipping away, for already most of the girls had vanished around a bend in the trail. They were all shackled to one another, stumbling on. While it was clear enough to see which of the men were trying to release them, it was not as easy to see who was slinging at the locals and bringing them down.

I made up my mind.

"Follow, Mako and you, Noki! You must fight!"

Then I was off, haring along the trail, dodging flung stones until, passing the struggling, shrieking girls, I reached the head of the column around the bend. The sea blazed before me, rippled with a breeze, glittering with the twin fires of the Suns of Scorpio. A large open pulling boat was drawn up on the sand. There was going to be no mistake now.

I went straight in at the three fellows hauling on the shackles at the head of the procession, dragging the girls along. They all dropped the ropes and slung at me. I dodged. Three blows took care of them. Against knives a fist is a useful weapon, lacking anything better. The unarmed combat disciplines hammered into me by the Krozairs of Zy also ensured I could take out a man armed only with a knife. As for the slung stones, they could break an arm or crack a skull. Two more slavers went down, their faces abruptly bloody, as they tried to jump me. And all the time I was leaping around like a frenzied fire-dancer, trying to present so shifting and erratic a target that the slingers would be bound to miss.

It all struck me as remarkably fatuous, not real, as though I was being run through a slow-motion reprise of what had gone on long ago in much more gory detail. But the truth was there in the blood and the screams and the agony. This was real enough. The missing factor was twenty-one years away from scenes of Kregen, I was the one at fault.

What I had left, only moments before, still seemed more real to me. The Parisian hospital, the Prussian guns, the balloon, the blood there. Already, because one of the slavers twisted his knife as I struck him down and spitted himself, I had blood on my hands. Blood. Is blood, then, so inseparable from life?

"They climb into the boat!" screeched Mako.

"Don't just stand there shouting about it!" I bellowed at him, running down the beach. "Stop them!" I did not have the heart to use the great word *Jikai*, and I think I was right.

An older man ran across as I started. A knife slash had brought blood in a line across his side. He was panting. "Let them go," he said, his chest heaving. "They may kill more of us."

I ignored him. His was the word of wisdom, of course, for the girls had been saved and the last of the slavers were evidently only too anxious to push off and row away. But I had other ideas. It was through no blood-thirsty madness that I acted as I did; I simply needed that boat. I did not know where I was but, by Vox, it was a long way off the beaten track.

The younger element was anxious to follow my lead. In a last affray in the surf, where, I admit, I stood back at the end and let them get on with it, the last of the slavers were seen to. Up on the beach the people on whose side I had fought were going around carefully slitting every living slaver's throat.

The girls, their shackles torn off, played a lustful part in that butchery too.

Presently I was able to go back to the older man who was being seen to, his wound stanched by a pad of leaves. No one produced a kit of acupuncture needles. Truly, I was out in the boondocks. Something about the light at last demanded my full attention, and I looked up. Yes. Yes, up there the huge red sun preceded the smaller green sun across the sky. In the forty-year cycle, which is never really an exact forty years by virtue of Kregen's Keplerian orbit about Antares, the suns had met and eclipsed and parted again. I thought of Magdag. What did they get up to on that occasion in that infamous city, when the green sun passed in front of the red? Could the smaller sun even be seen against that massive somber red glow?

"We owe you our thanks," said the older man, who said his name was Mogo the Wise.

I still remained on Kregen so I must have done the right thing.

Looking at the people here, the girls hysterical in their relief, the men comforting them, and now a stream of other people, old men and women, youngsters, coming running along the path from the village, I wondered which of them the Star Lords had wanted preserved. They did not seem a likely lot of prospects for a great destiny on Kregen. That was not my concern. Exchanging polite greetings with the headman was not my concern. I wrapped a fawn breechclout around my nakedness and possessed myself of a knife, a poor thing with a bone handle and a bronze blade, indifferently made. These people were poor. I cut through all the chatter.

"Tell me where this place is," I said, then, quelling their inquiries, I added, "for I have been shipwrecked and am lost out of the sea."

The head-shaking at this, the lip-pursing, made me wonder what they ordinarily did to shipwrecked mariners.

"Why," said Mogo the Wise, screwing up his eyes. "This is Inama. Everyone knows that."

In my screaming desire to know, to return to Delia, I wondered what fool had ever called this fool wise.

"And where is Inama? What is the next island called? The nearest mainland?"

"The next island is where those devils of Yanimas come from. As to any other large island, there cannot be any as large as Inama or Yanima, although there are smaller. And, as for what you call mainland…" Here he turned to his people and lifted his hands to his temples. Whereat everyone laughed. I kept my temper—just.

"Do any ships call here?"

"Of course. But they come to kill us or take us prisoner. They sail from the Ice Floes of Sicce. We run and hide. Sometimes they leave things behind." He held out his knife. It was of iron, with an ivory handle. "This is a great knife, left by a ship."

Of one fact I felt relief in my dangerous impatience: these poor people talked of the Ice Floes of Sicce. That particular version of a Kregan hell, perhaps the most famous, was not the only one. I took heart from this talk of hell.

I said: "I will take this boat."

The headman looked dubious at this, with much pulling of his lower lip. One or two of the young bloods fingered their knives. I said, "I have saved your girls. I would like you to place water and food in the boat." More head scratching and eyes turned to the sky. "By Vox!" I said. "And would you wish the Yanimas to find a boat of theirs here when next they call?"

That was a two-pronged argument, but Mogo the Wise took the point as I had intended.

"That would make them very angry."

"And they would kill many of you. Put food and water into the boat and I will leave you."

So it was settled.

The hideous anticlimax, the dread truth, the damnable situation in which I had been placed screamed at me, screeching with impending madness in my skull. Here I was, back on Kregen, and I had absolutely no idea where. I was lost. And all I had for transport was a mere rowing boat. Truly the Star Lords—if they had pitched me back here—took their revenge harshly.

But lost or not, rowing boat or not, I would set off to find Valka and my Delia. To the Ice Floes of Sicce with the Everoinye!

Seven
Lost on Kregen

Some experiences in one's life one would wish to forget. Certainly I rate that little boating excursion as among that group of experiences I would do a very great deal never to repeat.

By the position and altitude of the suns I could make a fair stab at latitude; longitude remained as much a mystery as it used to be on Earth before John Harrison gave the deep-water mariner a chronometer that would keep time with incredible accuracy. I had two alternatives and neither appeared over-appealing.

Despite the fact that Kregen possesses a much greater land area than Earth, there is still a vast amount of water. Here I was, in a cranky, stubborn rowing boat, adrift somewhere on the waters of Kregen and with every direction on the compass to choose for my direction.

The other alternative, simply allowing the winds and currents to push me where they willed, in the anticipation that I would be cast up on a frequented shore, I dismissed. By more bargaining as the food and water were brought down I obtained a sheet of cloth—that fawn material the women made up from the fibers of a cottony plant—and cut down a tree to make a mast and spar. Fashioning a crude dipping lug and stepping the mast as well as I could, I determined to sail where I was going under my own power.

The little dipping lug reminded me of the muldavy of the Eye of the World. This boat was a rough and ready affair, split logs being bent to shape, secured with treenails and with quantities of hair packed in with clay. It was more of a raft than a boat, but it would serve. It would have to serve.

With clumsy pottery crocks filled with water, a supply of cooked chickens and strips of bosk, dried in salt, and piles of various fruits of which palines formed a sizable proportion, I set off.

No doubt the islanders thought me mad. This island of Inama was clearly situated dwaburs off the shipping lanes, and my task was to find either a ship or land as speedily as possible. It would not be easy.

I could go east or west and be sure of striking land eventually. But if I was to the east of Havilfar and sailed east I'd be voyaging into an empty sea until I struck the lands of the other continental grouping from which came the shanks. And if I was to the west of Turismond and sailed the boat west, the same thing would result. The problem was a knotty one.

If I sailed north I fancied I'd stand the best chance. Southward would take me toward the equator and therefore away from Vallia.

In a similar situation on Earth there would be a strong possibility that a sailor would feel the ocean he sailed: the blue of the Pacific, the raw gray of the Atlantic, the sense of the Mediterranean. I had had no experience of these far outer oceans of Kregen, so I sailed north. The breeze veered toward the east and, accepting this as the kind of fate that had dogged me, bore away toward the northwest. The lug sail pouted, the boat more forced its way through the water than glided along, and I maintained a most strict rationing of the meager supplies.

The day came when I could not prolong the supplies by any artifice whatsoever; I had none. I do not intend to labor overlong on the rigors of that voyage; suffice it to say I caught fish and slit them open for their small quantities of fresh water. I drank a few handfuls of seawater per day for the moisture, knowing I could tolerate that small amount of salt, and I ate fish, which I detest, not only because of the damned fishheads from around the curve of the horizon.

Whether or not I could have survived without that immersion in the Pool of Baptism in Aphrasöe I do not know. But the day came when, almost out of my head and scarcely believing what I saw to be true, an argenter appeared, backed her maintopsail and so picked me up.

The hands that lifted me from the boat, the faces that stared down on me, were all a shining lustrous black. I knew I had fallen into the hands of apims from Xuntal, people of the same race as Balass. I had always found the Xuntalese to be firm, thoughtful, generous, fierce when they had to be. It seemed wise to appear in worse case than I was. So they carried me below decks and I flopped in a peculiar bunk built into the side of the ship and went to sleep. Water, food, everything I needed of bodily comfort was provided when I awoke.

There is little else to say about the argenter. She was *Scepter of Xurrhuk,* much after the style of those broad argenters of Pandahem, although, I fancied, not quite so wide and stubby and with another knot of speed in a fair breeze. She was painted in brilliant colors of many tones and shades and her sails were all of purest white, which delighted and amazed me, an old salt accustomed to the drab tawny sails long exposed to the elements of my own vessels.

Her master, a tall, imposing man wearing dyed blue garments of the finest ponsho wool, invited me to his cabin. The sweep of the aft windows brought back memories. I sat and drank a very fair Maxanian, straw-colored, light on the palate, and the master introduced himself as Captain Swixonon.

"You are a lucky man, dom."

"Aye, Captain. Xurrhuk of the Curved Sword smiled."

His craggy face regarded me gravely. "You are not of Xuntal."

"No. But I count at least one Xuntalese as a good friend. Tell me, Captain, where are we bound?"

"We sail from Mehzta to Xuntal."

"I know a good friend from Mehzta also."

"You are a much traveled man?"

I did not laugh but I said, "No. I met them far from their homes. I cannot pay you now for a passage, but I know ships. I can work. Later, when I am home, I will remit payment through the Lamnias."

"Very well." He was a captain, a man who made his mind up rapidly.

"Thank you."

"And your name? And your country?"

"I am Dray Prescot, of Vallia."

He raised his eyebrows. I did not think he had heard of me. After all, Kregen is a large place and my doings, although making a stir in the countries I had been, would mean little elsewhere.

"I am pleased to make a connection with Vallia. Maybe we can arrange something later."

He was shrewd. Trading over the oceans is a chancy business. There are fliers on Kregen, as you know, but most of that marvelous world's commerce is carried on by ship or canal or animal transport. Fliers—as I well knew—are often rare and precious objects, completely unknown over many and many a highly civilized land. Havilfar holds her secrets well.

With that in mind, I said, "I would like to hire or charter a flier in Xuntal. The Vallian embassy is still open?"

He looked puzzled. "Why should it not be, dom?"

"I have been away... politics. I shall be glad to be back, by Vox!"

In his shrewdness I fancy he read more into me than I intended to give away. He asked no questions about my arrival in a small boat, but he must have seen her and noted her lines. The rest of the journey I acted as a simple seaman and, I swear by Zair, despite the pressing urgency forcing me on, I recognized that the argenter could go no faster so I took some pleasure from the tasks of shipboard life again.

To pass very rapidly over the next few weeks is to bring me to the Vallian ambassador in Xuntal, that island off the southern promontory of Balintol, the large subcontinent of Segesthes. Mehzta, from which came my good comrade Gloag, lay off the northeast coast of Segesthes. Here in Xuntal I was about the same distance southeast of Valka as I was of Zenicce, where Gloag ran my House of Strombor. Yet, because of Delia, it was to the Vallian ambassador I went and not the Stromborian. Between Xuntal and Mehzta lie the Chulik Islands. Between Xuntal and Vallia lie the islands of Undurkor. At least I knew where I was on Kregen.

There was a little trouble in my seeing the Vallian ambassador. The embassy, a splendid and imposing building as befitted the Empire, lay along a shady avenue of other magnificent buildings housing various embassies and consulates. I barged right in and told the flunky I wanted to see the ambassador and to jump. I realize now that I was at fault. But I'd been away for twenty-one miserable years and I was in a hurry. They offered to throw me out.

Eventually, carrying one guard under an arm, four or five others holding aching heads in a trail on the floor in my wake and the last and most gorgeous of them, in golden robes, thrust along ahead with my hand around his neck, I presented myself before the Vallian ambassador.

The room was ornate, filled with light, expensive. I heeded none of it. The ambassador rose to his feet from the chair behind his desk. He had been talking to a shifty-looking Rapa who still sat, lifting his vulturine head to observe the proceedings.

"What do you want? Get out! Rast, out!"

I pitched the golden-robed flunky to one side.

This ambassador was one of your red-cheeked, pouchy-eyed individuals, all choler and bile. He wore decent Vallian buff-leathers, but a fancy decoration of black and white looped around his collar. I knew those colors in Vallia. He was a member of the Racter party, the most powerful political party of Vallia, and a gang who had given me trouble before and were to give me trouble again—aye, so much trouble I wonder any of them are still alive, by Vox!

I said; "Cramph! Your name! Instantly!"

He saw my face. I did not know him. I do not think he had ever seen me in Vallia before. But he saw my face and some of the color fled from his cheeks.

"Guards!" he screamed, waving his arms.

I picked up one of the flunkies' rapiers. I swished it around. I said, "I shall not ask you your name again."

Maybe there is something in me, in that stupid, thickheaded Dray Prescot, which guarantees that the yrium—the charismatic power that I detest and yet cold-bloodedly use when I have to—can shine through despite my lumpen ways.

"I am Vektor Ulanor, the Trylon of Frant! You rast, you will rue the day you—"

"I am Dray Prescot, the Prince Majister. You need not abuse yourself or show fear, for you could not know me. I need a flier at once. Let there be no delay. *Jump!*" He gaped at me.

I said: "I shall not ask you again. A Trylon? As ambassador to Xuntal? Very proper, for we value the Xuntalese. But you may well not be a Trylon for very much longer, Ulanor. You might not even be a noble at all, not even a Koter. You might be allowed to sweep the road of zorca and totrix droppings, in the great Kyro of Drak the Victorious in Vondium—if I am minded to be merciful."

Well, it was all most unpleasant and distasteful; in the end I secured the flier and supplies and bid a much shaken Trylon Vektor remberee.

Even then, as I sped through the clean air of Kregen, I wondered what this ambassador Ulanor had been up to with a Rapa in Xuntal. The Rapas, those diffs with the strong vulture-heads and fiercely curved beaks, are not often found in the guise of merchants. If plots were being hatched I would have to attend to them the moment I had assured myself everything was shipshape at home. Trylon Vektor had given me a brief rundown on the situation in Vallia. I gathered little had changed in my absence: the Emperor still ruled with his iron, despotic sway partially tempered by his Presidio, the Racters were still in strong opposition to his plans—this I had gathered by what Vektor Ulanor did not say and by his facial tic—and Valka, as far as he knew, had not sunk into the sea.

He conveyed the impression that he would be particularly pleased had my island done so.

After that first heated exchange he would have done as I commanded him; only afterward would he doubt his sanity and believe me an impostor. Luckily for him—I didn't care—one of the grooms in the embassy had been in Vondium with another employer and had seen me there. He was able to assuage the Trylon's fears as to my identity.

I gave them no explanation whatsoever of my presence in Xuntal or of my absence, about which they were well informed. I did give instructions that a fair passage money with a bonus should be paid in broad golden talens to Captain Swixonon, with my thanks. I also advised him, privately, to go for business to the Stromborian embassy and to say the Lord of Strombor had sent him. I added I did not think the Vallian ambassador would be of any use to a friend of mine.

Now I sent the little airboat racing over the surface of Kregen under the Suns of Scorpio.

She was an unhandy little craft and not overly fast, being capable of little more than eight dbs.[1] So as I urged her on and we passed over the sea dropping Xuntal astern, I settled down to the long haul ahead—if the flier did not break down. The flying furs wrapped me against the slipstream. At last the dim and faraway blue and brown flicker of islands to starboard told me I was passing the Undurkers. Northwest I went, over the suns-glittering sea, northwest as the suns sank and Kregen's primary moon, the Maiden with the Many Smiles, shone forth in pink and golden glory. A few clouds wafted against that glowing orb, for the moon was almost full, and I expectantly looked back to the east to see a sight I had never seen on Earth. Soon the fourth moon, She of the Veils, rose and the two moons rolled along above me, casting down their fuzzy pinkish light, most wonderful, most gorgeous, most comforting. Two of the lesser moons hurtled across, as though in welcome to see me again.

I am an Earthman, a terrestrial, and yet on Earth I had found having only one moon in the sky a most unsettling experience. How quickly we adapt and change, how quickly we grow accustomed to the bizarre... and yet isn't just one moon as bizarre as seven? My Delia would have thought so.

At this speed it would take me over a day and a half to reach Valka.

That journey proceeded with nightmare slowness. As I journeyed nearer and nearer to Valka and all the place meant to me, I grew more and more irritable, more agitated, more apprehensive. The closer I came the more I feared. All manner of phantasms rose to torture me. Anything could have happened, anything could have gone wrong. Twenty-one years! The idea of invisible, near-omnipotent Star Lords directing me and controlling my destiny sickened me. My own estimation of myself, my own foolish achievements, all meant nothing beside the enormity of their power.

My Delia! She must be there, waiting for me, smiling, running to greet me with outstretched arms!

Close to dawn I knew I must be entering the areas of my former life on Kregen. Below me, as the first ruby fires flickered over the eastern horizon, must lie the dark outlines of islands I knew. First rose Zim, that great crimson sun that is called Far in Havilfar, and has many and many a name over other parts of Kregen. I roused myself and stared ahead in that rosy dawn. The sea sparkled empty before me. I cursed. When the vivid emerald fires of Genodras, the smaller green sun that in Havilfar is called Havil and likewise has many other names, rose to drench the bloodlit sky, I saw a faint smear on the northwestern horizon. I was gripping the wooden rail of the flier like a drowning man. My head jutted above the little windshield and the breeze roared in my face, streaming my shaggy mop of brown hair, bringing water to my eyes.

I wore an old red-and-white checked shirt and a pair of breeches that barely fitted. Around my waist in a cheap leather scabbard and belt hung a rapier and main-gauche I had borrowed from Trylon Vektor. I stared ahead and I could feel my heart thumping. This—this homecoming was what I had craved for twenty-one unendurable years on Earth.

Islands flashed past below. I saw the cream of surf, the windblown trees, here and there the orderly signs of cultivation. Villages and towns flashed past and then more open sea. Ships sailed down there, toy models with swelling sails. I looked ahead. Valka! Yes—there rose the high battlements of the Heart Heights, those inner mountains where the freedom-fighters had rallied to oppose oppression. Now I could see the coastline, the whole fantastic sweep of the Bay, with Valkanium dotting the bright slopes with white and multicolored buildings. The high fortress of Esser Rarioch atop its hill, the banners and streamers, the brave red and white of Valka, the suns streaming their glorious mingled rays upon all that vivid scene; it was a fusion of color and movement and brightness as the voller swept in a lancing curve to land on that high terraced platform.

I stepped out.

I looked around.

By Zair!

Home—home after twenty-one years and four hundred light-years. I felt dizzy, dizzied with the sheer ache of longings fulfilled.

People came running.

Many I knew. Many I did not know. There rose a babblement of voices. I laughed. I, Dray Prescot, laughed. Up above my head a patrol of flutduins curved, those famous saddle birds of Djanduin with my riders of Valka perched on them. A voller swung away, assured by the people below that all was well.

Panshi came forward, smiling, holding his great staff of office, full well understanding the importance of this occasion.

"Master!" he said. He looked at me and I saw the expression on his face and I clasped him by the hand, mightily shocking him and yet perfectly conveying the impression of welcome and homecoming we both experienced.

"The Princess Majestrix! Prince Drak and Princess Lela! Prince Segnik and Princess Velia! Where are they?"

"My Prince!" he said.

And I chilled.

"Prince Drak is in Vondium with his grandfather, the Emperor. Princess Lela and Princess Velia stay with the sisters of the Rose. Prince Zeg is gone to a far-off place that must exist, for he has been there and returned, but it is beyond all men's knowledge."

My hands were gripped together. I was aware of the throng pressing, the shouts as the word passed: "The old Strom is back!"

I hardly understood what they said. The *old* Strom.

"And the Princess Majestrix?"

I did not like the look on old Panshi's face. But he was a good and loyal man. He straightened up.

"She too is gone, my Prince."

"Gone!" I was shouting. "Gone where?"

He waved his hand before his face. The great staff of office shook against the flagstones.

"I do not know, my Prince, I do not know. But she is gone."

Eight

"And so the Princess Majestrix went alone?"

My private rooms, my inner sanctum, were smothered in dust. Dust and decay harbored here. I smashed the rapier flat against a chair and the dust flew. Sitting, I stared at Panshi, who had followed me here. All others I had waved away.

"Fetch me food and drink, Panshi. Send for it. You must tell me all that has passed."

"Yes, master."

A Fristle fifi I did not know scurried in with refreshment, looking frightened. When she had gone I said: "You said Prince Zeg?"

"Yes, Prince. He is no longer Prince Segnik." Then Panshi revealed he was still the same old retainer, for he added in a more sprightly voice: "He said he would not have the *nik* added to his name any longer, and he fought Prince Vanden, whose father visited here, and gave the brat—I beg your pardon, my Prince—gave the young lord a bloody nose."

That sounded likely. This young Prince Vanden's father was that same Varden Wanek, Prince of the House of Eward of Zenicce, a good comrade to Dray Prescot, so something at least of the old alliances continued.

"Go on, Panshi." I spoke more calmly now. This was not the homecoming I had expected, hungered for. The emptiness in me rang hollow with mockery of my hope. But, after so long, how could I expect everyone to be home waiting for me?

"Prince Segnik went away—to a place—and when he returned he called himself Prince Zeg."

I fancied I knew where Segnik had been, and you who listen to these tapes will have no difficulty in understanding just where he had been and what he had been about.

"And the Princess Majestrix has gone there too?"

"I believe so, my Prince. But I cannot be sure."

"Tell me."

"Men came. Strange men. They were closeted privately with the Princess, and Turko the Shield had to be told by me most stringently that she was not to be disturbed. We waited and fretted and when the Princess bade the men remberee she looked—I crave your indulgence, master—she looked sad and tired. We wanted to help; but she would not confide in us."

"Didn't Prince Drak have anything to say?"

"He was in Vandayha over a matter of a silversmith who had adulterated his metal. There was a scandal and Prince Drak—"

"Yes, yes." I saw then that young Drak had been carrying on my government while I had been away. Well, wasn't that the proper function for a dutiful son?

"The young Prince and Princess—" began Panshi, but in my impatience I interrupted.

"And Turko and Balass and Naghan, Melow the Supple—they are all with the Princess?"

He looked thoughtful and adjusted the upper hem of his robe, for he had somehow managed to find the time to dress himself in his full regalia so that he looked at once imposing and faintly ridiculous, an eminently practical appearance for the Chief Chamberlain. "I do not know for sure, my Prince. They were called away with the Elten of Avanar to—ah—attend to the disturbances of the Strom of Vilandeul. He conceived the idea that he was entitled to the lands west of the Varamin Mountains and led an expedition—"

I felt not so much the shock of that as the annoyance. The Elten of Avanar was my old blade comrade Tom Tomor ti Vulheim. He was my Chuktar in command of the army of Valka. If the Strom of Vilandeul, a Strom governing his Stromnate on the mainland of Vallia, conceived that land in my island of Can Thirda belonged to him, there was going to be trouble. The shock, when I thought about it, was the wonder that the trouble should occur at all in the Empire of Vallia. Surely the Emperor was not so decayed as to be unable to maintain law and order? This was a matter that must be looked into. But not now; now I only desired to find my Delia. The children were quite clearly making their own lives. It was my Delia I must concern myself with.

"In this trouble, the young Prince would have been—" started Panshi.

"And so the Princess Majestrix went alone?"

He did not like my tone. He lifted his thin shoulders. "She would not listen, my Prince. We tried—she left when the Strom of Vilandeul played a false tune. I think, if I may be permitted to say this, my Prince, that when the Princess went the Strom fancied his chances."

"But Tom will fix him," I said. With Vangar and the air fleet, the cavalry and aerial cavalry and the superb Archers of Valka, my Stromnate should be able to resist this upstart Strom's plans for conquest and occupation.

"Master, men did go with the Princess, a small bodyguard she agreed to take, and Melow the Supple—"

"Ah!" I said. At once I felt more reassured.

Staring about the dusty room with the furnishings so carefully chosen, I wondered. As Panshi poured a fresh cup of tea—that superb Kregen tea on which I dote—I prowled around the familiar room, seeing that the weapons adorning the walls had all been most carefully greased, noting the books in their serried ranks, the pictures, the banners, marking all the old items, domestic and flamboyant, that made this room and these chambers a place to feel at home, to relax, to laugh and enjoy life.

"Why is the room dusty, Panshi?"

"The Princess would not allow anyone here after you—ah—went away, my Prince. There were some who whispered you were dead. But we who know you knew better. The young Prince, of course, did not—"

"Was a message entrusted to you?"

"Only that when you returned you were to be told what I have told you. I think, Majister, another message may have been left."

I thought so too. So I prowled, going to the writing desks and the bookshelves and all those peculiarly Kregan furnishings that make a Kregan home a place of color as well as comfort. I did not find a message from Delia. Well, I knew enough. There remained one item to learn, one remaining fact I hesitated to ask, dreading the answer. But one must accept the needle, as they say on Kregen.

"When did the Princess leave?"

"Seven months of the Maiden with the Many Smiles."

Over a year ago, in terrestrial reckoning! The Kregans' measurements of time are a vastly complicated affair, with their seasons and their months calculated to the phases of the three major sets of moons and the passages of the suns. I felt again that heaviness at my heart, that hollowness within me.

"You will have messages sent to Prince Drak and the Princesses, Panshi," I said, with as firm a voice as I could muster. "I have no time to write. Say I am returned and gone to seek their mother." I began to strip off the old red-and-white checked shirt. "And I will have a fleet voller readied, well provisioned and weaponed. I will select the weapons myself."

"I will do all you command, master. And the young Prince?"

"Since he is probably where I am now going I shall be able to speak with him myself."

I saw Panshi's eyebrows lift a tiny fraction, then he nodded and bustled off to prepare what was necessary.

There was no time to take the Baths of the Nine, for though Delia might have left over a year ago, I did not wish to waste a mur. As for weapons, I plundered the armory and took a fine selection. For clothes I had a whole wardrobe in a wicker basket placed in the chosen flier and made sure a quantity of scarlet cloth was included. I was traveling where men fought in different fashion from men in Vallia and Zenicce and Pandahem. And, to be truthful, in a way that was both advantageous and disadvantageous.

The state of Valka and my other lands was sketched by Panshi: the army as I had seen was in fine fettle; the shipyards prospered; we were recovering from a poor samphron-oil crop; the Princess Majestrix had trouble in Delphond, but the leader of the high assembly of Valka, grim old Tharu ti Valkanium, continued to shoulder the burdens of office. I remembered him with affection.

As always my mind turned towards my comrades, men and women of Kregen I counted as friends. Seg Segutorio, for whom young Segnik had been named—and how had he taken this changing of his given name, I wondered—knew where I would be going. I felt I could count on him to assist me. And Inch too would assuredly come. I must make time to write them. The pen squealed over the paper, for there was no time for the fine Kregan brushwork, and I stated to them both very simply that I was back and needed their help; I added that Inch should first contact Seg and they should journey together.

Then I crossed out the Kregish word for *should* and substituted a euphemistic expression that conveyed the idea of a request and a gracious permission on their part. After this lapse of time they would be deeply immersed in their own affairs. How could I expect them to drop everything and go flying across Kregen after a harebrained onker like me, rushing headlong into adventures again, as we had in the old days?

For I knew as surely as Zim and Genodras ruled the daytime sky that fearsome adventures loomed ahead. This was no picnic on which I embarked. And my Delia had gone—alone!

Well, not quite alone. I was marvelously cheered at the thought of a ferocious jikla, a Manhound of Faol, pacing at her side with slavering fangs ready to rend any who would harm her.

When I saw the flier Panshi had provided I could not prevent a tiny droop to my lips. She was not one of the best. He saw my face and hurriedly said, "Master, all the fliers save a very few have been taken, as I have told you. Even the sailers. San Evold and San Khe-Hi are with Prince Drak."

I knew what he meant. Nothing more had been done about deciphering the secrets of the silver boxes that powered vollers.

It was necessary for me to observe the fantamyrrh with great care as I stepped aboard the voller. This I did.

A young Hikdar of the Valkan Archers looked up at me. He bashed his red-and-white banded sleeve across his chest.

"My Prince! I would like to go with you. I and a choice band from my pastang."

I looked at him. Yes, I knew him. He had been a waso-Deldar when last I'd been in Valka. Now he wore the insignia of a shebov-Hikdar of the Fourth Regiment of Valkan Archers. In twenty years he had gone from the fifth rank in the Deldar structure to the seventh rank in the Hikdar. Even when men live for two hundred years there is still promotion when there is fighting to be done.

"I am sure your pastang is a credit to the Fourth, and to the Valkan Army, Hikdar Naghan ti Ovoinach. But your duty lies here, to protect

Valka, as you have been detailed."

His face lit up at my remembrance of him, and showed sadness at my words. But he bashed me another salute and stepped back to where his pastang, a full eighty superb bowmen, lined up. I saw that a strong hand had been running the army, at least, while I had been away. As the voller soared up into the limpid light of the suns I guessed that strong and guiding hand to belong to my son Drak. How odd to think that, even though I was chronologically over ninety years of age, my son at thirty-two was an older man than I. I had been thirty when I'd taken that dip in the Pool of Baptism.

Although no one had mentioned it, I knew well enough that he was regarded as the Strom of Valka, that when I was mentioned it would be as the *old* Strom of Valka, Oh, yes, I knew.

I set the controls at due west and thrust the speed lever hard over. The persistent habit of driving vollers at their top speed had been growing on me. This was no time to make an exception.

Rising into the air, the voller swung west. I looked down over the rim where the lacing of leather to the wooden rib had frayed and threatened to rip apart in the slipstream. This was an example of the more common form of voller which, while being able to move of its own volition by reason of the two silver boxes, was yet susceptible to wind pressure. If this craft failed me somewhere over the sea... Well, that would be an end to Dray Prescot, onker of onkers.

Unless, of course, the Star Lords still needed me for their inscrutable purposes. The veil that had been partially lifted on the Everoinye, allowing me a dim glimpse of secrets to be discovered, had shown me potentialities for conflict that staggered me, courses of disaster I did not wish to steer.

Below me Valkanium vanished aft, with the peak of Esser Rarioch lofting, its pinnacles and towers ablaze with flags and banners, the wink and gleam of weapons very comforting as Hikdar Naghan ti Ovoinach and his pastang saluted my departure.

The voller whisked into the clouds and I was alone.

Once more I was set full on a fresh course for adventure and headlong action, hurtling across the surface of Kregen. The thought came to plague me that perhaps I was no longer the Dray Prescot who had first been transported here by the Savanti. Maybe I had lost my cutting edge. Well, as Zair was my witness, I would do all that I could for my Delia, and not reckon the consequences. No matter what perils I might encounter I would not surrender the fight until they shipped me out to the Ice Floes of Sicce.

Nine
Into the Eye of the World

I, Dray Prescot, Lord of Strombor and Krozair of Zy, flew for the inner sea of Kregen, the Eye of the World.

Since I had left the enclosed world of the inner sea with Delia, Seg and Thelda, much had happened to me and much time had passed. I had become all manner of fine fancy nobility, Strom of Valka, Prince Majister of Vallia, King of Djanduin and other titles in addition. I had become a father. I had been to Earth and back to Kregen. How could I, who still took real and genuine pride in belonging to the mystic Order of Krozairs of Zy, expect to recapture the sensations and excitements of my life on the inner sea?

As I flew through the clear and bracing air of Kregen I felt no doubts about what must be done. For I flew to find my Delia, my Delia of the Blue Mountains, my Delia of Delphond.

For her sake I would dare anything, anyone. I do not boast. I state a plain fact. I know too that she would dare all for me, and it is at that thought that I tremble.

At an average speed of approximately ten dbs the flier would take roughly two and three-quarter days to cover the distance from Valka to Sanurkazz. Despite all the urgency I felt, and the maddening impatience that tore at me, there was nothing I could do but wait for the time to pass as the voller soared across Kregen. Vondium, the capital of Vallia, passed away over the southern horizon. The ocean that is called the Sunset Sea all the way from Vallia to Segesthes flowed beneath the petal-shape of the voller. By the time the shoreline of the continent of Turismond appeared ahead I was almost sunk in an apathy induced by frustration, fretting and concern.

My Delia had passed this way over a year before. What had happened to her? Then, as Port Tavetus, one of Vallia's colonial cities of the eastern Turismond coast, passed astern, I found a few remnants of sanity returning. Now I was headed for the Klackadrin. The earth had moved here at some time in the past, opening up a long narrow lift from which noxious gases poured, vapors carrying with them hallucinogenic substances that ripped away a man's sanity. I had traveled here on foot. The experience is one I seldom dwell on. The Phokaym, those coldly hostile risslaca men, riding risslaca steeds, gripped the land on the western edge of the Klackadrin in a fist of iron. The experiences through which I had been dragged there must have left deep scars, for I know I held on to the voller and prayed it would not break down over that hellish place.

The enormous rent in the earth's surface stretched for dwabur after dwabur north and south. I could see steam and vapors lifting and I drove the voller higher. The ground stank with barrenness. Remnants of the proud roads once driven across from east to west by the imperial powers of the old Empire of Loh glittered in the dying light of the suns. Now the Klackadrin on the east and the stupendous mountain bulk of the Stratemsk on the west effectively closed off the land between, land men called the hostile territories.

Believe me when I say that however inimical the hostile territories are, I heaved a sigh of relief when I passed safely over the Klackadrin.

As for the hostile territories, somewhere down there Delia, Seg, Thelda and I had marched and sang as we fought our way on foot from the Stratemsk eastward. Looking back, I could be thankful about what happened, that my friends were spared the horrors of the Phokaym and the Klackadrin.[2]

At the time, mind you, I was a very angry man.

Down there Queen Lilah might still be lording it over Hiclantung, aping the ancient ways of the Queens of Pain of Loh. Without any feeling that the emotion was grotesque, I found myself wishing her well. She was merely what she was. At the least and for all its faults, Hiclantung was an oasis of culture in a sea of barbarism.

The changing face of the land below as it sped past gave no real indication of what was going on down there. One day, when safe means of crossing the Klackadrin had been found, the onward-pressing frontier forces of Vallia and the various nations of Pandahem would spill out into the hostile territories. The use of vollers alone would not be enough. I consigned these interesting prospects for the future to the Black Spider Caves of Gratz as before me rose the impossible bulk of the Stratemsk.

I have already spoken of the Stratemsk, the ranges of mountains extending north and south, defying reason, sprawling into the sky, cloaked eternally in ice and snow, cleft by deep humid jungle valleys, demanding everything of spirit and valor to dare. They shut off the eastern portions of the lands of the inner sea. I must cross them. My Delia had done so—three times. I had crossed them only once, and then we had crashed.

This was where I had first encountered flying animals and birds on Kregen of a size large enough to carry a passenger. Out in the hostile territories I had seen a few distant dots in the air and the speed of the voller had taken me past. Now I faced gigantic birds and animals in their natural state, untamed, ferocious, vicious, forever seeking food.

I fancied they'd find Dray Prescot a tough and sinewy mouthful; still, it behooved me to keep my old carcass out of their fangs and jaws.

The voller took me through the first of the foothills. Ahead the high peaks waited. Wending a way through the passes and gradually flying higher and higher, I skirted those ice-bound precipices, sped beneath the pinnacles of glistening rock and drove hard through whatever open spaces valleys offered. The air cut to the quick. Flying silks and furs were heaped over me.

I crouched in the voller with only my eyes and nose showing and my fist gripped around the hilt of a longsword. If a flight of impiters caught me, those coal-black demons of the air would rip the voller to pieces. I could not hope to be saved once again by a gorgeous myriad of tiny pink and yellow birds.

Straight on past two mountain flanks that seemed ready to topple inward and grind together, I sent the voller hurtling down over the saddle. The long valley ahead swarmed with birds swooping from the rocks. I held to the center. Mists coiled below. The farther end of the valley showed its V-notch and chill white-blue sky beyond. Due west, always due west...

The voller fluttered and dived.

Useless to bash the controls, to rave and curse. Down swooped the voller, down and down, plunging into the mists. I ripped open the panel which in this small craft covered the two silver boxes in their sturm-wood orbits. A single glance told me the mechanism was functioning correctly, the orbits moving one with the other on their bronze and balass gearing. So the trouble lay within the vaol box. If there was trouble with the paol box there was nothing I could do. To open that would release the cayferm and that box would never function again.

The idea that this voller's power source had reached the end of its useful life, when the silver boxes dulled, had given me a nasty turn; now I must land and dismantle the vaol box.

The mists coiled more thinly. Huge bloated tree trunks passed. I had the speed down now and felt confident of making a respectable landing. The muggy heat rose. Here in these deep valleys the air hung heavy and humid, ground heat and the greenhouse effect combining to make jungle miniatures within the mountain mass.

A confused jumble of orange-speckled yellow, of leprous growths with medusa-arms, of black and glistening trunks, swished away. The voller roared past a lichened rock outcrop, clipped yellow powder from hanging clusters of puffballs, making me sneeze, and came to a shaky stop amid tendrilous yellow ferns. All about me the spectral trees rose like a wall. Bloated, whiplike, fern-fanned, the variety of forms displayed a massive and frenzied struggle for life. Lianas draped everywhere. The smells were fetid and yet not overly unpleasant and I guessed the busy scavengers were at work breaking down every last fragment of refuse.

A bulky something moved ponderously among the trees. A glimmering white outline, immense, inhuman, something like a giant slug with orange horns, slid past between the trees. The longsword lifted, but the monster glided on, tearing at the branches.

Putting the longsword down close by, I ripped out the vaol box and carefully opened it. How often I had done this! Inside the box the minerals were clumped, packed mostly at one end with only a scattering of powder moving freely. I used a dagger to stir the powder free, to break up the clumps, to return the mix to its original loose condition. By the time the lid was back on the sweat poured from me; the humidity was murderous.

The vaol box was slicked with moisture and I knew that enough had been trapped inside to make the box unusable again before too long. It would have to get me through the Stratemsk. I reseated it within its orbit and reconnected the gearing train.

It was at that moment, straightening up, ready to hit the controls, that the xi lunged.

There was barely time to scoop up the sword and parry that first vicious thrust.

The xi whirred its diaphanous wings and backed off, chirring in frenzy. Its iridescent scales glimmered in the diffused light. The xi was something like a dragonfly, with four glistening wings behind a head that was a nightmare cross between a bird's beak and a snake's wedge. But all likeness to a dragonfly was lost when the xi whipped its sinuous snakelike body from side to side and coiled it for a stinging blow from beneath. Besides, the xi was ten feet long—a flying monster, aiming to skewer me and then devour me at leisure for lunch.

A single dominant thought obsessed me: I must dispose of this fellow before the rest of the swarm found me.

It darted in again and I ducked the lethal lunge of the tail, the longsword slashing down at his forward antennae. The keen blade sheared through the black furry feelers, surged on to gouge into the bright and staring eye on the left of that wedge-shaped head. The xi's wings fluttered madly. It whirred away, spinning, flying clumsily. From the longsword a green ichor dropped.

The voller went up cleanly. Up and up, past the tumbling, pathetic shape of the xi, up to burst through the mist and so bring me into the chill upper air.

"By Vox!" I said explosively. "I was lucky there!"

In those last few murs before the mist enfolded me I had seen the glittering swarm approaching, flying fast, a blurring mass of shining wings and iridescent scales, the lizards of the air, swarming to devour me!

There is a considerable variety of xi, and I had just met a type whose body had nearly evolved into a whiplike snake form, away from the original, bulkier lizard form. Whatever family they belong to, the xi are bad news.

And my Delia had flown this way!

Straight on I forced the voller. Like the end of a nightmare the last valley

81

opened out and all before me stretched the downward trending slopes of the westward face of the Stratemsk. Here fresh dangers lurked. The flying furies of the mountains might all be behind me, the impiters and corths, the zizils and bisbis, the yellow eagles of Wyndhai and the iridescent-scaled xi; now I must fly over the lands of the crofermen.

Savage, untamed, cruel and suspicious, the crofermen inhabit the outer reaches of the Stratemsk. They live an arduous life filled with peril, defending their ponsho flocks against the demons of the air, continually fighting among themselves, man-beasts of lowering aspect and formidable ferocity.

I, Dray Prescot, say this with all truth: I was lucky to be able to fly over them and not have to come to ground.

As you know I had been well informed that it was against policy to take an airboat into the lands of the inner sea. Delia had landed her flier some way off the eastern edge of the sea and had taken local transport when she had come searching for me before. The people of the Eye of the World had little if any knowledge that it was possible for a man to fly through the air.

Now I knew that interdiction must have come from the Empire of Hamal, which made and sold vollers, and the law had been implemented by the Presidio of Vallia because they did not wish to lose their franchise. Hamal would not sell vollers to Pandahem or Loh, and their lack had proved disastrous in the past.

I consigned Hamal and Empress Thyllis, with whom I had an outstanding debt, to the Ice Floes of Sicce as I bored on through the bright air of Kregen, angling to fetch up in Sanurkazz itself.

How often I had promised myself I would return to the Eye of the World! And how often fate had destroyed my intentions, one way or another, every time. I had planned to return on a joyous holiday, to take my Delia and the family, to revisit the haunts of my existence there as a Krozair captain and see my friends once again. Now I came in urgency and haste, desperate that Delia might be in peril.

My plans were very simple. I would go first to Sanurkazz, the chief city of the Zairians, and seek information. If I found nothing I would fly on to Zy, the island fortress of the Krozair Brotherhood, that order of which I was proud to account myself a member and which, I truly think, meant more to me, for all the tiny scope of its activities on Kregen, than anything else except Delia and my family.

The journey had taken the best part of three days. I had flown in as straight a line by the compass as I could contrive, a great-circle route that wasted not a dwabur of distance. The distance would have taken months to travel by land and sea. It had taken me month after weary month to travel in the opposite direction. As the land opened out below and signs of cultivation appeared, I felt those irritable, apprehensive, fearful sensations attack me once more as I neared my goal.

It seemed to me that Delia had come here because she had had bad news of Segnik—he who was now Zeg. I had pushed all that from my mind. But what other explanation could there be? I had discussed with Delia the education of our children many times. She knew that I intended Drak and, in his time, Segnik to go to the Krozairs of Zy. I believe the most profound education was possible with them. I had intended to take a hand to soften the teachings that emphasized the hatred for the Grodnims of the green northern shore. Oh, yes, as you know, I hated the overlords of Magdag and all the other Grodnims of the northern shore. But I felt mature enough to hold that feeling in its proper perspective. I had worn green clothes of late and I had met in friendship those to whom green and religions associated with the color were good and fine. It was the inner strength the Krozairs of Zy give, the spiritual teachings, the skill at arms, the knowledge of self, all those mystic disciplines that make a Krozair a man among men that I wanted for my sons.

Dealing with the religious beliefs of Kregen, it was in the pure and life-enhancing teachings of Opaz, the embodiment of the Invisible Twins, that I wished my family to be brought up. But nowhere else could the skill, the powers, the self-control, the mystic self-knowledge of the Krozairs be found than here, in the Eye of the World. To be a Krzy is a great and precious gift.

Then a twitch afflicted my grim old lips. Among all this high-level occupation of my brain the tickling thought emerged that I would see friends here who would bring me down to earth—or Kregen—with a bump.

I would again see Nath and Zolta, my two favorite rascals, my two oar comrades. By Zair! We'd roister all night in Sanurkazz! We'd have the fat and jolly mobiles falling over their feet as they tried to arrest us, dancing through the streets, a flagon of drink in one hand and a pretty tavern wench in the other! What a fool I had been not to return here sooner!

And there would be Pur Zenkiren to see, that upright, grim, but scrupulously fair Krozair who had been a good friend to me and who must by now be the Grand Archbold of the Krozairs of Zy, for Pur Zazz, who had then held that exalted post, had clearly almost run his long life on Kregen when I had last spoken with him.

Then, too, there was Mayfwy. All my pleasant thoughts of anticipation clouded as I remembered with great affection and pride my oar comrade Zorg of Felteraz. He had died under the lashes of the whip-deldars of Magdag. His widow Mayfwy, her son Zorg and daughter Fwymay had made Nath and Zolta and myself very welcome at the estate of Felteraz. Yes, I would like to see Mayfwy again.

So there were many places and people I must visit. But first I must assure myself that Delia was safe. To look back was agony. Twenty-one infernal years!

Because people of Kregen live to two hundred years or so, once they reach maturity they change only slowly. I held a vision of my Delia in my brain that could not have altered in any great particular. Our thousand-year promise of life meant a great deal to me, quite apart from the obvious, for twenty-one years' separation on Earth would destroy in time's remorseless flow the joys we knew. How I hated the Star Lords when I allowed myself to brood on their high-handed usage of me!

That, along with all the rest of the unprofitable pining, had to be thrust aside. I would go on in my old way. I knew what I was about. If Zair was with me—and Opaz and Djan too, to be sure—I must succeed.

Ten
I am cruel to Mayfwy of Felteraz

Brilliant, glittering, filled with color, the waters of the Eye of the World rolled before me.

The twin Suns of Scorpio hung in the western sky, drenching the world in color and radiance. The air smelled sweet, sweet with the fragrance of Kregen. Below, the tended fields passed in neat checkerboards of cultivation. Here there could be habitation close to the shore of the inner sea, for ahead the massive frowning fortress guarding the careless city of Sanurkazz offered sure protection. As I looked ahead over the windshield, I saw that smaller but no less dominating fortress of Felteraz rise into view.

Felteraz, with its lush estates and its town and its fortress, was built into the sheer rock over the sea. Memories of the view from the high terrace there swam into my mind. How alike and yet how vastly different was the view in Felteraz from that dizzy prospect over the Bay and Valkanium from Esser Rarioch! Yet I loved this place. As my course took me over the gray battlements with their freight of banners, a sudden shaft of cunning pierced me through so that I trembled with my own deceit and struck the levers that sent the voller swirling down through the bright air.

There was no impediment to an aerial landing in the lands of the inner sea, for they knew nothing in their daily lives of aerial armadas and saddle flyers. The cities of the hostile territories were festooned with anti-flyer defenses. I was able to make a swooping landing, still the voller, and step out onto a broad platform just below the highest terrace. People came running, astonished at the apparition of a man falling from heaven. I dare say many of them took the commonsense view that I was a visitor from Zim.

Bronzed faces surrounded me. I saw again the mesh link mail of the men of Zair, the white surcoats blazing with a device I knew. That symbol, stitched in red and gold, with a lenk-leaf border, represented a pair of galley oars, crossed, divided upright by a longsword. Oh, yes, I knew that symbol. Hadn't I proudly worn it myself as a Krozair captain of a swifter of the Eye of the World, that device of Felteraz?

I knew none of the faces.

A longsword's point hovered a knuckle before my breastbone.

"Your name and your business, dom."

"My name is Dray Prescot. My business is with the Lady Mayfwy of Felteraz."

Only after I had spoken did it occur to me that Mayfwy might be dead, another here in her place as chatelaine of Felteraz.

The few murs of hesitation before the guard Hikdar spoke caused me great uneasiness, which vanished in a flood of relief as he said: "The Lady Mayfwy is at home. I think I have heard of you, Jernu,[3] from my father."

He looked at me doubtfully and did not lower the longsword. I would have faulted him in his duties had he done so. And from his father! Well, it had been a half-century by Earthly reckoning since I had been here last. I do not smile easily, as you know, so I looked at him and said, "Probably, Hikdar. If you will inform the Lady Mayfwy—"

"At once, Jernu."

He dispatched a swod of the guard and remained on the alert, watching me. The ring of people, joined now by women and girls, kept respectfully back and none offered to go anywhere near the voller. That was a marvel. I saw a movement in the pressing ring of people, in the direction opposite that taken by the guard swod, and I looked, seeing men and women moving quickly aside. A woman stepped out before them, holding a long silver wand in her hand with which she had no need to touch anyone who lagged in moving. I did not know her. I stared at the girl—the woman—who followed through the opened path.

She did not look quite the same. There was about her sweet face a graver air, a shadowed resignation to life that greatly pained me. In all else, though, she was the same lively, spritely, elfin girl who had first welcomed Zolta and Nath and me as we drove rattling up in our ass cart. Her dark, curly hair gleamed in the slanting rays of the suns, her pert nose uptilted and that small, soft sensuous mouth trembled and opened on a gasp. Her eyes widened and fastened on me a look that thrilled me through, a look compounded of pain and gladness, of joy and abiding sorrow.

With not the slightest holding back, with not a heartbeat of hesitation, she ran forward, lifting her arms.

"Dray! Oh, Dray! You have come back!"

And then she was in my arms and clasping me close and I looked over her shoulder with the scent of her in my nostrils and I felt the weight of Kregen crush in on me and knew myself for the most evil of devils imaginable—as I truly was.

85

She would not cry. Even with the emotions filling her she would not break down before her people. She stood back and held my hands and looked at me. I saw the brightness of her eyes, the tremble of that soft mouth.

"You have not changed, my Lord of Strombor!"

"And you," I said. "Mayfwy, you are the same dear Mayfwy."

"Oh, no. No, I know better than that." She glanced at the robed woman with the wand. "We will go to the terrace, Sheena, and be alone. Bring refreshments, Zond wine, for Pur Dray, the Lord of Strombor."

"At once, my lady."

And so there we were, Mayfwy and I, alone on the terrace as the sulking suns painted opaline radiance in the air and drowned the cliff face in color. I saw and I ached. How long it had been, how foolish I was! Fifty years— and then some of the iron returned, for twenty-one of those damned years had been wrenched away from my power by the Everoinye. Mayfwy took up a goblet of wine, laughing, handing it to me, and yet I saw the deep pain in her eyes. I gravely drank to her.

"Dray, there is so much to tell."

"Aye, so much."

"But first there is news that will gladden your heart... strange news to come from us here..."

So I knew.

"Delia! She has visited here? You have seen her?"

A shadow nicked across Mayfwy's elfin face and passed, then she lifted her chin proudly and smiled.

"Yes. Delia has been here. She sought you."

I looked at her. My relief was obvious, for Mayfwy went on: "Yes, she crossed the Stratemsk in safety. There was a beast, a horrific beast, with her, that I swear would tear a leem to pieces. My men were uneasy until your Delia reassured them."

"Melow the Supple."

"That was the name."

"She will not harm you, Mayfwy. But tell me of Delia!"

How cruel that was, those words of mine, my whole demeanor, to this girl!

"You treat women harshly, my Lord of Strombor." She paused and lifted her goblet. Its ruby decoration in chains around the gold caught the light and blazed blood-red. "You say you love them and you leave them, for seasons on end. And should I call you Prince Majister now? Or even King?"

"You call me Dray Prescot, as you always have. It is not of my will that I left Delia—or you—without saying remberee. There are dark and evil forces in my life—but enough of this. Is Delia well? Did she speak of the children? Where did she go? Tell me, Mayfwy, for the sake of my dear friend and oar comrade, Zorg."

"Zorg." She drank then, and it was a benediction. "She is well and she says the children are well, although wild—well, we all know how wild our children are."

"Forgive me," I said quickly—me, that Dray Prescot who never apologized except to Delia. "Young Zorg and Fwymay. They are well?"

"Yes. They are well. Zorg is now a Krozair of Zy, which is as it should be, I suppose. He captains a swifter. He has much of his start to thank you for, Dray."

"Nonsense! A lad like that will forge his own way on Kregen."

She looked at me oddly. Well, not so long ago I had been standing in a Parisian hospital with the Prussian guns thundering and Kregen was four hundred light-years away. So I said: "The Zairians will always need men like young Zorg. And Fwymay?"

"She has made me a grandmother twice, the minx. She married Zarga na Rozilloi, who is a Krozair Brother, and a very pleasant young man."

I knew that this Zarga na Rozilloi must be of importance to warrant the *na* as his connective term, but he was not a Krzy. Had he been, Mayfwy would have said.

"He is a Krozair of Zimuzz." She was looking at me.

"A fine order," I said. But we both knew there was no other order as fine as the Krozairs of Zy.

Now the suns were almost gone. The purple shadows dropped across the terrace. Soon the Twins would be up, eternally revolving one about the other, to cast their mingled pinkish light down on Kregen. We moved into the inner room where we had often sat and talked and listened to the music provided by the citadel singers. The room looked just the same, except that a full-length portrait of a splendid-looking man had been added to the other portraits. This must be Zarga, for he wore the symbols of the Krozairs of Zimuzz. I ignored this new son-in-law and walked across, planted my feet on the thick rug and stood firmly looking up at the portrait of Zorg of Felteraz. Mayfwy moved silently away and left me. I looked at this painting of Zorg and I remembered, I remembered the warrens of Magdag and the rowing benches of the Magdaggian swifters, with Zolta and Nath, and I remembered our shared agonies and perils, the onions we had divided up, the lashes we had taken and, finally, Zorg's death, there in the stench and filth of a Magdagglan swifter. I remembered. And when I turned back to Mayfwy she put a hand to her mouth and did not speak for a moment. I suppose a great deal of what I felt showed on that ugly old face of mine.

Then, as though what she said had been jolted out of her by this reunion, by my abstraction, she said: "I used to hope I could place your portrait there, my Lord of Strombor."

I shook my head.

Then she cried.

Afterward I gave her another cup of wine and wiped her eyes with a clean cloth—she wore no makeup and had need of none—and said: "I must press on to find Delia. You know that. It is a fate I cannot—would not—deny. Until I know she is safe I cannot rest."

"I do understand. But please forgive me for saying... and for crying." She tossed her head back so that the clustered dark curls glistened in the samphron-oil lamp's gleam. "What young Zorg would say I do not know. No Krozair's mother cries!"

"I do not believe that. And Zorg, if he is a true Krozair as I know him to be, does not believe it either."

"If only he would get himself married and have children, they would be a comfort to me here."

There was more talk after that, and a fine meal which I knew had been especially prepared for me, and more wine—that smooth splendid Zond wine that Nath was so fond of—and Chremson if a difference in the tickle of the palate was needed. But Mayfwy could see the impatience burning in me. Truth to tell, I felt that Delia would understand when I told her that I had broken my journey to see Mayfwy, more so now that these two had met. How I had both welcomed and dreaded that encounter, for I desperately wished for them to be friends. But sober reality would seem to indicate the opposite. I would have to see what my Delia had to say.

I stood up.

Mayfwy rose, lithe as a neemu, her gaze wide on me, a hand to her breast. She wore what I remembered as being her favorite costume, a sheer gown of shimmering silk, white, simple, deeply cut, fastened at her shoulders by golden pins encrusted with rubies. They must be the same fibulae. They would be the same when we were all rotting in our graves or shivering in the Ice Floes of Sicce.

"You must go? So soon?"

"When I find my Delia we will return, Mayfwy. I shall not again be such an onker. Do you forgive me?"

As I said the word that must have cut her, that simple "my" Delia, I cursed myself again. It seemed I could bring nothing but pain into the life of this girl. And girl she seemed to me still, despite all the lonely length of time she had lived, for she kept up her appearance out of her pride in being the widow of Zorg of Felteraz, a Krozair of Zy.

Luckily I did not ask her why she had never married again. That would have been the action of a clod; while I am a fine full-bloomed specimen of a clod, I did see clearly enough that the question would have been a slap in her face.

We stepped out onto that paved square high on the flank of the cliff where my voller waited. A guard had been posted around the craft, but no one had ventured near. Perhaps this was the very first airboat ever seen in these parts. I didn't care if it was or not, and I didn't care for the Hamalians and their dictates either. There was no remorse whatsoever in me for stopping here. Mayfwy told me that Delia had said she would fly direct to the fortress of Zy to find me. She had not confided in Mayfwy why, after a space of twenty years, she had thus come flying into the Eye of the World. But Mayfwy told me that Delia appeared sad, confirming Panshi's story.

I would brook no longer delay.

"Delia came riding a sectrix," said Mayfwy. She put a hand out tentatively and touched the leather and canvas of the voller. Her hand trembled. "You will use this marvelous thing?"

"If Delia went by here a year ago and then took ship for Zy, I can catch her all the quicker by voller."

"Voller? Ah, the flying boat."

"Yes."

"There are many of these... vollers, in the outer world? In the world of Vallia and Valka, of Djanduin and Strombor?"

"Yes."

"It must be a marvelous place."

"It is, but in many things it is not as marvelous as the Eye of the World."

"We have our troubles. I fear for Zorg and for Zarga, my son-in-law. Those horrible greens of Grodno bear down our defenses. We are in parlous case, these latter days, my Lord of Strombor."

She went on to tell me in a small voice that the Grodnims pressed hard on the Zairians, that many battles had been lost; the Grodnim swifters might still be kept at bay; but the Grodnim armies swept on, irresistibly, it seemed, from victory to victory. Her son Zorg scoured the seas and gained success in single-ship actions—how my blood fired up at the thought!—but Holy Sanurkazz lay sunk in apathy, awaiting the stroke of doom. I could scarcely credit this. When I had left here the Zairians, under the command of my friend Pur Zenkiren of Sanurkazz, had been pressing on to victory along the eastern shore in alliance with the Proconians, a people distinct from the red and green.

"Proconia?" I said.

She made a little moue. "They keep themselves aloof. They resist any attack on their territory. They no longer wish to ally with us in the fight."

"Then Zair will see they do not ally themselves with the damned Grodnims,"

"That is what we all pray."

I did not tell her that with the politics of this region—politics I had previously regarded as simple and straightforward—if the Grodnims gained an upper hand the Proconians, aye, and all the other uncommitted peoples, would jump in to be on the winning side. Once the slide began it would gain speed with frightful force.

"Perhaps I will call in at Sanurkazz," I said as I stepped up into the voller, observing the fantamyrrh. "On our way back. There has to be an explanation for what you say."

"King Zo still rules, Dray. He will be pleased to see you."

I put my hand over the levers. The Twins rolled along above among a myriad of stars. The Maiden with the Many Smiles would soon be up and then She of the Veils. This would not be a night of Notor Zan, the Tenth Lord, the Lord of Darkness.

Felteraz lies about three dwaburs to the east of Sanurkazz and the distance in a flier's straight line to the island fortress of Zy from there is roughly a hundred and sixty dwaburs. At my voller's best pushed speed of ten dbs I ought to sight the island cone well before daylight. So I looked down on Mayfwy and she looked up. The fuzzy pinkish light played tricks with her features; but I knew she was not crying.

"Remberee, Mayfwy."

"Remberee, Pur Dray."

I thrust the levers home and the voller shot skyward.

To relate the events that now befell me is to relive a time of scarlet horror, a time when reason itself vanished from Kregen, a time when my reason for a while deserted me. My recollections tumble all confused and distorted, as the massive russet bodies of the chunkrah swim and haze when seen in the heat of the campfires of the Great Plains of Segesthes.

The voller did not fail me and I came at last in sight of the extinct volcanic cone that is the heart of the fortress of Zy. On the journey I had eaten and drunk of the supplies so liberally provided by Mayfwy, and I had slept. As I stared eagerly forward with the slipstream blustering in my face and saw that grim black pile harshly upthrust against the moons-glowing sea, I rejoiced. Soon, soon, I would clasp my Delia in my arms again and she would clasp me...

I sent the voller straight for the tall rock arch leading to the inner harbor. Only a few dim lights burned where I had been accustomed to seeing many lights blazing from the rock and the pharos lantern, swung from chains in the arch of the rock, casting its friendly greeting on the waters below. In a penumbrous circle of indistinct forms I dived for the entrance.

It is a commonplace experience, universally observed, that when a person returns to a place of his former abode everything in building and architecture and scale appears to him much smaller than the memories he had carried over the years. I had not experienced that in Valka. To a certain extent in Felteraz, yes, I had noticed, but then, it is the very smallness of Felteraz that enjoins so much of its beauty. Here, as I swooped the voller under the immense rock arch of Zy I felt only renewed awe at the grandeur about me. The water rippled gently below, pitch-black and runneled with the reflected lights of torches. Lights clustered on the dock. I touched down on the stones and stood up, stretched and cocked a leg over the side of the voller.

"Stand still! Declare yourself or you will be feathered."

That seemed perfectly proper to me.

"I am Dray Prescot, Krozair of Zy."

To say those words again, here in the very heart of all that made the Krozairs of Zy so formidable, so much a part of my life, in the very sanctum of the order, gave me a sweet, dizzied feeling of homecoming that marched with those other feelings of homecoming I had experienced in Valka.

"Climb down from your flying contraption, Dray Prescot. Do not touch your weapons as you value your life."

This was carrying precaution to an extreme. Still, I accepted. After all, eternal vigilance was part of the Krozair creed. I stepped from the voller to face the party of men who accosted me.

They wore the white surcoats over their mesh mail. The old familiar device glittered from the breasts of the surcoats, bravely shining in the light of the torches, the scarlet circle enclosing the hubless spoked wheel embroidered in silks of blue and orange and yellow. I saw the faces enclosed in the mail hoods, hard, fierce, dedicated faces, all a strong mahogany brown from the suns and the winds, with those arrogant upthrust black mustaches bristling. Yes, these were my Krozair Brothers.

I felt strange, outré, a stranger, in my decent Vallian buff. I wore a longsword, true, but it was not a real Krozair longsword, crafted by master smiths in the workshops here. Out of habit I still swung a rapier and main-gauche from my belt. I took a step forward, and a dozen longswords were whipped from scabbards and leveled at my breast.

"Lahal, my Brothers," I cried. "Lahal and lahal, in the name of Zair."

"There is no lahal for you here, Dray Prescot," said a Krozair Brother, a Bold, one of those dedicated to the most intense efforts within the fraternity, a man whose whole life was bound up in daily service to the order. "Forsworn! No longer are you Pur Dray, Krozair of Zy."

I gaped at him. I did not understand.

"Forsworn, Dray Prescot, less than nothing, Apushniad, ingrate, traitor, leemshead. You are no longer a Krozair of Zy."

Eleven
Apushniad

Apushniad!

That was a terrible word to a Krozair. Traitor, ingrate, leemshead, outlaw. A man cast off from the order.

A man denied fellowship, a man despised by those who had once been his fellows.

And I, Dray Prescot, had been dubbed Apushniad!

I stood within the Hall of Judgment. The room was small, holding only a double hundred of Krozairs, ranked in their pews along the walls, the banners hanging in the lamplight above, a dusky, glittering mass of gold and scarlet. Small, that Hall of Judgment was, hewn from the living heart of the Rock of Zy. Small, because it was so seldom used. Once, long ago, I had witnessed the ritual trial and banishment of a Krozair Brother, accused of a crime no Krozair could own to and remain a member of the order. The ceremony had created a deep and lasting impression. So I knew what I faced.

They had clad me in a white surcoat and on my breast blazed the great symbol of the order. They had hung a scabbarded longsword about my waist. It was my own sword, not a Krozair longsword, but a good workman-like blade fashioned in the armory of Valka at Esser Rarioch by Naghan the Gnat and myself. It had served me well before. Now I stood in the Hall of Judgment, robed and armed like a Krozair, and I had no memory of how I had come there, how I had been dressed, what had happened after those terrible words had suddenly fallen on my uncomprehending ears.

If I say that in the days and sennights, aye, and months that followed, I do not clearly recall all that happened, I think it no marvel. I was gripped in a stasis of horror that seemed to me impossible and that must vanish in the next heartbeat, yet it never left me as day succeeded day. So I stood there, facing my accusers. In the high throne sat the adjudicator, a Bold, a man in whose heart no mercy for the Grodnims could exist and therefore a man in whose heart no mercy for those who did not fully support Zair could exist either.

To one side, in a throne with a hooded carapace fashioned after the likeness of that mythical bird, the Ombor—for whose name my House of Strombor in Zenicce was named—sat the Grand Archbold.

I had thrown him a single despairing look, expecting to see my old friend Pur Zenkiren, expecting to receive some acknowledgment, some sign of understanding.

Pur Zenkiren did not sit in the Ombor Throne.

I knew the man who sat there.

He sat with bitter down-curved lips, this man, the Archbold. This man who had succeeded Pur Zazz held the destiny of the Krozairs of Zy in his hands. I remembered him as a bold, free, ruthless Krozair captain, a man who would ram his swifter into the very jaws of the Overlords of Magdag. This was Pur Kazz of Tremzo, but different. A ghastly wound puckered the whole left side of his face, taking out an eye so that only the socket glared forth, rawly red. His bitter mouth twisted in the tail of that terrible scar. He sat hunched forward, his scarlet robes drawn about him, and I saw his hands shaking.

A Krozair Brother lifted a scroll.

"Step forth, oh man who is called Dray Prescot, Lord of Strombor."

A longsword point in the small of my back emphasized the demand. I stepped forward, onto the round raised pulpit where cunningly arranged lamps shed a concentrated light. I felt dizzy. I forced my head up and stood straight bracing those wide shoulders of mine back with a conscious effort.

"I am here!" I cried. "And I do not understand! What—?"

The Brother with the scroll began to read, drowning my words.

As I listened I felt my spirit tremble and shrink. I, Dray Prescot felt the awful weight of what he said crush down on me and rend my ib so that I had to grip the lenken rail and hold on while all of Kregen rocked about me like a swifter in a rashoon.

I heard his words—vague snatches of them recur in times of nightmare. I feel that neither my walk from the Phokaym across the Klackadrin nor the coronation parade of Queen Thyllis in Ruathytu, when I stumbled along at the tail of a calsany, scarcely moved me more, could have been more terrible. There have been other awful experiences through which I have gone on Kregen; perhaps this being out of the Krozairs of Zy affected me more powerfully than any of them, although, when I think back, I now understand that I did not really believe what was taking place before my eyes.

The Call had been sent. The great Call had been sent out, the Azhurad, the Call to Arms which would bring every Krozair of Zy to fight for his order against enormous perils. Every Krozair of Zy had answered the Azhurad, as was his sworn duty, every Brother had come joyously to fight for Zair against the evil of Grodno, every single Brother—except one.

All except Dray Prescot had answered the Call.

I shouted: "But I did not know!"

The adjudicator leaned forward.

"That is a lie! You live, therefore you must know."

A Brother stood up at my right. He was a young man. He did not relish his task. But the Krozairs point a path of justice in their dealings; they do not punish without trial and reason. This man, this Pur Ikraz, had been appointed to speak for me in my defense.

He said: "It is true that any living Krozair must hear the Azhurad when the Call is sent. But is it not possible that, in this one instance, Pur Dray, somehow, in a manner we cannot guess, did not receive the Call?"

The Adjudicator said, "It is impossible."

Through the mazy sounds of that chamber I recalled speaking to Pur Zenkiren and to Pur Zazz, promising them that wherever I might be in Kregen I would answer the Azhurad. It had been explained to me. As part of the initiation ceremony I had been escorted down into the heart of the Rock of Zy and in a great cavern scooped from the living rock I had been shown the Horn of Azhurad. I knew nothing then of radio waves and of telepathy; I did know that when the Archbold set the giant bellows into action, pumping air through the myriad holes in the rock, the Horn would sound. The Azhurad would tingle with powers that could fling a note around the world, resonating in the skulls of every member of the Krozairs of Zy. Only through mystic disciplines of which I do not speak could a Krozair Brother hear the Azhurad, only one trained in the arts could understand. Hearing and understanding, he would joyfully don his surcoat with the hubless spoked wheel blazing within the scarlet circle, belt on his longsword and so go up with his Krozair Brethren against the foe.

I gripped the rail. I shouted over their noise: "And if I did hear the Call, am I not here? Have I not answered? I was in the world of Kregen outside the Eye of the World. It has taken me many months of travel to reach you here."

I was prepared to plead anything to avert the horror.

The Adjudicator placed a forefinger to his lips as he spoke. "So you did hear the Call?"

I would not lie.

"No. I did not hear the Azhurad. But I am here now!"

"It is known that it is impossible for a living Brother not to hear the Call. You stand condemned on two counts: if you did hear and did not come, you are condemned; if you did not hear that can only mean you were never properly a Krozair of Zy. You were not pure enough of spirit, your ib remained befouled with the dross of everyday life, so you stand condemned on that count, also, to be banished, Apushniad."

A thought occurred to me so despicable I winced at my own vileness. I lifted my head again and jutted my jaw out like the rostrum of a swifter.

"My son Drak! Prince of Vallia! He was to join the Krozairs of Zy! And my second son Segnik, he who is now Zeg, he was also to join the Krozairs of Zy!"

I could not go on. Not for myself could I use my sons.

The Adjudicator hissed between his teeth.

"Your sons answered The Call! They came with great gallantry and they fought with joy for Zair! But you—"

"They are safe?"

"They live still. It was they who told us you were not dead, as we had believed. They did not know where you were. Had you been dead it would have been better for you."

Now Pur Kazz, the Grand Archbold, lifted his golden rod. Everyone fell silent and turned to the Ombor Throne.

"When you did not answer the Azhurad, cramph, you were tried and condemned in your absence. Now you have the effrontery to arrive here crying and mewling. The sentence of that trial will be carried out. We stage this trial now in order to show you, who deserve nothing, that the Krozairs of Zy do not punish vengefully, out of spite, but out of law and order and love of Zair."

I stared at him. His voice slurred. His hands trembled. I remembered him as arrogant and brash and filled with vigor. The disfiguring scar must have addled his brains. Besides, he had called me cramph, which is a term of abuse. Not one other of the Brethren had descended to insults.

I shouted at him. "And my Delia! The Princess Majestrix of Vallia! She is here! I demand to see her!"

"You demand nothing!"

The Adjudicator's quick words were chopped by the bellow of rage from Pur Kazz. I could not understand what he said, and I do not think anyone else could either. But we were all fully aware of the passions of anger and enmity blazing in him.

"Let the sentence be carried out."

Pur Ikraz, the man to speak in my defense, started to plead in mitigation, but Pur Kazz waved his golden rod and brought it down with a crash and bellowed. My defense withered away.

I do not fully recall what happened next. I have memories, lurid, black, lightning-shot, of men coming forward and speaking ritually above me. Of others ripping the bright insignia from the white surcoat. A dull realization of why they had clothed me in the emblems of the Krozairs of Zy shook me then. I had been clothed so that I might be stripped, in humiliation and shame.

My longsword was lifted from the scabbard. I could see three different reflections of myself in tall mirrors, the Three Mirrors of the Ib, positioned to reinforce what went on in the mind of the accused, to make him see himself in all his shame.

As the sword whispered from the scabbard I swung back. I saw Pur Kazz leaning over the golden rail of the Ombor throne. I saw the torches and the lamps, the massed faces of the Brethren; I heard the chanting as they exorcised the evil; I heard and I saw and I do not remember anything else until I found myself standing in that cleared space below my pulpit, the sword grasped in my fists in that cunning Krozair grip, cocked. I heard myself yelling—wild, strange, mad words, tumbling out pell-mell—and saw the ring of watchful Krozairs, bearing their swords in grips like mine, waiting, circling, ready to destroy me.

I saw my reflection in the Three Mirrors of the Ib.

I saw a madman. I saw the huge rent in the breast of my white surcoat. I saw the face: that devil's face with the furrowed brow and the snarling ugly mouth, the eyes like leems', glittering, maniacal, mad. I saw a man I did not recognize.

But I knew the truth.

The maniac brandishing a sword here in the Hall of Judgment, who would not accept the dictates of his onetime fellows in the Krozairs of Zy, that man who had reverted to all the old intemperate ruthlessness I had tried so hard to overcome, that devil incarnate here in the seat of wisdom and learning and great devotion—that madman was me, plain Dray Prescot.

I threw the sword down with a clang.

"You cannot understand why I could not answer the Call! If I said I was in a place where the Call did not reach, you would not believe! If I say I prize being a Krozair of Zy above all else on Kregen, you would sneer! I have failed you in your terms! But I have always kept the faith, I have not failed! It is you, who do not believe in Krozair Brother..."

But I could not go on. How could they believe my wild stories about living on another world? How could they conceive of a world with only one sun, a world with only one moon, a world with only apims?

Then, truly, my reason left me.

Only vague and rending impressions remain.

Someone must have picked up my sword. It hung before me in the air, the lamplight striking a star from the tip, the blade gleaming straight and true. A crazy thought afflicted me: how would Naghan the Gnat relish what was being done to his handiwork?

For the sword was placed across the twin Stones of Repudiation. Basaltic blocks, hard and bleak and unforgiving, they hunkered like extensions of the very earth itself. The sword glimmered. I saw the Hammer of Retribution lifted. It rose high, poised in the muscular hands of a Krozair Brother whose title I will not repeat. I saw his naked arms flex. They bunched. I wanted to look away. I could not. The Hammer of Retribution smashed down. My longsword rang once, with a gong note, twisted, echoing, lost in the crash of sundering metal and the hammerblow against the rock.

In shapeless shreds my sword lay on the floor.

I cannot tell what happened next. I can only piece together those earlier memories of seeing a Krozair of Zy receive the Apushniad. It is painful. It is so painful I will leave that scene of desolation and horror. I was finally led away, head hanging, and although chains were placed on me they were unnecessary.

I do remember the hissing and vindictive voice of Pur Kazz, Grand Archbold of the Krozairs of Zy, shouting at my back.

"So goes he who once was Pur Dray, Krozair of Zy. Apushniad! Let no Krozair Brother's hand be lifted to help him. He is accursed. He is banished from our midst, as his sword is broken and his banner burned, and all the goodness of our hearts and faces is turned from him. Apushniad!"

It was finished.

Twelve
Conversation in a fish cell on the Island of Zy

No, I do not wish to dwell on those moments in the Hall of Judgment, nor on the days that followed. You who have listened to my story know how I would willingly, gladly, have given up all the tawdry, tinselly titles I had accumulated, every one, to remain a Krozair of Zy.

Apushniad!

Outcast, leemshead, I was thrust from the warm circle of the order, and yet there was still work I might perform, still a use to be found for my unworthy body.

I was not to be executed.

Oh, make no mistake, the Krzy would think no more of executing an Apushniad than they would of lopping the head off an Overlord of Magdag.

They knew my strength. Many in that small Hall of Judgment had fought with me in the long-gone past. They knew I had slaved as an oarsman in the galleys of Magdag. Now one of the minor points of the Zairians I had been forced to slide away from and overlook and condone was brought home: the men of Zair also employed slaves in their swifters.

So I knew my fate.

Down and down we went, the guard surrounding me with ready swords. They were expert swordsmen, as indeed they must be to become Krozairs at all. It would have been a great and bonny fight. It would have been a fight to warm a man.

But I knew as we went down the stairs with the water dropping milkily about us and the torches hurling black-bat shadows ahead, that I could not fight those who had been my Brothers merely because they would not understand my wild talk of an earth with one sun, one moon and only apims. No, I had found, as I caught that dramatic reflection of the devil-figure who was me in the Three Mirrors in the Ib, that I could not strike out in hatred at a man who was a Krozair Brother, who wore the hubless spoked wheel within the circle as his emblem. Maybe there were other reasons. Perhaps, after all, I had grown weak and flabby, lacking the will and the old cutting edge. I do not think I felt fear. If anything my feelings had been the reverse and I would have joyed to leap forward to my death.

Even then, though, even then I knew that I was still the old Dray Prescot, a stubborn onker who would never give up the fight but would always struggle on against despair and defeat.

They thrust me into a narrow cell whose walls glistened wetly and the iron bars clanged with that soul-destroying sound of finality.

Then they went away and left me to the darkness and the emptiness of self.

How long did I spend in that cell? It is of no consequence.

I was fed at intervals, washed, shaved, given a gray slave breechclout. My chains were checked and I was at last led out and up those long slippery stairs in the heart of the rocky Island of Zy beneath the gracious living areas of the extinct volcanic throat. Straight to the small harbor within the immense rocky arch I was led. It was night. The stars shone in spattering reflections on the water. There were no moons in the sky.

Among the guards I heard a muttering, as of a low-voiced discussion that could not easily be resolved.

Ahead I could see against the quay a long, low, impressive shape of power. There had been no swifters when I had flown in. There was no sign of my voller. Perhaps I would still not have made a break for it even if I had seen the airboat. I was down, beaten, face-first in the muck of life.

The moored swifter possessed two banks of oars and was lean and powerful. Despite everything, I found myself noticing that she was bereft of much of the ornate panoply to which I had become accustomed in the swifters of the Eye of the World. She had been stripped for action with a vengeance.

I heard one of the guards, a tough old bird with a scarred face, speaking hotly.

"To the Ice Floes of Sicce with him! He is Apushniad!"

And another, younger, with a strong determined face, spoke out.

"And yet she is very beautiful."

I reeled. I gripped the nearest Krozair and he grunted and shifted his sword hilt out of the way.

Mercy is a commodity in relatively short supply on Kregen. Zair does not teach mercy to a Grodnim. And Grodno teaches only implacable hatred for all Zairians. Even in my kingdom of Djanduin the pantheon of warrior gods led by the divine Djan must have the case for mercy argued and won before they deign to nod their heads in merciful acquiescence. For the religion of Opaz, the Invisible Twins, mercy is a guiding light, but that too is a mercy tempered with forethought for the welfare of those of Opaz. As for Lem the Silver Leem—they should receive the same mercy they show and they would all be extinct. For old Mog, the high priestess of the religion of Migshaanu, away there in Migladrin, mercy was a known and valued component of the religion, used with care as a precious unction.

I could expect no mercy from these men who had been my Krozair Brothers, men for whom I would have fought and men who would have given their lives for me in like manner, before I had been tried and judged and condemned.

I would not plead.

But through all the agony of spirit I felt the fire in my blood. The agony refreshed itself at the wellspring of a new agony.

I knew.

We hustled toward the rock of the side wall. The guards spoke in harsh whispers. "Keep quiet," and "Careful with the light," and "He should be thrown to the chanks." I stumbled along. A lenken door opened and closed, silently. An iron bolt dropped into place, silently.

A pitchy darkness confronted my groping fingers. My chains clanked. I heard a panel squeal and a voice, hoarse, say, "One bur only, my lady. Not a mur more."

A form moved. A soft pearly light shone across a littered floor of discarded impedimenta, fishing gear, a broken trident, crumbling floats, a scattering of canvas, wooden tubs and withy baskets. The light wavered.

I looked up.

It is a long time ago, I was in torment, I do not recall—I remember her soft arms, her lips, the touch of her hair, the thrilling whisper of her voice. Oh, I felt as poor and downtrodden and useless there as ever I have felt. That it should come to this! A beaten man, chained, thrown out of all he held dear, yet daring to clasp in his arms the most wonderful woman in two worlds!

"Dray, oh, my heart..."

No, I cannot tell more.

Delia—my Delia of Delphond, my Delia of the Blue Mountains.

Of all we babbled I remember little. She said these terrible Krozairs of Zy were incapable of being bribed. Nothing would move them to deny their duty. I could have told her that. There was no easy escape through gold here. She was well. She held a great pride in her sons and daughters. Krozairs, Sisters of the Rose, Princes and Princesses of Vallia. I could hardly talk. She wanted to talk of the youngsters, but I kissed her and we clung together, warm, warm, and again she wailed that there was no way of contriving my escape.

I do remember, in a pale pathetic reflection of my old arrogance: "I will win free, my Delia. I will. And I will tell you why sometimes I go away even if you do not believe."

"If you tell me I will believe."

I was charged afresh with a ludicrous determination. 'I will win free. I will prove I am a true Krozair."

She held me. "Yes, yes, that is what you will do. I know. They are wrong..."

"It is a thing I must do. I must."

How different this, from all my grandiose expectations! I had waited twenty-one dreary years, and all for this! My Delia, the most perfect woman of two worlds, how cruel that she should thus be tormented on my account. I held her close and my thoughts were clouded. I remember... I remember little then.

No, I cannot tell more.

The panel scraped and the pearly light strengthened. I held her close, but she was gone, gone, and the panel closed and the light darkened and I was alone.

The outer lenken door was flung back and rough hands grasped me and, with my chains clanking about me, I was led down to the stone quay and up the gangplank. So once more I entered on the life of a galley slave of the Eye of the World, which is the inner sea of the continent of Turismond on Kregen, spinning beneath the Suns of Scorpio.

A galley slave may survive if he can last out the first week.

My memory of that time remains hazy. I recall that the work came as a shock; I had grown slothful. My strength remained, but it was not as easy as I might have been forgiven for thinking. It took me some time to regain all my old toughness and hardness, to endure the incessant toil, and all that time I remained sunk in a spiritless slough. I cared little for anything. I even came to regard that dark meeting with my Delia as an hallucination. Had I really once more clasped Delia of Delphond in my arms? Could it truly have been my Delia of the Blue Mountains? Or was I gripped by the Drig-driven phantasms of the madness I know claimed me?

Reason had fled. I pulled my oar. I lived like a vosk sunk in swill. I endured.

Even thoughts of Zorg of Felteraz, and Nath and Zolta, my two oar comrades still living, penetrated like a nightmare, so that often and often I would call their names, thinking them laboring at the loom at my side.

As for the five other wights on the loom with me, I knew nothing of them nor cared how they regarded me. I was the madman of the benches. I shouted for Zorg when the swifter went into action, yelling for Nath and Zolta, cursing the Overlords of Magdag, pulling with frenzy so that I could drown out the blackness of a despair I had forgotten tormented me, or why, or how, sunk in the blazing mania of madness.

When I had been a slave in the Magdaggian swifters I had gradually surfaced from near-insanity. I had taken an interest in what went on, noting the galleys, their construction, their methods of working and sailing and fighting. Now I cared for nothing. I pulled. When the lash fell on me I yelled out in abandon, uncaring, all pride forgotten.

It is all a fragmentary scattering of scarlet memories.

One time we were rammed and the apostis crumpled in deadly splinters and the side caved in and three of the poor devils chained with me were crushed to red pulp. One time arrows sought down into the slave benches, for this craft was rigged anaphract, and I saw a shaft sprout suddenly from the back of the slave in front of me. I saw with perplexity and no sensations of pain an arrow pinning my foot to the deck. I wrenched the thing out with a jerk of my leg, seeing blood, feeling nothing, pulling, pulling, pulling. I must have been sent down to the sickbay and recovered of the wound. I remember nothing of that.

There was a space when I felt the rain and the wind on my face, and the heat of the suns, and then a space when I did not. Now I realize I must have been transferred from the upper bank to the lower; it made no difference to my madness.

Once, I dimly recall, I awoke to look up and see the immense arch of the rock harbor of the Island of Zy above my head and I cried out "Krozair!" in a terrible voice. I strove to rise and could not, for I was chained and manacled and the chains were stapled to the deck.

Now, later, I know it was after that experience that I was vaguely aware of people bending over me, of shadowy forms, of a shielded light, of whispers.

I recalled these fragments of the night as I labored at the oar by day. The suns scorched my back, my hair grew wild, I fined off the excess weight that being a prince and king brings. I know I was as hard and tough and enduring as ever I had been.

In the full circle of vaol-paol all things must come to pass.

One night I felt my chains shaking, and I cursed and turned over irritably, for sleep was a precious boon to a slave. I heard a whisper and a curse, and someone said, "Sleep, you Grodno-gasta!" and the soggy sound of a blow. Another voice hailed, it seemed from a distance. Closer at hand the first voice said with great viciousness: "May Makki-Grodno devour his intestines!"

The chains shook again, I heard a clink of metal, and then all was silent. I turned over and found a softer patch on the ponsho-fleece covered sack of straw and slipped back to slumber.

No use to ask me where the swifter in which I slaved sailed. I had no idea. I had no desire to know. I believe I did not even understand quite what this all meant, somehow regarding all the toil and agony as a part of a dream in which Zorg, Nath, Zolta and I slaved and labored through all eternity.

During the periods when the breeze blew fair and the square sails on the two masts could be set, the slaves might rest. On one evening when the suns sank into a metallic sea and sheened from horizon to keel in a single sheet of burnished bronze, I realized we were at sea. I thought Zorg must have the better share of our onion. Nath and Zolta would share theirs. We were down to half rations. As for water, a mere mouthful and no more must last us.

We pulled ourselves up on the benches as the sails were furled and we settled to the looms. The drum-deldar beat out his rhythm and, all as one, like beating wings, the oars dipped and rose to dip again. Silently we stole into the coast.

Nothing meant anything. When the final beat from the drum and the oar-master's whistle signaled a cessation to our labors, every slave drooped over his loom. I squirmed about for a softer spot on the ponsho-fleece, for without these sacks and the fleeces a man could never last at the rowing benches. I prepared for sleep and knew I would dream my nightmares.

I dreamed that Zorg was telling me how he had secreted a piece of cheese; he wanted to divide it between all four of us, but we must do it when the Rapas on the next oar could not see, for it had once been theirs and they could not understand where it had gone. Nath and Zolta had chingled their chains in one of the many signals we oarslaves used to pass messages.

The thing must be done furtively. Not only must we not alert the Rapas, but the whip-deldars walking the narrow deck would delight in any excuse to lash us with old snake at a time when we should be resting.

"Hold still, Stylor!"

That was Nath, breathing in my ear.

We spoke in whispers.

"Split it fairly, Zorg," I said, and instantly Nath said: "Quiet, Stylor! For the love of Zair! Quiet!"

And Zolta, strangely near for his apostis seat, whispered: "Hurry it up, you great fambly!"

And Nath, breathing hard: "It takes a man to do this, you nit of nits."

Well, they would always argue and insult each other, and each ready to hurl himself to death to save the other.

"Is the Grakki-thing free yet?"

"In a mur—in a mur—"

And I said, sleepily, "Make the cheese a nice juicy Loguetter, Zorg. In the name of Diproo the Nimble-Fingered, we've earned it."

"Quiet, numbskull!" And: "Clap a fist over his wine-spout, Zolta, while I"—grunt of effort—"finish this."

And, oddly, I felt a hand over my mouth. How, I wondered in my dream, could it be Zolta's? He sat at the apostis seat, almost fully over the water. But it was a dream; anything could happen in a dream.

The night breathed about us, a night of Notor Zan, when no moon shines in the sky of Kregen. In the darkness I dreamed that Zorg partitioned up his cheese and the Rapas had not seen. I reached out for my portion. I felt a fist under my fingers, a fist that spread into a hand that grasped my hand.

"Where—" I began, and the other hand clapped back over my face. I squirmed. My chains did not rattle.

I was being lifted up.

This was indeed a most miraculous dream. Was I astride a fluttrell or a mirvol or even a flutduin? I rose into the air and I felt hands grasping me and movement. I tried to turn over to find another comfortable place on the ponsho-fleece, but the hands gripped me so I could not move.

The strange swaying persisted. Then I was being passed down like a sack from a freighter. I felt a bump and something hard struck into my backbone. Before I could do anything or cry out a great evil-smelling canvas was thrown over me. I lay there, wondering when I would wake up and, however nightmarish the dream, preferring it to the reality of slaving on the rowing benches.

The softly swaying movement beneath me told me I lay in a small boat. Well, they might not ask me to pull an oar then.

I heard a voice, somewhere high overhead.

"Weng da!⁴ Speak up, speak up!"

From close by my head Nath bellowed back: "Provision party, sir!"

"Carry on then, Palinter."

I heard a low chuckle in the boat. Why should the officer of the watch call Nath Palinter? Palinter was the title for the fat and jovially wicked fellows who were the pursers in—but no matter. This dream intrigued me through my madness.

The boat pushed off. There were two oars, I could hear.

The stroke was steady, the kind of rhythm that only two old comrades who had slaved together could row. I moved beneath the odiferous canvas.

"Lie still, Stylor. Only a few strokes more."

I lay still. I wanted to go to sleep and sleep dreamlessly. But this dream persisted, it pursued me, it would not let me go. The boat grounded. The canvas cover was thrown back. The night sky blazed above. I stood up. Nath and Zolta gripped my arms and helped me from the boat.

"All very nice, Nath, Zolta," I said. "But where is Zorg?"

They looked at me.

"I need my sleep. Let me go back to sleep."

Nath took my arm. "This way."

"Grace of Grodno." I stumbled along after Nath, with Zolta supporting me from the side. My legs felt like smashed bananas. "Zorg will row." The dream began to coil in my head. I panted. I felt the pains in my chest, in my head. My legs weren't there. "Zorg! Nath! Zolta! We must row—must pull—pull—"

"Nearly there, Stylor, nearly there."

I tried to haul up but they pulled me on.

"Nearly where, you two rascals? Is it wine and a wench you are after? I know you two, two oar comrades, two great rogues…"

We passed through a screen of trees, dark, massive and mysterious lumps in the star-flecked blackness. A clearing showed, with an arm of water curving into it hidden from the sea. A rickety hut of leaves and branches leaned over the water. I stopped, thunderstruck by a thought.

"Why do you call me Stylor? You know my name is Dray—"

"Yes, Dray, but we knew you first as Stylor. Now you are Dray Prescot…" Then, in a lower tone, Nath said, "Into the hut with him before he wakes the whole damned crew."

"Where is Zorg?" I said again. And then the thought finally rooted. "Zorg is dead! We have roistered in Sanurkazz, many and many a time, with Nath and his wine and Zolta and his wenches—and Zorg is dead!"

"Aye, Dray, Zorg is dead—and so will we all be if you don't stop yowling like a chunkrah in calf and get a move on!"

I felt my legs then. I felt the ground beneath my feet.

I trembled.

I touched Nath. I touched Zolta.

They were real!

I wrenched away from them. I pawed my eyes. The trees, the hut, the stars, remained. I hit myself in the chest. I did not wake up.

They were staring at me, there in the starlight.

"Yes, Dray, who we called Stylor. You do not dream." Nath smiled in the old reckless way.

"By Zair, Dray Stylor! We've rescued you from the Krozairs of Zy and they'll have all our heads if they catch us!" And Zolta seized my arm and ran me into the hut.

Rescued? Rescued? *Rescued!*

Thirteen
Two rascals of Sanurkazz

The succulent palines dropped one by one into my mouth: luscious cherry-like fruits, palines, sovereign remedies for the black dog.

I lay back on the rough pallet of the hut and marveled.

I was alone. Nath and Zolta, giving me no time to express my wonder, my fierce pride in them, my joy, had whispered ferociously that I was to stay hidden in the hut and they would be back as soon as they could.

For the first time I noticed they were clad as Zimen, the lay brothers of the Krozairs of Zy. Their dull red tunics bore the Krzy emblem decorously on the breast and back. Thick belts cinctured their waists and they swung seaman's knives there. They did not carry swords. They looked just the same as I remembered them—and then they were gone, melting back into the starlight.

"If all goes well on *Zulfirian Avenger*," were Zolta's last words.

And Nath's were: "By Zantristar the Merciful! Zair would not will it otherwise!"

So I was learning. The name of the swifter was *Zulfirian Avenger*. Nath and Zolta were still alive, were Zimen, a fact which before my downfall I would have gloried to know, and were acting against all their vows to the Krzy in thus helping me, who was Apushniad.

The penalties they faced were real and dreadful.

The mere fact of freedom, for however short a duration, began in me a process of drawing back from that frightening and bottomless black pool of madness. I began to think again. Of course those two dearly beloved rascals had called me Stylor. That had been my name when we'd met, a name bestowed on me by the Overlords of Magdag in those festering warrens. But how had they come here? I knew it could not be by chance.

I began to think of that tragic meeting with Delia. I *had* met her. I *had* spoken to her there in that dark cell in the rock wall with its trash of litter on the floor. Yes, yes, I had! I began to think of things she had said, items of information spoken quickly, in whispers, while I held her in my arms and tried to blot out the grim prospect of the future.

The thought of her presence dizzied me. By Zair but she was marvelous!

Yes, yes, she had said Drak and Zeg had written that the Call was out. As Krozairs of Zy they had responded. She had been engaged in a legal struggle over encroachments on Delphond, Dayra had received a bad report from the Sisters of the Rose—who the hell was Dayra?—the trouble with the scheming leem the Strom of Vilandeul, the samphron crop had been particularly bad in Valka and she had had to arrange to buy supplies from Vallia, her father the Emperor had been complaining bitterly that she neglected him—a myriad things of importance had been claiming her attention. She had cast them all to the winds.

She had taken the fleetest voller to Esser Rarioch. There she had arranged as much as she could and, on the very night she was due to leave, she had been visited by Krozairs. They had sailed in a ship of Vallia all the way through the Grand Canal and the Dam of Days, around the west coast of Turismond and past Donengil, and so up the Cyphren Sea past Erthyrdrin and on to Vallia. From there they had flown to Valka. From this record of a perfectly ordinary sea passage of one of our galleons I knew the letters of my sons had been delayed. So now with two purposes, Delia had set out for Zy.

First, she knew in her heart of hearts I was not dead, so she knew I would answer the Azhurad. She would meet me in Zy.

Second, until I came she would plead my cause with the Grand Archbold.

I quelled all hatred for Pur Kazz. He had acted as his instincts, his vows, his duties prompted. I wondered if Pur Zenkiren, had he become Grand Archbold as I had expected, would have acted any differently. I would find out why Pur Zenkiren had been passed over. Could he be dead? No, I would have been told by someone in Zy.

The peripatetic Krozairs who had visited Delia knew where I was supposed to be found, of course, from my sons. They had wanted to know why I had not answered. Had I been dead, they would have known. That is a small part of the mysticism of the Krozairs. At that news my Delia had known so great a happiness that all else mattered little. Only the dire truth as she was told of my condemnation could penetrate, and even then she had scarcely been able to believe.

I was not dead. I would answer the summons to Zy.

By Zair! I had not done so in all ignorance and, in all truth, according to my vows, deserved to be condemned to Apushniad.

The suns declined over the trees. Nath and Zolta had warned me to lie close.

Rising, I went swiftly from the hut with many a careful scrutiny of the foliage and secreted myself among the trees. If Nath and Zolta were discovered and men came for me, I would be ready. Aye! And if my two oar comrades did not return I would go back to *Zulfirian Avenger* and seek those who constrained them.

They panted up, jog-trotting, bearing provisions and weapons. They saw I was almost back to the knave they had known, and we were able to greet one another in a seemly way, with much hugging and belly-punching, quite like my Djangs, and to drink hugely, eat and talk. They told me much which I will relate at its proper time in this chronicle of my life on Kregen. Suffice it to say the passage of fifty terrestrial years seemed to pass in that first starlit meeting.

They were Zimen, and proud of that, and I sensed that much of their pride came in remembrance of Zorg of Felteraz, who was a Krozair of Zy. I mumbled my lame excuses for not returning and then said, "I did not receive the Call. This is true. I have been banished from the order and I cannot tell you where I have been, or how. And yet you put yourselves in the path of peril for me. I am not worthy."

Nath chewed reflectively on a chicken bone. He belched. "You may not be worthy, Dray. I will not pretend the decision was easy."

Zolta frowned. "No, Dray. We have served the Krozairs of Zy long and faithfully. And we have not seen your face for many seasons."

Then they both chuckled and drank wine. Spluttering, Nath said: "But we hold you in our ibs and, anyway, you are an oar comrade. That is what counts."

"Also," said Zolta, and I glanced swiftly at him. He had the grace to smile as he spoke. "Also, we spoke to your lady."

"Ah!" said Nath.

My heart leaped. I made them tell me everything. I licked every honey drop I could as they spoke to me of Delia. She had waited in the fortress of Zy, quartered in the lay apartments on the outer face of the rock, unwelcome in many senses, yet in a peculiar and delicate position. When my two odd comrades had discovered what had happened they had seen her at once; without anything definite being said, the compact had been made.

"Now, Dray," said Zolta, "I understand why you left the Eye of the World. I would stride the Stratemsk for such a lady."

Nath belched again. "I would never touch another drop."

When we turned to other matters, after a time, I discovered we were on a small island near the western end of the Eye of the World in an area I had seldom visited previously. This was a small and secret watering place used by the Zairians. The Grodnims had at last achieved a significant ascendancy over the red southern shore. They had actually established outposts and brought troops across. They had won battles. Now they were pushing along the southern shore, from west to east. Nothing could stop them.

"That is when the Call went out. The Krozairs fought but they lost. The Zair-forsaken Grodnims strut on our southern shore and advance steadily eastward. Soon immortal Zy will be besieged."

"Aye! And then it will be the turn of Holy Sanurkazz."

We remained silent for a while, contemplating the impossible.

Nath took up a jug and upended it. The glugging did not stop until the jug was empty. He wiped the back of his hand across his lips.

"By Mother Zinzu the Blessed! I needed that!"

I chilled at his words. The lightheartedness had gone. The euphoria of my escape was fled.

I roused myself as Nath said they would have to be leaving.

"No suspicion attaches to you over the escape?"

Zolta shook his head. They were a pair of ruffians, with the black curly hair of Zairians, with the mahogany brown faces of sailors, with the merry eyes and reckless ways of those of Sanurkazz. But I marked them. The defeats were wearing them down.

"No, Dray. I am a chief varterist, and Nath, for his potbelly, is in charge of stores. We have a certain leeway."

"And a missing slave?"

Nath made a face and Zolta looked fierce.

"Slaves die. Slaves are replaced. We brought up a spare from below. They are mostly Magdaggians, criminals—"

"Criminals—like me!"

"Aye," they both said equably and went out. I saw them off. Their plans might work. They bid me remberee, but they would be back later on, either the next day or the following night. A boat was hidden in that curve of water. They had brought provisions. We would sail out and carve a fresh life for ourselves. I knew that my future, for all its darkness and somber brooding, could go only two ways.

There was much to brood on the following day and I took the same precautions when Nath and Zolta reappeared. They carried further provisions. This time I had taken a longsword into the trees with me.

"The swifter is due to sail tomorrow night, Dray. There are four of them and they plan a descent on a Grodnim convoy. News was brought in by a scout, a dinky little three-twenty swifter. It will be a notable blow."

They were still caught up in the struggle against the green here in the inner sea.

We sat and drank companionably. If they came with me my course seemed marked out. I welcomed them. I would shake off the whole world of the inner sea, forget it, drive from my mind any remembrance that once I had been a Krozair of Zy.

I said: "Did Delia tell you anything of what I've been up to in the outer world since I left here?"

They looked at me oddly.

Nath drank and wiped his mouth and declared roundly: "The Lady Delia is a princess! By Buzro's Magic Staff! She is a princess from the top of her head to the tips of her feet, and she says you are a prince—the Prince Majister of Vallia, no less."

"For my sins, Nath, old comrade."

"Aye," said Zolta, putting a finger to his beak of a nose. "And she says you are a king of some place called Djanduin. If that is to be believed."

"What, you great onker!" roared Nath. "Do you doubt the word of Lady Delia?"

"No, no, you great oaf of a chunkrah! I doubt that this poor fellow here, this Stylor, could ever be a king!"

Nath subsided, rumbling. By Vox! How I needed their fierce heart-warming clowning, but how hollow it all struck me as I insisted on contemplating the future I beheld.

"Yes. Yes, I am a prince and a king. They mean nothing."

I did not go on. They stared at me keenly, and then Nath slowly said: "Lady Delia told us to tell you." He stopped and glared at Zolta. "Well, you nit that crawls on a calsany's back! You are the lady-killer, you tell Dray what's what!"

Zolta put his jug of wine on the dirt floor. His fierce bold eyes sized me up. We did not know the history of Zolta, yet he carried the proud *Z* not only just in his name, but as the initial letter of his name. Much was to be known of Zolta. As for Nath, as the son of an illiterate ponsho-farmer from Zullia, which is a village to the south of Sanurkazz, his whole history was writ in his large and powerful frame, his weather-beaten face, his addiction to drink, his jovial rough-necking and his loyalty. Now both of them stared at me as though they pondered the wisdom of their deeds.

"Tell me, by Vox!"

"Vox?" said Zolta. "You have been away a long time."

I said nothing, only waited.

Zolta heaved up a sigh and fixed me with an eye like that of a fish on a slab. "Very well, then, but how you come to be married to so divine a creature…" Here Nath nudged him and he went on. Despite his inclinations the seriousness crept in to shadow his words. "Lady Delia has said that, in view of certain impending developments, she feels it her duty to return to—where was it?—Ester Rarok?"

"Esser Rarioch. It is my home in Valka."

"Valka. Oh, aye."

"Return home? Impending developments? Tell me, in the sweet name of Zair!"

Nath shuffled his feet. Zolta picked up his wine jug and put it down. "You saw her in some stinking fish cell in Zy?"

"Yes—yes!"

"So that's why she is going home."

I felt stunned.

Then Zolta said, "She is so well aware of you, Dray, knows you so well. You told her you wished to reinstate yourself as a Krozair of Zy."

"Did I? I scarcely remember. And I find I do not overmuch care now—"

"That's a lie!"

"Aye."

"So she wants you to do what you can. She believes in you. By Zair, you great fambly! If I had a wife like that…" And here Nath swelled his massive chest. "I'd be pretty damn careful about how I upset her, I can tell you, Makki-Grodno take me else!"

"Did I upset her?"

"It would take a very great deal," said Zolta, at last, picking up his jug, "to upset Lady Delia. She wants you to regain your rightful place as a Krozair of Zy."

"Yes, she was very particular about that. Tell him,' she said, 'tell him I wear the Krozair badge still, and will not unpin it until he returns home to Valka and tells me to take it off with his own lips.' That's what she said, aye, and she meant it too!"

They both nodded like those balancing birds dipping their beaks in liquid.

"Fight back! Fight for what you believe is the right of it!"

How well I could picture my Delia saying those words, proud, chin lifted, her eyes sparkling with a dangerous light that the uncouth might construe as unshed tears. How my Delia knew me! And yet was it so strange? I had made no secret to her of my attachment to the Krozairs of Zy, and she had sent her two sons there, without question, joying in seeing them go through the same stringent disciplines as their father had endured. She must see the good in the Krozairs. She must regard my Apushniad as a mere interruption, to be cleared up, a passing shadow.

My Delia is seldom wrong in matters of this kind.

I felt that no dramatic gesture was necessary. So I simply said, "It will not be easy. There are things I cannot explain. Things that no sane man would believe. But I will try! I will fight back."

They both beamed at me.

Nath slapped his knee and Zolta twirled his arrogant mustaches.

"Lady Delia said—well, no matter. She knew. She told us what you would say, almost word for word. You see, Dray Prescot, Lady Delia loves you as you love her."

Fourteen
The fight in the clearing

Soon the Zairian swifter *Zulfirian Avenger* would weigh and make for the sea in company with three others of her kind, long, low sea-leems of the Eye of the World, ready to fall on a Grodnim convoy and joy in battle and slaughter and destruction. As responsible Zimen, men devoted as lay brothers to the care and comfort of the Krozairs of Zy, my two oar comrades Nath and Zolta should sail in her.

They had aided me to escape from the rowing benches. So far they were above suspicion, or so they claimed.

One of the courses that had been open to me before they told me of Delia's words had been to take them back with me to the outer oceans, back to Valka, where I would heap honors on them and shower them with chunkrah herds and mineral wealth and broad kools of land and drown them in gold.

As Zair is my witness I did not then really know if that kind of life would suit them well or ill. They were rough, tough sailors, accustomed to the hardships of life afloat in swifters in the inner sea. How would they take to the ways of life of Vallia and Valka, of Djanduin and Strombor?

Then I reassured myself. They were adaptable. They would do more than survive. And with some of the pretty girls out there Zolta could be very happy, and Nath, I felt sure, would pronounce a good Jholaix as fine as his best Zond.

Well?

The truth was I did not intend to leave the Eye of the World until I was once more dubbed a Krozair of Zy.

The issue was perfectly plain.

I could not ask them to come with me on a mission of so much peril and of importance only to me. They would throw everything for which they had worked away, abandon their careers, which I now knew had brought them to the ranks of zan-Deldars, ready to make the all-important leap across to ob-Hikdars. One was a chief varterist, the other a Palinter, a purser of the lower rank. No. No, it would be foully cruel of me to snatch them away from their own lives into lives filled with cruelty and danger and death, merely to serve my own selfish ends.

I valued them far too much to do that to them.

So I thought then, as I sat in the miserable hut and planned what I would do.

They had told me that Pur Zenkiren, who had known them too well for their own comfort, had been passed over when old Pur Zazz had at last died and gone to sit in glory on the right hand of Zair in the paradise of Zim. The battles he had fought up along the eastern shores had slid and slipped away so that gradually Proconia had been lost to the allies of Magdag. Nath had said, with a round Makki-Grodno oath, that the Grodnims he called Yoggur-cramphs had rolled down from the north with huge armies of diffs. Chuliks, Rapas, Katakis—at which my eyebrows had lifted—Ochs and Naor'vils like clouds driven before the winds of heaven, rampaging down with their mercenary ibs uplifted by the gold promised by the Overlords of Yoggur, following the green banners.

"We stopped 'em, in the end. The place was a defile, a good defensive position." Zolta licked his lips. "I was told by a Deldar who lost an eye. The place was called Appar, from which the battle takes its name. This Deldar did not relish the telling. But Pur Zenkiren marshaled his forces and we fought and we stopped them, the rasts of Grodno and their Zair-forsaken beast-men allies."

This was a thing I had long noted, how the men of the red southern shore seldom employed diffs, and how very few of the myriads of marvelous halfling races of Kregen made their homes along the southern shore of the inner sea of Turismond. How important a factor in my life—aye! and the destiny of Kregen—this proved to be you shall hear.

Appar is situated south of Pattelonia, which is the capital of Proconia. We had lost much ground then. And because of this, with no thought given to his final heroic stand, Pur Zenkiren had not been elected to be Grand Archbold of the Krzy.

His presence on the Ombor Throne in the Hall of Judgment would have made no difference to the sentence passed on me. I had been tried in my absence and found guilty; the Krzy merely gave me the outward show, as my right as a Krozair, to witness my own condemnation. Zenkiren could scarcely have subverted justice. So I must see him. There were one or two plans I had in that direction. When I say the Krozairs have no mercy I must qualify the bald statement as, clearly, you will already have realized is necessary. I had been granted the boon of a short meeting with my wife. For this the Krozairs showed the compassion which made them human. Without this Zair-inspired gift I doubt if my allegiance to the Krzy and my willingness to place the education of my sons in their care could have existed.

The day passed slowly. I drank sparingly and ate well and sharpened up the best of the longswords my rogues had brought. They were not Krozair longswords, being of that pattern issued to the men who fought in the swifters. For all that, they were fine weapons. Naghan the Gnat would have sniffed at them, no doubt, as would Wil of the Bellows in far Djanduin, but they would serve.

As I had done before, I slipped out before the last of the glow of the Suns of Scorpio faded from the sky. From my leafy point of observation I awaited either Nath and Zolta, a party from the swifters intent on retaking me, or simply no one at all.

I saw the leaves moving alongside the trail and I frowned.

Whoever approached the hut was coming up from the other direction. I took a grip on the sword. This looked promising.

The last of that glorious streaming mingled light of Antares fell on the edge of the little clearing past the corner of the hut. It sparkled on the strip of water curving in and shone on the loose camouflaging cover of the boat hidden there.

A warrior stepped out onto the path, tensed, head high, his weapons ready.

He was a Chulik.

I did not need the green badges, the embroideries and studding of his uniform to know him. A mercenary Chulik in the employ of Grodnim yetches, he stood there alertly while he was joined by two of his fellows. I marked them well.

All wore their heads shaved beneath the helmets, with the long tails dangling down their backs, all dyed green, bright and ominous in the last emerald fires of Genodras.

Chuliks are born with two arms and two legs and possess faces which, apart from the three-inch, upward-reaching tusks, might have been human, except that they know nothing of humanity. Their skin is oily yellow and their black eyes are small, round and habitually fixed in gazes of hypnotic rigidity. They are strong, with bodies well-fleshed with fat, and they are quick. They are superb weapon-masters.

These three quite clearly were a scout party, sniffing out the secrets of the Zairians on this small island. Once they saw the four swifters they would report back. The projected attack by the men of Zair would be betrayed—betrayed and doomed.

No doubt the swifter from which they had come lurked on the opposite shore, ready to race back to the main fleet with news.

Well, I had been dishonored and condemned by the men of Zair. I had been rejected, considered fit for the fight only to pull an oar. I was a Valkan, a Vallian, Lord of Strombor, King of Djanduin. What were the petty squabbles of red and green to such a mighty man as I? These sarcastic thoughts passed through my head and were gone like swallows at evening. Surely this was a test, sent by Zair himself.

Slowly, comfortably, I stood up and stepped out into the clearing. The last shards of emerald light fell across the trees, turning them into jeweled marvels. The air sang with the sound of evening insects. The grass glittered with dew.

The Chuliks saw me.

I was still hairy although washed clean. I wore a brave old scarlet breechclout. They knew, as I knew, that we could not allow a survivor. They must slay me or I must slay them. The destinies of Grodno and Zair demanded nothing less.

With an absolute confidence that might have shaken less of a maniac than I am they advanced, their longswords ready.

The first Chulik surprised me.

"Cramph! Lay down your sword and yield, lest we slay you."

I overcame my surprise. This was not mercy. This was a mere device to take a prisoner and extract information.

I said: "You three are dead men."

Chuliks and I, we do not laugh often. A diff of another race might have thrown his head back and guffawed his scorn and merriment. These three spread out and came on, silently.

The green light would soon be all gone. The sword glimmered like ice in my fists. I did not use the cunning Krozair grip. I have spoken a little of this Krozair longsword grip, but there is much more to it than the mere spacing out of the hands on the handle, much more, including the angle of the hands, the placing of the thumbs, the delicate and yet brutal over- and underhand play—yes, much more. The Chuliks would know about Krozairs. They came on with sure purpose. After that first exchange it was all silent and deadly there beneath the dying green sun.

I leaped. I did not wait for them.

The sword chirred. In the moment of leaping, before I landed and gripped the bulk of Kregen beneath my feet and struck, I had shifted grips. The full force of the longsword flung by the cunning, twisting motion of the Krozair grip ripped the head from the first Chulik's shoulders.

Stupid! Wasteful! This was not the professional fighting man-killer Dray Prescot; this was the old savage and barbaric Dray Prescot of bygone years.

The second Chulik bored in, his sword thrusting for my belly; the third circled and slashed down at my head.

I parried the one and slid the other and whirled the sword back. The Chulik leaped clear, but I had aimed short and so was able to carry the blow around, low and dirty, and cut the ankles from number three. As I leaped back, the longsword snapping up into position again, I cursed. I was fighting with power and fury and letting my muscles do the work. I, who had been a hyr-kaidur of the Jikhorkdun! Passion and senseless ferocity marked me during that fight. I needed to bash a few skulls, the black blood in me seething to run foaming and free.

The second Chulik—now so dreadfully the last—did not back off. He was a fighter—well, all Chuliks are fighters—but he fancied his chances, seeing the massive anger I had put into my strokes. He would feint with me a while and then use his skill to slay me. So he thought.

The blades touched and rang and then shirred in that shivery sound of war-metal striking war-metal. He lopped and aimed to slash, shortened and thrust. I parried and then bashed him back. From the tail of my eye I could see the footless one crawling along leaving a trail of red. If I trod near him he'd reach up and spit me. I angled away.

The swords blurred. The shadows dropped down. It was all very quick in the nature of a fight and yet all the hallmarks of the slow, mail-crushing longsword fighting held us both. This Chulik might have done better with his shortsword against me, an unarmored man. He most likely would not have though, I think, looking back.

He fought well and then I had him. A neat parade and hand-rolling movement dazzled him long enough for me to clear space to swing back-handed at his neck. The mail hood erupted. This time I struck with force sufficient only to strike through to his neck bone. His head lolled off, most grotesquely, with the blood spouting onto his mail, fouling all the bright green insignia.

The crawler knew he was finished and slit his own throat.

I felt a tiny whisper of surprise at this; it was known, but rare among Chuliks.

I dragged the three of them back off the trail, out of the clearing. When I straightened up, the stars glittered in their hosts and She of the Veils floated serenely above, a new sharp crescent among the stars.

Removing their armor was not difficult and relieving them of their weapons was likewise easy. I would have to cobble the rents in the mail together. I took everything and the supplies from the hut down to the boat—a muldavy with a dipping lug—and threw them all in and covered them with a flap of canvas. I did not know if Nath and Zolta would return this night or not. If they did not come my relief would be genuine. If they did I would have to make sure they got back to their ship in time.

They did arrive, puffing, swearing, calling on Mother Zinzu the Blessed, and searched around. I had moved the muldavy. They found nothing. I heard them arguing and insulting each other. I had to restrain myself, hold myself back from leaping up and embracing them and pummeling them to once more recapture our old comradeship.

But my life held no joys for them.

Eventually, with many a Makki-Grodno curse and a wonderment at my intentions, they wandered off back to the swifter. I waited on the island until the four swifters and the small scout vanished into the darkness. One day, I vowed, and this time I meant to hew to the resolution with great tenacity, I would see them again and explain my ingratitude, so that once more we might go carousing in Sanurkazz and roll into the Fleeced Pon-sho, roaring for wenches and drink, skylarking, merrymaking, creating havoc until the fat and jolly mobiles with their rusty swords came wad-dling up, wreathed in smiles.

But all that could only happen if the evil green of Magdag was ban-ished, sent recoiling back to its foul warrens. If the Grodnims overcame the Zairians in the Eye of the World there would be no more lighthearted roistering in Sanurkazz for Nath and Zolta and me—or for any other who followed the red of Zair.

It is at this point that the last cassette finishes those making up the Rio de Janeiro tapes. Prior to this point, an event I had come somewhat to dread as denying us anything more of the fascinating and incredible story of Dray Prescot on the planet of Kregen under Antares, a further supply reached me. They were transmitted in the same way as previously, namely, in a packaged box addressed to Mr. Dan Fraser, sent by the executors of his estate to Geoffrey Dean and so to me. They had been dispatched originally from Sydney, Australia. This time there was no covering letter to explain their existence.

As usual with Prescot at the controls, the opening of the Sydney tapes is fuzzed with a fair amount of wordage completely lost or so distorted as to be indecipherable. It is possible to make out Prescot talking at some length on the tangled political situation of the inner sea. It seems clear he took the little muldavy and sailed her to the western part of the southern shore in pursuance of his plan to reinstate himself as a Krozair of Zy.

He also speaks—and here his deep voice rolls out—of a name which appears to affect him profoundly. The name is Pakkad.

We are supremely fortunate to be blessed with further cassettes from Dray Prescot and the manner of their arrival here together with the maps he appends is of less moment than their content. Now we may look forward to further adventures on Kregen beneath the red and green suns, and share with Dray Prescot the barbaric color and headlong action of his life under the Suns of Scorpio.

Fifteen
Duhrra

"Step up! Step up! All comers! Duhrra the Mighty Mangler challenges all comers! A golden piece against one fall! Step up, my fine Jernus!"

Torchlights threw lurid splashes of color across the scene. The soldiers and sailors and workmen crowded close among the tents and bales and packing crates, all the impedimenta of an army stores base. The streaming radiance of the Twins threw fuzzy pink shadows into the corners, but the flaring torchlights dominated the shifting, erratic patterns, throwing greedy reflections on lips and anticipatory gleams in crafty eyes. Here was where an army disported itself when out of the line.

"Come on, doms! Come on, Jernus! Duhrra the Mighty Mangler welcomes all challenges. Clean wrestling, with the first fall to count against a gold piece! Where's your pride?"

The speaker—or, rather, the shouter—was a thin weasely individual with the face of a wersting, all fangs and ferociousness. His thin body, incongruously clad in a flowing scarlet robe, cinctured by a trashy brassy-gold belt, looked scarcely capable of lifting a longsword. He wore a tall white and red mitered cap streaming with arbora feathers, and he kept tossing a gold piece up and down in the clawed palm of one hand. With the other hand he pointed with great meaning to Duhrra the Mighty Mangler.

"There stands Duhrra! Undisputed champion of Crazmoz!' Any swod of the army who can best him takes away a gold piece! Step up, Jernus, step up!"

The half-mocking tone in which this barker addressed the clustered crowd, calling them Jernus, lords, made them laugh. But they eyed the massive bulk of the wrestler, shuffled their feet and averted their eyes. No one seemed anxious to step forward into the marked circle.

I studied this Duhrra. A magnificent body, yet bulky, probably not as slow as he looked, with immense corded thighs and plated muscle over his chest—and a belly that would do well to accept a few flagons less of Zond or Chremson.

I was here on the tail of the army with a purpose.

Somewhere further west, engaged in fighting the Grodnims, was Pur Zenkiren. I had to talk to him. Yet I needed a mount, I needed food and drink—shelter could be found under the stars—and for all this I needed money.

Money was the one thing Nath and Zolta had failed to bring.

All kinds of coins circulated among the Zairians. There were the Zo-pieces, minted by King Zo in Sanurkazz. There were many other mints of other free cities of the southern shore. There were the coins of great mercantile houses, banks, lords of the southern shore. And there were the gold and silver oars of Magdag.

The price to engage in combat with Duhrra the Mighty Mangier was a bronze so. That is, a three-piece. I did not possess even an ob, a one-piece.

About to make my move, for I felt confident that I could take this man despite his massive body, I checked. A bulky dwa-Deldar of the varters stepped forward, flinging off his red cloak, baring his hairy chest, bulging his muscles. He tossed a so to the barker with a confident shout of: "I'll show this hunk of vosk-steak how to fight!"

"Hai!" they shouted. "Hai for Nath the Biceps!"

I studied the ensuing instructive combat.

This Duhrra knew his business. His head was shaved bald, with a small peak and a descending pigtail, somewhat after the manner of an Algonquian or a Chulik, but far less flamboyant. His face bore a blank, expressionless flatness, with a smudge of a nose, upturned upper lip, and a general air of idiocy I felt belied the keenness he would show in hand-to-hand combat. He uttered a low gurgling cry of pleasure as the dwa-Deldar surged forward to come to hand grips.

The dwa-Deldar circled, lunged, gripped, tried to hoist Duhrra and throw him, as doubtless he had done many times to unruly swods in his outfit. Duhrra grunted. He scarcely moved. His corded thighs ridged as he grasped this Nath the Biceps. I saw the smooth heavy face abruptly blaze with power, the small dark eyes suddenly filled with great joy. Then, with a mighty heave, the dwa-Deldar, Nath the Biceps, flew into the air to land with a dust-billowing crash on his back.

The crowd yelled. There were a few boos. But the gold coin continued to flick up and down in the clawed palm of the barker and he chuckled his mirth.

"Undefeated! Duhrra the Mighty Mangler, champion still, winner by a fall!" And then: "Step up, doms! Step up! A gold piece to be taken this night!"

The crowd began to drift away.

I sidled quickly to the barker and said, "You are losing their interest, dom. Your man wins too easily."

He flicked me a liquid glance.

"Aye, dom. I know. But Duhrra is a real champion."

Across the aisle between tents a brilliant concentration of torches lit a crude stage upon which half a dozen girls danced. They wore beads and feathers and they writhed enticingly. The soldiers gaped up, licking their lips. Further along a man kept swallowing balls and snakes of fire, helping them down with daggers. His barker bellowed louder than the one before me.

"I will wrestle with Duhrra," I said.

"Where is your so?"

"If I lose you shall have your so."

One swod with the patches of a sectrixman heard and swung back, calling to his comrades. I stared at this barker who let the gold piece fall to lie in his palm.

"If my old father could see me now!" he cried. "Me, Naghan the Show! Reduced to shilling for nothing!"

"Hurry!"

"He gonna fight or ain't he gonna fight?" demanded the cavalryman. The crowd hovered.

I made up this Naghan the Show's mind for him.

"I will fight," I declared and threw off my old red cloak. The belt with the longsword and the sailor's knife followed. Clad only in the old scarlet breechclout I walked into the marked space. Duhrra the Mighty Mangler eyed me. I saluted him.

"You are a man, my friend," I said. "I bear you no ill will."

His dull eyes sized me up. He said: "Uh... no, dom... uh... no ill will."

Somewhere a woman screamed, "Duhrra'll kill him!" And another, shriller still, joying: "No! Lookit him!"

I fancy my good comrade Turko the Shield, who is a very high kham

118

indeed in the syples of the Khamorros, would have disposed of the Duhrra with no less difficulty than I. The Khamorros are mightily dangerous men in the disciplines of unarmed combat, able to kill or maim with a blow. Yet I had proved my own disciplines of the Krozairs of Zy were superior even to the khamster skills of the Khamorros. Could this Duhrra have benefited from Krozair training? I did not think so.

That, as you well know, made me a cheat, for Duhrra stood little chance. Yet he was a massive man, ridged in muscle, iron-hard, with that bald domed head like a battering ram. I would have to be very careful indeed and imagine the mocking bantering eyes of Turko upon me all the time.

The fight is scarcely worth the chronicling, for I was minded to be merciful to Duhrra. He attempted to seize me as I advanced and I drew him on. Then, as we had done so many times in the unarmed combat drills in the fortress of Zy, and later as I had with Turko in our little practice area in Esser Rarioch, I took him and turned and twisted and for all his enormous bulk he rotated about the grip and flopped back, toppling, to fall ponderously on the flat of that massive back.

I could not stop myself from saying "Hai Jikai!"

But that was a saying from other places and times.

The crowd stood silently and then, suddenly, burst into roaring applause. I merited no applause. I reached down and took Duhrra's hand and hoisted him to his feet. I stared into his dark dull eyes and saw an expression there I recognized; I did not know whether to be joyful or shiver with the apprehension of a new responsibility.

Naghan the Show waxed highly indignant.

"The gold piece, Naghan!"

In the end he handed it over.

I had the thing, warm from his claw, in my hand, and was bending to don my cloak and belt when the first shrieks and screams laced the air with panic.

Everyone was running. Pandemonium broke out further along where the bulk of the piled stores cut against the stars. I heard the fierce warlike yells, the battle cries, and I heard again that hated shrilling of: "Magdag! Magdag! Grodno! Green! Green!"

The longsword shivered in my grip.

Naghan the Show was screaming. He ran. Duhrra scooped up a red cloak and ran with him. I followed. They ought to know their way about this showground outside the base store camp. The devils of Grodnim were raiding from the sea. They aimed to destroy the stores here, in the rear of the army. These civilians, the tail of the army, the camp followers, were mere meat to be butchered. They must flee for their lives. I was not minded to flee, but I wished to fight where I felt success would attend my efforts. To be killed now in a stupid affray would nullify all I fought for in the wider realities. I had to quell that perfectly natural feeling that I ran like a nulsh from a fight. A fighting man who does not pick his field usually does not last long. But I admit I felt the shame and the indignity of running before those hated cries of "Magdag! Grodno! Magdag!"

I owed the Overlords of Magdag. Once I had nearly defeated them with my old slave phalanx of vosk-skulls. Now I must find the guard detail here and form with them to bash these green sea-leems back to their ship and burn them there.

So you see I had changed from the old Dray Prescot who had once roamed and fought over the Eye of the World.

Or so I thought in my folly.

Naghan the Show panted out, "Into the ruins! There we may hide from these cramphs of Magdag."

Duhrra gave a low grunting cry, unintelligible. When Naghan stumbled he caught the slight body up and carried him as one would carry a feather pillow.

Behind us the sky began to light up as the Grodnims started their fires among the stores. Away to our right along the shore the dark masses of tents and the long sectrix lines remained silent. If the guards did not counterattack soon they might as well shut up shop. The crazed mobs of people were running every which way. Ahead up a slight incline, sandy and scattered with thorn-ivy under the light of the moons, lay the sere gray skeletal arms of the ruins.

"Careful of that damned thorn-ivy, Duhrra," I said.

"I will... uh... take care, master."

"I am not your master."

He did not reply but ran on, carrying the complaining form of Naghan the Show over one brawny shoulder.

Still no sign of the necessary counterattack. We had broken clear of a mass of people. There were soldiers in that mass. I stopped running.

"Damn it!" I burst out "This won't do! By Zair, I'm not running from some kleesh of a Magdaggian!"

Duhrra stopped also. His smooth massive head turned and that blank, heavy-lidded idiot-face gave me no inkling of what he thought or felt Then:

"I shall fight with you, master."

"There is no call. You are not a soldier."

"Yet I can fight."

"Aye. Aye, by Zair, you can fight, Duhrra."

He put Naghan the Show back on his feet. He patted the fancy clothes into place, perched the tall miter cap squarely on the narrow head. Naghan squealed.

"What are you trying to do, Duhrra? Ruin me!"

"Zair needs all our arms this night, master."

Turning back, I spread my arms and yelled, as I was wont to yell hailing the foretop in a gale of Ushant or bellowing at my Djangs in the arrow-storm, halting the running mob. Quickly I roared a dozen or so soldiers back to a semblance of their duty. One, stricken with fear, insisted on running. Him I struck senseless with my fist and gave his sword to Duhrra. Then, with little hope but with hard determination, we went back to face the leems of Grodno.

Fortunately, for the fight would have gone ill for us, the guard eventually turned out and we smashed and bashed our way against the hated green. In among tall piles of lumber, massive lenken logs needed in fortress construction by the army engineers, we fought and chased the raiders of Magdag, as they fought and slew us.

The erratic light from the Twins cast pinkish reflections from burnished armor, caught rosy stars in the twinkling weapons that withdrew darker red, made seeing difficult. Pursuing a group of Magdaggian swods—they were apims like me—up an alleyway between stacked lumber, I sprawled headlong over a corpse whose dark red blanket-cloak completely deceived me in the rosy glow. I cursed and stumbled up. Ahead of me and backed against the lumber a young man in red fought two Chuliks in green.

The young man was yelling—screaming—as his sword blurred this way and that. He would not last long.

He screamed in high desperation: "Dak! Dak! Aid me now! For the sweet sake of Zair, Dak, to me! To me!"

Past the Chuliks were three other Chuliks and two Rapas, their vulturine beaks gaping with the passions of battle. Ringed by these five stood a man whose white hair blazed with pink highlights and roseate shadows, an old man, a man past two hundred years old. Yet, as I staggered about feeling the effect of that sprawling fall, I saw this white-haired man surge against the nearest Chulik, duck the blow, strike the Chulik's legs, cut back against the nearest Rapa, screech his blade along the diffs side. The longsword whirled underhand. The white-haired man shouted, a high full voice that drew every ounce of effort from him.

"Hold, Jernu! Hold! I am with you!"

And then—it was wonderful, courageous, bold; it was the true Jikai—this man, this old white-haired man called Dak smashed his way past the two Chuliks, ripped the guts from the last Rapa and so hurled himself at the two opposing his lord.

He had no chance. He exposed his back as he struck shrewdly at the first. The blow was parried. I saw the slowness of this Dak's reactions, saw that the strength had been drained from him. He knew his end was come and he flashed his longsword before his eyes and so drank for the last time of a foeman's blood.

121

As he fell beneath the slashing blows he shouted for the last time.

"Zair! Jikmarz! Jikmarz!"

He fell.

The whole incident took practically no time at all, less time than it took me to scrabble up from the corpse and shake the infernal ringing of those famous Bells of Beng Kishi from my skull, take a fresh grip on my sword and leap forward.

The young man screamed now, screamed high and shrill like a dying leem with the long lances of my clansmen transfixing its lean and evil body.

"Dak! Dak! Sweet Jikmarz! *Dak!*"

"Hold!" I bellowed, surging forward. "I am coming!"

As I smashed into the Chuliks and the group of apims I had been pursuing, Duhrra came to my side. Together we fought against the foemen, seeking to save the young man. We slew until our arms ran red with Magdaggian blood, until the last Chulik fell with his body hacked and butchered before he would drop, but when we reached that young man, that Brother of the Red Brethren of Jikmarz, he was dead.

Duhrra, his plated chest expanding and contracting evenly as he drew in enormous lungfuls of air, regarded me somberly.

"You fight well, Dak. Yet is this boy slain."

That be called me Dak was a mere mistake of the moment, a chance that he understood the Red Brother of Jikmarz to be calling on me when he screamed for Dak. The amazement was in his way of speaking, with no hesitation, no idiot's repetition of the opening "duh" to every sentence, no slurring of speech. Was this only the result of battle?

"Yes. It is the will of Zair."

I looked up. The mass of lumber moved. A beam toppled, twisting, falling.

"Stand clear, Duhrra!"

I leaped back. Duhrra braced to spring and the side of the stack of timbers bulged as a grain sack bulges in the moment it is slit open. The enormous weight of the logs rolled smashing down on Duhrra. In the leaping dust I caught a single glimpse of his left arm outflung toward me with the moon-oval of his face glimmering pinkly through the shadows. I grasped his hand and pulled. His mouth opened, but in the rolling noise of toppling logs I did not hear him. He would not budge. A beam struck my legs away from me and I cursed and surged back, then, mercifully, the logs lay still. The dust plumed in the air and drifted down. There was a sickly smell of rotting vegetation puffing from the lumber. I looked at Duhrra.

He was trapped.

His body lay on the ground, with his right hand caught between two squared beams of timber. I knew, looking, that his hand would be squashed flat, ironed out, ground into a flat and useless pulp.

"I cannot move, master."

Bending to look closely, I was aware that I could see very well. A quick glance back showed me that the loose timber among the stacks was on fire, burning fiercely. The beams, thick and massive though they were, were tinder-dry. They would burn.

And Duhrra lay trapped in the path of the flames.

"It is finished for me, Dak. You had best leave—"

"Shut up Duhrra! I will not leave you."

"Then you too will burn."

Down past the spouts of flame shooting horizontally from the crevices in the stacks a shimmer of movement came closer, the wink of firelight on steel. I peered. In the red firelight the colors down there looked black. Green.

Turning his heavy round head Duhrra saw too. He licked his lips.

"Put my sword into my left hand, Dak, my master. I would die well."

"You are an onker, Duhrra! There is no need to die. I cannot move the beams—"

"Aye. I could not move one. Together we could not move one. And they are piled up on my hand."

"Yet is there a way, if you will take it."

His heavy-lidded eyes regarded me with the shock of a new idea forcing its way into closed and resigned determination.

"Another way? Besides striking until I can strike no more and so go down to the Ice Floes of Sicce?"

"Aye. If you will take it. Many men would prefer to die..."

"I see, Dak, my master. It is clear now."

"Well?"

He regarded me with a maddening slowness, almost complacency.

"It is for you to choose, Dak, my master."

"I'm not your damn master! And there is a saying where I come from: Where there's life there's hope. So that's settled."

Don't think I was unaware of what the decision meant to a man like Duhrra, a superb physical specimen—somewhat on the heavy and bulky side, to be sure—who had lived by wrestling. To any man the decision would be hard. But I had seen the way Duhrra had used his longsword in his right hand, all heavy swishings and smashings as though he cut down trees. With his great physical strength that method of using a longsword would serve, at least in the yelling confusion of a battle. He would not have lasted long against just one of the Chuliks with space to display technique and bladesmanship.

"The green sea-leems come on," said Duhrra. "I am no calsany in these matters. Why do you hesitate?"

"I would like to know you are resolved first."

"I am resolved."

The fires spurted closer; the green cramphs from Magdag approached with hungry weapons. Perhaps the choice was not as difficult as I had imagined.

From one of the corpses I ripped a strip of humespack and tore the cloth with vicious fingers. As I had seen the skilled doctors of Valka do so I bound a strip around Duhrra's arm and knotted it until I brought a dinting furrow between his eyebrows, all the signs of pain this man-mountain would condescend to show.

I stepped back and took up my longsword.

He said, "Do not tarry, Dak. The rasts of Magdag are almost here, and the fire burns."

The longsword slashed down.

I dragged Duhrra to his feet, leaving his squashed hand and a tiny portion of his wrist to burn away between the logs. The blow had been good, the aim true. Blood spurted, of course, but he would survive until I could have a doctor treat his stump.

The fires roared and crackled and the smoke beat down as the breeze blew. I held Duhrra. More figures appeared, men wearing the red. Now I deliberately moved away from a fight. A Hikdar shouted, high, triumphant: "We have the cramphs on the run!"

I did not grunt sourly at him that the Grodnim-gastas had done the work for which they came.

Together Duhrra and I went from that scene of carnage and fire and blood to seek a needleman to tend Duhrra's pain and stump.

He breathed a harsh intake of breath. "I do not think, Dak, that I would like men to call me Duhrra the Ob-Handed."

"If you insist they do not, they will not," I said peacefully.

"That is true."

So we walked away, and I ruminated that I had had the best of the bargain that night.

For Duhrra had lost a hand and I had gained a name.

Sixteen
I come to my senses

I, Dray Prescot, Lord of Strombor and Krozair of—No! No! I was no longer a Brother of the Krozairs of Zy. I must not forget that. I could not forget that. It was branded on my brain with a searing iron.

I, that same plain Dray Prescot who had born many names on Kregen under Antares, no longer a Krozair Brother, had to assume a fresh alias.

The reasons were plain and pressing: should a man calling himself Prescot be encountered among the army, here in the west, where there were many Krozair Brothers, then the word would pass, the retribution would be swift.

I obviously had to have an alias, and one had been given into my keeping. I would honor the name of Dak. The old white-haired man had proved a true Jikai. In my misery and determination I keenly felt the task of keeping the name of Dak unsullied.

The conceit must have moved me that I had used the name Drak many times before; it was the name of the mythical hero of Vallia, part-god, part-man, and it was the name of my eldest son. Drak and Dak. Yes, the conceit moved me.

The next day the wreckage of the base could be surveyed.

The Grodnims had wreaked great destruction, yet there was much left they had not touched. This had been a pinprick which, of itself, would not materially harm the armies of Zairians fighting in the west, but which, added to many other similar pinpricks, could place all that strenuous effort in jeopardy.

Still, no longer a Krozair, what business was this of mine? I held warm affections for Mayfwy and for Felteraz. I could see the patterns of warfare out here plainly enough. But I held to my own destiny. My Delia had given me my orders, fully understanding my own agony of spirit, the tearing torture I must have experienced in leaving the Eye of the World with all I had held dear there in the Brotherhood of Zy blackened and ruined. And yet... and yet. Was being a Krozair Brother so marvelously vital and important a part of my life when set against all that waited for me in the Outer Oceans? No. No, I was a fool, as usual.

For twenty-one miserable years I had not beheld my Delia, I had seen her for a mere bur, there in the fish cell of the fortress of Zy. Looking around at the ruined camp, seeing workers and soldiers hard at repairing, restacking and carrying away burned and ruined stores, I seemed to feel the scales drop from my eyes.

Pride. That was all it had been. Mere stupid pride.

I had felt my idiot self-esteem hurt, because the single body of men I held in most regard on Kregen had turned me out, disgraced me. And I even understood why they had done it, why they had acted as they did. As the Savanti had thrown me out of the paradise of Aphrasöe and I had felt no real animosity toward them, knowing I had transgressed against their laws, so this time I held no animosity, for in the understanding of Kregen I had again transgressed. No amount of arguing or pleading could possibly change a single Krozair's mind, let alone that of Pur Kazz, the Grand Archbold.

No. The answer was simple.

I had come to my senses.

I would not deny myself or Delia what rightfully belonged to us.

And that, by Krun, was that!

How vicious and cruel those damned Star Lords were! They had banished me to Earth for twenty-one years. And in all that dolorous length of time my Delia had waited for me. When I had previously been banished from Delia—as when I fought in the arena of the Jikhorkdun in Huringa, or when I made myself King of Djanduin—she had spent only a fraction of time in waiting. The Star Lords had created a time loop by some alchemy of their own, so that when, for instance, I fought in Valka and cleared my island of the slavers and aragorn, I had been acting in the past, and my Delia had not even known.

Because of that feeling that Delia was not at home pining for me—and the marvel of why so perfect a woman should ever bother her head over a bulk like me always escapes me—I had acted as I would have acted in a time loop. Then the agony of waiting had been for me alone.

Now my Delia shared that agony.

I was worse than a mere fool, an onker of onkers. I was an ingrate, a tormentor, a prideful villain, and I deserved all I got.

The decision was made.

I went to say goodbye to Duhrra.

His stump had been cauterized and bound up and he was cheerful enough, considering.

"It is remberee, Duhrra."

"I found Naghan the Show. His head had been cleft in twain."

"It grieves me to hear it."

"I cannot wrestle with one hand—"

"Come now! You could lay most two-handed men flat on their backs without blinking. And think of the billing! The famous wrestler fights with one hand tied behind his back. You would make a fortune."

"It no longer appeals to me."

"So what will you do?"

"You say you are going to the west? That is where the army fights."

"Yes. But I do not go to fight."

He regarded me with a lift of one heavy eyebrow. His thick shoulders rolled as he eased his arm, favoring the stump.

"They are going to fix me up with a hook."

"Is it Duhrra the Hook, then?"

"No!"

I said, "I go to find a ship. Maybe I will have to go as far as the Akhram."

"I have been there."

"It is on the green northern shore."

"True. But the Grand Canal and the Todalpheme of the Akhram stand aloof. As they must."

He still looked the same, still with that same heavy, doughy, expressionless idiot-face. His dark eyes looked at me with meaning. He could be highly useful.

I said, "The Todalpheme are very wise."

He said, "I think I will go with you. It will be strange not to stand with folded arms and a stupid expression and listen to Naghan the Show extolling my prowess. It will be strange to walk the world again. I am not a clever man, Dak. I know that. But, just perhaps, I am not quite as stupid as I once thought I was."

You couldn't say fairer than that.

The lightness of my spirit astounded me.

Now that I had made the decision the whole world of Kregen appeared to me in new colors. I did not laugh, of course, and I cracked but the one smile for Duhrra—and that pained—but I felt liberated, free, all that weight of despond sloughed from me. I had made up my mind. The very Suns of Scorpio blazed the brighter.

"I have but twenty-nine silver zinzers left, for I spent this morning on breakfast, and ate like a king."

How incredibly humorous that statement was. I *was* a king!

"Yes, Naghan always managed to welsh. He slipped you a smaller gold piece than the one he tossed up, I'll bet."

"A nikzo."

Half a gold Zo-piece. Only thirty instead of the sixty silver zinzers I had won by hurling Duhrra flat on his back. He surprised me. He reached into the flat leather wallet on its strap over his shoulder and I heard the clink of coins. His left hand brought out, with a wink and a flash, another nikzo, brother to that one I had broken in the refreshment tent, paying a whole silver zinzer for tea and vosk-steaks, followed by palines, that would never cost a dhem in Pandahem or a sinver in Hamal. Still, silver coins varied in weights, just as did gold and copper ones. At sixty zinzers to a full gold Zo-piece, you were bound to get less than for the fatter sinvers.

Duhrra saw my expression and misinterpreted it. I was thinking that the damn war was sending prices skyward, the bogey of inflation as much a specter on Kregen in areas where men were stupid enough to fight wars, whereas Duhrra took it for a reaction of pride to his generosity.

He held the nikzo out.

"This is rightfully yours. You floored me."

I wanted to be canny. "More by luck than judgment." I hoped that would pass. "Still, a bet is a bet, and I need the cash." I took the money. Pride and I had fallen out.

The truth of the matter was that I held for this big man the same admiration I held for a zhantil: the wild, untamed savagery on the Zhan-til's part matched by the controlled docility of the savagery on Duhrra's. The apparent dichotomy is only apparent. The idea that he would accompany me pleased me. But that was all.

Duhrra lifted his stump swathed in bandages and stared at it critically. "I must wait for my hook. Tell me what you think best. There is Shazmoz ahead, but it is besieged. They could fix my hook there."

My mind was made up in the time a zhyan strikes.

"We go to Shazmoz. There is a man there I must see. After that it will be the Akhram."

Seventeen
Of a Pachak hyr-Paktun and a Krozair

Making our way into Shazmoz was not going to be easy.

We eased our sectrixes on the rise and let them blow gently while we looked down the long slope toward the army of Zairians encamped below. The sea glittered blue to our right. Not a speck of sail broke that wide expanse. The sky lifted high, high above, blue and distant, and the radiance of opaline light streamed mingled down about us.

"I hear there are thirty thousand," said Duhrra.

"And how many have the Zair-forgotten Grodnims?"

He waved his stump, still wadded in bandages. "No one knows. Men talk. Uh... sixty thousand."

"But they must lay siege to Shazmoz and at the same time front our field army. It is not easy for them."

"May Zair rot their bones and turn their livers green."

Shazmoz itself was distantly visible at the end of an inlet, a vision of white cupolas and towers, long white walls baking under the suns. Over there the bestial scenes of siege were being enacted; below us the camp seemed to slumber in the light.

I had heard that the general in command here was a certain Roz Nath Lorft.[5] Men spoke well of him. He was not a Krozair. His task, relieving Shazmoz, appeared daunting and I held the shrewdest suspicion that this Nath Lorft would keep his army in touch, feeling the enemy, keeping them in play for as long as he could. Then, when Shazmoz fell, he would fall back. It seemed the Zairians had lost the ability to meet the Grodnims in the open field with any hope of success.

Scattered parties of men were about the eternal tasks of soldiers. Very few people chose to live close to the shore of the Eye of the World; from time immemorial raids have devastated the inland coasts. If there was no secure fortress very close at hand, the coastline would lie empty and deserted under the suns, so these men were totally dependent on the supply trains. They might try to send forage parties inland, but the hated green ruled there by virtue of its greater numbers and this devil-inspired confidence of winning any open encounter.

Duhrra waited my commands. His assumption of my mastery irked me. I found him dour and taciturn as a rule, which suited me as I was alike in the matter. But I wanted him to feel and act the part of a companion. This he was either unable or unwilling to do. I shook the reins.

"Let's go down and make a start."

The camp merits no detailed description, being an army camp, except for the one particular that it was a camp of men of the red southern shore of the inner sea, and therefore a camp of highly individualistic Zairians. I doubt there was one single straight row of tents. Higgledy-piggledy, set down in the best site available, to the Ice Floes of Sicce with regimentation—this was the attitude of the Zairians. Oh, they were formed up in formations as to title and number and function, and no doubt in some dusty office of the Pallan responsible papers were to be found with the details scribbled down. But the Zairians fought as they lived, sprawling, rambunctious, riotous, each man anxious to get to hand grips with his opponent. The cavalry would lower lances and charge the instant anything approached they considered chargeable. The footmen would rave and yell and boil over in their efforts to keep up. Only the varterists held some discipline, and this because the craft and science of their art demanded rule and order.

Swashbuckling—aye, that is a good word for Zairians.

We trotted our sectrixes down the slope. Duhrra had come into all of Naghan the Show's possessions, and the cash was used to buy what was necessary for our journey. I found I still did not like the sectrix. This was the first of that species of six-legged saddle animals I had encountered. The nactrix is found in the hostile territories. The totrix in the lands of the outer oceans. Poor Rees! What had happened to his regiment of totrixes? And to Chido? I must not think of them—twenty-one years must have destroyed the last vestiges of their feelings for Hamun ham Farthytu. I imagined Nulty at Paline Valley would be the Amak in all but name by now. These dusty memories enraged me, so I bashed the sectrix in the flanks and we went careering down the last of the hill and flying into the camp.

A group of men were formed into a ring and as I went up and down in the saddle to the awkward, cross-grained gait of the sectrix, I saw dust flying up from the center of the circle.

"Stand away there!" I bellowed. The sectrix was maddened now, its head rearing up and sideways against the bit. On we thundered. The backs of the ring of men came nearer and nearer.

"Out of the way! Stand clear!"

Now one or two faces turned my way. The noise was really rather wonderful. The swods yelled. The ring of red backs switched around. Faces contorted, mouths yelled, arms and legs swayed up and out—and I was rolling past in a bellow of noise. Then the stupid sectrix tangled all its six legs among the gang of men struggling over the open ground and down we all came in a whirling flurry of collapsing bodies.

Head over heels and away, rolling among a welter of red uniforms and naked chests and a Pachak's tail-hand gripping my arm and a pair of studded marching sandals beating a tattoo on my head and—I surged up, gulping for air, stood there with the Pachak bellowing angrily, the swods toppling aside, the dust and noise in the sunshine perfectly splendid.

"Silence, you pack of famblys!" I roared. I took my left hand to my right and removed the Pachak's tail-hand. He coiled his tail over his head and glared about ferociously.

His red uniform was torn. He had a few cuts on his face. I saw the faces of the swods, so I knew what was going on here.

"Who in the name of Zogo the hyr-whip are you, you rast?"

I jumped for the swod who spoke, took his throat in my hand, squeezed—only a trifle—and bellowed: "Who I am is my business, you nurdling onker. But you speak to me with respect, or I'll ring Beng Kishi's Bells so loudly in your skull your brains will spout out your ears."

A couple of the men liked that image. They laughed. I let the man go and stepped back. To the Pachak I said, "Now is your chance to walk off with dignity."

Pachaks are diffs of middle height, with two left arms, a whip-like tail equipped with a hand, straw-yellow hair, an intense loyalty and a fighting capacity that has caused great argument among the professionals of Kregen.

The Pachak said, "I shall stay and fight them with you."

I said, "I do not intend to fight them, dom."

"A pity."

Then Duhrra rolled up on his sectrix and started edging the animal in through the ring. The dust was settling. An ord-Deldar appeared and began bellowing, as all Deldars bellow, and the men shuffled off. They cast longing looks back.

"You," I said to the Pachak, "will have some recreation if those fellows get off early tonight."

"They are apims,"

I did not laugh. "So am I."

"True. But you have a heart that weighs its decisions."

The laugh was very near now, incongruously near. "If that were only so, then I would not be here."

"Nor me. I am Logu Pa-We. At the moment my nikobi is given to the Roz, Nath Lorft na Hazernal."

"I am Dak, and this is Duhrra." I let my glance dwell just long enough on the small gold zhantil-head he wore on a silk cord threaded through a top buttonhole. "You are a hyr-paktun, Logu Pa-We. We are honored."

His straw-yellow hair fell about him, ripped free of its braids in the fight. Now he swept it back over his forehead with a gesture of pride. Any man, no matter what race, who gains the coveted pakzhan, the gold zhantil-head that indicates his status as a highly renowned soldier of fortune, a notorious mercenary, will be proud.

"And you who call yourself Dak. You also are a paktun?"

I had to ignore his choice of words. "I have been a paktun in my time..."

"Then you still are."

"But I have never worn the pakzhan." I couldn't add that during my periods of mercenary service I had, indeed, worn the pakmort, for he would never understand why I had taken it off, unless I had been disgraced. It requires a court of fellow paktuns to bestow the pakmort, and a court of hyr-paktuns to bestow the pakzhan. As for that wild and feral beast, the mortil, he is almost as large and powerful as the superbly impressive zhantil; he is just as savage and free.

This Pachak hyr-paktun fingered his golden pakzhan. The pakmort is fashioned from silver but it is also worn on a silk thread looped through a convenient top buttonhole or on the shoulder knot over armor. "You will drink with me?"

"Aye, gladly," said Duhrra.

The Pachak glanced at him and curled his tail in a single cracking acceptance. I have a great deal of respect for the Pachaks as people. I like to hire them as mercenaries, for they are intensely loyal to their employers and will fight to the death. So we three went off to the nearest tent offering refreshment. I demanded tea, that superb Kregan tea, for I was thirsty.

We talked as fighting men will talk, a rapid shorthand of professional jargon that conveyed much information in few words.

The army here was in trouble. The Grodnims always seemed able to best the Zairians in battle. "They lack discipline," commented the Pachak, Logu Pa-We. "I think I will not renew my nikobi when the contract expires."

"You would fight for the Grodnims?" Duhrra showed his ignorance then, as almost all Zairians were ignorant of the diffs of Kregen and their ways.

Logu flicked his tail-hand around his jug, but he answered equably enough. "That would not be ethical."

"You great onker," I said to Duhrra, and drank tea.

"Yes, master."

"And I'm not your master, by the diseased intestines of Makki-Grodno!"

"I do not agree with you in that, Dak."

The Pachak, evidently summing us up as just two more unstable and highly unprofessional Zairians, drifted into more general conversation. I learned what I could. When I said we wanted to get through the lines and into Shazmoz he pursed his lips.

"You would run great risks."

"There is a man I must see there."

"And I need a hook."

"Yes, there is a man renowned for that there."

The contract the Pachaks entered into with their employers they called their nikobi. That is, it was a weak approximation to the obi which gave authority and working arrangements to my clansmen of Segesthes. It was half an obi. Chuliks and Rapas and Fristles worked a different system. The myriad different forms of human beings on Kregen never cease to fascinate me. They are as different in their bodily forms as they are in the working processes of their minds. Yet they are all human and share human attributes. It would need an insensitive clod of a very high order of cloddishness to regard them as freaks, as candidates for a zoo or a menagerie. They are men and women. How odd we must look, we two apims, Duhrra and me, in the eyes of this Pachak. He would regard us as being crippled. We had only one left arm each, and so would always have trouble in taking powerful blows on a shield. We had a bare bottom each, with no incredibly useful tail with its grasping hand. He would find it laughable and impossible that a whole world swung in space peopled by cripples like us. I had the notion, fed by thoughts about the Everoinye, that very possibly a world existed peopled only by Pachaks. It made sense. No, the multifarious forms call forth no slighting or disbelieving comments about inmates of zoos or menageries; menagerie men contribute to the life and color and adventure of Kregen. I would have it no other way, clods or no clods.

The drinking was now bringing out the singing. Men love to sing on Kregen, and women too, in their own way.

The suns were declining now and, in the casual way of the Zairian military, the soldiers had had enough for the day. The songs lifted. A group of Pachaks serving with Logu Pa-We sang too, but the apims of the southern shore sang alone.

Logu was telling us of that remote and eerily mysterious land of Tambu, off the southwest coast of the continent of Loh. He was one of the very few men I had heard claim they had been there. He was saying the experience had scarred him in his ib. He would never go back. He was as well aware of

132

the lands of the outer oceans as I was—better, probably—and it was clear he was now regretting his decision to bring his men into the inner sea. Or regretting that he had joined up with the reds instead of the greens. But his ideas of paktun ethics must be admired.

The Zairian swods were singing *The Destiny of the Fishmonger of Magdag,* a highly colored and lurid account and one calculated to bring mirth to the voice and tears to the eyes, with the crashing down of the jugs onto the sturm-wood tables on the refrain "For the fish heads came off red, came off red, the fish heads dropped off red, red, red."

The pang struck me then: what did these fine roistering fellows, snug in their inner sea, know of the fishheads of the outer oceans?

Panshi had told me there had been no further raids after the one in which I had gone wandering on my travels, as he had phrased it. But I knew the internecine battle between the red and the green, here in the Eye of the World, was of scant importance beside the greater conflicts waiting outside in the greater world.

That very snugness had, I know, been a great deal of the charm of the Eye of the World, of my affection for the Krozairs.

The Swifter with the Kink went up—how we all dreaded a swifter whose lines were not true, as with the galleys' inordinate length-to-breadth ratio they so often were! And then *the Chuktar with the Glass Eye* battered against the stars. Oh yes, the swods sang.

I caught Duhrra's eye and motioned. Logu caught the signal, for Pachaks are quick in these matters, and we three rose and went out, away from the campfires and the singing.

"So you wish to steal into Shazmoz?"

"That is our intention."

"Maybe a way can be found. You will need to be silent and quick... and to bear up."

I think Logu was going to say we would have need of courage, but he had the sense to halt himself.

"You must leave all preparations to me."

I thought it fair to warn him: "That is agreeable. But we shall keep our fists upon our swords and the blades loose in the scabbards."

He chuckled and his yellow hair glowed strangely under the light of the moons.

We went through the moons-lit darkness toward the shapes of tents which seemed in less of a muddle than the others. A small body of Pachaks formed about us, grim men with blades already gripped in their tail-fists. It took very little time before we were all mounted up and riding softly out of the camp. This army of Zairians comprised detachments from many free red cities of the southern shore and other lands from further south; there were parties of Krozairs and Red Brethren also. We were able to pass through the last picket lines—these were men from Tremzo, stalwart fellows with pickled hides from drinking of their own produce—and so walk our sectrixes slowly off into the no-man's-land between the contending armies.

"You are determined to get your hook?"

"Aye, Dak. As you are to see this man you prate of."

In a little dell we dismounted and the Pachaks opened their saddlebags. I did not make a face, but the sight of the green robes and the green feathers filled me with disgust.

"It is necessary," said Logu peremptorily, "that you wear these garments."

We did so without arguing. When we resumed our movement we were a returning patrol of Grodnim scouts. I thought perhaps we were a little early for that, but after we had passed the first sentries with quick and harshly intemperate words from the hyr-paktun who led us, I realized Logu knew what he was doing. The way led us through a well-packed road where the moonslight glittered on the ruts of wheeled traffic. Supplies and varters. The damned Grodnims were organized. I knew how well they could handle slaves; even the Katakis could teach them little in that nauseating department of economics.

The breathing mass of a camp showed on our left. A few lights hung in regulation intervals. We pressed on. After a time we angled sharply to our right, toward the coast Sand shushed and shirred beneath the sectrixes. A dark shape rose ahead to bar our path and the moons shone on a lifted spear. What Logu said in a whisper I did not hear, but we went on with the spear returned to the upright position and the sentry stepping back from our path. He was a Fristle, his cat-face and slanted eyes turning to watch us go. We passed in silence.

Presently Logu reined alongside me.

"My brother is near now. You swear that your mission has nothing to do with the armies here, with the fight we have?"

"Nothing, as Zair is my witness." It was true.

"And as Papachak the All-Powerful is mine, if you lie your tripes will spill steaming on the ground."

He meant it. I meant what I said. We understood each other.

His brother turned out to be cut from the same cloth. They conferred for a moment, their sectrixes close, and I caught the words "... paktun not in employment."

If you marvel that two brothers could serve in armies opposed to each other then the rigid system of mercenaries on Kregen has escaped you. If they met in battle these two would fight. That was a part of their mystique, why they were paktuns; if asked they would look puzzled and say, probably, "It is in our nikobi."

But they were human beings in these stark surroundings, and I saw the real affection these two grim fighting men bore for each other. Duhrra and I might pass on; Logu's brother would not, of course, in the ethics of nikobi, allow him to pass.

After that we were passed through and Logu's brother said in his gruff voice, "You had best leave your greens here."

We doffed the hated green and, once more clad in the brave old red, set forth into the darkness. In only a bur or so we came under the walls of Shazmoz and the first patrols. With many exclamations of wonder we were escorted into the encircled town.

The sight of a city under siege is unpleasant The place moved with a sluggish air most displeasing. The men looked gaunt. We passed fires made from smashed houses and saw women there, poor bedraggled creatures who held out their hands to us. When a few gold coins were tossed to them they spat and hurled them back. Of what use gold? One cannot eat gold.

A Hikdar met us under the lamp over the citadel door. Like any city that sought to exist on the coast of the inner sea, Shazmoz was heavily fortified, with a defended harbor. The citadel frowned on a hill above the nighted waters. I said, "It is necessary that I see Pur Zenkiren."

"Your business? You come from Roz Nath?"

"No. My business is private."

The Hikdar was not a Krozair. I wondered if I dared presume, but guessed the news of the disgrace of Pur Dray Prescot would already have been spread. He looked at us undecided. Duhrra moved uneasily on his sectrix and then dismounted.

"Hikdar, Is there one here called Molyz ti Sanurkazz? Molyz the Hook-Maker?" And Duhrra held up his stump.

"Yes. He is here."

The Hikdar made no move to admit us. A guard party hovered near, bows drawn. This was an anticlimax. And yet who could blame the Hikdar? Strangers coming in the night through enemy lines demanding to see the general in charge of a besieged city? This stank of treason.

So I spoke a few short words that, whispered in the ear of a Krozair Brother, would apprise him that one of his fellows sought audience. The Hikdar nodded. "I will see. Stay here."

The wait stretched. Then he was back. "Come."

Many and many a time have I marched through a grim gray castle surrounded by guards. Often they have been my men, as often perhaps they have guarded me. Our feet rang on the flags. Torchlight flared and marked our way with fleeting shadows. Up through the levels we marched, stairway by stairway, past guards who, every one, showed the ravages of hunger and privation.

Along a passage a carpet muffled the tramp of our feet, then we reached a lenken door bound in iron. The Hikdar bashed on the door; it swung back and we were ushered into an anteroom filled with aides, young dandified men wearing profuse red decorations. There was another door, another knock, a fresh entrance. I did not see the room. I did not see the furnishings. I was hardly aware of the guards crowding at my elbow, of Duhrra breathing hoarsely in my ear.

All my vision concentrated on the man who stood in the center of the floor, half turned to greet this importune Krozair Brother come so suddenly in the night.

Pur Zenkiren.

I stared at him. By Zair! I knew I had changed not at all in appearance from the man he had known and to whom he had bid remberee in Pattelonia far away on the eastern shore. But Pur Zenkiren! I felt the blood thump from my heart. Where he had been tall and limber, with a fine bronzed fearless face, now that face looked gray, with folds of sagging skin. The bold black mustache still jutted fiercely upward beneath the beak of a Zairian nose, but that nose was bone-fine, thinned down, razor-edged. His black curled hair was as profuse as ever. About Zenkiren there hovered the black vulture wings of defeat and despair.

He wore a long white robe and a Krozair longsword belted at his waist. The device of the hubless spoked wheel within the circle shone dimly on his breast, the threads dulled and the scarlet embroideries broken away. The hem of the white robe was caked with mud.

"You have important business with me?"

His voice had lost the firm ring of authority. In the lamplight—cheap mineral oil which stank in the chamber—he peered toward me. I stood positioned most carefully so that the shadow of the gross bulk of Duhrra fell over me, casting me into limbo.

"My name is Dak, Pur Zenkiren. I pray you"—and here I mentioned a word or two known only to the Krozairs—"hear me in private."

Whatever had befallen this man, he remained a Krozair. He waved his hand and the guards withdrew. He stared at Duhrra's stump.

"Yes, Jernu," said Duhrra, immense in the shadowed room, bending his head. "I seek a boon from Molyz the Hook-Maker."

"There was no need to ask me." He gestured at me, in Duhrra's shadow. "Stand you forth, you who dub yourself Pur Dak, and let me see you."

I said, "I did not presume to dub myself *Pur*, Jernu. But I must beg you to listen to what I have to say before you make a judgment. All men know of your wisdom and upright countenance. I humbly crave your indulgence."

This, I fancied, was how a man might think it proper to address a powerful lord who commanded a city, besieged though that city might be. I knew from old experience that Pur Zenkiren put as much store by flowery words as I did myself.

136

"You speak in riddles! Step forth so that I may see you. Instantly!"

There came the old hard smack of command.

Slowly I stepped into the light.

He stared at me for a long time.

Then he walked a few steps to a table cluttered with lists and maps and an empty bottle on its side, where the oil lamp trailed a thin plume of blue smoke. He put a hand to the wood; he did not sit in the broken-backed chair.

"Why do I not instantly call out for the guards? Are you broken from your ib and come to torment me? Is it you? No, it cannot be you."

"I stand before you, an innocent man adjudged guilty. Think back, Pur Zenkiren! Think back to the deck of a Magdaggian swifter running with the blood of the Overlords, and a slave with a brand in his fist. Think back to Felteraz and Mayfwy and the broad prizes brought into Sanurkazz. Think of Zy and loyalty and comradeship, and then tell me, face to face, man to man, looking me in the eye, tell me, Pur Zenkiren, if Pur Dray is or ever can be—"

He did not let me finish.

He lifted up his voice and shouted: *"Apushniad!"*

He had not let me finish; he had finished the sentence himself, and he had finished me.

Eighteen
A case for casuistry

A vision of Delia sprang into my head. Clear, distinct, infinitely appealing. My course was set.

The guards would come boiling in in the next mur. I leaped for Zenkiren and clapped a hand around his mouth and with the other pinned his right arm to his side. And I laughed. I roared with laughter, shouting my glee!

"Aye!" I roared. "Aye, Jernu, well may you laugh!"

Duhrra said, "Uh?"

I said, "Laugh, Duhrra, just a little." Then, in a heartbeat: "Thank you, Duhrra. Your laugh clinches all."

Zenkiren writhed. But his strength was wasted away. I held him. I bent and whispered in his ear.

"You will listen to me. We were friends once. We remain friends for my part. I know that if I said I would kill you if you cried out again for the guards, you would cry out, defying all, for the sake of the Brotherhood. This I know."

He rolled his eyes and we both knew I spoke the truth.

"The Azhurad was sounded. I did not come. I do not deny I failed. But it is the nature of my failure that needs examination." It is said on Earth that it takes a Jesuit to chop logic. Casuistry of itself forms little part of the techniques of dialectic of the Krzy, but intricately detailed arguments and debates that sweep away the confines of mundane limitations are a joy to them. The brain must be honed and sharpened to an edge keen enough to slip between reason and reason. I felt Zenkiren's interest as I went on to present the case. There were two impossibilities and each one negated the other. "I am—was—a true Krozair. I would slay any man who denied me that. And yet I did not hear the Call. How may such a dilemma be resolved, Zenkiren? And, in studying the problem, bear two things in mind.

"You must recall that day in Pattelonia when you asked me to help you in the fight in Proconia. You ordered out a liburna. We sailed and the storm rose and the thunder rolled and the lightning struck. You understood that at the time I was fated to journey east. You were to consult Pur Zazz on the matter. I do not know what he may have told you—" Here I felt a strong jerk from Zenkiren, as though he wished to speak. I gripped him fast and went on. "But it must be clear to you I am not like ordinary men."

When I said that I admit I felt like the cheating impostor I truly was. Duhrra let out a gurgling noise which I ignored. The stink of the mineral oil wafted across and the light wavered on the littered table, on the weapons in their racks, the draped alcove where Zenkiren slept.

"That is the first thing you must consider. And the second touches us both. Oh, yes, I know it is long and long since you and I met. I have been too many places and seen many wonders and done many things—aye, and many of them I would rather not have done. But through all my wanderings and in whatever place I have found myself, I have always thought of myself as a Krzy. Always. It has been the single most important fact of my life—always, as you will understand, after my Delia. You will not understand this, Zenkiren, but it is even of more importance than the Swinging City of Aphrasöe."

Even as I spoke I caught my thoughts treacherously swinging, as we used to swing from growth to growth, from house to house in Aphrasöe. After my Apushniad, how could this inner sea be of consequence to me? That was a garblish fool talking. It was not the Eye of the World that was important, it was the mystique of the Krozairs of Zy that grew to overtop the highest peak of the Stratemsk and their concepts of world-shattering import that drew me on. And they drew me on even then, even when I had appointed myself a meeting at the Akhram on the Grand Canal.

I moved Zenkiren, gently, preparing to ease him free.

"I mention this, but without weight in the argument or the dilemma. You may solve the dilemma how you will, riddle it how you may. But one thing I mention without influence: we were friends, Zenkiren, blade comrades. I have never forgotten you nor ceased to regard you with Brotherly affection. This may be a feather-weight, a passing cloud, a midge that lives a day—I can only speak for myself. For me it has been as the keel of a swifter that strikes cleanly through the seas."

Duhrra said: "Duh… by *Zair*, Dak! And you a—"

"Hold, good Duhrra. I love this old man, yet if he cries out to betray us he must be silenced."

The tides of my life on Kregen had moved me up and down, washed me this way and that, willy-nilly. Now I knew the ebb tide might turn. Now, perhaps, the flood might make.

I took my hand away from Zenkiren's mouth.

The presence of Duhrra could afford me no comfort now. I wondered if I could kill Zenkiren and knew I might have to silence him as I had before. He looked at me and slowly, slowly, wiped a hand across his mouth. His eyes melted into me.

"Pur Dray, and is there no lahal between us?"

"Lahal, Pur Zenkiren."

"A long time. I did not believe it could be you… and you Apushniad. That was no doing of mine, although my vote was cast against you."

"I knew it would be. You could do no other."

"But what you say… so long ago and yet only yesterday in vaol-paol. I imperil my vows talking to you, and yet is not talk better than skull-breaking?"

"Or ib-breaking. No, Zenkiren, you do not break your vows, for the judgment against me was false. I am still a true Krozair although unacknowledged and declared Apushniad."

Again Duhrra let go that gurgling grunt and again I ignored him. Telling him anything now would only complicate the matter.

"What you say is of surpassing interest, for there is indeed in it the classic case of two opposites…" We all know the various examples cited; here was another one. I knew the knot could not be untied but only cut, and dared I place the sword in Zenkiren's hand and indicate where he should strike? Would even *he* believe? I think, had I confided in old Pur Zazz, that he would have believed my story of Earth. He would have offered words of comfort. For better or worse I decided not to make Zenkiren the first person on Kregen I told of my Earthly ancestry. I knew who had the right to the first confidence. And if the knot therefore remained uncut and all that followed from it, then so be it. I was in a pretty ugly mood, I can tell you, and closer than I probably suspected to impatience and contempt of all the mighty and mystical Krozairs of Zy.

We talked for a while. No refreshments were offered. Shazmoz lay under siege and I knew Zenkiren well enough to know he would share the rations with his men. He said that among the Krzy present were none who had known me in the old days. Fifty years is a quarter of a man's life on Kregen. Despite their longevity, it is still a monstrous span of seasons. If I had not known who Zenkiren was, there is every probability I would not have recognized him. This dreadful alteration in his appearance was not so much the erosion of the passage of time, of course, but the immediate effects of the siege and the more subtle and far-reaching effects of his failure to be elected Grand Archbold.

He would not talk of that sad subject and instead launched into an impassioned tirade against this new leader of the Grodnims who led them from success to success. He was not an Overlord of Magdag. He had sprung up on the green northern shore like a weed that grows overnight and with leeching suckers strangles the plants that sustain it. And the name of this man, previously referred to by obscene and odiferous names in my conversations with the men of Zair, I now learned was Genod Gannius.

Genod Gannius.

I knew the name Gannius. I had held it in my memory against the day when I might begin to unravel the mysterious purposes of the Star Lords. Was this Genod Gannius connected with that Gannius I had first met in the Eye of the World?

My speculations on this point were shatteringly interrupted as I understood what Zenkiren was now saying. He had seated himself and he looked tired and worn, with only a flicker of that old martial blaze about him. Duhrra had gone to stand by the door, folding his brawny arms on his chest as he had done when Naghan the Show cried up his prowess. I realized Zenkiren had filed away the Krozair dilemma; he must have resolved the ultimate answer in my favor—for whatever reason—and would wait for a more opportune time to decipher the proof. Now he was talking about Genod Gannius and the armies of Grodnims, the forces he called the "new" armies.

As I listened my thoughts whirled and I felt the shattering effect of his words.

I will not repeat word for word what he said, although they lay graven on my brain. In effect, Zenkiren indicated that the Grodnims had developed a new and devastating form of warfare for which they owed nothing to the Overlords of Magdag. Whispers of it had seeped out. Then an army trained by this Genod Gannius had appeared and annihilated one of the typically sprawling, roistering, swashbuckling armies of Zairians.

The way of it was this: when the Zairians stirruped up and set spurs to their sectrixes they were met with a wall of enormous spears, held cunningly like a thickset hedgerow. When the infantry attempted to wade in with their swords flashing, the crossbows had loosed and the storm of bolts fell on them, piercing them through and mingling them with the wreckage of the cavalry. The crossbows had shot quarrel after quarrel. And then, at the end, a final deluge had strewed the field with red corpses. The green banners had flaunted high in victory.

And so it had gone on, on field after field, with the results that led up to the desperate straits the Zairians now found themselves in. When the red archers loosed their shafts they were deflected from the green ranks by that coward's trick, that despicable device, the shield.

I knew.

You who have heard of my previous sojourn here in the Eye of the World, and of my doings in the warrens of Magdag with my old slave phalanx, my old vosk-skulls, you will also know—and to my shame.

By Zair! I had trained the slaves and workers to beat the Overlords. I had given them pike, shield and crossbow drill. We had been in the very act of thrashing the hated Overlords when the Star Lords had seen fit to snatch me away from Magdag and dump me down in Upalion in the far east of the inner sea. It had taken me no time at all, on my return here, to know that all my fears had been proved right and that the Overlords had turned and beaten my friends, the workers and slaves of the warrens. They must have, else Magdag would have perished. And the inevitable had happened.

Blind! Onker! Stupid fool, idiot, idiot. A weapon given to my friends—a sharp, lethal weapon. Oh, what a cretinous object I was!

It had not needed a genius in war to seize on the devices used by the rebellious slaves, though from all I was to hear I think this Genod Gannius was a near-genius. It was Gannius, in his own hold, who had taken what I had given the slaves and molded it and trained his men and so taken Magdag. He had thrashed the Overlords, seized into his own hands all their power and wealth, and turned it to his own crazy schemes.

He had set himself up on the high throne in Magdag and all men bowed in the full incline before him.

"When I first heard of the new manner of war practiced by the rasts of Grodno," said Zenkiren, and he looked across at me with a slow reflective stare that made me extremely uncomfortable, "I was minded of a memory I had thought forgotten. I harked back to what I had been told of a Krozair Brother who roused the warrens in vile Magdag. It seemed to me he had told me something of training slaves to unseat Overlords in all their might and power, of sticking them through. I reminded myself of this, but I did not speak of it to a living soul."

"I had thought," I said, "that mayhap that was a further reason for Apushniad."

"No. To give sharp weapons wantonly to children is to invite being cut in return."

"Yet this dilemma of which I spoke is further enhanced by this… unfortunate… happening. For it is of a piece."

"I shall remember."

"There are powers, Zenkiren, over and above—I cannot speak of them even if I could, for I do not yet understand them." I would not tell him of my dreadful thoughts about this Genod Gannius. For the full horror of that I must wait until I learned the truth.

Duhrra was beginning to shift about, from one foot to the other, and he kept whistling thinly through his teeth, which were good and strong and yellow, so I knew he was thinking of his stump and the hook Molyz the Hook-Maker might fashion for him.

Zenkiren took up a pen—it was a quill and not a reed so he was keeping up some standards under siege—and wrote swiftly on the back of an old order, long since finished with and now in these stringent times pressed into service again. 'Take this to Molyz ti Sanurkazz. He is authorized to use the necessary leather and iron."

"Thank you, Jernu." Duhrra took the paper and looked at me.

"I will meet you at the gate by which we came in, in time to depart."

"Zair keep you." Duhrra went out in search of a surrogate hand. The guards joked with him in desultory fashion. Though they were under siege and likely to starve to death if they were not stuck through first, yet they were still Zairians who loved a good laugh. My heart warmed to them.

Zenkiren took the opportunity to transact some business. The siege had become by now a matter of logistics, of empty storehouses, of morale and only occasionally of fighting. I knew if he asked me to stay and fight I would have to refuse. So much more of importance waited outside, in the greater world. He did not ask me. For that I was grateful, having no pride left.

We talked at length, for much time separated us. As with the other news I had gleaned I will apprise you of what matters at the opportune time. Suffice it to say I heard more bad news and it all centered on the new devil-given powers of the Grodnims.

"We can sustain very few further attacks in force. At least the Grodnims' new method of fighting does not aid them in siegecraft." He tapped his columns of figures scribbled over and over and altered often on the sheets of paper scattered on the table. "We have held them. No doubt we could hold them until the Ice Floes of Sicce go up in steam if we could eat. Unless they ship a larger army across we will not go down beaten in battle; only our unfortunate desire to eat will destroy us."

He cocked an eye at me. "And does not Roz Nath strive?"

Feeling the eyes of the Pachak, Logu Pa-We on me, I answered: "I do not think you should hold any hope in Roz Nath."

"Ha!" he said, a bark of sound, whether a laugh or a sob I did not know. "I have never reposed hope in Nath Lorft to march in and rescue us. But he performs a useful function, for Roz Nazlifurn will find his task that much easier." He stopped himself from talking then, stopped himself visibly. He rustled the papers on the table with his quill and said at random, "We grow less every day, less mouths to feed. We will last out."

His motives were transparent. There was a secret about this Roz Nazli-furn. I was going out of Shazmoz, through enemy lines, and might easily be captured. What I did not know I could not tell.

As though seeking to throw me further off, he added in a lighter voice: "We Krozairs do not put much store by titles and ranks of nobility. Would you not willingly trade a prince's crown, supposing you owned one, for membership of the order?" He pulled his lips back in a parody of a smile.

I did not smile. He did not know my history. The question hurt, stung. I surely would have, before the Apushniad! And now... I rose from the chair and spoke politely. Now I had changed my priorities. I was hewing to my nature, as I then thought, doing the correct thing in difficult circumstances and to hell with anyone who thought otherwise.

"It is time to bid you remberee, Pur Zenkiren. I regret the long empty years. I made a mistake in not returning to the Eye of the World sooner. But bear in mind the Krozair dilemma. At the least, it will make a capital subject for debate."

He shook my hand as they do in the inner sea, and I felt again the old Krozair grip. He smiled, this time a real smile. "See, Pur Dray. I call you Pur and I give you the right hand of fellowship. I have decided the Apushniad was incorrect. Now it remains to prove it."

I felt this keenly.

"You do me great honor, Zenkiren. I have been an onker, and yet the slaves in Magdag... they are human and needed to be set free. I did what I thought correct, according to my lights."

"Zair holds dominion over all and if it is His will—" He shivered and plucked at his gown, feeling the emblem stitched there, making me plainly see why it was so threadbare and worn. "Good will come of all this. Zair would not will it otherwise."

"Remberee, Pur Zenkiren."

"Remberee, Pur Dray."

So I went out and through the nighted streets and soon found Duhrra walking up to the gate. He carried his right hand inside his folded blanket-cloak. The guards brought our sectrixes. They wished us well. We rode away from doomed Shazmoz with the star glitter high above and a small moon slamming past above our heads.

The Pachak hyr-paktun Logu Pa-We and his brother would see us safely back. There need be no alarms on that score. I rode the damned sectrix in his ungainly waddle and I thought.

I could live with what I had done with the old slave phalanx and my old vosk-helmets. Then we had fought for our lives and liberty. What followed later was not of our doing. But...

143

But when I had first been transported here into the Eye of the World by the Star Lords their clear command had been to save the lives of two young people from the hideous rock-apes, the grundals. This I had done. I had ensured that Gahan Gannius and Valima should live. They had lived. They had married and begotten a son. That son must be Genod Gannius. I, Dray Prescot, had directly brought doom and destruction upon my beloved Zairians!

Nineteen
A brush with risslacas and a sighting at the Akhram

My Deldars had been ranked, as we say opening a game of Jikaida, and now I must press on and push all the spidery shadows of past follies behind me.

By the Black Chunkrah! What a nurdling onker I had been! For all the kindness Pur Zenkiren had been able to show me, I knew, and this without rancor or disappointment too great to be borne, that he would in all probability be quite unable to resolve the riddle. The two impossibilities canceled each other out; the Krozair dilemma remained. I would remain Apushniad. I had resigned myself to that. And then, gladly, fiercely, I declared that it was not a resignation but a joyous awakening to the true values of my life on Kregen.

"Down there, master!" said Duhrra, pointing. "Zair-forsaken Grodnims, may Uncle Zobab rot their livers and fester their tripes."

I spoke somewhat sharply as we rode the high bluff trending toward the sea, with the suns' radiance all about us and the thin piping of birds to keep us company. "What color do you wear on your back, oh Duhrra of the Mighty Muscles?"

He looked suitably discomfited and resentful.

"The damned green, master. And an itchy, vile, mean and crawling color it is, to be sure."

I was not going to argue with him. We had said remberee to the Pachaks and ridden off, going west, wearing the green over our reds. Now we had almost reached the farthest point of the Eye of the World. Before us would soon appear the Grand Canal and the Akhram, and, if we went that far, beyond them the Dam of Days.

Our sectrixes paced on. We kept to the wending ridge of bluffs above the narrow coastal strip for, however much we might wear the green and pass ourselves off as mercenaries, the ever-present danger was that Duhrra would explode into action against the Magdaggians, and I would be scant murs after.

Green is a charming color and restful to the eyes. There are a number of fine uses for green: it is the color of rifle regiments, of racing cars, of Robin Hood; I have nothing against the color itself. Had the Grodnims chosen to wear red and the Zairians green, my sentiments would have remained as they were, against what would have been the cramphs of red Grodnims. I did not forget what went on in their monstrous ziggurats and megaliths during the time of the green sun's eclipse.

A war party below, trotting their sectrixes parallel to us, had seen us; we must keep steadily on and give them no cause for suspicion.

In Havilfar, that progressive and yet barbaric continent, one of the most widespread of religions was that of Havil the Green. Havil, named for the Havilfarese word for Genodras, the green sun. How, you might ask, could anyone worship the small green sun when confronted with the magnificence of the huge red sun? The answer is simple and yet profound, and one that has made me ponder long. During eclipse, the red swallows the green utterly. There is no longer a green sun. But, eventually, lo! the green sun emerges, newly born, fresh, refulgent, a bright new sun eternally young. Oh, yes, rebirth and recreation play as significant a part in the religions of Kregen as of Earth.

Duhrra began to hum softly, *The Chuktar with the Glass Eye,* and we rode carefully, shading the liquid gleam of our eyes as we looked down on the war party pacing us below.

I shook the reins. "I think we had best join them. They will wonder why we ride aloof in this dangerous land. You, Duhrra the Mighty Mangler, must keep a straight tongue in your mouth."

He grew affronted when I taunted him with that old title he tried to forget. He humped and grumped and then came out with: "And you, a Krozair Brother!"

"I may have been." He knew enough now to desert me or remain; he had chosen to stay with me.

"My twin was a Zairian to the Krozairs of Zamu. The zigging Grodnims captured him and tortured him and slew him. I do not forget that."

"I lost a good friend under the whips of the rasts of Magdag."

"Then let us join them as you suggest and as soon as we are able let us slay every one, every last cramph."

"If we have to, we will, but our purpose is to reach the Akhram. Your hook depends on it, you tell me."

"Aye." He favored his stump. "Aye, master, it does."

I licked my fingers and stroked my mustaches. "Pull those damn bristling mustaches of yours down, Duhrra. We will have to wear a hangdog down-dropping Grodnim pair if we are to pass muster."

We stroked the Zairian mustaches into hangdog Grodnim mustaches. It pained us, but it was necessary.

145

When a Grodnim strains tea or soup through his facial hair a good Zairian has to decide whether to laugh or throw up.

So we rode down the slope and joined the Grodnims. They were not Magdaggians, being from the free Grodnim city of Laggig-Laggu, a large and prosperous conurbation some twenty dwaburs inland of the northern shore of the Laggu River. Hard, businesslike warriors, they handled their sectrixes with confidence and I took note of their weapons. There were ten of them and their Deldar told us they were joining the Chuktar of the west. We nodded as though understanding.

Where we marched was the southern shore. It had belonged to Zair. Now followers of Grodno rode confidently there. From the very last western extremity of the Eye of the World right up to Shazmoz, the green flaunted triumphantly over the red. This area had always been relatively deserted, the haunt of wild beasts, used for hunting.

My own plans were now settled. Duhrra needed to go to the Akhram, for there were to be found associated with the Todalpheme, who monitored the tides, doctors of a higher quality than the usual. His stump was not yet ready to accept the chafing of a leather socket and hook, so Molyz the Hook-Maker had told him, and the doctors of the Akhram would advise him further. So that was why Duhrra rode. As for me, my plans envisaged waiting, and damned impatiently too, for a ship of Vallia to pass through the Grand Canal bound back home. The galleons from Vallia carried on trade with the Eye of the World, as I have said, and I was confident one would eventually arrive. The voller was gone, and riding, walking, climbing and, in the end, crawling, over the Stratemsk, the hostile territories, the Klackadrin and then eastern Turismond would take far, far longer, if I survived it.

"Risslacas!" shouted the Deldar, yanking his longsword out, sticking his stirrups in and racing away at the head of his squad. We followed, keeping closed up. On the ridge above us two risslacas hopped along. They were carnivorous and no doubt regarded us as juicy dinners. This was obviously their territory. They were big, with enormous rear legs and haunches, pear-shaped bodies with neck frills of spines, two small grasping forelegs apiece and heads that could gulp an entire sectrix.

The sectrixes knew it. They were terrified. They bounded along on their six legs, letting terrified snorts of panic blast from their open mouths, not conserving their energies to run. Damn stupid sectrixes. Had I been riding a zorca it would have flown like the wind, everything concentrated on galloping. Had I ridden a vove I would have had to restrain it from going up the slope and knocking the risslacas over.

"May Grotal the Reducer wither their bones!" yelped the man riding by Duhrra. Sheer panic hit these Grodnims. The enormous size of the risslacas and the sharp glitter from their teeth and eyes were enough to unman them. I cocked an eye up the slope, knowing the sectrix, maddened with fear though it was, would not put a foot wrong now. The fur of the risslacas, a slatey brown ocher, fluffed as they cooled their laboring bodies. Fur and feathers are used to protect from heat as well as to conserve it. The two main families of risslacas, the cold-blooded and the warm-blooded, are well represented on Kregen, as I have said. It is a fair scheme to assign dinosaurs a class of their own, distinct from reptiles, birds and mammals. Their expenditure of energy would heat their bodies quickly and then they would have to rest to dispose of all that body-heat if they were cold-blooded. The sectrix had no doubts what they were. It ran with its blunt head outstretched and its six legs pumping, pumping, its body convulsing with effort.

The men of Laggig-Laggu carried short bows cased at their sides. By some considerable effort I edged my mount alongside the man who kept calling on Grodno and demanding that Grotal the Reducer deform, wither, plague, the risslacas so that he might escape.

"Let me have that, dom." I slid the bow from the case and with it a hand-ful of arrows. The bow was a poor thing if one thought of the longbow of Loh—or of Valka now!—but it would serve. Duhrra saw what I was doing.

"No, master!" he bellowed. "You have no chance!"

"The risslacas were designed by—" Then I rephrased that, for the name of Zair instead of Grodno had almost slipped from my babbling lips. "They hunt sectrixes. That is how they eat."

He couldn't argue. The sectrix wouldn't stop no matter how much I banged it, so I did not try. I turned in that damned uncomfortable seat and slapped an arrow into the bow, prepared to see if I might win approval in the eyes of Seg Segutorio, who is, I believe, the finest bowman of Loh of them all.

I do not claim to be as fine a bowman as Seg. That would be prideful folly. We have shot many a round and sometimes I win. The lumpen, ungainly, impossible gait of the sectrix made accurate shooting almost impossible. By calculation, riding the humps and bumps, the yawing and swaying, I fancied I would hit a risslaca eventually! There were only two weak points, the eyes. There were too few arrows to risk the chance. When Duhrra saw me cock a leg over the high wooden saddle he fairly yelled in outrage.

"Go on, Duhrra and, if I live, make sure you come back for me."

I slipped off and the sectrixes were gone in a billow of dust before he could answer. I turned.

By Krun!

They were big! And they were close!

The first arrow spit from the bow. I would not miss at a time like this. Two arrows whipped from the bow and the leading risslaca went crazy,

147

screaming, pawing with his ridiculous little forelegs, waving that enormous head from side to side. From each eye an arrow sprouted. The second dinosaur came on. He was, if anything, larger than the other, and cleverer or luckier, for he moved as the third arrow shot and it chingled and broke against his snout.

He was almost on me, snorting, spurts of steam belching from his gappy nostrils, his mouth wide and cavernous and blood-red, ringed with fangs. I shot again and his left eye went black for him. There was time now only to leap to that side, into his blind spot. His head swayed. I ran off, turned, notched the last arrow. His head swayed around; he saw me with his remaining eye; he charged. The arrow shot spitefully.

He shrieked and ran, ran in circles, colliding with his mate. Then, maddened by pain and unable to see, the two dinosaurs fell on each other, biting, clawing. It was hideous and pathetic and disgusting. I felt no flush of victory. I felt sorry for them, for they had been hunting, doing what nature had intended they should do. It was their misfortune that they chose to hunt Dray Prescot.

Somewhat glumly I left them and walked on in the trail of the sectrixes. It took three burs before Duhrra came back for me. He was cursing and swearing and when he saw me he looked like a man who sees a ghost, a broken ib returned to Kregen, all ghastly and gibbering.

I mounted up.

"Thank you for coming back, Duhrra. There may be others."

"Those Grodno-gastas! Refused to return, said we were no business of theirs! Rode on, quaking, the cramphs!"

The sectrixes were still nervous, sweating, trembling. We galloped them a little, to ease their fears and to stop them from catching cold. They would have to be coddled this night.

"That rast of a Grodnim swod will have a good story to account for the loss of his bow."

"Aye, master. And I will have a story that tells of how a maniac called Dak acted like a—uh... no one will believe me."

"If the risslacas had not been stopped," I said, letting my mount gallop ahead, "no one would have told any stories."

"That is true, by Zair!"

So it was in a growing spirit of comradeship, for all that Duhrra insisted on slipping the odd "master" into his sentences, and occasionally letting fall that idiot's "duh," we came at last to the Grand Canal, after a long enough and tiring journey.

There was no sign on the southern shore of the Grodnim army.

The northern shore, as I well knew, had a thriving series of communities held together in service to the Todalpheme, those wise men who calculate the tides and send warning, causing the Oblifanters to issue instructions to the workers for the Dam of Days to be opened or closed. I had never seen the Dam of Days. My Delia had, for she had accompanied my sons Drak and Zeg when a galleon from Valka had brought them here to sail to Zy for their education. I would take ship and sail home to Valka, and if I never saw the Eye of the World again it would be too soon.

Missals grew brilliantly along the upper level of the Grand Canal where the grass was cropped short. I stared at a particular grove of the missals, seeing their pink and white blossoms, thinking back. Duhrra sensed my mood and remained silent.

Slowly, I walked toward the edge of the Grand Canal. The last time I had come this way, Waterloo had been less than a year gone.

How I remembered! The sweltering Bombay night, then Kregen, glorious Kregen with the streaming mingled sunshine, the air like nectar and a whole world in which to go adventuring. Well, I had been a long way since then and done many things and seen many wonders. Then I had been callow in the ways of Kregen. Now I felt myself not wise so much as indoctrinated. I knew in my heart that I was just the same nurdling onker who would rush headlong into incredible danger where the prudent self I now imagined myself to be would hang back. It is all in the situation.

Over there I had seen a dying Chulik stagger from the bushes, his face ripped off by the teeth of the grundals. Lower down the cliff face flanking the Grand Canal I had fought the grundals and so saved Gahan Gannius and Valima. Saved them at the behest of the Star Lords, for I had been in mortal fear lest the Everoinye fling back to Earth a pawn who disobeyed. I had saved them for the day they could marry, mate and so bring forth the suppurating evil that today was called Genod Gannius, the man who ate up the Zairians, their lands, beliefs and spirit. Truly the Star Lords planned long and long into the future. I stood there thinking back on my handiwork and I realized afresh that each person with whose destiny I had meddled at the orders of the Star Lords must play a part in the greater destiny of Kregen.

Even my own part, which I had then thought worthy, of creating a slave phalanx of my old vosk-skulls and thrashing the hated Overlords of Magdag, had been turned against my Zairians by the machinations of Genod Gannius. Perhaps the Star Lords had seen what I would do. I could not believe that, for it had not been a thing of careful edges; rather it had grown and accreted of itself. No wonder the Star Lords had snatched me away in the moment of victory. A puzzle that had been with me for many years and seasons on Kregen had been solved.

Duhrra coughed, a hugely artificial cough, and said, "The suns decline, master. If we are to reach Akhram before nightfall..."

"Aye," I said, somewhat heavily. "I have been thinking what a garblish onker I am, when the Deldars are ranked."

He didn't bother to reply and I saw by the way he twitched his stump he did not agree. We went down the staircase cut into the wall of the Grand Canal and our sectrixes followed down the angled sloping paths cut for animals and swam the blue water; we climbed the other stupendous wall and came to Akhram.

The top of the Grand Canal was five miles across, flanked by cut steps a hundred yards broad, a mile or so deep, with something like forty steps of varying heights around a hundred and fifty feet average. The sheer colossal size of this man-made artifact impressed me all over again, as it had before. The perspective dwindled out of sight to the west. At that end of the Grand Canal lay the Dam of Days. For the simple satisfaction of actually seeing it I knew I would go there very soon. Duhrra and I approached the portal of the Akhram on this northern bank. Once again I saw that confusing collection of domes and steeples and minarets clustered within the stone walls. Once again the bronze-bound lenken door opened and the Todalpheme in their blue-tasseled cords and yellow hooded robes approached, bearing torches, making us welcome.

Their smooth skins showed the ministrations of oils and strigils, their faces fleshed with good living and yet ascetic with the mysteries of their profession. The Tides of Kregen are monitored by the Todalpheme. It is an art and a science. They had asked me to join them and I had refused. The old Akhram, the leader, was dead, and a new old Akhram lived in the chief place in his stead, as he had told me would happen.

There is little to say of that night Duhrra and I were made welcome, appointed a chamber, given food, were sent packing to bed. I lay awake for some time, pondering long on what had happened to me since I had last been here. It was incredible, but it had all happened.

The following morning after breakfast I walked with the Akhram, trying to recapture those old feelings of mine. He remembered my walking with his predecessor for, after all, it had been merely a quarter of his life span ago. I glanced up as a shadow fleeted below the suns.

I gaped.

A voller speeded up there, a fast two-place scout, quick and nimble. It vanished toward the west, flying fast and low.

The Akhram folded his hands within the sleeves of his robe, his face smooth and yet knowing. "A flying boat, yes, of late we have seen it a number of times."

"You are surprised?"

"Yes. We know of Vallia and Donengil here, of Wloclef and Loh and Djannik and a few other places. We have heard tales of boats that fly."

I rubbed my chin through the beard I had let grow. I did not like the look of this. "You have heard of Havilfar?"

He regarded me gravely. "Had you asked me that question but a sennight ago, I would have answered no. Today I must answer yes."

I felt the black bile, the anger, the remorse that I had stayed so long here in the inner sea. My place, I thought then, was at home countering the wiles of Hamal, the rich and evil Empire of the continent of Havilfar.

"We Todalpheme, as you know, take no part in the struggles between the green and the red. Our own people support us, and wear brown. They are raided—you will, I think, remember one such raid?"

"Yes."

The Todalpheme, because of their vital function, were taboo subjects over most of Kregen. No man would strike one down, lest the next tide should sweep him, his family and home away to watery destruction. I glanced up. Clouds massed before the suns. The temperature dropped markedly as we walked back along the battlements of the Akhram.

Akhram went on speaking: "We hear that this Genod Gannius has enlisted new allies in his struggles against the Zairians. He has brought new fighting men and weapons, and he has asked for a quantity of these wonderful flying boats."

I stared at him. Again the sense of vast unseen struggles enveloped me. The shadowy purposes of the Star Lords had, it seemed to me, been made a little more plain. They had used me to save Gahan Gannius and Valima and thus ensure the creation of their son Genod. What Genod was doing, therefore, must be desired by the Star Lords. I did not know why they should wish the green of Grodno to overcome the red of Zair, here in the Eye of the World.

The Akhram was still speaking, his face shadowed as the clouds grew over the bright face of the suns.

"We predict a great tide and the representatives of Genod Gannius have asked us to make sure a convoy of ships bearing the flying boats is allowed through the Dam of Days before we close the caissons." He glanced obliquely at the clouds. Already I, an old sailorman, had sensed the gale brewing. "If the storm breaks with the tide the ships will be safely inside the Grand Canal. We could not refuse Gannius, for he brought an army with his request, and they guard the Dam of Days now, to enforce their orders."

If I seem to you particularly stupid in that I did not at once seize on these facts and construct an impressive theory, I must plead only that I had taken a savage whirling in the blasts of fate and now I only wished to turn my back on the inner sea. Yes, I would feel a terrible grief when the red of Zair went down, when Zy was destroyed and Sanurkazz ravaged. But they were merely small places in a small locale hidden from the rest of Kregen. My place lay in Valka and Vallia, maturing our plans to withstand the insane ambitions of the Empress Thyllis of Hamal, or in Djanduin with my Djangs, or taking hard steps to combat the raids of the shanks from around the curve of the world. I also had to visit Strombor in the enclave city of Zenicce and assure myself that my house prospered. And I would then go on a visit to my clansmen of the Great Plains of Segesthes, my wonderful clansmen of Felschraung and Longuelm. So there was much I must do in this marvelous and terrible world of Kregen. The inner sea shrank in my estimation of the important things in my life.

But Havilfarese vollers, here, in the Eye of the World! Manned by the cramphs of Magdag and all the other rasts of Grodnims, swooping down to destroy the red of Zair. How the Krozairs and the Red Brethren would fight! It would be a wonderful ending to all, to join them and roar out the battle songs for Zair and so go down fighting into the Ice Floes of Sicce.

Sanity returned. That would not help Delia. She might sympathize with my emotions, but I could not destroy her out of sheer warrior's pride.

Already I had spent far too long dillydallying in the Eye of the World when I should be actively seeking out a galleon from Vallia, not meekly sitting here waiting for one to sail past. There would be galleons in Magdag. I must go there, find one and give orders to her skipper, in my capacity as Prince Majister of Vallia, order him to bear me home to Vallia without delay. Yes, by Vox!

But I thought Delia would allow me one look at this marvel, this Dam of Days. Just one look. Then Magdag, Vallia, Valka, home!

I said to Duhrra: "On the morrow I visit the Dam of Days. After that I go where I fancy you will not wish to go."

Duhrra replied comfortably, "I do not think there is such a place, master."

Twenty
The Dam of Days

"Why do you call yourself Dak, when our records show your name to be Dray Prescot?"

Akhram looked up at me with his wise gaze frank and open. We sat in his study with all the old familiar paraphernalia of ephemeris, globe, table and dividers spread around. Here I had talked for many burs one time with his predecessor, the old Akhram. I had been invited to join the Todalpheme and had rejected the offer, hungering for my Delia.

I said: "There have been many events in my life since last I passed this way. The name of Dray Prescot is well known on the inner sea… well…" Here I paused, thinking I boasted. To correct that impression, I said: "I am a hunted man from one side and, if the other side knew I still lived and was here, I would be the target for instant destruction. The name Dak is an honored one. I do not treat it lightly."

"We are aloof from the red and green. But we understand the passions that rule men within the Eye of the World. And, yes, I will arrange for you to visit the Dam of Days. And, yes, you may rest assured your name will remain Dak with us."

"You are most kind."

So Duhrra and I and a small escort of three of the younger Todalpheme rode out astride sectrixes for the western end of the Grand Canal. We carried supplies carefully wrapped in leaves. By walking the sectrixes and not galloping hard the journey would take about fifteen burs. I thought Delia would allow me fifteen burs there and fifteen back out of my burning urgency to return to her. Looking back, I think I sensed more in this journey than a mere excuse to my Delia. So we rode.

You who have followed my story this far will know that some other and altogether more evil and more Dray Prescot-like motive inspired me. Those ships carried Havilfarese vollers. I fancied they would be Hamalese rather than Hyrklanan or some other of the smaller states of Havilfar manufacturing fliers. So there might be a beautiful opportunity for me, the old reiver, the old render, the old paktun, to steal away a voller and fly directly back to Delia. That would be like the Dray Prescot I hoped I still was.

The water in the Grand Canal was low, barely half a mile deep. That was the usual depth the Todalpheme, through their agents the Oblifanters who ran the Dam of Days, attempted to maintain. When the tide smashed in against the outer coast I knew from the defenses of Zenicce and Vallia the level could go up in a Bay of Fundy maelstrom. These matters are a question of science, the suns and moons acting together producing spring tides, the neap tides falling about a lunar quarter later. With seven moons acting with and against one another and the two suns, for this purpose calculated as a single gravitational source, the possibilities were fascinating, susceptible to interesting calculation and extremely fraught. The Todalpheme earned their inviolability from the crude external pressures of Kregen.

I had much to occupy my mind as we jogged on. Duhrra had been measured up for his hook and the doctors had pursed their lips over his stump, commenting acidly on the butchery of whoever had amputated. Duhrra had thrown me a comical glance and I had told the story, which brought forth, as I had expected, a genuine desire to overcome the handicap of botched work. If they had deemed it necessary to amputate further they would have. Luckily for Duhrra—and me—they did not.

So, in the fullness of time, we came in sight of the Dam of Days.

How to describe it?

In rhapsodic terms, glowingly referring to the size, the splendor, the majesty? In scientific terms, the cubic volumes enclosed, the tons of water passing, the mechanisms of the caissons? In economic terms, for although electricity was not generated here—and I knew nothing of it then—the megawatts available would have lit up the inner sea.

In artistic terms, when the suns shone on the stone facings of the rock fill and glowed with all the flowerlike glory of an Alpine garden?

The Dam stretched across the mouth of the canal, which had widened into the bay. The bay enclosed a vast sheet of water. The Dam towered in size, rising to a stupendous height, and yet, when the eye's gaze traveled along the length, from headland to headland, the Dam appeared a long low wall against the sea. I think a Hollander would have appreciated that great work, or any man who has worked on a dam, anyone, actually, who had heart and imagination for the work of man's hands. The Dam had been built by the Sunset People in the long ago. Now I had learned—on Earth, on Earth!—that the Savanti of Aphrasöe were the last remnants of that once proud and world-girdling peoples. They had built well and to last. Yet their cities were tumbled into ruin in many places of Kregen; in the Kharoi Stones of my island of Hyr Khor in Djanduin were to be seen the fragmented particles of their glory.

Yet the Grand Canal and the Dam of Days glowed with the newness of building. The Sunset People had loved them.

"You see the waterfall, tumbling down into the sea by the northern headland, Tyr Dak?" The young Todalpheme pointed. He was a novice, learning his trade. In a hundred years, perhaps less if he was astute, he might become Akhram. I nodded. The waterfall fell into the sea and beyond it, inland, there was the glitter of a lake.

"When the tide rises the water fills the lake, so the river has merely to top it up. That is the reservoir from which comes the power of the Dam of Days."

We jogged on. Camped on a wide flat area rose the tents and huts of a sizable force. They were Grodnims. Duhrra hugged his detested green robes closer to him. I knew that we stood in some real danger of being accosted as slaves or runaway slaves, and was ready to be unpleasant in any event to any damned Overlord.

The three Todalpheme, although entirely unconcerned for they were secure in their immunity, angled away before we crossed the Dam. They were upset that naked force had been used here, where the pure light of science, as they said, should reign supreme. I could tell them about science, thinking back to my frustrating experiences on Earth during that twenty-one years of torment. I could also tell them about the uses of naked force.

Across the Dam the vistas were immense. On our right hand the greenly gray sea heaved away to a wild horizon. The gale was surely coming. On our left hand the waters, although separated only by the bulk of the Dam, yet showed the bluer color of the inner sea. We crossed halfway and stood for a while, lolling on the high parapet, looking around, marveling, silent. At intervals the Dam of Days was pieced by openings. They were arranged to resist the push of water from east and west and not from one side only

154

like a lock-gate. They were fashioned in the form of gigantic cylinders rising and falling in open masonry guides. A modern analogy I can now give is to liken them to pistons. When water from the lake was introduced from valved pipes they sank and so effectively blocked the openings.

The lifting of these caissons, although essentially simple, demanded a level of technology beyond that of the current manipulators. That only one caisson rope of steel wire had ever broken is a tribute to the building of the Sunset People. Next to each caisson in the Dam was sited an enormous reservoir tank. This was free to move up and down in guides. Many steel cables passed over central pulleys from caisson to tank. When the tank was filled with water from a separate valved and piped supply from the lake, it would descend. Because the tank size was greater than the amount of caisson under the sea level, the tank would haul the caisson up as it sank. Vents in the caisson valved open to let the water run out. Because the caisson, when high and empty, was itself larger than the amount of water left in the tank after that level equaled the sea level, the caissons would fill and sink, thus hauling up the tanks. All very neat and economical, the power being supplied by gravity through the falling water.

Finally, I should say that the Oblifanters kept hordes of workpeople busy greasing everything to ensure that it ran sweetly. To allow the caissons to move up and down their guides against the enormous differential of water pressure, a whole series of wheels were fitted on each side, to resist pressure front and back.

This made me think. The Todalpheme gave their orders to lower or lift the caissons to regulate the level of water flowing into the inner sea. Usually the high tides would cause them to close the gates. Why should the Sunset People bother to arrange wheels to resist pressure from the back of the dam? I suspected that in those long-gone days the dam was employed for more than merely regulating the tides.

One of the young Todalpheme novices shaded his eyes, looking out to sea. "I believe..." he said, pointing. I looked.

This young Todalpheme was used to poring over papers indoors. My old sailor's eye picked out the familiar shapes. Argenters, their sails board-stiff, riding the brushing skirts of the gale, rushed headlong through the tumbling whitecaps. I studied them, the wind in my face, wondering how many of them would smash to pieces before they negotiated the gates of the dam.

I saw the flags fluttering.

Four green diagonals and four blue diagonals slanting from right to left, the blue and green divided by thin borders of white.

Menaham.

That made perfect sense.

When mad Queen Thyllis, as she was then, had invaded the island of

Pandahem she had overrun country after country until her victorious armies and air service had been stopped in the Battle of Jholaix. Of all the nations of Pandahem she had made allies of the Menahem. I had remorseful memories of my treatment of young Pando, the Kov of Bormark, and his mother, Tilda the Fair. They lived side by side with the people of Menaham, and they called them the Bloody Menahem. Even when Thyllis of Hamal had been forced back, made to conclude a peace with Vallia and those nations of Pandahem she had overrun, still she continued the alliance with the Bloody Menahem. Hamal possessed few ships. Pandahem was an island center of commerce, as was Vallia. So what was more natural than that Hamal should use ships from Menaham?

If you ask why bother to use large, slow argenters to transport vollers when they might fly, you forget the ways of Hamal, the cunning of those cramphs of Hamal and their treacherous vollers. I knew well enough that the fliers in those ships would work well for a while and then break down. Oh, yes, I knew that! Would the Hamalians risk a flight from Hamal to the inner sea in suspect vollers?

And, of course, Genod Gannius, like us in Vallia, would be so anxious to lay his hands on fliers he would accept the probable defects as part of the price he must pay. This was what Vallia had done, what Zenicce and all the others who bought vollers from Hamal had done. Otherwise, no fliers.

So I stood no longer lolling on the high parapet-walk watching those ships standing in. They were handled smartly enough and they negotiated the wide openings superbly. They rode the waves like great preening swans. All their flags fluttering, the sails cracking and billowing as the hands braced the yards around, the ships aimed for the gaps, the white water spuming away from their forefeet. They breasted the waves and sailed through the Dam of Days into the bay leading to the Grand Canal.

I walked across to the other side of the dam and watched them, their motion much easier in the enclosed water. They made straight for the canal. They would probably lie up in the harbor halfway through, or in the harbor at the eastern end, depending on circumstances. Then the vollers would be brought up from those capacious holds. The air service men from Hamal would give them a final check and hand them over. No doubt Genod Gannius had made arrangements for his men to be trained in their use. And then...

I had an apocalyptic vision of hordes of Grodnims descending from the skies, first to smash all resistance in Shazmoz, then other cities along the red southern shore, then on and on, razing Zy, on and on, finally taking Holy Sanurkazz.

Well, the vision was apocalyptic, but it was no further business of mine.

And Mayfwy and Felteraz?

I bashed my fist against the stone of that high walk. I cursed. Why must I remember Mayfwy and Felteraz now?

Of what value were they, set against my Delia?

But they were not set against her.

One value could not destroy another if there was no conflict of interest. Wouldn't my Delia tell me—demand of me—that as a simple man, let alone a one-time proud, high and mighty Krozair of Zy, a man who professed Opaz—when it suited him, to be sure—my obligation was to protect Mayfwy, who was our friend?

But I wanted none of the inner sea. I wanted to go home. Sight of those argenters of Menaham had kindled the spark of deviltry. I would sneak down there by the light of the moons, steal a voller and so fly back to Valka. I might set one argenter alight; that would be reasonable, though I did not think I would care to attempt to destroy them all. Genod Gannius struck me as the kind of general who would take care of such possibilities in his planning.

A brisker gust of wind blew against the back of my head. I turned. The sea was getting up and the whitecaps were now rolling in thickly, with here and there a spume lifting and billowing away downwind. The air was noticeably colder.

Men in the brown of the workers were crowding past, down on the main road across the dam. I saw an Oblifanter directing them, a tough commanding figure in brown with a good deal of gold lace and gold buttons, with the balass stick in his fist.

"We must return, Tyr Dak," said the novice. He shivered. "The tide is making. They will close the gates now that the ships have passed. We must go back."

"And about time, too," said Duhrra. He had no idea what those ships carried, that they spelled doom to him and his kind. "We have seen this marvel, Dak my master. Now, for the sweet sake of Mother Zinzu the Blessed, I would like to see about my hook."

Slowly I climbed down off the high parapet and trailed on after the others. The novice called me Tyr Dak—sir. And Duhrra called on Sweet Mother Zinzu the Blessed, the patron saint of the drinking classes of Sanurkazz. Wouldn't my two favorite rogues, my two rascals, my two oar comrades, Nath and Zolta, also be caught up in the catastrophe if these vollers fell into the hands of Genod Gannius, the Grodnim?

The coils of unkind fate lapped around me then. Uppermost in my mind, the tantalizing thought of Delia drove out all other thoughts—almost. Nath and Zolta, Duhrra... and Mayfwy. It was not fair. But then nothing in this life, either on Earth or on Kregen, is fair. Only a garblish onker would imagine otherwise.

When we had escaped from King Wazur's test, there on the island of

Ogra-gemush, Delia had had to instruct me. I had been all for leaving the Wizard of Loh, Khe-Hi-Bjanching, and Merle, Jefan Werden's daughter, in the pit. Delia had made me, all wounded and half dead as I was, climb down there and drag them out—twice. If Delia were here at my side now, wouldn't she demand the same chivalry, the same conduct, damned stupid though it might appear to one unversed in the mysteries of the Sisters of the Rose and the Krozairs of Zy?

That I was no longer a Krozair of Zy had nothing to do with it.

Cursing, in the foulest of foul moods, I stamped along after the others.

The tide was making rapidly.

The Oblifanter, a bluff, weather-beaten man twirling his balass stick, was most polite to the Todalpheme, novices though they were. To Duhrra and me he extended a distant politeness that reflected his opinion of Grodnims who sought to take his functions into their hands. We walked on. The wind blustered past above the parapet. Flags were snapping and then standing out stiff as boards. The sea must be covered in white now. Inland the bay remained calm. The argenters were sailing into the cut, the wind on their quarter, under reduced canvas.

A giant creaking, groaning filled the air, like the ice blocks of the Floes of Sicce grinding against each other.

The Oblifanter cursed and ran to one of the tall chain-towers. He was yelling, "Put some grease on the ropes, you nurdling onkers!"

I wondered, if he kept up that tone to a Hikdar of the Grodnims, how long it would take for him to lose his teeth and have his nose broken. The Grodnims are a barbarous lot.

When we reached the spot the noise had sensibly reduced. We could look over and see the brown-clad workers perched on a spider-walk tipping buckets of grease onto the thick steel cables as they passed over the pulley train. Close by, the monstrous bulk of a caisson lowered slowly into the sea, while on the other side the equally monstrous bulk of a counterbalancing tank lifted up in its guides. The whole spectacle would have delighted the very hearts and souls of all Victorian engineers, who doted on gigantism within the context of wrought and cast iron. I walked on.

It was no business of mine.

The image of Delia floated before me. Now that image looked scornful. Her glorious face filled me with the kind of feelings a rope's end might have after a manhound puppy has finished with it.

A rope's end does not have feelings, although it can impart them smartly enough in the fist of a boatswain's mate, and it would be in shreds after a manhound had finished with it, puppy or not. In much the same kind of shreds as my emotions...

The valves controlling the pipes to the caissons lay grouped together under a stone shelter, built as an integral part of the dam. I stopped there, watching the brown-clad workers turning the handles. The Todalpheme ahead swung around and motioned me to follow. The Oblifanter whisked his balass stick over the rump of a worker who was clearly not putting his heart into the work.

I said, "Oblifanter, you would oblige me by opening the valves to the tanks and closing the valves to the caissons."

He gaped at me.

I said, "Be quick about it, dom, for my temper is short."

He started waving his arms about. His face assumed that red sometimes seen in a malsidge trodden on in a dopa den.

"You cannot do that! The gates will open—the tide will flood through!"

"Nevertheless, that is what you must do."

"But the tide! The *tide!*"

"You will let enough through to do as I desire. When that has been accomplished you may lower the caissons again, so it will not be enough to sweep on through the Eye of the World. It will expend itself before it reaches Shazmoz." I thought about that, of the Grodnim ships hovering like sea-leems off Shazmoz, preventing communication. "We had best leave the caissons up until the tide reaches Shazmoz. Yes." I felt remarkably cheerful. I did not smile, but I felt amazingly active and energetic. "Yes, that will serve admirably."

"You are mad!"

"Do not doubt it."

"Here!" yelled the Oblifanter, his eyes fairly popping from his head. He shouted to a group of Grodnims sauntering off with the workpeople not laboring at the valves. "Here! You! Earn your keep, for what good you do here! Stop this madman—"

He said no more for I put him to sleep gently and lowered him to the stone-flagged roadway. I stared at the group of workpeople at the valves. Their faces looked back blankly, like calsanys'.

"Shut the caisson valves and open the tanks. *Jump!*"

They saw my face and they shivered and began to do as I said.

The Grodnims walked back, puzzled by the shouting, and saw what the workmen were doing. The Todalpheme stood to one side, quite unable to grasp what was going on. Duhrra looked at me hard and then sauntered across.

The day was darkening over, the clouds massing. The wind blew keenly. The gale would strike very soon now. And all the time the tide rose, one of those enormous Tides of Kregen that could wash away all before it like a tsunami, leveling and destroying, save where the hand of man placed obstacles in its path to protect his property and life.

"What's going on here?"

It so happened that there was a Jiktar among the Grodnims. A Jiktar has come a long way in the chain of command, for he commands a regiment, a swifter or a galleon; when he has worked his way through to zan-Jiktar, he may reach the highest military rank of all, that of Chuktar, above whom there exist only generals of the highest rank, princes, kings and emperors.

"Stand aside, rast!" He spoke quite matter-of-factly. He shouted at the frightened workpeople. "Shut the tank valves at once."

I said, "Open the tank valves."

The Jiktar did not hesitate. That was one reason why he was a Jiktar.

"Seize him!" he said, again quite normally. "If you have to slay him, you have to. But I would like to put the madman to the question."

He'd really like that, enjoying himself.

The Grodnims came for me with their longswords swinging. I was not overly fussy about how many got themselves killed.

There remained one item to be finalized, no, two, for I saw Duhrra start fumbling about under his blanket-cloak.

"Stand away, Duhrra!" I yelled. "Don't get yourself killed."

He did not reply.

What I must do was position myself in front of the workers so as to cow them and assure them of unpleasantness if they did not continue to fill the tanks, and I must prevent the Grodnims from getting past me at them. The fight looked promising. The immediate future appeared somewhat scarlet, lurid and highly diverting.

The impressions of the moment burn bright still: the wind beginning to build up into a howling torrent rushing across the high loft of the Dam of Days; the frightened workers in their brown smocks frantically turning the valve wheels as I glared at them; the clatter of the soldiers' studded war-boots as they ran on the stone flags of the walkway; the glitter of their mail and the bright sheen of their green as they advanced, ample excuse for swordplay; the sight of Duhrra hopping about beyond them, his face a maelstrom of emotions that in another place and another time would have proved comical in the extreme; the feel of the longsword hilt in my fist. This was a cheap weapon, not a Krozair longsword, with a cross-guard and grip of iron, the grip covered in sturm-wood, the blade true enough but the whole brand lacking the superb balance of the genuine article. The grip spanned only two hands' breadths so there was no chance of spreading fists in that cunning Krozair fashion. This sword was designed for the bludgeoning, hacking of men-at-arms in the melee. Well, it would serve.

The Grodnims at first thought simply to overawe me, so they rushed up swinging their swords, yelling, ferocious. It seemed unchivalrous, unsporting, not Jikai, to slay the first of them, so I parried his blow and cracked him across his mail coif. He went down like a log. The second pair came in together, abruptly shocked, ready now, in the swift way of the men of green, to slay me and have done.

Their blows hissed past and I cut once, backhanded once and leaped clear of a third who sought to drive his point beneath my breastbone.

My sword took off the side of his face. I whirled blood-drops at the workers who had stopped turning.

"Turn, doms, turn! Fill the tanks!"

The blood spattered brightly across them and yet, in the instant I swung back and engaged the next pair, that bright red darkened and dulled as clouds drove beneath the suns.

More men ran up, shouting, as the Jiktar, fairly foaming with not so much rage as the outrage he felt, bellowed them on. I cut down the two before me, finding the clumsy sweep of the longsword some impediment. I had used a longsword like this many times. Perhaps employing the magnificent Krozair longsword weakened a fighting man when he was forced to use lesser weapons. So I leaped and ducked and fought, hacking and thrusting when the opportunity offered, for these men wore mail. I had noticed on this second period in the Eye of the World that the Grodnims affected a second sword scabbarded at their waists, a shortsword. Perhaps this was the handiwork of Genod Gannius. If it was, he would have turned purple with rage that his men stubbornly stuck to their familiar longswords now. I was unarmored. A shortsword man might have been able to drive in under my longsword and finish me. The shortsword has, as I have said, advantages in some combats.

A Grodnim Deldar, raving to get at me through the press of his own men, abruptly stiffened, rearing upright, his eyes popping. I saw a sword smash down on that juncture between neck and shoulder where the mail spreads, battering its way through. The Deldar fell. Duhrra, the sword in his left hand whirring up for another blow, appeared bright-eyed, furious of face, yelling.

"Hai Jikai!" bellowed Duhrra, laying about him. "Hai Jikai!"

The wind blustered past above us. Mailed men screamed and fell as our longswords bit. Duhrra took a glancing slice on his right arm—only a slicing glance. In combat of this kind there are seldom wounded men, not for very long anyway. A blow from a longsword, which is really a sharpened length of tempered iron, will do a man's business for him with certitude. The longsword possesses awful smashing power. I took a man's arm off and whirled to deface his comrade, leaped and ducked and so roared in to get at the Jiktar.

He saw me coming and jerked his sword up. Two more men went down before we could meet. Duhrra took out another and then the stone-flagged walkway contained only the brown-clad workpeople, the three Todalpheme, the Grodnim Jiktar—and a quantity of dead Grodnims scattered about.

The Jiktar said, "You are assuredly mad and will die for this."

I would not have replied anyway, but as I closed I saw a wide-winged shadow on the stones. The sun had shafted through for an instant, the green sun, for the red remained swathed in cloud. If this was an omen I would have none of it. In that ephemeral shaft of green sunlight the shadow of a hunting bird lay at my feet. Before I looked up I leaped out of reach of the Jiktar's sword.

Yes. Yes, up there, the damned scarlet and gold raptor, the spying Gdoinye of the Star Lords!

The sight enraged me more than the fight had been able to do.

And then... and then!

A blue radiance began to seep in, to encompass me. The vague outlines of that giant Scorpion appeared before my eyes. I tried to scream out violently and managed a whisper, feeling myself falling. The blue radiance hovered. Someone—a long time ago and a long way away—had said that by willpower I might avert the call of the Everoinye. I tried. I struggled. I do not think that I could have succeeded alone.

The harsh bite of the stone flags against my knees told me I still remained on the high Dam of Days. There was still a fight to be fought and won, a Jikai to create. The blue radiance changed, swirling, coiling. I sensed an unease. A tinge of yellow crept into the blue. I did not ever remember seeing yellow when I was transmitted to and from Kregen.

"I will stay here, Star Lords!" I roared. I struggled to rise. I could hear a strange tinkering sound, as of water hitting a tin cup. "Leave me be, you kleeshes! I stay here!"

The blue wavered; the yellow prospered.

The enormous form of the phantom blue Scorpion assumed vast, grotesque proportions—and then it burst. A blaze of pure yellow exploded about me, with the sound as of cymbals clanging in the High Pantheon of Opaz in Vallia.

I knelt on the stone flags of the walkway across the Dam of Days. I looked up. The Jiktar was in the act of ferociously smiting at Duhrra, whose left arm lifted his sword at the last moment. Duhrra's sword showed a succession of savage dints along both blade edges. He was finding extreme difficulty in settling to a rhythm and swinging. That he had fought as well as he had with his left hand testified to his extraordinary physical strength and to the resolution of his will.

With a beast's roar, a roar as of the leems being let out into the Jikhorkdun, I gathered my feet under me and sprang.

The Jiktar's head flew high as his torso toppled.

"You are unharmed, Duhrra?"

"Aye." He panted now and lowered the sword. "I thought you done for, although I could not see..."

"No." I looked at this hulking man-mountain with the idiot face and bulging muscles and the useless stumped right arm. Very gravely I lifted my bloodied sword in the salute.

"Hai Jikai, Duhrra. Henceforth, I think, I shall call you Duhrra of the Days. Hai Jikai!"

He gaped at me, amazed. The reference to the Dam of Days was clear enough.

"If you…" He started over. "It is for you…"

I swung the sword at the pipe valve wheels. The workers, freed by the fight from oppression, had all run off. They had closed the valves down. I could not blame them. I walked across.

The moment I began opening the valves again to let water flow from the lake reservoir into the tanks and so lift the caissons and open the gates, the three Todalpheme hurried across. They had been shaken by the savagery of fighting men; but this business now, they conceived, concerned them.

I disabused them.

As gently as possible, I said, "If you seek to stop me I shall knock you all down."

They appeared to understand.

The flat rather than the edge sometimes works as well.

One said, "The tide is rising fast and the storm comes on apace. If you open but one gate the water will—"

I finished with the valves, for I had spun the wheels with savagery, and said, "The water will serve Zair. After that, you may close the tank valves and open the caissons'."

They knew I would stand by the wheels with a naked sword in my fist until I was ready. The blood had ceased to drop from the blade now, but the length was shining red and evil in the light.

Tremendous power was to be unleashed in the next few murs. Water from the lake reservoir ran through the multi-branching pipes and past the valves I had opened, filling the counterweighing tanks. The wind tore at us, streaming our hair, screaming past our ears. The roar of the waters mounted. The tanks began to sink. The weight of water pulled them down and the steel wire ropes groaned under the strain. Duhrra put his sword down and ran to slop grease onto the series of pulleys, using the flat wooden spatula with his left hand, the grease-bucket caught up under his right arm stump.

"Pour it on, Duhrra!" I bellowed in my foretop hailing voice. He barely heard. He upended the bucket over the pulleys.

The caissons began to rise. I knew that if they did not rise sufficiently for my purpose before the full weight of the tide bore against them they would not budge thereafter. On the coast of Scotland the measurement of breakers has revealed a stunning effort of six thousand pounds per square foot. So I stood while we opened a door to hell.

Clouds blew furiously overhead, drowning the faces of the suns. Up there the moons were lining out in that deadly conjunction which would certainly spell destruction and might mean death for many a seaport city around Kregen where the seaward defenses had been neglected. Even the three smaller moons, which hurtle frantically low over the face of the planet, were in conjunction. The first and largest moon, the Maiden with the Many Smiles, the two second moons, the Twins, and the third Moon, She of the Veils, all were exerting their gravitational pull together with the Suns.

When no moons are in the sky of Kregen—when they cannot be seen, that is—it is called a night of Notor Zan. When all the moons blaze at the full, when even the three smallest join with the major four, that is called the Scarf of Our Lady Monafeyom. We could see nothing overhead but the dark swirling clouds lowering down, but we knew what was going on out there as we knew how the waters of the ocean were responding to the titanic forces.

The Dam shuddered.

All that monstrous construction thrilled to the shock, alive with the vibration.

The wind tore the reason from our skulls.

The tide burst through.

The gale broomed its own violence and added to the pell-mell tumult. I hung onto the guardrail, my hair blown forward over my face, staring at the mouth of the Grand Canal.

The opening was small at this distance and the argenters appeared like dots in the gloom, but I have imagination and the whole scene was described vividly to me later by one who was there and saw it all at close hand.

Across the bay leaped the tidal bore.

A wall of water, tipped with the vicious fangs of breakers, towering, cresting, blowing, omnipotent in its might. How tall was the eagre?

The famous Severn bore rushes up at the equinoxes to heights of five to six feet. Good friends have told me that in New Brunswick they have seen the daily tidal bore roaring up the river from the Bay of Fundy in a mightily impressive sight: a genuine wall of water simply rolling up the river with the floodwater following directly behind. The rise and fall of the tide in the Bay of Fundy is known to every schoolboy. At the head of the bay the tidal height reaches a fantastic sixty-two feet and even halfway up, at Passamaquoddy Bay, it is twenty-five feet. The force and power of millions of tons of water rolling along with the fang-toothed eagre at their head are enough to convince the most skeptical of mortals that in sober truth nature is the lord and master of the worlds we inhabit.

All this power and smashing violence, the colossal movement of water—with only one sun and one moon! How high?

I stood there as the Dam thrilled to the vibrations of untold millions of tons of water smashing at its ancient structure, as the water spumed through the opening I had made, shuddering under the shrill of the wind. How high?

I saw the small shape of an argenter lifted up and up and up. It broke apart. It flew apart as a barrel flies apart when its hoops are broken through. Planks, timbers, bundles—dark, pitiful objects—whirling and smoking through the frenzied turmoil of the waves, with the spume covering all with a white confetti of death.

Horrible, terrible, malignant. I would prefer to pass lightly over that destruction of a fleet, for I am an old sailor who has a love for ships.

But the ships were broken and riven. Crushed against the hard stone of the terraced Grand Canal, tossed up like chips to fall, cracking open and spilling shrieking bloody things that had been men, the ships died. The wind lashed the sea and drove relentlessly on. The bore sliced through the Grand Canal and the waters boiled and roared and fought as they cascaded on.

On and on through the cut smoked the waters.

The tide had struck and destroyed, shouting in its strength.

How high? High enough for death.

High enough to claw up past terrace after terrace of the Grand Canal, filling the cut with the violence of unleashed waters, rolling remorselessly on and on over the wrecked remnants that had once been a fleet proud with flags.

So, I thought, ended Genod Gannius plans to use vollers from Hamal against Zairians.

The sight of those broad comfortable ships, those splendid argenters, being smashed to driftwood did not please me, even when I knew what they were and what errand they had been on.

I, an old first lieutenant of a seventy-four, am sentimental in these matters.

Against the shriek of the wind Duhrra's voice reached me thinned. "It is time we moved on, Dak my master. I see the green moving in the shadows beyond the Dam."

The darkness pressed down as the stormclouds boiled. The Todalpheme were anxious to lower the caissons once I gave them leave. I stepped past the body of the Jiktar. He had been a Ghittawrer, a Grodnim member of a green brotherhood that attempted to ape the ways and disciplines of the Krozairs. His sword would be of fine quality. Duhrra and I would leave the novices; we must find our own way out of this situation. I turned back.

"One boon I ask," I said to the novice. "The tide will reach Shazmoz but will scarce do further damage. Do not tell the Grodnims the names you have heard us use."

165

"Then what names shall we tell them? They are hard men and will be exceedingly angry."

"Say you heard us call each other Krozairs."

The Todalpheme's face betrayed his speculation through the continuing shock. "That will make them even more wroth."

Then I laughed. "I shall be sorry to miss that pleasant sight."

So, laughing, Duhrra and I ran rapidly from the Dam of Days.

Once we had slipped into the storm-shadows at the far end we were able to circle and mingle with the Grodnims, securing ourselves from all possible suspicion. We were merely two paktuns, serving Grodno the Green.

I had stooped to take the longsword from the Jiktar. It was a fine weapon. Its pattern was startlingly similar to a true Krozair longsword, but it was not. Its edge was dented in only two places, where Duhrra's common blade looked almost like a saw. He too possessed himself a fine new blade. All the common longswords bore on the flat of the blade below the guard the etched monogram G.G.M. I remembered that. The Jiktar's sword bore a device I knew, a lairgodont surmounted by the rayed sun. The lairgodont, a most ferocious carnivorous risslaca, is known over much of Kregen but is most numerous in northern Turismond. So I kept the hilt of the longsword, with its device and decoration of emeralds, hidden under a flap of green cloth, for that symbol denotes a green brotherhood devoted to Grodno.

We took our chances, Duhrra and I, and we passed through the encamped army of Genod Gannius, commanded by his Chuktar of the west, and so came at length free of them and to the east of the Grand Canal, on the northern shore.

"I am for Magdag, Duhrra. There I shall find a galleon, a great ship of the outer oceans. I shall bid you remberee."

"We shall see," he replied. He was altogether too complacent. He had said that idiot "duh" barely half a dozen times since I had dubbed him Duhrra of the Days.

Truth to tell, after the visitation on the Dam I had been hourly expecting the return of the damned Gdoinye and the apparition of the blue Scorpion. I felt sure I had not beaten the Star Lords and I expected them to whisk me away. If they chose to hurl me headlong into fresh adventure on Kregen, well, that had been the pattern of my life and I would do what I could to fight through and reach Valka and Delia. If they chose to toss me contemptuously back to Earth I felt I might truly go mad. I did not think I could face another spell of twenty years on the planet of my birth.

We had stolen three sectrixes and had enough plunder loaded on the third to last us. We rode gently, for we had a way to go. The gale had passed, scouring the sky. With a new day the Suns of Scorpio flamed above, casting down their mingled streaming light. We rode in an opaline radiance.

The sea glittered to our right and the deserted countryside about us testified to the savagery of man in the inner sea. Also, I realized, it indicated that the sea could turn savage and cruel if the Dam of Days did not regulate the Tides of Kregen. Ahead of us a little knoll posed the usual problem. I said, "We are two greens, Duhrra of the Days, lest you forget. We may ride up boldly."

"Aye, Dak, my master. But if they be not too many…"

I glanced at the stump. In his saddle bag he carried the leather attachments to buckle on, the hooks and implements given him by the doctors of the Todalpheme. We had paid for them with golden oars taken from a Grodnim who lay in the bushes with a slit throat.

"You must wait to test your new hook, Duhrra of the Days."

"May Uncle Zobab quickly smile upon my stump then, for I long dearly to… uh… prove…"

The sectrixes stopped in mid-stride. Duhrra sat erect in the saddle with his big moon-face arrested with down-dropping jaw. I looked at the knoll.

A scarlet and golden figure sat a zhyan there.

The enormous pure white bird with the scarlet beak and claws took to the air and with a few lazy beats of its four wings settled at my side. I gazed at the woman seated on the zhyan's back.

She smiled gently at me.

"Lahal, Pur Dray."

"I am no longer Pur Dray, Madam Ivanovna."

"And on Kregen I am not Madam Ivanovna. You may address me as Zena Iztar."

Her robes sparkled in the light of the suns. All scarlet and rose, crimson and ruby, with golden tissue vestments and sumptuous gems and trappings, she presented a dazzling sight to an old sailor who was no longer a Krozair of Zy. She wore armor, golden plates cunningly fashioned, fitted to her, making me see the full voluptuous figure, the strength, the lissomness, the lithe power in a seductive frame. I did not return the smile.

"Why do you seek me out, Zena Iztar?"

"Didn't the yellow overthrow the Scorpion's blue?"

"Aye."

"Do you not then owe me gratitude?"

"I waited three damned long years after you visited me in London."

"Aye."

We stared at each other.

Then, touching her red lips with a painted and gilded fingernail: "You are no longer a Krozair of Zy."

"No. It is of no consequence now."

"I think you lie."

I did not think I lied. "No, I do not lie. If those Zair-forsaken cramphs of

Star Lords do not catch up with me I intend to sail to Valka. There is where my labors are required."

The marvel, the magic, the sheer wonder of this visitation, this apparition, had no power to move me now. I was sullen. I knew what I wanted to do at last—about time too—and I suspected most evilly that I was to be prevented.

I repeated, speaking so that she gazed down haughtily at me, although she did not flinch by more than a slight shifting of her head: "I am for Valka."

"And what of the Eye of the World? What of your friends here? What of Zair?"

"I am Apushniad!"

"Yet we both know that Dray Prescot is a man who could alter that, if he willed."

"He does not so will."

"I feared this. I had hoped—"

"Look, Zena Iztar. I want to go home! I want to see Delia again. Is that so strange? I have been tossed around, made slave, pranced about with these disgusting greens of Grodno—now I want to go back to Delia again."

"She is safe and well in Esser Rarioch."

"Aye! And that is where I want to be also."

"Why did you open the Dam of Days and destroy the vollers from Hamal? Was that a rational act of a man who does not care?"

"I am not a rational man! I thought to strike a blow for Sanurkazz and Zy and Felteraz. That is all."

"It is not all. I must leave you now. But I will tell you this: in your stiff-necked pride and in your selfishness you will fail. You will not be allowed to return to Valka."

"By the Star Lords?"

"No."

Before I could roar out a fresh question, for I was exceedingly angry, as I felt I had every right to be, the zhyan clashed its four wide wings, raising a whirlwind of dust, and rose into the air. I watched it fly up. The scarlet and gold figure leaned out and down, looking at me until vision was lost. Even then, I suspected, this hulu of a Madam Ivanovna, this fancy Zena Iztar, could still see me, a hulking great fighting man, hot with the lust to bash something around because he could not go home to his wife and children.

"…uh… to prove I can take a swordsman with my right hand."

"Do what?" I said.

"Master! What is it?"

I forced myself to sit in the uncomfortable saddle, take up the reins and try to make the stupid sectrix behave.

"Nothing, Duhrra of the Days. A vision. It is passed. I still ride to

Magdag and I will still find a galleon. There is much to be done in the outer oceans. I will shake the dust of Grodno and Zair from my feet and say good riddance."

Much had been explained to me, if not in words, but a very great deal remained; there were yet mysteries to be solved. I'd think about them when I reached Valka and once more held Delia in my arms, my Delia of the Blue Mountains, my Delia of Delphond.

"Uh... I shall never say good riddance to Zair. But I think I will go with you across the wild and wonderful outer oceans."

I recollected myself. What the hell did I think Duhrra was going to do if I left him stranded in Magdag, the fortress city of the megaliths, the home of the Overlords of Magdag, the archenemies of all Zairians? I glared at him.

"Very well, the Duhrra of the Days. You come with me." I could not smile, but I said, "And right gladly will you be welcome."

"Uh," said Duhrra. "I think perhaps tomorrow I will try my new hook."

Renegade of Kregen

A note on Dray Prescot

Dray Prescot is a man above medium height with brown hair and brown eyes that are level and dominating. His shoulders are immensely wide and he carries himself with an abrasive honesty and a fearless courage. He moves like a great hunting cat, quiet and deadly. Born in 1775 and educated in the inhumanly harsh conditions of the late eighteenth century English Navy, he presents a picture of himself that, the more we learn of him, grows no less enigmatic.

Through the machinations of the Savanti nal Aphrasöe—mortal but superhuman men dedicated to the aid of humanity—and of the Star Lords, the Everoinye, he has been taken to Kregen many times. On that savage and exotic world he rose to become Zorcander of the Clansmen of Segesthes, and Lord of Strombor in Zenicce, and a member of the mystic and martial Order of Krozairs of Zy.

Against all odds Prescot won his highest desire and in that immortal battle at The Dragon's Bones claimed his Delia, Delia of Delphond, Delia of the Blue Mountains. And Delia claimed him in the face of her father the dread emperor of Vallia. Amid the rolling thunder of the acclamations of Hai Jikai! Prescot became Prince Majister of Vallia and wed his Delia, the Princess Majestrix. They are blessed with two pairs of twins, Drak and Lela, and Segnik and Velia. One of their favourite homes is Esser Rarioch in Valkanium, capital of the island of Valka, a part of Vallia, an island of which Prescot is Strom.

In the continent of Havilfar Prescot fought as a hyr-kaidur in the arena of the Jikhorkdun of Huringa. He became king of Djanduin idolised by his ferocious four-armed warrior Djangs. In the Battle of Jholaix the ambitions of the Empress Thyllis of Hamal were thwarted leading to an uneasy peace between the empires of Hamal and Vallia.

Then Prescot was banished to Earth for twenty one miserable years. His joyful return to Kregen was marred by his ejection from the Order of Krozairs of Zy. Now he is determined to forget the Krozairs of the inner sea and return home to Valka and Delia and the children...

Alan Burt Akers

One
We ride into Magdag

We rode, Duhrra of the Days and I, into Magdag. Magdag, the city of the megaliths, the chief city of the Grodnims, those devoted followers of Grodno the Green, stank in our nostrils, us followers of the true path of Zair.

"This place is a cesspit of vileness." Duhrra spat, juicily, into the dust of the roadway. "It should be smashed like my hand and cauterized like my stump."

"Amen to that, Duhrra. You know I am taking ship here for Vallia. You are gladly welcome to join me. If you wish to smash and cauterize Magdag, kindly give me time to go aboard and weigh."

He gazed at me, his big moonface sweating, his foolish-seeming mouth gaping.

"Duh—you're a hard man, Dak."

"Aye—and I should be harder. Now shut your black-fanged wine-spout. Here is a pack of Magdag devils in person."

We slumped in our saddles and half closed our eyes and let our heads droop on our breasts as we rode past a body of Magdaggian sectrixmen riding toward the west. I did not even bother to fleer them a searching glance as we lumbered by. Ahead lay the fortress city of Magdag, a place of great power and great evil, and I wished only to take myself as speedily as possible aboard a galleon from Vallia and tell her captain to sail me home as fast as his vessel could sail, home to Vallia and Valka.

Home—back to Esser Rarioch, my high fortress overlooking the bay and Valkanium, home to Delia and the twins!

The dusty road led straight to the western gate, an imposing structure of many levels, battlemented, loopholed, a tough nut to crack in any siege. The road itself thronged with people coming and going, for as a large and prosperous city Magdag demanded the unremitting toil of many hands to keep its belly fed. Here, on the green northern shore of the inner sea, those working hands would be slave.

Shadows of the gate dropped about us. The smells began in earnest. I intended to talk to no one. Straight to the harbor—the nearest of the numerous harbors of Magdag—and there seek information on the first ship of Vallia; yes, that was the plan. If I had to wait a sennight or so I felt I could just support the extra torment, for I had suffered much of late. The twin Suns of Scorpio streamed their mingled light upon the walls and battlements of the city, giving the evil place a spurious grandeur and glory.

All the light and color of two worlds cannot in the end disguise true evil. So I thought then and, by Zair, so I think now.

The stupid sectrixes with their six legs and their blunt stubborn heads sensed the ending of their day's labors and a comfortable stall and food, and they speeded up their lumbering trot. Maybe they were not so stupid after all. Jogging awkwardly up and down we passed the lofty pointed arch of the gateway beneath the hard, incurious stares of Magdaggian soldiery, hired mercenaries mostly, with a few Homo sapiens among them, and turned sharp right-handed for the harbor area.

The eternal sounds of a great city rose about us, mingling with the stinks. The shadows clustered.

"And remember, Duhrra. You wear the green. Think like a Grodnim. Look like a Grodnim. Act like a Grodnim."

"Aye, Dak my master. Uh—Think, look, and act like a devil."

"Aye."

He shifted the stump of his right arm, severed at the wrist, and folded swathing rags more securely to conceal his hook.

"I do not forget I wear the red beneath all this green."

"That is well. Do not forget and strip off and reveal all to everyone. In all else—forget."

He caught the tone of my voice and hawked and spat again and we cantered through the deepening twilight toward a certain sailors' tavern where news was to be had. The shadows lengthened.

A line of beggars along the decaying inner wall cried out and held up pitiful mutilations, rattling their wooden begging bowls. These were men who had been used by the overlords of Magdag in war, and being wounded or rendered unfit for further duty, had been cast off. They were not even of use as slaves.

Somewhere a few good days' ride back to the west lay the corpses of half a dozen devils of Magdag. The gold and silver oars that had once jingled in their purses made the same bright sounds in ours. Money has no cares over its owners. I drew out a handful of copper obs, that almost universal single-value copper coin of Kregen, and threw them, one by one, at the beggars as we passed. The act gave me no pleasure.

"Grodno bless you, gernu!" "May the delights of Gyphimedes be yours tonight, gernu!" The babbling cries lifted as we rode past. The gutter ran with slime here. "May you sup with Shagash, gernu!" "The sweet Greenness of Grodno upon you, gernu!"

I kept my ugly old face iron-hard as we passed. There was every chance, had this scene been enacted fifty years ago here, that some of those men might have come by their afflictions at the end of my longsword. Duhrra's sectrix pushed close.

"Waste of obs," he said.

"Aye."

My thoughts pained me. In Holy Sanurkazz, the chief city of the Zairians of the southern shore of the inner sea, sights like this, of maimed and blinded men piteously begging, were almost unknown. The various orders of chivalry of Zair saw to that. That was one of their prime functions besides the greatest function of all, which was their sacred duty, the destruction of everything of the Green and of Grodno upon the Eye of the World. My thoughts should not pain me. Once I had been a Krozair of Zy, a member of the Krozair Order held in highest repute. I had been ejected, ignominiously thrown out, declared Apushniad, my longsword broken. Of all the fancy titles I held on Kregen, only being a Krozair of Zy had meant much to me. Now I must push all thoughts of the Krzy away. I was for home, for Vallia and Valka. And, too, I do my wonderful four-armed warrior Djangs a grave injustice if I say I did not hold being their king as of high importance and meaning in my life.

The names of places that have special significances to me ring and resound in my head. At that time apart from Felschraung and Longuelm, which were not places but the names of my wild Clansmen of Segesthes, a number of names could move me.

Strombor. Valka. Djanduin.

Yes, and Felteraz, too, here in the Eye of the World where I had been cruel to Mayfwy, widow of my oar-comrade Zorg. I can remember my thoughts, triggered by that pitiful line of broken men, mulling and jangling in my skull and giving me not so much a headache as an infernal feeling of wishing to get home to my Delia and finding some sense in this beautiful and horrific world of Kregen. I was just thinking that, too, under my alias of Hamun ham Farthytu, Paline Valley in Hamal had meaning for me, when I caught the suppressed breathing from the shadows of the next archway, the incautious chink of steel.

The reins tautened under my fingers and I slowed the eager sectrix. Duhrra reined in alongside me.

"I came here in order to take a ship and sail away. I did not seek trouble." My right hand crossed my body and fastened on the hilt of the longsword scabbarded at my waist. "But sink me! If any cramph wants to make trouble I will accommodate him!"

Duhrra's long exhalation of breath sounded like a benediction. His big face gleamed in the erratic light of a distant torch bracketed to a slimy wall. "I knew there could only be trouble in vile Magdag. By Zair! Right happy this will make me—"

"You take the left-hand rasts, Duhrra."

"Aye, master."

Duhrra could swing a longsword with his left hand. I knew.

We rode another half a dozen yards and the tall pointed archway rose over our heads carrying either a cross street or a house above the harbor road we followed. The shadows blacked out the forms of the men waiting. I did not think they would be stikitches—professional assassins—but more likely would be desperate men ready to kill for money, and men of that stamp are to be found wherever men congregate together.

Well aware they could see me, I did not draw.

Surprise is a useful weapon. So is a longsword. Even the sword I bore, taken from the body of that Grodnim Jiktar who had attempted to stop me opening the caissons of the gate of the Dam of Days and so destroying a convoy of foemen's ships. I held the hilt that was almost the hilt of a true Krozair longsword. The blade bore the device of a lairgodont, a most ferocious carnivorous risslaca, surmounted by a rayed sun. That device denoted a Green Brotherhood devoted to Grodno. The sword had served me well since we had left the Dam of Days and the Grand Canal at the extreme western end of the inner sea. Now it would serve again.

The lesten-hide grip over wood and iron ridged firmly into my hand. This thing would have to be quick—quick and deadly. I saw the shadows move.

The thieves made the mistake of shouting. No doubt they sought to frighten us. As they leaped so they screeched.

"Gashil! Gashil! To Sicce with you!"

Duhrra bellowed a fruity oath and his sword blurred up and down. My blade leaped for the throat of the first attacker. He staggered back, trying to scream, with the black blood spouting. Twice more I struck as the leems of the sewers leaped. One reeled back, sightless, faceless, dying. The other, a Rapa, skewed his sword across and partially deflected the blow so that the blade sliced through the crest atop his gray vulturine face. He stopped screeching "Gashil," the legendary patron of bandits, and screamed out a string of Rapa oaths. But, for all that, his sword lunged in again. I leaned out and over, looped the weapon in a shadowy blur, lifted it, and so slashed down. The Rapa dropped his sword. He took a step from the shadows into the pink moonlight, his hands to his head. He had been cleft down to the bridge of that big vulturine beak. Only then did he fall. Rapas are fierce opponents and worthy to be called warriors, even if they do stink in the nostrils of apims like me.

Duhrra's sectrix backed and collided with mine. I swung a swift glance toward him. The one-handed man's sword skittered up into the air, spinning, catching the slanting rays of pink and golden moonlight. I saw beyond his sectrix the lithe vicious shape of a numim closing in for the kill.

"Look out!" I yelled, trying to kick my beast into action and so close. I would be too late.

The numim, his golden lion-face a single blaze of ferocious pleasure in the moonlight, which slanted narrowly above the eastern roofs, leaped for Duhrra, a longsword upraised. I felt that my comrade was doomed. I reversed the sword ready to throw, and—

A bar of steel twinkled cleanly in the moonlight. It thrust straight at the numim. The lion-man's leap ended in a shriek and a gurgle. He slumped to the ground. He tried to rise and run, and collapsed, and lay, groaning and cursing.

Duhrra turned his big face toward me. He looked more like an idiot than ever.

"The rasts," he said. He lifted his right arm.

Where he usually wore his hook, fitted for him by the doctors attached to the Akhram by the Grand Canal, now a brand of steel flamed black and gold in the moonlight. I knew why he had carried what I supposed was his hook concealed in rags, for we had wished to prevent news of a one-handed man being bandied about. Now I realized he had concealed more than a mere hook.

He waved the blade at me, socketed into leather and wood over his stump, and his great idiot face showed pleasurable delight in a new toy.

"They did not expect this, Dak. They didn't like it."

He slid a leg over his saddle and jumped to the ground. I was very conscious of the shadows about us, the darkness of the pointed archway in which the ambush had taken place, the comparative brilliance beyond as She of the Veils rose higher and cast down her light. Eyes could be watching us; but that was a thing I could do nothing about.

The wounded numim lay gasping on the ground. He had rolled over and so lay on his back, gasping and cursing, and glaring up at us. Blood stained his golden mane. I had known a numim who had been a great man and a good friend, even if he had been a citizen of hostile Hamal. I stopped as Duhrra bent.

"You, rast," said Duhrra of the Days, "may receive a boon at my hands. You may go to roister with Gashil, to sit on the right hand of Grodno in the radiance of Genodras. You are equally doomed, cramph. For Grodno is the true devil."

And Duhrra sliced the cripple-blade across the numim's throat and so slew him.

He stood back and turned to me.

"He had seen my hook—or, rather, the blade. He would have talked. I do not think you would care for that, Dak, my master."

All I could say was, "No."

Methodically, Duhrra cleaned the cripple-blade and its tang which fixed into the socket of the stump, turning with a cunning twist to lock. He unlocked it and cleaned the tang and the socket as we rode on, for we did not wish to tarry with the street cumbered with dead bodies. Magdag has a force of hired mercenaries to fight with her own people, and she had the night watch, who delight in catching thieves and ne'er-do-wells, for each one gains them a bounty when sent to slave at the oar benches of the galleys.

Presently Duhrra, his stump once more concealed, said, "You seem to know this devil's nest passing well, master."

"Aye. I once lived here for a space—in good times and evil. And must I keep on telling you I am not your master?"

"No, master."

"What does that mean?"

A hurrying group from an alehouse passed, men and women of a number of different racial stocks, all swathed in dirty green garments, with link-slaves to light their way. They passed the sectrixes like a flood, opening out before and closing aft. I twisted in the awkward wooden saddle to stare after them. The torchlights scattered red and orange reflections. The shadows grew darker and swooped down, writhing. Silently, with only a rush of sandaled feet, those people passed us.

"Are they phantoms?" Duhrra's face showed no shock, but I saw the coverings over his stump moving.

"No, you great fambly! They are workpeople going to their hovels after drinking as the suns set. They go in a group with torches because—"

"Yes. Well, there is one little lot who will not disturb them this night, by Za—"

"Onker!" I bellowed.

I had no need to say more. But Duhrra, who looked like a great muscle-bound idiot, could play games, also.

"By Grodno the Green!" he said loudly. "You call me onker, master!"

I glared at him. Neither of us would smile. The moment was amusing. I shook the reins and we cantered past the alehouse with its sign of a broken pot—broken by skylarking children, I shouldn't wonder—and so turned into the Alley of Weights which would take us to the main waterfront of Foreigners' Pool. The alley lay in darkness, but from the waterfront the sounds of rollicking and roistering lured us on. I had no real fear of another attempt on us so close to the clustered taverns of the waterfront, but we rode with swords in our hands, just in case. As to the carousing— the sounds rose thin and few. I had fancied the Pool would be jumping; perhaps it was too early.

She of the Veils had risen clear of the roofs now and as we reached the end of the Alley of Weights and saw the dark water before us a jaggedly rippling ribbon of pinkly golden light stretched, as though to welcome us back to the sea. Lights shone from the taverns and alehouses, for sailors' work is thirsty work. Again I fancied business was slack. The tavern I wanted, known to be the favorite of the Vallian seamen who had sailed here all the weary way across the Outer Oceans, was called *The Net and Trident*. I knew little of it, for, as you know, my former residence in Magdag had been once in the slave warrens and once in the Emerald Eye Palace.

In those old days I had spied out a deal of Magdag, as I have mentioned, with a true Krozair's eye for weaknesses in the defense against the great day when the call rang out and we of Zair went up against the hated men of Grodno.

Well, the call had gone out, and I had failed to answer the Azhurad, and so had been ejected, was no longer a Krzy, was Apushniad. I'd been on Earth at the time, banished for twenty-one terrible years; but how to explain that to a man of Kregen?

A couple of drunks staggered past. Our sectrixes let a silly snort escape their nostrils, and I kicked the flank of mine to remind him his work was not yet done. The third sectrix with our dunnage strapped to his back tailed along in the rear.

There were damned few ships tied up. I saw an argenter, one of those broad, stubby comfortable ships, probably from Menaham, although her flags were not visible in the harbor. Beyond her lay three of the broad ships of the inner sea, dwarfed by the argenter. Seeing both types of ship so close together gave me a true idea of the impressiveness of the ships of the Outer Oceans. The little merchant ships of the Eye of the World would never brave the terrors outside the inner sea.

There was no galleon from Vallia moored up.

I looked hard as we reined up outside *The Net and Trident*. No. No, it was sure. I could not see a single Vallian ship.

Well, I was annoyed. It meant I must wait until one sailed in from the Outer Oceans, sailing in through the Grand Canal and along to Magdag. I would wait. There was nothing else to do.

We tied the sectrixes to the rail, at which they showed their spite. Later, when I had asked the questions boiling in me, we could stable them properly. We pushed into the tavern and stood for a moment adjusting to heat and light and noise.

The place was not overly full, and the patrons were mostly sailors of the inner sea, with a mercenary guard or two, and at a table beneath the balcony of the upper floor a group of men who might be merchants in a small way of business.

A few serving wenches—I dislike the name of *shif* commonly given to these girls—moved among the tables and benches. We moved farther into the room, letting the door swing shut at our backs. My right hand hung at my side, ready. The sawdust on the floor showed itself to be old and in urgent need of replacement. The odors of old grease and burned fat and sour wine clung about the room.

Nodding to a table in a corner where no one was likely to get at our backs, I went over and Duhrra followed. His right arm was buried in his green cloak. We wore the mesh mail beneath our green robes, but we had removed our coifs earlier. We sat down and stared about, rather as two hungry and thirsty travelers might do. And, in truth, that was what we were.

One of the girls hurried over, plastering a smile on her face. She was apim, and not happy, worn out and tired already even though the night's drinking had barely begun.

Duhrra began an argument about the wine she might serve, and he went dangerously near perilous ground by asking if they had any Zairian wine recently come in from a prize. She tossed her hair back tiredly and said they had none, and she could recommend the local Blood of Dag which, she said, as a wine was, as was proper, a bright and beautiful green. Duhrra's face did not express his distaste. But he started to speak.

"Excellent!" I said loudly. "And a rasher or two of vosk with a few loloo's eggs. And pie to follow—malsidge, if possible, or squish."

"Malsidge?" said Duhrra, not too pleased. "Make mine squish."

"We are taking a long sea voyage," I said. "Malsidge."

"Malsidge is off," said the girl. She wiped her mouth and smeared the red stuff over her cheeks. "Huliper pie today."

"Very well." I put my hand in one of the pockets of the robe beneath the cloak. I made a habit of carrying money spread out over my person. I let a little silver chink show through my fingers. Her brown eyes fixed on the silver as a ponsho fixes his eyes on a risslaca's eyes.

"Tell me, doma, what is the news of the ships from Vallia?"

She would know all the gossip, I guessed. Whether she willed it or not her life would be bound up with the men of the inner sea and their vessels. She would hear them talking.

"Vallia, gernu?"

Her tone had changed markedly since the gleam of silver between my fingers.

"Ships from Vallia sail into Foreigners' Pool. When is the next one due? Has she been signaled yet?"

She shook her head. She looked frightened. Still she had not taken her eyes away from that gleam of silver.

"No, gernu. Not for a long time. The ships from Vallia no longer sail to Magdag."

Two
The flash of a Ghittawrer blade

As I have said before, there is nothing intrinsically wrong with the color green. It is a charming, restful color. Our green vegetation makes of our Earth a marvelous place. I know that if green suddenly vanished from the spectrum we would all be immeasurably the poorer for that. But as I sat there, in that squalid tavern on the waterfront of Foreigners' Pool in Magdag, so overwhelming, so bitter, so malefic a hatred for all things Green overcame me that I shut my eyes and gripped onto the inferior earthenware pot so that it smashed into shards and the bilious green wine ran and spread over the table.

"Gernu!" cried this poor serving wench.

Then sanity reasserted itself. Of course! She did not mean that Vallian ships never came to Magdag. The inner sea lies at the western center of the continent of Turismond. It is separated from Eastern Turismond by a devilish cleft in the ground from which spurt noxious and hallucinatory vapors, and also by The Stratemsk, so monstrous a range of mountains that men believe their summits reach up to the twin glories of Zim and Genodras, the red and green suns of Antares. There was no way, as all men knew, across The Stratemsk on foot. And—there were no airboats in the inner sea. Equally, it needed a ship of the Outer Oceans to navigate in those stormy seas, all the way from the Dam of Days in the west, south and so past Donengil, and then north up the Cyphren Sea, sailing with the Zim Stream and so passing the northern extremity of the continent of Loh, and so at last due east for Vallia.

No. No, this girl did not mean the galleons from Vallia no longer sailed to Magdag.

She meant the seamen from the galleons no longer came to her tavern, *The Net and Trident*.

I told her this, in a gentle voice, but still she flinched back.

"Indeed, no, gernu. I speak sooth. Since King Genod, may his name be revered, told them not to sail here, they have not come back."

"He did *what?*"

"Gernu…" Her voice sounded faint.

The door opened and on a gust of fishy, fresher air, men bulked in, apims, diffs, laughing and talking, scraping chairs and tables, bellowing for wine.

The girl cast one last longing look at the silver between my fingers, and fled.

I sat like a loon.

Of course, I could take passage in an argenter. Sail to Pandahem. But—but there was no other answer. That is what I would have to do. I did not like it. There was no other way.

Pandahem, the large island to the south of Vallia, had always been in trade and military rivalry with the empire of Vallia. Pandahem was divided into a number of different nations. I had friends—rather, I used to have friends—in Tomboram. This new and evil king Genod Gannius here in Magdag had arranged a treaty with my enemies in Menaham in Pandahem. He wanted to buy airboats from Hamal and use the Menaheem to transport them to Magdag and so gain an invincible sky force to crush the Zairians. I had put paid to that scheme, at least for now. No doubt he would try again. By then I would be well out of the Eye of the World, back home in Valka, my island off the coast of Vallia. But... in order to sail home I would have to ship in an argenter from Menaham.

By Vox! How the Bloody Menahem would crow if ever they discovered they had the Prince Majister of Vallia in their hands!

Duhrra was looking at me.

He put that moonface of his on one side, and a frown dinted in the smooth skin of his forehead. His scalp was bald and gleaming, with that small pigtail dangling down his back.

"You show nothing on your face, Dak. Yet is not this news bad? It is not what you expected."

"No. It is not."

"Then you cannot return to your home in Vallia. You will have to return with me to Sanurkazz—or Crazmoz, which is my home—and we will have fine adventures on the way."

I could not answer.

This Duhrra, whom I had dubbed Duhrra of the Days, did not know all there was to know of me, even here in the Eye of the World, where years and years ago I had been a Krozair Brother and the foremost swifter captain of the inner sea. Those cramphs of Magdag had trembled at my name. I knew it to be true. Nursing mothers lost their milk, strong men blanched, maidens screamed, if they thought themselves in danger from me, from Pur Dray, Krzy.

Duhrra called me Dak, for that was a name I had adopted in all honor, even though I believed he had heard me addressed by my real name. He never referred to it. The Krozairs are a remote and exotic breed of men, even among their own countrymen who have not aspired to the honor and glory of becoming Krozairs.

The serving girl bustled about seeing to the ribald and vociferous demands of the newcomers. They were mercenaries, and even seated at table they swaggered and boasted. Presently she brought our vosk and loloo's eggs, and the huliper pie, together with a fresh jug of that ghastly green wine, the Blood of Dag.

I flipped the silver oar up. It glittered in the lamplight.

"You forget this."

She bobbed a quick curtsy, the same kind of submissive dipping of the head and bending of the knee as one saw on Earth, and caught the silver coin and dropped it safely down her blouse.

"Thank you, gernu. May Grodno smile on you."

Another man might have thought, *Zair certainly is not.* But I thought only of a scheme to return to Vallia and Valka and once more clasp my Delia in my arms, my Delia of the Blue Mountains, my Delia of Delphond.

"Eat," said Duhrra. "Eat, my master, and afterward you will feel better."

He was partially right, of course. I ate. The stuff tasted foul. I took up a handful of palines, for they are usually—although not always—to be found in a dish on every tavern table, and I munched moodily. Palines are sovereign cures for a headache, cherry-like fruits of exquisite taste, sweet firm flesh, and are an item sadly lacking on this Earth, this Earth of my birth four hundred light-years from Kregen under Antares.

This disastrous news had shattered me.

I had been through horrific experiences before, many times. But this feeling of being trapped numbed me. I had been trapped when the Star Lords had banished me to Earth for twenty-one years. Then there had been no possible way for me to do something and return to Kregen. I had made attempts and had scared up some response from the strange woman who called herself Madam Ivanovana on Earth and Zena Iztar on Kregen. But now I was actually on Kregen, my duties for the Star Lords for the moment discharged, and willing and able to travel at once to the only woman who means anything to me—and I was prevented by mere geography. Distance and time separated me, as I then thought.

So be it. I remember I sat up and found myself looking at one of the mercenaries at the adjoining table. I would make my way back to my Delia, as I had before, and I would do so come hell or high water.

With that decision made and already plans for that damned Menahem argenter forming in my mind, I was aware of the mercenary rising from the table.

Duhrra sucked in his breath.

The mercenary was a Fristle. His powerful humanlike body was clad in the mesh mail. His catlike head, with the striped fur and the slit eyes and the bristling whiskers, lowered on me most evilly. He advanced from his table and he loosened his scimitar, which all Fristles use no matter what other weapons they chance to be issued with.

"You are looking at me, dom," said this Fristle, very menacingly. He was vicious and tough, that was evident. "I do not think I like that."

I knew what had happened. So wrapped up in my thoughts had I been I had allowed some of my anguish and my anger to show on that iron-hard face of mine, thereby destroying any illusion I might cherish of being an iron-hard man. The Fristle had seen this and with his quick catlike temper had taken this as a deliberate affront, a challenge.

I sighed.

"You are mistaken, dom," I began. "I was not—"

That was a mistake, to start with.

"You are calling me a liar?"

"Not at all." I searched around for words. This situation was not quite unparalleled. I had acted the coward and the ninny as Hamun ham Far-thytu in Ruathytu, the capital of Hamal. Now I wanted to avoid trouble. For Duhrra's sake as much as mine, I wished no brawling here. "No, dom. I would not call you a liar—unless you were, of course."

"Cramph!" he said. Even in the simple word *cramph* he insinuated a cat's hiss into his voice. Then, splendidly, hissing out into the tavern room and bringing everyone's attention to center on us: "Rast!"

A rast is a six-legged rodent disgustingly infesting dunghills. I have used the word a few times in my life.

I stood up. I stood up slowly.

"I was not looking at you with intent. In that you lie. You call me a cramph. You lie. You call me a rast. You lie." My right hand slowly crossed my waist toward the sword hilt. "It seems, dom, you are a chronic liar."

"By Odifor, apim! His scimitar flamed. "I must teach you your place!"

His comrades lolled back in their chairs, laughing, mocking, catcalling, telling this mercenary, whom they called Cryfon the Sudden, to be gentle with me and only knock one eye out and not to stick more than two fingers' breadth of steel into me and so on.

He had no fear of my longsword. In these confined quarters with tables and chairs to entangle legs, the quick and deadly scimitar would do its work wonderfully well. His Magdaggian longsword, no doubt with the initials *G.G.M.* etched into the blade, hung disregarded, scabbarded from a baldric.

I moved to one side so as to give myself room and whipped out the long-sword. The lamps cast their glow upon the blade, for it had been newly cleaned and it shone lustrously.

The mercenaries at the table suddenly fell silent.

The Fristle, who a moment before brandished his scimitar with every intent of giving me a good thrashing, short of slaying me, stopped stock still. His breath hissed between that catlike mouth.

"By the Green!" he said.

Duhrra moved at my back and I guessed he was swathing up his stump again.

"Gernu!" said this Fristle mercenary, Cryfon the Sudden. "I did not know—I had no idea. Your pardon, gernu, a thousand thousand pardons."

Where before he had been calling me rast and cramph, as well as dom, which is a friendly salutation, now he called me gernu, which is the Grodnim way of saying *jernu* or lord.

One takes one's chances on Kregen.

"I was not staring at you with intent."

"Indeed not, gernu. In that I lied. I lied most foully, as Odifor is my witness."

One of the mercenaries, a bulky numim whose golden fur glowed gloriously in the samphron oil lamp's gleam, called, "You always could pick the wrong 'un, Cryfon." The numim rose, bowing to me. "Gernu—you will pardon the poor onker and take a sup of wine with us?"

He was a Deldar, and the leader and spokesman of this little gang. I turned to face him and realized I still held the looted Grodnim longsword. I swished it in a little salute and sheathed it. Its flash was scabbarded. But in that movement I caught at some of the meanings here. The device! The lairgodont and the rayed-sun emblem. At the time I'd picked it up on the Dam of Days, with its headless late owner sprawled by the valve wheels, I had considered the problems of that device. I'd chipped out the emeralds and given the device a rub with a rough stone, but the quick eyes of these men had picked it out, and recognized it—and, too, no doubt, they had seen the condition, the lack of jewels, and had drawn conclusions from that consonant with a Green Brother patronizing a low-class drinking tavern like *The Net and Trident*.

Even a Green Brother, a Ghittawrer of Grodno, down on his luck was a man not to be trifled with. And, too, it was not only because of the longsword, which they now knew would have chopped the Fristle mercenary, Cryfon the Sudden, very surely, scimitar or no scimitar, close quarters or no close quarters. Also, there was in these men's shocked deference to a Ghittawrer Brother the subservience to power and authority vested in mystic disciplines, the force of religion, the aura of invincibility.

I had seen similar, although not so violent, reactions in Sanurkazz when an unthinking carouser came face to face with a Krozair Brother. But the Zairians are a ruffianly lot anyway, and they tend to joke more and to make rough good humor out of the mystic disciplines—making very sure first that no Krozair is within earshot. These Grodnims, in line with their religious character, took a more narrow view. They believed more fanatically. They were more fervent in their observances. For them the Green was all.

Was this, I wondered, one reason why now the Green rose in ascendancy over the Red?

"I thank you, Deldar," I said, speaking stiffly, as a Ghittawrer Brother would. Truth to tell, I had been speaking as a Krozair might, and that seemed to serve. "You are kind. But I must go about my business."

He nodded at once, quickly. "I understand, gernu. May the blessed light of Grodno go with you."

"And with you."

Well, if he meant it—so did I!

We threw down coins to pay for our meal and wine and went out. Duhrra took a tremendous breath once outside, under the stars, with She of the Veils rising up into the night sky.

"A po-faced lot, these Grodnims!"

"Aye. And you had best be, too."

He rumbled and moved his wing, but he remained silent.

We had come out of that well. But I determined to get rid of the device. I would not care to part with the weapon, for it was the finest I was likely to get my hands on for some time.

Those mercenaries in there came from the galleys in the adjoining harbor. No doubt they found *The Net and Trident* more hospitable since the withdrawal of Vallian ships. There would be more room and better service, and a discount, too, I shouldn't wonder. But they were hard, tough men. I had fought their like on the Eye of the World. How long would it take them to arrive at the truth? That the insolent apim who had fronted down their comrade, Cryfon the Sudden, had merely found the Ghittawrer sword? Stolen it, most likely, with a knife in the back of the Brother in Grodno.

Even if they reached that conclusion I fancied they would not be too anxious to rush out and test it.

The power of the Green Brotherhoods is long and terrible, in ways quite foreign to the powers of the Krozairs.

Then I thrust all this petty business away.

Here I was, aching to return home, and stranded in the inner sea, thousands of miles from Valka.

The thoughts tortured me. We mounted up. I had no real idea what to do now, for all my plans had envisaged my going aboard a Vallian galleon this night. I had not even seriously considered the alternative I had thought on, that I would have to wait a sennight or so.

Now, no galleon would come at all...

We rode past the argenter.

I said, "It seems, Duhrra of the Days, that we shall have to take passage in her."

"I will still sail with you, Dak."

"Aye." Duhrra had been earning a living as a wrestler when I first met him. I had a good idea he was no stranger to the sea. "It may well be I shall have to pay passage money."

"That seems just. Use the money you would have paid the Vallian captain."

I humped along on the sectrix for a space, avoiding all the usual impedimenta of a waterfront. Then: "There will not be enough for a captain of Pandahem." I could not explain that as the Prince Majister of Vallia all I needed to have done was convince the Vallian master that I was who I was. I could do that, all right.

"It would seem, master, that the Pandaheem are more greedy than the Vallians."

That was a reasonable assumption on the facts.

"Probably. Let us find an inn and get some rest. I will talk with the master of the argenter in the morning."

"We must slit a few throats and gain ourselves some gold."

"Let us talk to the master first, and discover his price."

"As you say, master."

I reined in and Duhrra's sectrix snorted and shied away. Both animals we rode and the pack animal were annoyed they had not been fed and watered, rubbed down, and bedded for the night.

"Listen to me, Duhrra of the Days. You act the part of a Grodnim here in Magdag. You understand that reason well enough."

"Aye. They'd draw out our tripes if they discovered—"

"When we go aboard the Menaham argenter, forget all mention of the word Vallia, except to give the place a round curse every now and then. Menaham and Vallia do not get on."

His heavy-lidded eyes regarded me in the flaring torchlight from over a nearby dopa den.

"I see. That makes the problem a little clearer."

"Just remember—it's my neck as well as yours."

We slept that night at the hostelry of *The Missal Tree* just off the waterfront but still in the harbor area. We were merely two weary travelers seeking a bed. The sectrixes were seen to by a lame Relt, one of that race of diffs who are cousins to the Rapas. The Rapas seem to have taken all the ferocity, the Relts all the gentleness. We turned in and, as I say, we slept. Old campaigners both, this Duhrra of the Days, and me, Dak.

Duhrra's stump was well concealed, and the Ghittawrer emblem likewise was covered with a flap of green cloth.

The argenter captain did not ask our business or why we wished to sail out of the Eye of the World, for which I was grateful, for I had been cudgeling what brains I have to find a reason that would stand inspection. He stroked a hand through his broad black beard and stared at us with sober calculation showing on his heavy, seamed face. He wore a gold ring in each ear, which offended my aesthetic sense. He was a hard man, as he would have need of being, and he drove a hard bargain.

When we left him amid the bustle of his ship's company preparing for sea, with the seabirds calling, those ill Magbirds of Magdag, with the mixture of stinks of tar and oil and seaweed in our nostrils, and went down the gangplank, Duhrra favored me with a look that spoke volumes.

On the quayside and heading for the tavern three along from *The Net and Trident*, Duhrra said, "A large sum, Dak."

"We will find it."

"Oh, aye, I never doubted that."

We found the money, and a couple of overlords of Magdag awoke with thick heads and a garbled tale of assault in the night as they rode beneath an archway, so I guessed, for I had not cared to slay them, realizing the furor that would cause. With their gold we bought passage, for they had been staggering home well loaded after a night's gambling. Their luck was now our luck. The link-slaves had run, screaming, at the first sight of sword-twinkle.

A fair northeasterly breeze bore us on bravely after the towing boats had cast us off. With all plain sail set—and the argenters had only plain sail—we creamed along, leaning over only a little on the starboard tack. Our cabin was as well-appointed as one might expect. It was, to tell the truth, luxurious by many of the sea-standards I have known. The twin suns shone, the sky lifted high and blue above us, the seabirds were dropped astern, and ahead of us lay only the Grand Canal, the Dam of Days, and then the long haul south and east and north, to Pandahem. From thence I would find a way to reach Vallia.

When the first of the black clouds appeared, boiling on the southern horizon, I felt the sudden gripping sensation at my heart. When I had been living in the inner sea before and had attempted to sail to Sanurkazz and to Felteraz, the Star Lords had sent a most violent rashoon. Rashoons, those sudden and tumultuous gales of the inner sea, are known and accepted as part of life. What the Star Lords sent was greater and more vicious, huge black clouds swirling, winds that tore canvas to ribbons, that smashed a ship over onto her beam ends.

The hands took the canvas in smartly enough. We snugged down. I recalled that the woman—so marvelous in her scarlet and ruby and gold clothing, astride a white zhyan, the woman whose use-name was Zena Iztar—had promised me I would not leave the Eye of the World just yet. She had said I would be prevented, and when I had asked if the Star Lords would prevent me, she had answered no. I stared at those ominous clouds, hanging dark and angry, and I cursed.

The master, Captain Andapon, appeared confident. His beard lifted arrogantly.

"It is only a rashoon. That is a mere nothing to a sailor who has sailed the Outer Oceans."

He was right, if it was only a rashoon, a local storm.

"It will pass, never fear."

And he *was* right. The black clouds rose a hand's breadth into the sky above the horizon. The light shone strangely over there. I stared. The clouds were dwindling, were thinning, were withdrawing. I stared harder. A white speck appeared, diving down on the argenter. The ship wallowed. Captain Andapon bellowed and his men swarmed aloft to cast loose the canvas. The air felt still and warm, the breeze dying. Still that white speck flitted nearer. No one else aboard appeared to have seen it.

The suns shone on that flying dot. And as I looked up so I recognized the white dove of the Savanti. Long and long had I seen this white dove, the Savanti's counterpart to the bird of prey sent by the Star Lords to be their messenger and spy. I gripped the rail. I could not look away.

The white dove hovered. I knew the Savanti, those mysterious men, mortal but superhuman, of the Swinging City of Aphrasöe, were once more taking an interest in me. They were the ones who had first brought me to Kregen. They had wanted to make of me a Savapim, an agent to work for the humanization of the world. I had failed them because I had cured my Delia; her baptism in the Sacred Pool of Baptism of the River Zelph in Aphrasöe not only cured her crippled leg but conferred on her, as it had on me, a thousand years of life.

What could they want of me now? Why did the Star Lords stand aloof? Was this what Zena Iztar had meant?

The argenter, *Chavonth of Mem,* wallowed and rolled in the windless sea. The sky cleared. The suns blazed forth and no speck of cloud obscured that wide expanse.

"This will not last for long," said Captain Andapon. I had to admire his hard grittiness, even though he was a member of the country I familiarly knew as the Bloody Menahem, those people who had allied themselves with Hamal against Vallia.

The watches changed and the bells rang and the lookout screeched from the maintop.

"Sails!"

"They bring a wind, Pandrite be praised!"

We all stared up uselessly at the lookout. He pointed to the south. His voice reached us, hoarse with yelling. "Swifters!"

Captain Andapon stamped upon his own deck, and swore.

"May the vile Armipand take 'em! Swifters!"

He meant they would be pulling, using their banks of oars, sailing independently of the wind. We were still becalmed.

The men of Menaham had no fear of the bitter struggle between the Red and the Green, for they were neutrals. Swifters flying the red or green flags would treat them merely as passing strangers upon the sea.

Soon the swifters hove into view over the horizon. As they neared it became clear they had seen us and were bearing down to investigate this lone ship. That made sense. Captain Andapon bellowed and the Menaham flag rose up not only to the mizzen, but also to the main and foremasts. I looked at the colors: four blue diagonals and four green diagonals from right to left, divided by thin white borders. I thought back to the Battle of Jholaix when the yellow saltire on the red ground, the colors of the empire of Vallia, had borne down and trampled the colors of Menaham along with those of Hamal.

Now those colors would protect me from the Red and the Green; for to the Greens I was a hated enemy Krozair, and to the Reds I was Apushniad, an unfrocked Krozair.

The lookout bellowed again.

Captain Andapon leaped nimbly, for all his bulk, grasped the larboard shrouds, and climbed a dozen ratlines. He shaded his eyes and peered at the swifters. Before he descended to the deck he looked down at us, all standing there and looking up at him. His voice cracked, flat and brutally.

"They showed neither red nor green. They are small craft, less than ten oars a side. You all know what they are." His voice smashed at us. "Beat to quarters! Stand to arms! They won't take us without a fight"

So I knew, too.

Renders, pirates, sea-wolves of the Eye of the World. They took and looted and burned Zairian or Grodnim; it was all one. This fine fat ship of Menaham, all becalmed and idle, would be served up to them, like ponsho on a plate!

Three
Ringed by renders

If it was not the Star Lords, then the hand of the Savanti lay in this. This contrivance was not beyond them. Superhuman, their powers. They possessed powers I had not thought about overmuch and perhaps I had neglected a duty in that. If the Star Lords—of whose powers I knew so little it amounted to nothing apart from their capacity to hurl me like a yo-yo from Earth to Kregen and back—could hurl a sudden thunderstorm upon a ship, then surely the Savanti could attract a pack of sea-wolves to a becalmed ship. It would take very little to do that.

The renders pulled on. Now they were clearly visible. Four big, open pulling boats they were, scarcely swifters at all. The swifter is your true galley, lean and deadly; these boats, although slender of build, hauled their single bank of oars over the gunwales, in closed rowlocks of rope and thole pins, and they possessed neither ram nor beak that I could see.

"You look a fighting-man," said Captain Andapon. "But your man—?"

Duhrra was standing near. "He is not my man," I said. "He is my comrade."

"Can he fight—with one arm?"

"I will fight with one arm," said Duhrra of the Days. How anyone could ever imagine him an idiot—even with that idiot's face—amazed me then.

The master nodded briskly and went off shouting to his crew. The Bloody Menahem are accustomed to fighting. Thinking about that statement makes me realize that most nations of Kregen are accustomed to fighting, and there are many fighting-men; but not all men fight, as you know. Perhaps there is a greater proportion of warriors on Kregen than on this Earth in these latter days.

This would be a bloody affray. If Captain Andapon struck without a fight the renders would probably butcher us all. There was the chance they might offer us the choice. If we fought I did not think we would win, for they outnumbered us. But from the tenor of the crew's voices, and the way they handled their weapons, I knew they would fight.

The men were talking among themselves and I overheard the way they called on the Gross Armipand to blight, wither, and destroy these rasts of renders. The name of Opaz was called on, also, with pleas for a successful outcome. How strange it is that a man can feel fellow feelings for men who are supposed to be his mortal foes! I did not like the Bloody Menahem. But I felt a surge of spirit as these Menaheem prepared for battle. If we were all slain we would all go down to the Ice Floes of Sicce together—blade comrades. Odd—odd and unsettling, those feelings that would not be denied.

The four boats pulled up and then separated out of varter range to take us on the two quarters and bows. The crews of the varters were busily engaged in greasing and winding and coddling, and selecting their best chunks of rock, their straightest darts. A kind of ballista, the varter, with great penetrative and smashing power, hurling a dart of iron, or a rock, in a hard, flat trajectory. *Chavonth of Mem* was not equipped with catapults. Their higher trajectory and longer range might have been useful; I could see artillery in the boats and so the varters would have to be adequate until the renders closed and boarded.

Then it would be cold steel

I had no bow.

Standing higher out of the water, *Chavonth of Mem* could shoot her varters earlier than the boats might. With that thrilling screeching clang the first varter loosed. The rock plunged into the sea alongside the first boat, raising a water spout. The other three followed, and the rocks flew. Very quickly the varters in the boats opened up and scored. A rock flew to thud most messily onto our deck, smashing two men and a boy into red ruin. How this brought back the memories!

There were no grand concussions as the great guns fired, no leaping rumble through the decks, no swathing clouds of gunsmoke. But in all else—oh, yes, I had not been a sailor in Nelson's navy for nothing!

The boats came on. One drifted away, her larboard bank of oars ripped and idle, water slopping inboard, men tumbling out and swimming desperately for the nearest boat. A Deldar of the top spun about, there on the deck, clapped a hand to what was left of his face, trying to scream and only gurgling. Lines parted aloft and blocks spattered down. A bowman fell from the maintop screeching like a leem pierced through with a lance. Blood stank on the air, bright in the sunshine over the deck.

"Prepare to receive boarders!" bellowed Andapon. He swaggered aft to his poop-ladder, clambered up, and so pushed through the afterguard clustered there to the starboard quarter. He wore a back and breast, and a huge helmet adorned with a mass of blue and green feathers. He swirled his rapier widely. I followed him, for the first boat to touch us was almost here.

Duhrra said in my ear, "It is said, sometimes, it is wiser not to wear mail when fighting at sea."

"So it is said. But you wear the mesh mail, as do I."

"I think, if I fall into the sea, it is too far to swim in any case."

"You must do as you think fit."

"Aye, I will—master."

His big, sweaty idiot moonface loomed above me. I turned back to face what might come. He had never once remarked that I had upended him and dumped him down flat on his back and thereby won myself a gold coin when I'd been starving. He'd had two hands, then...

So deeply had I been thinking about the Savanti and the Star Lords, and giving a part of my mind to Duhrra, and, as I have indicated, doing some not inconsiderable boasting to myself, I had neglected what was staring me in the face. I had simply thought of this affray as just another fight. I had given it no thought. When Andapon yelled in baffled fury and his party with the huge rock perched over the quarter ready to drop on the boat yelled also, I woke up.

I raced forward along the poop, leaped down the ladder, belted for the break of the quarterdeck, yelling and waving that damned Ghittawrer longsword above my head. I was almost too late. A torrent of yells and shrieks burst from forward and the men posted there on the forecastle tumbled back in ruin. There were no gangways so I ran along the deck, leaping onto the hatches and jumping down, taking the starboard side. Now more men appeared over the forecastle. If I knew the ways of renders they'd be in through the foreports, into the forecastle.

Men rallied with me. We charged forward and met the pirates face to face, hand to hand. They were wild, hairy men, clad in remnants of armor, some bare-chested, swirling their weapons with a will. Gold and silver glittered about them. Immense lace-knots and feathers flaunted above them. There were women among them, fighting alongside their men. That was unfortunate. The struggle broke free as our impetuous rush, reinforced by a clamor from our rear telling that Captain Andapon had realized how nearly he had been fooled, carried us on. We smashed them and drove them back, over the beakhead, down and into the sea.

A man crawled up onto the foot of the bowsprit, yelling. He backed up, his face filled with horror. Six arrows struck him simultaneously and with a pitiful howl he fell off to splash into his watery grave.

"Below!" I bellowed.

Swinging about to lead a rush down the forward hatchway I realized Duhrra was no longer with me. He'd followed me good and hard, breathing hotly down my neck. In the press we had been parted. By Vox! If these miserable renders had done for Duhrra of the Days I'd do woe unto them.

Captain Andapon bellowed a group of his men about him. He saw that I was prepared to take a hand below. His second in command had been killed. A rock flew low over the deck, parting lines, but, thankfully, missing everyone. One of the render boats had resumed shooting then. Andapon would deal with the fellow trying to get aboard over the quarter. One boat had been sunk. So that left one to be accounted for.

"Where away that other Pandrite-forsaken boat!" I yelled. The Menaheem jumped. One shouted back from the waist. I did not think the pirates would attempt to board from there and the man pointed forward on the larboard side. In the next instant an arrow took him through the throat and, silently, he toppled back.

"Come on, lads!" I yelled, quite like old times, and went bashing below.

In the dimness shot through with vivid streaks of sunlight through the scuttles—and also through a rock-smashed hole—the outlines of men appeared, struggling, flaming with the wink and glitter of steel.

"Chavonths!" I shouted as we ran forward. I had no wish to slay a Menahem or to be slain by one in the confusion. Truth to tell, for I was most annoyed by this time, the latter consideration far outweighed the former.

At that instant a gleam of sunlight speared through an opening where a man leaped down onto the deck. The light glanced off a gleaming, sweaty bald skull, highlighted a dangling scalp lock of hair.

"Duhrra!"

"You're just in time! They're breaking in like leems!"

The last boat's crew poured in to help those of their fellows who had smashed in during the attack we had repulsed up on the forecastle. Now we faced them in the semi-gloom and, by Krun, there were a lot of them.

In among the rough furnishings of the forecastle we struggled hand to hand. It was all a dimly seen business of cut and thrust, of muffled chokes and gasping grunts, of men abruptly shrieking as the steel bit red.

They were sure of themselves, these renders of the inner sea.

My stolen Ghittawrer blade flamed. Men leaped and shrieked and died.

Men were falling about me as the sea-wolves cut their way through. Duhrra and I stood together and presently we were back to back, our blades dripping red.

I'd fought with Viridia the Render, up along the Hoboling Islands of the Outer Oceans. She and her crew of cutthroats would have been at home here. So we fought. Step by step we were forced back, back to the low wooden door leading from the forecastle into the waist. I swirled Duhrra around so that I faced the pirates.

"Dak!"

"Get outside and chop the first cramph who follows me."

He ducked through without another word.

I leaped, slashed three quicktimes, left, right, left, dropped three of the screeching hellions, then turned and bolted for the door. As I shot through so Duhrra's bulky shadow blotted the suns.

"Hold, Duhrra!"

"Aye! Do you think I'd take off your head?"

And down, swish, thwack, squelch, came his longsword, neatly decapitating the first render incautious enough to thrust his head and shoulders through after me.

The door could not be shut.

Other renders leaped through, swirling their blades, shrilling in triumph.

I fancied that familiar victory yell would die in their throats now we had room to swing a blade.

Duhrra and a few of the mercenaries of the ship—Rapas, Brokelsh, Womoxes—bashed in again. We held the pirates for the moment. The wind hung breathless. The suns burned down. The deck became slippery with spilled blood. And still our brands flamed and cut and thrust and kept that vengeful seeking steel from our own throats and guts.

For a short space the pirates drew back.

Duhrra appeared a gleaming mass of crimson.

"I think it will not be long now, Dak."

"We'll have 'em yet! Look at their hangdog faces!"

" 'Ware shafts!" The cry went up from the mercenaries.

Arrows flew.

I spread my fists on the Ghittawrer blade as best I could, ready to ward off the arrows. Three I batted away and then the fresh howls shrieked to the brilliance of Zim and Genodras at our backs. I risked a quick glance aft.

Captain Andapon and the remnants of his crew were being bundled forward, struggling and laying about them. But the renders had broken through aft. Now the crew of the argenter was trapped between the two render parties, and, as Duhrra had said, it would not be long now.

"By the Black Chunkrah!" I said. "We'll take a fine crew of 'em to sail with us across the Ice Floes of Sicce!"

We were ringed in.

Now the renders ceased loosing shafts for fear of hitting their own men. I sized up the men opposite me, selected a likely looking Kataki with his steel-armed tail, his low-browed face fierce and leering upon us.

I sprang.

"Hai! Jikai!" I bellowed.

He swung his blade up and I sidestepped, caught the vicious stab of his tail in my left hand, pulled. He staggered. I took the time to slash right-handed at a fellow who tried to cut me down from the side and then brought the longsword blurring around to chop through the mailed junction of the Kataki's neck and shoulder. He dropped. I dropped his tail, cut savagely left and right, and so leaped back to the ranks of the crew.

If I was going to take that last trip to the Ice Floes of Sicce, then this little affray was going to be a true Jikai. I'd see to that. I dislike using that great word *Jikai* except when the fight is a Jikai—if this was a mere pirate's brawl on the inner sea, all well and good. If it meant the end of me, then it was damn well going to be a high Jikai.

The renders hesitated, hanging back.

The crew around me, no doubt heartened or depressed by that flashy show-off charge of mine, prepared to go down fighting. The renders yelled—deep wolfish howls and shrill wolfish howls; they were all one in the bedlam—and charged.

We met them fiercely. Blurred, scarlet impressions flashed before me: of smiting and hacking, of thrusting and ducking. Against mail a good solid meaty blow is necessary. I gave plenty of those. Now one or two strokes slid in from directions where a comrade should have been standing. I felt a smash against my left side and before the Brokelsh could recover my blade lopped his arm. I had to leap wildly thereafter to keep off a Rapa who insisted on engulfing my blade with his throat. He fell. Another took his place. The deck slipped and slimed in blood.

"Hai, Jikai!" someone was yelling.

"Fight, you cramphs!" I bellowed.

Captain Andapon was down, still shouting, weakly trying to flail his sword up against two men who would have taken his head had Duhrra and I not stepped across and spitted them both.

There were precious few of Menaham left.

A squawking shrill lofted. The renders, still struggling, fell back. No one, for the moment, understood the meaning of the hail. Then a woman, high on the poop, shrilled and pointed.

We all looked. For the moment the fighting stopped and we all gaped out to sea like loons.

Smothered in green flags a swifter pulled in toward the argenter, white water smashing away from her ram. Armed men crowded the narrow deck aft of her arrogant prow and the beak was lifted, ready to be dropped and run out. The three banks of oars rose and fell, rose and fell like the wings of a great bird of prey.

"Swifter!" yelled a render. And then, immediately, "Magdag!"

Thereafter we could watch the educational sight of the renders madly rushing from the sinking argenter, clambering down to jump and sprawl into their three boats, and to push off frantically. The crew began to row. Their oars worked in a frenzied manner, hauling the three away in different directions.

"Saved!" said Duhrra. "And by Magdag."

"Thank the good Pandrite they came up when they did," said Captain Andapon. He had staggered up and now, gripping his wounded side, stared hungrily at the swifter.

What followed was even more educational than seeing renders fleeing a sinking ship.

Whoever commanded the swifter knew his business.

Every oar blade rose and feathered together, every oar in unison. We could hear the double roll of the drum-Deldar as he banged out the rhythm. White water creamed away from the long, low bronze ram, that cruel rostrum that could degut a ship and leave her shattered and sinking. Now the Magdaggian swifter captain swerved his ship as though on tracks, lined up on the first render boat. We all saw the ram hit, saw the planks fly up, bodies go pitching into the water.

The swifter did not halt. One bank of oars backwatered and the other pulled ahead. The swifter spun. Like a great leem pouncing on lesser predators she smashed the second boat. The third knew it could not escape. The oars faltered and came to a clumsy halt. Men were standing up in the boat, waving rags. The swifter did not hesitate.

Straight over the boat ran the galley, her sharp bronze ram crunching timber and flesh, strewing the sea past her lean flanks with wreckage.

We heard the yells and then the peculiar double *rat-tat* of the drum. Whistles blew. Every oar dug in and held. The swifter came to a stop in an incredibly short space. A boat lowered. Another boat swayed out from her center deck space. One boat went to pick up the half-drowned wretches of renders, the other pulled for the sinking argenter.

The argenter's crew, or what was left, babbled with near-hysterical relief. Men were running below to bring up their possessions. Captain Andapon

196

had quite forgotten he had just been saved from death, had near enough forgotten his wound. He raved on like a maniac.

"My ship! My beautiful *Chavonth of Mem!* Those rasts have sunk her!"

He glared about, distraught, one hand in his hair, tugging, his eyes wild.

"You've your life, Captain."

"My life! My life! And my goods! The profit on the voyage! Oh, why has Opaz forsaken me now?"

Well, it was understandable. He'd be stranded in the inner sea, too.

The boat from the swifter hooked on and men came over the side, hard, tough men, overlords of Magdag. I nudged Duhrra.

These newcomers took in the scene: The deck cumbered with dead men, running with blood; the few survivors frantically hauling out their dunnage; the captain raving and moaning about his beautiful ship and his lost fortune; and two hard-faced fellows, smothered in blood, who stood where the fighting had been the thickest.

I realized we must stand out, must be noticeable.

"Get some of our dunnage up, Duhrra. Act like the others."

The Hikdar with the green robes and the gleaming helmet and the mesh mail picked his way delicately between the corpses and sidestepped the worst patches of blood. He saluted the captain.

"Your ship is sinking, Captain. You will accept the hospitality of our swifter."

He looked at me.

Again he saluted, his arm raised in that particular Grodnim way. I replied.

"You wear the green, dom. You are of Magdag?"

"No," I said. I had to say something. "I am of Goforeng." It was one Grodnim city of which I knew a little, having raided there and made myself a nuisance—many and many a year ago—and it was a damned long way away to the east.

"They breed fighters in Goforeng it seems."

I knew the correct answer to that.

"You are too kind. But it is we who must thank you for saving us. We were nearly finished."

"So I see." He did not look about him to underline his remark. He was probably the swifter's first lieutenant, a Hikdar being a nice middle-of-the-hierarchy rank. "You had best come aboard at once. This vessel has not much longer to live."

"My beautiful *Chavonth!*"

"Yes, Captain. Now, if you will go..."

So he chivied us over the side and into the waiting boat.

Duhrra brought our effects. I hoped if by any chance a scrap of our breechclouts showed the Magdaggians would think them only drenched in blood. Duhrra had his right arm wedged into the front of his robe. I helped him with the dunnage. The Hikdar's black eyebrows rose. He was a most supercilious young man.

The boat pulled across to the swifter. Captain Andapon could not take his eyes off his ship. The argenter, *Chavonth of Mem*, went down in a last froth of bubbles as we climbed up onto the swifter's quarterdeck.

Oh, yes, the memories gushed up for me, who had been a slave in a Magdaggian swifter, and then a captain of a Zairian swifter, the foremost corsair upon the inner sea.

We were escorted below and to the captain's cabin. The men would be quartered on the upper deck, well away from the oar-slaves. Captain Andapon and I stepped into the ornate elegance of the aft cabin, and entered a world of luxury and wealth, of power and the naked display of arrogance and riches.

Aides and orderlies sprang instantly to do the bidding of this swifter captain of Green Magdag. We were waved to comfortable upholstered chairs, wine was pressed into our hands. What the blood was doing to the upholstery seemed to give no one any cause for second thoughts. No doubt another raid would amply repay the cost. The captain walked in.

"Lahal, gernus. You have wine? Good. Now tell me the essentials."

Captain Andapon was not only a tough hard seadog, he was also a man who had had dealings with the overlords of Magdag. He did not beat about the bush.

"Lahal, gernu. We were caught in a calm. We fought. They would have had us but for your timely arrival, for which I thank you from the bottom of—"

"Very good." This captain waved Andapon down. He looked at me. "My ship-Hikdar tells me you fought well. He says you are from Goforeng. I warn you I can smell untruths many dwaburs off. I want the truth."

How typical this was of overlords of Magdag. And, too, how refreshing! I'd been getting soft of late.

I still sat as I spoke.

"Lahal, Captain. If you do not choose to believe I am from Goforeng, that is your concern."

I heard the horrified gasps from his aides. Andapon drew a little away on his chair, as though to disassociate himself from this ungrateful and suicidal madman.

Before anyone could say any more, I said, in what I considered a reasonable tone of voice, "You have not told us your name."

Again the gasps from the aides. The ship-Hikdar, who had come in with some importance, half drew his sword. I glanced up at him. "Why do you draw your sword, dom? Do you wish to die?"

The Hikdar's face flushed with painful blood. He blazed out at his captain, "Gernu! Is this to be tolerated? May I have the pleasure of chopping this—"

"Softly, Nath, softly. There is more here than we supposed." He bent a frowning glance on me. I recognized it as a practiced expression designed to overawe. His black curly hair was bunched on his head, oiled and scented. His long green robe was belted in at the waist, and he wore a shortsword there, on his right side. His face was hawklike, bold, arrogant, two blue bolts for eyes, the chin of a swifter's ram—yes, these were the externals. But in that face there was not only the consciousness of power, there was real power also.

"I think," he said, "that you should tell me your name before I tell mine. That would appear equitable."

It was so, on the face of it, according to ship custom.

"Dak." I paused for only a hairbreadth of time. I had to think of some convincing name, and fast. "Dak ti Foreng." I stared up, my ugly old face hard and uncompromising. "And you?"

The Hikdar bustled forward, outraged by my conduct and yet unwilling to allow the pappattu to be incorrectly made.

"You have the honor to be in the presence of Gernu Gafard, Rog of Guamelga, the King's Striker, Prince of the Central Sea, the Reducer of Zair, Sea-Zhantil, Ghittawrer of Genod..."

All the time this Hikdar Nath rattled off the titles, and there were many more in the wearisome way of Magdag, this Gafard sat watching me with a small ironical smile playing upon his lips. In this, if nothing else, he recognized the follies of panoply and pomp. But I fastened on one fact, one single vital item in all that long imposing list. He did not bear a surname. No man with the power and rank he had, starting from that rog—which equaled the roz of the zairians; the kov or duke of the Outer Oceans— would willingly stride the world's stage without a surname. I knew him for what he was then.

The anger and bitterness in me ought not to be present, save as a general principle. I had made up my mind to quit the inner sea. Why, then, worry my head over its intrigues, its deceptions, its treacheries?

When the ship-Hikdar finished and stepped smartly back to his place, this Gafard bent his eye on me and said, "Now you know."

"Aye," I said.

This man was no true overlord of Magdag. Had I spoken to an overlord as I had to him I'd have been run outside and something diabolical would be happening to me, had I not done as I intended and broken free among the slaves chained below. This Gafard had prevented me from doing that, whereat I cursed within me, impotent to do what I wanted. No novel situation, I know, by Zim-Zair!

Gafard said, "I wish to speak to this wild leem alone. Clear the cabin. Nath, stand close beyond the door with a guard. Come running at my hail."

"Your orders, my commands, gernu!" bellowed the Hikdar, saluting, turning, bellowing the others out. We were alone.

He sat for some time at the long shining table before the stern windows, his hands limp on the balass wood, his gaze unwavering, direct, on me. Then—

"You take terrible chances, dom."

"It is necessary."

"Do you not think you might raise a gernu?"

I had made up my mind as to my tack. It was a chance, but I fancied this Gafard would be in need of what I offered—or would seem to offer, to my shame.

"What do titles mean to such a one as you?"

"Ah!" He rose and walked about the cabin on the soft rugs, his hands at his back, his head jutting forward so that his arrogant beaked nose looked even more ferocious.

"And suppose I give the orders and you are stripped and thrown below, chained to slave at the oar benches."

I did not shrug. "You might try."

He sucked in his-breath at this.

"I need men like you," he began.

I felt a premonition that the banal words might cloak a real meaning, that I was on the way to winning. He could see I read the meaninglessness of his words, for he went on, "You say you know who I am. Very well. I own it proudly! The name of Gafard, the Sea-Zhantil, is known upon the Eye of the World. I am rich, wealthy beyond your dreams. I fight for King Genod. I am a Ghittawrer in his very own Brotherhood. All these things I am, but in Zairia I was nothing! Nothing! There was no Z in my name. I fought for the Red—aye! Fought well, and nothing was my reward. I was prevented from joining the Krozairs, from joining any Red Brotherhood."

"So you turned renegade."

"Aye! And proud of it! Now I take what is rightfully mine upon the Eye of the World!"

He stood before me, alert, his right hand resting on the hilt of the shortsword. He turned, ready to draw. It would be a fifty-fifty chance whether or not he could draw and present the point at my throat before I could get out the longsword. I would not attempt to draw...

"You do appear to be doing well. And I compliment you upon your swifter handling."

He saw the arrogance in my words. Yet he smiled.

"You know I am not an overlord of Magdag by birth. But I am an overlord now, by right! Any other Grodnim gernu would have had you chained to a rowing bench by now."

"Yes," I said.

"You wear the green. You carry a Ghittawrer longsword with the device removed. You fight well—or so I am told. Do you not think to ask yourself, you who call yourself Dak ti Foreng, why you were not thrown below, chained, whipped at the looms?"

I looked up at him. "Why?"

His smile mocked me.

"I am a renegade, yes, once of Zair and now of Grodno. And you—you were of Zair, also!"

Four
Gafard, the King's Striker, the Sea-Zhantil

The secluded courtyard of the Jade Palace echoed with the clash of combat, the quick breaths of fighting-men, the spurting gasps of effort. The streaming lights of Antares flooded down to illuminate the yellow stone wall and the vines rioting in gorgeous colors on their trellises, sparkling in the upflung jets of water from the stone lips of stone fishes surrounding the lily-pool.

I switched up the shortsword and felt the shock of Gafard's point hitting just below my breastbone. We were both stripped to the waist. Gafard's muscular body glistened with sweat. He bellowed to me.

"Again, you fambly! You do not have a great long bar of steel in your hand! You have a shortsword—a Genodder, the great slayer—fashioned by the genius of King Genod himself!" He stamped his right foot and lunged at me again with every intention of spitting me once more. I clashed the wooden sword across and this time I deflected his lunge. I had to force my muscles to lock. I had to stop myself—with some violence—from doing what was natural and looping the sword and riposting and so dinting Gafard in the guts, as he so delighted in dinting me.

He slashed at my head and I ducked, he sidestepped and I let him drive his wooden sword into my ribs. It was damned painful. I thought I had done with this kind of tomfoolery after those days I had acted the ninny among bladesmen in far Ruathytu.

Gafard leaped back and saluted me, ironically.

Slaves advanced to take his sword, to sponge him down with scented rose water, to press a glass of parclear into his hand, to fan him, to fuss about him as dutiful slaves should fuss about a kind master.

"I am a longsword man," he said, sipping his sherbert drink, and then with a single swallow downing the lot. Slaves handed me a glass of par-clear, for which I was grateful. I do not usually sweat a great deal. I had had to leap about in the sunshine to work up a glow. Gafard threw the glass casually over his shoulder. A nimble numim girl caught it before it hit the flags. I wondered what the slave-master would do to her had she missed. Now this Gafard, this Rog of Guamelga, this Prince of the Central Sea, this man of many ranks and titles, this man of enormous power and wealth in Magdag—this renegade—looked at me and repeated: "I am a longsword man. But I recognize the power of the shortsword. The Genodder is a for-midable weapon."

"Aye, gernu," I said. I wiped my gleaming body with a soft towel. Gafard had narrowed his eyes when I'd stripped off. "It is a knack, surely."

"A knack you must master if you are to be of use to me."

Only a few days had passed since Gafard and his swifter *Volgodont's Fang* had rescued us from the renders. Much had happened in that time, but all the hurry and bustle amounted only to the one important thing. Duhrra and I, as one-time adherents of the Red, were now followers of the Green.

Duhrra of the Days, and I, Dak, had turned renegades.

The scene in which I had tried to convince Duhrra of the wisdom of this course still had power to make me bristle. Of course I was right, and of course Duhrra was right. We'd been standing, facing each other, in the center of the bedchamber allotted to us in Gafard's Jade Palace. The room was wide and tall and sumptuously furnished and we'd almost hit each other.

"Turn traitor! Bow and scrape to Grodno! You are mad!"

"Not so, and for the sweet sake of Zair do not shout so!"

"I am prepared to go out and cut down these evil rasts of overlords until I am cut down in my turn."

"You may be. I am not."

Duhrra eyed me. He was more worked up than when he'd lost his hand.

"I do not believe you lack spirit, Dak. But you talk like a mewling woman, heavy with child, with another at her breast, whining for mercy."

I compressed my lips. Then, unable to restrain myself, I burst out, "Sink me! Of course I'm after mercy, you great fambly! I'm long past the day when I will fight for the pleasure of fighting, or resist when resistance is hopeless! Have you learned nothing? To turn renegade now and pretend to follow the Green will not only save us from the galleys, or save our lives, it will give us the chance to escape—you great onker!"

"Now who's shouting?"

Before Duhrra had finished his sentence I'd crossed the soft carpet in long vicious leem-strides and wrenched the sturmwood door open. The corridor beyond lay pale and empty, with a tall table bearing a jar of Pandahem ware, the cold sconces upon the tapestried walls, bars of mingled sunlight streaming in past barred windows at the end. I turned back and slammed the door.

"By the Black Chunkrah! I won't shout if you will not shout."

"Duh—who's shouting?"

I breathed hard, through my nose.

"You know where I want to go. We've won through so far. If we are to escape this little lot with our lives we have no choice but to do as Gafard wishes. He's made a good thing out of it, by Krun!"

And, as I said that, I saw a ruse I had overlooked. Well, you who have listened to these tapes will know what the ruse was and how I might have employed it in the argenter. As it was, it was too late now.

So, here I was, a guest in Gafard's Jade Palace, awaiting ratification of my application. King Genod welcomed with open arms all defectors from Zair. He took a dark delight in that. I didn't have to be told that.

We went inside and Gafard insisted I play Jikaida. I like the game. We played jikshiv Jikaida, which is a middling size, for Gafard had an appointment later and could not spare the time for a larger and longer game. As usual we ranked our Deldars and set to. The game proved fascinating, for this Gafard had a cunning way with him that, if I was honest, was not so much cunning as straightforward ruthlessness applied cunningly.

[Here Prescot goes into some detail of the Game. A.B.A.]

Rising, Gafard motioned for a slave to clear the board. He looked not so much pleased by his win as puzzled. He nodded.

"Come into my chambers while I dress. I would talk with you."

I followed him.

The rooms were furnished with a sumptuousness and display of luxury that clearly indicated cost had formed no part of the designer's plans. Everything was of the finest. I did not go through into the bedchamber, and sat in a gilded upholstered chair as Gafard dressed. Silks and satins, gold lace, swathing artful folds of green and gold—gradually his clothes were built up. I noticed that he wore a fine mail shirt under his tunic of green and gold. That mail had never been made in the inner sea. That must have come from one of the old, old countries clustered around the Shrouded Sea, in southern Havilfar. He saw my interest, and smiled that slight, down-drooping smile that betrayed so much.

"Yes, Dak of Zullia. Only the best."

My short-lived pretense of being a Grodnim from Goforeng, naming myself as Dak ti Foreng, had given place to my naming myself from another well-known location. This time it was the small ponsho-farmers' village south of Sanurkazz from which hailed my oar-comrade Nath. We had taken a trip there, Nath, Zolta, and I, riding lazily through the warm weather, drinking and singing. Nath had felt the urge to visit the haunts of his youth. One oldster—a man two hundred years old, with a white beard—recognizing Nath, had called him "You young rip Nathnik."

Zolta had near bust a gut laughing. "Nathnik!" he crowed, slapping himself on the thigh, rolling about.

I can tell you, Nath and Zolta lost no opportunity to score off each other in the most outrageous ways, for all that each would gladly lay down his life for the other. They were far-off days now, long, long ago...

So it was that I felt some confidence in naming Zullia. If Gafard had ever by chance been through the place and if by an even greater chance he remembered it, I could answer up.

A long white robe was lifted and set so that the shoulders projected on small wings. Gold chains blazing with gems were draped over his chest. Slaves belted on a broad emerald and gold creation, glittering and gorgeous, and from it hung the jeweled scabbard of a brightly shining Genodder. The baldric for the longsword swung over his right shoulder; the scabbard, brilliant with gems, depending on the left. Finally, two things: the iron helmet swathed in green velvet and silk, with flaunting green and white feathers, and a last sprinkling of scented water.

Gafard, the King's Striker, was ready for audience.

He would be carried there in a preysany palankeen, with link-slaves, and body slaves, and a strong guard party of his men clad in his personal livery. He affected the golden zhantil as his emblem. I sighed.

"The Sea-Zhantil," I said.

"Aye. It is a proud title. It is one I cherish. A certain man once carried that title upon the Eye of the World. A great corsair of the inner sea. A Krozair—a Krozair of Zy. He was the Lord of Strombor."

"I have heard of him," I said. But my heart thumped.

Gafard, in the usual way of Kregans, showed no real indication of age, and could have been anything from thirty to a hundred and fifty or so. I fancied he was much less than a hundred. I, for all that my physical appearance had remained much as it had been when I was thirty and had taken the dip in the Sacred Pool of Baptism, could subtly alter the planes and lines of my face, as I have said. I could make myself look different enough to fool a lackluster eye. But beside the bulky magnificence of Gafard I looked the younger of us two—which I was, of course, as entropy if not chronology goes.

"Yes," he said, following my thought. "He disappeared from the inner sea before you were born, I imagine. A great man. The greatest Krozair of his time, this Dray Prescot, Lord of Strombor."

"So I have been told."

I did not say that I practically never used the title of "Sea-Zhantil" conferred on me by King Zo of Sanurkazz. I believe I have not even bothered to mention it in these tapes. It was of no consequence. No title could mean anything in the inner sea beside the simple, dignified, immortal Krozair of Zy.

Instead, I said, "So you, a follower of Grodno, relish using the title of a Krozair of Zy."

He flashed me a look. I wondered just what I would do if he considered I had gone too far. But he boomed a laugh and gripped his longsword hilt where the gems blazed gloriously, and strode for the door.

"A title lost by the Zairians! A title won by the Grodnims! I glory in it! And, for another reason, another reason far too precious—I am behind my time. Practice your Genodder work with Galti. He is quick and strong and will test you well."

"Your orders, my commands, gernu!" I bellowed as they did in the Magdaggian service. I learned quickly when I wished.

He went out to his appointment with King Genod and I took myself off with Galti to bash around some more with the rudis.

Galti was quick and agile, clever with the shortsword. His chunky body was made for sharp in-fighting. His broken-nosed face with the scar over the left eye danced before me as I parried and shifted and swung and withdrew. I found myself realizing that in my contemptuous dismissal of that boastful title, Sea-Zhantil, I had allowed something of the old feelings about the Krozairs of Zy to come to the surface. The Krozairs of Zy had thrown me out and declared me Apushniad. It seemed that Gafard did not yet know this. So why should I condemn him for taking the title, when it meant nothing, when the Krozairs of Zy no longer meant anything?

Thus thinking as I fought Galti with the rudis I was aware of a blade flashing for my stomach. I found myself doing what I normally do when that happening happens. The wooden blades clashed once, my wrist turned over, my arm straightened, and Galti went backward with a thunk and a yell as the blunt wooden point punched into his belly.

"By Tangle, master! That was a shrewd blow!"

I did not reach out a hand to help him up, as I would ordinarily have done. I must think and act as a damned overlord of Magdag if I were to join their detested ranks.

"I must have slipped, Galti. That will be enough for now."

"Yes, gernu. Grodno have you in his keeping."

"And the All-Merciful, you."

He went out, casting back a look at me and rubbing his stomach. It had been a fair old thwack.

The best thing I could do now was to have the bath I had promised myself, when Gafard had been bathed before dressing, and find Duhrra and make sure he did not drink so that his brave Zairian tongue wagged too much.

My mind had been made up, my course set. I wanted nothing further to do with the Eye of the World and the tangled politics of Red and Green. I was for Valka and Delia. Some way must be found. Already I had thought up a dozen impractical schemes. A ship of the inner sea would never successfully survive the long sea-journey back home. There were no fliers. But—this maniacal King Genod would probably bring in fresh fliers from Hamal. When that happened I would steal one. This time I would let my head rule my heart. Zair, Red, Krozairs—all meant nothing to me now.

So why did I feel a continuing repugnance for this Gafard, despite his friendliness, his help of Duhrra and myself, his obvious strength and power and tenacity of purpose, the clearly evident geniality of his personality behind the grim facade of authority he must maintain in his position? He was a renegade.

He had destroyed all credence. Once a man of the Red, he was now a cringing cur of the Green.

But—Red and Green meant nothing to me now...

All this talk of the great Krozair, Dray Prescot, Lord of Strombor, had unsettled me. That was a long time ago. Now I was a Vallian and wanted to go home.

Finding Duhrra in our room with an opened bottle of Chremson I slumped into a chair and reached out my hand. Duhrra slapped the bottle in. This Chremson was not Grodnim wine; it had been looted from a sinking prize. For all his protestations, Gafard still preferred good Zairian wine.

"Good stuff, Dak."

"Go drink with moderation, Duhrra." I glared at him. "I am still concerned about you and your hook. If word comes back from the Akhram that they fitted a man with hooks and cripple-blades, and that information is joined with the novice Todalphemes' account of what transpired on the Dam of Days, we could—"

"We could find ourselves with a coil of chains about us and our tripes being drawn out! Aye! And we might also find ourselves with brands in our fists smiting down these cramphs of Magdag."

"Your black-fanged wine-spout gapes too much."

"Aye, master, you are right. I will be a good Grodnim."

I did not laugh. But the invitation was there as I said, lifting the bottle, "Then you'd be a dead Grodnim." The expression, crude and cruel, is known on Kregen as on Earth.

Later a slave summoned me over to Gafard's chambers. He was in jovial mood as his slaves disrobed him. He had been drinking and the flush in his hard face and the sparkle in his eyes told me that the drink was only a preliminary for the night's activities.

"I spend the night in the Tower of True Contentment," he said, flinging his green tunic off himself so the slaves might unlatch the mesh shirt. "But, before I go, I have great news. The king accepts you! You have an audience on the morrow. You will be gladly enrolled."

I nodded, not wishing to speak. He took that as a favorable sign, an indication I was moved with joy.

"You will do as I have done. Once I was Fard of Nowhere. Now I am Gafard, a great Ghittawrer, a rog, Prince of the Central Sea. You will take the name Gadak. It is as Gadak that you join the ranks of the Green, serving Grodno, a true Grodnim!"

Five
Zena Iztar advises me in King Genod's palace

I had been a seaman in the late eighteenth-century navy of England, Nelson's navy, and an education does not come much harder than that. I had been a slave, whipped and beaten and slaving all the hours of the day. I had been a prince, living in luxury, a king, even, leading my ferocious warriors to victory.

Also, I had been a spy, acting a part to steal away secrets from a hostile nation.

As Gafard critically appraised the preparations made for my dress and appearance, and counseled me, sagely, on how to conduct myself during the audience, I reflected that I had had enough experience to pass off this coming ordeal without trouble.

But for all my protestations to myself, for all my newly won wisdom, for all my concern lest I had lost that old cutting edge, I did feel the dangers ahead. I might break out with a furious roar of "Zair! Zair!" and go on bashing skulls until they hacked me down and dragged me out by the heels.

I might.

There was too much at stake for me to allow myself that luxury.

My island Stromnate of Valka, a part of the empire of Vallia, would soon be locked, I felt sure, in another bloody struggle with the evil empire of Hamal. My duty lay to Vallia. My Delia, the glorious Delia of Delphond, Delia of the Blue Mountains, awaited my homecoming. I could not jeopardize all that for the sake of the heady satisfaction of swinging my sword against the hated Green. And—I was no longer a Krozair of Zy. Why then did I fear so much what I might do?

My kingdom of Djanduin had not seen their king for many a long day. Strombor, my noble house of the enclave city of Zenicce, no less than my Clansmen of Felschraung and Longuelm, must feel deserted by me.

No.

No, I must mumble and scrape and humble myself to this maniac, this Genod Gannius.

He would never know that it was only because I had obeyed the dictates of the Star Lords on that long-ago day by the Grand Canal and saved the lives of his parents that he had been born at all. But for me he would never have been. I had brought woe to all Zairia with that action, all unknowingly, moved only by selfish aims, for I had dearly needed to continue upon Kregen...

Immense and awe-inspiring is the city of Magdag. Enormous walls defend the many harbors. Tier upon tier rise the costly houses above the waterfront. Many glittering temples rise to Grodno, and the place is forever a babblement of people about the business of a great city.

The single stupendous fact about Magdag, which marks it off from most other cities, is the incredible area devoted to the megaliths. For dwabur after dwabur they stretch along the plain, colossal blocks of architecture, striding with the insensate hunger of continual growth. Thousands of slaves and workers toil ceaselessly, forever creating new halls and courts and pavilions, raising fresh towers and cupolas to the glory of Grodno the Green. Always, in Magdag, there is building as the overlords indulge their obsessive craze. As a slave, as a stylor, I had worked there, and, too, I had been caught up in the dark mysteries revealing the reasons for this fraught building mania.

As Gafard in his preysany litter and I, astride a sectrix and riding abaft him, made our way through the crowded streets, those enormous blocks, the megaliths of Magdag, fractured the far skyline. Dominant, impressive, brooding, they lowered down over the city of Magdag.

The reception at King Genod's palace proceeded much as I had expected. There were all the usual panoply and pomp and circumstance, the frills and the rituals, the protocols. We were escorted through court after court, up marble stairways, and through immense arches in the tall pointed fashion of Grodnim. Everywhere stood guards, ramrod stiff, on duty, only their eyes moving as they watched every arrival and departure. They wore a variety of fancy uniforms, and I stored away details of armor and weaponry against future need.

The chamberlains in their green tabards and golden wands went before us. Trumpeters pealed a blast as we passed that was designed, I felt damned sure, to make the suppliants to the throne jump out of their skins with fright. On we went and, at last, came to the anteroom to the reception chamber. Like many of the palaces of Kregen of which I had knowledge, this Palace of Grodno the All-Wise contained a maze of rooms and chambers and secret ways. I held myself erect and I looked about openly, as would be expected; but I had loosened my longsword in the scabbard and my right hand remained limp and flexed, ready for instant action.

Trumpets pealed again, the anteroom doors were flung back, and preceded by the chamberlains, Gafard and I marched into the gleaming brilliance of the reception chamber.

Light, color, glitter. The sight of waving fans, bare shoulders, silk and furs, armor of iron and steel, and everywhere the green, that green, shining and refulgent, here in the reception chamber of King Genod Gannius of Magdag.

Designed to impress, the chamber weighed down on my spirits. What was I, who had once been of Zair, doing here, even if the Krozairs of Zy had rejected me?

The device of the lairgodont appeared in many places. Guards with spears and swords, in glittering mail swathed in green robes, stood dumbly along the walls. I marked their helmets. Atop each burnished helm rose the sculpted form of a lairgodont, in the round, fashioned of silver, shining and winking in the light streaming through the clerestory above. The artist who had created the master image had caught all the violent, vicious character of the lairgodont, portraying him with a half-turned head so the wicked fangs in that gap-jawed mouth showed prominently. The body scales were delineated to perfection, the spiked tail curled high and menacingly, the skull-crushing talons gripped like vises of death.

We marched down the marble length of floor to the throne at the far end. There were three thrones and in the center, higher throne, sat King Genod.

Our studded sandals rang on the marble.

Gafard presented a formidable picture of a fighting-man, loaded with honor and wealth, harsh and cruel, superb in his strength.

I, this same Gadak, marched a half-pace to his left rear. Over the mail shirt he had given me I wore a white robe well splashed with the green decorations, with a green sleeveless jacket embroidered in silver over that, the Genodder scabbarded high on my right side, the longsword swinging from a baldric at my left.

Past the watching lines of guards we marched, past the crowds of courtiers and officials and high officers, past the clustering women who arranged, every one, to wear their flaunting green feathers in ways individual to each. The light streamed in above, the mass of gems and feathers and precious metals formed a chiaroscuro of brilliance, and over all the hated green prevailed.

We halted where a golden line in the marble pavement indicated the distance by which we must be separated from the king and his magnificence. I halted, still that half-pace to Gafard's rear, and the chamberlains wheeled to the side and stood, their heads bent, facing the throne. Deliberately, I looked at the smaller thrones.

The right-hand chair of gold held the small, shrunken body of a man I judged to be well past two hundred, well past the age he should have gone to the Ice Floes of Sicce or, in his case, up to sit in glory on the right hand of Grodno in the green radiance of Genodras. His role, I judged, would be that of court wise man, perhaps wizard, and his lined, pouched face and those dark darting eyes, like lizard eyes, confirmed the shrewd intelligence of the fellow. His frail body was so smothered in green and gold no indication of his figure was possible; I fancied he had little longer to spend on Kregen.

In the left-hand chair sat— My breath sucked in and I forced my ugly old face to remain a carved chunk of mahogany.

Oh, yes, I knew her.

She had changed since I had last seen her. Plumpness had softened the lines of beauty in her face, making her appear more petulant than ever. But she remained superbly beautiful, still lithe and lovely. Her dark hair had been dyed the fashionable green. Her kohled eyes regarded me and I kept my face blank. The last words we had exchanged—so long ago here in Magdag as my old vosk-skulls surged forward to the victory that was surely theirs, that victory so cruelly denied—had been words of anger and unfulfilled yearning. She had said I looked ridiculous, standing there with an old vosk skull upon my head. She had slashed at my face with her riding crop, and I had ducked and the blow had glanced harmlessly from the vosk-skull helmet.

The princess Susheeng.

Oh, yes, I knew her.

Would she know me?

How she had recoiled when she had learned I was a Krozair of Zy, the Lord of Strombor!

I stood dumbly and looked away, daring in the parlance of the overlords of Magdag to lift my eyes to the radiance of the king.

He was a man, this king Genod. I saw at a glance the fire in him, the fierce energy, the deep-banked fires of genius that could flame and flash as he led his men, driving them, leading them, inspiring them with all the magnetism of his powerful personality. And yet in those deep dark eyes I saw the callous cruelty of a leem. I saw in the bladelike nose, the arrogant jut of jaw, and the thinness of the lips signs that, brush them aside as you will, denote the man who puts himself and his own purposes always foremost in all he does.

He sat brooding upon us, and all the gaudy glitter of his clothes and jewels and arms paled beside the sullen power of that face.

"Lahal, Gafard."

"Lahal, majister."

That was all, between these two. Yet I swear I understood a little more of the bond between them. Master and servant, brain and tool, they complemented each other. Between them they could take the inner sea and wring it dry.

The princess Susheeng, who had once knelt weeping, beseeching, supplicating before me, naked but for the gray slave breechclout, did not move. I flicked her a quick glance and saw no outward change in her demeanor. It had been a long time, and that notorious Krozair Brother, the Lord of Strombor, was long dead and gone to his grave. And, perhaps I, too, had changed over all those years.

Also, Gafard's shadow from the clerestory windows fell across me, and my green silken turban wound around the plain iron helmet draped half across my face. I breathed more easily.

Impossible to imagine she would recognize in this new renegade seeking admission to the king's armies a man she had once known so long ago and who was now dead.

Gafard had warned me that this audience would form the public initiation. From this time on I was Grodnim. Later the king would see me privately, and there I might form a better opinion of what was required of me.

I recognized that Princess Susheeng had achieved much of her heart's desire. She and her brother, that devil prince Glycas, had planned and plotted to raise themselves even higher in Magdag. Now this storming genius Genod Gannius had appeared on the scene and had led his armies in triumph over Magdag and ruled here in the city of megaliths. And he had chosen Susheeng as his consort. She, at least, had achieved much.

The thought that Glycas must be here, if he was not dead, made me realize the latter alternative to be far more preferable.

The short ceremony of admission was about to begin.

The chamberlains unhitched the Genodder from the high belt and carried it toward a Chuktar, a Chulik, who stood enormous and impressive in armor and green. He took the sword.

After some mumbo-jumbo, the Genodder would be blessed by the priests, waiting in their green robes at the side, the king would kiss it, and I would receive it back, to kiss it and so hang it once more upon my person. The admission would have been completed.

So I stood there, waiting for the next move in this charade.

No one moved.

No one stirred.

I looked hard at the king. His right hand was half lifted in the sign to begin. That hand did not move, did not waver, did not tremble. The old wise man's mouth was half open. That mouth neither opened nor closed. Susheeng's hand turned at the wrist and fondled a golden brooch upon her breast. Nothing moved.

So I knew.

Not a sound rose from the mass of courtiers in the bright reception chamber, not a person moved.

I shuffled my feet and turned around, nastily, to face the tall double doors. Now, I said to myself, now what does she want?

Zena Iztar walked in through the opened double doors and past the lines of petrified people. She looked, as always, supremely imposing. She wore her crimson and scarlet and golden robes, with a narrow green sash, and the jewels flamed from her to drown in magnificence the suddenly tawdry splendor of King Genod's glittering reception chamber.

She halted a little way off from me. She shook her head.

"Dray Prescot!"

"What do you want, Zena Iztar?"

"I seek to know what you do here."

"It is obvious."

"Not to me, not to the Star Lords, not to the Savanti."

"Then are they—and you—of little wit."

That calm face, imperious, proud, beautiful yes, all those things, but also maternal and wise and sorrowing, did not smile. Again she shook her head and the jewels of her headdress flashed and sparkled. "If we used our wits, as you suggest, we might believe you did an evil thing here."

"Of course it's evil!"

A tiny line dinted between her eyebrows.

I said, "We have met three times, Madam Ivanovna, Zena Iztar. Do you not yet understand I am an evil man?"

"Yet were you chosen by the Savanti and after they cast you off, by the Everoinye, the Star Lords."

"That was not of my seeking."

"Yet were you chosen."

I wasn't fool enough to ask why I had been chosen. The Savanti, those superhuman men of Aphrasöe, the Swinging City, selected many men from Earth and subjected them to a test and so, accepting them, trained them to become Savapim and go forth upon Kregen to uphold the dignity of apims, of Homo sapiens. I had been found wanting and so had been kicked out of paradise. I had fought and worked and created my own paradise upon Kregen. All I held dear lay with my Delia. The Star Lords used me when they willed for their own ends. The reasons behind the selection of myself were obvious; the ramifications of the conflicting desires of others were the causes of the way my life had gone upon Kregen. I had no stupid delusions that I was in any way special, destined for a great and glittering fate in this world four hundred light-years from Earth.

"I warned you, Pur Dray," said Zena Iztar, "that you would not be allowed to leave the Eye of the World."

"I am no longer Pur Dray."

"That is sooth. But I would like you to become Pur Dray again, once more to take up your rightful place as a member of the Krozairs of Zy."

"I'm finished with all that!"

"You will never leave the inner sea until you do."

All along, all during the time of my boasting and planning, when I had ridden to Magdag, when I had taken the argenter, all the time, I must have known—had known—that I could not leave the Eye of the World. Those vast and implacable forces operating outside of the time and space I knew held me fast caught. Until what they desired occurred I must remain here, a free man within the confines of the inner sea, but imprisoned here as I had been imprisoned on my own Earth.

"The Krozairs of Zy mean nothing to me now. I am Apushniad. Had you forgotten?"

"I do not forget important things so lightly."

"It's not important! Not any longer!" I was shouting. "I have put the Krozairs behind me, cast them off, shed them as a snake sheds a skin. There are other places of Kregen I hold more dear."

She bent her gaze upon me. "As a snake, you said..."

"Well, then? I am evil, so a snake will serve. Although I detest the things, even though they live according to their natures."

"The man of your Earth called Shakespeare had a word for your conduct now, Pur Dray."

"He had a word for everything."

"And I have a word for you. You are held here. When you are once more a Krozair of Zy, then perchance you may return to your Valka—"

"And Delia?"

She put one long white finger to her lips. Those lips, red and soft, parted and I caught the gleam of white teeth. She cared for herself, this Zena Iztar. "You know your wife. You know her mettle. She is safe, as happy as she will ever be without you—poor soul!—yet will she risk all to find you again."

"And you condemn her to that!"

She was very brisk about that. "I condemn no one to anything. Men and women have suffered since the beginning and, assuredly, will suffer until the end."

"You told me I would face a choice, a hard choice—"

"Not this petty business, serious though it may be." She brushed my words aside. "The choice will come later. Also, I said that even Grodno might play a part, that stranger things have happened."

"I remember. That was the first time, in my chambers in London, before the séance—"

"And when I saw you for the second time, by the banks of the Grand Canal, I warned you afresh. You have a part to play. I would you would play it with all your heart."

"When I am parted from Delia, that I cannot do."

"I see that, and I believe it. Then I say this to you: you must pursue the path with every part of you that you can. Put as much of yourself into your struggle as you can possibly spend. I know whereof I speak. I salute you as Pur Dray."

I nodded my head at the thrones. "And if Susheeng recognizes me?"

"I do not think the—the princess Susheeng will know you. For her the Eye of the World revolves about the king. And she will not wish the king to know she once abased herself to you and that you spurned her."

"Aye. She didn't relish that, by Vox!"

"But you did?"

I flicked up my evil old eyes to glare at her. "Sharp, Madam Zena Iztar! No, I do not think I relished seeing a silly hulu make a fool of herself. I do not think I took pleasure from that. But had I done so, I could have understood myself passing well."

"I have no more to say to you now."

I knew that in a moment she would walk off and the silent, motionless people all about would wake to life and the ceremony would proceed. Already the Chulik Chuktar, he who held my shortsword, had the piece of red cloth extended, still and unmoving. There were very many things I wished to ask this woman, and every time she sidestepped them and we got into an argument. I said, "Not the Star Lords, not the Savanti, then who, Zena Iztar?"

She saw my eyes and looked where I looked and saw the scrap of red cloth in the fingers of the Chuktar.

"They will make you—"

"Yes, I know."

"And it will mean nothing?"

"Nothing."

"Remember what I have said. Your only way out. Remember."

"But—tell me who you are and why—" But she was walking away with that lithe swinging gait, going out the doors. She had passed along all that long expanse of marble with supernatural speed; yet she appeared to be only walking naturally. The double doors closed of their own volition—or so it seemed. She was gone. The piece of red cloth in the Chulik Chuktar's fingers jerked as he finished ripping it from his pocket. He held it up, ready for the king's signal.

Silver trumpets pealed. The high room filled with the sigh and murmur of hundreds of people gathered together to witness the repudiation of the Red and the acceptance of the Green. The king finished making his signal.

So the sorry charade was gone through, when I spat on the red cloth—it was an old swifter flag—and trampled on it. I made various promises which, as they were made in the name of Grodno, meant nothing—and all the time I heard those ominous words clanging about in my vosk skull of a head.

"To leave the inner sea—you must become a Krozair of Zy!"

Six
Gadak the Renegade rides north

"Such plans the king has!" said Gafard, guiding his sectrix past a broken tree stump in the forest trail. "Such plans, Gadak, as gods must surely dream!"

I wasn't fool enough to point out that the king was no god.

"You may rest assured, gernu, that I will do all I can to help the king." I looked at him as he rode, a tall, strong robust man with that iron profile eager and aimed always for the heights. I decided to take a chance. "I think, gernu, all I can for the king—after you."

He turned his head to regard me. His Zairian face glowered. Then the sheer infectious bubbling of his good spirits broke down that overlaid Grodnim severity. "Aye, Gadak—I know what you mean, and I joy in it, for that is why I chose you. But, for all our good and health, never say it again."

"Your orders, my commands, gernu."

"Remember it!"

We rode for the northern mountains. We rode for battle. The leem-sheads—outlaws—had allied themselves with the barbarians of the north and King Genod had arisen in his wrath and dispatched his favorite general to put down the disorders and to drive the barbarians back away from Magdaggian land and to hang all the leemsheads he could lay his iron hands on.

At the least, I had not, for my first task, been called upon to fight against Zairians.

A sizable little force we were, a full ten thousand warriors, led by the overlords of Magdag. And, leading them, a renegade, this Gafard, the King's Striker.

I wondered just when the moment would come when I would have to strike him down.

That, it seemed to me then, was the only course left open to me.

The reasons why he had taken to me, helped me, secured my admission as a Grodnim to the service of the king through him, were perfectly plain. He had many enemies. Many and many a proud overlord of Magdag hated and despised this upstart renegade. That would be inevitable. So he looked for friends, men he could trust, allies in whom he could repose confidence. And of all his friends, bought by bribes and high office and the ear of the king, none would be more faithful than men like himself, once of Zair and now of Grodnim, traitors, turncoats, renegades.

One very simple and effective way of ensuring their loyalty had been spelled out to me by Gafard himself.

"My name is anathema to all Zairians. They know of me only too well. Rest assured, Gadak; your name also has been passed to the king and his nobles in Sanurkazz, to the Krozairs, to the Red Brethren. There is no return for us. Now we are of the Green. I do not believe you plan treachery against me, for I am your good friend and master; but think what will be your fate should you return to Zairia."

Well, that was the rub. That kind of fate did not bear contemplation, and yet according to Zena Iztar it must be dared. How arrogant her display of power, there in the sumptuous reception chamber of King Genod! She had chosen her moment well. How clearly she had shown me my own puniness, the driveling paucity of all men, of Red and Green, here in the inner sea!

There was the other side of this coin of forwarding names of renegades. The Grodnims kept long lists of the names of Zairians who had wounded them. These rolls had been diligently searched and no record of one Dak of Zullia had been found thereon. Gafard had shown his relief.

"Had they found your name on the rolls, Gadak, you would have had to answer for your crimes against Grodno, after you had renounced Zair and taken the Green. The secular and the divine laws catch you between them, like Tyr Nath and his hammer!"

He also took the opportunity to tell me, in a strange tone of voice, that not one of the names on the Grodnim Rolls of Infamy bore a longer list of crimes than the name of Pur Dray, Krozair of Zy, the Lord of Strombor.

His attitude puzzled me. It seemed that he admired this Pur Dray and tried to emulate him from the Green side of the inner sea. More than once he used expressions that I could only construe as envy of the renown and prowess of that foremost corsair of the Eye of the World. "Yet he is dead and gone these many years," he said, as though ramming home a debating point.

We rode together near the head of the army, with a scouting force well ahead and covering parties of sectrix-men to the flanks. The flaunting green banners flew over us and the silver trumpets pealed ever and anon to give orders. In a long toiling column the infantry marched, men of many races, with the varter artillery spaced out, and at the rear trundled the strings of calsanys packed so heavily it was a marvel they could walk. Carts rumbled, harnessed to dour and shaggy krahniks, that special kind of tiny chunkrah, and following all that came the camp followers.

There appeared to be no quoffas, that large and patient draft animal of the Outer Oceans lands. The cavalry right out ahead in the scouting party rode the four-legged hebra, a saddle animal recently adopted from those very barbarians we marched out to chastise. Although not as heavy and stubborn as a sectrix, and that beast, as I have indicated, is barely up to the work imposed on it of carrying a mailed man, the hebras were quicker and more spirited. The whole *trix* family of six-legged saddle animals is not much to my liking: the sectrix of the inner sea; the nactrix of the Hostile Territories and elsewhere; the totrix of Vallia and Pandahem and Havilfar. I prefer the zorca, the superb four-legged, close-coupled nimble-footed animals combining marvelous fire and spirit with an endurance topped only by the legendary vove.

But all the same the hebramen cavorted about in fine style and could whoop up a rousing gallop to go haring away to investigate every plume of smoke or wisp of dust, every knoll and defile on the line of route.

We had left the inner sea far to the rear, marching north northeast. We had crossed the River Dag twice as it curved in one of its huge lazy arcs in its long journey from the distant mountains of The Stratemsk. The enormous river effectively contained the immediate hinterland north of the inner sea. There were many other rivers and mountains; none reached the size of the River Dag and The Stratemsk.

Our march would take us for the best part of a hundred and forty dwaburs. We would cross the River Daphig, which flows southwest from the Mountains of Ophig and joins the River Dag almost due north of Magdag, a hundred dwaburs away. At the junction stands the important trading city of Phangursh. We would cross the River Daphig close under the Mountains of Ophig, some hundred dwaburs east northeast of Phangursh.

Depending on the difficulty of the way and the feet of the swods, the journey might take as much as a month of the Maiden with the Many Smiles.

The camp followers were not allowed to impede our progress. If they could not keep up that was their business.

Among the leaders of the camp followers a huge and ornate palankeen, a veritable house slung between thirty-two preysanys, swayed along. The drapings were of gold and green silk; the curtains were kept always tightly drawn. Beautiful apim and Fristle slave girls served the occupant of the palankeen. No lewd soldier eyes would ever behold the glories of the fair occupant. Every night a gorgeous, sumptuously large tent was set up in a reserved space, marked out and guarded by Gafard's personal bodyguard. Every night he would bathe and change into crisp clean clothes, smothered with jewels, adorn himself with scents, and so, perfumed and handsome under the moons, would go into this magnificent tent and the flaps would be let down and no one would see him until reveille.

As we rode in the long journey he took more and more to calling me up to ride at his side. I was uneasy. This sign of favor marked me among his retinue. Duhrra accompanied me and we slept lightly in our little two-man tent at night when we were not on guard duty.

Gafard summed it all up in a phrase. "I need men like myself, men I can trust, about me. I see in you, Gadak, a man who can go far. Your loyalty is what I ask."

I assented with the usual words. But I knew well enough that he had other men in his retinue who would dispatch me without a qualm if I angered him. Autocratic, absolute power—well, I knew all about those baubles and the paths they led a man's feet into.

For my own good, perhaps, my periods of absolute power on Kregen had been heavily broken up by periods when I was the recipient of harsh authority. Although, as you know, I react with vicious hostility to most forms of authority when they are manifestly unjust.

We crossed the River Daphig at last, a brownish swirling flood running through eroded banks, and pressed on into the disputed territory. We had long left the cultivated areas behind, the enormous factory farms of Magdag, the immense pasture lands, the vast expanses of head-high grasses. Now we ventured into a sparser land, broken, where water became precious. Our goal was an outpost from which we would seek out the leem-sheads and the barbarians after we had rested and recouped.

That night Gafard said to me, "I hunt on the morrow, Gadak. You will ride with me."

"Your orders, my commands, gernu."

"Aye."

Of his immediate retinue there were a number of men, not all apim, with whom I rubbed along, quelling my distaste for the Green, consoling myself with the reflection that I planned for the future when the Red might once more rise.

On that morning Gafard rode out hunting. With him went five of his favorite officers, two women, and me, Gadak.

The beaters, simple swods earning a few obs, ran ahead crying up the game, and we rode slowly along after. We all carried the short simple bow of the inner sea. There were, I had noticed, no Bowmen of Loh among the mercenaries of the army. And another thing I took note of—this little army was composed of overlords to command, of mailed men-at-arms to obey and act as cavalry, and of mercenary swods, cavalry and infantry, some mailed, some not, some apim, some not. There was not a single sign of the superb fighting army created by Genod Gannius on the model set him by the slave phalanx of Magdag.

We rode along, bright and glittering under the lights of the Suns of Scorpio. I rode easily, looking about for quarry. We hunted what there was to find, for some would offer good eating and the others would offer the challenge of predators disturbed in their own hunting grounds.

Presently I found I had trended to the left, going through a rocky defile where the sand puffed beneath my sectrix's hooves. A shout from the rear brought back my attention.

Gafard rode up with one of the women, sitting her sectrix in the fashion that told me she was a rider, for all she wore a long green robe concealing her and—most unusual in Turismond—a heavy green veil.

Loh is the continent of secret walled gardens and veiled women.

I guessed this woman to be Gafard's paramour, the woman of the sumptuous palankeen and luxurious tent. He made no offer to introduce me, and, with a bow, I went to fall in at the tail.

"Ride with me, Gadak."

So I reined in to his left. The veiled woman rode on his right, which is a privilege given to very few. I disliked anyone walking or riding on my right.

Even out hunting he could not desist from talking.

"The king's plans, Gadak! I tell you, with our army we can sweep the southern shore of all the Red! We can turn the whole inner sea Green."

"If that is Grodno's wish it will surely come to pass."

"You have not seen the army of the king. This is a mere rabble, a mercenary host hired to put down the leemsheads and barbarians. Down on the southern shore—that is where the battles are."

I risked a question.

"And Shazmoz?"

Shazmoz, one of the last frontier seaport fortresses of Zair, had been heavily besieged. Pur Zenkiren, a Krozair Brother, now broken because of ill health and disappointment, held it against impossible odds.

He made a gesture of irritation. "It holds, still." The woman remained silent, but I knew she listened. "That old devil Pur Zenkiren holds the city. His days are numbered. Prince Glycas leads the army on toward the east, on to the fortress of Zy, and on to Holy Sanurkazz itself."

So that was where the evil rast Glycas had got to...

I did not venture to ask why, if Gafard was the king's favorite, he was not down there, leading this formidable army. Perhaps the king preferred him closer to hand.

We walked the sectrixes slowly, hearing the calls and shrill hunting horns of the beaters ahead and to our right. We were for the moment alone. Gafard went on talking.

"The king has fashioned an army like no other upon the inner sea—save for a contemptible slave army fashioned by this Pur Dray." Perhaps this would explain his obsession with the Lord of Strombor. I had learned that Genod Gannius, fruit of that Gahan Gannius and the lady Valima whom

I had saved at the Grand Canal, hailed from Malig, a powerful but small fortress city of the northern coast some twenty dwaburs along from the Akhram. That explained the presence of his parents there on that fateful day so long ago. All that area lay under the sway of Magdag, the city of the megaliths. Even the important conurbation of Laggig-Laggu, near twenty dwaburs up the Laggu River and twenty dwaburs from Malig, owed allegiance to the king in Magdag. It also explained how I, knocked on the head and captured by overlords, had been shipped to Magdag. They took tribute of everyone for dwaburs about their city.

Gahan, it seemed, had been in Magdag when I had led my old slave phalanx of vosk-skulls against the overlords. He had seen and he had remembered. The old king had been only too thankful that this dangerous insurrection had been crushed. He, like the Magdaggians, put his trust in mailed men riding sectrixes, armed with the longsword.

So Gahan had experimented and fashioned an implement. But it had been his son, Genod, who with all the ardent fire of youthful genius had seized on the implement and turned it into the most formidable fighting machine yet seen, who had used it to take Laggig-Laggu, to overturn the mercenary hosts of Magdag, to humble the overlords, and, eventually, to make himself king, the All-Powerful, the Revered, the Holder of Men's Hearts.

I knew that fighting machine. The solid ranks of armored pikemen, the halberdiers and swordsmen in the front ranks, the wedges of crossbow-men shooting in their sixes. And, because the fighting-men of Segesthes and Turismond commonly derided the shield, the shield-protected phalanx could simply march forward and topple all the mailed chivalry sent against it.

"It was this same Pur Dray, the Lord of Strombor, who created the first phalanx. He was defeated and slain. And Genod Gannius now rules in Green Magdag."

"But suppose," I said, feeling the emotions in me boiling up in a rage comical and ludicrous, "this same Dray Prescot was not slain?"

He reined in his sectrix with a lunging thump of hooves.

"What mean you?"

"Only, gernu, is it certain sure he was slain?"

He eyed me. He licked his lips above the black beard.

"No," he said, at last, reluctantly. "No, it is not certain."

"And has there been no news of him since?"

He smiled, that ironic half-smile. "I can say what is common knowledge, that men tell stories of two Krozairs of Zy who claim this Dray Prescot as their father."

How my heart leaped!

"And do they speak false?"

He flicked the reins and kicked in his heels. "Who is to say what is false and what is real? I would that it was true, though, by the Holy Bones of Genodras!"

"Aye," I said. "So that we might go up against this great Krozair and measure swords with him."

"Not so, Gadak!" He spoke too sharply. He saw my expression and kicked in, harder, and sent his sectrix bounding off. The woman spurred up, also, and raced after him. I was left looking at their flying animals, and their tensed bodies, their capes flying, and wondering.

Well, there are none so blind as will not see. But, by the Great and Glorious Djan-kadjiryon, how could I be expected to see then?

I shook up the reins and cantered after them, the sectrix's six legs going in that damned ungainly lumber. The hunting horns had shrilled and died; the cries of the beaters dwindled and faded to silence. The sectrix lumbered along. I heard a scream. I rammed in my heels and we picked up speed and came galloping out onto a scene that in all its ugly drama made me furious and, had I known it then, would have made me go cold with horror.

Gafard had shot cleanly and had dismounted to dispatch his kill, a small tawny-colored plains ordel. The hunting lairgodont had caught him totally unprepared. The sectrix had wrenched free of its reins and bolted. The woman's sectrix, equally terrified, bolted also and bore her off. After that first scream, which I suspected had been ripped from her when Gafard and she had first seen the lairgodont, she remained silent, wrestling to keep her beast under control.

Gafard stood there, his longsword out, his feet spread apart. Dust puffed as the lairgodont drew itself up ready to charge.

Not so much large in their strength, the lairgodonts, as vicious and quick and damnably difficult to kill. Scaled and clawed, sinuous as to neck and back, with those skull-crushing talons and those serrated, steely fangs in the gap-jawed mouth, the lairgodont presents a terrifying spectacle of feral horror.

Scarlet gaped the fanged mouth of the lairgodont. Pricked ears lay back on its scaled head. Hissing, it advanced, one taloned claw after another. That long forked tail rippled high. When that tail straightened and became a rigid bar...

I was minded to let Gafard, the renegade, go to his fate unmourned.

I knew I could not make the sectrix advance any farther. It pawed the ground, trembling, arching its neck and shrilling in fear. Hastily, I dismounted and hitched the reins to a projecting rock. If I was slain the sectrix would provide a fine second course.

Yes, Gafard, arch-traitor, a man who had betrayed the Red of Zair, yes, why not? Why not let him be pitched to the Ice Floes of Sicce under the fangs and talons of this vicious monster?

The bow in my hands spat four times as fast as I could draw string and let fly. The four arrows struck. Two bounced away, broken. The third penetrated one staring eye. The fourth took the lairgodont in the belly, for it leaped with the shock, not charging. I lugged out my longsword and ran in, yelling.

"Hai! Lairgodont! Your dinner is this way!"

It whipped about so that Gafard went into its blind side. Then its forked tail lashed sideways and knocked Gafard head over heels. There would be no support from him, then...

What an onker I was! Charging into this mess when I should have wheeled my mount away and let nature take its course.

"The ordel is not yours this day, my friend," I said, and I leaped.

Seven
The Lady of the Stars

I leaped.

The longsword is a cruel weapon.

Even this longsword, this Ghittawrer blade Gafard had allowed me to keep without comment, could do its work with cunning and smashing power in the hands of a Krozair Brother.

And, as I leaped, I even shouted: "Hai! Hai!"

The sword licked across the beast's near foreleg and almost severed it, crunching into bone. I leaped nimbly away. The tail hissed above my head. Again I leaped and as the vicious head struck at me so I came down and went on, rolling, to come up with the sword blurring for the other eye. The eye vanished in a gout of blood and slime. A blow like—well, a blow like a ripping slash from lairgodonts talon—raked down my side. I thanked Opaz I wore mail this day, even for hunting.

I was knocked over and flying, landing in a spout of dust. I heard Gafard's yell, feeble and coming from a long way off.

Somehow I jerked the sword up and thrust and the lairgodont screeched and hissed and drew back. Blood flecked its snout above the fanged mouth. I got to my feet, drew in a breath, cocked the blade. Then, again, I leaped.

A clawed leg lashed blindly at the sound. The beast's other leg, half severed, collapsed. It toppled forward. I was able to brace myself, feel the ground under my feet, my legs hard, and swing the blade with full force. Full force from all that length of steel...

The lairgodont hissed once. Its head hung askew. Blood spouted from the hideous gash in its sinuous neck. It tried. Yes, it tried. Incredibly vicious and tough, the lairgodont. It tried to scrabble up to get at me and so, once again, I slashed. It fell. It rolled over and blood pooled away. Its body fell flaccidly. For the space of a few heartbeats I saw its belly heaving; then it slowed and stopped.

Gafard was there. He looked ghastly.

"Hai, Jikai!" he said, and then: "My heart! My love!" He glared distraught after the bolting sectrix bearing the girl away. He staggered and gripped his side. "The pearl of my days! She is doomed!"

I looked. I saw. This lairgodont had a mate. The mate, hissing and screeching, pursued the girl in swift, agile bounds.

There was time for no words, no comment, nothing besides leaping astride my sectrix, freeing the reins, a violent dig with the heels, and a jolting, bouncing, breakneck race to save the girl from certain death.

As I went hurtling past, spouting dust, I heard Gafard yelling, but his words were lost. He called the woman of the palankeen, the woman of the tent, by the tenderest names. But not her name. The endearments might mean anything. But I knew he felt all he could ever feel for a woman and so, too, knew that if I failed I had best never return to the patronage of Gafard, the Sea-Zhantil, the King's Striker.

Head down I galloped, the neck of the sectrix outstretched. It would run for me, lairgodont or no damned lairgodont. I used the flat of my sword, all bloody as it was, on the back of the animal and it responded gallantly. We flew over the ground trailing a long plume of dust. Hard rattled the hooves of the sectrix, a drumming staccato that echoed the hoofbeats of the girl's mount. The lairgodont kept up a hissing shrill that would have unnerved, as it was designed to do, the prey on which it lived.

This Zair-forsaken risslaca was the emblem of the Ghittawrer Brotherhood founded by Genod. I cursed him, too, as I cursed everything else as I thundered along.

The thing would have to be done nip and tuck.

I gained on the risslaca as it gained on the girl. Again and again I hit the poor sectrix—and I felt sorry for the beast then—and we roared on. A sharp cry from the girl, the only one she had uttered since the first, heralded the plunging collapse of the sectrix. It went over in a sprawl of six legs and a wild confusion, dust spouting, the girl flying off to land with a crunch against rocks. I cursed for the last time, stood up in the stirrups, and swung the longsword high over my head.

We galloped madly up to the running risslaca, who was a mere half-dozen strides from the crumpled form of the girl. The long bloodily gleaming blade high above my head blazed as the head of the crazed sectrix reached the tail of the lairgodont, reached past its flank, panted and gasped alongside the very fanged head of the monster itself.

Side by side we raced those last few strides, and then the longsword fell with all the weight I could put into it.

It struck shrewdly, just abaft the head on that sinuous neck.

The shrill the lairgodont let loose rattled the stones of the hills.

I swung back with a wrench, prepared to strike again, and saw there would be no need.

The monster swerved in its dead run, collapsing, toppling, its head flopping, and skidded in a long swathe of dust on its belly before it swiveled about, its legs spread, to come to a stop, tail limp, stone dead.

I hauled up the sectrix and jumped down, keeping the reins in my left hand. I rammed the bloodied longsword into the ground and knelt by the girl.

The risslaca had sprayed blood as it skidded past. She was drenched. Her green veil was torn away. So I looked down on her as she lay there.

I saw the full firm beauty of her form in the green riding gown, splashed with blood. I saw the beauty of her face, superb beauty, a perfection of features such as is seldom seen—but I must not maunder. She opened her eyes as I gazed. Her face in all its blood-splashed purity tried to smile.

She licked her lips, those soft, sweet perfect lips.

"The monster—?"

"The lairgodont is dead, my Lady. There is nothing to fear."

"Then you—" And she raised herself, turning that imperious head to look. She saw the lairgodont. She saw me holding the reins of the sectrix, and she smiled.

"Yes," she said. "Yes, it is all right now. Hai, Jikai!"

"Perhaps, my Lady," I said. "It was a small Jikai."

Her hair was a deep glossy black, curled in the fashion of the inner sea. A shadow crossed her face and her brown eyes widened on me. She reached a small firm white hand and gripped my arm.

"My lord Gafard! He is—he is—?"

"He is safe, my Lady." I felt the enormous attraction of this girl, a sensation I could not understand or explain. I thought she would respond to a small jest. "Judging by his shouts he is very sound of wind and limb—my Lady."

She stared at me, a long, level look. "Yes. Yes—I have seen you about the camp. I think I can trust you. You are this Gadak of whom my beloved speaks?"

"I am Gadak."

"And you are—as is he—"

I interrupted, always a rash thing for a mere soldier to do when speaking with a highborn lady. "Yes, my Lady. We are both. But it does not matter—you are safe."

She was a highborn lady. I felt that. I picked her up and felt her firm and warm in my arms and so carried her to the sectrix, who stayed calm now that it could smell dead lairgodont instead of ravening lairgodont. I did not

224

wish to put the longsword all bloody back into the scabbard, even though this scabbard had not been made up for me by my beloved Delia...I noticed the way she spoke so unaffectedly of Gafard. Perhaps, after all, there was a real affection, a deep love, between them?

How painful it must be for her, then! I knew nothing of her history, but if she was Grodnim by birth, then a love for a renegade would reduce her in the eyes of her family. If she was Zairian and had been captured, perhaps made slave, then how much more painful it must be to receive wealth and privilege and love from a man who had turned his back on Zair.

I looped the bloodied longsword through a rear strap and let it dangle. If it thwacked the beast a little it would help it along. It had done well. I would revise my opinion of sectrixes in its favor. Its name was Blue Cloud, and it was expensive, a gift from Gafard.

I took the girl in my arms again and mounted up, a trick I knew well from the days when I rode with my incomparable Delia. I held the girl close to my breast, supporting her, feeling her warm, firm body against mine, and she placed her slender arms about my neck. So we rode back to Gafard.

We spoke but little, silly inconsequential stuff, for she was a great lady and the shock of her experience had not all worn off, although she affected to regard it as a mere incident. A fold of the veil tangled about her waist and the hunting gown were all of green, yet the lairgodont's blood had splattered them with red. I felt the enormous attraction of this girl, for I judged she was still very young, and the perfection of her beauty would set any man mad and inflamed with passion. Yet I felt a strange otherly feeling for her in which my own profound and abiding love for Delia formed an inseparable part. As we rode back over the dust and left the dead monster behind, I thought about the many beautiful women I have known upon Kregen and of them all—even Mayfwy and certain others—none would have moved me had I never known Delia. But this girl might have...Had I never met my Delia, then this girl, I thought, might have come in her time to take my Delia's place. And this, I thought, as I reined up, was blasphemy.

Gafard had limped out after us, raving. He had seen most of what had gone on. Like a warrior he had brought his sword with him. He was shaking. His face showed dirty gray beneath the bronze suntan.

"My heart! My heart!" He limped forward, desperate.

I set the girl upon the ground and she tottered.

"My beloved!" she cried.

Gafard dropped his longsword. The gleaming blade and the ornate hilt encrusted with jewels, all the symbolic power of the weapon, went into the dust. He took the girl in his arms. They held each other close. I walked away.

Yes, I thought, yes, there is genuine love here.

I, a grim old fighting-man, can understand love.

After a space, when I looked back, I saw that Gafard had adjusted what was left of the green veil, drawing it up to hide the glory of the girl's face. He called her his pearl, his heart, the beloved of his days. He did not use her name.

That, too, I understood.

When, after a time, others of his retinue found us, he became all harsh authority, damning and blasting, calling down the wrath of Grotal the Reducer upon the beaters. He shouted passionately for his guards to take the head beaters and flog them and if they would not die to draw out their bowels until they did. Old-snake, torture, hideous death, would be their portion for allowing for a single instant any danger to his divine beloved. He desisted in his anger against them only when the girl pleaded for their lives.

"Jikaider them!" shouted Gafard, incensed, holding the girl as she held him. "Punish them so that all may know their crimes!"

Flogging them jikaider, with a right-handed and a left-handed man to wield the lash, was horrific punishment. But Gafard was at pain to point out why he was merciful. "You deserve to be shipped out to the Ice Floes of Sicce! But my Lady of the Stars has interceded for you, and I deny her nothing within my power! Thank her, you cramphs! Her orders are my commands! Go down on your bellies, you rasts, grovel to show your gratitude to the divine—to my beloved."

The beaters flopped down, howling, crying, wailing out their gratitude that they were to be flogged jikaider.

They were flogged most thoroughly, jikaider, and that night their howls sounded uncannily over the camp, stopping the cowardly and the guilty from much rest. That vicious crisscross flogging opens up a man's back to the bone. Mere raw lumps of meat, the beaters, by morning. But they would have unguents applied and they'd be carried in litters and, after they'd recovered, would go back to the ranks. Tough, the swod of Kregen, the ordinary common warrior soldier. I wondered if they'd be paid the few obs they would have earned beating for the hunt. The beating had been of a very different kind, poor devils.

And yet, thinking that, next morning as we prepared to get under way again, I realized I'd have done exactly as Gafard had done—more, probably—if harm had come to this girl he called the Lady of the Stars.

In only a few more days we would reach the area in which our operations could start. Then it would be man's work once more. The hebramen scouting ahead kept more particularly alert, for these wild barbarians were notorious for their cunning and skill in ambush in this hard and sere region. Farther north the land of the tall forests led on and on until, at last, the land of everlasting whiteness was reached. I had no desire at all to journey there. What I did now was a part of the plan I had formed. Duhrra followed me still because I had promised him I knew what I was doing and he had had evidence of that in the past.

"We will for a time act the part of Grodnims, Duhrra of the Days. We do not fight Zairians—"

"No! Mother Zinzu the Blessed forfend!"

"Yet when we reach the Eye of the World again we will have proved ourselves of the Green. Then we may escape."

"Duh—let us crack a few skulls before that, Dak, my master."

"I am Gadak now."

"Aye! And they call me Guhrra, may Zair rot their—"

"Easy, easy. The camp has ears."

Duhrra had been about the camp, ears cocked, picking up all the scuttlebutt that forever circulates where fighting-men congregate. I wanted to know about this girl, this Lady of the Stars. There was precious little to know. The men speculated on the mysterious occupant of the palankeen and the great tent, of course, in the scabrous way of warriors. The story that had gained the most currency said that she was a Zairian, from Sanurkazz, and had been taken in a swifter by a squadron commanded by Gafard. He had found her in the aft state cabin and from that moment on no other man had seen her face.

"In a swifter?" I said. "Passing strange, for a woman to be in a swifter in action."

"It is known."

"Aye. It is known. And is that all?"

"None know her name, none know her face. Four men—trusted men—have been flayed alive by Gafard's orders for trying."

The majority of the personal bodyguard maintained by Gafard about the tent were not apims. That would greatly reduce the dangers, of course, although no sane man trusted a woman to the protection of some races of diffs. Gafard chose wisely.

The moment came to which I had been looking forward with an interest that had led me to keep Blue Cloud always in perfect condition, a bag of provisions knotted to his harness, to sleep lightly and to have the edges and points of all my weapons honed razor sharp.

The summons reached me carried by one of Gafard's aides. I went with him to the campaign tent in which Gafard dictated his orders and kept his official being. Only when he had discharged his duties would he dress and anoint himself and go to the great tent where the Lady of the Stars awaited him.

Among his retinue I had, as I have said, made no real enemies apart from his second in command. This was a certain man called Grogor. He was a renegade, also. The situation was obvious. Grogor feared lest I, the new friend of Gafard's, might oust him from his position. I had been at pains to tell the fellow that I had no intentions of doing any such thing. He had not believed me.

Now Grogor, a bulky, sweaty man, but a good fighter, motioned me into the campaign tent. Gafard sat at a folding table affixing his seal to orders and messages. He looked up and waved me to sit at the side and wait.

His stylor, a slave with privileges as a man who could read and write, was, as was common, a Relt. The Relt gathered up all the papers and their canvas envelopes in his thin arms and, bowing, backed out. The flap of the tent dropped. Gafard lifted his head and looked at me. I had not been called to ride with him since the episode of the lairgodont and the hunt.

"You have been wondering why I have been cold to you in the last few days, Gadak?"

It needed no quick intelligence to understand why. I said, "Yes, gernu."

He put his hands together and studied them, not looking at me as he spoke.

"I owe you my gratitude. I do not think I would care to live if my beloved no longer lived and walked at my side."

"I can understand that."

He looked up, his head lifting like the vicious head of a striking lairgodont itself.

"Ah! So you are like all the rest—"

There was no way out of this save by boldness.

"I saw the face of the Lady of the Stars. Yes, it is true. You have had men flayed for less. But when a lairgodont rips at one, and the green veil is already torn away, there is not much choice."

He still stared at me. He measured his words. "Have you ever seen a more beautiful woman in all the world?"

I have been asked that question—and most often by silly women seeking to gain power over me—many times, as you know.

Every time, every single time, the answer was automatic, instant, not needing thought. No woman in two worlds is as perfect as my Delia, my Delia of Delphond. Yet...

I hesitated.

He thought I feared, perhaps, to speak the truth, hesitated for the reason directly opposite to the truth.

Often, although my own feelings needed no thought to arrive at the truth, that none could compare with my Delia, I had temporized—most particularly on the roof of the Opal Palace in Zenicce. Now my hesitation held none of calculation.

I said, "The lady is more beautiful than all women—save, perhaps, for one."

He seized on that.

"Perhaps?"

"Aye. But beauty is not all. I know nothing of the lady's perfections—and I do know a lady whose perfections are unmatched, in her beauty, her spirit, her love of life, her courage, her wisdom, her comradeship, her love—"

He sat back. That small ironic half-smile flitted on his lips and vanished.

"I do not think you lie. You speak too warmly for lies."

Here there was no need for me to go on. He would decide what to do with me. If he decided against, then I would decide if he must be killed at once or if I dare leave him merely gagged and bound.

Perhaps something of those wild leem thoughts showed in my face, although I own I would have been extremely wroth had I thought that possible: perhaps he realized more than I gave him credit for at the time.

"You know little of my history, Gadak."

"I know little, gernu. Men say you were a Jikaidast. If that is so it is no wonder you always win."

His smile broadened, became genuine, warm. "Were I not so busy—with this and that—I would call for the board at once, the grand board. Yes, I was a Jikaidast, in Sanurkazz."

These Jikaidasts are a strange lot, strange in the eyes of ordinary men who love the game of Jikaida and play when they can. A Jikaidast lives only for the game. As a professional he plays to earn a living, and these men are found all over Kregen earning their living from the highest to the lowest levels. The greatest of them even aspire to the title of *San,* which is given to great savants, wise men, and wizards.

There is much to be said about Jikaida and Jikaidasts, as you will hear. The odds would be against the manner of the master's winning, not if he would win. Handicaps would be set, a simple matter of removing a powerful piece, say a Paktun or a Chuktar, or of giving the privilege of extra moves.

Gafard, the King's Striker, said, "I was known as a Jikaidast who could win after having surrendered my Pallan from the call of 'Rank your Deldars'."

I resisted the temptation to fall into the deadly trap of talking Jikaida. That way lies the engulfment of many burs of a man's life.

"You were a hyr-San, gernu. But of aught else, I know nothing."

He showed his pleasure. This was the first time I saw him as a human being apart from those traumatic moments when he had clasped his lady to him after the hunt of the lairgodonts.

"There is little to tell, as a Zairian. My home was too small, the people too small, my opportunities too small. When I fought for Zair men smiled. I was taken by the Grodnims. I did as you have done. I think the decision

229

hardened me, made of me different flesh. I am a man among men now, the keeper of the king's confidence, his Striker."

"And Sea-Zhantil," I said.

I couldn't resist that little dig. He nodded. "Aye. I value that. You know it. It was borne by a man who—" He glanced up sharply at me, and I saw he felt his own surprise.

"You were brought here to listen to me, Gadak. I tell you this because I have taken a liking to you. But treachery is rewarded by a knife in the back, just under the ribs."

"Aye. Perhaps that is all it deserves."

Again that probing look. If I was to take him seriously, for he was a mortal powerful man in his own surroundings, I would have said, then, that he was puzzled by my attitude, realizing he dealt with a man who might be of more use to him than he could have imagined.

"That is sooth." He picked up a dagger that threw scattered shards of light from the gems packing the hilt, and he twirled it as he spoke. If there was a meaning here, he was underlining it too obviously. "I am a king's man. King Genod is a wonderful man, a genius at war, commanding, powerful—he has the yrium. I do not forget that. But—" Here he again broke off and flicked the dagger into the ground. The sharp blade struck and stuck, the hilt vibrating just enough to fill the tent with leaping colors. "But he demands women. He takes women and uses them and discards them. It is his only weakness; and, for a man such as he, it is not a weakness."

"I can see that. But the princess Susheeng?"

"She carried much weight when King Genod defeated the overlords of Magdag and took the throne. She supported him and in return is his official queen—although, well, it is all in the loving eye of Grodno. I tell you this, Gadak—" He interrupted himself yet again, rising and prowling about the tent, his fierce face thrust forward. "It is all probably common knowledge. Susheeng has her powers. She must tolerate Genod's caprices. Do not whisper this in your cups, for you may wake up minus your head."

"I believe I understand, gernu. The veil, the concealment so that no man may see her face—yes, I understand."

"Be sure that if you do understand you tell no one."

I felt it was about time he eased up from this fraught excitement. And, anyway, confidences like this were damned dangerous secrets. So, to goad him, I bellowed.

"Your orders, my commands, Gernu!"

He turned on me, saw me standing bolt upright, my ugly old face blank, and he caught himself and lowered his hand.

"Yes, yes you are right, Gadak. That is the way it must be. Regulations. Just remember. I let you live even though you have seen the face of the Lady of the Stars."

"I shall not fail you."

"I do not think you will. I would have you slain out of hand, you know that. And yet I would feel sorrow were that to be so."

As I went out I said to myself, rather obviously for all it was the perfect truth, "Not half as sorry as I would be, dom!"

Eight
Concerning the mystery of the escaped prisoners

There followed a short campaign that, although viciously and bloodily fought, contained nothing of interest apart from a demonstration of the overlords' methods of maintaining order in their own lands and of dealing with incursions over their borders.

The people who lived beyond the river were mainly nomads, although cities existed as well, built by settlers in favored positions. No one knew very much of this whole vast area of Northern Turismond, and we were much less than two hundred dwaburs into a space of land stretching, it was estimated by the Todalpheme, for six hundred dwaburs to the pole.

These nomads did not remind me of my own Clansmen.

Oh, they possessed vast herds of chunkrah, and they lived in magnificent tents, and when they moved they shook the earth. I do not think the land was as rich here as it is in the Clansmen's areas of Segesthes. These folk had their ways and their customs, traditions and folklore, and pretty and fascinating it all was to me at the time, to be sure. These people called themselves the Ugas, in their various tribes, and many races of diffs formed the tribes and nations. They had no zorcas. They had no rarks. Their weapons were inferior longswords and small bows. They did have the hebra, which I have mentioned, and a form of dog I believed they called *ugafaril*—the derivation is obvious—but which the Grodnims called rasts and cramphs and all manner of obscene things, for the dogs kept watch and alerted the camps and it was damned difficult to carry out a neat smart raid.

In all this I acted my part with as good a grace as I could muster. Duhrra, rumbling like a vessel of San Evold's boiling with the cayferm, followed.

I will not weary you with the details of the campaign. We caught leemsheads who were very dreadful men with atrocities upon their heads, so that I had no compunction about dealing with them. The Ugas were another matter. But they were worthy foemen and after they caught a strong party of Grodnims and slaughtered them to a man the atmosphere eased. And, anyway, I did not see much fighting, being used by Gafard as an aide, a messenger, a trustworthy conveyer of orders and instructions.

231

One day we surprised a war party of Ugas, and Duhrra and I had a taste of the reckless charge, swinging our swords, going up and down on the sectrixes, lumbering into a bone-crunching collision with the Ugas. Hebras went down. Swords whirled. The dust rose in driven clouds. When it was all over we inspected what we had captured.

This had been a slave caravan. The Ugas required slaves, as was common over Kregen except where Delia and I had stamped out the practice, and we were happy to release a number of Grodnims who fell on their noses and upended their bottoms and gave long howls of thanks to Grodno for their rescue.

Among the slaves I saw a group of men and women with stark white hair.

I thought, as was natural, that they were Gons, that race who habitually shave their white *hair* religiously until they are bald, out of shame.

"Not so, Gadak," said young Nalgre, the son of an overlord of Magdag on Gafard's staff, and therefore one day to be an overlord himself and so a candidate for the edge of my sword. He would have been a smart young man had he worn the red. As it was, he had no chance to learn what humanity meant. "They are the Sea-Werstings. Best we slay them all, here and now, and so save trouble."

"Are they so dangerous?"

"Little you know, renegade." They liked to rub our noses in it, these puppies, when Gafard was not around. "They are a sea-people and they should be sent sailing to the Ice Floes of Sicce, by Goyt!" He half drew his Genodder, scowling at the huddled group of naked white-haired slaves, and thrust the shortsword back into the scabbard with a meaningful snap.

Later there was a chance to talk to these Sea-Werstings, for Gafard had issued orders they were not to be slain but were to be kept awaiting his pleasure.

Their language was but little different from the universal Kregish, an imposed tongue, and it would have been easy to talk with them even had I not been blessed by Maspero's coded genetic language pill given to me in Aphrasöe, the city of the Savanti.

I selected a strong man in the prime of life, who sat with bound hands and feet in a protective fashion by the side of a woman who, although not beautiful in the accepted sense, was firm of body and pleasantly faced, with a fineness about her forehead where the white hair had been cut away.

"You have fallen on hard times, dom," I said, sitting at his side and offering him a piece of bread soaked in soup. He opened his mouth sufficiently to speak, and shut it at once.

"Thank you, master. Give it to my woman."

I did so and then gave him a second piece from the earthenware bowl. I kept my weapons well away from his bound hands, just in case he had been working on his bonds.

"You are Sea-Werstings?"

He scowled. "That is the foolish name given to us by these barbarians, and by you ignorant Grodnims."

"Then what is your name, and where is your home?"

As we talked so I fed them soup-soaked bread, and gave also to the others nearby.

"We are the Kalveng. We are a seafaring folk, with havens all along the western coast of Turismond. When our long-ships breast the foam and our weapons glitter across the dark sea, then all men tremble."

"I have never been there. Is it very cold?"

He looked at me as though I were an idiot. "No more than a warrior may bear, wearing mail and wielding a sword."

"And a woman?"

"They, too, are handmaidens of Veng."

We talked more. It seemed to me the spirit of these people would not be broken by fetters and chains. Had I been a king ruling a country menaced by their depredations, I fancy I might have heeded well the advice of that young puppy Nalgre, the Magdaggian overlord's son.

This Kalveng, Tyvold ti Vruerdensmot, clearly a proud and stubborn character, told me much of the unknown lands of northwestern Turismond. In the map I roughly sketched out I indicated that coast with a mere scrawl, a line of no meaning, for the coast there had no part to play in my story then.⁶ The inner lands are riddled with vast lakes and inlets of the sea; there are fjords and rapids and marshes, a whole vast area aswarm with life and people on the move and people in their keeps and towns. As the folk of the inner sea face inward, to the Eye of the World, so the nations of the northwest hold themselves aloof from others!

"What is your name?" said this Tyvold ti Vruerdensmot.

"I am called Gadak."

He looked astonished.

"And is that all?"

"Aye."

"You do not trifle with me, for sport?"

"No. You are bound and I am free. There is no sport in that."

"I have seen it, though, when the slaves ran and the torches flew and the brands bit. You are a man with a secret."

I stood up, easily enough, and stretched my shoulders under the mail and the white tunic and the green sleeveless jacket. I looked down on Tyvold.

"And if you escaped this night... would you return home direct?"

The hunger in his face moved me.

"Aye!"

"Direct?"

233

He took my meaning. "Aye, master. Direct."

I said no more and turned away, leaving the empty bowl.

That night a thief broke into a stores tent and a quantity of food and clothing was taken. Also, in the morning, a Rapa guard was discovered unconscious but otherwise unharmed where the Sea-Werstings had been chained to stakes driven into the ground. The Sea-Werstings had vanished, every one, and a search failed to discover any trace of them. Gafard entrusted the leadership of the search party into the hands of his fellow-renegade, Gadak; and Gadak, although he searched diligently to the north, failed to find a single trace of the escaped slaves. With that, amid a smother of curses, the affair was forgotten.

As Nalgre said, lifting his manicured fingernails to the gold lace at his throat, "They do not make good slaves. We would have had to slay them, in the end." He couldn't leave it alone, for he added with selfish venom, "A fine opportunity for sport, lost!"

I did not answer, but walked away. I wondered what that cold northland of the Kalvengs was like.

When the Grodnims said the Sea-Werstings would not make good slaves I knew what they meant. Some races seem destined to be enslaved and one must fight for them and put iron in their backbones, for no man is born slave in the eyes of Zair or Opaz.

Of the diffs of Kregen, the Xaffers are a case in point.

Other races breed men and women who will not tolerate slavery, and these simply will themselves to death, or seek release at the hands of their masters in the final death. I will not speak of these races now.

And there are races of people with a stiff-necked pride that bends ill beneath the yoke. There are many of these. My fearsome four-armed Djangs will accept slavery if forced upon them; but they make their masters damned uncomfortable all the time these masters are foolish enough to enslave a Dwadjang.

I had been slave many and many a time, as you know. So had my Delia, to my shame. I wondered how my children would tolerate slavery. I had last seen my eldest twins, Drak and Lela, when they had been fourteen, just at the time when they were burgeoning into manhood and womanhood. Now they were all of thirty-six. Prince Drak ran my island Stromnate of Valka and was a Krozair of Zy, and was a powerful man. Lela had refused the offers of marriage five times—at the last count. My other twins, Segnik and Velia, would now be twenty-five years old, and I had last seen them when they'd been three, running and laughing upon the high terrace of Esser Rarioch, forever plaguing Aunt Katri, joyous, gorgeous, wonderful children; and now Segnik would have himself called Zeg and was a Krozair of Zy, and Velia had received the same education as Lela with the Sisters of the Rose and was no doubt in her turn refusing offers of marriage. I wondered what they were like now, and if I would ever see them again, and so that made all the dark powerful forces of obstinacy rise up in me.

I would play out this hand and act like a Grodnim and so use that as a springboard to escape with Duhrra and once more become a Krozair of Zy. Oh, yes, I'd set my hands to that task. I'd become a Krozair of Zy again, for only by doing that would I escape the Eye of the World and once more clasp my Delia in my arms, see my twins Drak and Lela, and my twins Zeg and Velia.

As to the Red Brotherhood of Zy—the Krozairs—I swung a Ghittawrer longsword at my waist now and wore the green and swore luridly by Grodno. Nothing mattered besides escaping and going home to Valka and my family.

When the last barbarian chief in this area had been captured and had his head removed Gafard said we would return to Magdag. A strong force would be left against future disorders. None of these Grodnims seemed to realize that the Ugas were not barbarians. There were savages in the north, we all knew that, but they lived farther off, and they cut up the Ugas cruelly. One day, no doubt, the barbarians of the northern hills would foray down south, past the tribesmen and the citizens, past the Ugas, and come rolling down to find out what pickings the Eye of the World might offer.

History and destiny follow their own paths, on Kregen as they do on Earth.

On the march south a messenger rode up on a foundering hebra and was instantly escorted to Gafard, where he rode at the head. He had remained cold to me, reserved, but not hostile. Shortly thereafter Nalgre summoned me. Gafard looked at me stonily. He had given orders that closed up a bodyguard, ready to ride.

"Orders, Gadak, from the king. We ride for Magdag and must reach there faster than the wind." He bent closer from his mount. "There is serious trouble in the inner sea. I want you at my side, for I smell treachery." He lifted himself in the stirrups, a powerful, compelling figure. He waved his sword. "We ride! On for Magdag!"

Nine
Museum pieces

The red sun of Antares, Zim, preceded the green sun of Antares, Genodras, across the heavens. A small but powerful body of men rode hard across the plain kicking dust in a straight line for the northern gate of sinister Magdag. All about on the plain stretched the megaliths, monstrous edifices, cutting enormous blocks of darkness against the radiance of the suns.

When the red and green suns passed in eclipse awful rites took place in those megalithic chambers, which only the highest of the land might see. The ordinary folk must huddle in their hovels and shudder at the wrath of Zair upon the land.

Always, Genodras would emerge from the pierced flank of Zim, and thus proclaim that Grodno still ruled.

We rode hard. The suns were drawing apart again in their cycle and were about a quarter of the way through that outward and inward movement. Our cloaks flared in the wind of our passage and our sectrixes labored with snorting nostrils, for they sensed the stables ahead and knew the journey was almost over. There was no time to reflect on the mysteries of Grodno and Zair within the spider-webbed shadowy chambers of the megaliths.

The sky held a high, drawn look, streaked with ocher clouds, and a few magbirds fluttered and cawed, whirling spots of blackness against the light. Heads low, trailing dust, we raced for the northern gate of evil Magdag.

Among our company, surrounded by Pachaks, rode a figure in armor and green robes glittering with precious gems. She was clad and accoutered like a warrior, but I could not mistake the erect, graceful carriage of the Lady of the Stars.

I was grateful that her protection had been entrusted to Pachaks. They are intensely loyal, honoring through their own system of nikobi the obligations of their hire; mercenaries whose code places them above the common herd. Two left arms has a Pachak, so that with a shield he is a formidable fighter. A long, sinuous tail equipped with a strong hand has a Pachak, so that he may slice you down from aloft or spit you clean as the blade leaps between his legs. Oh, yes, I employed Pachaks whenever I could.

There were no Rapas among our company.

The hooves of the sectrixes rang loud on the stones beneath the gate. Passing archways with that pointed Grodnim shape, we saw the alert forms of guards and watchmen, the slanting rays of the suns bright on their weapons. The echoes bounced from the yellow stone walls and the dark granite walls as we clip-clopped along. People scattered from our path. A basket of gregarians overturned and the ripe fresh fruit rolled, squishing.

Straight to the Jade Palace we rode, and Gafard, lost in thought, led us, his head sunk upon his breast and his powerful body lumbering along in time to the ungainly gait of his mount.

As in any well-run palace everything was prepared against the master's homecoming.

In the hullabaloo and uproar as slaves ran and men bellowed, Duhrra and I took ourselves off to the small chamber we had been allotted for our personal use. This lay under the roof to the rear, overlooking a courtyard where daily vast amounts of sweat were spilled by swods drilling. When Gafard needed us he would call. In the interim we spent the time arguing, as was inevitable, here in Green Magdag, about the best ways of getting back to the Reds.

I felt sure that Duhrra had either completely forgotten or had never really understood just who I was. After all, there had been only the scraps of quick conversation between Pur Zenkiren and myself, there in besieged Shazmoz, to afford any inkling that I was not the Dak I claimed to be. For Duhrra the task was simply that of escaping from Magdag and returning to the Zairian side of the inner sea.

For me, of course, there awaited slavery at a galley oar in Zairia, for I was an unfrocked Krozair, Apushniad.

After we had bathed and eaten a huge meal and were thinking about emptying a few pots, the call came.

I took care to dress in my mail and to bear my arms as I followed the Relt messenger along the corridors and so down to Gafard's private suite, secluded in a separate wing of his palace with the windows cunningly angled so that the occupants might not be overlooked. The suns had long set and She of the Veils rose over the steep roofs and the flat roofs, set alternately in pleasing patterns. The long shadow of the Tower of True Contentment lay across the last corridor. The shimmer of golden light at each end burned unfocused. The Relt hurried on, silent on his foofray satin slippers, and I in my mail clumped on after in my studded sandals.

This was not a private audience. A number of Gafard's chief officers crowded the anteroom to his study. Grogor, of course, was there, to favor me with a scowl as I entered. The others looked up without speaking and then went back, as I considered, to biting their nails. They knew far more than I of the intrigues festering in Magdag; whatever news Gafard had brought back from the king was not good. The close, oppressive atmosphere as we sat in silence and waited told me that.

We were called in at last and trooped through the green velvet-draped doorway and so came into Gafard's study. There were books here, papers and charts, maps and the paraphernalia of the fighting-man by both sea and land. Also on separate tables lay spread out six separate games of Jikaida, all in different stages of progress. Gafard waved us to seats.

We sat, expectantly, waiting for him to speak.

"Gernus," he began, and so we knew this was a serious business, for he used the usual euphemism, calling us lords. They do not go in for *koters* and *horters* in Green Magdag. They fancy *kyrs* and *tyrs* are below their gernus—as, indeed, they are—their overlords of Magdag.

"There is serious work afoot. I have to tell you the king is highly displeased with some of the recent actions over against the rasts of Zairians. Shazmoz is not taken. Shazmoz is relieved."

There was a stir at this, a buzz, a murmur of speculation.

"Yes, well may you be astonished. For was not Shazmoz closely ringed, besieged, due to fall like a ripe apple? And now the king, may his name be revered, tells me that not only is Shazmoz undefeated, it is relieved, and the cramphs of the Red press on to the west."

I own I felt perky at this news. Mind you, I had given up any concern over the outcome of the internecine strife between the Red and the Green; but I own I felt a lift of the heart at this news.

"What, gernu, of Prince Glycas?" Grogor, Gafard's second in command, spoke up.

"Aye, well may you ask, Grogor! The king has heard ill words of Prince Glycas, who commands our armies there against Zair. But the disaster cannot be put down to him. He was to the last, pushing ahead, when two things happened that deprived us of Shazmoz."

If Pur Zenkiren, who commanded in Shazmoz, was still the powerful force I had known, for all he had sadly fallen away after he had been passed over in the elections for Grand Archbold of the Krozairs of Zy, then I was not at all surprised at what miracles he might achieve.

Gafard went on speaking, and he ticked off two points on his fingers.

"One, a new, fresh strong force came up out of the hinterland and caught the besiegers of Shazmoz unprepared. They were led by a damned Zairian noble, a Roz Nazlifurn. He coordinated his thrust with the commander of their eastern army, Roz Nath Lorft."

Now I understood what Pur Zenkiren had stopped himself from saying, and I rejoiced. How the Krozairs must be laughing!

Gafard went on, "And, two, a freak tide swept away the shipping. We lost a great deal of supplies. Explanations are being sought from the Todalpheme, whose task it is to prevent such catastrophes in the Grand Canal."

I kept my hard old face straight. So the tide had reached Shazmoz and had swept away the damned Grodnim shipping! Well, that was good news. No doubt, also, the tide had created havoc on its way, and many a good man had lost a boat, a shed, a house. I felt sorrow, I felt the guilt I carried, but most of all I felt some deep pleasure that the tide I had created had not only swept away the Menaham argenters carrying King Genod's damned vollers, but had also contributed to the Zairian victory at Shazmoz.

"So we are for the southern shore, gernu?"

"Aye. We take a swifter squadron, and broad ships with mercenaries and men-at-arms. We make a landing and we strike at the rear of the combined Zairian army. The king, whose name be revered, is confident we can restore all that has been lost."

Here, then, was a task set to the hand of the king's favorite general and admiral.

Preparations were already well under way under the aegis of the king's hyr gernu admiral—his lord high admiral. He was a man past a hundred and seventy who would be only too grateful not to have to command the expedition, for he was a hedonist much given to the daily inspection of the bottoms of many glasses. He held the titular rank, to keep up the face and the pretense for the overlords of Magdag; it was Gafard, the King's Striker, the Sea-Zhantil, who held the real power.

In all the bustle, as the final details were attended to, I had to take serious stock of my position.

For Duhrra, the future was clear. The moment he reached the southern shore he would break free and rejoin his comrades. With contempt he would hurl the name Guhrra back in the teeth of the Grodnims, and as Duhrra would joyfully embrace Zair.

I said, in the privacy of our room, "The Grodnims have sent your name to Zo, the king in Sanurkazz. You are renegade."

He swelled his enormous plated chest. "Maybe so, Dak—Gadak—but I shall explain. As you have explained to me. The king will understand, for he is wise and just."

I hadn't seen King Zo in fifty years; I did not smile.

"As to his wisdom, it would be impolitic to doubt that. But his justice—you will run a mortal danger."

"I know. We both will. But I have faith in the justice of Zair."

You couldn't say fairer than that.

What I did say, and at that merely giving expression to a thought that had been building for some time, was, "And if when we were thrown down before King Zo, crying piteously for mercy, we could bring with us, in chains, this same Gafard, the renegade?"

Duhrra turned slowly to stare at me. His idiot-seeming face bloomed with blood, a flush seeping from forehead to neck. He half lifted his good left hand, and let it fall slowly to his side. His hook trembled.

"That would be a deed, by Zair!"

"Think on, Duhrra of the Days."

He surprised me.

"I hate the Green as any man of the Red must hate the Green. I do not forget my brother. All my friends who are dead and gone. But, yet—for all his villainy, I would not joy in delivering up my lord Gafard to his enemies."

I looked at him. He was sincere. He shared my thoughts.

In so many ways the early life of this Gafard—who had then been Fard—paralleled my own. From a humble birth he had faced a life completely without prospects. He had striven to improve his lot and had become a

239

Jikaidast, and a good one. Then he had fought for the Red, and fallen foul of Zairian justice—from what I gathered he had knocked the teeth out of a Red Brother—and had for a space served in the galleys and then had been taken by the Grodnims. As he had said from the moment he had changed his allegiance, aiming for the main chance, his fortunes had dramatically improved. Would I, having served a similar apprenticeship, not have embraced the Green? Was I not a newly converted enthusiast to Zair? All my early convictions remained unimpaired, merely overlaid with newer convictions of Kregen.

"No, Duhrra," I said. "He is a man, for all he is a renegade. He is very likable, for all his villainy. And, do not forget, the Lady of the Stars loves him dear."

"There must be good in him." Duhrra rubbed his hook flat over his bald head, a trick that, at first, had quite turned my stomach. Now I was used to it. He put his thoughts awkwardly into words, reverting to his old ways. "Duh—I wonder if his good outweighs his bad. A rogue, yes, but I believe his heart still belongs to Zair."

He could have said "his heart is still in the right place," but that would not have conveyed the flavor of his thoughts.

"Then," I said, "he has sent a damned lot of good Zairians up to Zim to spy out his welcome."

"That, of course, he will pay for."

For my own plans to prosper I needed something like the enormous prize that Gafard would represent. If I could haul him in at the end of a chain and dump him down in the Krozair Isle of Zy, display him a captive to Pur Kazz, the Grand Archbold, might not that win me back my place as a Brother of the Krozairs of Zy?

I believe the sight of my Lady of the Stars affected my decision, even then. I had seen her face, and talked with her, and I felt this spiritual attraction, and I felt absolutely confident she loved Gafard as he loved her. And there was the man himself, confident, hard, but likable, generous, friendly. The two halves of his personality were not any the stranger than the two halves of my own.

The thought of betraying him so basely, after his extended hand of friendship, despite all the hidden threats, sickened me.

I'd do it, of course, like a shot, for my Delia.

Nothing could remain undone for Delia.

Even this Lady of the Stars could not stand against Delia, could she...?

My unforeseen, too familiar brush with the Lady of the Stars led Gafard to appoint me to a task of some honor on Kregen. I have indicated how the banners and standards of armies and ships are regarded with deep veneration—not the tawdry bit of cloth, but the meanings the bright colors and symbols contain—and men have had their arms hacked off rather than give up the standard. This is known on our Earth, also. In certain armies men vied to carry the standard into action and when honored prepared everything for their own deaths. The honor of bearing the banner into action was so great they were prepared to give their lives, for they knew as everyone knew that the standard-bearer was the target for the most violent attack. So they would dress themselves in their full-dress uniforms, clean and smart, would go through their necessary religious observances, make their farewells of their friends, and then take up the standard and march into battle, expecting to die. Usually they were not disappointed.

Summoned to the presence of Gafard, I found him lounging in a long white silk robe, his concerns for the moment thrust aside. He had chosen one of the luxurious saloons of his palace, with padded walls and soft furnishings, mellow lamps and many potted flowers, the scents heavy in the close air. There was a great quantity of different wines from which to choose. He waved the majordomo away and beckoned me in. I wore mail and my weapons, a custom I had faithfully followed since I had turned Grodnim.

"Sit down, Gadak—wine? There is a matter I wish to tell you, and, after that, another matter."

"I await your commands, gernu."

A Fristle slave girl dressed in bangles and pearls poured wine. Gafard waited until she had finished and then waved her away. We were alone. He handed me the wine goblet; it was all of gold with great rubies set about the bowl and stem. I sipped, making the sign to him of salutation and thanks. It was Zond.

"When we used to drink this, gernu," I said, wishing to get him started on this interview, "we would say: 'Mother Zinzu the Blessed! I needed that.'"

"Those days are best forgotten." He drank quickly. He looked not so much agitated as keyed up. "You, Gadak, will carry the standard of my Lady of the Stars."

I gaped at him.

"Close your mouth, you fambly, and listen."

I shut my mouth with a snap.

"My Lady will accompany me on this expedition. She will dress and travel as a man, a great gernu. This for reasons that need not concern you. Arrangements have been made for her cabin in *Volgodont's Fang*. She will not be seen. But, as an overlord, she must needs have her deviced banner. This will be your charge."

I knew what was required of me. I bowed my head, and then looked up. "The honor is undeserved, but I will serve till death."

To a Green Grodnim, such a promise meant nothing; it was rote.

"Good." He stood up. "I have taken a liking to you, friend Gadak. After this expedition, who knows, you may well be Gadak of some honorable title. Come—there is that I would show you."

He led me toward a tall single door, which he unlocked with the bronze key on his belt, and we went through into a tall narrow room lit by lancet windows. The room flamed' with color.

Red!

Banners and standards of all kinds hung from the walls. There were stands of arms of Krozair manufacture—although there were no Krozair longswords I could see—and I looked.

"Aye, Gadak. This is my trophy room. These are the trophies of my battles and actions."

I swallowed down hard. I recognized some of the devices.

There was much there I was dismayed to see. This man, this King's Striker, had roamed the inner sea like a leem. I walked slowly along, looking up. At the far end in a small alcove stood a balass-framed glass case. The light struck across it and lit its contents. I looked.

A scrap of red cloth, not eighteen inches square, with faded gold embroidery, and, along one edge, a strip of yellow cloth. Also in the case lay what was clearly a fragment of mesh mail. Also a main-gauche…A main-gauche? The left-hand dagger was not a familiar weapon in the inner sea, for they were not rapier-and-dagger men.

I looked back at Gafard. He stood there, one hand to his beard, staring at the case with an expression I found hard to read.

"You wonder at these pitiful relics, Gadak?"

"Trophies of your first action?" I suggested, doubtful.

He smiled. "No, Gadak. My first victim sank in a bubble and all was lost." He came closer and stood looking down at the red cloth, brooding. "No. These are precious to me. Most precious. You will not understand, and yet, I sense in you a spirit, a spark that can ignite if fanned with skill."

"Swifter actions are violent and bloody—"

"Aye! And the man who owned this red flag, and this mail shirt, and this dagger, was violent and bloody above all."

So I knew.

I looked closer.

Well… the bit of red cloth with the yellow edging could be a quarter ripped from my flag, that yellow cross on a scarlet field fighting-men call Old Superb. The colors were faded and, like museum pieces, gave a fusty, dusty faded look. The mesh mail, a scrap from a left shoulder and breast, might also have been mine. As for the main-gauche—my mind went back fifty years…

Yes, I was almost sure it was one given to me by Vomanus, the young man who had so recklessly come seeking me in the inner sea because he had been told to do so by Delia. He was Delia's half-brother. He was now Vomanus of Vindelka. I thought he was a good friend. Yes, it could be his.

A spot of dirt about the ornate hilt where the metal had corroded bore that out, for he was always careless of his weapons.

And damned funny it was, to be sure, to stand and look down at bits of one's own belongings all solemnly laid out in a glass case in a museum, relics to be sighed over with awe.

I tapped the case lightly. "How can you be sure these belonged to Pur Dray?"

He smiled, and the smile was neither ironic nor wolfish; it was the smile of the collector who has paid a price for a dearly desired object of his affections.

"I know them to be. I have been given proofs."

I decided I had best display some of the chauvinistic ignorance of the warriors of the Eye of the World.

"This dagger. It is of strange design." I put my hand on the glass and twisted it about—my right hand. "You would hold it, but with difficulty."

He laughed. This, the first genuine laugh I had heard from him, for he could contort his face to a polite grimace when the occasion warranted, sounded light and happy and carefree.

"Your left hand, Gadak."

So I went through the pantomime of putting my left hand on the glass and holding the main-gauche. I was suitably amazed.

"You have heard of Vallia? The king no longer desires to trade with them, for now we are allied to the empire of Hamal, wherever that may be, and the ships of Menaham ply here. But there are many things of Vallian make in Magdag. This dagger is one, and it was owned and used by the Lord of Strombor."

He did not offer to take the precious objects out of the glass case. I hadn't the heart to ask him. I could feel the weight of all those years rolling down on me, like the peaks of The Stratemsk toppling upon me, and I felt my spirit reducing, as though Grotal had me in his grip.

Truthfully, I, an Earthman, had not yet adjusted to the normal and accepted life-span of two hundred years usual to the people of Kregen, let alone the thousand years that stretched ahead. To Gafard as well as other Kregans, the past fifty years was like twenty to an Earthman.

And I knew what twenty years trapped on Earth was like, Krun rot the Star Lords!

Gafard was speaking again, and I roused myself to listen.

"...honor of the most high. She will be waiting in my saloon now. Show no surprise, Gadak, I caution you, for she has chosen this from the Vallian goods I have told you of. It is a bauble, but it augurs well for your future with me."

Not quite sure what he was talking about I cast a last look at the scraps and relics of what once were mine, and went with him back to the saloon.

My Lady of the Stars waited for us.

I bowed deeply, very deeply, going almost into the full incline, and this I did without conceit or embarrassment.

"Rise, Gadak, for I think you would be a friend to my lord Gafard and to me."

Her voice, musical, filled with light, entranced me.

"I will serve you, my Lady. Your standard shall never be dishonored."

She wore no veil. She was dressed, as was Gafard, all in white. Her black hair was piled in ringlets upon her head, and she held that head erect and yet, although she held herself with pride, there was nothing of arrogance in her. I looked at her, drinking in her beauty, and then looked away, for I felt the desolation within me.

"I wish you to wear this, Gadak. It is a trinket, a foreign bauble from some unknown place far over the Outer Oceans. Yet it has value. I would wish you to wear it in remembrance of me, and as a thanks for your Jikai with the lairgodonts." She held out a golden chain. "And, for what is far more important, you saved the life of my beloved."

I took the bauble. From the golden chain swung a miniature made from bright enamel and precious gems. Red and white. The semblance of a tiny bird in red and white, with spread wings and beak agape. A valkavol. This bird, this tiny harmless bird, could become frighteningly ferocious when attacked or if its young are threatened. I knew the valkavol passing well. Native to my island Stromnate of Valka, in far Vallia, the valkavol had been adopted as the emblem set atop my warriors' standard poles.

I looked at it, there in my hand, a tiny scrap of gold and red and white. I was to be her standard-bearer and she, all unknowingly, had given me the very symbol that decked my Valka's standards.

"I thank you, my Lady..." I could say no more.

Gafard boomed his laugh again. "I can spare you two burs. Then my Lady and I return to the Tower of True Contentment."

I have absolutely no idea of what passed during those two burs. I regret that now, regret it bitterly, as you shall hear.

Ten
Of red sails and green banners

The crushing power of Magdag reached out a mailed arm across the Eye of the World.

Ten top class swifters, the smallest a hundred-and-twenty swifter, escorted a hundred and fifty broad ships carrying twenty-five thousand troops, infantry, cavalry, artillery. The force was sizable, well-balanced, the varters brand-new, and their equipment did credit to the slave armories of Magdag.

I would as lief have seen the lot at the bottom of the sea, save for the swifter *Volgodont's Fang,* which carried my Lady of the Stars.

That flagship carried me, also, but I am an old hand at shipwreck, and so did not count myself among the blessed.

We sailed on southerly with a fair wind and a calm sea and the oar-slaves were relieved from their intolerable burdens of pulling, eternally pulling, and the breeze blew their stinks away from the functional quarterdecks and high ornate poops.

To me, who had once been a Krozair of Zy and devoted to the Red of Zair, the sight of all those miserable naked slaves came as an affront, but a subdued one. I could never have sat still and done nothing previously. Now I accepted what fate had to mete out—or nearly always—and reflected that I, too, had slaved at an oar not only for the overlords of Magdag but for the Krozairs of Zy as well.

One day, Zair willing, I would return to my true allegiance. Now, I was Grodnim and intended to play that role until the bitter end. Poor Duhrra scarcely ever showed himself on deck. We had a little cubby under the forward part of the quarterdeck—the half-deck of a seventy-four—and I, too, stayed there for long periods.

The standard for which I was responsible hung racked with the others of the overlords in the great cabin aft, blazes of green and gold and white about the cabin. My Lady of the Stars had chosen—or someone had chosen for her—a plain white and green banner with a gold device of a zhantil, a rose, and three stars.

I harbored no thoughts that she might be from Earth, thus explaining the familiar name given to her, that was not her real name. She was a Zairian, as the tightly clustered, shining jet-black curls showed.

She kept to the suite of cabins allotted to her. The king had appointed an agent—a kind of Crebent—to sail in the flagship, and we all knew his eyes were everywhere and full reports would go back to the king. We were all on our best behavior during the voyage.

This galley, *Volgodont's Fang,* proved to be an exceptionally fine craft. She was an eight-six-three hundred-and-eighty swifter. That is, she had three banks of oars, thirty to a bank, each side. On the lowest tier there were three men to an oar. The middle bank rowed six to an oar, and the upper bank eight to an oar. These men were stripped stark naked and, as we had recently cleared the ship sheds of Magdag, every man's head was shaved as smoothly as a loloo's egg. They had no need to wear the conical straw hats, dyed green, that rowers in an open-decked swifter were issued with, for this swifter was cataphract, decked in to give protection and space for the fighting-men to operate.

Although Gafard had shown signs of haste during' the fitting out in Magdag and the final clearances of the mole, now that we were on course he gave orders for the slow cruise speed to be maintained. Only one bank of oars was manned and the slaves took turns to pull, thus conserving their strength.

The swifter still carried only one mast, I noticed, and I wondered yet again why the overlords did not do as the Zairians did and give their galleys two masts. Both types carried the forward boat-sail, a kind of sloping bowsprit not unlike the artemon of merchant vessels. The sail was square and reefed from the deck and was dyed a brilliant emerald green. At its center the golden device of the zhantil, rampant, glowed and glittered in glory for the Sea-Zhantil, Gafard, the King's Striker.

The breeze remained fair and we reached the various tiny islands that lay on our course in good time each day before the suns sank. Because war vessels must be as light as possible commensurate with the strength they require, their bottoms are not sheathed in lead or copper. So they must be hauled out of the water as often as possible, otherwise the old devil teredo will go to his devastating work. I knew that the teredo worm was nowhere as active or vicious on Kregen as on Earth and warships for all their cunningly light construction lasted longer than the flimsy vessels of the Ancients of Earth. The Ancient Greek penteconters and triremes and the Phoenician biremes were manned with one man to one oar; but there is room to conjecture that the quadriremes and quinquiremes of later times had four or five men disposed pulling one or two oars. Certainly, this makes more sense than to suppose there were four or five banks vertically separated. As for the later giants of Classical times, these must have been crewed with more than one man to an oar—and, indeed, as we know, there were giants in the Mediterranean in those days.

The Roman dekares probably crewed five men to an oar with two banks barely separated vertically, the distancing being done laterally and fore-and-aft. This is a neat system, for it reduces the height needed to contain the oarsmen and also gives the chance of a decent freeboard. This is, as I have said, always a problem with galleys. Before I'd left the inner sea all those years ago a squadron of these dekares was being built up in Sanurkazz and trials were planned in competition with swifters of comparable power in oarsmen.

The major disadvantage of the dekares is the necessity for adjusting the beam. Kregan galleys are notoriously long and slender craft, for all the controversy over the short-keel and long-keel theories, and there were shipwrights who swore that five men above five men, giving that desirable narrow beam, were better than five men side by side with five men. As you know, I'd left the inner sea before any of this could be worked out.

So when I say that Gafard's swifter *Volgodont's Fang* was a fine craft, you must understand me to mean it was a fine craft of its class.

The two projecting platforms in the bows were armed with large and impressive varters. They were not, of course, as powerful as the gros-varter of Vallia, but they would hurl a rock with power enough to smash into light scantlings. I walked forward and studied the weapons, thinking back to wild times with Nath and Zolta, my two oar-comrades, my favorite rascals.

Gafard found me there, leaning on the rail, watching the break and spume and the white water curling below.

He came straight to the point.

"I spoke to you of treachery, Gadak."

"Aye, gernu."

He leaned back against the rail and swept his gaze across the decks. People moved about their business. We could not be overheard. His bronzed face scowled and his right fist gripped onto the hilt of his Genodder.

"I tell you, Gadak. For all I do for Magdag, and the king, the overlords would gloat to see me torn down and brought low."

"Yes, I can believe that."

"After we left the army it was surprised in the night by raiders wearing black clothes. My belongings were rifled, the great tent belonging to my Lady of the Stars destroyed."

"But why?"

"Why do I bring my Lady always with me, on campaign, where there is no fit work for a lady's hands?"

He was making an opening for me. I took it, taking a chance as usual. It would be a damned long swim from here to the next island on our course to the southern shore...

"The king sends you on errands and when you take my Lady with you he sends men to surprise you and steal her away."

What reaction I had expected, and been ready for, mattered nothing. For this man, this bronze-faced, black-haired, fiery-eyed renegade boomed a huge laugh. He spluttered.

"By Genodras, Gadak! You take the chunkrah by the horns!"

I said nothing.

He wiped his eyes and then said, sharply, "You are right. It would be your head to repeat it."

"Aye."

"I like you. There is something—I cannot put a name to it—that appeals to me in you. You would have been strung up by your entrails by any other overlord long before this. I do not understand why I listen to you—"

"If the certain person we know of wishes to take my Lady from you, I do not think there is a place in all Grodnim you may hide."

He scowled blackly and swore. But it was true.

"Then must the guard be at all times ready. If they slay men skulking by night, clad in black, no man can point the finger at me. I am a loyal king's man. Aye, by Goyt! Despite all, I admire that man, for he is a true genius in war and statecraft, in all things, save this. And in this he has the yrium to do as he wishes and make it the right thing."[7]

I wondered, privately, however much yrium Genod possessed, if he took the Lady of the Stars from Gafard how that violent man would console his conscience for his master. Or would he take sword and seek to redress his wrong, authority and power or no damned authority and power?

Next day we all knew we faced a long haul ahead. The warships were run down into the water, the slaves in their chains whipped on into putting their backs to it. They merely labored to float the ships that were their floating prisons. The suns shone. The sky lifted high and blue, with a few lazy clouds. There would be little wind today, although I fancied a breeze would get up toward evening and if we were unlucky would be dead foul for our southerly course.

There are many small islands dotted all over the inner sea, which is often a very shallow sea; but this day we faced a haul that would take us through the night and well into the morning of the day following before we sighted Benarej Island. Here we expected to be joined by a squadron of swifters for the final passage to the southern shore.

Well, the day limped along. The rowers pulled. The suns shone brassily, mingled jade and ruby, streaming down on the decks and casting strange-colored splotches of light through the awnings. Everyone sweated. The thought of the slaves below and the agonies they were enduring as they took their tricks at the looms made me fidgety and irritable.

Had I been still a Krozair of Zy I would have found an excuse to go below, would have slain the whip-Deldars and would have freed the slaves and so taken the ship back for Zair. But that, by itself, would not be enough to reinstate me. That would be the simple, ordinary, and obvious thing for any Krozair to do. And I was no longer a Krozair. So I sweated and was unpleasant to Duhrra and took myself off to stand in the bows and watch the bar-line of the horizon, burning against the sky.

That sky changed subtly in color. I watched. This might be a normal rashoon, one of those suddenly explosive storms of the inner sea, or it might be the far more sinister manifestation of the Star Lords once more taking a hand in my destiny.

"It would have to strike us now, when there is no lee to run under."

I turned.

The ship-Hikdar, Nath ti Hagon, had walked forward to stare with great animosity at the growing storm. He did not like me still, and who could blame him after that scene in the aft cabin when I had first come aboard *Volgodont's Fang?* But the annoyance of the moment made him speak.

"We are in for a blow," I said, feeling that the calmest and most obvious thing to say. I turned away ready to go aft. He stopped me by speaking in a low, hurried voice.

"You know I do not like you, Gadak. But hear me in this. If you prove false to our lord in anything I shall surely slay you."

Shock, pleasure, annoyance? The emotions clashed in me.

I said, "I do not need you to teach me my duty, Nath ti Hagon. But, for your peaceful heart, I am charged to protect my lord. You see that you do not fail him." And I stalked off.

He said no more and I guessed he was staring at me with baleful eyes and wishing to tear me to pieces as I walked aft. Hagon, his home town, lay in one of the huge looping bends of the River Dag, some sixty dwaburs north of Magdag as the fluttrell flies, although more than twice that far if you followed the curves of the river itself. Guamelga, of which province Gafard was rog, lay some eighty dwaburs to the west of Hagon, still on the same river, which looped sharply north and east, going upstream. Phangursh lay fifty dwaburs farther upstream, to the northeast. In all our operations across the River Daphig, to the east, Gafard had never troubled himself to ride across to the west and visit in his rognate of Guamelga.

That made me think of all my own fair lands in Valka and her nearby islands, in Strombor and in Djanduin, and I cursed and hurled off below to make sure everything in our cabin was tightly lashed down against the force of the coming blow.

The swifter herself was snugged down. Gafard, who had been a swifter captain for a long time, knew how to handle ships on the inner sea. His first lieutenant, this Nath ti Hagon, had already proved to be a tough nut, able to run a trim swifter. I had no real fears we could not ride out the rashoon.

This displayed another facet of Gafard, for a man in his position as king's favorite, Sea-Zhantil, would act as an admiral and have a captain under him to run the ship. Not so Gafard, the King's Striker. He ran his ship like a captain, and joyed in the doing of it. Not for him the sterile and removed glories of admiralty.

The rashoon swooped down on us and the suns vanished in gloom as the dark cloak of Notor Zan enveloped us. The wind screeched and white-caps ran and were blown away across the tumbling sea. A galley is no ship to ride in during a blow. Men were frantically baling, and I took a hand, with Duhrra, cursing and swearing. The boat-sail was torn to shreds. In the gloom and the heaving movement, the wild shriek of the wind, the roil of the sea, I took a savage and bestial delight in battling those natural native elements, for the Everoinye had no part of this.

When, at last, the rashoon blew itself past, its violence intense and short-lived, we saw the scattered mess in which the convoy had been left. Mind you, Duhrra had a hard time not to crow aloud in his glee.

"Keep your black-fanged wine-spout shut, Guhrra! And that stupid grin off your chart-top!" I was harsh with him, for his own good, as he knew.

We had in sight across the still tumbling sea some fifty or so of the broad ships. They were scattered, but already sails were breaking out aboard and they began to straggle back into formation. I scanned the horizons; past the sails of the convoy, around over that islandless sea, and could make out not a single other swifter. Well, I knew *Volgodont's Fang* had been handled superbly. She had kept up to the wind, being as weatherly as any lubberly galley ever can be, and the other swifters had all been blown down to leeward.

They'd row back when the breeze finally died. We set about sorting the convoy and heading on for our destination on Benarej Island.

"Sail ho!" bellowed down from the lookout perched on the high prow beside the beakhead swivels. Then: "Red!"

Swifters of the Eye of the World commonly carry three sets of sails, white for normal duties, black for night work, and red or green for business, depending on which side of the sea they harbor. I felt a thump of the old heart, at that call of "Red!" I can tell you.

Many of the Zairians ship blue sails as well as red, for red is a color not conducive to slipping up unseen, and their hulls, too, are often blue instead of red. It is a matter of common sense. When the strange sail showed, gleaming a bright ruby-crimson in the opaline light, I saw moments later the long, lean hull show up with the same brave color.

This fellow was a fighter, then...

A tremendous bustle and scurry thundered along the three rowing decks of the swifter as the slaves were rousted out and the spare slaves brought up for extra power. They were whipped and rope's ended along to their benches and shackled down. Every oar would be in use and every loom would be fully manned. The green sail came in, in a booming rustle, and was fought into a long sausage-roll shape and stowed. Soldiers poured up onto the upperworks from their quarters on the open upper deck. The varters were cast loose and the men bent to the windlasses.

Gafard, the Sea-Zhantil, appeared on his quarterdeck gorgeous in white and green, with an enormous mass of feathers in his helmet to mark him. I stood nearby, ready to hand, with my green feathers in my helmet.

The drum-Deldar, in obedience to the orders of the oar-master in his tabernacle, raised the beat. The double note sounded, treble and bass, thumping out the rhythm. Now the whistles all stilled. The sound of water hissing past the sides reached everyone. The creak of the woodwork and the rush of water, the long groaning sigh of the slaves as they pushed and pulled, the sounds of the oars grinding, made a pattern of sound very familiar. Also familiar, dreadfully so, were the sharp, vicious cracks as the long whips snapped over the backs of the slaves. A snapping crack and a jerked shriek, and then the usual sounds until another lashing blow produced another agonized screech.

The whip-Deldars of the swifters of Magdag are skilled with old-snake.

And, too, there sounded the shouted word I hate, the vicious, sadistic bawling of: "Grak! Grak, you cramphs! Grak!"

Grak means work and slave and jump to it until you can work no longer and are dead. Grak! Oh, yes, I have heard that foul word many and many a time on Kregen, and many and many a time in evil Magdag and on her hellish swifters.

"Wenda!" bellowed the ship-Deldar, bashing his fist against the quarterdeck rail. "Wenda!"[8]

Gafard stood still, his head lifted, grand in his armor and blazonry. He looked across the starboard bow. Over there the square red sail still bore on with the wind. But even as we looked so it shriveled, shrank in size, became distorted and so disappeared to be rolled and stowed out of the way, as we had stowed our green sail.

Very quietly Gafard said to his ship-Hikdar, Nath ti Hagon, "Break 'em out, Nath."

"Your orders, my commands, gernu!"

Nath bellowed his orders and the hands ran. I watched, fascinated, for it had been a long time.

From the masts raised along the sides of the swifter's apostis broke the green flags of Grodnim. Two parallel rows, those flags enclosed the ship in a box of green power. With an apostis some one hundred thirty feet in length and the flag-masts set at ten-foot intervals, there was room for some twenty-eight flags. This coruscating mass of green and gold and white fluttered in the dying breeze, magnificent, really, bold, daring—and damned well green.

I saw that the standard of the Lady of the Stars had been placed right forward on the larboard side. The standard of Gafard matched it on the starboard. I looked at Gafard and caught his eye as he turned to survey his quarterdeck, and I nodded my head, hitched up my sword, and started off forward.

I was used to fighting an Earthly ship from the quarterdeck. In swifters and swordships it was often preferable to fight them from the beakhead itself.

The Norsemen of Earth, those hard, tough warriors and their enemies called Vikings, held to the tradition of the fighting-man being right forward. They called the warrior selected to fight in the prow *stafnbui,* stem-fighter; the Kregans call him *prijiker,* which is much the same thing.

As a stem-fighter I could wish to have Nath and Zolta with me. But what they would say of me now, as I went forward with every prospect of coming to hand-strokes with men of Zair, I did not care to contemplate.

As for Duhrra, I had spoken to him most severely. If he could get across to the Zairian without being killed he would do so, win or lose. Otherwise he would stay close in his cabin and hope to escape detection, and failing that—and it was a remote chance—must plead illness, an old wound, his stump giving him trouble. I knew he would never strike against a Zairian. He would hope to escape among his comrades. I just did not know, as I strode past all that panoply of the Green, just what I would do.

I thought of the Lady of the Stars. She had entrusted her standard to my care, and had given me a little valkavol symbol as a sign. If a tough, care-free Zairian sailor tried to slash that standard down and carry it back to Sanurkazz or any other Zairian town in triumph—what would I do? Could I cut him down? Could I let the standard go? For the sake of my Lady, who trusted me, I really believe I might have cut a Zairian to pieces. I thought of Delia, and I knew my decision would not be affected.

Across the narrowing stretch of water the Red oar blades all lifted and fell as one. The swifter came on as though on tracks, every oar parallel, rising and falling like the red wings of a great raptor of the air.

The bronze rostrum cut through the water with a swirl of blue and white, curling into a white line tumbling and flowing past her sides. That cruel ram would rip the guts out of a ship. Above it the center wales curved to join at the proembolion, which would force the rammed ship off and thus prevent her in her sinking from dragging down her victorious enemy with her. The beakhead was lifted and men in the brave red worked there ready to drop it with stunning force onto our deck, or to run it out ready to form a boarding gangway. The two forward varter platforms showed busy activity, as did ours.

The first darts flew, massive, long bolts of wood tipped with iron. Soon bolts entirely of iron would be used as the range, closing minute by minute, dropped. And then the chunks of rock, which would smash and rend their way through wood and flesh alike. A dart hissed in to pierce a varterist near me clean through. Blood burst from his back, spraying everywhere as he gave a last screech and spun and toppled overboard. He went under the thrashing lines of oars. Another man of the Green stepped up to take his place at the windlass. The varter clanged and a wicked bolt flew off in reply. The air filled with missiles as more and more varters and bows could be brought to bear.

The two swifters bore down on each other, their whip-Deldars frantic with lashing, their drum-Deldars banging out the stroke, the oar-masters bellowing the time, and the two opposing captains watching and waiting for the first glimpse of intention in their enemy. One or the other must sheer. The diekplus might be used, the ram-to-ram, the straight shear. The time for decision was running out with gathering speed. And then I, an unfrocked Krozair of Zy, deciphered the devices of those red flags. I

252

stood ready to engage in bloody combat with a swifter of the Krozairs of Zy themselves.

Could I, even Apushniad as I was, fight and slay my Red Brothers in Zair?

Eleven
The *Golden Chavonth* leads us a dance

The two swifters leaped across the last gap of water at each other like sea-leems.

The answer to the question that formed in my mind was: Of course I damned well could! I was an old mercenary, an old reiver. When men sought to slay me no matter who they were—by the Black Chunkrah!—I'd slay them first! And there was the green standard of my Lady of the Stars to consider. Was a man's life, the life of a Brother Krozair of Zy, worth more or less than a scrap of green silk given into my care by a girl? How could such idiotic and callous thoughts even occur to me? Had this girl, this beloved of Gafard, this Lady of the Stars, addled my wits?

There had to be a way—a way of honor.

The arrows rained down about me now and I cursed the stupidity of the men of the inner sea, no less than of Vallia and Segesthes, that they despised the shield as the coward's artifice. Turko the Shield should be with me now, his great shield upraised, deflecting the arrow storm.

I flicked away two arrows that would have pierced me.

An officer at my side, a Chulik mercenary and a man with long experience in artillery, in command of the bow varters, coughed gently to himself. He pulled an arrow from his arm where the keen steel head had bitten clean through his mail. He threw the two halves to the deck, with a Chulik curse.

The gap of blue sea between those two closing rams narrowed with dreadful rapidity.

I stared wolfishly at the Red swifter. She was two-banked and the two tiers were set closely together. Her beam appeared broader than I would have thought necessary. I could see the heads of the men clustered abaft her forward breastwork, across the forecastle. The beak remained aloft, ready to drop down if her captain chose to board. Our beak likewise remained lifted. Both captains considered this to be ram work.

How quick would Gafard be?

He was a fine swifter captain—he must of necessity be so to have earned his reputation. He was called the Sea-Zhantil, a name taken from the

Zairians, a name taken from the renowned Krozair, the Lord of Strombor. He measured himself against that long-dead Krozair, did Gafard. Whatever Pur Dray had done, Gafard, the King's Striker, would do better—or die in the attempt.

The hail from aft reached me attenuated and thin. The breeze had almost died after the rashoon. The order of command from the Red swifter reached me as clearly.

Both swifters hauled out, spinning. I had thought the Zairian would try the diekplus, the maneuver in which the attacking swifter abruptly swivels and turns so as to smash her ram hard against the leading oars and the apostis forward frame, what the Ancient Greeks called the epotis. As I have said, in the swifters of the inner sea this framework remained a supporting member and, forward, a true cathead of substantial construction, designed not only to secure the anchor but also to smash on down the line of oars, was fitted with that intention. The diekplus was thus rendered less of a formidable weapon than of yore. In a ram-to-ram the stronger cathead would win the day, provided the attacker's oars could be hoicked up out of the way, and this presented difficulties.

I had thought that a two-banker would not try the ram-to-ram against a three-banker.

I was right in that. And I was wrong about the diekplus. Gafard had thought the same and had sought to take his vessel into the accepted method of attacking defense: a rapid wheel and a reversal so he had the enemy's tail in front of his ram.

But the Zairian went on spinning. She turned past the ninety-degree point, turned more, and then all her oars went down as one and she shot off, away from us. Gafard's vessel, still turning, the water a welter of white along its sides, was left facing at an oblique angle. I could hear Gafard raving as he bellowed his orders to bring the swifter back on line.

As the Zairian thus impudently fooled us I saw the bows flash past, turning. I had seen the men there, close. And I had recognized the Krozair Brother in command, the prijiker in command of his party of prijikers. Their hard bronzed faces in the glittering helmets turned as they flew past. Arrows crisscrossed, but no man flinched.

That was Pur Kardazh over there, one of the five Krozair Brothers who had been accepted into the Krozairs of Zy at the same time as I was. I would have thought he would have reached higher in the hierarchy than a prijiker commander, no matter the glory and honor of such a position. Perhaps he had taken the world-stance, as had I, and the call had brought him back to the service. As the swifters bore on I pondered. Could I slay an old friend, Pur Kardazh, for the sake of a scrap of green silk?

The ship-Hikdar, Nath, came running forward again, bellowing. He was not satisfied with our bow varters' performance. That the Chulik in command had an arrow wound in his arm meant nothing. In that, of course, he was right.

"The cramph! You see what he is after!"

Indeed, I did see, and I felt most pleased.

For the Zairian was not after a fight with the Magdaggian. He was after the plump chickens of the convoy. As the breeze dropped so conditions became impossible for the sailing broad ships and ideal for swifter work. The Red swifter made no attempt to take prizes. With *Volgodont's Fang* on her tail there was no time for that luxury.

Sharp cries of anger rose from the men. They were filled with rage that they were standing idly by. For long, graceful streamers of smoke rose from the Red swifter, arching over, curving to land with precision on the decks and in the rigging of the broad ships. First one and then another burned. We were flying along at full speed, every slave hurling every ounce of his being onto the looms. But the Red swifter kept ahead, and the fire-pots blossomed from her, and she left a blazing wake of ruin as she went.

"By Grodno! I'd like to drop our beakhead on her quarterdeck now!"

"That would prove interesting," I said.

Nath shook a fist at the Krozair swifter.

"Krozairs! The bane of Grodno! They are damned and doomed to all eternity! May the Green strike them."

I didn't bother to reply. I now realized what had puzzled me at first about that double-banked galley as she had pulled toward us. I'd lost a great deal of the sharpness of a swifter captain. The two banks of oars had been lifting and falling at a speed much below that of *Volgodont's Fang*. I had assumed that to be because not only was Gafard's swifter in perfect fighting trim with a trained crew, but more probably because the Krozair swifter had been newly commissioned with an inexperienced crew. More than ship quality, crew quality can win an action.

Now the Red swifter's wings beat in furious tempo.

In a bur or so the slaves being lashed by Gafard's whip-Deldars would be unable to keep up the stroke. His spare oarsmen would be insufficient to make up the numbers required to propel the swifter at her top speed, and the time taken to change rowers would disrupt her smooth effort. But the Red swifter's oarsmen were fresher. She could outrun *Volgodont's Fang*, that was certain.

And, too, I had noticed that the Zairian, with the figurehead of a chavonth, had possessed no less than thirty-six oars in each of her banks. I had counted them quite automatically as she flashed past, as I had recognized Pur Kardazh, as I had stood under the arrow hail. She was of the long-keel construction, then. Slow to turn, perhaps, although her spin when she broke and fooled Gafard had been executed smartly enough. She would be very fast. It was clear that Gafard had come to the same conclusion.

The oar-master shouted, and the drum-Deldar subtly smoothed his frenzied banging and the bass and treble rang out with a slower rhythm. The Green swifter plowed more slowly through the calm blue sea.

Now Gafard showed his seamanship.

The contest presented itself to me as a problem. The Krozair swifter had cut through the convoy in a straight line. Now she was beginning to turn. Gafard followed, more slowly, and pulled out free of the convoy flank. Orders rattled and the whistles blew and the oars came up, level and still.

Like a faithful rark guarding a flock of chunkrah, the Green swifter hovered, ready to dart larboard or starboard to catch the Red swifter in the flank as she bore in again.

The oars in the Krozair swifter leveled. Both vessels drifted.

If this was a waiting game, then every advantage lay with Gafard. As though to confirm that a hail reached us and the news flashed like wildfire about the swifter.

"Swifters! Coming up fast!" And, then, "Green!"

The Krozair captain made out the fresh vessels at about the same time. Immediately he put up his helm.

"He's running! May Grotal the Reducer grind his bones!"

By the time the Green swifters, four of them from the scattered squadron, hove up, the Red swifter was a brilliant dot on the horizon. I gazed after that speck of color, and I sighed. I wondered who her captain might be. He had struck a shrewd blow for Zair. He had struck like a leem and destroyed, and had vanished the moment the odds altered. He had acted as a proper ship captain and not as so often the Krozairs did as a crusader willing to die for no good purpose.

I would remember that golden chavonth figurehead. Maybe I might live to shake that Krozair captain's hand.

Gafard was livid with rage. He looked dangerous.

"The rast! Twenty good broad ships—burned! And I'll wager he has no more than twenty casualties, if that."

We had thirty dead and wounded.

Later, when Gafard's anger had cooled—and this was after he had spent a bur with the Lady of the Stars—I said to him, when it was safe, for I had no wish to puncture the boil of his anger again and drown in the suppuration: "An interesting vessel, that Krozair swifter."

"You must have seen them, as have I. They play about with their ship specifications, the shipwrights of Sanurkazz. I'd say she was a seven-seven hundred-and-forty-four. Double banked, shallow draft, broadish in the beam, but quick and deadly."

"I saw the oars, gernu. Seven-seven, you say?"

"Not tiered—raked. A diabolical design. But, given a fairer margin, I'd say *Volgodont's Fang* could catch her."

Yes, I said to myself. Yes, I'd risk that. The speed of turning had been found in a greater beam for length ratio; maybe there was more than just the one controversy in Sanurkazz these days. Maybe the short-keel people had gone over to the long-keel argument and then given their ships a broader beam and so regained their original position.

She'd been low in the water, long and deadly, and I knew she was a highly tuned precision fighting instrument.

As she'd cut through the sea a deal of spray had flown over the prijikers, wetting my old comrade, Pur Kardazh.

Where I had stood the spray had flown clear.

Maybe the swifters of the inner sea were developing faster than I had given them credit for, for with a man's life-span extending to two hundred years, change was bound to be slower on Kregen than on Earth.

"The *Golden Chavonth?*" said Gafard, pulling his black beard. "Aye. Aye, I'll remember her."

For the rest of that day we went on our way, slowly gathering up the convoy, for the breeze I had expected got up. I wondered how the captain of *Golden Chavonth* would have dealt with a hundred and fifty of the broad ships instead of the fifty he had met, and of which he had destroyed twenty.

The swifters closed up, the sails were set, and we passed the rest of the night on course for Benarej Island. We were late for the rendezvous; but we met the other squadron, fifteen swifters of various sizes, and, after a day spent recovering, we all weighed or were slipped for the southern shore.

By Zair, though! Hadn't that Krozair swifter presented a grand sight with all her flags red and glorious under the Suns of Scorpio! And hadn't her captain led Gafard, the King's Striker, the Sea-Zhantil, a right merry dance!

Twelve
Of Duhrra, dopa, and friends

I, Gadak, a Green Grodnim of very dubious reliability, watched moodily as the army disembarked. There seemed to be no end to the lines of marching men, the strings of sectrixes, the rolling thunder of the varters on their wheeled carriages. There were hebramen, also, and the Grodnims considered these would give them a decided advantage in scouting against the Zairians.

So I stood on the quarterdeck of *Volgodont's Fang,* where she had been pulled up onto the shelving beach, and I brooded.

Duhrra stood with me and he breathed harshly through his opened mouth, his hook hidden within his green robe.

"You are sure he did not recognize you, Dak—Gadak?"

"No. Anyway, I had a fold of white cloth about my face. I fancy it is a precaution we could both do well to adopt all the time. The sand in the wind here gives ample excuse."

I had not told Duhrra that it was a Krozair Brother I had recognized and he no doubt took it that I referred to one of the seamen, one of the prijiker party, or the varterists. I fancy he wanted to know nothing about Krozairs. They are regarded as men apart, dedicated, austere, giving their whole being to fighting the Green for the glory of Zair. Those Brothers who choose to take the world-scene, as had I, achieve this sense of awed mystery when they adopt the Krozair symbol no less than the Bolds, who are men dedicated for every single mur of their lives to the Krozair Brethren.

That symbol had been displayed in *Golden Chavonth:* the hubless spoked wheel within the scarlet circle. That device had stirred me. I felt uneasy. I had been ejected and I must regain my place in order to leave the inner sea and I was doing precious little about it. That there was precious little I could do at the moment had no importance in the sense of nagging frustration.

My plans depended on a great stroke, a High Jikai.

I was kept running about on errands for Gafard.

He provided me with a hebra, a spirited little animal, for all it was no match for a zorca, and I grew to like it. Its name was Grodnofaril, and I thought it inexpedient to change that, so I called it "Boy" and left well alone.

We had landed on the main southern shore in a deeply indented arm of the sea some twenty dwaburs to the east of Shazmoz. The east. About twenty dwaburs across country to the east of us rose the Zairian fortress town of Pynzalo. It goes without saying that any town or city on the Red or Green shore must be strongly fortified if it lies within a day's march of the sea. These frowning battlemented places must be strong. Most towns and cities are inland, well away from raid and foray.

King Genod's idea was simple enough. Reputed a genius at war, he demonstrated some of the necessary qualities of genius by issuing instructions to his subordinates that were easy to comprehend. Their execution would be another matter, of course.

After Shazmoz had been relieved the combined Zairian armies had fought on to the west, rolling up some of the Grodnim defensive positions, for they had been weak, every mind being set upon advance to the east. Now the advance had stalled and both armies lay in stalemate.

Our descent onto the rear like this would seriously disrupt communications, at the least. We had already caught a supply column—and there was nothing I could do about that. Even ships that coasted along the shore could be snapped up. Once the fleet of broad ships had discharged the army and supplies for a period they left us, to return to Magdag. They were expected again very shortly, bearing the main supply buildup. So, here we sat, astride the Red communications, and very ready to strike in any direction.

More fleeting raids by Zairian swifters had bothered us, but since that destructive onslaught by *Golden Chavonth* nothing so damaging had been achieved against us. I fancied that Gafard might not wait for his full supplies. They had been faced, the king and the King's Striker, with the alternatives of dispatching half the army with full supplies, or all the army with limited supplies. In my view, given the caliber of Gafard, the king had chosen correctly. One must always remember the slowness of armies when men march on their feet, and draft and pack animals carry their gear and supplies and there are no mechanical contrivances for transport.

I fancied Gafard would strike east, at Pynzalo.

With that fortress reduced and its supplies captured, and with his swifters dominating this whole stretch of coast through their use of slipways and bays and beaches, Gafard could then form a firm rear on Pynzalo and turn west. With Prince Glycas to the west, they would have the Zairian forces caught like a nut between crackers.

Just how long it would take for Sanurkazz to realize the position and scrape up another army to fling against Pynzalo could, for me, remain only conjecture. I did not know how far the treasury's resources had been depleted. I did know that both sides had expended vast amounts of treasure on this internecine warfare. Red and Green! Well, I was supposed to have grown to a more mature wisdom, but I own I still felt the old surge when Red rose up to challenge Green, still the blood thumped quicker through my veins.

One night after I had been all day chasing hither and yon carrying orders—and, incidentally, coming to know the composition of this army, its strengths and its weaknesses—Duhrra rolled into the tent we shared, not so much drunk as fuddled and annoyed.

"Tonight," he said, slumping down on his cot with a crash. "Tonight, my Gadak of the Green—I escape!"

I took the bottle from his hand and sniffed. Dopa. I threw the thing into the moon-shot darkness and I followed it out to the hanging water bottle and I took that into the tent and sloshed the entire contents over this Duhrra of the Days and his cot. He spluttered and roared and I reached down and put a hand over his mouth.

"Duhrra of the Days," I said, in that kind of penetrating whisper that smacks of drama. "If you wish your entrails to be drawn out, then by all means continue to shout of your intentions."

259

His eyes glared up at me over my hand.

He put his left hand on my wrist and tried to draw my hand away. I resisted. I did not let him take my hand away.

I said, "If you wish to go over the hill you must plan. There must be food and water, a mount, a plan of escape. Onker! Think on, Duhrra of the Days."

I took my hand away.

He dragged in a harsh breath. His eyes were bloodshot.

"Aye, Gadak of the Green! You argue well and shrewdly. Yet you do nothing to escape. I begin to think you really love these zigging Grodnims. You wish to stay with them forever. I do not think—"

"No, Duhrra, you do not think."

"Duh—I do, so!"

I shook my head. I know I wore that old evil expression on my face in the moons-glow, for he flinched back.

"I do not intend to escape, meekly run away, like a cur with its tail between its legs. When I go, I go in style, in a way all men may see, and say—'That was a Zairian!'"

"Fine words."

"Aye."

He still did not know what to make of me. Of late I had been your true dyed-in-the-wool Grodnim. The religious observances that amused me had been dealt with faithfully. I think that Duhrra did doubt me then. And he had every right so to doubt, for I doubted myself.

All my life I have been a loner. With the exception of my Delia I have never revealed myself. And yet I have good friends, as you know. Seg Segutorio and Inch—great men, fine blade comrades, true friends. And there were others you have heard me speak of—Hap Loder, Gloag, Prince Varden Wanek, Kytun Kholin Dorn, and Ortyg Fellin Coper. And there were my friends who lived in Esser Rarioch: Turko the Shield, Balass the Hawk, Naghan the Gnat. And I included here Tilly and Oby. There were others of whom you know. There was most particularly here in the Eye of the World Mayfwy of Felteraz. How could I face them with the knowledge I bore? I do not make friends easily. When I do make a friend I tremble lest I destroy that friendship through one of my typical, stupid tearaway actions.

Not for me the easy assumption that friends remain friends no matter what atrocities I commit.

How would Rees and Chido regard me? They were of Hamal, the empire ruled by mad Queen Thyllis, and were deadly foemen to Vallia. Yet during my days as a spy in Ruathytu, capital of Hamal, I had found true friendship with Rees, Trylon of the Golden Wind, and with chuckling, chinless, popeyed Chido, a courtesy amak. I had been tortured by the decisions forced on me, the honest attempt to rationalize the friendship I felt for Rees and

Chido and the numbing knowledge that our countries fought and hated each other.

Duhrra punctured my problems with a new brashness owing much to dopa.

"So, Gadak the Great Planner. When is this to be?"

"As soon as the right opportunity offers." I did not smile at his words. But this was much more like it—much more a cheerful companion, this Duhrra who chided me for my lapses from grace, my omission of good works. That to him these good works could exist only in labor for the Red of Zair meant only his vision was scaled to the Eye of the World. Maybe I had been slack of late. But, despite all, for me, still, it was Red and not Green. The conflict in the Eye of the World might be of tiny dimensions when compared with the dramas of the Outer Oceans. When a fellow was caught up in them they tended to reduce visibility to the immediate horizon.

Duhrra possessed the appearance of that kind of superbly built idiot calculated at first glance to deceive. I have met your true moron from time to time, and usually give him a wide berth. They do not amuse me, as they appear to amuse so many people, these slack-faced giants with muscles of gods and brains of calsanys. Duhrra was basically right in his desires to go and *do* something for Zair.

My problem was that what I did must rank as a High Jikai, a world-shaking feat of arms that men would talk about and nod their heads over sagely and consider to be worthy to stand in the legends of Kregen along with the other high feats of achievement. That it would be damned difficult to do I knew. Maybe I overmatched myself against fate.

"We will strike for honor, Duhrra, but I do not believe I shock you when I say that honor is a poor substitute for life."

"Duh—you threw away my bottle!"

"Aye—now get some sleep. I must think."

But my thoughts coiled around my friends and my shortcomings.

These feelings of dissatisfaction with myself prompted me to the reflection—which I try always to keep somewhere near the forefront of my mind—that a man must work hard at keeping friends. At least, I know this was so for me. I did not feel that no matter what I did my comrades would remain loyal to me forever and ever. I know this is the counsel of perfection, the David and Jonathan summit; and I knew, too, I would never lose my affections for Seg and Inch and the others just because they were foolish at some time or other, or played me false out of a lapse from the counsels of morality we all accepted in our own ways; but I felt always that I was under trial. If this proves me lacking in understanding, as I suppose it does, it also proves that I am a true loner.

I would not have understood had someone at this time pointed out to me that—in my assumptions that no matter what my friends did I would forgive them but if I erred they would not forgive—I did my friends a grave injustice and imputed a higher value to my friendship than I was prepared to extend to theirs. I knew, then, I was not worthy of my Delia, and, also, not worthy of the friendship extended to me by Seg and Inch and the others. This is what I believed.

So, with Duhrra as with Melow the Supple, with Vomanus of Vindelka, with all my comrades, I chose to hew to the line of rectitude—and as always the savage barbarian that is the true me, I often think to my shame, would break out and I'd go raving off doing all the things that should, if my philosophy was correct, have resulted in the cloak of Notor Zan falling on me from a great height.

Kytun Kholin Dorn—that magnificent four-armed warrior Djang, a kov—and Ortyg Fellin Coper—a wise and learned Obdjang statesman, a Pallan—ran my kingdom of Djanduin in the southwest of Havilfar for me when I was away. I had been away on Earth, banished by the Star Lords, for twenty-one Terrestrial years, and since my return and all this imbroglio in the inner sea I had not been back to Djanduin. I had no doubts whatsoever, no doubts at all, that Kytun and Ortyg ran the country with all the efficiency and honesty we had built up between us. I was still the king of Djanduin, and when I returned I would be greeted as such. Provided, of course, they were both still in power and no further revolutions had taken place. Against a warrior of the caliber of K. Kholin Dorn and the statecraft of O. Fellin Coper, I did not fancy the chances of new revolutionaries, for we carried the people with us. I give this example to illuminate my tangled feelings about friends.

Twenty-one years' absence and then a cheerful "Lahal, Ortyg. Lahal, Kytun," and I would resume the throne as though I had not been away. Blind I was in those days, for although I gave thanks to Zair—or, in this case, to Djan—for my friends, I did not fully understand the quality of their friendship, and how blessed I was in the receiving of it.

All of which led to a very subdued Duhrra, with a hand to his bald head, crawling out of the tent on the following morning and moaning for a handful of palines.

"Dopa," I said.

"Aye, master. Dopa. Duh—a fearsome drink."

"And suitable only for those who wish to become as calsanys."

"There are many bottles in the infantry lines. I was led astray."

Dopa if drunk in sufficient quantity is guaranteed to make a man fighting mad. Did Gafard, then, need dopa to whip his splendid army to fighting pitch? I was surprised.

When I was summoned to the usual morning briefing ready to begin a day astride my hebra, Boy, carrying messages, Gafard appeared to be wrought to a high pitch himself, as though he, that hard, practical, seasoned warrior, had been drinking dopa.

"Gernus," he said to the assembled officers and the aides standing respectfully in the rear. "Great news! We are highly honored. The king himself, the All-Highest, sends news he will pay us a visit—we must expect him today."

Later I saw the arrival of King Genod. He flew in by voller.

The moment I saw the petal-shape of the airboat flitting in over the camp from the shining sea, I knew the instrument had been placed into my hands.

This, then, would be the means of creating a High Jikai.

Thirteen
King Genod reviews his army

A considerable bulk of the army drew up on parade to greet the arrival of their king, this Genod Gannius, genius at war.

In my capacity as aide to the general in command here I rode my sectrix, Blue Cloud, and clad in mail and green, waited respectfully among the ranks of the aides, well to the rear of Gafard and his high officers.

The trumpets pealed, the flags flew, the twin suns cast down their mingled opaz radiance, sectrixes snorted, and the mailed ranks stood immobile, splendid, imposing, their pikes all slanted as one, the suns-light glittering from their helmets.

There were two vollers.

One was the small two-place flier I had seen over the Grand Canal, before I'd released the tide and so swept away the vessels carrying the consignment of vollers from Hamal.

The other voller was larger, higher, with three decks and varter positions, with room for a crew of eighty men—a pastang. As she flew in I was forcibly reminded of the power an aircraft must possess over the earthbound fighting-man marching on his own feet.

Rumors had floated about sufficiently for me to know that these were the only two vollers Genod possessed. I took no pride that I had deprived him of the squadron supplied by Hamal; the relief I felt was tempered by the knowledge that with these two alone, against totally unprepared Zairians, he could do a great mischief.

The reception went off smoothly enough—I was sorry to see—and with the bands playing and the flags fluttering and the swods marching in perfect alignment, King Genod made his way into the camp of one of his armies upon the southern shore.

There was no doubt as to the polished drill of these swods. There is a great difference between your wild warrior and your disciplined soldier, for all they are both fighting-men. The mercenaries Genod had hired were not on parade. He was being welcomed by the army he had helped create, the killing instrument with which he had won his victories and carried the Green triumphantly to the Red southern shore. This was a family reunion, as the long ranks of pikemen marched past, with the halberdiers and swordsmen leading, and the wedges of crossbowmen, closed up to march, followed, their crossbows held all in strict alignment across their chests. Each man in the ranks with his green plumes and insignia, I felt sure, owed a special and personal allegiance to King Genod. Genod had forged his army and it was his, in his hand, to do with as he willed.

He trusted this army, out of the greater army he had created, to Gafard, the King's Striker.

There was a deal of affectionate greeting, and much bowing and saluting, the pealing of trumpets, the curveting of sectrixes, the green flags proud against the sky.

A little breeze had ghosted up, and this added a fine free atmosphere to the occasion, a zephyr breeze foretelling the great wind of destruction that would sweep the Green to victory over the Reds all along the coast.

The king and Gafard and a sizable body of their immediate officers and retinues disappeared into the tall pavilion erected against the king's coming. Treasure was being spilled here. Yet for this genius king, this superman with the yrium, such attendances were not only expected and demanded—they were essential to his life-style.

A powerful Pachak guard surrounded the two fliers, and the gaping swods were kept well away. I stood in the crowd with that fold of white silk across the lower half of my face. Many soldiers affected the style, for here the wind carried stinging sand. I stared at the two vollers.

For my money they would both be first-class specimens. Hamal habitually built and sold inferior specimens to foreign countries. That had been one cause of a war that, while it lay in abeyance for the moment, was by no means over. The Hamalese had supplied these two vollers as examples, and on their performance the balance of the order might rest, although I knew well enough that any nation which did not manufacture fliers was only too pleased to buy examples from Hamal even if they were less than perfect.

"Real boats! That fly through the air!" observed a swod, his full-dress uniform now changed for his fatigues. The other pikemen and arbalesters were likewise changed. Full dress was costly and reserved for occasions like this grand parade and, ironically, for battle.

"I'd never have believed it, if I hadn't seen it with me own eyes!" declared a dwa-Deldar, wiping his nose with his fist.

"Gar!" said a wizened little engineersman, spitting. "They be just ordinary boats, fitted with the power o' Grodno, if you ask me."

"Nobody's asking you, Naghan the Pulley."

They would have wrangled on, in the press, amicable in this off-duty period as swods usually are. I moved away with Duhrra. I would see all I wanted of the positions of the vollers. I did not like the guards being Pach-aks. That complicated matters.

In less than a bur I would be on duty again, and just before Duhrra and I went to dress into our mail and greens, a fresh interest cropped up in the army. Two swifters came in bringing with them a captured Zairian swifter.

We all trooped down to the beach to look and jeer and shout mocking obscene threats as the Zairian prisoners were marched ashore in chains.

The two swifters were from Gansk, a powerful Grodnim fortress city of the northern coast opposite Zy itself. The Zairian was from Zandikar, a fortress city up the coast to the northwest from Zamu. So, of course, the Ganskian sailors and marines were cock-a-hoop over their victory and very mouthy about it to the men of Magdag.

Duhrra spat. "Zandikar," he said. "I've been there myself! I fought a bout there and won two zo pieces. I think they fought well before they were beaten."

The sight of those chained men displeased me. Zandikar, the city of Ten Dikars, was nowhere near as powerful or wealthy a city-state as her next-door neighbor, Zamu; but her small fleet was considered smart and effective and she had a reputation for her archers and her gregarian groves. There was no order of Krozairs associated with Zandikar, not even a Red Brotherhood, but she was of the Red and of Zair, and an ally.

The two Gansk swifters were six-five hundred-and-twenty swifters. The Zandikarean was a five-three hundred swifter.

There must have been great slaughter, for far less than a full swifter's crew trudged ashore. As for the oar-slaves, they were sorted out, Green and Red, and sent the one to recuperate and rejoin their fellows, the other to further slavery on the oar-benches of Grodnim swifters.

After this excitement Duhrra and I had to be quick about dressing and reporting in for duty. There were more messages on this afternoon than there had been for the entire previous three days. The king had stirred things up, although I had no feeling that Gafard had been dragging his heels. Strong scouting forces had already probed east and west, and weaker patrols had gone south to check out if the Zairians had yet returned to the villages of Inzidia, which had been evacuated earlier when the Grodnims had advanced. I knew that the scouts going east would have to halt long before they reached Pynzalo, for the base camp at which I had met Duhrra, and where he had lost his hand, lay in their way.

From the nature of the messages I carried it was perfectly clear that the king endorsed Gafard's view that a strike to the east, the quick capture of Pynzalo, a consolidation on that strong line, and then a chavonth-like spring to the west represented the best strategy. They both agreed with my views, then...

As the suns were dipping into the sea to the west with the nearest of the confused mass of islands known as the Seeds of Zantristar—the damned Grodnims called them the Seeds of Ganfowang—black bars against the burning glow of sea and sky, it chanced that Gafard called me into the inner compartment of his campaign tent. I went in and saluted and noticed he looked keyed up. He paced about, as he spoke, over the priceless carpet, well pleased over some matter.

The imposing many-peaked tent provided for his lady had been taken down long before the king arrived, and the tent, the lady, her retinue, and a strong guard of Pachaks had left the camp, no man would say where. I had seen the king's Crebent wandering about looking exceedingly bilious. He was one Grodnim among many we could do without.

"Such news, Gadak!" Gafard greeted me. "We are on the move. The king approves—but these are matters not fit for the ears of a mere aide. Look—" He gestured to a side table. "Help yourself to a drink. It is all Grodnim stuff."

I refused politely. He'd had to stock Grodnim wine when the king came here.

"The King also brought me an item of information interesting to him; an item of supreme importance to me!" He was expansive; I had never seen him more febrile, alert, restless, pacing about, a flush beneath his mahogany suntan giving him even more of that voracious carved beakhead look I know so well from the mirror.

"Yes, gernu?"

"You asked me once if it was sure the great Krozair, Pur Dray, the Lord of Strombor, was surely dead. And I answered it was sure. Well, Gadak—" Here, he stopped pacing and turned and glared at me with a look of unholy triumph. "There is news, sure news! The king's spies brought it; it cannot be doubted. Pur Dray has reappeared in the inner sea from—from where no man knows. He is still alive!"

"You honor me with your confidence—" I began. He brushed that aside.

"It is no confidence. The news will soon circulate. The greater the news the faster it travels. But, Gadak, there is more... Pur Dray has been ejected from the Krozairs of Zy! He is Apushniad!" Gafard shook his head in bewilderment. "I cannot understand how they can be such fools, such stupid idiot onkers; but the fact remains."

"Then if he is Apushniad," I said, speaking slowly, sizing him up, "you think, perhaps—?"

"Aye, I do! There is a certain matter between us. I must meet him. Now that I know he is alive and not dead I am overjoyed!"

How badly he wanted to overmatch the old reputation of that Krozair of Zy who was dead and was now alive!

I said, "You would seek to come to hand-strokes with him, to slay him, to prove yourself a greater Ghittawrer than he is a Krozair?"

He looked at me as though I were a mewling infant, or a crazy man screaming at the lesser moons to halt in their tracks. He opened his mouth, but the tent drapings ripped up and Grogor, his second in command, appeared, throwing a quick salute, butting in, interrupting: "Gernu! The king! He calls for you—at once, gernu!"

Gafard's mouth snapped shut. He whipped up his green cloak and threw it over his shoulders. His longsword clanked once as he strode past me. He said, "Get about your duties, Gadak. Serve me well and you will be rewarded."

"Your orders, my commands, gernu!" I bellowed blankly.

That small incident had shown me in more revealing drama the situation between these two, between King Genod and Gafard, the King's Striker. For all the talk of brain and hand, of genius and executive, still when the king whistled Gafard ran. Gafard was tough and strong and ruthless and high-handed and all the things a man needed to be to survive upon Kregen and attain a position of comfort—quite apart from power and wealth—and his authority within the army was unquestioned. Still, King Genod whistled and Gafard ran.

Then I checked. Did I not run when Gafard whistled?

The answer to that question should be satisfactorily answered this very night.

After the suns had gone down and the Maiden with the Many Smiles began to climb the heavens, I found Duhrra thinking about wandering down to the infantry lines after more dopa, and told him what I was going to do.

His broad idiot face broke into one huge grin. "About time, master! Huh—I'm with you, by Zantristar the Merciful!"

I said, "We will take both the flying boats, for that will be easier. The little one will rest on the big one's deck."

We gathered up all our fighting gear we would ordinarily use on duty and left our sleeping silks and spare clothing scattered about as though we had just left casually. I wanted to leave a bolthole in case the damned voller was not a first-class example and played up. That is a thing anyone of foresight would do, even though I did not expect to see this place again for a long time.

The Maiden with the Many Smiles, Kregen's largest moon, gave more light than we needed for a desperate enterprise of this nature. But I would not wait. The king might leave on the morrow after his inspection. And my impatience had now boiled over. Rashness and recklessness—they are a mark of my own stupidity, I own.

Acting perfectly normally we walked through the moon-drenched shadows to the edge of the bluffs overlooking the beach. In one of the curved beach hollows fenced on its seaward side the Zairian prisoners had been lodged. They would be chained and the chains stapled to stakes driven deeply into the sand. Here lay one chance; the sand would give more easily than earth. I had brought a length of iron filched from the engineers' stores, just in case. As it turned out we were lucky here. One of the Rapa guards, who toppled over after Duhrra hit him on top of his crested head, carried keys on a large bronze ring. Cautioning silence, we went among the prisoners, releasing them. They gathered about me in the pink and golden shadows, breathing hard, hardly believing.

"You are men from Zandikar. I salute your prowess. Now we strike a blow for Zair and we strike in absolute silence!"

"I am Ornol ti Zab, ley-Hikdar, third officer of *Wersting Zinna*." The man looked squat and hard, a real sailorman, his black curly hair smothered in sand, with the black dried blood crusting about a wound. "We are with you in this escape. But—you and this giant with one hand wear the green."

"Aye," I said. "Aye, Hikdar, we do. And if there is a scrap of red about we will gladly wear that! By Zair, yes!"

There were dead men in the dunes. Red cloth was to hand. I wound the crimson about my loins, over the green, draped an end over the green tunic. There was no time for more. We all stole silently across the sand. The Hikdar halted as I put my hand on his shoulder and whispered in his ear.

"Not that way, Hikdar."

"But," he whispered back, "that way lies our swifter, our fleet *Wersting Zinna*."

"There is a greater Jikai tonight. You are a ley-Hikdar.[9] Success this night will leap you at a bound to Jiktar. I promise you. Your king Zinna will do no other.

He looked doubtful. I did not blame him. I could be a part of a trap, devilish sport of the Grodnims with Zairian captives.

"King Zinna is an old man now, dom. He would sooner see his swifter back in the ship-sheds of Zandikar."

"Yet the way I show you will deliver up a greater prize. Did you not see the flying boats land?"

He gasped. "Aye—aye! This will be a great Jikai!"

So we went on through the moonlight in the way I directed. Of course, King Zinna must be old—I'd last seen him fifty years ago and he'd been middle-aged then. The cities and states of the Red southern shore hang together in a sketchy alliance against the Greens, but they are touchy of their national honor. I didn't care to which Zairian city-state the voller went just so long as I stopped off at Zy first.

Although, come to think of it, my allegiance should go to Mayfwy of

Felteraz and through her to King Zo of Sanurkazz. That was, if I had any allegiances left.

The night guard on the two vollers had been changed from Pachaks to Fristles. No doubt apims and Chuliks and any other diffs on the roster might have been used as required. My sea-leems of Zair dealt with the Fristles; the cat-faced diffs swiftly disposed of, the Red swamped over the Green.

The moon glistered on the ornate scrollwork gilding of the sternwalk. The hull bulged with power. Yes, this was a fine handy craft, equipped with varters, decked, a superb fighting machine of the air. We swarmed up like ants, climbing up onto the deck and taking by surprise the remnant of the guard sleeping off watch there.

With brands in their fists, with their blood up, these men of Zandikar showed their mettle.

Their captain and ship-Hikdar had been slain in the battle with the two swifters of Gansk. Many of their comrades had gone up to sit in glory on the right hand of Zair in the radiance of Zim. Now they sent a covey of Grodnims down to the Ice Floes of Sicce without compunction.

Some noise fractured the night in that swift struggle. That was unfortunate but seemingly inevitable. I belted for the control deck shouting to Duhrra to make sure everyone was aboard safely. The controls were perfectly familiar to me. I hit the levers and we went up in a smooth, swooping rise, a rush of power. The smaller voller was not in its mooring place and so King Genod must be sending more messages. I chilled.

Suppose he had taken the voller himself? But no—no, Zair would not play that trick on me. I did as I had planned and brought the voller to earth again in the first spot that appeared suitable from the air. I knew this terrain from carrying messages and had selected a number of deep gullies where the voller might be hidden. I double-checked the best place from the air as we slanted down, and was satisfied she would not be spotted if the two-place flier nosed over.

Hikdar Ornol ti Zab organized his men into throwing the scrubby branches of nik-nik bushes over the deck to shield her. The nik-nik is a nasty plant and the men were scratched. They did not care. My plan appealed to them.

But, Hikdar Ornol and Duhrra both said to me, growling: "We shall come with you, Gadak."

"Not so," I said. "I am able to pass easily where you would have trouble, Duhrra, and you, Hikdar, could not pass at all."

They fumed and argued, but they knew I was right. The voller had to be secured first. Now came the tricky part.

I started to leave them and as I did so Hikdar Ornol said to me, "There is one among our company who claims to have seen a flying boat before. He even says he can fly one through the air like a bird."

The urgency in me, I now admit, made me gloss over this information that would normally have been startling. The Hikdar went on, speaking in his growly graint voice: "If you do not return within two burs of dawn we shall decide—"

I knew what he was going to say. I stopped him.

"You will get this young fellow to fly the boat out. You will all be trapped if you return. You know this to be true."

"Aye." He spoke surlily, a warrior deprived of a fight. "It is sooth. But we are loath to do this thing."

"I shall not say Remberee."

"Hai Jikai!" he said to me, and so I went back toward the camp and to King Genod and Gafard, the King's Striker, the Sea-Zhantil.

There was a quantity of confusion going on about the vanished voller. Guards ran and shouted and torches flared. This was all to the good. I ran in as though most busy about my work, and almost forgot to rip off the red cloth. I bundled it up and stuffed it inside the green tunic over the mail.

"It must be cramphs of Zair!" men bellowed. "Rasts of the Red!"

In all this confusion I ought to be able to take Genod and Gafard. At the least, I ought to be able to do that. So I planned as I ran and shouted with the rest and worked my way around to the tent of the king.

How man proposes and Zair disposes! Or Opaz or Djan. I wouldn't give the time of day to Grodno or Havil or Lem. I ran through the moon-shot darkness. This was where I let rip all the frustrations, where I really hit back, where I at last created a High Jikai that would reinstate me among the ranks of the Krozairs of Zy.

All the stupid pride flooded me, onker that I was. What would that oaf Pur Kazz say when I landed with a magnificent flying boat of the air, with rescued Zairians, and with the enormous prize of not only Gafard, the Sea-Zhantil, the most renowned Ghittawrer of the Eye of the World, but his liege lord also, his king, this same king Genod, the genius king of evil Magdag!

Well, onker I was and onker I remained.

The king's tent was flooded with light. Orderlies and sectrixmen waited outside, nervous, fidgety. I marched through as bold as Krasny work, up to the tent flaps and the guards.

I thought—well, that would be to reveal too much. Suffice it to say I thought it could be done and I could do it. I think, now, in all sober truth, I could have done it. It was, after all, a thing I had done before and was, as you shall hear, a trick I was to pull off again, more than once.

But could the Star Lords have had a hand in this? The Savanti, perhaps? I did not know. I do know that as I bluffed my way past the guards and entered the first of the canvas-sided anterooms leading into the king's quarters a number of what I then considered impossible events occurred.

There were far too many men here to be accounted for by the loss of the voller, serious though that was. These were men who should be out hunting for the king's airboat.

I heard a man shouting: "I tell you it is sooth! I saw him. I saw him as he climbed up the side of the flying boat and the moon shone on his face. He wore the red. I would know that devil's face anywhere, for did he not give me this scar on my own face, these many years ago!"

I halted in the press, at the back, unable to pass through, cursing to get on and yet halted by these words.

"It was the infamous Krozair himself! Pur Dray. The Lord of Strombor! Come back from the dead!"

Other men shouted that how could Golitas be sure, and this Golitas with the scarred face bellowed that, by Goyt, he knew the most renowned Krozair of the Eye of the World when he saw him!

This made it more tricky. Golitas must have come in with the king, for he had not been about the camp. Had he been he would no doubt have taken longer to recognize me for the circumstances would have been far less dramatic. I had best place my white scarf about my face again, but my groping fingers encountered nothing where the scarf should be. Of course, I'd lost the damned thing somewhere along the way.

This was bad enough. But then—and I swear I was in so ugly a mood I might have done something I would have regretted for all the thousand years of life vouchsafed me—I heard two voices I just could not believe in, could not, for they were of another life and another place many dwaburs removed from the problems of the inner sea.

The first voice boomed out in a great Numim bellow.

"What a gang of onkers, by Krun! Can't even guard a voller the empress Thyllis sends out of friendship!"

And the other voice tripped up and down the scale: "This is a wight leem's-nest, Wees! We can't walk all the way home, now can we, dear fellow?"

Fourteen
I avoid old comrades

Rees and Chido!

Incredible. Impossible. But true.

The crowd swayed as guards opened a path through. In the uproar that roaring Numim voice of Rees's blasted out again. He was upset. He didn't mind who knew.

But—Rees and Chido! All the way from Ruathytu in distant Hamal, to the Eye of the World. They must have been with the voller. No other explanation was possible. I stood back, no longer pushing forward.

They had not seen me for over twenty years, but I had no doubts that I would be recognized. They'd know me. They'd be as thunderstruck as I was myself.

They'd know me. They'd know me as Hamun ham Farthytu, the amak of Paline Valley. They did not know their friend Hamun whom they had tried to make into a bladesman was the Prince Majister of Vallia.

What thoughts tumbled pell-mell through my dizzy mind! I had stepped back purely involuntarily. The onker Golitas was still babbling on about it being sure that he had recognized the notorious Krozair, the Lord of Strombor, and over that Rees's lion-roar blattered against my ears.

"By Krun! What a bunch of onkers! Chido, old fellow, this is a right leem's-nest!"

And Chido's light voice, turning all his R's into Ws, a mode of speech I seldom attempt to reproduce, saying: "I suppose you can't blame 'em too much, Rees. If this fellow who stole the voller is as good as they say—"

And a rumble from Rees, indicating to me that he had been learning wisdom in the years separating our last meeting. By Krun! But was I glad to know he and Chido were still alive! After the Battle of Jholaix in which Vallia had smashed the Hamalese Army of the North, anything could have happened to them. Maybe they were even back in the good books of the empress Thyllis. If they were, they were even more of an enemy to Vallia...

The swirls in the crowd as the closely packed men reformed to let the high dignitaries through pushed me against a wooden post holding a peak of the side wall. I could see past the heads and shoulders of those moving in front. I saw Rees and I saw Chido.

They looked just the same.

Well, of course, twenty-one years made little if any difference to the appearance of a man on Kregen, once he had reached the age of his maturity. They looked great. The flaming golden mane that marked Rees for a Numim, a lion-man, glowed in the lamplight. His broad, powerful lion-face scowled and those tawny eyes caught the light and glittered. And Chido, just the same, popping with excitement, spluttering, his chinless face and pop-eyes bringing back the memories. Dear old Chido!

If they saw me they would call out in huge surprise. What explanations had they thought up to explain away to themselves the vanishment of their comrade and fellow bladesman Hamun?

I caught a quick glimpse of a black-browed fellow with a hard, blocky face beyond Rees. Across this fellow's features an old scar showed livid as the blood flushed.

This must be Golitas.

If he saw me the next few murs would be exceedingly tricky and complicated. They might be interesting, too.

Maybe, maybe I might have risked it. For if this Golitas hauled out his
sword and ran at me, and Rees and Chido saw that, might they not shout in
shock and run to stand with me?

They might.

Somehow, I did not think they would.

My shock had been great at seeing them. They might put two and two
together. I had plans for Hamal and I wished to preserve my identity as the
amak of Paline Valley.

I turned my head away.

Yes, I, Gadak, turned my head away.

A table lay cluttered with cloaks and capes and scarves dropped by the
officers and aides as they had entered. A green scarf, snatched up, covered
my face. I do not disguise my own feelings of contempt for myself. But
much, much more depended on my actions now; my freedom meant more
than the freedom that has so often been denied me—it meant getting out
of the Eye of the World and back to Delia. That must come first.

There seemed to me to be more than an inkling in my head why these
two, Rees and Chido, had come to the inner sea with the voller for King
Genod. I guessed they had fancied the adventure, no doubt feeling at a
loss in peacetime Hamal. Had Rees's estates of the Golden Wind all blown
away yet? Was he now merely the owner of an empty title? How was Saffi,
his daughter, that glorious lion-maiden I had rescued from the Cripples'
Jikai, snatched from the Manhounds of Faol?

The interruption in my progress, the check as the crowd surged back
making way, the shock of seeing old comrades again, all conspired to
thwart my plans.

Chido gesticulating violently, and Rees stalking on arrogantly, they
passed through the crowd and on into the moonlight outside. I roused
myself. The idiot Golitas would follow soon. After he had gone, would
there be a chance to snatch Gafard and the king? "Ah, Gadak! Just the
man!"

I whirled about and my hand fell to my longsword. Gafard stared at me,
and past me at the others in the canvas-walled anteroom.

"All of you! Out searching! The king is most wrathful. The flying boat
has been stolen and stolen by no less than Pur Dray, the great Krozair. Stir
yourselves!" He saw the movement of my hand. "Yes, Gadak. It is a time for
swords—but only when we find the flying boat"

"Yes, gernu."

How easily I slipped into the ways of Grodnim that had encompassed
me these past months!

My prime responsibility was to Delia. I had to get out of the inner sea and back to her. I had to get back alive, for she had warned me, long and long ago, that she would be cross with me if I got myself killed. Beside her anger at that kind of foolishness on my part, the anger of King Genod over the loss of his voller was as the mewling of an infant.

There were many men, both apim and diff, in the anteroom of the king's tent. A guard party of bowmen stood with bows held up and arrows nocked, a part and parcel of the king's security. Word that the Lord of Strombor had been seen was enough to make every man stand to arms and tremble, sweating in anticipation.

The events that had taken place since I had bluffed my way in here to hear Rees's great Numim bellow to the moment when Gafard ordered me to join the search had taken practically no time at all. Words and thoughts and actions had tumbled one over the other.

My plan had failed.

There was no chance at all to take Gafard and less chance, even than that, to take the king.

If I put a sword-edge to Gafard's throat and forced my way in to the king the bowmen would feather me, and if Gafard died as well that was the price Grodno exacted. I remembered, here in the very Eye of the World, the callousness with which Prince Glycas, the embodiment of all that was evil in the overlords of Magdag, had told me that I could slay his guard-commander, but that he would surely slay me, anyway. The only life with which to bargain with King Genod was the life of King Genod himself.

"Don't stand about, you calsanys!" bellowed Gafard. No doubt he had had the rough edge of Genod's tongue. His fierce face showed all the venom I might have shown in a similar situation. "Schtump!" He used that coarse and abusive word to these officers, the word that conveys in such a vivid way "Get out! Clear off!"

"Schtump!" roared Gafard, the King's Striker. "Find the flying boat of the king!"

Even then, as the men elbowed out carrying me with them in the press and I saw the tall, scar-faced form of Golitas approaching Gafard, the King's Striker had not made any evil promises as a reward for failure. He was canny enough to see the apparently obvious. If the flying boat could sail through the air faster than a galloping sectrix, then she would be away and gone and no torchlight search in the darkness would find her again.

As we mounted up I had to stop cursing. My hands did not shake, but in all else I felt myself to be the greatest rogue in two worlds. My nerve had not failed me, for I knew it was Delia who had restrained my hand. But I knew what my conduct would appear to my comrades, to my Brother Krozairs—I had failed in my plans and had not taken the opportunity to cut down all in my path until I died still striking out with the cry of Zair on my bloodied lips.

That, of course, was the maniac's way, the battle-lover's way, the berserker way I had renounced with disgust.

But—would that not have been a Jikai?

Possibly, but a damned little one in my view.

I gave up making excuses for my feeble conduct and spurred off into the darkness with the others, the link-slaves astride preysanys lighting our way, and precious little chance we had of finding the voller, I can say.

The torches flared their blazing hair over the shadows and we rode and men shouted and there was much hullabaloo. I took the first opportunity to ride off and lose myself in the darkness.

The Maiden with the Many Smiles made that difficult, for the darkness was a matter of a pink-lit radiance, gloomy only in comparison with the glory of the daytime suns; the torches emphasized the darkness. I slipped away at last and cantered along to where I had left the voller. No one followed.

I had miserably failed in the main elements of my plan. I did not return with the king and Gafard. But the second part of the scheme could still work. I would take the voller and we'd fly out over the inner sea and when the convoy bearing the supplies for the army appeared off the coast we would swoop down and sink and burn the lot.

Yes, that would at least salvage some part of my Jikai.

With a voller of the quality of the airboat we had captured under my command I would be master of the situation.

Grandiloquent ideas burned in my mind. I felt the power of madness and of supernal power flowing through me.

With the airboat I could be master of the coast, and destroy utterly all Genod's plans.

He had no varters that could deal with vollers. The armies of the Hostile Territories and of Havilfar contained high-angle varters, artillery designed to hurl bolts upward and so bring down the flaunting ships of the air. These devices were unknown in the inner sea. I would be unchallenged. I would be unchallengeable.

So it was that with the hateful word "I" ringing in my head I reached the place where the voller had been hidden.

Approaching cautiously, for there had been weapons aplenty in the flier and I did not want an arrow through me, I gave a low-voiced hail.

"Duhrra! Hikdar Ornol!"

The camouflage had been well done. The nik-nik bushes concealed all. My sectrix lumbered on, his hooves near soundless on the sandy soil. The pink and golden moonlight flooded down and away from the interference of the torches' glow I could see well. I called again, louder.

No answer. Nothing.

The sectrix slipped and skidded down the incline. I was enclosed by the bushy walls. I looked about.

The voller was not there.

I looked again, and shouted, and spurred up and sent the sectrix crashing down into the bottom of the gulley.

Nothing. The voller was gone.

Just how long I rode up and down, flailing at bushes with my sword, yelling, bellowing, I have no idea.

At last the realization reached me that, in truth, the voller had flown. I could not curse. For the last time I galloped lumpily across the sandy soil, flailing away, and bits of bush flew into the air, spinning in the moon-drenched darkness. The smell of night blooms hung strongly in the air.

Nothing.

No voller.

Duhrra and the men from Zandikar had gone.

I was alone.

Now, if ever, was the time to remember that I, Gadak of the Green, was not and never could be Gadak of the Green.

Fifteen
My Lady of the Stars wields a dagger

"The onkers rush upon their own destruction," said Gafard with great satisfaction.

We sat our sectrixes upon a slight eminence in the nik-nik covered bluffs. The sea sparkled bluely away to our left. The land to the right trended, flat and uninteresting, to a far horizon where heat shimmer broke outlines into blue and purple ghosts. Blown by the wind, drifts of sand swathed the scene below.

Below us and less than half a dwabur away marched the hosts of Zair, advancing to the west. How marvelous they looked, with their many red banners fluttering, the suns striking back in gleam and glint from armor and weapons. Sectrix cavalry trotted on the flanks. Infantry marched at the center. On they came, proud in their might, a splendid army gathered from the fortress cities of Pynzalo and Zimuzz, from the inland towns of Jikmarz and Rozilloi, and from many of the villages of the fertile inland territories.

In all those brave banners of the Red I saw the proud devices, and recognized many of them. Justice and hope marched there, pride and honor. On the right flank, their sectrixes' hooves sometimes cutting through the surf, trotted a contingent of splendid cavalry on whose red banners the device of the hubless spoked wheel within the circle blazed and coruscated.

Only a small contingent of Krozairs of Zy there were. I guessed that the bulk of the Krzy would be far to the west, fighting with Pur Zenkiren and the two generals of the combined armies there.

My heart lifted when I saw that grand and formidable array advancing toward the massed green banners before me.

Gafard, the King's Striker, sat his sectrix and chuckled and ever and anon he pulled that black hawk-beard of his. He had given no further orders after those that had drawn out the army of Magdag into its allotted positions.

Two sennights had gone by since my disastrous debacle on the night the king's voller had been stolen by the famous Krozair, the Lord of Strombor. Although a strict watch was kept against the flyer's return, no more had been seen of her.

I had hoped she would be flying over the host of Zair when they marched to the attack. The Zairians had worked like demons to collect this army to reinforce the armies of the west. Now we had appeared unexpectedly in their path. They attacked recklessly. This was the way they reacted to the descent upon their coasts of the Green of Grodno.

The king and Gafard had been highly delighted.

All thought of investing Pynzalo had been abandoned. The garrison of the city marched in the host fronting us. Gafard had said, "They save us much labor and casualties." He had slapped his thigh with his riding glove before throwing it to a slave and taking up the metaled war-gauntlets he would wear for the battle. "You ride as aide to me, Gadak. Nalgre and Nath and Insur, with Gontar and Gerigan, will be all I need. Once the battle is joined there will be little need for messages. The army of the king knows what to do!"

"One wonders," said Gontar, who prided himself that his father was an overlord of Magdag who owned estates requiring ten thousand slaves to run, "if that cramph the Lord of Strombor is with the onkers this day."

"One," said Gafard, Sea-Zhantil, "sincerely trusts he is not."

They took that to mean the obvious, but I glanced at Gafard—and away smartly, to be sure—and guessed he meant he hoped Pur Dray would not be there to be slain by a casual pike-thrust. Gafard wanted to cross swords with the great Krozair in person, so I said to myself, pondering imponderables.

I admit, in all fairness, that I was not only coming to share these damned Grodnims' obsession with Pur Dray, Krozair, and regarding him in the third person, but also was still much surprised that his legend persisted so vividly after fifty years. I could scarce credit that no other Krozair had risen to a similar eminence in the Eye of the World.

The truth was that Gafard so hungered after a similar renown his well-known obsession fostered the persistence of the stories and tales of the Lord of Strombor. Now that Pur Dray had returned to life, had been declared Apushniad by the Krzy and had actually been seen back at his old activities, no wonder speculation and rumor buzzed around the camp like flies over the carcass of a chunkrah slain by leems on the plains.

Also in this fascination with a Red Krozair must be the dread knowledge in the minds of the overlords that Pur Dray had witnessed the private, terrible rites that went on in the utmost secrecy within the megaliths at the time of the Great Death, when the red sun eclipsed the green sun.

I suppose, trying to think about it logically and restraining myself from taking the amused and cynical line that was too treacherously easy, there was a terrible and malefic aura about the name and deeds of Pur Dray, the Lord of Strombor, Krozair of Zy.

The hosts of Red marched on, their banners flying. The ranks of Green waited calmly, silent, and their green banners flaunted no less vividly under the suns.

Gafard was eyeing the distances. We could all see the restiveness in the Red cavalry on the wings. They would charge at any moment, a torrent of mailed men bursting down on the ranks of Green footmen. Those footmen were fronted by a glittering, slanting wall of pike-heads.

I knew the heart of that formation down there below us on the sandy soil. I had created it myself. The serried mass of pikes in the strong phalanx to take the shock of the cavalry change. The halberdiers and swordsmen to protect the pikes from swordsmen. The wedges of arbalesters shooting with controlled rhythm. And the shields—that cowards' artifice—the shields to protect the men and deflect the shafts from the short, straight bows and the crossbows of the enemy. Oh, yes, I had designed that fighting machine to destroy mailed overlords of Magdag. And now those same devilish overlords used my fighting instrument, remade by them with their own swods, to destroy my comrades in Zair. I tell you, my thoughts were bleak and spare.

I hoped that the Zairians would win.

I knew the worth of my work and the genius of Genod Gannius, whose parents I had saved from destruction, and I knew, darkly and with agony and remorse, the inevitable outcome of the battle.

What I would do was already worked out. I knew that despite all, I could not stop myself.

The red cloth was stuffed again within the breast of my tunic. I would don the red, draw my longsword, and so hurl myself into the rear of the pikes as the charges went in. Perhaps there would be a little chance for the Krozairs, for the Red Brethren, for the warriors of Zair.

That chance was slender to the point of nonexistence.

But, despite all, I could not stop myself.

Sharply, a shadow fleeted over the ground and we all looked up and there, skimming through the bright air, flew the two-place voller with Genod Gannius gorgeous in green and gold leaning over and encouraging his troops.

If he had fire-pots up there...

The army of the Green let out a dull surf-roar of welcome and greeting to their king. Very pretty it was. And in defiant answer rose the shouts from the Reds.

"Grodno! Zair! Green! Red!" The shouts rose and clashed. "Krozair! Ghittawrer!" The yells twined in the brilliant atmosphere. And, a new shout, a shrill screeching: "Genod! Genod! The king!"

The Zairian cavalry charged, a torrential mass of steel and red bearing down on the massed pikes. I reined Blue Cloud a little way back of the other aides. They were all standing in their stirrups, craning to look down from our eminence onto the drama spread out below. Now was the time to don the red and so charge down and make a finish.

It might not be a Jikai, but with those Krozair shouts ringing through the air and the brave scarlet fluttering I could do no other...

A shadow flitted into the corner of my eye and I turned, quickly, the red half drawn from my green tunic.

A Pachak with only one left arm, and a bloody stump where the other should be, rode frantically up to Gafard, his hebra foundering. He yelled at Gafard. I heard his words, caught and blown by the wind; I saw Gafard's hard mahogany face turn abruptly gray within the iron rim of his helmet.

"My Lady—treachery—we were surprised—slain—black—men in black—my lord..."

The Pachak fell even as his hebra collapsed.

Gafard lifted his head and screeched.

I thrust the red away and kicked Blue Cloud over.

"Gadak! You I trust! Find Grogor! Find Nath ti Hagon! Take men—anyone—ride, Gadak, ride! My Lady of the Stars—my pearl, my heart... ride, Gadak! Ride as you love me!"

I didn't love the devil. But—my Lady of the Stars!

What do I know, now, of my thoughts, my emotions, and my feelings? I know I knew the Zairian army below me was doomed, for I had wrought the instrument of their destruction. But there would come another time, another field, and another battle. Now all my blood clamored that I save my Lady of the Stars.

I rode. I did not ride wearing the red. I rode not for my lord Gafard, the King's Striker, the Sea-Zhantil—but for my Lady of the Stars.

Even now, after all that happened, I do not regret that decision.

If only some easy power of sorcery had been open to me!

If only by some magic formula I could have prevented what was fated to occur.

But I am a mortal man and the fantasies of wish-fulfillment belong to the myths and legends of Kregen, not to the hard reality of that beautiful and terrible world beneath the Suns of Scorpio.

Yes, there is seeming magic on Kregen, and the wizards practice mighty sorceries, but they are of a piece, following ordained paths. The wonder and mystery of Kregen can never be denied, but it is men and women with hope and courage who flesh out the true fantasies.

I rode.

Grogor, Gafard's second in command, that surly man, did not hesitate a fraction. He screeched a savage order to a squadron of sectrixmen, all picked men-at-arms, apims and diffs, and wheeled his mount and was away with streaming mane and flying feathers. We picked up Nath ti Hagon, Gafard's trusted ship-Hikdar, and then, in a compact body, we rode from the battlefield. Sand blew from our sectrixes' hooves. The wind of our passage blustered in our plumes and scorched into our faces. So we left the action, the battle, that debacle for the Red, which the mad genius king Genod called the Battle of Pynzalo.

Wherever Gafard had hidden his beloved, the rasts of men in black had found her. I had one hope. The voller had been flown by Genod himself and it had flown over the battlefield. We had to deal with men mounted on sectrixes like ourselves.

In one item of my reading of the situation I was wrong.

We went flying through the near-deserted camp, sending the camp followers stumbling out of our way, only the green of our plumes and dress able to convince them they were not attacked by a raiding party of Zairians. We belted past the lines of tents. I had nudged Blue Cloud gently to the head of the pack, for although I wished to conserve him for what I thought would be a long ride, I still felt the mad desire to hurry on like a maniac and be the first there to rescue my Lady of the Stars.

The Pachak of her guard who had escaped to warn Gafard must have been a most intelligent as well as a brave man. He must have fought until he saw there was no hope left and then, instead of going on fighting and throwing his life away, had turned and raced for the King's Striker. Out past the camp we saw the flurry of green cloaks. I looked closer. A party of sectrixmen was picking its way down the sandy slopes toward the beach. A swifter waited there, her stern ladder erected, one end on the quarter and the other on the beach. Beneath the green cloaks I saw—instead of the expected white, or green, or the flash of mail—black.

Grogor saw, also, and shrilled and we all pelted along, hurling ourselves madly over the bluffs and so roaring down the sandy slopes in great clouds and smothers of sand.

Somehow Blue Cloud kept his six legs under him. We were on the beach. I yanked out my longsword, that Ghittawrer blade with the device removed, and whirled along the packed sand.

The black-clad men saw us coming.

There was a struggle in their midst.

Grogor and Nath were neck and neck with me. Our three swords thrust forward, three-pronged retribution.

The black-clad men tried to face us.

There must have been few men who could have stood up to us in that frenzied moment.

In the moments before we hit I saw my Lady of the Stars.

She wielded a long, thin dagger in her white hand, and she toppled one kidnapper from his saddle and whirled on another who tried to spit her through. She parried—it was marvelously done, marvelously!—and riposted and stuck the rast through the eye. He screamed and fell and then we were upon them.

Our rage was terrible and genuine.

The longswords whirled and glittered, split and cleft, and whipped aloft again for the next blow, dripping red.

Blade clanged against blade. My Ghittawrer longsword sang above my head. Aye! It sang as I whirled it up and down. I smashed with full force, seeing a head spin off, seeing a black-masked face abruptly disappear into a ghastly red mask, seeing an arm spin up and away as a back-hander curled beneath a blow. It was all over in scant murs. We panted. I dragged in a great lungful of air and then, dismounting, walked over to my Lady, who lay in the sand. Her green veiling remained in place, for she had one hand to it. But she knew me.

"Gadak! So you rescue me again."

"Aye, my Lady. You are unhurt?"

She stood up. She put a hand on my shoulder. Her left hand. In her right hand, smothered in blood, she still gripped the slender, jeweled dagger.

"I am unharmed. They tried to—at the end—when they saw you coming. But—"

"Yes, my Lady. You yourself created a Jikai, I saw." Then I smiled—I, who am a surly beast and with a face like the ram of a swifter. "I am minded of another lady, my Lady."

"I would not have thought—" she began, and then stopped and threw the dagger to the sand. She took her hand from my shoulder and drew herself up. She put that clean left hand to her hair. Typically, the next words she said were, "And my lord? How goes the battle?"

"The battle will go well enough."

She sighed.

She, like myself, had been Zairian once.

"I returned to the camp, Gadak, and they were waiting for me. Men in black. Stikitches—kidnappers for a space—but real stikitches, nonetheless."

"Aye."

My men were inspecting the corpses. The swifter was gone, pulling madly out to sea.

Grogor turned one body over with his foot and then cocked an eye at me. I looked down.

The brown face with a livid scar all across it showed where Golitas, who had received that scar from the hands of Pur Dray, had died in agony.

"It would be best to heave these carrion into the sea." Grogor took out his knife. "But first—My Lady, would you please retire for a space, for there are things that must be done."

She understood well enough. A warrior maid, for she had fought magnificently, now she was a practical lady with a man to protect. So we disfigured the corpses so that they would never be recognized and heaved them into the sea. When we had finished we escorted my Lady back to camp and had anyone challenged us he would have been a dead man.

We had saved my Lady of the Stars for Gafard, Sea-Zhantil; we had saved her from the clutches of King Genod himself and no one to point the finger of accusation at us. Also, a man who knew my face was dead. Besides the safety of my Lady that was of no importance at all.

Sixteen

Grogor surprises me

Black magbirds flew overhead. To larboard the lesser Pharos passed at the end of the mole. The stones gleamed in the slanting lines of masonry, and the curve of stonework opened out into a broad view across the outer harbor. Two swifters rode to their moorings here, their yards crossed, and the last preparations caused a bustle on their long, lean decks as they were readied for sea. *Volgodont's Fang* glided on, the oars pulling with a slow, steady rhythm that drove our stem through the water with a low musical chinkle.

The frowning stone gateway to the cothon, the inner basin, lined up directly with our ram. Nath ti Hagon stood staring directly ahead, lining up the ship, giving quick, direct orders to the oar-master in his tabernacle and to the two helm-Deldars at their rudder handles. These two old tarpaulins turned the curved steering oars with cunning, smooth movements that kept the swifter dead on track.

The group standing with me on the quarterdeck included Gafard, but he was in this matter quite content to let his trusted first lieutenant conn the ship. Hardly a breeze ruffled the still surface of the water in which reflections stood out in perfect mirror-images.

The entrance to this cothon had been excavated widely enough to accommodate the spread wings of a swifter. Many cothons have narrow entrances, so that a galley must be drawn through by pulling-boat or, more usually, by gangs of men hauling hawsers from the dock side, all heaving together at the crack of a whip and the yell of "Grak!"

We glided on smoothly. I had no doubts that Nath would take the ship fairly through the center of the narrow channel with not a single oar splintered. Swifters habitually carry as many as half the number of oars again to replace broken oars, for breaking oars is a familiar hazard to the swifter captains of the inner sea.

Once we were fairly through the whistles shrilled and the drum-Deldar tapped his peculiar terminal notes and every oar lifted and remained level. Swifters of the size of *Volgodont's Fang* are reasonably stable in the water, unlike the smaller swifters that rock so much a man must step lightly and the oars must rest in the water to ensure stability.

How familiar the details of bringing a vessel into port!

I watched, storing away the nostalgic memories and refusing to become maudlin. The sides of the cothon were lined with the long, slanting ship-sheds, narrow structures, two slips to a roof, inclined toward the water. Ingenious capstans and pulleys were arranged so that the swifters might be drawn up out of the water and gangs of slaves whipped to the work. The open fronts of the sheds with their ornate columns and Magdaggian arches could be closed by wooden doors in inclement weather—of which there is, thankfully, very little in the Eye of the World—and as they clustered closely together they presented a compact, crowded nesting effect. Little over the width of a swifter, probably not one being more than forty feet wide to accept the apostis, they were long, a hundred and eighty feet or more. This was not the king's harbor. Over there the sheds were, of course, larger. The massively impressive building rising to the rear, sculptured almost like a temple, was the Arsenal of the Jikgernus—the warrior lords—and there were kept the multifarious stores demanded by the swifters. The smell of that place could waft me away and away four hundred light-years in my mind's eye.

Farther to one side and lifting grandly over the ship-sheds, the bulk of a real temple glittered in the suns-light. All smothered in green tiling, ceramics of the same high quality that decorated the megaliths, the temple of the sea-god, Shorush-Tish, sparkled and glistered in the light. Set at the apex of its many-peaked roofs the marble representations of swifters, one third full size, leered down over the mariners and marines and slaves who crowded the narrow streets, busy about the sea business of Shorush-Tish.

It is a remarkable fact—at least, at that time it was remarkable to me—that the blue-maned sea-god, Shorush-Tish, is shared by Grodnim and Zairian. In all else they clash in their beliefs, for all that they sprang from the same original religious convictions. Temples to Shorush-Tish are obligatory on all the seafronts of all the ports of the north and south, the Green and the Red. Even the Proconians erect altars to Shorush-Tish. Even the many races of diffs who live up in the northeastern areas of the Eye of the World—and particularly around the smaller sea known as the Sea of Onyx to the apims because of the many chalcedony mines around its shores—build their temples to their halfling representations of Shorush-Tish. Even the Sorzarts who live and reive from their islands up there respect the power of the universal sea-god of the Eye of the World.

It would be a foolish and reckless captain who did not make an offering to Shorush-Tish before he observed the fantamyrrh boarding his vessel.

For all my own dogged beliefs I complied with the custom, and many were the rings and cups I had given to the blue-robed priests of Shorush-Tish in his great temple on the waterfront of the inner harbor at Sanurkazz.

Over by the near wall as we glided on, busy gangs of workmen swarmed over an old swifter of that class rowed in the fashion the savants call *a terzaruolo*. I have mentioned that the extra power gained by using a number of men on one oar rowing over an apostis in the *a scaloccio* system had reached the inner sea; but, like the swordships up along the coasts of the Hoboling Islands, the older system still clung on. This swifter with her five men to a bench, angled to the stern, each man pulling on one oar, could not hope to match the speed of a modern swifter of the type of *Volgodont's Fang*. Yet she had been built well and the teredo had not got her, and her timbers were still sound. She had been a fairly large example, rowing five men to a bench each side and with thirty-two oars in each bank. This gave her a total of three hundred and twenty oarsmen and three hundred and twenty oars.

When I say she would not reach the same speed as the more modern examples, I mean essentially the same sustained speed and the same driving power. To improve her it would be necessary to place the five men of each bench all pulling on the same oar, and to increase the length and strength of that oar out of all recognition of the smaller loom and blade hauled by a single man.

This is exactly what the workmen were doing.

When completed, she would be classed as a five sixty-two swifter. I looked to see if they were building a second bank, but saw no sign that this was proposed in her rebuilding.

We went through all the usual formalities of landing. The slaves were herded off to their bagnios. They would very quickly be pressed into service again, for, as the conversion of the old swifter of the *a terzaruolo* system showed, Magdag was scraping up all her resources to fling into what everyone here must consider as the final stages of a victorious war.

The omens looked propitious for King Genod and the overlords of

Magdag as for the whole of the Grodnim alliance. I had more or less recovered from the smart of that series of disasters on the Red southern shore. Now we had come back to Magdag, For all the others here this was a homecoming. For me it was the chance to further my plans—those plans that envisaged the king, Gafard, and a voller.

King Genod had duly won his Battle of Pynzalo. There had been few prisoners, and while I was glad of that, I knew the truth lay buried in the sands or running back to Pynzalo and beyond. That, I tell you, was one battle I was glad with a heartfelt gratitude to have missed.

Gafard did not tell me of what passed between him and Genod.

After all, I was as far as he was concerned merely a fellow renegade he had befriended and given employment and who had by chance come into contact with his beloved in ways that, hitherto, he had rewarded with death. I did have a privileged position of a sort, that was clear, but it did not extend past the concerns of his household and domestic matters.

He had thanked the group who had rescued the Lady of the Stars, thanked them profusely and with gold. We were only too well aware of what we had done; but the squadron under Grogor was composed of picked men, every man loyal to Gafard personally. No possible blame could attach to the King's Striker for having his men cut down black-clad assassins and kidnappers.

All the same, at the first opportunity, Genod handed over command of the army to Genal Furneld, the Rog of Giddur, and called Gafard back to Magdag. A gloss was put on this by the announcement to the army that soon Prince Glycas would take over command of the combined armies and Gafard, the King's Striker, was required for further duties.

This Genal Furneld was of the usual cut of unpleasant overlords of Magdag and I avoided him. Giddur was sited on the River Dag in one of the great sweeping bends south of Hagon. He had arrived on the southern shore breathing fire and slaughter and having fifty men of a pike regiment punished for dirty equipment. I thought the army was welcome to him. Gafard had said, lightly, concealing his feelings, that Genal Furneld could sit down in front of Pynzalo and freeze for all he cared. No one imagined that he would carry the city with the same panache as the Sea-Zhantil. That had cheered me a little.

Little time was given me for moping.

My Lady of the Stars returned to her apartments in the Tower of True Contentment and Gafard called me in to tell me that he had decided, if I was to earn my keep now that he no longer commanded actively, that I was to stand guard with the others of his loyal squadron. I do not like guard duty. But I accepted this charge with equanimity.

"The matter is simple. Grogor will give you your orders. Do not fail me, Gadak. I am a man of exceeding wrath to those in whom I have reposed trust if they betray me."

So, I bellowed, "Your orders, my commands, gernu!" and bashed off to see what unpleasantness Grogor might dream up for me.

He surprised me.

He sat in the small guardroom in the wall hard by the entrance to the tower. It was plain and furnished with a stand of weapons of various kinds, a table and chairs, no sleeping arrangements, the toilet being outside, and was a harsh and unlovely room.

"Now, Gadak, who was once a Zairian, listen to me and listen well."

I was not prepared to strike him, so I listened. I had plans. I thought Grogor as a vicious killer was not worth my destroying what slender chances my plans possessed. But, as I say, he surprised me.

A bulky, sweaty man, this Grogor. He said, "You told me you did not aspire to take my place in the affections of our lord and I did not believe. I was wrong. I do believe you now." He reached over a leather jack and drank with a great blustering of bubbles. He started to say "By Mother—" and stopped, and swore, a rib-creaking oath involving the anatomy of Gyph-imedes, the favorite of the beloved of Grodno.

I said, "It is hard, sometimes."

"Aye."

"I serve my Lady," I said. "As you know well."

He slapped the jack onto the scarred wooden table. His sweaty, heavy face lit up. "By Grodno! But it was a good quick fight, was it not! We tore them to pieces like leems."

"Yet you missed the battle."

He looked up at me, for he sat while I stood. "Aye. What of it?"

"Nothing. Except that you strike me as a man who enjoys a good fight."

"I do." He nodded to the interior door leading into the tower. "And if anyone save the lord or people bearing his sign attempt to pass that door, it is a fight to the death."

"I understand that."

"Good. It is well we understand each other."

There was no doorway at ground level leading into the tower from the outer four courtyards around the base. The only ingress was through the guardroom in the wall. And we guarded that room and that wall and that door.

A second chamber lay alongside the guardroom in which the guards on duty but off watch might sleep and clean their tack. This room smelled of spit and polish, of sweaty bodies, of greasy food. One day, Gafard said, he would have a fresh chamber constructed and so separate the various guard functions. As it was, our prime duty was to guard my Lady.

I sent in a formal request to see Gafard. When he received me, it was in the armory, where he was inspecting a new consignment of Genodders of a superior make. They would bear the Kregish block initials *G.K.S.M.*

in Kregish. This, quite obviously, stood for the sword from the armory of Gafard, King's Striker.

"You want to see me?"

"Aye, gernu. I guard the tower and am happy to do so—honored—"

"Get on with it!"

"We guard the door. But the roof—we have all seen a certain flying boat—"

He slapped a shortsword down so the metal rang.

"By Grodno! No honest man would think of such a thing—which proves you are no honest man and therefore of great use to me. By Goyt! We'll fix any onkers who try to fly down like volgodonts onto my roof! We'll impale the rasts!"

All this meant, of course, was that he had not lived, as had I, in a culture where vollers and flying animals and birds are regularly used. It was a thing he would not have thought of in the nature of his experience. But he sealed the roof as well as any roof was sealed in the Hostile Territories.

Kregen is a harsh and cruel world for all its beauty, and there a man must protect his own, a woman protect her own. I had done precious little of that, lately, but I had supreme confidence in my Delia. She, at the least, would give me firm assurance that I did the right thing in thus helping to protect this unknown Zairian girl, this Lady of the Stars.

I felt sure I was right in this, and yet could give no real reason to myself. I have tried to explain as best I can the effect this maiden had on me, and although I intended to knock Gafard on the head when I could get him and the king together with a voller, I fancied I'd think of her as I hit him.

One night I went on duty earlier than usual, because I was fretful and wanted to get away from some of the diffs of the squadron who were playing dirty-Jikaida (a game I do not care for), and so I wandered along by the wall thinking of Delia and all manner of distant dreams. The guardroom door was open and I went in and almost stumbled over the body of young Genal the Freckles. His neck had been cut open.

The longsword was in my hand, a brand of fire in the torchlight.

The inner door to the off-duty room was shut and logs jammed it.

Three men in black swung about as I stumbled. They lunged at me. I shouted before I bothered to deal with them.

"Guards! Guards! To the tower! Treachery!" Then the blades met and rang in a glitter of steel. These three were good and they used Genodders. They would have had me, but I whipped out the shortsword and with that in my left hand fended a little, foining as I would with rapier and main-gauche. With a longsword and a shortsword this is not easy; but the second man dropped with the longsword slicing his throat out, and the third man screeched and tried to run as I chopped him as he turned.

The first man was clawing up from the floor, the shortsword still transfixing his throat where I had hurled it. He collapsed in blood and then Grogor burst in from the courtyard.

"Aloft, Grogor!" I bellowed.

We kicked the logs away and the men inside, alerted by the scuffle and baffled by the jammed door, poured out. In a living tide of fury we went up the stairs. The fight was not long. The kidnappers had posted three of their number to watch the guardroom and sent three aloft. We had no mercy on them. We did not wish to hold them for questioning. We knew who had sent them.

I did not see my Lady then, for she had taken her dagger and gone to her private rooms beneath the roof. We caught the kidnappers, but not before they had slain a beautiful numim maiden, her glorious golden fur foully splattered with her own blood. I cursed. When we trooped downstairs again, assured by an apim girl, a handmaiden to my Lady, that all was well, we took the three bodies and disposed of them along with the first three.

Gafard, livid, twitching, raced up the stairs without a word. He came back furious. I wondered what he would do. I knew there was nothing he could do—save send the girl to the king with a handsome note, a gracious gift.

"This is becoming expensive for the king," he said.

That was all.

I think I admired him then, as much as ever I'd done.

We kept the guard even more alert after that.

Three days later I had occasion to go into Magdag on an errand for Gafard. This was all a part of my duties as his aide. He was ordering a pearl necklace of many strands, an enormous pearl choker for his lady, and I was to deliver gold for the fittings and clasps. He trusted me in this.

The souks of Magdag are strange places, filled with all the clamor one expects of markets where all is bustle, but yet completely lacking the bright, cheerful sounds of markets in Sanurkazz. Dour people, the folk of Magdag, resting on a slave foundation for labor, giving orders and whipping and shouting "Grak!" and taking the profits for themselves. They have this marvelous way with dressed leather, as I have said, although the best leather comes from Sanurkazz. I found the jewelers' arcade and the right shop, with its barred windows and narrow door, and transacted my business. Awnings stretched out overhead and the suns' glare was muted into gentle saffron and lime and pink. The sounds of the souks penetrated in a buzz. The walls were yellow and bright, but few vines or flowers grew, where in Sanurkazz in such a place the whole area would have rioted in blossom.

I came outside, bending my head to duck under the low Magdaggian door, and a dagger presented its point to my throat, a hand gripped my arm, and a voice said, "We mean you no harm, dom. Just come quietly with us."

In the normal course of events I would not have abided this. To slide the dagger was not all that easy, for the point pricked just above my Adam's apple; but I did so, anyway, and kicked in the direction of the voice as I gripped the hand and twisted up and back.

Then I was outside the door, dragging one screaming wretch over the stones, seeing another reeling away—most green and bilious and vomiting—and staring at a third who held a crossbow spanned and loaded and pointing at my guts.

"We said we would not harm you, Gadak. We are on the business of a man you would do well to heed. You will come with us."

A fourth man, dressed like the others in the usual green and white robes with tall white turbans, approached and bent to say in my ear: "You are an onker! This is king's business."

The moment he spoke I saw the next few burs in all clarity—and damned awful they would be, too.

If I had been recognized—but this was very much an outside chance. As we went along the crowded streets where it would have been easy for me to slip away, I did not do so. I had already convinced myself that scar-faced Golitas had recognized me only because of the stark illumination as I'd climbed up into the voller. The corner of the eye and the quick, illuminating flash can often reveal far more than the long stare. So, as I went along, I wetted and pulled my moustaches down even more into that ugly soup-straining fungus the Magdaggians think of as proper moustaches. No—I did not think the king wished to see me because I had been recognized as the arch-enemy of Magdag, the notorious Krozair, Pur Dray.

In that—about the king seeing me—I flattered myself.

Everything was conducted in the chilling, efficient way of machine governments. The house to which I was conducted was not a villa, not a hovel. It was nowhere near the king's palace. The king would not dirty his hands with the details of his desires. The man who told me what he wanted me to do was puffy and limp-fingered, with a green-swathed paunch, bloated eyes, and moustaches so long and thin and black I felt he could tie green ribbons in each side.

He did not condescend to tell me his name; he told me I might call him *gernu*, and if that was not sufficient, when I received my pay I might address him as Nodgen the Faithful.

It did not take a genius to understand what these cramphs wanted.

I was to arrange to open the guardroom doors, to arrange to let the kidnappers in, and this time when we jammed the door we would stand guard with more spirit and at a proper time. Of course, this Nodgen the Faithful had no idea of what had happened to his party of kidnappers. I told him, simply, they had all been slain.

"Then this time it is your neck, Gadak. We know you, renegade. You will sell your ib for an ob."

I might sell my soul for a penny—but not on Earth or Kregen.

"And young Genal the Freckles? Will you serve me as you served him after I open the door, as he did?"

"He was an onker. He would have talked."

"And I will not?"

He looked annoyed. I realized I had best not pursue that line too far, otherwise he would release me from the contract prematurely—with a free passage to the Ice Floes of Sicce. So I agreed. They had a lever.

"If you betray us, be very sure you will end up on the oar benches, pulling your guts out in a swifter, flogged... you will not relish that, I assure you."

"How would you know?" I began to say. I did not add, as I would have done were I not meditating great, evil joy, "You fat slug!"

We agreed terms. Fifty golden oars. A large sum. I managed to get them to give me ten golden oars on account. No doubt they thought they would take them back from my dead body after I had opened the doors to them. Arrangements were made, the day was set, three days' time, and I was taken away and left in the souk. It would be useless to return to the house. That was a mere convenient place to meet; the owners were probably bound and gagged in the cellars. I returned to Gafard's Jade Palace. As I went in I glanced up at the Tower of True Contentment. I did not smile. But I thought of my Lady.

Any man would do anything for the king to escape the galleys.

What was a mere slip of a girl besides my freedom to pursue my quest in the Eye of the World, to return to Delia?

Would not any sensible girl rejoice in the wealth and luxury the king would heap on her in return for her favors? The princess Susheeng was out of Magdag, visiting friends in Laggig-Laggu to the west. The king had a free hand. Would not any girl leap at the chance to become the king's favorite, and use her wits to keep her head on her shoulders when he tired of her? Wouldn't any beautiful girl of spirit leap at the chance?

I thought of the very real affection I knew existed between Gafard and the Lady of the Stars, an affection I fancied to be as true a love as any man and woman could be happy and fortunate enough to find on Kregen.

They loved each other. Whether or not Gafard deserved the love of so fine a lady I cared not. She wanted him. He might want her; that did not count. What she wanted mattered.

The king must be an onker of onkers to imagine he could tame so free and fiery a spirit as hers!

Seventeen
"It is him! I know! Pur Dray, the Lord of Strombor!"

I, Gadak the Renegade, spat juicily on my harness and laid into it with a will with the best polishing cloth. Tack and gear lay spread about on the old sturm-wood table. Others of the men in the loyal squadron likewise polished and spat, spat and polished. We all felt we needed to look smart when the hired kidnappers of the king came calling.

Gafard had smiled that smile of his that was nowhere ironic but all grinning leem-grin.

"So you come to me, Gadak, knowing the king very likely can send you to the galleys?"

"If that is to be Grodno's will, that is to—"

"Aye, aye! And how do I know you have not made another bargain with the king's man—this Nodgen the Faithful?" Here Gafard curled his fist in contempt. "The conceit of the rast. He gives himself a name that is an anagram of the king's. Truly, he must be faithful, the cramph."

"I made the bargain I have told you of. I am to do as poor foolish Genal the Freckles did. To put poison in the wine of the guards and to open all doors."

Gafard's fist made a circle in the air.

"And so ten of my best men are dead, poisoned, and Genal the onker is slain."

"And they will stand a better guard this time and it will be at the midtime, when no guard changes take place."

As I spat and polished I thought of what Gafard had said, and I did not marvel that he had reached the position he had, Ghittawrer, King's Striker, Sea-Zhantil. For he had produced a plan that should be foolproof—for a time.

In essence it was simple and brutal.

I was to do all that the fat cramph Nodgen the Faithful commanded. Except, I was not to poison the guards; they would feign sleep and death. But I was to open the doors and then stand well clear.

"You will have men hidden, to slay the black-masks?"

"No." He was enjoying himself. Had the stakes not been my Lady of the Stars, then I know for certain that Gafard would have enjoyed this game of stealth and wits with his king as much as Genod clearly did. "Oh, no! A slave wench will be bought from the barracoon, privately, before she is put on show for all to see. A beautiful shishi. A Zairian captive, no doubt I shall treat her with great kindness. I shall call her my Lady of the Stars. She will think herself most fortunate to be thus chosen by the King's Striker."

I said, "And this girl will be taken by the king's men?"

"Yes. If she holds firm to her story, and she is beautiful, the king will be happy. I do not hold it against him as a king, only as a man. He has the yrium, and what he does he does."

So I spat and polished and thought on about my part in this.

I must report in to Nodgen that all was ready for the day.

If there was room for any pity in my bleak old heart I do not think I spilled over much for the girl slave bought from the barracoon and taken straight up into the Tower of True Contentment. If all went well she would be the king's mistress. If she pleased him, who knew how high she might aim or what her influence might be? Certainly, she would be far better treated than in many of the dumps and dives she might have been bought into.

Of course, if she failed to act her part and the king flew into one of the tantrum rages of which he was so terribly capable she might be strangled out of hand. But then, that was a risk, the risk of death, that everyone runs.

Thinking these and other equally odiferous thoughts on the next day, I made my way to the appointed rendezvous, a wineshop in the Alley of a Thousand Bangles. The gewgaws tinkled in the breeze off the sea, bright and sparkling, cheap and cheerful, and there were many women admiring the bangles and bartering for their purchase. The wineshop lay in a curve of the souk and I waited outside. If there was to be double treachery, I wanted a space to run and swing a sword.

Nodgen sent the same pack who had brought me to him. They eyed me with evident desire to get their own back. I said, "It is all arranged. Give me the poison."

They handed over the vial and refused my request for more gold, repeated their threats, and so strode off, pushing the girls out of the way. I turned and went in the opposite direction out of disgust and so found myself crossing an open area I had scarcely ever visited before, where they sold calsanys. No one loves a calsany except for his stubborn strength in carrying burdens—oh, and, of course, for another calsany.

The animals were quite peaceful, which was useful for the salubriousness of the quarter, and I went quickly along past the auctioneers and the crowds of men—merchants, traders, caravan owners and drivers—making their bids in the quick, incomprehensible ways of auctioneers two worlds over. The whole scene was alive with the movement of commerce and the glitter of money changing hands. The breeze puffed a little dust into the air. I reached to pull up the white scarf.

A voice burst out from a crowd around an exceptionally large man flogging calsanys.

"By Grodno! It is him! I know! Pur Dray, the Lord of Strombor!"

I hauled the scarf up and took a running dive into the middle of a pack of calsanys.

It was damned unpleasant.

But in the hullabaloo, the shouting and yelling, the braying and honking, the dust flying up, and the general effluvium upon everything, I managed to get out the other side, knock over a stall covered with calsany brasses and bells, and disappear running up an alley. People turned to gawp. I yelled "Stop, thief!" and pointed and one or two turned out to run with me. Earth or Kregen—it is a useful ploy.

I may make this sound lighthearted, with calsanys doing what calsanys always do when frightened and pots and pans rolling and people yelling and running, but it was a deucedly serious business. By the Black Chunkrah, yes!

I did think that after fifty years people might forget what my ugly old face was like. But fifty years to a Kregan is not like fifty years to an Earthman. And some of those people had cause to remember Pur Dray, the most renowned Krozair upon the Eye of the World. It was not so surprising, after all. But it was most inconvenient. I think, also, that so many rumors of the return from the dead of Pur Dray had swept over Magdag that people's nerves were keyed up. Certainly, the very next day, the day before the plot was to go into operation, some poor devil was shouted up as Pur Dray and set on and stabbed to death in the Souk of Silks. When he was dragged out by the heels, his green tunic a mass of bloody stab wounds, inquiries revealed no one anxious to own to the first shout of alarm. A lesson had been learned there by all Magdag.

So the day dawned.

Gafard said to me, standing in his armory with the wink and glitter of his priceless collections of arms upon the bare walls, speaking harshly: "Is all prepared?"

"Aye, gernu. The poison has been poured down a drain. The guards know their parts. Grogor—"

"I will answer for his conduct this day. I do not wish to miss this charade. Perhaps, one day soon, the king will relish the telling at a party. He must one day realize the position and relinquish this pursuit of my Lady."

He didn't sound convinced.

"As for the greater news," he said, and he fired up at once, as he always did when he spoke of the notorious Krozair, "I believe Pur Dray to be in the city! It must be. He is a man who will be up and doing, always scheming, working for Zair."

How mean and small he made me feel!

"I must meet him. Somehow it must be arranged. There is a matter between us."

Nowadays I would have been reminded of the famous if fatuous walk up the High Street at noon. As it was, he reminded me of a bull chunkrah pawing the ground and tossing his horns, ready to face the challenge of who was to be top chunkrah of the herd.

I said, and not altogether to goad him, "You as a Ghittawrer, gernu, have the lustre now. All the accolades won by Pur Dray lie in the past, sere and shriveled. There have been no great Jikais done by him since he returned from the dead."

He stared at me.

"You speak of things you do not understand, Gadak. You do not understand. Pur Dray was the greatest Krozair of the Eye of the World. No one doubts that or seeks to challenge it. And, today, I am the greatest Ghittawrer of the Eye of the World. Any who seek to dispute that will feel my heavy hand."

"Yet is one of the past and the other of today."

He clapped me on the back, at which I forced my hands to remain clamped at my sides.

"You mean well, Gadak. You mean well. Yet there are matters of honor that are past your comprehension."

If he meant he wanted a good ding-dong with Pur Dray to prove who was the better man, I understood that. But I was beginning to think it was not as simple as that. There was more to it than a straightforward confrontation. Gafard was fighting a legend. That is always more difficult than fighting a flesh-and-blood opponent.

So, in my cleverness, I worked it all out.

Stupid onker, Gadak the Renegade!

If only...

But, then, we'd all be rich and happy on *if onlies*.

Looking back as I do speaking to you into the microphone of this little machine here in the Antipodes, I try to visualize it all with calmness. I try to maintain a balance. I blamed myself bitterly for many and many a year afterward. I took the guilt. I did not luxuriate in guilt, as some weak people do. And yet, today, I know I was not to blame, not really, not when the situation was as it was.

Gafard had no doubts.

"The king is a wonderful man, Gadak. He is built in a different mold from Pur Dray and myself. He has the true genius for war, the yrium, the power over us all. Yet he has this weakness, this fault—which is not a fault, for has he not the yrium, and does not that excuse all?"

If ever there was a man trying to make excuses to himself for some other cramph, there he was now, talking to me.

"Gernu," I said. I spoke with seriousness, for the answer to my question intrigued me. This man revealed more of himself to me than he realized. And, I did not forget that he was loved by the Lady of the Stars. "Gernu.

What do you think would happen were the king and Pur Dray to meet, face to face?"

He did not let me finish. A little shiver marked his shoulders and he put a hand to his face. Then he rallied. "It would be in the manner of their meeting. Were it blade to blade, or sectrix to sectrix, or in council chamber, or wherever it might be, I—" He pulled down his moustaches, for, like the Zairian moustaches they were, they insisted on growing upward and jutting out arrogantly, like mine. "I would give everything I own both to be there and yet never to have to witness that confrontation."

Around about then he remembered he was a rog and the King's Striker and a great overlord of Magdag, and I was a mere renegade looking to him for everything. He bade me clear off and make sure my Genodder was sharp for the night, just in case.

My orders were simple, for I was to open the doors and then make myself scarce. Gafard knew as well as I that the king's kidnappers might seek to slay me to silence me. My own plans called for a somewhat more ambitious program. That plan, however, would go into operation only if the king himself came with his men. There was little chance of that, but this Genod was a man of mettle, even if he was an evil rast, and the adventure would appeal to him.

Stealth and secrecy and wild midnight journeyings by the light of the seven moons of Kregen—yes, they have all been my lot on that wonderful world. I had spied in Hamal. I had made friends of Rees and Chido. Now they had left in an argenter, going back to Queen Thyllis with a story of the inefficiency of King Genod's guards, no doubt, and I regretted I had not plucked up the strength of will to confront them and so joy in a reunion I felt they would relish as much as I. This night might see me once again in action, taking a king and his favorite back to Zy.

The emerald and ruby fires of Antares slipped below the horizon past the jumbled roofs of Magdag, casting enormous, elongated shadows from the megaliths across the plain. The guard details changed as usual. The life of the Jade Palace went on normally. The thought of Rees and Chido calmly setting sail and leaving the Eye of the World, sailing back around the world to Hamal, filled me with the kind of baffled fury the prey of the Bichakker must feel when he unavailingly tries to climb the sloping sandy sides of the cone, and slips down into the hideous jaws waiting for him below. I was not sure who had created the sandy slopes that kept me imprisoned in the inner sea. But imprisoned I was. Any argenter in which I sailed would never pass through the Grand Canal, never reach the Dam of Days.

Gafard remained aloft with his beloved when the king's men came. The doors were open. I watched them through a chink in the inner door and saw them carry their logs and wedges to hold within any guards I had not poisoned thoroughly. This time there were no less than ten of them. Five remained to guard the escape; five went aloft. They returned very quickly bearing the shishi wrapped in a black cloak. She had ceased struggling. I saw with relief that no one carried a bloodied sword; all the blades remained in their scabbards. Silently, the black-cloaked men fled into the moon-shot darkness.

After a time Grogor came down and opened the door for us, kicking the logs and wedges away.

"It is done," he said. The evil smile on his face made me think of him in a much warmer light.

So we went back to our regular guard duties, for there were many other perils in Magdag besides the lusts of the genius king Genod.

The next day I went along to the rendezvous to pick up the balance of my pay, the other forty golden oars. No one turned up. I waited some time and then, with a fold of green cloth over my face, went back to the Jade Palace.

Nodgen the Faithful had proved himself damned faithless, the cramph.

Eighteen
At the Zhantil's Lair

Of course, it had been obvious from the first that King Genod would not do his own dirty work. He would never descend to padding about one of his nobles' palaces snuffing out a girl for himself. He was the king. He had the yrium. He would never come to me. So I had to go to him.

That was settled.

I am sure I have not adequately conveyed my feelings of desperation and frustration during this time when I was Gadak the Renegade. My heart felt sore and bruised. My mind shrieked for me to be free of this evil place and to leave the Eye of the World and return to Valka and race up the long flight of steps from the Kyro of the Tridents and so burst shouting joyously into my fortress palace of Esser Rarioch and once more clasp my Delia in my arms, my Delia of the Blue Mountains, my Delia of Delphond.

Before that devoutly longed-for resurrection could take place I must once more be accepted as a member of the Krozairs of Zy.

A High Jikai seemed to me to be the only way.

Truth to tell, as the days passed in Magdag and suns arched across the heavens and the duties came and went, I felt I cared little for the Krzy. I wished merely to use them to escape.

If this is brutal, callous, mean, and vengeful, then this is also me, to my shame.

Sometimes I would see my Lady of the Stars riding in the grassy park expanse, for the Jade Palace is large and sprawling among the buildings and palaces of Magdag, and she would graciously incline her head as I stood respectfully looking at her. She invariably wore the green veil.

Then I would feel the tiny gold and enamel valkavol on its golden chain about my neck. I detest chains and strings and beads. They give a foeman a chance to grip and twist and so drag your head down ready to receive the final chop.

I wore the little valkavol, except when on duty, for then danger and instant action might occur at any moment.

Occasionally Gafard would foin with me in the exercise yard. He was very good. He was a skilled man with the shortsword, and his Genodder work made me use all my skill to let me lose to him gracefully.

Although it seemed to me in my frustration and misery the time sped by superhumanly fast, as time is measured on Kregen very little elapsed before the announcement of the excursion was made and busy preparations immediately got under way.

We were to form a happy holiday party and visit Guamelga, Gafard's enormous estates up the River Dag forming his rognate.

I said to Gafard that if he could spare me I would wish not to travel with the party. It was not that I was reluctant for a holiday. Truth was I wanted to stay in Magdag and work on my plans to take this evil king Genod and pitch him facedown in the muck and so, binding and gagging him, lug him off to a safe place. Then, I fancied, it would be comparatively simple to do the same to Gafard.

"What, Gadak the Renegade! Lose the chance of a holiday!"

"If it please you, gernu."

"It does not please me. My Lady of the Stars will go with us. She travels as she has before. But I need all my loyal men. Has Shagash got at your guts, and you are sluggish and bilious?"

So there was nothing for it. I decided I would have to take Gafard and then see about the king. It would be more difficult that way around.

One thing I felt sure of. This time there would be no Chido and Rees to halt me in my tracks.

Although at the time of our taking of the one-pastang flier I'd felt annoyed we'd missed the little two-place voller, now I saw the enormous benefit of that. The small flier remained in Magdag. Once I had the king I'd put the voller to good use. It would carry the three of us. I'd make it damn well carry the three of us. Its lifting and propulsive power, carried in the two silver boxes, would be ample. If necessary I'd hang the two devils in straps from the outside and let them freeze in the slipstream...

With that decided I put a bold face on the matter. I would have to act as a man delighting in the excursion, the picnics and the hunting parties.

Everyone meant to enjoy every moment. We all surmised this was a last holiday before Gafard, the King's Striker, was dispatched on new missions for his master the king.

Before we left Magdag I carried out the last of my reconnaissances of the king's palaces. He possessed many residences in Magdag, the largest and most gorgeous of which, the Palace of Grodno the All-Wise, he used the least. This was reserved for official functions and contained the reception chamber where I had been received as a Grodnim. Two things must coincide for my plans to work right. The voller was seen over the city from time to time and people would look up and shout and no doubt think how mighty and powerful was their king. Sometimes a green-clad arm would wave. I had been unable to discover at which palace the damned thing was kept.

If it was moved about, then that made my arrangements just a little more difficult, for—by Krun!—they were difficult enough as it was. The voller and the king must be in the same place at the same time. Anything less would be not only suicidal, but downright stupid.

This genius king was very highly security conscious. I knew that after he had successfully won his battle against the overlords of Magdag and taken over here there had been plots against him. The overlords are a malignant lot. But he had weathered the troubled times and now kept his apparatus of guards and watches and sentinels and werstings in full order, for his genius, no doubt, told him this was a prudent course.

The next palace I reconnoitered, the Palace of Masks, looked promising. It was small, or at least small as any building of a palatial kind could ever be in Magdag of the megaliths. It hugged the crest of a hill to the east of the city just within the walls, built of yellow stone and yellow bricks. I say that it looked a charming spot, and I say that genuinely. There were more flowers and blossoming trees here than is usual in bare Magdag. I hung about looking at the guard posts and the sentry boxes, eyeing the roof with an evil glint, figuring angles and possible places for climbing and descent. If voller and king coincided here, I would strike.

Walking back to Gafard's Jade Palace I found myself wondering how that little shishi was faring with the king. If she kept her head—and I meant that figuratively, although it had as much force literally—and maintained the fiction that she had been with Gafard for some time as his Lady of the Stars, she might become a person of extraordinary importance in Magdag. Even the princess Susheng might have to look very carefully before she struck back.

As for Susheng—if I never saw her again on Kregen it would be too soon.

That night all was bustle and laughing preparation within the Jade Palace. Opaz knows, the overlords of Magdag were a vile, villainous bunch; but even for them, and more particularly their women, a holiday ranked as a capital time to slough off all cares. We, the men of the loyal squadron, would ride our sectrixes fully armed, armored, and accoutered. I had had a small piece of good fortune one day in the Souk of Trophies, one of the open-air markets that should, by rights, have been called the Souk of Loot. Here the stalls were heaped with booty from Zairian prizes. I recalled when I had bought a piece of cut chemzite, a handsome trinket, to take to Vallia, and the princess Susheeng had thought it for her, and of my dark knowledge later that when she discovered it was not for her the scene had saved my life. Well, I found there not a piece of jewelry but a South Zairian hlamek, a wind-and-sand mask used by the people living on the skirts of the vast South Turismond deserts. It consisted of a metal skull, a finely crafted piece of hammered iron, well-padded with soft humespack, to which were appended four long and wide white humespack panels. From the upper side of the left-hand panel a broad square of silk was hinged in such a fashion that the left hand might take the top corner and hook it to the right side. It would cover all the face below the eyes, crossing the bridge of the nose. As a protection against wind and sand it was first rate, loose and soft enough to keep the wearer comfortable. All the brave scarlet stitching had been stripped away, but the basic fastenings remained intact.

As a facemask it offered opportunities I could not refuse.

So the hlamek went into the saddlebag along with my toilet necessities, the book I was reading *(How the Ghittawrer Gogol Gon Gorstar Conquered Ten Kingdoms of Zair to the Glory of Grodno),* my eating irons, and the golden drinking cup, one of the set presented to all those who had rescued her by the Lady of the Stars. We drank deep and long to her health in her golden drinking cups, for she had had the forethought to include a notable quantity of wine with her gift.

In a glittering procession we rode out of Magdag early on the following morning only murs after Zim and Genodras cleared the eastern battlements of the city. Each sectrix had been rubbed down, its mane curled and decorated with green ribbons, its hooves polished. The harness burned in the light. Green banners fluttered. Following the lord came his staff and retinue, his aides, his loyal squadron. The overlords who owed him allegiance rode with their wives and families. Following after came the long lines of wagons stuffed with good things, their krahniks in the shafts and hauling on the traces as scrubbed and shining as the sectrixes and hebras of the escort. After them came the calsanys, loaded down with enormous swaying baggage packs, linked head to tail by caravan ropes dyed green.

Yes, we made a goodly spectacle as we rode out of evil Magdag.

Although the slow-moving River Mag was perfectly suitable for river navigation, Gafard had chosen to ride. We could cut across the vast lazy curves of the river and cross by the ferry services provided on this, the direct route to the north. Once free of the delta we could swing to the northwest and so leave the river entirely and march through fertile country, past the chains of factory farms run in so meticulous a fashion by the overlords of the second class and journey on until we reached Guamelga in its loop of the river.

Hikdar Nath ti Hagon received special permission to leave us to ride to the east to his home town for a visit. He would rejoin us at Guamelga later.

Among our bright company there rode the Lady of the Stars, accoutered like a warrior. Gafard rarely left her side where they jogged on at the head of the column. Perforce, I was left to trundle along in the ranks and meditate on my plans.

A hunting party of a similar kind in Havilfar, if they did not fly by voller, would have flown astride any of the marvelous saddle birds or animals of that continent. With a mirvol under me, or a fluttclepper, I could have breasted into the breeze and the slipstream would have blown the cobwebs from my mind. I do not think, as I have said, I would choose a zhyan, for all that Zena Iztar had appeared to me astride one of those snow-white birds. Best of all is the flutduin in my opinion, the flyer of my warrior Djangs, and a magnificent flying creature I had introduced into Valka. It seemed to me, jogging along toward Guamelga and a holiday that would be a farce, that King Genod would very soon receive another consignment of vollers to replace the ones I had smashed up in the tide released from the Dam of Days. If the empress Thyllis meant to do a thing, she did it come hell or high water—and she'd had the high water, by Vox! So I would have to provide the hell. That, in my mood, seemed a singularly pleasant prospect.

Still and all, during my enforced imprisonment on Earth I had missed the high enjoyment of sweeping through the sky astride a giant flying mount. Even a fluttrell with its ridiculous head vane would have been like water in a desert to me then.

The city of Guamelga itself was small, gabled of roof, of no particular distinction, walled—for it was near enough the lands of the Ugas for raids to be counted on—and dominated by the harsh stone bulk of the castle, the Goytering. We did not stay in the castle or the city for long, Gafard being anxious to get away from all cares, and so we went deeper into the countryside away from the cultivated areas to one of the hunting lodges he kept up. The one he chose was the Zhantil's Lair. A comfortable enough place set in woodlands with wide-open prospects of tall grasses beyond, it would not accommodate all his people and of those he kept with him I was one. I was pleased about this. I wanted the rogue under my eye.

Days of hunting followed. There was all manner of game, and there were leems and chavonths and, once, a pair of hunting lairgodonts. The hunting party was in sufficient strength to dispose of them. The trophies were brought back in triumph.

The Magdaggians do not go in greatly for singing. Oh, yes, they do sing, of course, and we had a few sessions around the fires of an evening. It is an odd fact that the Magdaggian swods when they sing on the march habitually bellow out only two or three songs, not caring for many others. Of these the most common is a song I find tiresome, going as it does with the beat of the studded marching sandals—"Ob! Dwa! So!"—One! Two! Three!—followed by a doggerel verse about Genodras or Goyt or Gyphimedes or Grodno. *Ob, dwa, so,* as intellectual subject matter for a song, seems to me somewhat below what is necessary. Still, it takes all kinds to make a world, particularly the world of Kregen. As was to be expected, this song was known as the "Obdwa Song."

When some idiot started up this song in the wood-paneled dining room, I stood up, swaying a little to color my appearance of fuddlement. "Ob, dwa so," they sang. "We're a bloodthirsty lot, as Gashil is our witness. Ley, waso, shiv, we'll slit throats and empty purses. Shebov, ord—"

I wandered out into the paneled hall and made my way to the kitchens in search of a drink of fresh water from the pump.

The room was brilliantly lit at the far end, down by the ovens and the preparation tables, but where I had come in to get at the hand-cranked pump, shadows fell. I heard a noise and instantly, for the noise was a slither, I put my hand on my shortsword and padded forward silently. I heard a low voice, a very low voice, singing a song I knew.

It is impossible to translate the song as a poem from the Kregish to the English, as I have already mentioned. But the meaning of the words was something like: "If your swifter's got a kink, my lads, your swifter's got a kink. You'll go around in circles, boys, in circles around you'll go. Your ram will pierce your stern, old son, your ram will pierce your stern. You'll vanish like a sea-ghost, dom, a sea-ghost you'll become—"

At this point the soft singing stopped and I heard the evil scrape of steel on steel as a blade cleared scabbard.

A harsh voice, kept low and penetrating, bit out: "Weng da!"

At the formal challenge of *Weng da* I said, "It is only Gadak the Renegade."

For I knew who this was and I knew the next words of the song, that famous old Zairian song, "The Swifter with the Kink," were highly uncomplimentary to the Green of Grodnim and most satisfyingly urbane about the Red of Zair.

I stepped forward into the light.

If Gafard wanted to make an issue of this, well, now was a time I would not have chosen; but it was a time I would make serve. I saw the silver glitter run up and down his blade.

"Gadak! You heard?"

"I heard 'Ob, dwa, so,' gernu. That is all."

The reflections of the blade shimmered and then were engulfed in that scabbarding screech.

"Make it so." The slur in his voice was barely noticeable.

I made no formal bellow of loyalty.

I said, "But, all the same, it is hard."

He did not bite.

Instead he answered me in a way that showed he had thought about this thing and had reconciled himself.

"I am Gafard, Rog of Guamelga, the King's Striker, the Sea-Zhantil. Few men carry the honor I command. You would do well to think of who your just masters are, Gadak the Renegade."

My hand rested limp and relaxed, ready to whip the Genodder out in a blur of steel.

"You told me, gernu, that no overlord would treat me as you have done. This I believe. I think had you been an ordinary overlord of Magdag one of us would be dead by now."

He stepped into the light and smiled. He was not quite perfectly composed. "If that were so, I think it would be you who lay stretched in his own blood on the kitchen floor."

"Yet you did not strike."

"My Lady has said—it is a thing I marvel at—" He put something of his old imperiousness into his words. "She has taken a fancy to you, Gadak. For that alone many an overlord would have you done away with."

"Yet this business with the king—it is a worry."

He lost his smile and scowled.

"I have said before, this is no matter for you to concern yourself with. I am the King's Striker! The king has the yrium! That is all there needs to be said."

"That is all—until the next time."

"You step dangerously near the bounds of impudence, of insubordination. If one of us accused the other of singing 'The Swifter with the Kink,' who do you think the overlords would believe? Riddle me that, Gadak!"

"You are secure in your power, gernu. Yet—" I stopped.

"Yes. Yet?"

"I will say no more. I serve you and my Lady. You know that to be sooth."

"I know it is sooth now. Let it remain sooth."

If I clouted him over the head now I'd have the devil of a job hauling him back to Magdag and then of taking the king and the voller. Better by far to grab the king first, with the voller, as I planned, and then bundle up this Gafard after. Yes, far better.

As I stood there with him in the kitchen I thought how dark and dangerous and powerful a man he was. I would then and there have joyed in

302

hand-strokes with him, for he was a doughty fighter. But I let the opportunity pass.

"When, gernu, do we return to Magdag?"

"You are tired of this holiday? Aye, it palls." He stretched and yawned. "Give me the thrust of a swifter, to stand as prijiker in the bows, to bear down in the shock of the ram—aye! That is living."

"It is," I said. I believed the words as I spoke them.

"We will roam the Eye of the World, Gadak! We will create many a High Jikai! Soon all men will forget that Pur Dray existed—he will be a name, lost and forgotten with Pur Zydeng, the greatest Krozair of five centuries past. Dead with the great Ghittawrer Gamba the Rapacious, who went to the Ice Floes of Sicce these thousand seasons gone. Aye!"

"And yet, gernu, you speak always of the Lord of Strombor. I know you have no fear of him. But your interest interests me. I am fascinated not by Pur Dray but by your fascination."

He had forgotten to be imperious. His eyes held a long-lost look of a man sinking in a death-race of the sea.

"The Lord of Strombor was the greatest Krozair of his time. Greater than any Ghittawrer of Magdag. I would prove I am his match—and there is more. For this matter between us—and I speak to you like this only because my Lady smiles on you. I shall be sorry, tomorrow, and you may tremble lest I have your head off for it." He was, I could see, more than a little fuddled with wine. He was not drunk. I never saw him drunk or incapable. But he had had his tongue loosened.

Irritation at his petty problems flooded me. Perhaps I might have flamed out, in my stupid, prideful arrogance: "Sink me! You stupid onker! I am Pur Dray and what is this matter between us you prate so of?"

But I did not. I do not think, had I done so, it would have made any difference.

He probably would not have believed me, anyway, then.

He pulled himself erect and slapped his left hand down on his longsword hilt. "Enough of this kitchen talk! I came here to—to vent a little spleen. I want no more of them in there this night. Attend me to my room."

"Aye, gernu."

We went up the back stair to his suite of chambers in the Zhantil's Lair. They were lavish and expensive, as one would expect, hung about with trophies of the chase. A lounge had been furnished by a man's hand. But through the inner doors lay the apartments of my Lady of the Stars.

He slumped down in a chair and bellowed for wine.

"You, Gadak the Renegade. Have you ever been outside the Eye of the World? Out to the unknown, improbable lands there?"

I poured him his wine and pondered the question.

"Yes, gernu."

"Ah!" He took the wine. The shadows of the room clustered against the samphron oil lamps' gleam. "You have never seen my Lady—before you met me?"

"No. I swear it." This could be dangerous. "I respect her deeply. I feel I have proved that, yet I would not in honor speak of it."

"Yes, yes, you have served. And you swear?"

"I swear."

"And she is very tender of you. She was much impressed when you slew the lairgodonts. That was a Jikai. You trespass where no man has trespassed before—and lived."

"I am an ordinary man. I know my Lady has the most tender affection for you. Do you think I would—?"

"What you, Gadak?" He drank the wine off, and laughed, and hurled the glass to smash against the wall, splattering a leem-skin hung there with dregs and glass, shining in the light. "No, Gadak, for I recognize you. You are the upright, the correct, the loyal man. You know which side your bread's buttered. With me you have the chance of a glittering career. You may be made Ghittawrer soon."

"If the king's man, this Nodgen the Faithful, does not have my head for the king."

"No. No chance of that. The king and I—we play this game, but for him it is a game. For me the stakes are too high. I do not know what I would do if my Lady was taken from me—" He bellowed for fresh wine then, to cover his words.

"She must not fall into the king's hands." He drank deeply. I had never seen him drunk; he was in a fair way to showing me that interesting phenomenon for the first time. "She must not! He would do what I should do—should do—and, by Green Grodno, cannot, will not—will never!"

I saw clearly that some oppressive matter weighed on his mind. As a renegade he was not fully accepted by the overlords. He believed in the king and yet in this matter he could not talk to the king. He desperately wished to confide in someone, as is a common practice among people, I have noticed. If he decided to tell me, I wondered if that would make my position more secure or destroy me utterly. I rather thought it would be the latter. Yet this man fascinated me. I could feel the strong attraction he exerted despite the evil of him. He was a mere man, as was I. He would pay for his crimes. Was the changing of allegiance from Red to Green so great a matter anywhere but on the inner sea? I found it hard to condemn him as I knew him now, as I had found it easy to condemn him when I did not know him.

"Riddle me this, Gadak. Which is more important, the good of your lady or the good of your country?"

"That has had many facile answers, and every case is different."

"But if it was you—you! Your answer?"

"No man can answer until he has faced the situation and the question."

"Do you know that my Lady of the Stars and I are married? No—only a very few know. Grogor knows. We married permanently. Not in the rites of Grodno—" He picked up his glass and spilled most of it. He barely noticed.

"Then the king would honor a legal and sanctified marriage."

"Fambly! He has the yrium. And the rites were not the rites of Grodno." He chuckled. "Even though there were two ceremonies, neither was that of Grodno." And he drank and let the glass slip through his fingers.

I felt a prod might bring him back to reason. For so strong and powerful a personality he was letting go of his will, was allowing this matter that tormented him to undermine all the strength he possessed, and so I knew this was no ordinary matter that so obsessed him. I spoke carefully.

"If the king succeeded in taking my Lady, would your men fight to regain her? If the fact was over and done, would they risk treason against the king? In that situation would not their loyalty to the king transcend their loyalty to you?"

He struggled to rise and slumped back, panting.

"So that is how you answer the question of loyalty to your lady and loyalty to your country!"

"You should know better—if this is the case you present, then—"

"It is the case! Grogor would go up against the king for me, I know! And I picked you, for I thought you would be loyal—even if I could not, for the king has the yrium, even if I could not—you—"

If that was his problem I fancied the stab of an emergency would quickly make up his mind for him.

As though Drig himself had heard me and mocked me, on that thought the door opened and Grogor burst in. He looked ghastly. Both Gafard and I knew, at once, almost word for word what he would say. Gafard lumbered up, screeching, drawing his sword. Swords would be useless for a space, I fancied.

"Gernu! She is taken! Stikitches—real assassins in metal faces, professionals... They ride toward the Volgodonts' Aerie!"

The Volgodonts' Aerie, another hunting lodge like the Zhantil's Lair, stood some three burs' ride away in the woods. That, we could not have foreseen.

Gafard's face appeared both shrunken and bloated. His eyes glared. All the drink he had taken made his face enormous and yet the horror of the moment shriveled him. He gasped and struggled to breathe. I caught him and lowered him into his chair. Grogor stood, half bent, expecting an avalanche of invective. Gafard croaked words, vicious, harsh words like bolts from a crossbow.

305

"We must ride, Grogor! Have the sectrixes saddled up. Gather the men. We must ride like Zhuannar of the Storm!"

"Rather, master, call on Grakki-Grodno—"

I knew what he meant. Grakki-Grodno was the sky-god of draft-beasts of Magdag. So for all his brave talk, he had failed the test.

But Grogor said, "The king has taken my Lady and she is now his. He is the king and he has the yrium. The men would have fought for you—*have* fought for you, master—when she was rightfully yours. Now she is rightfully the king's. No man will raise his hand against the king." Then, this bulky, sweaty man, a renegade, drew himself up. "I would ride, my lord. Would you have me ride alone against the king?"

He had a powerful point. Gafard looked crushed. The strength and power oozed out of him. I felt a crushing sorrow for the Lady of the Stars. Evidently the little shishi had failed to convince the king. Spies had done the rest. There were those in Gafard's household who did not love him, that was certain, and we had made a splendid spectacle riding out of Magdag. There was no point in my offering to ride. If Gafard roused himself, if Grogor rode, that would be three of us against a band of professional stikitches. The assassins of Kregen are an efficient bunch of rasts when they have to be, and on a task of kidnapping they are no less ruthless. No, sorrowful though this made me, I would have to go with the majority.

My own concerns for my Delia must come first. My Delia—ah! How I longed for her then... How could a pretty girl, even a girl with the fire and spirit and charm of the Lady of the Stars, stand for a moment in my thoughts against my Delia!

The shadows in the corner of that masculine room—with the harsh trophies of the hunt upon the walls, the stands of arms, the pieces of harness and mail, the tall motionless drapes—all breathed to me of softer, sweeter things: of Delia's laugh, the sight of her as we swam together in Esser Rarioch, the love we had for our children, all the intimate details that make of a man and a woman, make of a marriage, a single and indivisible oneness.

No, I would not throw away my Delia's happiness for my Lady of the Stars.

Gafard was breathing in hoarse, rattling gasps. The drink, the shock, the fuddlement, had left him bereft of that incisive command. He had been stricken down.

"The men will not ride!" He shook his head, hardly able to believe and yet knowing the stark truth of it. He turned to me and stretched out a hand. "And you, Gadak the Renegade, the man I chose and pampered—will you, Gadak, ride for me this night?"

"No," I said.

He fell back in the chair. His face sagged. He looked distraught, wild, near-insane.

Then he proved himself.

"Then to Sicce with you all! I will ride myself, alone, for I know well what my Lord of Strombor will say!"

I felt no shock, only puzzlement.

He staggered up, waving his arms, casting about for his mail. I gripped his arm and Grogor jumped. I said, "What is this of the Lord of Strombor?"

Gafard swung a wild, sweaty face upon me. The sweat clung to his dark, clustered curls and dripped down his face. The lines in that face were etched deep. His beard bristled.

"You onker! If the king takes my Lady—Pur Dray is in the city! He has been seen in Magdag, it is very sure." He spoke down from that high screech, as a man explaining a simple problem to a child. He put a hand on my hand. "Let me go, Gadak, traitor, ingrate! I will save my Lady for Pur Dray and then I will deal with you."

I held him. Grogor moved and I swung my head and glared at him. "Stand, Grogor, as you value your life!" I shook Gafard, the King's Striker. "Listen to me, Gafard! You prate of Pur Dray, the Lord of Strombor. What has he to do with this matter? Tell me the matter that lies between you, Gafard! Tell me! What has the Lord of Strombor to do with the Lady of the Stars?"

Some semblance of sanity returned to him. He was Gafard, the Sea-Zhantil, and he was not to be shaken by a mere mercenary, a renegade, a man he had made!

"You cramph!" he said. He spoke thickly. "You are a dead man—for you sit and let my Lady go to certain death—hideous death—death by torture for what she knows, and, before that, to humiliation and the baiting of a trap."

"Tell me, Gafard, you nurdling great onker! *Tell me!*"

He shrieked as my fingers bit into the bones of his arm.

He twisted and glared up, his fierce, predatory face close to mine and so like my own, so like my own.

"You fool! Pur Dray, the greatest Krozair of the Eye of the World, is here, in Magdag. And King Genod takes the Lady of the Stars! When he finds out, as he will find out—for he has the yrium, he will find out—then—and then—"

I shook him again. I bore down on him, all the hateful ferocity in my face overmatching his own. Grogor took another step and I said "Grogor!" and he stopped stock still.

"When the king finds out what, Gafard? What is this trap? Tell me or I will break your arm off!"

He shrieked again and foam sprang to his lips. He tried to pull away and Grogor moved once more so I swung Gafard, the King's Striker, about, prepared to hurl him at Grogor. I could feel his bones grinding under my fingers.

"Now, Gafard, now!"

"You are a dead man, Gadak! For King Genod has taken Velia, who is the daughter of Pur Dray, the Lord of Strombor."

Nineteen
Stricken by genius

Gafard screamed it out, foaming, as I hurled him into the chair.

"The king has taken Velia, Princess Velia, daughter to Pur Dray, the Lord of Strombor, Prince Majister of Vallia!"

Everything blurred.

I remember colliding with Grogor on my way to the door and knocking him flying. There were stairs. There were people shouting and milling. Men stood in my way and were suddenly not there. There were softnesses under my feet. The air was suddenly cool and fresh. Stars blazed. The moons were up, gliding silently through the starfields. The sectrix stalls lay shrouded in darkness. Harness—no time, no time—bareback! A sectrix beneath me. A vicious kick, more vicious kicks. The lolloping six-legged gait. Hard, merciless kicks, the flat of my sword, then sharper, more urgent bounding. The dark flicker of tree branches overhead. The dazzlement of the moons. The harsh, jolting ride, the clamor of hooves, the rush of wind, the pain, the agony, the remorse—

Velia!

My little Velia!

Fragments, I remember, of that night ride with the horror gibbering and clawing at me, the ghastly specters obscenely taunting me, mocking me—

I knew what this kleesh of a King Genod would do when he discovered he held in his hands the daughter of Dray Prescot, the Lord of Strombor, the notorious and dreaded Krozair of Zy.

I would consign all the Krzy to Sicce to save my daughter.

What would Delia say? What would be her agony?

I galloped and galloped and I galloped as a man who has no heart, has never had a heart, and is never likely to find a heart in this wicked world.

Velia... Velia... The sectrix hooves beat out her name on the hard forest paths, over the rippling grasslands silver and pink and gold beneath the moons, the breeze swaying them as a breeze ruffles the inner sea.

Years and years ago I had last seen her. I had not recognized her, and she had not recognized me.

Yet—was not that strange feeling I had suffered now explained, the weird compulsion in me to do nothing to destroy the happiness of the Lady of the Stars? Now I knew why Gafard, the King's Striker, was not bundled in a blanket and safely in the hands of the Krozairs upon the fortress isle of Zy.

If we had not recognized each other's faces, and our names had been strange and false, had not the blood called, one to the other? Oh, maybe that is sentimental nonsense, maybe it is mere wishful thinking; but there *had* been some deep psychological force drawing and binding me to my daughter. Perhaps the racial unconscious, if there be such a thing, is most pronounced and powerful in relatives, and the only bond as powerful as that of a father to his daughter is that of a mother to her son.

The sectrix's hoofbeats echoed in my ears, a strange triple echo. I twisted about. In that streaming moonlight a second sectrix followed me, bounding along, its rider's cape flaring in the golden light. The man rode like a maniac. He rode as I rode.

I recognized Grogor.

I smashed at my mount again and he responded. We flew out into a clearing of the tall grasses and splashed across a stream. On and on—the stikitches would take my daughter to the king at the Volgodonts' Aerie. There was every chance he would have flown here in the little two-place airboat. If he had I would take his voller. Somehow I did not think I would bother to take him back to Zy.

Looking back now, as that mad ride brought me raving across the wild country to the Volgodonts' Aerie, I recognize my headlong foolishness. I had been denied many of the best years in which a father may see his children growing up. Velia had been three when the damned Star Lords had whirled me back to Earth for a miserable twenty-one years; she would be twenty-five now. What had her life been like?

Fragments, impressions, the jolting of the sectrix, the blustering of the wind, the pain in my jaws, and over all the moonshine, streaming gold and pink and glorious upon the nighted face of Kregen, mocking the blackness upon me. For every moon shone in the sky, full and gleaming, in that tiny period when the three smaller moons in their hurtling passages coincide and form with the Maiden with the Many Smiles, and the Twins, and She of the Veils; that magic time of the Scarf of Our Lady Monafeyom.

Brilliant the light, brilliant and yet soft with the exquisite delicacy of moonlight.

The land lay as though enchanted.

And through that magic midnight splendor I rode with the devils gibbering at me and ghastly phantasms tormenting my mind, for I knew that this genius king planned no pleasure for my Velia.

Through a screen of trees I flung the sectrix, striking away branches and leaves, silver and gold and rose in the radiance, and bore out onto a meadow where a stream ran, liquid bronze under the moons of Kregen—and there lifted the Volgodonts' Aerie.

Stark and many pinnacled, it rose against the stars like a stretched and piercing claw of a volgodont itself.

The sectrix was not as fine a mount as Grogor's. Now Gafard's second in command was up with me. The two animals galloped neck and neck. I did not speak. I could not speak. I stared ahead as a leem stares, entirely vicious and feral, without mercy.

Grogor shouted. "We will never save her—only us two! The lord follows. Gadak, this is madness!"

I did not answer him, but hit my failing beast with the flat of the sword.

"The lord bid me say he would forgive you, Gadak, only if you humble yourself to him—he follows—Gadak!"

Still I did not answer. We raced on. I feel sure that you who listen to my story will long ago have realized who the Lady of the Stars was, that she was my daughter. Now, with hindsight, it seemed obvious. But, to me, plain Dray Prescot who had so little experience of daughters to go on, how could that stunning truth possibly be easy? I had not known, had had no remotest idea. How could I?

Sectrix riders trotted out into the clearing to front us.

I saw their green cloaks, weird in the moons' radiances, and the blackness of their clothes. Pinkly golden glitter reflected from their steel facemasks. They wore mail.

Grogor saw and cursed.

I did not halt the laboring sectrix. The animal lunged straight ahead, gasping in convulsive effort, the steam jetting from his nostrils. The stikitches lifted their swords. There were six of them, I believe. I did not count. I recollect the jar of blade on blade, the quick and deadly cut, and the vicious thrust. I lopped and chopped. I spitted. The facemasks splintered in shards of flying metal. I whirled that Ghittawrer weapon and I sliced those damned assassins, and there was no real time or reason in it beyond the swirling madness in my brain, the crazy viciousness of insanity driving me on.

The six of them, if there were six of them, lay sprawled upon the grass of the meadow, their black and shining blood dribbling in pools from their mutilated bodies. I did not spare a single look, but hit the sectrix and galloped on. I did hear Grogor screaming: "You are a devil!" That was true. Why remark on it?

"We are too late!" Grogor was yelling and hauling his beast up. He almost collided with me, the six-legged animals struggling together and staggering sideways.

"Get out of my way, rast!" I said, hauling my mount up, driving it to stand and run although it was almost done. "Look!" Grogor pointed. He pointed up. I looked. If the king was away in the voller it would be over.

A great winged shape lofted from the top tower of the Volgodonts' Aerie. Against the radiance of the moons the fluttrell soared up, his wide pinions beating in that long, effortless rhythm of the saddle bird.

Grogor yelled in openmouthed disbelief. The truth was plain. More argenters had arrived from Hamal and as well as vollers they carried saddle birds. The fluttrell was the most common saddle-mount of Havilfar. Thyllis had spared a few to please the whim of King Genod and he had mastered the knack of flying and had come here, in person, to show off his prowess to his new conquest, the Lady of the Stars, who had once been the lady of Gafard, the King's Striker, and was now the lady of the king—for a time.

"The devil from the bat-caves!" yelled Grogor. My sectrix staggered with exhaustion. Grogor hauled out his bow, drew and nocked an arrow, lifted and let fly. I reached out to him, dropping the blood-choked Ghittawrer sword. But his fingers released the string and the shaft flew. If he hit Velia...!

The fluttrell winged up, its pinions beating. I did not see the arrow strike. I saw those wings suddenly flap limply; they beat off-rhythm; and the bird swerved in the air.

Grogor's arrow had wounded the fluttrell, yet it could still fly. I saw it curve around in a mazy, sweeping circle. It was dropping. The wings beat erratically. The bird extended its legs, talons spread wide.

Grogor hauled out his sword. He yelled, high and fierce. He sent his mount charging for the point where the bird would land. I could see two figures on the fluttrell's back, abaft the wide head vane. Two figures, struggling. I held my breath.

The king must have newly learned the art of flying a saddlebird. I guessed my Velia—my Velia! My daughter!—would be an expert in the air, trained by my Djangs astride flutduins. She would not thus foolishly struggle as a bird planed in for a landing.

Grogor's sword blurred in the mingled light of the Scarf of Our Lady Monafeyom.

The king saw us below him. I saw his face, a pale blur in the light, saw it lift and stare past that other face so near his hateful features, stare and look past me. I turned. A body of men rode in the shadows of the trees. It was difficult to distinguish them, save for the green and the mail and the glitter of weapons and war harness. I did not think they rode on behalf of Gafard. But they might. Gafard, himself, might ride at their head.

This is what the king thought.

I swung back. Grogor was bellowing and shaking his sword.

The bird made a last effort. It beat its wings and tried to rise. The two faces up there were close together as the bird tried to lift and fly in obedience to the frenzied flogging from Genod's goad. It tried to beat its pinions and rise up, and could not. I saw those two faces—then there was one face only above the fluttrell's back and a white-clad form pitching headlong from the air.

King Genod, the genius, had thrown my daughter from the fluttrell, thrown her to the ground beneath.

Relieved of the extra weight the fluttrell beat more powerfully and rose. Its wings thrashed the air. It lifted and soared up. Grogor's second shot fell far too short.

I saw all that from the corner of my eye, not heeding.

I saw the spinning form of Velia, her white dress swirling out, pitch down through the empty air. She fell. She fell to the ground. She fell. She fell on the ground.

I was riding hard.

How often I had picked up little Velia as she tottered on her chubby little legs, there on the high terrace of Esser Rarioch, learning to walk, determined, clambering up and trying again, to tumble down again in a sprawl of her short white dress.

I rode on.

An arrow whipped in past Grogor's ear. He swung his mount about, yelled, high: "Overlords! We are dead men! We must run!"

He stuck in his spurs and was away, the sectrix hurtling along low over the ground, its shadows spreading about it, undulating eerie blobs of half-darkness.

The overlords of Magdag trotted over the meadow toward me.

I galloped and I did not care what the damned overlords did.

The six legs of my beast skidded and splayed as I reined it up. I was off its bare back. It just stood, waiting for me to remount.

I knelt.

She lay crumpled, her white dress spread out, with no sign of blood anywhere. Her eyes were open, those beautiful brown eyes I could see now were those of a Vallian; beautiful brown eyes like my Delia's. Her glowing brown hair was dyed black and artificially curled, in imitation of a Zairian. That was so.

"Velia," I said, and I choked.

"Why, Gadak," she said. "You know my name." As she spoke a tiny line of blood trickled from the corner of her mouth. "I—I like that, Gadak, for I have always been fond of you."

"Velia—" I took her hand in mine as I knelt. It was cold. "Velia—I am not Gadak. That is not my name."

She smiled up. Now I could see my Delia in her face—my glorious Delia reborn in a subtly different way, as glorious, as wonderful—and thrown callously through the air by a genius.

"You will look after me, Gadak? And my lord? He is safe?"

"He is safe, my heart. Listen—I love your mother as no man has loved a woman. There in Esser Rarioch we were happy, and we joyed in our twins, Segnik and Velia—"

She stared at me, her soft mouth curling in puzzlement, for she felt no pain.

"What do you say, Gadak? What of—Esser Rarioch, and Valka? And—my mother—you—I have no father. He is gone away, a long way away, a long time ago."

Those Star Lords! If I'd had one under my hands then, he would never more play cruel tricks on plain men.

"Yes, Velia, you are my dear daughter, for I am your father, and I have sinned—it is all my fault—and—"

"Father...?"

"Yes."

I did not know what she would do. Had she cursed and reviled me I would know she was right.

She said, "Gadak—you do not say this—to please me? Where is my lord? Has he told you to say this?"

I held her hand and it was cold. I touched her lips with a silk kerchief and wiped away the blood. I smoothed her hair. We spoke, then, and I told her little things, things that she would understand Dray Prescot, the Strom of Valka, would understand. She could not move. She smiled and I saw in her face that she forgave me. I did not deserve that, but she forgave me. We talked—and I took her into my arms and held her and smoothed her hair and looked down upon her face. Her pallor gave her an ethereal beauty there in the light of the moons of Kregen as the Scarf of Our Lady Monafeyom gleamed in pure brilliance against the stars.

"Father?" She understood I spoke the truth. "I wish my lord were here. We are married. In the rites of Zair and Opaz. He is a fierce man, proud and brave, but very gentle. He means well."

She moved her head slowly to one side, and then back, nestling in my arms, and looked at me. "There is a child. My little Didi. Gafard—my lord, my beloved—keeps her well hidden. She will love her new grandfather."

I had to close my mouth. I could not speak.

"I came with Zeg to the Eye of the World. He is a great Krozair, Father, a famous Krozair of Zy. And—and I was taken. I fought them with my dagger as Mother knew I would. The Sisters of the Rose... but it was Gafard, my lord. I knew, even then, and he knew, too." She breathed a long, shuddering sigh and I looked down on her, but she went on speaking in that small girl's voice through the gathering darkness about her. "The king—Genod—is evil, Father. Drak and Zeg have told me. Now he has vollers and birds. The overlords—they laughed when the king flew off with me. If only Gafard—"

The mists were closing down over her eyes. She stared up, trying to see me clearly. "Father—where is Mother? Where is my lord?"

"They will soon be here, Velia, my heart. You will soon see them. And little Didi."

Now I could hear the trampling of sectrixes and the clatter of harness. The overlords of Magdag were riding up for me. A strong party galloped in pursuit of Grogor. They left their comrades to deal with the willful girl and this uncouth man of Gafard's. They approached slowly, confident in their might. My sectrix still stood, head drooping, reins dangling, waiting for me to mount up and ride.

I held my Velia in my arms, her head against my breast, and I would not move.

"It is very dark, Father. Is this the night of Notor Zan?"

"Yes, Velia. The Scarf of Our Lady Monafeyom is all rolled up and put away, and the dark cloak of Notor Zan is unfolded. You will sleep for a while. Then Mother and Drak and Lela and Segnik and your Didi will come to see you."

"I long to see them again, and Jaidur and Dayra and—" Her soft whispering voice gathered strength. "And my lord?" She tried to move in my arms. "And my lord Gafard? He will come to see me. He is safe—Father! He is safe?"

"Yes, Velia my daughter, Gafard is safe."

"You will like him, Father. I wished you could have known him. He is a very good man and he loves me so." Her eyes were wide open, not seeing me. "It is very dark. When will Mother come to see me? And Gafard..."

The overlords of Magdag trampled nearer in their iron and their might.

I, Dray Prescot, with a host of stupid titles, sat and held my daughter Velia in my arms.

Shadows fell across the bright faces of the moons.

Toward the end her sight cleared. She looked up as I held her cradled and she saw the tiny gold and enamel valkavol she had given me.

"The valkavol!" she said, and the dark blood ran down her white chin, thick and thicker. "Father—it will be all right..."

I did not care if the whole of Kregen heard her. The overlords meant nothing. The metallic rattle of their war harness sounded loudly now, the stamp of sectrix hooves iron-hard on the turf.

She lost that brief spurt of luminous reason. She lay back in my arms, as she had when I had first held her, looking up from her tiny face to the glory of my Delia beyond, smiling. Her hands and her face were ice-cold.

"My lord..." she whispered. "My love..."

She was slipping from me.

"Mother," she said. "Here is Father."

The pallor of her face, the coldness of her, and that ugly red dribble from her mouth...

"Father—" she said again. And then: "Gafard." She spoke his name three or four times. At the end she said, "Oh, to be home in Val—"

The overlords of Magdag rode up to take me.

I sat on the ground holding the broken body of my daughter in my arms as they came for me—as my Velia died.

Krozair of Kregen

A note on Dray Prescot

Dray Prescot is a man above medium height with brown hair, and brown eyes that are level and dominating. His shoulders are immensely wide and he carries himself with an abrasive honesty and a fearless courage. He moves like a great hunting cat, quiet and deadly. Born in 1775 and educated in the inhumanly harsh conditions of the late eighteenth-century English Navy, he presents a picture of himself that, the more we learn of him, grows no less enigmatic.

Through the machinations of the Savanti nal Aphrasöe—mortal but superhuman men dedicated to the aid of humanity—and of the Star Lords, the Everoinye, he has been taken to Kregen many times. On that savage and exotic, marvelous and terrible world he rose to become Zorcander of the Clansmen of Segesthes, and Lord of Strombor in Zenicce, and a member of the mystic and martial Order of Krozairs of Zy of the Eye of the World.

Against all odds, Prescot won his highest desire and in that immortal battle at The Dragon's Bones claimed his Delia, Delia of Delphond, Delia of the Blue Mountains. And Delia claimed him in defiance of her father, the dread emperor of Vallia. Amid the rolling thunder of the acclamations of *Hai Jikai!* Prescot became Prince Majister of Vallia and wed his Delia, the Princess Majestrix. One of their favorite homes is Esser Rarioch in Valkanium, capital of the island of Valka of which Prescot is Strom.

In the continent of Havilfar, Prescot fought as a hyr-kaidur in the arena of the Jikhorkdun in Huringa. He became King of Djanduin, idolized by his ferocious four-armed warrior Djangs. In the Battle of Jholaix the megalomaniacal ambitions of the empress Thyllis of Hamal were thwarted, leading to an uneasy peace between the empires of Hamal and Vallia. Then Prescot was banished by the Star Lords to Earth for twenty-one miserable years. He caught up with his education and learned a great deal during this time.

His joyful return to Kregen was marred by his ejection from the Order of Krozairs of Zy. On Earth he had been unable to answer their Call to Arms, when the fanatics of Green Grodno swept all the Red of Zair before them in irresistible conquest. Determined to forget the Krozairs of the inner sea and return home to Delia and their children, he is told by Zena Iztar, who saves him from being banished back to Earth, that he must again become a Krzy before he can return home to Valka.

The genius king Genod of Magdag, using a new army modeled on one created years ago by Prescot, is sweeping victoriously across the inner sea. Gafard, the king's right-hand man, was—unknown to the king and to Prescot—married to Prescot's second daughter, Velia. Now, in order to escape on a wounded saddle-bird, King Genod has callously hurled Velia to her death. Prescot, using the name Gadak, is left holding the dead body of his daughter in his arms as the overlords of Magdag ride up to take him.

This is where the last volume, *Renegade of Kregen*, finished. Still known as Gadak the Renegade, Prescot picks up the story as he is dispatched to the horrific fate of an oar-slave in the swifters of Magdag.

This volume, *Krozair of Kregen*, brings to an end the "Krozair Cycle" and with the next volume, *Savage Scorpio*, Prescot is confronted with a monstrous challenge on the planet of Kregen under the Suns of Scorpio. Because most, but not all, of the action takes place in Vallia, I have called the next cycle of Prescot's headlong adventures on Kregen the "Vallian Cycle."

Alan Burt Akers

One
The chains of Rukker the Kataki and Fazhan ti Rozilloi

The lash curved high in the air, hard, etched black. I, Gadak the Renegade, grasped the harsh iron chains that bound me so savagely to this coffle of slaves, and which made of us one miserable body. We stumbled down the dusty streets under the lash toward the harbor.

The people of this evil city of Magdag barely noticed us, did not even bother to spit at us or revile us, for we were but one small coffle among many. The iron ring about my neck chafed the skin raw and driblets of blood ran down onto my chest and back.

"By Zair!" the man on my left, for we were chained two and two, gasped, his face a scarlet mask of effort. "I swear the cramph won't be happy until he's had my head off."

"He will not do that. We are needed to pull at the oars."

The overseer, careless in his authority, slashed his thonged whip and my companion yelped and stumbled. I let go of my own chain to help him up. The fellow in front, a giant of a man with the black body-bristle of a Brokelsh, surged forward. The length of chain between us straightened and, by Krun, it felt as though my own head were the one being wrenched off.

"Thank you, dom," the Zairian I had assisted was saying.

Ignoring him, I lurched forward and made a grab at the chain so as to ease the ring about my neck. A voice at my back bellowed in vicious temper.

"Rast! Keep steady, you zigging cramph!"

There was no point in turning about and chastising the fellow. We were all slaves together and I might have yelled as he had done if my own pains had not been caused by myself. The uneven lurching carried back like a wave along the coffle. The air was rent with blasphemies. Listening, I used this occurrence to learn about my fellow slaves, for we had merely been hauled out willy-nilly and chained up together for the walk from the bagnio to the harbor and the galleys.

The stones of Magdag under our feet and rising in wall and terrace and archway all about us held no more pity for our plight than the hearts of the Magdaggians. From the curses and prayers that went up, I knew we were a mixed bunch: Zairian prisoners, Grodnim criminals. And, in truth, I the renegade—who had once been of Zair and who said he was now of Grodno—hardly knew to which of these gods to cleave for the injuries that had been done me.

We were being whipped down to be taken aboard a galley and there enter upon hell on earth.

I knew.

The glorious mingled suns-light poured down in radiance about us, the streaming mingled lights of Zim and Genodras, the red and green suns of Antares. We stumbled along with our twin shadows mocking us, forever chained to us as we would be chained to our rowing benches.

"If I get my hands on that rast..." The Zairian at my left side, with his red face and perfectly bald head, showed a spirit to be expected of a Zairian. I wondered if he would be broken by the torments ahead of him, of all of us. All our heads had been shaved as smooth as loloo's eggs. We wore the gray slave breechclouts, which would be taken from us once we were shackled to our benches. All this I had endured before. This time, I vowed, I would make a positive effort very early on and escape.

The enormity of the death of my daughter Velia still had a stinging power to wring my heart. I had known she was my daughter for so pitifully short a time. I had known her as my Lady of the Stars for a short space before that, and we had talked. But I had found her and then, it seemed in the same heartbeat, she had been taken from me.

This mad king, this genius, this king Genod, who ruled in vile Magdag, had thrown her from the back of his fluttrell as the saddle-bird, winged, had fluttered to the ground. Genod had been in fear of his life then, and had thrown a girl for whom he had planned an abduction out to her death. If there was one thing I intended to do upon Kregen under the Suns of Scorpio, forgetting anything else, that thing would be to bring King Genod Gannius to justice.

We passed beneath the high archway leading through the wall of the inner harbor, that harbor called the King's Haven. The cothon, the artificially scooped-out inner harbor, presented a grand and, indeed, in any other city, a noble aspect.

Like all building in Magdag of the Megaliths, the architecture was on the grandest scale. Enormous blocks of stone had been manhandled down to raise these walls and fortifications, to erect the warehouses and ship sheds. Every surface blazed with brilliantly colored ceramics. The tiles depicted stories and legends from the fabled past of Kregen. They exalted the power of Grodno and of Magdag. And, of course, the predominant color was green.

Nowhere was a speck of red visible.

The overseer with the lash bellowed at us, using the hateful word I so detest. "Grak!" he shouted, snapping his whip, laying into the backs of the slaves. "Grak, you Zairian cramphs!"

The lash was of the tailed variety, designed not to injure us but to sting and make us jump. The Kregans have their equivalents of the knout and the sjambok, as I have said, made from chunkrah hide. With these they can pain, maim, or kill. We dragged along in our chains in the bright light of the twin suns, the smells and the sounds of the harbor in our nostrils and ears, the sight of the galleys motionless by the yellow stone walls. I looked at everything. For I had once been a Krozair, and this place was the arch-enemy of all Krozairs, all the Red Brethren, and knowledge conferred power. Mind you, I might possess a vast amount of knowledge right now; I was still chained up in a coffle of shuffling, whipped slaves.

The particular slave overseer entrusted with the task of bringing us down to the galleys was a Chulik. A Chulik has a yellow skin and a face that, although piglike, is recognizably Homo sapiens in general outline, save for the two fierce, upward-thrusting three-inch tusks. A Chulik will normally shave his head and leave a long rearward-descending pigtail, braided with the colors of whomever happens to be hiring his mercenary services at the moment. I will say here, at once, that my comrade Duhrra, an apim like myself, wore his hair shaved and in a short tail at the rear; I had never thought to compare his shaved skull with a Chulik's. A Chulik may possess two arms and legs and look vaguely human; that is all he knows of humanity. I eyed this specimen as he strode past slashing with his whip and I guessed he was taking what he could from the hides of the slaves before he reported back to the bagnio.

"I'd like to—" began the Zairian to my left.

"Shut your mouth, onker!" came that fearsome bellow from my rear. I had not seen who had been chained up aft of me and I'd been too careful of my neck in that damned ring to care to turn to look.

The Zairian bristled. We passed into the shadow of a warehouse wall, past slaves hauling bundles and bales for the swifters moored alongside the stone wharves. I fancied the swifter for which we made lay past the galley ahead of us. She looked large. If I was shoved down in the lower tier, to slave in almost nighted gloom in that airless confined space, I'd really go berserk. I had been holding myself in admirably, looking for a chance. Not a single chance had been given me. Chuliks and the overlords of Magdag form a formidable combination in manhandling. Like Katakis, who are ferocious slave-masters, they leave no easy chances for escape.

The hoarse rumbling voice at my back sounded again.

"Onker! You make it worse by your prattling."

The Zairian's red face turned even more scarlet, if that were possible. He started to speak, and I said, smoothly and swiftly, "Lean a little this way, dom—quickly!"

He was struck by my tone of voice. He leaned in, bringing the chains with him. We remained in the shadow of the warehouse wall, marching beside the edge of the wharf where the galleys waited. We were almost on the low-slung ram of this swifter, just passing the forward varter platform on her larboard bow. Beyond the ram stretched a space of open water, before the upflung stern of the swifter I fancied we were destined for closed that open space. I stumbled.

The Chulik was there. He had been waiting to get a few good lashings in with his right arm before he signed us over to the oar-master of the swifter.

His arm lifted and as I sagged against the chains the Zairian at my side sucked in his breath. The Chulik lashed. I took the first blow and then the bight of chain looped his ankle. I straightened and heaved, and the cramph sailed up and over, I had hoped he might bash his head against the stones. As I flicked the chains and so released his ankle, he toppled, screeching. The lash sailed up. He went on, staggering backward, his arms windmilling, his legs making stupid little backward steps. He wore mail. He went over the edge of the wharf and the last I saw of the rast was his flaunting pigtail, streaming up into the air in the wind of his fall, and the damned green ribbons flying.

We all heard the splash.

We had remained absolutely silent.

We all heard the beautiful sound of the splash, and then helter-skelter, willy-nilly, dragged by the frantic ones up front, we were pelting for the far side of the warehouse.

"Haul up!" I bellowed.

"Stop, you rasts!" boomed that vast voice at my back.

"Halt! Halt!" cracked from the Zairian, in a voice of habitual command.

But nothing we could do just yet was going to stop that panic.

The Brokelsh in front of me was screaming and running.

We rounded the corner of the warehouse in full cry, a crazy fugitive mob of men chained together. This was no way to escape. Anyway, the high wall surrounded the dockyard and harbor, enclosing the arsenal and the ship sheds, and there was no way over that, and certainly no way through the guarded gateways. I wondered if the Magdaggians would feather us, for sport, or if their war-machine was so desperate for oar-slaves that we had, grotesquely, become valuable.

The bellowing voice at my rear smashed out again.

"You! Dom! Throw yourself down!"

The Zairian and I immediately dropped down. I held on to the chain in front with both hands. The Brokelsh went on running. The jolt was severe. I felt the chain haul out and I tugged back, the Zairian doing likewise.

Then—I swear all thoughts of my being a slave for that moment were whiffed from my mind and I was once again a fighting-man confronted with a hated enemy—the tip of a long and sinuous tail curled under my arm. The tail looped the chain that was held by my hands, so the three gripping members formed a lock on the metal. I felt at once the physical power in that tail. The strain sensibly slackened. We skidded over the stones in our slave breechclouts, and then more men at the rear must have stumbled over the Kataki at my back, or thrown themselves down, either because they saw the sense of that or because they expected the arrows to come shafting in.

In a tangled, cursing pile we came to a skidding halt.

The guards surrounding us appeared with mechanical swiftness. They were not gentle sorting us out. I did not see the Chulik among them.

In a welter of blows and curses we were thrashed along to the swifter and pitched aboard. I tried to see all there was to see, for, even though I am cynical about power and resigned about knowledge, still, as I have indicated, knowledge is power, even to a chained slave, even in his abject condition. It might not do me much good right now; but, although still in a partial state of shock after the death of my daughter, I held tenaciously to this idea of an early escape. Then knowledge would be vital.

If I do not for the moment mention the swifter it is because her arrangements became important later on. The chains were quickly struck off, to be returned to us in the form of chains binding us to the rowing benches allotted. As we filed from the entranceway forward I counted. We were conducted below, whereat I cursed, for this swifter was three-banked, and I had no desire to heave my guts out among the thalamites.

The thranites already sat at their apportioned places on the upper benches, eight to a bench. We passed below them down narrow ladders where the chains clanged dolorously. This was like descending a massive cleft, the sky-showing slot between the larboard and starboard banks, with the grated deck aloft.

I blinked and peered along the second tier. I cursed this time, cursed aloud and cursed hotly.

"By the stinking infamous intestines of Makki-Grodno! Every zygite is in place." I shook a fist upward, the chains clashing. "The bottom for us! The bilge-rats! The thalamites!"

The Zairian said, stoutly, "We will survive, dom."

The Kataki, above him, his tail looped about a stanchion, leaned over. "This is a strange and doomed place—you know, do you, apim, whereof you speak?"

"Aye," I said, descending into the bottom tier. "Aye, I know."

I did not wish to address him, and I wouldn't call him dom, which is a comradely greeting. I did not like Katakis.

The whip-Deldars were there to welcome us.

They cracked their whips and herded us along and I saw one poor devil, a big fellow, tough, a Brokelsh, strike out at them. They surrounded him like vultures. They carried him away. I knew what would happen. Later on he would be used as an example to us all. He was, and I shall not speak of it.

The whip-Deldars were backed by marines with shortswords naked in their fists, their mail dully glimmering in the half-light. We were sorted into fours. The Zairian, the Kataki, and I shuffled up and were clouted into a bench. The fourth who would row on our loom fell half on top of the Zairian. He was a Xaffer, one of that strange and remote race of diffs of whom I have spoken who seem born for slavery. He looked shriveled. As the smallest, he was shoved past us to the outside position. The Zairian sat next. Then came myself—to my surprise, really—and, outside me, the Kataki. The locks closed with meaty *thwunks*. The chains and links were tested. We were looked at and then, the final indignity, our gray slave breechclouts were whipped off and taken away.

Bald, naked, chained, we sat awaiting the next orders.

For the moment I could think. The oars had not been affixed as yet. That would be the next operation and was being done with us in position so as to show us what was what, how the evolution was carried out. I felt a surprise I should not have felt. Normally, oar-slaves would serve a period of training aboard a dockyard Liburnian with her two shallow banks of oars. Now that the Grodnims of the Green northern shore of the inner sea were carrying forward so victoriously their war against the Zairians of the Red southern shore they needed every craft they could put into commission. There was just no time to go through the protracted period of training when oar-slaves were weeded out. The vicious weeding-out process would take place in this three-banked swifter, and the dead bodies would be flung overboard. Already, after us, the batches of spare slaves were being herded down and stuffed into the holds and crannies where they would wait and suffer until required. This swifter was a good-sized vessel. There were a great number of slaves forced into her, and we were packed tightly.

The chanks, those killer sharks of the inner sea, would feed well in the wake of this swifter, whose name was *Green Magodont*.

The noise from the slaves echoed and rebounded from the wooden hull. For the moment the whip-Deldars were leaving us to our own devices. Once the oars started to come aboard they'd show us the discipline Magdag required of her oar-slaves.

The Zairian said, "My name is Fazhan ti Rozilloi, dom."

I nodded. The *ti* meant he was someone of some importance in Rozilloi. And that city was known to me, although not particularly well...I knew Mayfwy of Felteraz must have sad thoughts of me, still, for I had used her ill. Her daughter Fwymay had married Zarga na Rozilloi—and the *na* in his name meant he was, if not the most important person of Rozilloi, then damned well high in rank.

"And your name, dom?"

Well, I'd been called Gadak for some time now and had been thinking like Gadak the Renegade. But this Fazhan ti Rozilloi was a crimson-faril, beloved of the Red, and so I deemed it expedient to revert in my allegiance to Zair. Truth to tell, I'd never seriously contemplated abandoning the cause of Zair and the Red; but recent events had been so traumatic—to use a word of later times—that I had been so near to total shock as to be indifferent to anything. Tipping that damned Chulik into the water had been not only a gesture of defiance, it signaled some return of the lump of suffering humanity that was me to the old, tearaway, evil, vicious, and intemperate Dray Prescot I knew myself at heart still to be.

"I am Dak," I said. I did not embroider. I did not wish to involve myself in dreaming up fresh names, and I had taken the name Dak in honor from a great and loyal fighting-man upon the southern shore. And, too, I was growing sick of names, sick of titles. This is, of course, a stupid frame of mind. Names are vital, names are essential, particularly upon Kregen, where so much is different and yet so much is the same as on this Earth four hundred light-years through interstellar space...

This is true of names. As to titles, I had collected a hatful already in my life upon Kregen and was to gather many more, as you shall hear. Of them all I had valued being a Krozair of Zy the most. And the Krozairs of Zy had ejected me, thrown me out, branded me Apushniad. No, I would not tell this Fazhan I had once been Pur Dray, the Lord of Strombor, the most feared Krozair upon the Eye of the World. Anyway, he wouldn't believe me. Since I had taken a dip in the Sacred Pool of Baptism with my Delia I was assured of a thousand years of life and a remarkable ability to recuperate rapidly from wounds. This Fazhan betrayed the usual ageless look of Kregans who have arrived at maturity; he could be anywhere from twenty to a hundred and fifty or so.

"Dak?" He looked at me, and then away. Then, seeing that we were to be oar-comrades, he said, "I salute you, Dak, for dumping that Zair-forsaken Chulik in the water."

325

He made no mention of Jikai in the matter, which pleased me. Too many people are too damned quick to talk of some trifle as a Jikai. A Jikai is a great and resounding feat of arms, or some marvelous deed—the word should not be cheapened.

"And I am Rukker na—" boomed the Kataki, and stopped, and looked at us, with his evil lowering face dark with suppressed passion. "Well, since you are Tailless Dak, I am Rukker." He lifted one massive hand. "But I shall not like it if you call me Tailless Rukker."

The recovery had been swift. But he'd said *na,* and then checked. Whatever place he came from, he was its lord.

Carrying on his recovery, the Kataki swung his low-browed, furrowed face toward the Xaffer, looking past Fazhan and me. Katakis usually grease and oil and curl their black hair so that it hangs beside their faces. Their flaring nostrils curl above gape-jawed mouths. Their eyes are wide-spaced and yet narrow, brilliant and cold. They are not apim, like me; they are diffs. Perhaps their greatest physical peculiarity and strength is the tail each one can sinuously twirl into vicious speedy action, and with a curved razor-sharp blade strapped to its tip bring slicing and slashing and darting in against his opponent. No, I did not like Katakis, for they were aragorn, slave-managers, slavers, slave-masters.

"Xaffer!" roared this blow-hard Kataki, his dark-browed face fierce. "And what is your accursed name?"

The Xaffer surprised me.

"You are a Kataki," he said in that whispering, hushed, timid voice of a Xaffer. "Your devil's race has brought great misery and anguish to my people. I hate Katakis. My name is Xelnon and I shall not speak to you again."

The Zairian shifted his eyes from the Xaffer to look at me, shocked. I looked at the Kataki, this ferocious Rukker. The blood pulsed in his face, veins stood out on his low forehead, his eyes looked murderous. "Cramph! Were we not chained you would not speak thus! Mark me well, Xelnon the onker! Your day will come and I shall—"

"What, Rukker," I said loudly. "You will beat and lash and enslave him, as you are undoubtedly a Kataki and that is what Katakis are so good at doing."

His shocked gaze shifted to me. We sat next to each other, with the steps of the bench lifting him a little higher than me so as to reach the loom. He glared at me. His chains rattled.

"You—apim—" He swallowed down and his thin lips showed spittle.

"Do not fret, Rukker the Kataki. Your tail is safe from me. If you do not cause me trouble."

He bellowed then, raving. I kept a sharp eye on him, for I knew a little of chain fighting by slaves, and I had no desire to be strangled or have an eye flicked out. He reached down to grab me with his right hand, for we sat on the larboard side. This confrontation was no sudden thing; it was long overdue. He tried to seize me about the neck, for the iron rings had been removed after our walk here and tame-slaves were going about with pots of salve made into paste to ease us. The blood on my neck and back and chest was congealing. If he did as he intended he'd not only open up the sore places, he'd squeeze my throat into my neckbones, and if he did not choke me, he'd give me a damned sore throat and head. So I took his right hand with my left. His face convulsed. Struggling silently, for a space we held, he pressing on and I resisting him.

He glared with a mad ferocity upon me. Vicious and feral and violent are Katakis. This one thought to overpower me and subdue me and punish me for my words. Yes, Katakis are all those terrible things. Confident in his power Rukker bore down. It was his misfortune that the man upon whom he happened to choose to release his own frustrations labored under torments he knew nothing of. It was his hard luck, as a vicious, feral, and violent man, to meet a man who was more vicious, more feral, and more violent. I do not say these things in any foolish state of inverse pride. I know my sins. But, here, violence met violence and recoiled.

His eyes widened. I bore back harder, twisted, and so brought my right hand up to block the savage blow of his left. As for his killing tail—I stomped it flat against the planking of the deck, whereat he yelled.

"Desist, Rukker, or I shall break your arm off."

"You—apim—I'll—I'll—"

"Do not think I would not do it, Rukker. You are a Kataki. Do not forget what that means."

"I do not forget, you rast—"

I twisted a little more, and as his left fist still looped around at me, I took his wrist in my right hand and jerked most savagely.

He let a gasp of air puff past those thin twisted lips.

"You cramph! You'll pay—"

A lash struck down across his broad naked back and he snapped upright. A whip-Deldar, sweating in his green, his dark face sullen, lifted for another blow. "What's this?" he shouted. "I'll discipline you—you—"

"Whip-Deldar," I said, speaking quickly and loudly enough to make my words penetrate. "There is no trouble here. We were testing the height and the stretch of the loom."

The odd thing was that our motions might have been taken for a practice evolution. The whip-Deldar lowered his lash. He looked tired, tired and spiteful.

"You dare talk to me, you rast!"

"Only to save your trouble, whip-Deldar. The oar-master would not welcome damaged oar-slaves now."

The whip-Deldar glowered, flicking the lash. He might be a poor specimen of humanity anywhere, let alone in evil Magdag, but the sense of what I said penetrated his sluggish brain. He gave me a cut with the lash, stingingly, just to show me who was in charge here, and went off, cursing roundly.

I do not laugh, as you know, nor smile readily. I kept my ugly old face as hard as a bower anchor as Rukker, the Kataki, said, "He was flogging me, not you, apim."

"If you wish him to continue I will call him back for you."

"By the Triple Tails of Targ the Untouchable! Were you a Kataki I would understand!"

Fazhan leaned forward and looked up past me. "But for this apim Dak, you would have been beaten, Rukker."

"I know it. But it would be best if you did not mention it again."

"Ah," said Fazhan ti Rozilloi, "but it is worth the telling, by Zantristar the Merciful!"

The swifter shook and a shudder passed through her fabric. In the next instant, to the accompaniment of distant hailing above decks, we all understood we had pushed off from the wharf. A long, slow gentle rocking made us all aware that we had been cast off into our new life. Until the oars were in, the swifter would possess this gentle rocking motion, for she was of large enough build to remain steady in the water without her wings.

Rukker the Kataki and Fazhan ti Rozilloi glared for a space longer at each other, then I stuck my old carved beak head between them and said, "If we are to pull together it will be easier if we do not try to fight one another all the time."

Rukker nodded. He was a man accustomed to instant decision.

"You say you understand these infernal things. Tell me."

"You have never sailed in a swifter?"

"Aye, a few times. But I sat in the captain's cabin and drank wine and the way of the vessel did not concern me."

"It concerns you now," said Fazhan.

"Aye, that is why I would learn of it."

"All you need to know," I said, and I spoke heavily, "is that you will pull the oar, and go on pulling the oar, until you are dead. All else will mean nothing."

"Where are these oars, then?"

"We are being towed out from the cothon through the narrow channel. It is too narrow otherwise. Once in the outer harbor we will receive our oars from the oar-hulk. They will arrive soon enough, bringing misery and torment, and for some, a happy release in death."

Rukker mused on this. His dark Kataki face scowled.

"You appear to me to be a man, Dak—of sorts. I will allow you to assist me in my escape."

Fazhan gurgled a little cynical laugh; but it was not a laugh a refined lady would recognize. Oar-slaves do not often have either the opportunity or the reason for laughing.

We bumped and the swifter rocked, and then we bumped again and remained still. We had been moored up to the oar-hulk. Noises began from forward, spurting through the confined space, hollow, echoing. Hangings and scrapings, and at least two shrill yells. It was common for a slave to be crushed or injured when the oars came inboard. We waited for our turn and we did not have long to wait, for we pulled six oars from the bows. A sudden shaft of suns-light speared through the oar port as the sliding cover went back. Sailors busied themselves—hard, adventurous, callous men—hauling the oars in, adjusting the set and balance, cursing the slaves who brought down the round lead counterweights. The oar shoved past Xelnon the Xaffer, past Fazhan ti Rozilloi, past me, Dak, and so past Rukker the Kataki. The loom end was inserted into the rowing frame, which was hinged up to receive it, and locked, and the counterweight was hung on and locked in its turn. The four of us sat, looking at that immense bar of wood before us. The carpenters followed to affix the manette, which we would grasp, for the loom itself was of too great a girth.

I had noticed immediately on boarding the swifter that she smelled clean. She smelled of vinegar and pungent ibroi and soap.

She was not a new vessel, this *Green Magodont;* but she had been in for a refit and was now as sweetly clean as she would ever be. All that was about to change.

Amid the usual barrage of curses and yells, slaves came running along the grated decks and hurled sacks of straw and ponsho fleeces at us. Men scrabbled for well-filled sacks, for fleeces that did not appear too mangy. Rukker hauled in half a dozen and the slave yelped; Rukker knocked him back and examined sack after sack. He took a fine-filled one and as he discarded the others, I snatched up the best and threw them along to Xelnon and Fazhan. The fleeces were likewise gone through, and the slave, jittering with fear, reviled by the other oar-slaves opposite us, squealed at Rukker to let him have back those he did not want.

"Quiet, kleesh," said Rukker, and the slave shook.

A marine, his shortsword out, walked up along the grated deck and I looked forward, not without interest, to a little action; but Rukker hurled the last sack back and cursed. The marine chivied the slave along and he went off to throw the fleeces down to the next set of oar-slaves. We were all busy spreading the fleeces over the sacks, arranging them. Already I had nipped three nits under my thumbnail. *Green Magodont* was no longer a clean swifter. I glanced up at Rukker.

"You were allowed the pick of the sacks, Rukker, because you have a tail. I understand that. But do not think to take the best of everything the four of us are issued with."

He might have bellowed his head off then; but a whip-Deldar ran along, not hitting us but cracking his lash in the air with a sound most doleful and menacing, violent and frightening. He impressed us poor naked slaves, he impressed us mightily.

"Silence!" shouted the whip-Deldar. "The first man to speak will get ol' snake—I promise you."

I did not speak.

No one else spoke.

We had learned one elementary lesson we would not forget.

A deal of confused shouting bellowed down from aloft. I, who had been a swifter captain of the inner sea, could understand what was going on—but only to some extent. I knew these oar-slaves with me on the lowest tier, the thalamite bank, were raw, untrained, useless. I could not understand why the oar-master had ordered our oars fixed and threaded—that is, placed in the rowing frames. Presently, amid a deal of noise and confusion, fresh sailors and slaves poured below and took the oars from the rowing frames, slid the oar-port covers back, and we all had our first lesson in pushing the oar looms forward so that the looms lay as close to the hull as they would go, which brought the outer portions and the blades close to the outside hull. The thalamites were not trusted to pull yet, and *Green Mago-dont* would begin her journey with only the two upper banks pulling.

We heard the orders, the whistles, the sudden deathly silence in the ship. Then the preparatory whistle, and then the twin beat from the drum-Deldar, the bass, and tenor, thumping out. We heard the creak of the upper oars, the splash of water as they dug in. We all felt the swifter surge forward, slowly at first, but gathering momentum. All rocking ceased and the swifter struck a straight, sure path out through the harbor, out past the Pharos, out from vile Magdag into the Eye of the World. Wherever we were going, we were on our way.

Two
Oar-slaves in the swifters of Magdag

We rowed.

We oar-slaves pulled at the massively heavy looms of the oars, up and back and down and forward and up and back and down and...

A week. Give a galley slave a week, more or less, and he will be either dead or toughened enough to last another week, and then another, and then perhaps, if his stamina lasts, to live. If the existence of a galley slave can be called living.

The Xaffer, Xelnon, lasted five days.

He would have died sooner, but *Green Magodont* caught a wind Swinging out of Magdag and so we slaves were spared much of the continuous hauling that is the killer. But he died.

He did not tell us what he had done to be condemned to the galleys. Usually Xaffers are given the lighter tasks of slaves, household chores, secretarial work, record-keeping. Most often they, along with Relts, are employed as stylors. But he was here, with us, slaving, and then he was a mere cold corpse, blood-marked by the lash, a bundle to be thrown overboard to the chanks.

A Rapa took his place, brought up from the slave-hold. His gray vulturine face with that brooding, aggressive hooked beak and the bright feathers rising around his crest fitted in with the stark horror of our situation.

We spoke rarely. We learned the Rapa's name was Lorgad, that he had got himself stinking drunk on dopa and had run amok in the mercenaries' billets. Exactly what he had then done he did not say, presumably because he could no longer remember. He pulled on the loom with us and we labored and sweated in the stink and dank darkness of our floating prison.

On the day after Xelnon died we beached up on a small island, one of the many small islands that smother the larger maps of the Eye of the World with measle spots. The swifter was hauled up stern first onto a beach of silver sand. I have said that the old devil the teredo worm is nowhere as fierce on Kregen as upon Earth and often the swifters are not sheathed in copper or lead. Often, especially in the cases of the larger types, they are. *Green Magodont* was not sheathed, and so despite her size her captain had her hauled up out of the water as often as he could. The task was formidable; but we slaves, still chained, were flogged up and over the side and so set to work hauling the drag ropes.

The island glimmered under the distant golden fire of two of the moons of Kregen; the Twins, eternally revolving one about the other, smiled down upon our agony.

We were herded back into the swifter and chained up, for in the ship lay the best prison for us.

In the normal course of events the gangs on a loom remained together in duties of this kind; but the captain of *Green Magodont,* although undeniably a cruel and vicious overlord of Magdag, was of the school that liked to rotate his oar-slaves between tiers. Once the agonies of learning how to pull correctly to the rhythm of the whistles and drums and to conduct the necessary evolutions smartly and promptly had been hammered into our skulls and muscles, we thalamites of the lower tier were rotated to the center tier, where the zygites pulled.

Green Magodont carried on the short-keel system eight men to her upper bank, six to her middle, and four to her lower. We did not aspire to the center tier until some time; but, at last, we were deemed sufficiently proficient to be rotated.

We had left that island where we had gone ashore to work, and since then, although the swifter had touched land each night, we had not gone ashore again. As to our journey and its direction, apart from my guess that we were headed southwest, I knew nothing. Oar-slaves are not consulted on the conning of the ship.

"Will they really let us onto the middle deck, Dak?"

"Once we can be trusted to pull correctly, Fazhan. Aye."

Rukker the Kataki grunted and turned to find a more comfortable position, his tail curled up and looped over his shoulder. We rested this night, as we rested any time, chained to our bench. "Do we ever get up onto the upper deck?"

"Only when we are considered fully proficient." I did not want to talk. More and more I had been thinking about my daughter Velia, of the tragically short time I had known her and known she was my daughter, of the manner of her death. "I can tell you that if I captained this damned swifter this loom would remain in the thalamites forever."

"You!" scoffed Rukker. "Captain a swifter!"

"I said *if*."

"And yet you know about Magdaggian swifters, Dak." Fazhan had lost much of the scarlet in his face; he had thinned and fined down on the food we ate, on the daily exercise. "I was a swifter ship-Hikdar before we were taken. But I know little about Grodnim swifters."

"I have been oar-slave before," I said, and left it at that.

Fazhan grunted and turned his head on his arms, spread on the loom. But Rukker showed instant interest. "So you escaped?"

"Aye."

"Then you will certainly assist me when we escape."

"I escaped," I said, "when we were taken by a swifter from Sanurkazz. A swifter captained by a Krozair of Zy." I said this deliberately. I wanted to probe Fazhan—and Rukker, too. For the martial and mystic Order of Krozairs of Zy is remote from ordinary men on the Eye of the World, strange, and dedicated to Disciplines almost too demanding for frail human flesh.

Fazhan turned his head back quickly.

"The Krozairs!" he said. He breathed the word as a man might in talking about demigods.

The Rapa, Lorgad, snuffled and hissed. "Krozairs! We fought them—aye, and we thrashed them."

"Thrashed?" I said.

The Rapa passed a hand over his feathers, smoothing them. "Well—it was a hard fight. But King Genod's new army won—as it always wins."

"But one day it will be smashed utterly!" said Fazhan. His voice blazed in the night, and surly voices answered from the other rowing benches in the gloom, bidding the onker be quiet so tired men might sleep.

I had learned what little Rukker would tell me of his story, and I knew Fazhan's, that he had been a ship-Hikdar in a swifter from Zamu. Yet he was not a Krozair Brother, not even of the Krozairs of Zamu. As for Rukker, as he said himself, he was essentially a land soldier, and knew nothing of ships and the sea. As a mercenary he had hired out his—And then he had paused, and corrected himself, and said he had been hired out as a paktun to Magdag. I knew, if I was right and he was a gernu, a noble, that he had taken a force of his own country to fight for Magdag for pay. Now this was, to me, passing strange, for my previous experience with Katakis had been of them as slave-masters, slavers who bartered human flesh. There were a number of races of diffs living up in the northeastern seaboard of the Eye of the World, notably around the Sea of Onyx. Rukker had said he came from an inland country there, a place he had once referred to as Urntakkar, that is, North Takkar. He did not refer to it again.

I said, "Have you heard of Morcray?"

"No."

So I let that lie, also.

But if the Katakis were moving out from their traditional business and becoming mercenaries, then the future looked either darker and more horrible, or scarlet and more interesting, depending on the hardness of your muscles and the keenness of your sword.

We sailed in company with other swifters; just how many we thalamites in our stinks and gloom could not know. We anchored for the night and then took a wind and so rested the next day, and on the following day, the wind fell and we pulled. That was a hard day. Another ten slaves were hurled overboard, either dead or flogged near to death. Those who remained hardened, and the replacements from the slave-hold were those who failed.

That night we once again hauled *Green Magodont* out of the water. I saw six other swifters being hauled up, and also there were signs of a wooden stockade being constructed on the shore into which the slaves might be herded. I knew that Magdag, no less than every other Green city of the northern shore, was utilizing every possible sinew of war. Slaves were now becoming valuable, even though many a poor devil had been captured by the new army of King Genod, the genius at war.

In the stockade only a few fights broke out. Most of us wanted to stretch out—and what a luxury that was!—and sleep. I did not stay awake long. The four of us—for the Rapa, Lorgad, was accepted by us as an oar-comrade—slept together. The morning came all too soon, and with many groans and stretching of stiff joints, we rose and were doused down with a vile concoction of seawater and pungent ibroi, and then we gobbled the food thrown to us. This was a mash of cereal, a torn hunk of stale bread, and a handful of palines. For the palines everyone gave thanks to whatever gods they revered.

The whip-Deldars stalked among us, the lashes licking hungrily, sorting us out amid a great clanking of chains.

"I believe," said Fazhan, staring about, "that we are to go up to be zygites this day."

It certainly looked like it. The dust from the stockade compound rose thickly as hundreds of pairs of naked feet stamped. The blue of mountains rose inland, and the sky showed that hint of fair weather that heartens the hard-bitten soul of a sailorman. I wanted no trouble. We had been working on our chains. I had experience to go on. The Kataki had the experience of the master slaver, the man to whom the guiles of slaves seeking escape were known as a part of his business. And Fazhan and Lorgad worked at our directions. So I wanted us to stay together, and not to create problems.

We waited in long rows, our chains clanking as men shifted position. The Suns of Scorpio rose over the hills and flooded down their mingled streaming light. I stretched and felt my muscles pull. I was in superb physical shape; but I could have done with more food, as could all of us. A commotion broke out among the slaves to our right.

I heard a bull voice bellowing, and abruptly a whip-Deldar catapulted into the air, turning over and over, his whip thonged to his wrist whirling. He landed flat on his back amid a splash of dust. The slaves cheered. The smashing voice shouted:

"By Zogo the Hyrwhip! You zigging cramph! I'll break your back! Duh, I'll rip your guts out and—"

Dragging the other three, I was running.

The bellow smashed out again, louder, roaring with fury.

"Duh—by Zair! You'll not walk again, rast!"

"Hold, Dak—what is it?" And, "You rast, haul back!" And, "By Rhapaporgolam the Reaver of Souls, you are mad!"

The three of them, I hauled along. The dust, the yells, the confusion, the stink... I bundled headlong into the thick of the confusion.

A second whip-Deldar screamed with gap-toothed mouth, glaring unbelievingly at his left arm, which dangled with broken bones protruding pinkish white. Slaves stumbled out of my way. I bashed on to the center and there—standing like a mountain, like a mammoth beset by wolves, a boloth beset by werstings—stood Duhrra.

His bald head already grew a bristly fuzz like all of us. His dangling scalplock had gone. His naked body showed all the splendid musculature of the wrestler. His idiot-seeming face was contorted into a hideous scowl, and I sighed, for Duhrra was normally the most peaceable of men unless someone upset him. Once riled he was like to tear your head off. On the ground at his feet and chained to him lay a young man. A youth; barely come to his full growth, his body showed the promise of a superb physique. He was not unconscious, but a thread of blood ran from one nostril.

I threw a Rapa away, chopped a couple of apims, kicked a Brokelsh, and so grabbed Duhrra by the arm. He whirled, ready to smash my face in, and I said, low and hard, "Duhrra! Calm down, bring the boy, come with me. *Jump!*"

He picked up the boy in a single fluid motion of that massive body, and we turned and plunged back into the throng of shouting, excited, dust-stirring slaves. I had to break the neck of the whip-Deldar who reared up, flailing his whip with his right hand, his broken left arm dangling. He had seen us. I knew what would happen if we were detected. As for the other whip-Deldar—I saw a Brokelsh jump full on him and guessed his back-bone would not stand the strain.

With Rukker, Fazhan, and Lorgad trailing on the chain, with Duhrra carrying the youth at my side, we bashed our way through the mob until we reached the line as yet undisturbed. I watched for guards, whip-Deldars, and anyone who showed too much interest.

"Put the boy down, Duhrra."

I bent and scooped up dust, spit on it, wadded it.

"Stand up, lad! Hold yourself straight!"

I shoved the chunk of spittle-wadded dust up his bleeding nostril and then wiped away the blood, licking my fingers. When he looked presentable, and we had knocked the dust from one another—all of us—I said to them all: "Stand and look stupid. By Zair! That should not be difficult! We know nothing of the disturbance."

"Duh—Dak—" said Duhrra.

"Quiet, you fambly. Tell me later."

Rukker, the Kataki, said, "You think fast, Dak, for an apim."

"Shut your black-fanged wine-spout, Rukker. Here come the guards."

We all stood there, in our chains, and looked suitably stupid. There was a considerable quantity of confusion lower down, and shouting, and the sound of the whips lashing. Some of the slaves were too stupid in all reality to run off. When order was restored and we were sorted out, the six of us were herded back into *Green Magodont* and chained down in the middle tier. We were to be zygites, six to a loom, and if the oar-master of the swifter discovered he had two slaves too many, he would give thanks to Green Grodno and smile. As for the swifter from which Duhrra and the lad had come, her oar-master would curse and rave—and I felt damned sure that the oar-master of *Green Magodont* would continue to say nothing and smile even more broadly. As the quondam first lieutenant of a seventy-four I knew only too well the avariciousness of shellbacked sailormen in the matter of ship supplies—and in the Eye of the World of Kregen, ship supplies included slaves.

Green Magodont, as I had previously observed, was broad enough to accept six oarsmen abreast on a loom. Above our heads on the thranites bank the men were arranged to push and pull, the eight men forming a convenient pattern. This tended to cramp them a little more than us lower tiersmen; but the shipwrights of Magdag had done their sums well so that the leverage and power required on the differently sized oars evened out. So we sat at the loom of the zygite oar. The six of us, from the apostis seat, the outer seat, were: Lorgad the Rapa, Fazhan ti Rozilloi,Vax, Dak, Duhrra of the Days, and Rukker the Kataki.

"Duh—master," Duhrra had said to me as we sorted ourselves out, "I should take the rowing frame."

He was fractionally bigger than Rukker.

I said, "Fambly! With that newfangled claw of yours! Next to the gangway! Where you will get lashed more easily!"

"Yes, master."

"And, for the sweet sake of Mother Zinzu the Blessed! I am not your master!"

"No, master."

As always when arguing with Duhrra on this point—for he had attached himself to me on the southern shore, when he had lost his right hand, and since then we had had a few skirmishes together and were good comrades—I gave up the argument in a kind of helpless mirth. Even an oar-slave may feel that at times, in the ludicrousness of his position; for, to all the names of the gods in two worlds, it is not a position a sane man can regard without recourse to the black humor of absurdity.

Some bustle attended our departure, and we were forced to throw our backs into the work. The captain was evidently in the devil of a hurry. The stockades and the cooking fires were left on the shore so we guessed we'd be back tonight. We pulled. We heaved up on the oar, those on the gangway sides of the long rows of men shoving up, standing up, and then with all the weight of the body and bunched muscles, hurling themselves frenziedly backward onto the bench. The hard wood had to be covered by the straw-stuffed sacks and the ponsho fleeces. Had they not been we would have been red raw in no time, and unfit for rowing. This is not a luxury the overlords of Magdag extend to their oar-slaves, in the matter of ponsho fleeces and sacks; it is a matter of economics and slave-management.

The swifter squadron pulled about, it seemed to me, quartering in different directions. I guessed the courses were not set at random. We either searched for another ship, or we wasted a deal of energy. Nothing—apart from the eternal damned pulling—occurred, and we eventually and to our surprise heard the terminal whistles and the final double drumbeat. The oars lifted and were looped and held, locked in the rowing frames, and we slaves slumped, exhausted.

Before lethargy could drug us into stupefaction, we were flogged out and herded up into the job of hauling the swifters out of the water. The wood from which swifters are built must have been placed on Kregen either by a god or a devil. This flibre, as I have said, possesses remarkable strength for a remarkable lightness. We would scarcely have shifted the ships had they been built of lenk. But flibre gives a large vessel the shrewd feather-lightness of a much flimsier vessel. As I say, flibre was put on Kregen either by a god or a devil—a god, in order to lighten the drudgery of slaves, or a devil so that the damned ships could be manhandled out of the water at all.

At last, fed, exhausted, we flopped down on the hard ground of the stockade and slept. If anyone had wished to tell the story of his life to me at that time, and paid me handsomely to listen, I'd have consigned him to the Ice Floes of Sicce, and turned over and slept.

The next day the swifters remained high on the beach and we oar-slaves sprawled in the stockade, still chained, but able to stretch out and rest our abused bodies.

Parties of hunters went inland toward the mountains and later as the suns began their curve toward the horizon we slaves were issued with steaming chunks of vosk. How we grabbed and stuffed and ate! Provisioning swifters is invariably a complicated process, and the large numbers of men involved demand ready access to vast quantities of food. Usually we subsisted on the mash—there are several varieties—the base of which consists of mergem, that rich plant stuffed with protein and vitamins and iron that has the blessed quality of fortifying a man against his daily toil. But for mergem, which provides so much nourishment in so small a bulk, we would have been a gaunt and hungry crew and quite unfitted to haul on our looms. Onions were provided—how Zorg and I had debated the dissection of a pair of onions!—and some cheese and crusts and palines.[10] The palines helped keep the insanity levels within toleration.

We devoured the boiled vosk with the voraciousness of leems. Then we lay back with bloated bellies, burping contentedly, to sleep the night away.

Duhrra at last found time to tell me what had happened since we had stirred up the camp of King Genod's army and stolen his airboat. He had had to be overpowered by the Zairians from Zandikar when I did not return in time, for he would have gone to find me. He spoke of this with some spirit of contempt for himself that he had been thwunked on the back of the head when he should have been alert not only against the cramphs of Green Grodnims but also, apparently, against the Red Zandikarese.

"When I woke up, Dak—duh! We were flying in the air!"

"You cannot blame the Hikdar—Ornol ti Zab, I believe his name was—he had a duty very plain to him."

"Maybe so. But we flew away and left you."

He and the lad Vax had shipped back from Zandikar and their vessel had been taken. It was becoming more and more dangerous for any vessel of the Red to venture into the western parts of the inner sea these days. The Grodnims had placed swifter squadrons at sea, which carried all before them. Only a very slim coincidence had brought us together again, and to Duhrra it was absolutely inevitable that we should meet up once more. As for Vax, he told me the youth was a fine lad, and potentially a good companion; although he would swear so dreadfully about his father, and Duhrra was strongly of the opinion that if Vax hadn't run away from home to escape the continual beatings, he'd have killed the old devil. Or, so Duhrra believed.

I gave him a brief—a very brief—résumé of what had happened to me after we'd parted. He expressed a desire to twist Gafard's neck a little. We had both been employed by Gafard, the King's Striker, the Sea Zhantil, who was the hateful King Genod's right-hand man, when we'd been renegades, as Gafard himself was a renegade. When I told Duhrra that the Lady of the Stars had, at last, been kidnapped by King Genod's men, he thumped his left fist against the dirt and swore. When I told him that the Lady of the Stars was dead, callously hurled from the back of a fluttrell by the king when the saddle-bird had been injured, and Genod thought himself about to die, Duhrra simply sat on the ground. He ran a little dust through his fingers onto the dust of the ground. His head was bowed.

At last, he said, "I shall not forget."

I did not tell Duhrra of the Days that this great and wonderful lady, who had been called his Heart, his Pearl, by Gafard, and who had loved him in return, was my own daughter Velia, princess of Vallia.

My Delia, my Delia of Delphond, my Delia of the Blue Mountains, waited for me in my island Stromnate of Valka, that beautiful island off the main island of Vallia. I yearned to return to her. Yet I was under an interdiction. Until I had once more made myself a member of the Order of Krozairs of Zy I would not be allowed to leave the Eye of the World. Whether or not it was the Star Lords or the Savanti who chained me here, I did not know, although Zena Iztar had indicated it was not the work of the Star Lords. Well, I would become a Krozair of Zy once more and escape from the inner sea and return to Valka. Before I did that I fancied I would bring this evil king Genod to justice. So, having done all these marvelous and wonderful feats and proved just how great a man I was, I would go home. I would go home and race up the long flight of stairs in the rock from the Kyro of the Tridents, leap triumphantly onto the high terrace of my palace of Esser Rarioch overlooking the bay and Valkanium and I would clasp my Delia in my arms again. Oh, yes. I would do all this. And then—and then I would have to tell her that her daughter Velia was dead.

It is no wonder that on this dreadful occasion I found less thrusting desire to go back to Valka and Delia than I'd ever experienced before. I must return. I must tell my Delia and then comfort her as she would comfort me. It was not just a duty, it was what love prompted. But it was hard, abominably hard.

Duhrra was telling me about his new hand and I roused myself. I had to plan and think. My thoughts had run ahead. Here we were, still chained oar-slaves in a swifter of Magdag.

"...locks with a twist so cunning you'd never know. Look."

I looked. Duhrra's right stump had been covered with a flesh-colored extension that looked just like a wrist and the hard mechanical hand looked not unlike a real hand. He could press the fingers into different positions with his left hand. He kept it hooked so that he could haul on the manette of the oar loom. I felt it and the hardness was unmistakable.

"That's a steel hand, Duhrra—or iron."

The doctors of the inner sea are not, in general, quite as skilled as those of the lands of the Outer Oceans. They are good at relieving pain and can amputate with dexterity. But I did not think they were capable of producing prosthetics of this quality. Duhrra had seen Molyz the Hook Maker and this kind of work would have been quite beyond him. Duhrra had been attended to by the doctors attached to the Todalpheme of the Akhram, the mathematical astronomers who predicted the tides of Kregen, and they had fitted his stump with a socket and an assortment of hooks and blades to be slotted in. But this work here was beyond them, also. Duhrra waxed eloquent for him.

"In Zandikar, it was, Dak. Right out of the blue. This lady says she can fix me up properly. Wonderful woman—wonderful. Gentle and charming and—well, you can see what she did."

"You saw her do it?"

"No. Somehow—duh, master—I do not know! She looked into my eyes and then she laughed and told me I might leave and I looked down—and it was all done."

"And her name, this wonderful woman?"

"She said she was the lady Iztar."

I did not answer. What was Zena Iztar—whose role so far had been enigmatic in my life although I felt I owed her a very great deal—doing in thus helping Duhrra? Her machinations, I suspected, might not jibe with those of the Star Lords or those of the Savanti. She it was who had told me I might never leave the Eye of the World until I was once more a Krzy. I believed her implicitly, had not thought to question her. She, I felt, I hoped, wished me well. That would make a remarkable change here on Kregen, where I had been knocked about cruelly by Savanti and Star Lords moving behind the scenes and exerting superhuman forces. So I admired Duhrra's new hand and thought on.

Then the selfishness of my thoughts mocked me. It was all "I"—Zena Iztar could have helped Duhrra because he was Duhrra.

Tame-slaves threw in malsidges and we ate them, for they are a quality anti-scorbutic. We settled down to sleep and I had a deal to think about; but, all the same, I slept.

Sleep became a rare and precious commodity during the next couple of sennights, for we were employed pulling at night as well as day. The swifters called at islands for short periods and then weighed again, and once again we threw our tortured bodies against the looms of the oars. Food was short and we hungered. Men began to die. I fancied Duhrra would last this kind of punishment well, and the Kataki had reserves of strength on which to call. For Fazhan ti Rozilloi the work became harder and harder; but with all the gallantry of a true crimson-faril he struggled on, refusing to be beaten. The young man Vax stuck to his work with stoical fury, sullen, with a smoldering anger in him hurtful to me. We were not flogged more than any other set on any other loom. But we lost Lorgad the Rapa. One day he could not pull any more, and the flogging lash merely made his dead body jump. He was unchained and heaved overboard, and a fresh man took his place.

He was short, and he took the apostis seat, chunky, and with a black bar look about the eyebrows, and a pug nose that was of the Mountains of Ilkenesk south of the inner sea. Yet he was a Zairian, an apim, and he contrived to give Rukker the Kataki a cunning slash with his chains as the whip-Deldars bundled him across.

Rukker bellowed and shook his chains.

I saw the chain between him and Duhrra pull taut. The chain between Duhrra and me began to pull. The link on which we had been working bent. It began to open. I cursed foully, loudly, unable to get at Rukker past Duhrra.

"Sit back, you stinking Kataki cramph! You tailed abomination! Sit down or I'll cave your onkerish head in!"

He swung back to glare with murderous fury at me. The whip-Deldars bashed away at the new man's chains. Duhrra tried to sit back as well, to release the pressure on the chains. It was a moment when all hell might have broken loose.

One whip-Deldar flicked his lash—almost idly—at me and I endured it. I bellowed again, something about Katakis and rasts and tails, and whispered to Duhrra, "Tell him, Duhrra! Get the gerblish onker to sit down!"

Duhrra leaned across and his rumble would have told the whole bank if I had not started yelling with the pain of the lash. It was not altogether a fake. Vax looked at me in surprise. I yelled some more. And then Duhrra must have got the message across, for Rukker slapped himself back on the bench, whipping his tail up out of the way, and the strain came off the chain.

When the whip-Deldars had gone, he started to rumble at me, "You called me many things, Dak, and I shall not forget them—"

"You would have ruined all, Rukker. You must think and plan if you wish to escape the overlords of Magdag and their slave-masters. Onker! I did what I did to make you sit down."

Duhrra said, "Had you ruined our chances, Rukker, I would not have been pleased—duh—I would have been angry."

Rukker glared at me again. Duhrra lifted the chain between us. Rukker looked.

Duhrra's metal hand had worked hard and well. The bent link was on the point of parting. Rukker whistled.

"Well, you onker! Now do you see your foolishness?"

He did not like my tone. But he was a Kataki.

Rukker said, "I understand. I will not speak of it again."

That was Rukker the Kataki. He had this knack of putting his own mistakes and unpleasant experiences into a limbo where he chose not to speak of them. The idea of apology never entered his ferocious Kataki head.

Three
Of Duhrra's steel hand

"Well, Dak, apim, when is it to be?"

Rukker's words whispered in his growly voice in the darkness. *Green Magodont* lay anchored somewhere or other—we oar-slaves had no idea where we were after all the comings and goings of the past days. We knew only that if we searched for a ship we had not found her.

I said, "There is the question of this Nath the Slinger."

"I shall break his neck the moment I am free," said Rukker, in a comfortable way, perfectly confident.

Nath the Slinger turned his pug-nosed face our way, looking up from the apostis seat, and scowled. He looked an independent sort of fellow, who would as soon knock your teeth out as pass the time of day. Rukker had not liked the slash from his chains.

"We can free the link tomorrow. But we shall not let you go, Rukker, if you—"

He bellowed at that, raising a chorus of curses from the oar-slaves about us in the darkness, weary men trying to sleep.

"You are a nurdling onker, Rukker—why not shout out and tell the captain? I am sure he will be happy to know."

In the starlight and the golden glow of She of the Veils the zygite bank showed enough light for me to catch the look of venomous evil on Rukker's face. But it was dark and shadowy and I could have been mistaken; I did not think I was.

"I do not wish to discuss that, Dak. If it is tomorrow night, then—"

"We will release you only if you swear to fight with us. Your quarrel with Nath the Slinger must wait."

"I'll rip his tail out and choke him with it!" said Nath the Slinger, in his snarly voice.

I sighed.

Anger and enmity—well, they are common enough on Kregen, to be sure. But when they interfere with my own plans I am prepared to be more angry and be a better enemy than most.

"When we have taken the swifter, you two may kill each other," I said, pretty sharply. "And curse you for a pair of idiots."

A voice from the bench in front whispered back.

"If you all shout a little louder—"

"We already said that," said Fazhan nastily.

"Then we will join you. The oar-master has the keys."

Duhrra rolled his eyes at me.

"They must think we don't know what we're about."

"They are slaves like us. Now the word will be all over the slave benches. If there are white mice among the slaves we may be prevented before we strike."

"White mice" is an expression from my own eighteenth-century Terrestrial Navy, meaning men among the hands who will inform to the ship's corporals and the master-at-arms. On Kregen these men are called *maktikos* and may sometimes be discovered among slaves who appear and disappear without apparent reason on a tier of oars, moving from bench to bench. I had wondered if Nath the Slinger might be an informer. There were plans to insure his silence once we had begun the escape. The only way to insure our safety before that was to note if he spoke to the overseers or the whip-Deldars. I fancied an apostis-seat man would experience difficulty in that.

"Why not tonight?" rumbled Rukker. "Now?"

"The link must be further bent."

"I would snap it with one wrench."

"You may try—but for the sake of Zair, do it quietly."

Rukker leaned over Duhrra. He took the chain in his right hand and tail and heaved. The link strained open, as it had when he'd surged up before; it did not break.

The veins stood out on that low forehead, his face grew black, his eyes glaring. He slackened his effort and panted. "Onker, Duhrra! Help me! You too, Dak!"

So we all pulled.

The link would not part.

"Tomorrow," I said.

Duhrra said, "You were told, Rukker. Now do you believe?"

Rukker said, "I will not speak of that."

I did not laugh. We were going to escape, I was certain; but I could not laugh—not yet. There would be time, later...

The next day during those periods in which we were not called on to fling every ounce of weight against the looms, Duhrra used that marvelous hand given to him by Zena Iztar. The steel fingers prised against the link like a vise. Even a steel hand that gave the hard pressure necessary would not have accomplished the bending without the superb muscles that Duhrra could bring to the task. I helped as best I could, taking the strain. We had to work surreptitiously. The bent link was camouflaged by a mixture of odoriferous compounds I will not detail and it passed the daily inspection, for a strong pull on it resulted merely in the usual melancholy clang. The whip-Deldars suspected nothing. They were always on the watch, for slavery makes a man either dully stupid or viciously frenzied.

I said to Rukker, "Once we are free, everything must be done at top speed. The slaves will yell and cry out and demand to be freed. You will not be able to silence them. They have no idea at all, in moments like that, beyond the hunger to strike off their chains. So we must be quick."

"I'll silence—"

"You will not. You will take the whip-Deldars. We need weapons. I will see to the oar-master."

"I give the orders, Dak. This is my escape."

"I don't give a damn whose escape it is. But if you foul it up I'll pull your tail off myself."

I had warned him, earlier, not to be too free with his tail. He could have upended a whip-Deldar easily enough. They did not carry the keys, as the onker of a slave in front of us had said. If a Kataki used his tail too much in a swifter the overlords would simply chop it off. I had told Rukker this. He had heeded my advice.

So we planned out our moves exactly, each man assigned his part. I listened as Nath the Slinger spoke, in short harsh sentences. I came to the conclusion that he was not a maktiko, that he might be trusted.

The day seemed endless. *Green Magodont* pulled frenziedly in one direction for a bur; then we rested on our oars for another. Then we set off at slow cruise in a different direction and suddenly we were called on for every effort, and as suddenly relieved and sent back to slow cruise. I fancied we were dodging about among islands and shooting out past a headland in a surprise attack that resulted always in nothing. If the Grodnims sought a ship, as I suspected, her captain played them well in this game of hide-

and-seek. Duhrra told me he had come from the swifter *Vengeance Mortil*, where he and Vax had been the two slaves chained together to push against the loom. I did wonder if Gafard's *Volgodont's Fang* led this squadron, for our swifter was not the flagship.

One item I should mention here, for it would affect our manner of escape, showed how either development was taking place in the swifters of the inner sea, or the overlords of Magdag were running short of iron; or, very likely, were conscious of the need to lighten their galleys. There was no great chain that connected all the chains of the inboard slaves. We would have to release the locks of each set separately. This would take time. There would be no release of the locks of the great chain thus freeing all the slaves the moment the great chain had been passed through their chains. It was a factor to be figured into my calculations.

"By Zinter the Afflicted!" rasped Nath. "Is the work finished?" We lay on our oars as the gloom deepened about us and *Green Magodont* rocked gently with the evening sounds from an island nearby reaching us mutedly—the cries of birds, mostly, with occasionally the coughing roar of a beast of prey, and then, sometimes, the shrill scream of its quarry, telling us we were anchored well into the island up a river mouth. The chinks of light that streamed their opaz radiance into our prison waned as the suns sank.

"We will escape," said Vax. He spoke seldom and he was, as we all could see, obsessed by some consuming inner torment.

"Then praise Zair," said Fazhan. "I do not think I could last another day." He coughed, too weakly for my liking. "My old father would weep to see me now."

Vax let rip with a rude sound, and a coarse observation about fathers in general and his devil cramph of a father in particular. The venom in his voice gave me hope that he would fling some of that diabolic energy into the coming fight.

"I do not care to hear you talk thus of your father—" began Fazhan. It was clear to me that Fazhan had been brought up in the best circles of Rozilloi and was, in the terminology of Earth, a gentleman, although the peoples of the inner sea have a trifle different set of gentlemen from the horters of Havilfar and the koters of Vallia.

"You did not know my rast of a sire," said Vax, most evilly. "And neither did I, for he died just before I was born."

This did not accord with what Duhrra believed; but it was of no moment then as the whip-Deldars ran screeching among us, lashing with their whips, and the whistles blew and the drum-Deldar crashed out his double-beat. In the gathering gloom the swifter made a last try to trap the elusive vessel that caused the Grodnims so much trouble and us oar-slaves so much agony.

Green Magodont did not catch the quarry.

"I do not know," Vax had said as we bent to our loom, "if I wish my foul father was here with me now. I would not know if I should slay him at once and thus purge his evil crimes, or if I should allow him to live so that he might suffer as I suffer."

"Let the rast suffer, dom," said Nath the Slinger and then we flung ourselves into the task.

The Suns of Scorpio set in a last blaze that penetrated our prison in a mingled veil of colors and gradually died to an opaline glow. Presently the chinks of light through the gratings took on a pinkish golden tinge as the Maiden with the Many Smiles lifted above the horizon and shone down upon us.

Duhrra kept up the work on the link. I helped.

At last I said, "You must sleep, Duhrra. We will have much to tire ourselves on the morrow."

"I am sure it will give—"

"Then all the more reason for sleeping."

We composed ourselves. Rukker's hoarse whisper, cruel and sharp in the night, pierced the darkness.

"What are you onkers doing? There is no time for sleep. Keep working, rasts, or I will—"

A whip-Deldar on watch walked along the gangway between the rowing frames and Rukker had the sense to shut up and drop his head on the loom. Although the swifter's slaves were washed out twice daily with seawater, we still stank. Our hair was growing back in bristles, giving us an outlandish appearance. The Deldar passed on, humming to himself—the stupid "Obdwa Song," it was—and Rukker lifted his head. I caught the gleam of his eyes in the slatted chinks of light from the gratings.

"Shut up, Rukker, and get some sleep. I shall see how you fight on the morrow—or before, if I decide."

"You—"

A ship is never silent. There are always the same familiar sounds, at sea or at anchor. Through that quiet threnody of water splash and creak of wood, the murmur of distant voices, I whispered, "You are becoming tiresome, Kataki. I know you are a fighting-man. Just do not keep on trying to prove it all the time. And remember who it is you fight—the overlords, and not the slaves. Dernun?"[11]

A marine bellowed some order or other high on the quarterdeck, and Rukker made a visible effort. His moon-shadowed face scowled with the effort as he controlled himself. "After, Dak the High-Handed," he said. "After we have the swifter—"

"Yes, yes, go to sleep."

I heard a low gurgle—hardly a laugh—from Vax, at my right. Duhrra was already fast asleep.

"If my evil rast of a father had been tamed by someone like you, Dak, I might have let him die under my hand, instead of letting him suffer."

A most vicious and intemperate young man, this Vax.

Toward morning, with the innate sense of rhythm of an old sailorman that even the oddities of Kregen and the stresses of being an oar-slave could not break, I awoke. Soon Duhrra was hard at work on the link. Vax yawned when I nudged him, and bid me clear off. "Schtump!" he said, most malignantly.

"Wake up Fazhan and Nath. Jump!"

He gave me a look, all shadowed and dark, that was unmistakable. But he leaned down and gave Fazhan a crack in the ribs. When Fazhan was awake he woke Nath. We yawned, still tired; but I knew they were keyed up to the work ahead. If I have glossed over this period of my servitude as an oar-slave it is because I do not care to remember in too vivid a detail a time of great agony and fatigue upon Kregen. Suffice it to say I may appear to be callous about serving as a slave and lax in escaping; the truth was I wanted out of that hellhole as fervently as a man dying of thirst needs water.

Duhrra let a low whispering sigh pass his lips. His powerful body eased back. The snap of metal echoed in the night

We all sat perfectly silent.

Presently, when I was satisfied no other ears had picked up that sharp snip of sound, I eased the chain off. Duhrra clawed himself up and I put a hand on his shoulder and pulled him down.

Without a word, not moving the chain that lay limply on the deck at our feet, I stood up. The gratings above let down a patterned splotching of pink and gold. The long rows of naked feet and legs of the thranites glistered in the light. Here and there the coil of a chain shone dully. A whip-Deldar approached.

Silently—silently—I eased up. The Deldar passed. In one leap, touching Rukker's bench with foot and springing on from there, I reached the central gangway. A hand clapped about the Deldar's mouth. He went limp and I eased him to the gangway.

He had a knife.

This I passed down to Rukker.

I saw the Kataki's face.

"No noise, Rukker," I whispered. "Until we are all free." By all I meant the six of us on the oar. "This end is up to you, now. I'm for the oar-master and the keys."

He would have spit some surly remark; but I padded off along the gangway. The slaves slept and I did not fear discovery from them. Only one more whip-Deldar fell before I had reached the after end of the gangway. I looked up. Up there past the thranites the little tabernacle in which the oar-master sat and blew his whistle and controlled the drum-Deldars and made sure the motive power of the swifter functioned perfectly lay in darkness. I went up like a rock grundal. The oar-master would be asleep in his cabin. The keys were neatly racked on their hooks ready to be issued to the whip-Deldars when the slaves must be taken out of the ship. I scooped them up, reading the labels, made from leather, going back down again to the zygites. From then on the process would be one of progression.

Fazhan met me on the gangway. He shook. He looked elated and yet filled with a dread fury he might not be able to control. There was no sign of Rukker or Duhrra. Vax and Nath took the keys I handed them and began to awaken the slaves.

Fazhan said, "I will go aft, Dak."

I gave him the thalamite keys. I pointed down.

"When you come up again, Fazhan, bring men who will fight with you."

"Aye, Dak."

I shooed him off. Nath was working forward. A noise and a stir began to whisper in the hollow hull of the swifter. In a few short murs all hell would break out. The time for silence was almost gone.

I started off aft again, and Vax threw his keys to a slave three benches forward. He hit the poor devil over the head and awoke him and whispered fiercely in his ear and then clapped a hand over his mouth. I warmed to the young man. He might be intemperate and malignant in his ways, but he knew what he was doing. He looked at me. I was aware that the light was growing and that I could see him quite well.

"I will come with you, Dak. I need a sword."

He merely echoed my own thoughts.

Together, we stole silently aft, aiming for the quarterdeck, aiming for swords, aiming to wrench this swifter from the grip of the hated overlords of Magdag.

Four
Nath the Slinger collects pebbles

The sweet fresh night air greeted us as we climbed up onto the quarterdeck. The false dawn lingered with fading radiance upon the deck and the bulwarks, the ship-fittings, the ropes and gilding. The men of the watch were sleepy; they'd been hard at work the previous day as had we. There could be no thought of mercy. Truth to tell, for all the grand talk of mercy here on this Earth, in some situations mercy would be cruel. We were going to take this swifter. I had no doubts. What would happen to any overlords,

347

any ship-Deldars, any marines, when they were caught by the released slaves would make their swift, painless deaths now merciful to them.

There was time for me to observe this young tearaway Vax in action. I liked his style. The men on watch were dealt with on the quarterdeck. As the last sailor slumped, a shout ripped from the forepart of the swifter. The long narrow length of her lay dim in the tricky light. Shadows moved. Men were stirring. Catching the crew just before dawn might have been good planning, even in a ship. It was doubly clever in that the slaves themselves would be sluggish and slow to understand their own liberty. I had known this before. The slaves would not suddenly snatch up chains and wooden beams and go raving into action. It would take time for them to understand. But as the first shrill yells broke out and the sounds of fighting, I knew some, at least, understood.

Vax and I burst into the quarterdeck cabins.

An overlord completely naked with sleep still on his face tried to stop us and I knocked him down and kicked him as I went past.

"In here, Dak!"

Vax was pointing to the first cabin.

"You go—if you wish. I'm for the captain's quarters."

Vax cursed and followed me. We ran down the corridor leading from the double doors that gave ingress from the quarterdeck. These cabins lay under the poop. I went straight into the aft cabin, seeing the light hazy and unreal through the sweep of stern windows where the gallery overhung the curved stern. Up above, the high upflung stern post, curved and decorated—with a magodont, of course—would hover over the poop. I wondered where Rukker and Duhrra had got to and if they were up there. The cabin was empty, as I had expected it to be. The sleeping cabin's door ripped open under my blow and I leaped in.

The captain tumbled out of his cot—this was a fashion to be followed more and more in the larger swifters—roaring. He snatched up his shortsword. He stood lithe and limber, instantly awake, a true captain. I jumped for him.

The shortsword blurred forward.

"Die, you rast!" bellowed the captain.

He should have saved his breath and concentrated on his swordsmanship.

I slid the blow, not allowing the blade to touch me, and drove a fist into his mouth. I kicked him and as he went back I twisted his right hand with such force the wrist-bones broke. Then the Genodder was in my own grip. It felt fine.

The captain staggered back, blood from his mangled mouth dripping down his chin. His eyes were wild.

Vax said, "Why do you not finish him?"

"He may be useful. Deal with him—but do not slay him."

I barged out of the cabin and almost at once was fighting for my life. Marines ran down the corridor, yelling first for the captain, and when they saw me, yelling blue bloody murder.

I accommodated them.

The Genodder was a fine example of a shortsword in the fashion of the inner sea, invented by King Genod and named after him. I swished it up and thrust, cut and jumped, and, in short, had a fine old time. Normally I do not enjoy fighting unless—well, you must be the judge of that. Suffice it to say that on this occasion my pent-up fury broke out. That red haze did not fall before my eyes, for I kept a cool head and my wits about me—at least, I think I did—but there are few memories until I was at the double doors again with a trail of dead men in my rear.

The clean tip of a longsword appeared at my side, from the back, and I whirled and the Genodder hovered inches from Vax's throat.

"You onker," I said, speaking reasonably. "That's the way to get yourself killed." I had not heard him over the noise from the swifter. "You move silently. That is good."

"I—" he said. He looked more than a little taken aback. "I did not expect—"

"Expect everyone to attack you all the time. That way you may stay alive." I looked at the longsword. He had selected a good specimen, although it was not a Ghittawrer blade. "Can you use that?"

"Aye."

"Then let us see what we can find."

"Right gladly. I need—"

I shut him up and we ran out. I knew what he needed.

That fight contained a number of interesting incidents. But then, each fight is different in details, even if they all may seem to be merely a blind scarlet confusion of hacking and thrusting. For instance, Duhrra, who appeared laying about him with a longsword, used it in his right hand, the steel fingers closed and clamped about the hilt. Rukker had spared the time to strap a dagger to his tail. With that bladed tail he could cut a man up in a twinkling. And Vax fought superbly. He did know how to use a longsword. As I barged my way through the knot of marines who came tumbling up from their deck above the rowers, I saw Vax elegantly dealing with his men in a way that made me think he might be a Krozair. He was very young, it was true; but given that the blade he used was a common longsword with a short hilt, he contrived quite a few Krozair tricks. I stuck with the Genodder, for I allow that a shortsword can, in the right circumstances, nip inside a longsword in unskillful hands. I fancied a shortswordsman would be at a disadvantage against this young ruffian Vax.

Duhrra was thoroughly enjoying himself. His great voice boomed out, "Zair! Zair!" and other men took up the call. Rukker fought silently, as did

I and Vax. Fazhan and Nath appeared, bearing swords, and threw themselves into the fray. The upper decks covered with struggling men. There were naked men with weapons against men roused from sleep with weapons. We must do this thing quickly, even though there were perhaps seven hundred and fifty slaves against a couple of hundred sailors and marines. I had no desire to swamp the Grodnims by sheer numbers, for that would be mere brutalized force. I wanted the thing done quickly and in style.

Rukker had cleared his area and was about to lead a hunting party to roust out those still below. I bellowed in his ear, for the released slaves were creating one hell of a racket.

"Rukker! Try not to slay too many. We need oarsmen, too!"

He glared at me, aroused, the blood-lust strong on him. He took a great draft of air.

"Aye—aye, Dak the Cunning. You are right—and do not forget we have a score to settle, you and I."

"Let us secure the swifter and chain down these damned Grodnims and then we may talk."

Only after he had gone roaring back into the fray did I realize he had been hired by and had been fighting for the Grodnims. But if he came from the northeast corner of the inner sea, as he said, the chances were he did not worship Green Grodno in quite the same way as the Grodnims of the Eye of the World. Anyway, I was in no state to accommodate him no matter what his inclinations.

The light had dimmed after the false dawn. But as the sounds of combat flared over the swifter so the light strengthened. Soon Zim rose in a crimson glory, at which all the Zairians yelled mightily. "Zim! Zair! Zair!"

And, inevitably, when green Genodras rose, and we waited for the shouts of Grodno to echo around the ship, and none sounded, we roared our good humor.

Rukker stormed among the released slaves, cuffing them out of his way, giving them orders, bellowing...

Duhrra was not sure what to do, so it fell to Fazhan to see about chaining down the new prisoners, those who had been spared.

I prevented a mob from tearing apart a couple of Grodnim sailors in their rage, and bellowed at them, "Would you wish these two rasts to go up to Genodras, to sit on the right hand of Grodno? Of course not! Chain them down to the benches, make them pull at the Zair-forsaken oars!"

"Aye, aye!" screeched the ex-slaves. 'To the thalamites with them!"

So we managed to save a few men to pull for us.

There would be the problem of what to do with the Grodnims who had been enslaved with us. The oar-slaves were mostly Zairian prisoners; there was an element among them of Grodnim criminals. There could be no half-measures, of course.

I climbed up the mast and took a look around.

Green Magodont lay in the mouth of a river, with low vegetation-choked banks to either side. The mountains inland of the island looked blue and floating in the early morning mist. Downstream lay two more swifters. People were running about them. The noise and confusion in *Green Magodont* needed, it seemed to me, little explanation.

We weren't out of the woods yet.

I looked down.

Two large and powerful looking men, both apims, were arguing. They both carried swords, they both had snatched up scraps of clothing to cover their nakedness. They had been slaves, miserably chained to the bench; now they were arguing over who was in command.

"I am a roz and therefore outrank you, fambly!"

"I am a swifter captain, you onker, and know whereof I speak!"

I watched Rukker. He walked toward them. He bellowed.

Other men crowded around on the upper deck. They could be called slaves no longer—or, perhaps, for a space no longer if we did not do something about the other two swifters. Rukker yelled.

"I am in command here! Get about your business!"

The two men turned on him, hot in their anger and pride, a pride so newly returned to them. Their swords flickered out.

One of them dropped with a sword through his guts, the other could not screech. His throat had been ripped out by the Kataki's tail-blade. I sighed.

"I, Rukker, command! If any more of you rasts wish to die, then step up."

Duhrra, at the back, started to rumble and shove forward. I went down the mast with some speed and jumped to the deck.

"What! Dak! And so you wish to challenge me." Rukker waved his tail above his head. The blade glittered.

"If you are in command, Rukker, which I doubt. What do you think we should do about the two swifters that will surely pull up here to retake this vessel? Come on, man. Speak up."

"I do not wish " he began. But the other slaves—ex-slaves—were running to the rail and pointing at the swifters downstream and caterwauling.

I said, "You may not wish to know about them, Rukker. But that won't make them go away."

"One day, Dak the Cunning, I'll do you a mortal injury."

"You may try. Until then you had best listen to what I say."

"I am in command!"

"You command nothing, Rukker the Kataki. This is no swifter fit to fight. You could not tackle those two. Think, man—" I did not take my gaze from him, and I watched that treacherous tail as a ruffianly sailor-man watches a Sylvie as she dances the Sensil Dance.

But he was, I felt sure, a high noble of one kind or another, and he could think quickly when he had to. "And what do you, oh wise and cunning Dak the Proud, think we should do?"

It would have been easy and cheap to have said, "But you are in command, Rukker."

The men had broken out the wine now and would soon be helpless. At least, some would, for the supplies wouldn't stretch to better than seven hundred thirsty ex-oar-slaves. I looked downstream again. The oars were moving in the swifters. They would back up to us, and their men would be armed and armored and ready. But drunken men can fight if they have a bucket of cold water soused over them and know that if they do not fight they will be killed if they are lucky, and go to the galley-slave benches if they are not lucky. But it must be done quickly.

In that uproar it was difficult to make myself heard. I turned to Duhrra. "Go and bash on the drum, Duhrra."

"Aye, master."

When the booming banging went on and on the men gradually quieted down and turned to look at Duhrra as he bashed away where usually the drum-Deldar beat the rhythm. I held up my hand. Duhrra stopped banging the drum and the silence fell.

I bellowed. I am able to let rip a goodly shout, as you know.

"Men! We must fight those swifters! There is no other way out for us. We can win easily if we stick together and fight for Zair!" This was mostly lies, of course. We could have run into the island and hidden. That would have been better than slaving at the oars. And as to winning, it would not be easy. But, Zair forgive me, I needed these men and their flesh and blood to further my own plans. I own that this makes me a criminal—a criminal of a kind, perhaps—but there was nothing else I could do, impelled as I was.

Vax shouted, before them all, "Aye! Let us take the two swifters to the glory of Zair!"

So they all bellowed and stamped and then it was a matter of finding weapons and clothes and armor and of seeing that not too many men fell down dead drunk.

We would have to wait for the attack until the last moment.

I said to Fazhan, "You are a ship-Hikdar. Can you organize from these men a crew to run the swifter?"

"Aye, Dak."

"Then jump to it. If we have to man the banks with our own men, they will have to do it. By Zair! They should be proud to row for Zair! We'll cripple those rasts out there!"

I turned to Rukker, who during all this had stood glowering, with his tail waving dangerously. I felt he would not strike just yet. He was too shrewd for that. "You want to be in command, Rukker. But you know nothing of swifters. Let Fazhan run the ship. Once we have those other two, we will have three alternatives."

He started to say something, thought better of it, and swung away. I bellowed after him, "Go and command the prijikers, Rukker. That is a post of honor."

The two swifters made no attempt to turn in the narrow mouth of the river. They could have done it. No doubt their captains wished to get up to us as fast as they could. I fancied they erred in this. I hoped I judged correctly.

The water rippled blue and silver, with jade and ruby sparks striking from it as the suns rose. The birds were busy about the trees. The day would be fine. I sniffed and thought about breakfast.

No time for that now. Men were arming themselves from corpses and from the armory. I went down and had to push my way through a throng crowding along the quarterdeck and so into the cabins. Men gave way for me, for they knew I was Dak, and Dak had freed them. They had been told this by Duhrra, although some still thought Rukker had organized the break. It did not concern me.

We could find no red cloth anywhere, and no one seemed over keen to wear green. Not even the Grodnim criminals, who kept very quiet, with good reason.

With seven hundred men or so to arm there was no chance of my equipping myself with a longsword to match the Genodder, and any man with two weapons had, perforce, to give up one to a comrade who had none. I bellowed for bowmen and soon all the men who said they were archers clustered on the deck where all the bows we could find were issued. As for arrows, these were brought up in their wicker baskets and likewise issued. There were insufficient bows to go to all those who clamored for them.

I saw Nath. He had a piece of cloth. He saw me and waved and then stood on the bulwarks and dived cleanly into the water.

One or two men yelled and they would have started an outcry.

"Silence, you famblys! Nath the Slinger goes to collect pebbles."

A few other men turned out to be slingers and they went off to collect ammunition. Rukker turned up again; he was growing tiresome, but I wanted to humor him, for not only did he intrigue me, I needed his bull-strength in the bows as a prijiker when the attack came in. And that would not be long now. He wore a mail shirt and a helmet. He carried a longsword. He looked exceedingly fierce.

"I do not know why I suffer your impertinence, Dak. But after we have taken those ships—"

I turned to Vax.

"Why have you not put on a mail shirt, Vax?"

"Because they are all taken already."

That was the obvious answer to an unnecessary question.

But Rukker took the point. His face went more mean than ever, and he began to bluster. I pointed forward. "They are almost here."

He swore—something about Targ and tails—and stormed off to the bows. He had selected a strong prijiker party, those stern fighters who were the cream of a crew.

Again I went a little way up the mast. Grodnim swifters still had only the one mast, apart from the smaller one for the boat sail forward. I studied the oncoming swifters. Their tall upflung sterns towered. Men clustered their quarterdecks and poops, armed and armored men, anxious to revenge their fellows in *Green Magodont*.

I called down to Fazhan standing on the quarterdeck.

"Get under way and aim for the rast to larboard."

He was a merry soul, this Fazhan ti Rozilloi, when not being flogged at the oars.

"I have ample volunteers to act as whip-Deldars, Dak. But not many oar-slaves."

"We do not need a great speed. Just enough to get our beakhead onto his quarterdeck."

"That I will do."

Vax met me as I reached the deck.

"And the cramph to starboard?"

"If Rukker can handle his swifter, I'll take that one."

"Then I will stand with you."

I lifted an eyebrow, but did not comment. Truth to tell, at that moment I was pleased to have him with me in the fight. Rukker had his party poised, and I saw he had about twenty Katakis with him. Again the incongruity of Katakis actually being slaves, instead of slavers, struck me.

We could all hear the steady double drumbeat from the oncoming swifters. Their helm-Deldars kept them sweetly on course, going stern first, and I fancied they would both be smart ships. This was not going to be as easy as many of the ex-slaves seemed to think, screeching their joy at freedom and their malefic hatred of the damned Green Grodnims.

Duhrra said, "The one to starboard is *Vengeance Mortil*, Duh—just let me get aboard of her..."

Vax lifted his handsome, fine-featured face, with the blood staining under the skin. "It will give me exquisite pleasure to chastise her whip-Deldars."

I said, "And each time you strike you will strike at your father, no doubt."

He flung me a scorching look.

"It is likely, for he and they have much in common. He has done me a great injury and I shall never forgive him."

"My old man," said Nath the Slinger, walking up dripping wet, carrying a leather bag filled with stones, "used to knock the living daylights out of us kids. But he meant well, the old devil."

"Back in Crazmoz," said Duhrra, fussing with his hand, "my father was always chasing the women. My mother used the broomstick on him right merrily. Duh—how we all ran!"

My father had died of a scorpion sting, back on Earth; but now was no time to consider how that had affected my life.

"Just so long as we get onto the deck. By Zair! We hold the Grodnims in play and the men slide below and release the slaves. That's the only way we'll win."

It was not the only way, of course; but it would be the easiest. And I wished this fight to be over so that I might resume my tasks in the Eye of the World.

A brief inquiry among the men as the two swifters hauled up to us established the second galley as *Pearl*. She was smaller, a two-banked six-four hundred-and-twenty swifter. She was not a dekares of the *Golden Chavonth* type. I eyed both of them as they backed up. Fazhan had those men of ours who had not found weapons at the upper tank looms. A little byplay had ensued there, for a group of ex-slaves without weapons had protested vigorously at taking their places on the rowing benches. I strode up, mighty fierce, not happy but knowing what I did was right.

"Give us weapons'" bellowed the men. "We will fight!"

"You will row," I said. "That will be your fighting."

I did not say that by not already snatching up weapons they proved themselves less able than their comrades who had. But I glowered at them, and spoke more about the glory of Zair, and shook the Genodder, and finished with, "And two last things! Once we strike the damned Grodnims you will have weapons in plenty. And if you do not row I shall beat you most severely."

They were convinced.

My friends, even, say that sometimes I have a nasty way with me. This is so. And even if I deplore my manner, it does get things done in moments of crisis. As I went back to the station I had taken on the quarterdeck, Vax gave me a dark look, sullen and defiant.

"You are a right devil, Dak."

"Yes," I said, and went off bellowing to a party of men to sort themselves out, with the bowmen in rear, a great pack of famblys, asking to be slaughtered.

Rukker looked back. The gap narrowed.

I yelled at him: "Get your fool hands down! They'll be shooting any moment."

As I spoke, the first shafts rose from the two Green swifters.

"Get the ship moving, Fazhan!" I swung about and roared at the two men who had taken the helm positions. "Bring her around to starboard! Put some weight into it!"

Green Magodont's wings rose and fell. We could put out only a few oars; but these gave us sufficient way to take us out into midstream. I judged the distances. Arrows struck down about us. The helmsmen looked at me, hard-muscled men, hanging on to their handles, waiting my orders.

"Hard over! Larboard!" I bellowed at Fazhan. "Every effort, Fazhan! Make 'em pull! Speed! Speed!"

The oars beat raggedly and then settled and the swifter's hard rostrum swirled to larboard and cut through the blue water. We surged ahead, aiming for the starboard quarter of the larboard vessel, *Pearl*. Our stern swung to starboard. We formed a diagonal between the swifters. Arrows crisscrossed now. I saw Nath leap up and swing his cloth about his head, let fly. I had the shrewd suspicion his stone would strike. The swifters neared. Any minute they would strike.

"Ram! Ram! Ram!"

The bull roar bashed up and men tensed for the shock of impact.

We struck.

The bronze ram gouged into *Pearl*. Both vessels shuddered and rocked with the impact. Men were yelling. I bawled out to Rukker; but there was no need. With his knot of Katakis about him, a compact force of devils, he leaped onto the swifter's deck. Instantly a babble of brilliant fighting ensued. Our stern swerved on, still going.

"Rowed of all!" I screamed at Fazhan. Our oars dropped.

The stern hit.

Somehow I was first across, scrambling over gilding and scrollwork, hurling myself onto the deck of *Vengeance Mortil*. Like a pack of screeching werstings my men followed. The blades flamed and flashed in the light of the twin suns, and then we were at our devil's tinker work, hammering and bashing, thrusting and slicing.

Vax followed and Duhrra leaped at my side. We swept a space for ourselves and then flung forward; for to stand gaping was to invite feathering.

"Below!" I yelled and men darted off to drop into the stinking gloom of the rowing banks and begin the task of freeing the slaves.

A monstrous man in green and gold fronted me, swirling his longsword.

This kind of work demanded a longsword; but I made shift with the Genodder, dropped him, and with no time to snatch up his sword engaged the next man with a clang. Swords flamed all about me. Men screamed and dropped. The rank raw tang of blood smoked on the morning air.

"Grodno! Grodno!" rang the shrieked battle cries.

"Zair! Zair!" the answering screams ripped out.

Mailed men boiled across the quarterdeck. For the next few murs the mere strength and solidity of packed men would tell. I cursed the damned shortsword, for its premier advantage in the thrust availed little against mailed men, although I gave a couple of fellows sore ribs before I got the point into their faces. I swung the Genodder in a short blurred arc and bashed through a mailed shoulder. A longsword hissed past my ear. It was a case of duck and twist and to the devil with the so-called dignity and art of fighting. I chunked a Fristle's eye out and slashed back at a Rapa, who spun away, screeching as Rapas do screech. The very fury and frenzy of the fight pushed us back and forth across the deck. But we had men, many men, and soon more swarmed up from below as their chains were struck off.

Five
Vax

The sheer pressure at our backs drove us on. The hideous sounds of mortal combat shocked into the sky. Blood ran greasily across the deck and men coughed or screamed or said nothing as they died. In the press the shortsword proved of value, but I caught a distorted glimpse of Duhrra swinging his longsword and clearing men from his path as a gardener hews weeds. Vax drove on with him. I cursed and beat away a spear-point, thrust short and sharp, and brought the blade back to catch a longsword sweeping down at my head and felt the jar smash along my muscles.

I made a grab with my left hand at the longsword and after one fumble, during which I kicked a fellow in the guts, the longsword was mine. It was a common one with a small hilt; but it would serve. I swapped with a feeling of release.

In the next mur I had leaped after Duhrra and Vax. Together we cut a triple furrow through the Green ranks. Duhrra fought as he always did with a sword, using tremendous sweeps, enormous bashes, and mighty slashings to hew down his opponents. I felt vast relief that he had found and donned a mail shirt, for he left himself dangerously exposed. Vax fought with the trim economy of the trained swordsman. I saw the way he handled his blade and again I wondered if, at his age, he could be a Krozair.

We reached the double doors leading from the quarterdeck into the passage under the poop. *Vengeance Mortil* was a longer vessel than *Green Magodont,* rowing thirty oars to a bank against the latter's twenty-one. The poop over our heads was now the scene of fighting. We could hear shrieks and the thumps of feet on the deck. Most of the cabins were empty and we tore straight on toward the captain's cabin.

He was not there, and I recalled the large man I had felled at the instant of boarding. If he had been the captain, then his crew fought well without him. Satisfied that the cabins here were all empty, we turned to dart out and finish the fight. I stopped stock still.

Duhrra and Vax halted in the doorway.

"Come on, Dak!"

A glass case stood against the bulkhead. A shaft of mingled light struck through the aft windows and illuminated the contents of the case. Crimson blazed. A long blade of steel shafted back gleaming light.

"Trophies," said Duhrra. "Some poor devil of a Zairian—"

I swung the sword at the glass and smashed the case open.

I took the longsword into my fists. It balanced beautifully.

A Krozair longsword. The genuine article. I saw the etched markings, the Kregish letters in flowing script: *KRZI.* So this was a longsword of the Krozairs of Zimuzz. The red cloth was a flag. I ripped it down and swathed it about me. I drew it up tightly between my legs and tucked in the end. I picked up the Krozair longsword.

"Now I'm ready to finish this little lot."

We belted back down the passage. Our backs were secure. We had only to surge forward along the swifter and take or slay all the Green and the ship would be ours.

A dead marine lay at the corridor entrance. I bent and ripped off his belt and buckled it up about the red flag I used, without blasphemy, in all honor, as a loincloth. We went into the fight like leems. I felt rejuvenated. How ridiculous and petty it must seem that a piece of red cloth could wreak so great a change! But the true change was wrought by the Krozair longsword. The blade flamed. The balance was perfect. I felt the power in my fists and I battled forward, bellowed for my men, and together, yelling, "Zair! Zair!" we catapulted the Greens from the quarterdeck, drove them along the upper gangway. More and more slaves poured up from below, whirling bights of chain.

The uproar continued.

I took time to step back as a Grodnim dropped under the blade, and darted a quick and savage look at *Pearl.* Yes, the fighting there flowed forward, as did the fighting in *Vengeance Mortil.*

A perverse desire grew in me to clear this swifter before Rukker cleared his. I shouted again and roared on, cutting into the last resistance. The

Krozair brand sheared through mail where the shortsword would have bounced. We tore into the dying remnants of the resistance and, suddenly, we were on the forecastle with the beakhead lifted, and there were no more adversaries to taste our steel.

The men in the swifter at my back began cheering.

I looked across the gap of water at *Pearl*. Fighting boiled across her forecastle where a knot of men in the green resisted to the end. I saw the Katakis—fewer of them now—battling in the front of the struggle. Rukker was there, a giant figure striking with sword and tail-blade.

Springing onto the bulwark, I put my left hand to my mouth—my right was bloodier than my left—and I lifted up my voice and shouted in right jocular fashion.

"Hai! Rukker! What's holding you up?"

He heard.

The Kataki devil heard. I saw a Grodnim head fly into the air and Rukker stormed onto the starboard bulwark, springing up to glare across at me.

"We have cleared all! There are no skulkers at our backs!"

"And no slaves to pull the oars, either."

He didn't like that.

"We have taken this Takroti-forsaken ship! That is what matters."

"You may have taken her—but have you slaves to man her?"

"I do not wish to discuss that."

I heard a gurgling laugh and looked back and there was Vax holding his guts and laughing. Well, it was funny, of course; but I had no desire to be stranded without oar-slaves by that Kataki idiot over there.

Anyway, there was every chance that our ram had done *Pearl* too serious a mischief underwater to make her seaworthy. That must be looked at, at once, and the man to do the looking was Fazhan ti Rozilloi, ship-Hikdar. I bellowed to Duhrra to sort out the men here, told Vax to see about chaining up the new slaves who had so lately been sailors and soldier-marines of Grodnim, and took myself off aft. Fazhan was cleaning his sword. I had had no time. The beautiful Krozair blade gleamed red in the lights of Antares.

"Hai Jikai, Dak!" Fazhan greeted me.

I pondered for perhaps a half mur. Was this a Jikai?

Perhaps.

It was most certainly not a sufficiently high enough High Jikai to enroll me once more in the Krozairs of Zy, that was for sure.

"Is *Pearl* seaworthy, after we struck her?"

He saw my face. "I will see, at once." He ran off.

In the nature of things there was a great deal of confusion. Released slaves, all naked and screaming, surged about, and I knew there would be no Grodnim whip-Deldars to chain down to the rowing benches. I saw men I thought must be of some importance—or, rather, men who had been important before they'd been captured—and tried to bash some sense into them. Our own slaves from *Green Magodont* had by this time some idea of what was needful in this situation. Soon all the men of Zair would come to an understanding. For the moment sheer exuberance and wild release of fettered spirits would make of the three swifters hell-holes.

So I will pass quickly over the ensuing scenes. I took myself off back to *Green Magodont* and met Rukker storming back. He looked savagely delighted with his morning's work. He saw my red breechclout and the sword, and he made a face and began to make some kind of snarling remark; but he did not. His tail quivered and shot erect over his head, the tail-blade gleaming, for he had cleaned it off.

"The ships are ours, Dak. You have served me well. Now I will resume full command."

The Katakis formed a bunch at his back. He had them well cowed. They were extraordinarily formidable. I hefted the Krozair longsword. I opened my mouth and Vax appeared at my side, laughing, saying, "Give me your sword, Dak, and I will clean it off for you. It is a beautiful blade."

"I clean my own sword."

He looked offended.

Rukker bellowed, "Now we carouse and make merry."

The released slaves would do that, anyway.

Some onker was bellowing that *Pearl* was stuffed with wine. He carried an armful of bottles, waving one above his head, the rich red wine spilling out over him. He was already half-seas over. I did not consider long. Maybe I could have halted the debauch that followed. Maybe not. I did not try. I wanted to talk to Rukker and see if the way I planned to handle the Kataki devil would work.

He had taken a good long look at the three swifters. Fazhan reported that *Pearl* had taken a nasty crack, but that the sharp sheer of her stern had been enough to prevent our ram from driving home, and that she would be fully seaworthy when the planking had been repaired. So Rukker could tell me in his lofty way, "I will take *Vengeance Mortil*. She is the largest. You may have either of the others."

I said, "Bring a few bottles to the cabin. We can talk there. If you wish to fight, here and now, I shall accommodate you. Otherwise, no fighting until we have decided what to do."

Now that he had won and was in a strong position, he no doubt thought to show a facade of magnanimity. I do not think I do Rukker an injustice if I say that because he was a Kataki he was, by his religion and customs and mores, what other people would call an evil man. He could not help that; like the scorpion, it was in his nature. But I found that he had a gift denied to most other Katakis. He had a streak of humanity in him that, at first, because I did not believe it possible, I found disconcerting.

"Surely, Dak the High-Handed. We will drink together. But there is no question of our deciding." He emphasized the "our." "I have decided what we will do."

I did not answer but barged off to the cabin, snatching up a couple of the bottles the idiot from *Pearl* had dropped—for he had passed out, beaming idiotically, on my quarterdeck.

My quarterdeck.

Ah! How we arrogate to ourselves, arrogant in our pride!

Nath the Slinger appeared. He wore bits and pieces of finery, and carried a Genodder as well as his sling. He saw Rukker. He started to say something, but Rukker chopped him off.

"We talk, Nath the Slinger. Afterward, I may take from your hide payment for your insolence."

Nath said, "I think the people may set fire to the swifters."

That was a very fair chance.

Rukker bellowed at this, and in a twinkling, a dozen of his Katakis ran out along the gangways, roaring. That was one thing I could count on. Rukker would command obedience from his own people, and I could trust them to stop a parcel of drunken ex-oar-slaves from foolishly setting fire to the swifters they so much hated.

"Tell 'em to make sure they don't kill too many Grodnims," I said to Rukker, sharp.

He bawled it after them. Then he took a bottle from a man near him, who did not argue, and rolled off to the aft cabin, swinging his tail in high good humor.

Fazhan looked at me, uncertain.

"You did very well, Fazhan. Now come and have a drink."

"We should set a watch—there were three other swifters in the squadron."

"The Katakis will do that. Or Rukker will have their tails."

As I went along aft I admit I felt it most strange that I should be working in collaboration with Katakis. But, there it was. Those of us who had been architects in the escape gathered in the great aft cabin of *Green Magodont* to talk about our futures.

I will not go into all the discussion, although to a student of human nature it proved fascinating, revealing not only the desires of frail humanity but revealing very clearly the different traits of the differing racial stocks. The problem could be broken down into one of allegiances. The released slaves fell into four main classes. There were the Zairians who wished only to return to their homes of the southern shore. There were the Grodnims who, as criminals, could go neither to Zairia nor to Grodnim.

There were the mercenaries who didn't care who they fought for so long as they were paid and who, because they slaved for them, must have fallen foul of the overlords of Magdag. And there were the Zairians who, for one reason or another, could not return home.

Of the two latter classes, Rukker and I were representatives.

Long were the arguments and sometimes bitter the wrangling. But, in the end, it all boiled down to a decision by Rukker and most of the others, to join the Renders. These pirates infested many portions of the inner sea, of course; but they were particularly strong in the southwestern end, where many islands gave them shelter. As for the Zairians who wished to return home, they might take a swifter that Rukker did not want.

I said, "That does not dispose of all."

"There is no one else, fambly!" Then Rukker, sprawled in a gilt chair, an upended bottle to his lips, roared out, "By the Triple Tails of Targ the Untouchable! No one would wish to go to Magdag!"

"I do," I said.

He gaped at me.

"There is a certain matter I have left unfinished there."

"Well, you will find not a single man to go with you." Then he squinted at Duhrra—enormous in the corner, watchful—and grunted, and said, "Except that mad graint, of course."

"And me," said a young, firm voice, and I turned, and Vax stepped forward. "I wish to go to Magdag, for I have business there, also."

Well, I fancied whatever his business was, it boded no good for some poor devil.

Vax had been drinking. His face flushed heavily and he did not walk steadily, even though *Green Magodont* remained still.

Nath the Slinger had been drinking, also, and he snarled, "No doubt it has to do with your rast of a father."

Vax turned sharply, and nearly fell. I do not like to see young men the worse for drink—or any man, come to that. Vax spoke in a cutting, nasty way. "Yes. For my father has done me a grave injustice. He has finished all my hopes in the Eye of the World. Yes, he bears a part, the cramph. But it is not for him I wish to go to Magdag, but my sister—"

"Well, go to the Ice Floes of Sicce for all I care!" boomed Rukker. He roared his mirth. "Three of you, to run a swifter! Ho—one to pull at the oar, one to beat the drum, and one to steer! Ho—I like it!"

Certainly, the image was a lively one. But I did not smile.

Vax looked as though he would be sick at any moment, if he did not fall down. I judged he was not used to heavy drinking. I stepped over to him and sniffed. I looked down at him.

"You young idiot! Dopa!"

Duhrra said, "Duh—dopa! I know, master—I know."

Dopa is calculated to make a man fighting drunk; Vax had not yet drunk enough to turn him berserk. I saw the bottle in his hand, and I took it away. He tried to stop me. I broke the bottle over a handy table and showed him the serrated edge. "This is what you deserve, you gerblish onker."

He staggered and would have fallen. I grabbed him and propped him upright.

"You're coming with me to a cabin where you can sleep it off. I have work to do." I dragged him out. "I'll see about you, Rukker, when I've seen to this hulu."

I half carried him along to the ship-Hikdar's cabin and tossed him down on the cot. As I say, cots and hammocks had previously been unknown in swifters, because they usually came ashore at night. No doubt the war was changing many things since the genius king Genod had taken over in Magdag. Vax snorted and tried to rise and I pushed him back and the hilt of the Krozair longsword slid forward. He blinked at it owlishly.

"I was to have been a Krozair," he said. He was growing maudlin. "Yes, I trained. Not Zimuzz, though. I worked and all I wanted in this life was to be a Krozair like my brothers."

"Yes," I said, lifting his legs onto the cot. "Get some sleep and you can talk about this later."

He grasped my arm and glared up into my face.

"You don't understand. No one here does. How can they?"

He enunciated his words carefully, as a near-drunk sometimes does; but he made sense in what he said. He was pretty far gone, and he just didn't know he was saying what he was saying.

"My father—"

"Look, son. We all had fathers, and they all failed us at one time or another." That was not true; but the intensity of this lad's hatred for his unknown father hurt me, thinking of my own father and the love I bore him.

"My father failed my mother. He ran away—ran away—"

"You said he died."

"I always say he is dead, out of shame. But he was alive, all the time. All the time. He ran away and left my mother in mortal peril, and she was carrying me at the time, and he ran away and left her. They nearly got her—she told me, and she laughed—but—but I knew. He wouldn't answer the Call, the Azhurad, and it is im-impossible for a Krozair not to answer the Call. So they made him Apushniad. And serve the rast right. And I was training to be a Krozair of Zy—and they—they— So I left them, ashamed. My father, Apushniad—destroyed me. Destroyed me! Me, Jaidur, Jaidur of Valka, ruined my whole life, and if I find the kleesh I shall surely slay him."

I just gaped, stricken.

363

Six
Renders of the Eye of the World

The Renders of the western end of the Eye of the World made us welcome. They welcomed reinforcements of tough and ruthless fighting-men. They were not so sure of the three swifters we brought, for they habitually used small, fast craft, which could slip into a convoy and cut out the fat prizes. They said they could no doubt pick up enough oar-slaves for the swifters. But we would to a great extent be on our own. Rukker boomed his great laugh and swished his tail and said he'd show these people what real rending was about, what a fighting Kataki could do in the piracy business.

He had found a competent ship-Hikdar among the ex-slaves to run *Vengeance Mortil* for him. I ran *Green Magodont,* and a tough and experienced swifter captain, a Krozair of Zamu, took command of *Pearl.* Once we filled with oar-slaves we would be a hard little squadron, and carry some punch in the Eye of the World. The Krozair of Zamu, Pur Naghan ti Perzefn, would sail *Pearl* back with all the Zairians who wished to return home.

These Renders were a cutthroat lot. Consisting of escaped slaves, criminals, men who could find a home neither north nor south of the inner sea, they carved out their own destiny. If you ask why I was with them, instead of pursuing my schemes in Magdag, the answer is surely plain.

My son!

Jaidur—that same name that Velia had spoken, and I had not understood, when she had been dying in my arms. So my Delia had been pregnant when we'd flown off to chastise the shanks attacking our island of Fossana, where the damned Star Lords had sought to make me do their wishes. I had refused out of stiff-necked pride and fear for Delia, and so had been banished to Earth for all of twenty-one miserable years. There had been twins again, twins of whom I had known nothing. The girl, Dayra, the boy, this same Jaidur who called himself Vax out of shame.

He had rambled on a little more before falling into a drunken stupor. He was quite unused to dopa. He had known that any son of Dray Prescot, the Lord of Strombor, would receive scant shrift from the overlords of Magdag, and he had been on his way there because his sister, Velia, had been missing, reported captured by a swifter from Magdag.

Velia had, indeed, been captured. But she had been captured by Gafard, the King's Striker, the Sea Zhantil, and they had fallen deeply in love. I believed that to be true. I believed it then, and I am sure of it now. Gafard owed complete allegiance to King Genod, and even when the king sought to abduct the Lady of the Stars, the name by which Velia was known, for the same reasons that Jaidur called himself Vax, Gafard had been unable to blame him; for the king possessed the yrium, the mystic power of authority over ordinary people.

King Genod had, in the end, taken Velia. And because Gafard's second in command, Grogor, had shafted the saddlebird the king flew, and because the king was abruptly in fear for his life, the genius king had thrown Velia off, to fall to her death. Yrium or no damned yrium, when I caught the cramph I'd probably have trouble stopping myself from breaking his neck before I dragged him off to justice. I know about men who possess the yrium. As I have said, I am cursed with more than one man's fair share of the yrium.

All this I, alone of our family, knew.

I could not tell Jaidur—or Vax.

I could not tell him.

I had not told him I was his father.

How could I?

There had to be a kinder, better, way of breaking that horrendous news to him.

He was in very truth a violent young man. How could I lift a hand against my son in self-defense? And yet how could I stand and let him slay me? For I thought he very well might try. That would be a sin not only for him but for me, also.

His hatred was a real and living force.

Mind you, if I told him and then invited him to try to carry out his avowed intent, and so foined with him and disarmed him—no, no, no... That would shatter his self-esteem, would turn hatred for me into contempt for himself. And, anyway, he was a remarkably fine swordsman. He might finish me. I share nothing of this silly desire to call oneself the greatest swordsman of the world—or, in my case, of two worlds. That way lies not only paranoia, but a mere killing machine without interest or suspense. Each fight is a new roll of the dice with death, a gamble of life and death.

I had decided to go to join the Renders with Rukker because had I gone to Magdag, Vax would have gone with me, and in evil Magdag he might all too easily be slain or enslaved. I did not want that and would stop it. So I had turned aside from my purpose.

A scheme occurred to me whereby I might turn Vax from his path, also. It would give him pain; but nothing like the pain he would be spared.

We sailed out on a few raids and caught Magdaggian shipping and so fought them and took them and built up our stock of oar-slaves. Our base lay up a narrow and winding creek in the lush green island of Wabinosk. When I say *green* I refer to the vegetation. The island boasted a large population of vosks; but they were kept down by an infestation of lairgodonts. I had no further wish to meet any more lairgodonts, for the risslacas had caused problems before and, anyway, the things were the symbol of King Genod's new Order of Green Brothers. The islands in this chain were, in their turn, infested by pirates, and we had one or two set-tos with Renders who fancied our prizes. But with Rukker booming and bellowing away we kept what we took.

One day Duhrra started talking about Magdag to Vax, who was most anxious to learn all he could. I listened.

The people we had released from oar-slavery had settled down into a pattern, taking up tasks for which they were suited. Those Zairians who wished to return home had gone in a captured broad ship. Now we had smallish crews, but we were building, and our motive power was almost up to strength. I planned to leave at the earliest moment I could; I had to be sure of Vax first.

"Zigging Grodnims," Duhrra was saying, sharpening up his sword on a block, taking care over the work. "All they do is build monstrous great buildings. Rasts."

Vax egged him on to talk about Magdag. And as I listened so I caught an echo of the way Duhrra saw the rousing times we had spent as pretended renegades. "The king in Sanurkazz has our names down on his roll of infamy—and we innocent."

"When King Zo hears what you did, Duhrra, I am sure he will pardon you. Was the Lady of the Stars, then, so beautiful?"

Duhrra spit and polished meticulously. "Indeed she was!" Duhrra rolled his eyes. "No maiden more fair graced the earth, they said."

I felt a pang. Roughly, I said, "Did you ever see her face, oh Duhrra of the waggling tongue?"

"No, master. But I know she was. Duh—everyone said so."

Here was a chance. I felt a pain in my chest.

"Yes, she was beautiful. Gafard loved her truly, and she loved him truly." I did not look at Vax. "I think that does mean something important." I leaned closer. "And here is something Gafard told me that must go no farther than the three of us." I turned and glared directly into my son's eyes. "Do I have your word?"

"Yes, Dak. I will not speak of it."

"Good. Then know that this Lady of the Stars was the true daughter of Pur Dray, the Lord of Strombor."

Before I had finished the great word *Strombor,* my son Jaidur, whom I must think of as Vax, leaped up. He let a terrible cry escape him. Then he turned—I saw his face—and he ran to the ladder at the stern and fell down it and so raced like a maniac into the bushes of the shore, vanishing out of sight.

Duhrra stared after him, a powerful frown crumpling up that smooth, seemingly idiot face. "Duh, master! What did I do?"

366

"You did nothing, Duhrra. And I am not your master."

"Yes, master."

I walked away, feeling the desolation in me. This was not my idea of family life. But, then what did I know of family life? I had been privileged to know my eldest twins, Drak and Lela, for periods off and on until they were fourteen. My second twins, Segnik and Velia, had been three when I'd been so mercilessly hurled back to Earth. And now Segnik was Zeg and a famous Krozair of Zy, and Velia was dead. Of Dayra I knew nothing, and of her twin, Jaidur, I must see him every day and speak with him, and call him Vax, and bear the agony; for he hated the memory of his father, a father he knew nothing of—or, at least, knew nothing good of.

I did know one thing of Dayra. Delia had told me she had been giving trouble at school, with the Sisters of the Rose, of course. And I remembered old Panshi talking of the young prince and of my assumption he meant Segnik, when he meant Jaidur. Old Panshi had had a little frown of puzzlement. Why couldn't I be just an ordinary simple man? But then, if I were that, I would never have won Delia, the Princess Majestrix of Vallia, at all.

We sailed out on a raiding cruise the next day, hopping from island to island, and I was exceedingly beastly to the Magdaggian shipping we caught. The three swifters acted together, for it seemed the natural thing to do, and Rukker was getting the hang of sea fighting. On this cruise we took a small swifter by a ruse, and boarded her and slew or enslaved her Magdaggian crew. Her slaves joined our ranks. She was sailed back to Wabinosk in triumph.

That night we caroused as Renders do. I had run through all my memories of carousing the nights away with Viridia the Render on the Island of Careless Repose, in the Hobolings. She had been youngish then, and with the normal two-hundred-year life span of the Kregan, I had no doubt she was still at her piratical tricks. Would I ever see her again? Would I ever see any of my old comrades—and enemies—again?

The coveted High Jikai appeared to come no nearer.

But my words with Vax—I must think and talk of him as Vax—bore fruit

Fazhan, who acted as my ship-Hikdar, told me the swifter we had taken was of Sanurkazz. She had been taken by the Magdaggians and converted to their use. As in the wooden navies of the eighteenth century of Earth, the ships of the contending nations were of so similar a type they were fully interchangeable. She had the name arrogantly painted on her bows and under her stern—the sailors of Kregen follow this fashion more often than not—and I read this aloud. "*Prychan*. A suitable name."

"Yes," said Fazhan. He reached out with his knife and scraped at the green paint. "Yes, as I thought. See, Dak, underneath. Her real name, carved as is proper; but blocked up with this damned green paint."

We removed the offensive paint and saw the original name of the galley.

"*Neemu*. Yes, I see." You know that a neemu is a black-furred, near leopard-sized killer, with a round head, squat ears, slit eyes of lambent gold, and runs ferociously upon four legs. A prychan is a very similar beast, sharing the same characteristics, but having fur of a tawny gold. I studied the lines of *Neemu*.

She was two-banked, a four-three seventy-two. Although she had only eighteen oars to a bank, they were concentrated in the usual way of swifters, giving her an exceptionally long forecastle and quarterdeck. She was narrow in the beam, so narrow I ordered her oars kept in the water to keep her upright. She was fast. I tried her in maneuvers and found her cranky so that she did not respond as well as—for instance—*Green Magodont*, which was a much larger craft, a three-banked hundred-twenty-six. *Green Magodont* was of that class of swifter designed to sail in the front rank in a battle, agile so that she might spin about and deliver the diekplus, shearing away an opponent's oars. Then the second line would come in to take on what was left. This *Neemu* was clearly a scouting vessel, designed for high speed, yet powerful enough to tackle reasonably heavy opposition.

Vax said, "I would like to take all those who will come and sail back to Zandikar."

There was now a fresh batch of rescued Zairians wishing to go home.

I said, "Why Zandikar?"

He said, without shame, "There is a girl—"

"Oh," I said.

So the brutality of my ruse had been worth it. Vax had decided not to go to Magdag to search for his sister Velia. He knew she was dead; he did not know the manner of her dying. I had told no one that I had held Velia in my arms as she died, and of how the overlords had trampled up to take me. They had not caught Grogor, Gafard's second in command; but he it was who had shot the arrow into the king's fluttrell; he it was, they thought, who had slain the stikitches employed by the king. I was a mere pawn, Gafard's man, and me they had dispatched to the galleys.

"Very well—" I started to say, when I was interrupted by a harsh and ominous screeching.

I knew exactly what that raucous shriek from the sky was, and I did not look up. The Gdoinye, the great golden and scarlet raptor of the Star Lords, the magnificent bird of prey they used as a messenger and a spy, had sought me out once again. Duhrra was talking to Vax about taking *Neemu* back to Zandikar, and trying to urge him to go on to Sanurkazz, for that was nearer Crazmoz. Vax cocked up his head.

"What is that bird?" he said.

Duhrra looked up, also, his idiot-face peering.

"Duh—I see no bird."

I glanced up, casually.

The confounded Gdoinye was up there, planing in wide hunting circles, screeching down. The thing spied on me for the Star Lords, that was sure.

"Up there, Duhrra, you fambly!" said Vax. He pointed. "Surely you see it? A great red and gold bird."

"Vax—you've been at the dopa again."

Vax shouted hotly at this and swung to me. "Dak—you see it?"

I looked up at the Gdoinye circling up there, watching me, telling the Star Lords what I was about

"No, Vax. I see no bird."

"You're all blind!" shouted Vax, and stamped off. I felt sorry for him. I wondered what he was thinking.

But I thought this must be an omen. I must stir myself, or I might be thrust back across four hundred light-years, to Earth, and never get out of the Eye of the World. First, I must make sure my son Jaidur, who called himself Vax out of shame, was safe.

Seven
We strike a blow for Zairia and for Vallia

On a fine Kregan morning as we pirates swaggered down to the swifters hauled up onto the beach, I said to Duhrra, "You want to talk to this young tearaway, Vax. Probe him about his father." I saw Duhrra glance across at me. "It is not good that a young man feels this way."

"I agree. But it is a powerful hatred he bears."

"Talk to him."

"Duh—master—it will be all too easy. He will deafen my ears with his anger."

Our plans for departure had been interrupted by this capture of *Neemu*. There was no question of the ship being given to Vax. He was far too young and inexperienced on the Eye of the World. I did not say this. It was freely spoken of by the other Renders. Among their ranks were men who knew the inner sea, men who had fought for many years upon the sparkling blue waters, men who understood the ways of the Eye of the World. Pur Naghan ti Perzefn had not taken *Pearl* back. Those Zairians who wished to return home had sailed in a broad ship. Pur Naghan, Krzm, realized he could strike resounding blows for Zair in thus rending with us. As a Krozair of Zamu his vows impelled him to struggle with the Green at every opportunity. Our plans called for us to sail back together, *Pearl*, *Neemu*, *Crimson Magodont*, as a squadron.

369

No Krozair, not even an ex-Krozair, could command a swifter with *Green* in her name.

Green Magodont was now *Crimson Magodont*.

Rukker, waving his bladed tail in a typical Kataki fury, had bellowed, "I spare no oar-slaves! If you wish to fill your banks you must take the rasts yourselves. And *Vengeance Mortil* sails with me." He was in a right old fury.

I recall this particular day with some brisk satisfaction as demonstrating a neat double-hander in my dealings on Kregen. Occupied though I was by affairs and mysterious dealings in tie Eye of the World, I was still aware of the vaster problems awaiting me in the lands of the Outer Oceans. Out there that great and evil empress Thyllis planned to hurl all the military resources of her empire of Hamal against my island of Vallia. Out there intrigues and treachery and double-dealing blossomed like the black lotus flowers of Hodan-Set.

So, on this day, when our squadron sighted sails on the horizon, and the whip-Deldars flew about with ol' snake licking, and bellowing, "Grak! Grak!" and the swifters flew over the waters, I found a profound joy in me as I saw those sails resolve into the typical shapes of the canvas of argenters from Menaham.

Menaham with her argenter fleet was used by the empress Thyllis of Hamal to trade with the overlords of Magdag. She sold them airboats and saddle-flyers. Judging by the course of the argenters, which bore on bravely with their three masts clad in plain sail straining, I would find out what King Genod paid the empress Thyllis in return.

I pushed away disappointment. I would have preferred to have captured the argenters on their way to Magdag. Then I would have taken vollers and flyers. As it was, this blow would more directly damage Hamal. But that mad genius Genod would suffer, too...

In any kind of breeze the swifters would never have caught the argenters. But the Eye of the World, like the Mediterranean, is a fluky place for wind. Oared vessels reign there except—and this I say with pride, for the pride is not for me—for the great race-built galleons of Vallia. We pulled in for the kill.

Sails billowed and fluttered as the breeze fluked around. The argenters wallowed. We could see their people running about the decks and a pang struck through me, for I remembered when Duhrra and I had stood in an argenter and watched the Renders pulling in for us. That made me make sure that lookouts with keen eyes were aloft to spot the first hint of Green slicing toward us over the horizon.

"They scurry like ponshos before leems," observed Vax with bloodthirsty satisfaction.

We stood on the quarterdeck. I looked at my son.

"Do you so hate them, then, Vax? They are not of Magdag."

"I have reasons for hating them. You would know nothing of my reasons. But, believe me, they are very real."

Much though I was dismayed at my boy's bloodthirstiness, I was cheered by his evident concern for the affairs of his own country. And, anyway, on Kregen a modicum of good honest skull-bashing is often the only antidote to poison. I deplore this; but while it remains true I prefer to have other people's skulls bashed. The truth also is that I have done a great deal on Kregen to lessen the incidence of skull-bashing and bloodthirsty fighting in these latter days. I speak now of a time when the famous old Bells of Beng Kishi regularly rang in many and many a thick skull over the length and breadth of Kregen.

Just to get Vax going a little more, I said, "And these marvelous reasons, Vax. I suppose your cramph of a father is mixed up with them—oh, but he's dead, isn't he?"

He shot me a murderous glance. I did not know how much he remembered of what he'd maundered on about to me; I fancied he had precious little idea of what he had said.

"My father—" He scowled and gripped his sword-hilt. "He did fight the Bloody Menahem. I will give the rast that."

Duhrra was looking at both of us with an expression that on his gleaming idiot-face looked most comical.

"So you have something good to say about your father, then?"

"By Vox! No! I believe he fought only through others, that his friends did the fighting, while he—"

"Rukker's going ahead!" bellowed the lookout.

I was rather glad of the interruption.

Fazhan bellowed down to Pugnarses Ob-Eye, our oar-master, who might boast only one eye but who ran a taut six oar banks.

We heard Pugnarses' whistle blow and then his full-blown voice telling the whip-Deldars interesting facts about their physiognomy and antecedents and probable destinations in the hereafter, and the beat of the oars quickened. No one on the quarterdeck or on the forecastle thought overmuch of the pains of the oar-slaves. We knew exactly what they were going through. Exactly.

As Mangar, our drum-Deldar, increased the beat in response to the commands from Pugnarses and the oars thrashed faster, so we began to pull back the distance Rukker had surged ahead.

Three swifters ravening down on four argenters. I found by chance that I would line up on the third ship from Menaham. Rukker would hit the lead ship, and Pur Naghan the second.

There would be time. I said, "It's surprising to me, Vax, that any man with a father like yours would bother to get born at all. I suppose you will spend the rest of your life hating him?"

"And if I do, it will be spent gladly."

The first varter shots were coming in. Our varters up forward replied. Soon the bows would sing. I could not leave well alone.

"Of course, if your father died before you were born, you have only the words of others. You don't know yourself."

"I know enough! I know what being Apushniad means—" He checked himself there, and glared about. He wore mail and a helmet and he looked young and bold and vigorous and—and frighteningly vulnerable with his flushed face and scowling lips. He whipped out his longsword. "I fight with the prijikers today and show the world I am not as my father!"

"No!" The word was shocked from me. I could not stop it.

He glowered at me, half turned, ready to storm off to the forecastle and be among the foremost of the prijikers who would swarm along the beakhead when it thumped down onto the argenter's deck.

"No? I am a fighting-man. I am—I was, nearly— What do you mean, Dak; *no?"*

I couldn't explain. He was my son. I didn't want him in the forefront of the most dangerous part of the attack. A prijiker, a stem-fighter, joyed in his honor and glory and danger. I reckoned they were all more mad than other sailors. They bore the most wounds; from their numbers the most men made holes in the sea.

"I want you to be at my side."

"But why? Do you deny me the glory?"

"There's no damned glory in getting killed in a stupid render affray!" I roared at him. "It's only loot out there. Are you so greedy for gold you'd throw your life away?"

He drew himself up in that faintly ridiculous way a young man indicates that he is grown up in his own estimation.

"You cannot stop me from fighting with the prijikers. If I get killed that is my affair." He swung his sword violently at the argenters. "Anyway, they are enemies of my country."

We were closing now and the arrows were feathering into the palisade across our forecastle. The beakhead swayed with the onward plunge of the ship. Men crouched up there, ready to spring like leems onto the decks, ready to smash in red fury to victory.

"And is that your marvelous reason?"

"It will do for now!"

And he swung off along the gangway. I glared after him. I knew practically nothing about the way he would act. He was a headstrong and violent youth, suffering under a sense of shame and outrage, carrying a heavy burden of hatred that ate at his pride. But as the fight developed and we smashed into the argenter and the beakhead went down and we roared across her decks, I had to understand that I could not do as I had unthinkingly sought to do. I had acted, I conceived, as any father would act. I did not want my son to go off fighting. But I could not hold him back. His own instincts, his pride, his youthful folly, all impelled him to rush headlong into the thickest of the fight.

Can any father thus shield his son from reality and expect to produce a man?

Sometimes the burdens of fatherhood are too heavy for a simple man to bear. Sometimes, I think, nature should have invented some easier way to carry on the generations. I did not enjoy that fight. I drew the great Krozair longsword and I went up the gangway after Vax, and I bellowed back to Fazhan to conn the ship, and I plunged into the fray like the madman I am, striking viciously left and right, thrusting and hacking, carving a bloody path through those poor devils from Menaham. We took the argenter all right. I had known we would take her. Everyone knew we would take her. It seemed idiotic to me that my son should imperil himself in so obvious a way over so obvious a fight.

But he did.

He was my son.

He was just as big a fool as I am.

When it was over and the flag came fluttering down in a blaze of blue and green and the shouts of "Hai!" rose, I saw that Vax, although splashed with blood, was unharmed. He had fought magnificently. I had been near him and there had been no single time when I had had to intervene. He could handle himself in a fight, that was plain. I knew he had been under training with the Krozairs of Zy. Their wonderful Disciplines had molded him well. He must, I guessed, have been very near to the time when he would have been accepted into the Order as a full member and have been allowed to prefix that proud *Pur* to his name.

But, all the same, despite his prowess, I was mighty glad when the fighting ceased.

Vax it was who spotted the danger to *Pearl*, ahead of us. He sprang onto the forecastle of the argenter and waved his sword.

"*Pearl!* Pur Naghan's in trouble!"

The swifter had wallowed around and broken a number of her starboard oars. The fighting on her decks looked confused. Men were spilling over into the water. There was no time to be lost.

We pulled up and launched ourselves afresh into the fray, battling up with *Pearl's* men to take the Menaheem by surprise and so overpower their last resistance.

"Thank Zair you appeared, Dak!" panted Pur Naghan. His mail had been ripped and blood showed on his shoulder. "They fight well, these Menaham sailors."

"Bloody Menahem," said Vax. "I owe them."

"You owe a lot of people, it seems, Vax," I said.

He scowled at me, his brown eyes bright, his face flushed.

"Do you mock me, Dak?"

"Mock? Now, why should you think that?"

"If you do—"

Duhrra appeared, immense, his idiot-seeming face creased.

"You do—uh—seem to poke fun, master."

I knew that Duhrra regarded Vax as an oar-comrade, and this gladdened me. I realized I had gone far enough.

I glanced over the side.

"And while we prattle Rukker has boarded the last argenter."

The cunning Kataki had taken the first ship, and then pulled out and dropped down to the last. Now he had two prizes.

Pur Naghan said, "We will share this one, Dak, of course."

Vax favored me with a scowl and took himself off. I bellowed the necessary orders and we took possession of our prizes. There were only three. Rukker's first impetuous attack with the ram had so holed the argenter that she was visibly sinking. A great deal of hustle took place as the goods were brought up and whipped across to the swifter. Chests and boxes, for they contained treasure, were favored over merchandise.

Soon the three swifters and the three argenters began the voyage back to the island of Wabinosk. We called in at our usual island stopovers and met with no untoward incidents.

We pulled with a fine reserve of manpower.

The argenters were sailed by scratch crews and we held fair winds almost all the way, only having to tow the sailing vessels twice in calms.

At the island hideout we inspected our spoils. The ship taken by *Pearl* and ourselves contained mostly sacks of dried mergem, whereat I felt greatly amused. This seemed to indicate Thyllis was in want of food for her people. Our ship contained a quantity of the fine tooled and worked leather for which Magdag is famous. As well there were sacks of chipalines and also, to my surprise, many wicker baskets loaded with crossbow bolts. These were uniformly of fine quality. I guessed they had been manufactured by the slaves and workers of the warrens, those people who, downtrodden and accursed, I had attempted to free, only in the moment of victory to be whisked away by the Star Lords and to leave them to defeat and continued enslavement. I picked up one of the iron quarrels and turned it over in my fingers. Yes, this was a fine artifact, and it should by rights be driven from a crossbow to lodge in the black heart of an overlord of Magdag. Had we not intercepted it, the bolt might well have battered its way into the heart of a Vallian.

Of the cargo carried in the ship Rukker had taken we were concerned only with the treasure.

374

It seemed fitting to me that all gold and silver and precious gems should be heaped into a great and glittering pile and then be shared out equally, portion by portion according to the Articles.

Maybe I was naive in this belief. Rukker's ship had carried the majority of the treasure paid by King Genod for the Hamalese fliers and flyers. The saddle-birds and vollers had fetched extraordinarily high prices. I lifted a heap of golden oars and let them trickle through my fingers back to the glittering mass within the iron-bound lenken chest. This was what Thyllis needed. Her treasury must have been sorely used by the war and now, twenty-odd years after, she was busily building up her reserves so as once again to send sky-spanning fleets against Pandahem and Vallia.

With these thoughts in my mind I went to the meeting with Rukker and the others of our people in positions of authority and found myself not one whit surprised that the Kataki claimed all the treasure he had taken for himself. I was not prepared to argue. I wanted to place my son Vax in safety and then see again King Genod. Only after that could I begin to think again about what to do to free myself from the prison of the inner sea.

"You may keep what you claim, Rukker. If you can maintain your hold on it. For I do not renounce either my claim or the rightful claim of my people."

He did not sneer at me; but his look, brooding and dark, held calculation. "I take note of your words, Dak the Proud. But I think you will be hard pressed to take what you claim."

Vax bristled and shook off Duhrra's hand and barged forward.

"I do not renounce—" he began.

"Keep quiet, Vax," I said.

"By what right do you—" he blustered.

I looked at him.

Duhrra said, "The master speaks sooth, Vax." And then the old devil added, "I think you needed a father to teach you the ways of life—duh! You will get yourself spitted if you go on like this."

"Should I care, Duhrra?"

When my son said those words I felt the hand of ice clench around my heart.

Rukker broke the awkwardness, booming out in his coarse Kataki way, "You sail for Zandikar. Well and good, for, by Takroti, I am sick of all this quibbling." He glared around, yet he was in a high good humor. "I will sail with you and from thence back to the Sea of Onyx. With this treasure I can alter certain events at home."

So it was settled. The local Renders were only too pleased to see us go, for not only had we beaten off their attacks on us, after the first flush of welcome, in our operations we had shown them up almost humiliatingly.

The four swifters and the three argenters made a nice little squadron, sailing east, cutting through the blue waters of the Eye of the World, sailing for Zandikar.

Eight
Rukker does not speak of his seamanship

A man who has but two score years and ten to look forward to, and perhaps a little longer for good behavior, is filled with the thrusting desire to be up and doing—or he should be if he has any sense. To a Kregan with about two hundred years of life to use to explore experiences on his wild and wonderful planet, the desire to be up and doing burns no less strongly; but the Kregan can contemplate with equanimity the passing of a few seasons in doing something outside the mainstream of his life. Rukker the Kataki, as vicious and intemperate a Kregan as they come, made nothing of spending the time we had among the Renders of the inner sea. These little side excursions transform life for a Kregan. I, too, with a thousand years of life to use, shared much of that attitude, even though I had not thrown off the ways of the planet of my birth.

This trip to Zandikar to see my son Vax safe was a mere side-jaunt. I did not forget that in this jaunt Delia, Vax's mother, would concur wholeheartedly with what I was doing.

So we sailed past those mist-swathed coasts of mystery. The Eye of the World contains many areas that remain unknown, shores of faerie and romance, as well as shores of danger and horror. We pulled across the blue waters, from island to island, dropping down to coast most of the way in easy stages, venturing out across wide bays where the portolanos told us we would fetch the opposite headland in good time. I felt no sense of frustration. I was fascinated by Vax. This journey would have been a good time to become acquainted. How I longed to ask him for all the details of his life!

Even the man I was then understood that children have their own secret areas sacrosanct from their parents' understanding. But I hungered to know more of Vax, and through him, more of my other children. And, of course, most of all, to hear about my Delia.

I might explore the Eye of the World. I was debarred from exploring my son's life.

Duhrra did as I asked and would often regale me with tidbits of information he had gleaned. I slowly built up a picture. Vax would freely admit he did not come from the inner sea, and once he had indicated to Duhrra that he had learned much from the Krozairs of Zy and would soon have been admitted to membership of that august Order; he did not tell anyone he came from Vallia and Valka.

"Whatever his father did, Dak," said Duhrra, pulling the fingers of his right hand into the right shape to clasp a flagon of Chremson, "Vax felt he could no longer continue with the Krozairs. Duh—anyone who gets that close must be remarkable. The Krozairs—" He picked up the flagon but did not drink, looking thoughtful, as is proper when mention is made of the Krozairs of Zair. "Duh—they put ice and iron into a man, by the Magic Staff of Buzro! No wonder he detests his old man."

"No wonder," I said, and turned away.

A commotion boiled up in Rukker's *Vengeance Mortil* and we all looked across the bright water. The sail billowed and crackled and then blew forward. The mast bent and bowed and came down with a run. We could hear the passionate yelling over there. I said, quite gently, to Fazhan ti Rozilloi, my ship-Hikdar, "Put the helm over, Fazhan. We must make a beaching. Rukker has proved once again that he is no sailor."

"Aye, Dak," said Fazhan, with a laugh. Rukker might be a ferocious and malevolent Kataki—with yet a spark of common decent humanity surprisingly in him—but, all the same, an old shellbacked sailorman would laugh at him for his woeful lack of seamanship and understanding of the sea.

Vengeance Mortil might quite easily have continued under oar-power and certainly Rukker would have no thought for the well-being of his oar-slaves. We had ghosted through the islands and were now making southerly toward the southeasterly sweeping arm of the inner sea past Zimuzz. Astern we had left Zy, that famous extinct volcanic island cone set boldly within the jaws of the Sea of Swords. The coast here was seldom visited. A triangularly lobed bay southward received the waters of the River Zinkara, running from the Mountains of Ilkenesk. On the Zinkara stood the city of Rozilloi. Fazhan had heaved up a sigh when our calculations showed us we passed that longitude special to him. Zandikar lay some sixty dwaburs farther to the east. We could hope for a wind. So we set about beaching the swifters and anchoring the argenters and removing the weights. We made camp and prepared ourselves for what might come.

Far inland, low rolling hills showed that purple-bruise color of distance, and on the sandy plains between only straggling trees grew. A party would have to push some way before they found a tree that would yield timber suitable for a mast. The made-masts of my own old Terrestrial navy were known here on the inner sea; but usually a single stout tree trunk was employed in swifters.

We had stationed a lookout and he bellowed down.

"Swifters! Green! Six of 'em!"

The curve of the bay where we had beached concealed us from seaward observation—an elementary precaution—and the lookout could see without being seen. The nearer headland under which we sheltered contained a mass of ruins, ancient stones, time worn and weathered, tumbled columns and arches, shattered walls. Up there I had a good view. There were six swifters, medium-sized vessels plowing in line ahead with their oars rising and falling in that remorseless beat. They pulled into the wind, long, low lean craft, evil and formidable. We waited carefully until they were past.

Rukker said, "I will stand guard on the camp and the ships."

"Very well," I said. "It will be a nice task to select the proper tree for your mast"

So it was decided. If those six Green swifters returned or if we were beset by unexpected foes, then Rukker and his men would defend the camp with ferocious efficiency. I took my sailors and a gang of slaves to drag the timbers, and set off inland.

We spent the rest of the day as the suns declined searching for the right tree, and when we found it and cut it down and dragged it back, two of the lesser moons sped past above in their crazy whirling orbits, and She of the Veils smiled down in fuzzy pink radiance. We had seen no signs of life apart from the spoor of mortils and the bones of their prey, and the high circling of warvols, the vulture-like winged scavengers waiting for the mortils to finish. Once upon a time—or, as Kregans say, under a certain moon—this land had been lush and fertile, filled with the busy agriculture and commerce of the People of the Sunset. Now they had gone, and the land gleamed sere and empty under the moons.

The moment we arrived back in camp we were greeted by news that filled me with amusement and filled Vax and the others with heated fury.

Old Tamil told us—a cunning rascal, quick and sly, who had appointed himself Palinter in *Crimson Magodont*. As our Palinter, our purser, he could be relied on to wangle extra supplies for us in his accustomed tortuous dealings with the common resources; in looking out for himself he looked out for us.

"That cramph of a Kataki!" spluttered Tamil, his off-center nose more than ever like a moon-bloom in the pink radiance of She of the Veils. "Took the treasure and sailed off!"

Howls of execration broke out at this. But then those howls changed to jeers of derision as we looked where Tamil pointed.

Less than an ulm offshore *Vengeance Mortil* lay becalmed in the water. She was down by the head. She stuck there, solid and unmoving, clearly held fast by fangs of rock piercing her bow.

"So the rast took our treasure and sailed off and ran himself aground!" bellowed Fazhan. He looked as offended as any of them there. They were running down to the shore and waving their arms and brandishing weapons. It was a fitting sight for a madness. It was, also, somewhat humorous—at least, it seemed funny to me at the time.

The treasure meant nothing, of course. It did mean something to these ragged rascals with me, and so that made it important to me because of them. But, all the same, the idea of a great and ferocious Kataki lord sweeping up all the treasure and loading it into his ship and sailing grandly off, only to get stuck on a rock, struck me as ludicrous and something to raise a guffaw.

The old devil had cut down his own mast, of course, to get us ashore in this lonely spot and send us sailormen off on a wild-goose chase. When he had run aground—what must his thoughts have been? He had been thrown by his own varter, as the Kregans say. Boats were ferrying his men back. There was a sublime amount of confusion and argument; but no one came to blows. The first flush of anger dissipated in the sense of the ridiculousness of the Katakis.

I said to Fazhan, "I will wager Rukker's words will be: 'I do not wish to discuss this' or 'I will not speak of this again.'"

"No bet," said Fazhan, being a wise man.

Pur Naghan was highly incensed, although seeing the humor of the situation, for he was bitterly annoyed by the evident lack of honor in Rukker's actions. Honor—aye, the Krozairs set great store by that ephemeral commodity.

Rukker stormed ashore in high dudgeon. At least, that seems to me an evocative way of describing his malevolent scowls, the way his tail flicked irritably this way and that, the dark glitter of wrath in his evil eyes. He was on the verge of a killing mad.

He said in his surly hoarse voice, "I shall not speak of this in the future."

At this a howl went up. And, thankfully, among those howls sounded many a guffawing belly-laugh. I felt relief. I watched carefully. But I think the sheer ludicrousness of it all saved an eruption, for plenty of men there would have chopped Rukker given half the chance. But the heat evaporated from the moment. Wine went around. We ate at the camp fires. We were, after all, a bunch of daredevil Renders, comrades in arms, for the time being. Tricks like this must be expected in such company.

The Maiden with the Many Smiles lifted and flooded down her golden light and we sat and drank and some of us sang. On the morrow we would fashion a new mast for Rukker and so sail off with the breeze toward Zandikar. We sang "The Swifter with the Kink," of course, and "The Chuktar with the Glass Eye," for they are fine carefree songs full of opportunities to expand the lungs and bellow. The firelight leaped upon our faces, on gleaming eyes and teeth, on mouths open and lustily bawling, on long bronzed necks open to the air. The red southern shore is populated by apims almost exclusively, and these apims, I had noticed, were contemptuous and intolerant of diffs. But it takes all kinds to make a world.

Here some of the Zairian apims found that for all the tricks of the Katakis the other diffs of our company were human men, after all, and not mere menagerie men.

A little Och sang "The Cup Song of the Och Kings," sending the plaintive notes welling out into the light of the moons, a yearning song telling of great days and great deeds, filled with the throbbing resonances of nostalgia. Then, as seemed always to happen when an Och sang that song, the moment he finished he pitched forward on his nose, out to the wide.

We all roared and cheered. At the other fires others of the Renders caterwauled to the skies. A Gon leaped up, his skull shaved clean of all that white hair of which Gons are so ashamed, to their misfortune, and started in to sing a wild, skirling farrago, filled with spittings and abrupt, deep reverberations, of hints of horror, all accompanied by dramatic gestures evident of extreme terror. This was the song sometimes called "Of the Abominations of Oidrictzhn."[12]

A man—an apim, a Zairian—leaped clear across the fire, singeing the hairs on his legs, and screaming. He tackled the Gon with a full body-cracking charge, smacked him in the mouth, and so knocked him down and sat on his head.

"You get onker!" screamed the apim, one Fazmarl the Beak—for, in truth, his nose was of prodigious proportions. "You wish to destroy us all!"

We hauled him off and the Gon, Leganion, sat up, highly indignant. "It is a good song and will make your flesh creep."

"Yes, you rast! Do you not know where we are?" Fazmarl the Beak swung his hand violently to point at the moonlit ruins crowning the headland, frowning down above us. "You prate that name—here! Onker!"

One or two other men challenged Fazmarl, and he spluttered out a long rigmarole of weird doings and nightly spells and sorcery, there in the ruins of the Sunset People. He would not bring himself to repeat the name. But he made it very clear that the ruins harbored some malefic being in whom he believed and yet whose existence he must deny in the pure light of Zair.

"Superstitious nonsense!"

"Fairy tales for numbskulls!"

Oh, yes, those fierce Renders caterwauled bravely enough as the pink and golden moonlight flooded down and we sang and drank around the camp fires. But I saw more than a few of them cast up a quick and surreptitious glance at the pale stone-glimmer of the ancient ruins.

In the very nature of these men, for there were no women with us, fights broke out. These must be settled according to whatever code of honor and conduct was acceptable to both parties. I have not mentioned the detailed protocols involved in challenges and combats of Kregen, outside of a few remarks on the obi of my Clansmen, and the formal dueling of Hamal. But now, and with horrific suddenness, the finicky demands of honor and the protocol of fighting became of supreme importance to me.

It began with Vax, who had sworn off the dopa, swearing away, as was his wont, about his cramph of a father. One of the Katakis, no doubt as bored by Vax's obsession as the rest of us, bellowed some remark and tossed back his wine. This Kataki was Athgar, called the Neemu, and it was whispered he chafed under the yoke of Rukker's authority. Vax stood up, limber and lithe, and I caught the flare of madness in his eyes.

"You said, Athgar?"

No one had heard what Athgar had spoken; the moment could have been allowed to lie, and so dwindle and die.

But Athgar, wiping a hand across his face, bellowed out a curse to Targ the Untouchable. His low-browed, narrow-eyed face, as malignant and devilish as are all Katakis' faces, even the dark face of Rukker, bore down on the slim erect figure of Vax.

"If your father was the rast you claim him to be, then your mother must be a stupid and unholy bitch to have married him in the first place and so give birth to—"

That was as far as he got.

There was no heroic posturing from Vax. He did not bellow out; he did not request Athgar to repeat his words. My son Vax, who was Jaidur of Valka, Prince of Vallia, simply lashed out with his fist and knocked Athgar the Kataki, called the Neemu, head over heels into the fire.

When the uproar subsided and Athgar was held by Rukker's Katakis, and Vax was held by Duhrra and Nath the Slinger, the ritual challenges and responses were gone through, the lines drawn and the demarcations between edge and point, between death and maiming, the rules and observances were finalized with all due solemnity. The rules of Hyr Jikordur would apply. I stood still and silent, watching, for the matter was passed from the hands of mortal men and lay now with the gods. Honor and passion ruled all. Words had been spoken. A blow had been struck. Now the answer, in the whims of the gods, must be found in steel and blood.

Moon-mist lay over the camp and the fires flared strangely.

In the sand the lines were drawn out.

Men ran from the other fires to form a great circle of intent staring faces. A Jikordur happened every now and then and gave fuel for gossip for sennights thereafter. The matter was grave and full of a prestigious death-wish, filled with blood and death.

Instinctively, in the very moment a challenge had become inevitable, I had stepped forward to take Athgar the Neemu on and so shield my son. But that was impossible. Ideals and honor, however misplaced and distorted, now dictated all actions.

381

This was to be a Hyr Jikordur. I made an effort. I said, loudly, "Let no life be taken. Let the result be adjudged in the first blow."

Athgar sneered back his thin Kataki lips. "If it be first blood, Dak the Tenderhearted, then I will take the cramph's head off."

And my son said in his ferocious way, which a calmness made all the more vulnerable and bitter, "Let it be to the death, for, by Zim-Zair, I do not care."

At that Krozair oath all my defenses went down. I must stand and watch my son fight a predatory member of a feral and cruel race, vicious, fully armed and accoutered, equipped with a deadly bladed tail. I must stand and watch. To do anything else would impugn the strict codes of conduct, bring the Jikordur into disrepute, and as well as insuring my own death, bring my son humiliation and disgrace.

The Jikordur meant nothing to me. My own death little more. And I would so contrive my interference that Vax was spared that humiliation...

Rukker checked his man. He favored me with a slow glance that I felt meant more than he cared to say. I stood before Vax. I drew the great Krozair longsword. I tendered it hilt first. Vax looked up, and something got through to him, for his lips compressed. Then he smiled.

"I thank you, Dak."

A sword-blade struck a helmet like a gong. The combat began.

Nine
Blood in the Hyr Jikordur

Pachaks have been blessed by nature—or the dark manipulations of genetic science—with quick and lethal tail hands. Katakis must strap their steel to their whip-tails. I am partial to Pachaks, as employed mercenaries, as friends. In long talks with them around the camp fires on the eve of battles I have learned much of the art of tail-fighting. There are tricks. As the gong note clanged with grim promise from the sword-struck helmet, I leaned down to Vax and said, "His tail may be numbed by—"

"I know," said my son.

They always seem to know, these cocky youngsters. I stepped back. I did not waver from my resolution to court personal dishonor and destruction if they were necessary to save my son. The chances were he would know. Planath Pe-Na, my standard-bearer who carried Old Superb into action, must have known Vax as the lad grew up into manhood. Along with all my friends of Esser Rarioch—Balass the Hawk, Naghan the Gnat, Oby, Melow the Supple, the Djangs who were a regular part of the people there;

all must have contributed their knowledge toward the education of Vax no less than they had to Drak and Segnik—no, I must call him Zeg now. And, of course, there were Seg and Inch and Turko the Shield. If Vax had taken in what they had to tell him then the combined knowledge should make him a formidable fighter—and he was, indeed, as I had seen, a bonny lad with a sword.

Planath must have told Vax of the tricks an apim might get up to with the tail of a Kataki. Planath would have relished the telling.

With no more relish in myself at the idea of this fight, but with some feeling of relief, I watched as Athgar stalked forward—arrogant, completely confident—to knock over and slay this slim and supple apim lad.

I cannot do justice to that fight, for I was far too intimately concerned for my own good. I had picked up the look from Duhrra and he had slipped me his longsword. I held it ready, and I must give thanks that the fight occupied the attention of the men there, for had they seen my face in the firelight glow and the radiance of the moons, they would no doubt have run shrieking.

Athgar launched himself, his sword blurring, his tail-blade high and deceiving. Vax lunged right, checked and reversed, came back. The two combatants passed. Now was the danger! The tail hissed around. Vax jumped. I let out a grunt of relief. Vax dropped down hard. He made no attempt at that cunning tail-numbing trick. Athgar had expected him to duck, as would be the instinctive response to the threat of that arrogant high-held blade. Athgar struck low. Vax jumped. And the great Krozair longsword flamed.

Athgar shrieked.

The tail spun and looped away, the strapped blade glittering, flicked like a limp coil of rope into the fire. It sizzled.

Blood pumped from Athgar. He stood disbelieving. He stood for perhaps two heartbeats.

Rukker yelled, "Athgar the Tailless!"

The Neemu screeched and swung his sword in a ferocious horizontal sweep. Vax met the blow, slanting his brand, and let the blades chink and screech in that demoniac sound of steel on steel. His broad back muscles tensed and bunched, drew out in a ripple of massive power. The blade struck forward. The point burst through Athgar's throat above the mail, smashed on to eject itself in a spouting gout of blood.

Without a word, Vax withdrew and stepped back. He looked on silently as Athgar dropped his sword and gripped his crimson throat, his eyes glaring madly. He choked, trying to say something. Then he fell. He pitched down to sprawl at Vax's feet.

Vax looked down. He was my son. Without a word he spit on the corpse. Then he walked away.

No one said a word.

It was left to Vax, turning to speak over his shoulder, to say, "I will clean your sword, Dak, before I return it."

I wanted to say—how I wanted to say!—the words hot and breaking in me... I swallowed. I said, "Jikai—keep the sword, Vax. It is yours."

For a moment he stood, silent, limber, lithe and young, staring at me. The firelight painted one half of his face ruby; the moons shone fuzzily pink and gold upon the other. He nodded. Again he did not speak. He just nodded and lifted the sword, and saluted, and so walked into the darkness beyond the fires.

I handed Duhrra his sword. "Take Nath. Follow."

"Yes, master."

Duhrra and Nath melted into the moon-drenched shadows. Other men of my crew followed. They would see that Vax came to no harm. They were good fellows. If I do not mention them overmuch, surely it is obvious that concern for my son dominated all my thoughts.

Rukker said, "There is no need for that, Dak."

"No."

He looked down at the corpse. "He was my man and yet he was not my man. I think this Vax Neemusbane is your man and yet not your man. It was a Hyr Jikordur. There is no blood between us."

"None," I said. "And you are right about Vax. I think he has done you a favor."

"Probably. But I do not wish to discuss that."

It amuses me now to think how Rukker regarded me. He treated the other Renders sharply enough, and they respected or hated him for it, according to their natures. But he must have come to terms with his own ruthlessness in his dealings with me, or so I think. Maybe he did not forget our first meeting, or the way he would have been flogged on the oar bench had I not spoken. As I say, Rukker possessed a scrap of humanity.

All the same, I meant to repay him for his trick when he had loaded all the treasure aboard his swifter and attempted to sail away. He might not wish to speak of that in the future; I had a few words on the subject—and these words would not be spoken but acted on.

In any company on Kregen one feels naked without a sword. A weapon is needed most everywhere. Even the unarmed combat skills developed by the Khamorros of Havilfar, and the Krozairs of the Eye of the World, cannot fully compensate for the lack of a weapon if the unarmed combat man goes up against an opponent skilled in his weapon's use. And it does not have to be a sword, of course; but legends and myths cluster about swords.

In our reiving over the western end of the inner sea we had built up an armory and in my cabin in *Crimson Magodont* a useful array of weapons I had taken a fancy to awaited my inspection. As I went up the ladder I turned and saw in the moons-light Vax and Duhrra and Nath walking back to the fires, and already Vax was working away at the blood on his new sword. Satisfied, I went into the cabin. There was no real choice before me; just the one sword I fancied. There had been no other Krozair blade come into our possession; but I had taken a fine Ghittawrer blade. The Grodnims produce fine weapons and, as in the case of the Zairians, the finest are made by and for the Brotherhoods of Chivalry of the Green. This Ghittawrer sword had borne the device of the lairgodont and the rayed sun and I had had them removed. I picked it up and swirled it a trifle, feeling the balance as being good but not as perfect as the Krozair brand I had given my son, honoring his Jikai.

That thrice-damned king Genod, self-styled genius at war, had insti-gated his Ghittawrer Brotherhood, the lairgodont and the rayed sun. The blade was good. It would serve to lop a few Green heads and arms.

A shouting on the beach, and a distant calling from higher up, drew me to the deck. The night lay calm and sweet under the stars and moons; yet mists trickled down like thickened waterfalls from the headland. I looked up. Lights speckled the ruins. Many torches flared among the aeons-old walls and columns.

"What is it, Sternen?" I shouted at the watch.

"I do not know, Dak. But whatever it is, men have gone up to find out." He shivered. He was a tough apim with a scarred face and quick with a knife. "By Zogo the Hyrwhip! Those screams never came from a human throat!"

About to check him roughly, I paused. The shrieks from the ruins sounded unnatural. Sternen made several quick and secret signs. These were rooted in a time before Zair and Grodno parted into enmity. I slapped the Ghittawrer blade into the scabbard, for the Grodnims attempted to copy the dimensions of a Krozair blade, and rattled off down the ladder. Many men were running up the steep track in the cliff toward the ruins, carrying torches, bearing weapons. Renders out to prove they feared not a single damn thing in all of Kregen. I followed.

Panting up at my side Nath the Slinger said, 'The lights up there aren't ours."

I halted. Duhrra and Vax appeared. Some way beyond them a knot of men I knew would be loyal not only to Zair but to me pressed on, I shouted at them, intemperately, and they clustered around. Before I spoke I looked up. In the lights of the moons the mass of Renders ascending into the ruins looked apelike, crowding up, bearing torches. The Katakis were there. I looked at Vax and Fazhan and Duhrra. I told them what I wanted them to do. I did not mince my words.

"And if there's a watch," I said, most unpleasantly, "knock him on the head and spirit him away. Do not kill him, though."

Duhrra rumbled a hoarse chuckle.

"Duh—master! A fine plan!"

"Aye," said Fazhan. "Just rewards, by Zair."

"And if there is a fight," said Vax, half drawing his beautiful new sword, "I shall joy in showing this boastful Kataki Rukker he may join the cramph Athgar."

"You will not fight him unless I tell you." I looked hard at Vax in the streaming moons-light. "He will not succumb so easily as Athgar."

"Yet is he a Kataki, and Katakis have tails."

"And with them they rip out throats of young coys."

He was beginning to know a little of me, enough to understand that I might argue with him in some matters, and in others he had best obey, schtump. All the same, he looked daggers at me.

"Take Tamil the Palinter with you. He is adept at weighing and measuring."

"Aye, master."

"I shall entertain Rukker until you signal. Now, jump!"

I intended to be scrupulously fair. What I intended was perfectly obvious, of course; but if my men did not do a quick clean job there would be a fight. Renders habitually quarrel and fight; it is all a part of their image, Articles or no. As they took themselves off I wondered if I was doing this out of mere irritation with myself, out of a sense that time was rushing by and I had made no progress, and played this trick not so much out of evil boredom as out of self-contempt.

Then I ran lightly up the trail in the cliff toward the ruins of the Sunset People and the mysteries that might await me there.

Ten
Among the ruins of the Sunset People

From the concealment of a screen of bushes we looked upon a scene at once hideous and horrific. The Renders had extinguished their torches and they did not speak above an awed whisper. The lights illuminating those time-weathered stones were not our lights. The flaring torches wrapped tendrils of golden brilliance about the old columns and arches, lit gray walls and time-toppled cornices. Shattered domes like eggshells smashed wantonly glittered starkly in the pink moons-light. We crouched silently and we stared upon that pagan scene.

Next to me crouched the trembling form of Fazmarl the Beak. I could feel his body shaking against my shoulder.

"I warned them, the fools," he whispered to himself, and I could feel the tenseness in the words he scarcely knew he uttered aloud. "It is Oidrictzhn himself! The Abomination!"

I nudged him. "Silence, you fambly. Is this all you know?"

He glared mutely at me and shook his head.

I drew him down farther into the shadows.

'Tell me. And speak low."

"Oidrictzhn!"

I clapped a hand across his mouth and shot a glance over the bushes. The figures prancing in the torchlights were concerned over their own pursuits and we did not appear to be observed; but I fancied they'd have someone on the lookout. I shook Fazmarl the Beak.

"You bear an honored name. These Abominations. Is that what they're up to out there?" I released his mouth.

He drew in a whooping gulp of air. "Yes. It is old, older than anyone knows. Long before Zair and Grodno, whose name be cursed, separated out of—"

"Yes, yes. I know that. Will they slay the girl?"

"Assuredly. They have come from many little villages inland and they would travel to the west of us. I know, for I lived in one of those small villages, like a vosk in swill—and all knew the old stories of Oidrictzhn and his Abominations."

"You do not mind saying his name now."

He did not laugh; but he emitted a sour grunting kind of cough. "No—for it is too late. The evil one has arisen from his sleep. He has been conjured. Do you not see his gross form, there, where the shadows cluster, although the torches shine the brightest?"

There *was* a puzzling splotch of shadow against an ancient gray monolith where the torches shone, where one would expect light and the reflections brilliant against the masonry.

"How?"

"Who knows? No one owns to knowledge. Yet all know there are those who possess the secret powers. The Abominable One has risen and he will not return until he is sated."

I was not prepared to dismiss all this as fear-induced madness.

On Kregen as on Earth there are the darker myths, hideous stories of hideous beings from out of time and space. Normally one gives no credence to them. But to hear of them among tumbled and time-shattered ruins, ancient before ordinary man ventured to tame fire and crouch at his cave-mouth brandishing a stone hand-ax, with the shifting light of the moons streaming across a scene of naked savages—for rhapsodic belief had turned these people savage—screaming and chanting, circling a stake whereon hung the bloody corpse of a ponsho, closing nearer and nearer to a raised stone slab on which lay a young girl, ripe for the sacrifice… as I say, to hear these horrendous myths of demons and devils in circumstances like those is to make belief all too easy.

The Abominable One had been driven away when the true light of Zair had risen in the land. But he was not dead. He slept and awaited his call. He could be raised up and he would not be satisfied until he had drunk of the blood of a virgin. That it must be a female virgin was not specified; but it seemed appropriate. I had to hold on to the levity that wanted me to rush out there and lay about with the Ghittawrer blade. I do not totally condemn these feeble-minded stories; a little care for one's ib is as proper as care for one's flesh-and-blood hide.

"The Zair-forsaken cramphs of Grodnims advance from the west. They destroy all who oppose them. King Genod's army is invincible. Soon they will be here. All the little villages to the south will be enslaved—aye!—and the great cities also."

"You may be right, Fazmarl. But I think you wrong. And these deluded fools seek to raise up a long-dead god of evil to protect them? They are mad."

"Yes, they are mad. But madness is easy in these times."

Rukker crawled over. He looked as fierce as ever; but I sensed he was unsure. Why else did he crawl?

"What is this onker chattering about, Dak?"

I told him that out of fear of the Grodnims the locals were raising from his long-sealed vault a monster of evil, out of time and space, a being who might sweep us all away with the power of his breath. Rukker grunted and stilled the impatient swish of his tail.

"If the ancient god is in the likeness of an apim—"

Fazmarl let rip a hysterical giggle at this, a tiny sound of horror in a greater scene of horror.

"His shape is more awful than anyone—"

"Yes," I said. Fazmarl quieted. "It is not of our business, Rukker. Do you agree?"

"I agree. I think I shall not speak of this later."

"Yes," I said. "Yet the girl…"

"She is apim," said the Kataki.

"Oh, assuredly. Had she been a Fristle, or a numim, a sylvie, or a girl from Balintol, I do not think it would make overmuch difference."

Fazmarl, quaking, said, "They would mean nothing."

I did not hit him. I must come to terms with this detestation of diffs that was so widespread among the apims of Zairia. I had hardly remarked it during my previous sojourn on the inner sea. I had changed, not the Zairians, that was all. And, anyway, Fazmarl and Rukker would have no idea where Balintol was. I lifted a trifle and peered over the bushes. The blasphemous ceremony drew to its gruesome climax.

Couples were dancing out there in the streaming torchlight, going widdershins, letting abandon carry them away in frenzy. The dread weight of evil bore us down. The sense of evil among the stones shivered through the torchlight, and a coiling mist melted the gold and pink moonbeams. Fazmarl shivered. He began to crawl back, away, shaking his head, his lips slobbering.

I let him go.

I said to Rukker, "It seems to me a little Jikai might be created here, Kataki."

"You may. By the Triple Tails of Targ the Untouchable! This is no business of mine."

"You would not trust your Targ against this Oidrictzhn the Abominable?"

"There is nothing supernatural there. It is a man, dressed in a skin, with a chimera for a head."

"So why hang back?"

His tail started to twitch. I drew my sword. He saw it. He said, "You may get yourself killed if you wish. Do you not see the archers?"

"Aye. That proves they fear physical as well as occult powers."

"Then, by Takroti, you may test them yourself."

He would have left then, calling his people about him. I could feel the evil in that place. It is a difficult thing to say. There was some suppurating spirit of demonology flaunting itself against the gray stone wall, drinking the light of the torches. I held Rukker. The people out there, abandoned, most half gone on dopa probably, clustered close to the stone slab.

"Would it not be a Jikai to go out there and deprive them of their enjoyment? Would not depriving other people appeal to you, a Kataki?"

Under my hand his arm quivered. I could feel the bunch of muscle below the mail. He hissed the words as a Kataki can hiss. His face was demonic as any devil's, almost as devilish as my own. "Take your hand off me! I shall spit you for this, apim!"

"Then you will have to catch me, Kataki," I said, and stood up, and ran forward into the torchlight toward the stone slab of sacrifice and the girl bound helplessly upon its scarred surface.

Hideous yells burst from the corded throats of the people dancing and clustering about the slab of sacrifice. They were possessed. Drugged on dopa or any one of a variety of narcotics, or on sheer fear-driven hysteria, they capered and screeched and sought to drag me down with clawed raking fingers. I pushed them aside. There was no time to feel either anger or pity for them. I got in among them with vicious speed and the archers perched on the crumbling lichenous walls shafted two poor devils instead of me.

The aura of horror swelled nearer that splotch of utter darkness on the

389

gray wall. In a tangle of naked arms and legs I pushed forward toward the slab. I did not use the edge of my sword; the flat sufficed.

The girl was not unconscious. She lay on her back, strained over by thongs from wrists and ankles that were knotted to iron rings stapled into the stone. She wore stockings that reached to mid-thigh and were banded by red-glinting gems. The stockings were black, a fitting counterpoint to the darkness that hovered over her. Her body gleamed pink and golden in the moons-light, looped with gems, strings of jewels chaining her breast-cups of gold and twining around her stomach and legs, linking her ankles and wrists. Her hair of that midnight black of the Zairians of the inner sea glistered with gems and silverdust. Her face seemed only a pale flower, her mouth and eyes mere dark bruises.

A man leaped on my back and I bent and hurled him away. The sword slashed the thongs of her ankles, sliced the right wrist-thong. I moved to reach the left thong and someone grabbed my ankles. I kicked. A screech like a lost soul in torment cheered me. The sword licked out. I put my left arm under the girl's head, lifted her, slid my arm down to her neck, her back, and took her up as one might hoist a sack of cereal.

She felt light and soft and warm, and she trembled all the time with a fine shivering that tingled against my hand.

Now I would use the edge, if I must.

An arrow splintered against the slab. The scarred surface showed ancient evil stains. Just beyond the slab a pit in the ground covered by an iron grating drew my alert attention. People were dragging the grating up, screaming in ecstasy and fear, throwing the iron grille down and then running, running...

Anything could squirm out of that dank pit...

"Slay him! Strike him down! Immolate him!"

The shouts grew in frenzy. With the girl caught up to me and dangling her strings of jewels and chains of gold, I began to run back. I looked over my shoulder, just to check my rear, as was my custom—and I saw the dread shadow against the stone move.

At that moment of impending horror an entanglement at my feet brought me pitching to earth. I held on to the girl and as we both slammed into the ground she did not cry out. Her eyes were wide and brilliant and fixed on me hypnotically.

I looked up.

A Thing moved among the shadows.

A Shadow moved among the things.

The screeching and shouting died to a whimper and faded. The breeze stilled. Mists coiled before the moons and the light changed with dread subtlety from gold and pink to a drenching shower of blood-rubied radiance.

I looked up.

Something ancient and evil slithered against the stones. Something... There was only one name that could be given this bestial monstrosity from out of the dead ages of time—Oidrictzhn—Oidrictzhn the Abominable!

The Shadow rose and lifted and became monstrous, huge, blotting out vision and reason. A chilling slithering, a hissing, a feral, hateful mind-numbing hissing whispered from the shadows clustered about the Shadow.

The Beast from Time slithered out from the shadows to devour me.

Eleven
The Beast out of Time

Apim, the thing was, fully ten feet tall, gray and leprous of skin, marked by the splotches of foul disease. Its skin hung from it loosely, fold on fold of repulsive gray mantling, dripping with the festering slime. And its head! Domed of head and yet with leprous crawling skin patches supplanting all hair, with deeply sunken eyes that glared now as mere red slits. Red, red, those eyes, twin pits of fire, burning down on me. I rolled over above the girl. I saw the thing's mouth. Arched and black, it gaped obscenely, and from its upper jaw tendrils of slime hung like oozing living stalactites. Green ichor dripped. The thing lifted gaunt arms from which hung like living gray curtains the hideous folds of flesh. Skeletal the fingers, curved, harsh, bony webs of taloned destruction. Now I was on my feet. The girl lay in her tawdry jewels and gold, winking flashes of fire in the torchlights and that dropping blood-red light, splendid against her flesh in that moment of horror.

The thing advanced farther from the shadows. The slithering hissing of its progress sounded from nameless horrors hidden in the shadows thickly pressing around its legs and feet. Its arms lifted like bat wings, its skeletal talons reaching forward. The red eyes blazed from their deep pits of hate, and the green slime dripped from its mouth. The fetid odor of the thing near drove me back; but I gagged and lifted the sword.

The girl spoke.

"If it touches you with its claws, you are doomed."

"Then, my lady, I shall have to see it does not touch us."

Her gasp was a pretty diversion; but the horror moved on and the contrasts of the moment must be forgotten. This was no mere mortal monster. I did not think a mere mortal man hid behind this obscene facade. This was a real true and *live* ancient evil one, from beyond Time, summoned up and demanding his sacrifice.

How old was this ancient thing? From what pits of hell had it been raised?

The slime dripped from its ghastly mouth and its head bent forward, so that the ruby eyes sank into mere furnace slits.

How could I spare pity for it? It should have died long and long ago, no longer needed by mankind, forgotten and allowed to sink into its tomb. But superstitious humanity had dabbled blasphemously in the black arts of Kregen and had drawn forth this horror. So a simple mortal man must drive it back from whence it came.

"It is Oidrictzhn the Abominable!" The devotees had regained their voices. They were shrieking in rhapsody, falling onto their knees, their arms uplifted in supplication. They prayed in an obsessed fervor to this Abomination. "All praise to thee, Oidrictzhn! Lahal and Lahal to the Abominable One!"

The thing slithered nearer.

And the lassitude and the weakness crept up my sword arms. I held the Ghittawrer blade with both fists, one unhandily near the other, for the hilt was not a full Krozair hilt. I struggled to think of the Krozairs then. Of Zair, of Opaz, of Djan. I tried to form words and hurl them at the Beast of Time. I wanted to shriek out that it should return to its ghastly haunts in the name of Zair; but I could not croak a word.

The sword felt impossibly heavy. My arms trembled. My calves shook. My head drooped. I struggled savagely to lift my head, to lift my arms, to still the agonized trembling of my body.

And the thing spoke!

Serpentlike, the hissing words garbled out through that obscene mouth.

"Puny mortal man! Foundling of Time! I demand my due!"

Only my body betrayed me. I knew what I was going to say. Oh, yes, I knew what I'd shout at the obscene thing. But it had the power, it possessed the ancient evil powers out of time and it held me in a stasis so that all my muscles could not move my body, my arms could not uphold the sword.

The blade drooped and sank.

The girl struggled to her knees, her golden breast-cups jangling against the golden chains, the gems over her body glittering. She clasped my knees. But I was of no use to her.

I think then, I really think, that I, Dray Prescot, lord of many titles and many lands, would have marched on my last long journey to the Ice Floes of Sicce. I really do...

I fought against occult powers that I dismissed as being the enfeebled ravings of children and idiots. But who may say what festers in the past of Kregen? Who deny the reality of that moment of horror?

The sword drooped and the point struck the ground and I leaned forward. In moments only I would topple helplessly to the ground.

And all the time the ruby fires of the thing's eyes glared furnacelike upon me and the green ichor dripped from the gaping arch of its mouth.

I could not speak; but my mind formed words.

"Sink me!" I burst out. "A stinking slimy half-dead monstrosity with all the black arts of Tomborku to see me off with my own thirty-two-pound roundshot for company! By Zair! A fine fool I'll look when the gray ones greet me among the Ice Floes!"

I felt the tremble in my arms. I remembered what a lady had said. The Star Lords—well, they would probably laugh to see me in this plight, for all that they could have aided me had they wished. So I thought then. As for the Savanti, they were mere mortal men, even if superhuman in their powers. They would not aid me now. Only I could aid myself, so I thought, in my usual blind arrogance and pride.

And the tremble persisted and I felt the sword's weight again and I lifted. The hilt felt incredibly good in my fists. I raised my head. The thing did not advance. Against the shadows a radiance grew. A yellow light. A yellow light that limned that ghastly head with the dripping fungoid growths depending in place of hair, that shone upon the gray walls and drove away the black shadows. Yellow. A yellow radiance.

"By God! Zena Iztar," I said. "But you are very welcome."

And I lifted the sword against the tearing shriek of my muscles and I struck at the leprous shape before me.

It stumbled back. I caught it a glancing blow and it keened a shrill whine. The shadows writhed and coiled and lambent blue sparks spit from the darkness. But they spit and recoiled as that glorious yellow glow strengthened. Again I lifted the sword and took a pace forward and struck. The thing shrieked again and stepped back and back. I could feel nothing, now, in my arms. Twice I had struck and twice I had missed. I, Dray Prescot, swordmaster, bladesman, Bravo-fighter, had missed this shuffling, lumpy, ichor-dripping obscenity not once but twice.

I knew then that Zena Iztar could aid me only in some way, some not-so-small way, that lifted the occult power of the force that enchained me. But I could not move forward. I was held by unnameable powers. The sword glittered in the mingled lights; it could not be impelled against that hideous shape of horror.

"By Zair! Give me but the strength for one last blow!"

Willpower, the striving, the desire, the determination, by these I might stand against the Star Lords, Zena Iztar had told me. I must summon up all my willpower and force my reluctant muscles to power my body forward.

Oidrictzhn the Abominable leered upon me with his furnace eyes of ruby fire. He saw. He moved forward and his claws raked around. One touch was death. One touch of these webbed and taloned claws would doom me for all eternity. This I knew.

I burst the bonds even as the claw raked at my face. I swung the brand and the steel shrieked and bit and green slime spouted.

The thing screamed. It staggered back.

I have scoffed at the word eldritch. But in that moment I knew what an eldritch scream sounds like.

It sounds with the insane terror of pure horror.

The yellow glow began to fade.

The worshipers of this vile thing had dared not to approach. The archers had not dared to loose. The Beast from Time lurched. One claw still made feeble raking passes as it staggered back. The other claw lay on the ground at my feet and even as I looked so it gathered itself to it, and like a webbed scorpion scuttled for the shadows against the gray stone. I let it go. I know about scorpions.

"You have failed me!" the thing's voice whispered now, weird and out of Kregen and altogether blasphemous. "I shall leave you to your fate. Oidrictzhn returns to the Abominations from which it came."

The shadows rushed together as bats swoop about a church steeple. A noxious odor made me retch. The shadows paled and wafted and there were left only the shadows flung from the torches and streaming behind the moons' radiance.

An arrow flicked past my ear.

I hoisted the girl. I was myself again.

I ran. That was a fair old run, a scamper across the sand and sward between the ruins until I had reached the tumbled columns and so run on, safely now, into the bushes.

Only one man stood there to welcome me.

I said, "I salute you, Rukker. And the others?"

His booming laugh rang somewhat hollow. "They scuttled."

"Then let us go down to our ships and push off. This is an evil place."

Twelve
News of the Red and the Green

The mingled streaming radiance of the Suns of Scorpio filled the Eye of the World with light and color. Our little squadron bore on over a sparkling sea, with the wind in our canvas and the spray lifting whitely from our forefeet. Often I have spoken of that glorious opaz radiance of the twin suns of Antares, but seldom have I so luxuriated in the brilliance of the Suns of Scorpio as on the morning following that ghastly nighted encounter with Oidrictzhn of the Abominations.

That part of the southern shore of the inner sea is called the Shadow Coast. The name is apt. Of all the men who had climbed so boldly up to the ruins all but one had fled away. Now I stood on my quarterdeck and watched *Vengeance Mortil* as Rukker urged her along. The new timber for the mast had been pitched aboard and no one had questioned our sailing before the new mast was stepped.

The plan was for us to beach up well away from the Shadow Coast and then step Rukker's new mast. But the Kataki lord had other ideas. Fazhan commented acidly, and Duhrra let fall a few astonished Duhs. Vax looked on Rukker's swifter with compressed lips. For *Vengeance Mortil* and the argenter Rukker claimed as his prize and manned with his own men curved away to larboard. Our course to the east carried us on with the wind. Rukker bore away to the northeast.

"Does he mean to leave us, then?" said Fazhan, peering under his hand.

"It seems so."

Vax laughed nastily.

Duhrra said: "Duh—when he finds out!"

My men had done a good job, so Fazhan said. With old Tamil the Palinter there to weigh and assess, we had deducted our shares of the treasure. Rocks had been placed at the bottom of the chests, with canvas over that and the fair proportion of treasure belonging to Rukker spread artfully to conceal all. Rukker, believing he carried all the treasure, bore away from us. I wondered if he questioned why we did not follow.

One of the hands began laughing. He was a prijiker and stood on the forecastle now in his accustomed place, leaning against the overhanging bulk of the beakhead. Others of the men began to laugh.

"Nath the Berkumsay!" I bellowed. "Belay that caterwauling."

He looked back and I saw the puzzlement chasing the laughter in his face. I turned to Portain, the ship-Deldar, and said with some irritation, "Go forward and tell Nath the Berkumsay to shut his black-fanged winespout. If he wishes to bring Rukker back tell him to swim after *Vengeance Mortil* and tell the Kataki personally."

"Quidang!"[13] bellowed the ship-Deldar. He bustled forward and very shortly thereafter no one laughed at Rukker as he sailed away with his fair treasure shares, and the rest merely rocks.

"When he finds out," said Fazhan, with some glee, "I am wondering if he will summon the calmness to say that he will not speak of this in the future. Ho—it is indeed a great jest."

These men had not been up in the ruins of the Sunset People, they had not witnessed the Beast from Time; I felt glad they had been spared that. But, all the same, I wondered if they'd be quite so merry and carefree this morning had they seen what I had seen.

Rukker's two ships disappeared over the horizon rim and we settled down to the haul to Zandikar.

Toward evening as we began to look out particularly for our expected landfall for the night, a tiny island called the Island of Pliks, the lookout sighted a sail and hallooed down.

We flew red flags.

The vessel, a small coaster, bore a red flag, also.

We made the Island of Pliks together and after all had been seen to in our camp a party from the coaster came across. They were either incautious, brave, or they did not care. Red flags may be flown by anyone in the inner sea.

After we had drunk tea and sat in the light of the moons eating palines, the coaster captain heaved up a sigh and said, "If you sail to Zandikar, dom, you sail to destruction."

"What?" Vax's lean hard face looked exceedingly dangerous in the ruddy fire-glow. "Spit it out!"

The coaster master, a weather-beaten old salt with a massy beard and a face graven by wind and wine, cocked an eye at this highly strung stripling with the wide shoulders and lean powerful look of the fighting-man.

"Be careful they do not spit you out, son, if you venture there."

Duhrra put his steel hand on Vax's arm. The touch seemed to calm the lad. Maybe it was Duhrra's hand, maybe Vax was learning tact and discretion; whatever it was, he said, "I would like to know what passes in Zandikar. There is a girl—"

"Ah," said the master, who called himself Ornol the Waves. "A girl, is it? Well, King Zenno is partial to young girls."

"King Zenno? Who is he? King Zinna reigns in Zandikar."

I listened, as we all listened. This was news.

"King Zinna is dead, slain by the very hand of King Zenno. Since the siege the city is—"

"Siege? Zandikar is under siege?"

The coaster master, Ornol the Waves, flicked a finger of palines into his mouth, and grunted as he chewed, speaking offhandedly. "You are strangely ill-informed, doms."

"We have been faring in the western sea, taking Grodnim devils. Tell us of the siege and of King Zenno."

"As to the siege, there is little to say. That rast, Prince Glycas, sits down before Zandikar and throttles the city."

There rose sounds of disgust and of anger from the ranks of my men, who were red Zairians. This news was bad, very bad.

"And King Zenno, who was a reiver called Starkey the Wersting, slew the old king and with his paktuns took the city and dubbed himself Zenno— out of mockery or politics, it is all one."

Pur Naghan ti Perzefn started up at this. He looked incensed.

"The rast dares to arrogate the 'Z' to himself? No man may take the letter unless he is born with it already, or unless he creates a hyr Jikai. No one!"

Men were calling out, demanding to know more; others were

blaspheming away about Prince Glycas and the Grodnims; others cussing away about the paktuns. I did not smile; but I felt the nudge of amusement that Pur Naghan, a Krozair of Zamu, should feel more concern over a man taking to his name the letter "Z," which as an initial letter is hard come by, hard won, given seldom without a hyr Jikai.

An idle thought occurred to me that the Krozair Bold who had ousted my friend Pur Zenkiren for the position of Grand Archbold, this Pur Kazz, did not proudly own the initial "Z," that he was Pur Kazz and not Pur Zakazz. Well, he had done what he had out of a fanatical belief in his power and authority and in the Krozair-given right to judge. He had judged wrongly, and because of that I was expelled from the Krozairs of Zy, was Apushniad. I had not thought of this matter for some time, and now I rose and shook the black thoughts from me, and went walking quietly in the fuzzy pink moons-light, pondering.

If Zandikar was besieged, would our plans have to change?

There was further information I must have. At the fires Ornol the Waves expatiated on the plight of Zandikar, the city of the Ten Dikars. Prince Glycas had the city in a death-lock. His Grodnim army defeated all who sought to stand against it. It was only a matter of time before he took the city. The Grodnims, led by the overlords of Magdag but drawn from many cities and towns of the northern lands, had leap-frogged once more. They had avoided certain fortress-cities of the southern coast and had landed before Zandikar. They had, in particular, avoided a head-on confrontation with Zy. I could visualize the position with a clarity made all the more awful by the directness of the threat. In this the hand of the genius king Genod was clearly apparent.

Pur Naghan had the gist of it, also.

"I am a Krozair of Zamu!" Here was no time for a strange and mystic reticence, a blanket of aloofness that is usual with Krozairs in non-Krozair company. Here was a time for strong leadership. "Zamu lies a mere twenty-five dwaburs from Zandikar, by the land route. By sea there are many islands and the coast curves strongly in the Nose of Zogo and the way is difficult for an attacker. We must sail to Zamu and join the army that will march to the relief of Zandikar."

Ornol the Waves had finished his palines and was drinking our wine. He swallowed, the wine wet on his lips above the beard, and he said, "I told you. Prince Glycas and his army are invincible. The relief expedition from Zamu is destroyed."

Pur Naghan sagged back, stunned.

The hubbub increased. All now understood the peril.

"The rasts can march from Zandikar and take Zamu. The cities will fall, one after the other. And from Zamu they can march across the base of the peninsula of Fenzerdrin, across the River of Golden Smiles."

"Aye!" shouted others. "And before them lies Holy Sanurkazz itself!"
Holy Sanurkazz!

The sea journey is laborious, and in the name of Zair rightfully so, for in this lies devious protection to Sanurkazz, the chief city and holy place of Zairia. But Prince Glycas and the Grodnims would be marching with their invincible army, securing their rear with Zandikar and Zamu, marching across the base of Fenzerdrin, to attack Holy Sanurkazz from the land.

It was a plan that would work, given the deadly tool with which King Genod would put it into operation.

And—a few dwaburs east of Sanurkazz lay Felteraz, beautiful Felteraz, the home of Mayfwy, the widow of my oar-comrade Zorg. I had done much, I would do much more, to protect Mayfwy.

I stood up and glared upon that ruffianly assembly, all gesticulating and arguing and thumping balled fist into hand, and gradually they looked up at me and fell silent.

"We sail for Zandikar. It is there we can smash the kleeshes of Grodnims. We sail with the dawn."

I walked away. I did not wish anyone to argue, for I would have had to cut him down.

Later I sought out Pur Naghan.

"Yes, Dak, I agree with the plan. I would dearly love to go to Zamu for— But you are right. We must stop them at Zandikar."

"Yes, Pur Naghan."

"You are a hard man. Yet the men follow you. Sometimes I find that strange. I am proud but I am also realistic. I know a man—it is to me the men should look, as an avowed Krozair; but I follow you as willingly as they. It is passing strange."

"If you wish to lead, Pur Naghan, I would not challenge you."

He favored me with a strange, lopsided look.

"I believe you. I do not understand; but I believe. No, Dak, I am content as we are. You are a leader. You have the yrium. As for me—" He moved his right hand in a vague gesture, quite at variance with the man I knew he was. "I am Pur Naghan. I have not yet become Nazhan. I sometimes wonder if I ever will, and the thought of being Pur Zanazhan eludes me."

"Naghan is an ancient and honored name on Kregen." I thought to snap his spine erect. "And in Zandikar, by Zair, you should find deeds worthy to place the 'Z' in your name."

"Aye, Dak," he said, his hand clenching. "Aye!"

It should be remarked here that the Zairians in their use of that truly honorable name of Naghan softened the hated "G" into a "J."

The coaster skipper, Ornol the Waves, had not put into Zandikar. He had picked up trade among the islands as was the custom and was making for Zimuzz. That great fortress-city, home of the Krozairs of Zimuzz, had been bypassed by Prince Glycas. Before we sailed on the next morning one of his men was brought to me by Duhrra. This man bore the short straight bow of the inner sea; but I noted it was somewhat longer than the average, and stouter. He appeared limber and with the bowman's strength of shoulder, and his nut-brown face creased up around his eyes. This was Dolan the Bow, and I knew a man did not achieve that soubriquet unless he had earned it.

"This man, Dolan the Bow, wishes to go with us," said Duhrra.

There was no need for hesitation. I guessed he was a Zandikarese from the bow. "You are very welcome, Dolan."

He smiled. He did not say much. But Seg would have got on with him, I knew that, and it cheered me.

As we pulled steadily past the last headland of the Island of Pliks we saw considerable activity in the coaster's camp.

Dolan the Bow smiled again, his face crinkling up like a crickle nut, brown and rosy and filled with goodness. "Ornol will be disappointed," he said. Then, "I will show you the safe channels into Zandikar. The Grodnims have wrecked many swifters there, Zair be praised."

We bore on along our easterly and four days later we pulled in for our last landfall. Dolan had suggested we should make a long hard night's pulling of it for the final leg, bypassing the usual stopover. I agreed. Swifters' speeds vary and we had the argenters, subject to the fickle vagaries of the winds if we did not tow them, and the journey was long and tiring. The two men we had chosen to skipper the argenters had by now sufficient experience of them to be able to handle them with reasonable confidence. They were bluff sea dogs of the Eye of the World, and they did not mince their words when they accosted me on the quarterdeck of *Crimson Magodont*.

The gist of their argument was that they would be perfectly happy to drive in, in a swifter; but they doubted the capacity of the argenters. I told them they would be towed for the last dangerous part; but they remained somewhat reluctant.

"These argenters will not answer among the islands off Zandikar Bay. And there will be Magdaggian swifters."

"Aye," I said. "There will be. We shall tow you. I shall tow you, Robko, and Pur Naghan will tow you, Mulviko. If we run into Grodnim swifters we may have to cast you off to fight them. I shall expect you to sail in. We will protect you. It is spoken."

They wanted to argue. They saw my face. They did not argue.

As they went over the stern ladder I called to them.

"Be of good cheer. Before the twin suns rise on the morrow we shall be in Zandikar. Then, my friends, the real business will start."

Passing a towing line at night is always a tricky business; but the wind was with us, a fresh westerly, and I wished to conserve the strength of the oarsmen as much as possible. Under the canopy of stars we sailed toward the east and Zandikar and ventured into the waters patrolled by the hostile swifters of Magdag. Occasionally the dark bulk of islands occulted the horizon stars. The Twins rose, revolving eternally one about the other. They bear many and many a name over Kregen; but the Twins is what I call them most of the time. They cast down too much light for our purpose; but Notor Zan was not on duty this fateful night, and we ghosted along with our wind under the stars, with the chuckle of water passing down the side and the creak of wood and the slap of blocks an unheard accompaniment to our progress.

Dolan stood with me on the quarterdeck. When the closer time came he would go forward with the prijikers and signal helm orders from there. I, who had sailed impudently through the waters of the approaches to Brest on the unending duties of blockade, felt the keen zest of a seaman's enthusiasm for a difficult technical task. I had no doubts. We would go through.

The time came for the tow ropes to be passed. The difficult evolution went through without a hitch, save that young Obdinon squashed a finger and cried out and was instantly told to stopper his black-fanged winespout, the silly fambly, and get on with the job.

Following my orders against just such a need, we had saved the hated green flags of the swifters. Colors are seldom flown at nighttime; but I had the green bent on and ready, just in case. The sense of mystery and taut-breathing expectancy held us all as we pulled on, going cautiously across the dark and subtly moving expanse of the sea. Night birds passed above us on wings that sighed and creaked like unoiled hinges. We watched the stars and the black bulks of islands and not an eye closed in any of the five ships.

We turned starboard, to the south, and soon the sweet scent of gregarians on the air told us the fabled gregarian groves of Zandikar drew near. Now all those superb groves would lie under the callous hand of Grodnim. We pulled on.

Deeply into the southern shore bites the Bay of Zandikar. South we rowed, and we watched the horizon for the first hint of a long, low predatory outline to tell us we faced instant action and perilous encounter.

When, as I had half known we must, we saw that lean rakish shape of a Magdaggian swifter, I own I felt a stab of disappointment. Magdaggian swifter captains do not relish night sailing. But Zandikar lay under siege, and Prince Glycas was there, I knew, and mayhap the king, also, waited impatiently in the encirclement for the city's fall. Perhaps Gafard, the King's Striker, was there. I felt no recognizable emotions over an encounter with him. I knew very well—or thought I did—what I was going to do to this genius king Genod when I caught up with him, this insane war genius who had callously murdered my daughter Velia.

"Weng da!" bellowed the challenge across the dark sea.

The pink and golden moonlight misted visibility and made accurate vision tricky. I lifted a speaking trumpet to my lips and shouted back.

"*Strigic of Grodno!* With supplies for the prince."

For a mur or two the silence hung; then the voice from the low quarter-deck of the swifter answered.

"Lahal and Remberee! Grodno go with you."

"And with you. Remberee."

The leem shadow vanished under the moons' shadows and was gone.

Water chuckled from our ram and passed rippling down our sides. The oars rose and fell, rose and fell. We glided on.

"I have sailed to Zandikar before," said Nath the Slinger. "But not by night. But it cannot be too far now. Bolan the Bow guides us well—for an archer."

"I pray Zair," said Fazhan, my ship-Hikdar. "I pray the argenter does not pull the bitts out entire."

"She will not and we will reach the Pharos," I said.

"The lantern will be dark."

"Aye."

A hand ran aft from the forecastle and panted up at us.

"Dolan says three ulms only, Dak."

"Good."

One ulm passed. I swear, although an ulm is about one and a half thousand yards, that ulm seemed to me the full five miles of a dwabur. A shape appeared ahead, athwart our course. One minute the sea shimmered empty in the moons-light; the next the lean, low ram-tipped bulk of a swifter lay there, broadside on, beginning to turn. The water frothed pink from the oars.

The hail, this time, was sharper, harsher.

"Weng da! Heave to! Back water!"

Now the swifter's bronze rostrum swung into line. I yelled back, "*Strigic of Grodno!* Do not make us lose way—we are towing supplies for the prince."

"Orders of the king! Heave to!"

"But—"

*Heave to or we ram!"

Thirteen
"Ram! Ram! Ram!"

"By Zair!" I said, enraged. "The cramph means business." Moons-light shone on the bronze ram of the swifter ahead. She had turned directly into line. Her oars lifted and remained level. Our own wings continued to beat on. Once again the hail reached us, and this time there was no mistaking the violence of the shout, the decision taken on that swifter's quarterdeck.

"Your last chance! Heave to or we smash your oars!"

I said to Fazhan, "Signal *Neemu* to come up. Drop the tow."

"Quidang," he said and was off.

I shouted in a voice pitched just to reach Pugnarses Ob-Eye, our oar-master. "At the signal, Pugnarses. Full speed."

We had a few murs' grace. The swifter ahead, two-banked, fast, designed for patrol and scouting duty, still held her oars leveled. In those few murs we must cast off our tow and hope *Neemu* would be able to retrieve it and continue to haul in the argenter. I turned sharply as Vax said, a little loudly, "Tow rope cast off."

"Now, Pugnarses! Full speed! Use ol' snake!"

We all heard the drumbeat abruptly break, then rattle, and finally settle into a swift and demanding rhythm. The oars thrashed and for a moment I thought they'd lost it, and the rhythm had been broken—and then the blades churned the water all in line, level as though on tracks, and through our feet we felt the forward surge of *Crimson Magodont*, that exhilarating onward bounding like a zorca under a rider careering wildly across the plains.

"Starboard!" I yelled at the helm-Deldars.

The forecastle of the swifter moved out of line with the swifter ahead. I could see in the moons-shimmer her oars quiver and then fall, all together, and in a macabre counterpointing echo to our own I heard her drum rattling out the time.

For a couple of ship-lengths we surged on and then I shouted to the helm-Deldars to bring her back to larboard. *Crimson Magodont* was of that style of swifter short-coupled, chunky, yet still retaining the long, lean lines of a true galley. She could turn on a golden zo-piece. Her starboard bank continued to pull frenziedly and we could hear through the ship noises the sharp sizzling cracking of whips, the shouts of that hateful word, "Grak! Grak!"

The larboard bank dug into the sea. *Crimson Magodont* spun.

Then every oar smashed into the water, the blades churning, and we leaped as a leem leaps.

"Ram! Ram! Ram!"

We took the Grodnim swifter on his larboard bow. We smashed and bashed down a full third of his length. The pandemonium racketed to the starlit sky. I did not think what was going on among the slave benches of the swifter. We spun into the Magdaggian and we wrecked a third of his oar banks and then we eased a fraction to starboard and so ripped away the remaining two thirds before we turned to free our own blades.

The noises from the Magdaggian obliterated the shouts and yells of our men. Those noises spurted hideously against the pink moons' glow. I held my jaw shut and I could feel my teeth punching into my gums, aching.

Arrows arched. The varters let fly. There would be no boarding. The Magdaggian drifted past, wallowing, one entire wing ripped from her. And here came Pur Naghan! Driving on astern of us, flanking our argenter, he bored on with all his oars thrashing. *Pearl* surged ahead, like a living lance. Her rostrum struck the Grodnim swifter full abeam. The rending sounds as bronze sheared through wood racketed out. What they were doing aboard the argenter that *Pearl* towed I could only guess; but she went clear. *Neemu* had the first argenter's tow secured and was going ahead. I stared around in the moon-drenched darkness.

There were no other Magdaggian swifters I could see.

"She's going!" said Vax. He held the hilt of the Krozair longsword and I knew the young devil longed to dive into the fray and use that terrible weapon.

The Magdaggian wallowed lower.

I said, "We cannot abandon the Zairians in her. Take us alongside."

It was madness. It was folly. The arrangements had been that if attacked *Neemu* would take our tow and *Pearl* would continue on. Nothing had been agreed about what to do with any victim of our ram.

Fazhan said, "If there are other rasts of Grodnims abroad, the noise—"

"Aye, Fazhan. We must be quick."

We were quick. I commanded a crew of men who had been Renders, who knew how to raise a swifter's oar-slaves against their masters. We ravened onto the Magdaggians deck. Arrows flew. I saw Dolan the Bow calmly shooting from the forecastle, sending shaft after shaft in a flowing rhythm into the ranks of the Greens clustered to receive us. And from the quarterdeck, Nath the Slinger flung his deadly pebbles and lozenges of lead, trying to match the speed of Dolan. I drew the Ghittawrer blade and led the charge that cleared the foeman's quarterdeck. *Pearl* had ripped a ghastly hole in her side. She'd be gone very quickly.

The slaves were pouring up from below, waving their chains, raving. Many a poor devil had been crushed by his loom, those who had neither the knack nor the knowledge to duck under as the cruel ram smashed down in the diekplus. Our successful diekplus had smashed the first third of the larboard banks; from these benches came very few slaves to join us.

There were plenty of others, though, to join us as we dispatched the Grodnims. The freed slaves leaped joyously onto the deck of *Crimson Magodont* as the Magdaggian swifter sank in a smother of bubbles and breaking timbers.

Neemu and *Pearl,* with their tows, had pulled ahead. We followed. I let the scenes of frantic joy blossom on the gangway and forecastle as we pulled in toward the Pharos of Zandikar. Any man released from slavery at the oars of a swifter from Magdag is entitled to leap and cavort, to shout and bellow, to scream his thanks to Zair.

Many men fell to their knees and banged their heads against the flibre of the deck in utter thankfulness.

I did not tell them, yet, that they were entering a city under siege, that when their bellies hungered they might yearn for the slop and the onions and crusts thrown to them on their oar benches.

Among the sailors of the inner sea the saying runs: "Easier a thorn-ivy bush than the Ten Dikars."

Truly, the maze of channels threading between islands and headlands leading to Zandikar are confusing and treacherous. We had come safely through, thanks to Dolan, and now as we reached a broad calm stretch of water the city rose beyond and patrolling Zandikarese swifters nosed in to attack. Now we did not mind heaving to. The swifters assured themselves we were who we said we were—well, who some of us said we were at the time—and very soon scenes of riotous joy spread from our decks and gangways to the battlements and quays and streets of the city itself. Torches burst into flame as hundreds of emaciated people flooded down to the quayside. I frowned.

"Fazhan—anchor out in the center of the harbor."

He nodded. If that lot of crazed and starving people sought to board we'd be done for. Now the mergem carried in the argenter proved of inestimable value. The ship carried enough to supply Zandikar's normal population for a season, possibly; the war and the siege had wasted away at the people; they would not starve now. As well, the chipalines would prove of great value, and the corps of crossbowmen welcomed the bolts. I told my men to let the provender go freely into the town. No one could argue over that. If it flushed out rasts, I would be happy.

The Todalpheme who lived in a small stone house by the Pharos came aboard and were fervent in their thanks. These wise men who monitor the tides are protected by protocol and taboo from any harm from another man. They were indignant that in the siege Prince Glycas had starved them, too. We gave them mergem and sent them away, praising Zair, although I was coming around to a belief that the Todalpheme of Kregen worshiped no gods that other men worshiped.

The rasts were duly smoked out.

They came aboard on the following morning as the business of unloading went on. Fazhan and Pur Naghan had organized well. Boats pulled to the shore loaded with sacks of mergem. On the shore my men and the harbor crossbowmen formed a hollow space with the crowds pressing outside, shouting and screaming and raising a dust and tearing their clothes—but all with joy upon their faces. The sacks were handed out. All who asked were supplied. Any boats approaching the argenter were kept off with pointed bows. I knew that everyone of besieged Zandikar would eat well this night, even if it was only mergem, and no one would starve.

The rasts came aboard, having shouted their own importance, and strode across my quarterdeck.

I looked at them. Oh, yes, they were familiar faces, their bearing was familiar, their manner of talk. I did not know one of them; but I knew what they were. I had met in my career on Kregen aragorn, slave-masters, overlords, great nobles, masters of the arena, Manhunters—in them there glowed the same self-satisfied and preening knowledge of self-importance.

Their leader, a Ztrom,[14] flashily attired, adorned with many gems and much gold lace, carrying a Krozair longsword, marched up and I noticed how his right hand crossed his body among the ruffles of gold lace to rest on the hilt of the longsword. There was no doubt in my mind he could use the weapon, gold lace or no damned gold lace. His face, as I have indicated, showed quite clearly he was for Cottmer's Caverns when he was at last put where he belonged. I own I am intemperate in these matters.

"You are the master of this vessel?"

"Aye."

"You address me as *jernu*. We shall take over now."

A commotion began on the quay. Armed men, mail clad, bearing swords, were beating the crowds away. They were not overlords of Magdag; but from their demeanor and behavior they might just as well have been.

There were six of them on the deck, and in their boat alongside waited a dozen more with the oarsmen. I turned back as the Ztrom snarled—very adept at snarling are these people, the high and mighty of the land—and drew that great sword. The blade flamed before my eyes.

"Cramph! Answer when I speak to you!"

I said, "If you do not send your men away, you are a dead man." I did not draw my sword.

He gaped. He just did not believe his own two ears.

"Rast! I am Ztrom Nalgre ti Zharan, the king's councillor! All Zandikar does my bidding."

He swung about to order his five men. He stopped, abruptly, as a foolish ponsho stops when it butts its head against the wall. A dozen archers, and chief among them Bolan the Bow, drew their shafts back and held their glittering points upon the five.

I said, very gently, "Secure them all. Bind them well. You, so-called Ztrom Nalgre, I do not believe are a Ztrom at all. You are a jumped-up devil, a sewer-rat, a cramph who steals food from starving people."

He struck then.

I slid the blow, stepped forward, and drove my fist into his belly. As he fell I took the sword away. One thing was for sure, he was no Krozair.

He retched on the deck. I stirred him with my toe. "Him, too." Over the side the men in the boat were shouting. I walked calmly to the bulwark by the quarterdeck varter. A rock rested in its beckets, like a shot garland, ready. I leaned over and shouted.

"Go back to your cramph of a king and tell him if he touches the food for the people, his Ztrom Nalgre ti Zharan will be hanged in the sight of all. Schtump!"

One of the fools loosed a shaft. I moved my head. The arrow flew past. They just did not believe anyone would cross them, deny their wishes. They had to be shown, and shown quickly. I lifted the rock over my head in both hands, bent back, and then catapulted forward. It was a nice little throw. It took the bottom out of their damned boat.

The next second they were in the water all caterwauling and yelling. We threw ropes down to them and hauled them out and ran them down to the lock-up, a tiny brig that soon filled, and so we had to chain them down on the gangway of the thalamite tier. Some of the oarsmen swam for the quay. I bellowed my words after them. But so far, not so good. I had not done enough.

"No more sacks ashore, Fazhan—tell the argenter."

Very soon thereafter the crowds dispersed. The mail-clad riders dismounted and stood watching us. They were mostly apim, although a few Rapas and Fristles were in evidence. The walls of the city here along the shore remained firm, at the least. Those walls, all of a grayish-white stone, gleamed under the suns. The jumbled red roofs of the city, the spires and towers, clustered behind those walls. I could not see the farther walls inland; but that was where the siege was going on. If this newly appointed king did not make haste my own patience would be gone. I had not come here to act as a Palinter, important though that was.

Pur Naghan had himself rowed across and came up onto my quarterdeck looking somewhat perturbed. I reassured him.

"Normally a central rationing point is essential. But we have so much mergem that is not necessary. We must get the people and the warriors fed and back in health and heart again. I must get up to the walls."

"This king will not take kindly to you."

"I've already taken unkindly toward him."

"Aye," said Pur Naghan, who was a man not averse to a hearty chuckle, like any Zairian. "I had noticed."

Presently a party of sectrixmen cantered down to the jetty and there was a deal of flag-waving and shortly thereafter a fat and sweaty Pallan was rowed out to us. He stood on the quarterdeck, panting, patting his face with a lace kerchief—prepared to be nasty, as I saw, or prepared to be reasonable, as I hoped.

"The king bids you attend him in his palace at once."

"Does he not inquire if Ztrom Nalgre is dead or alive?"

"Let us not be hasty—give me your name and style and we may talk."

This fellow's robes, although originally of red, were so smothered in gold and silver and chains and tassels as to make of him a tapestried object of ridicule. He wore a wide flat red cap, much folded, sporting feathers secured by a gold buckle. He stood and I let him stand. His pouched eyes rolled in search of a chair.

"You are the visitor in my ship. It is for you to open the pappattu."

His fat and greasy face regarded me and I saw something there I had not expected. He made a small bow.

"I am Nath Zavarin, Battle Pallan to his most exalted and puissant majister, King Zenno, on whom—"

"Yes," I said with coarse rudeness. "I suppose like any jumped-up paktun he adorns himself with titles." I own I knew I smiled away inside my skull like any fambly—me, Dray Prescot, badgering on about amassing titles! But there are ways and ways. I had decided what to say. "I am Dak of Zairia."

That said all and said nothing, and this Zavarin knew it.

"Do you think, Captain Dak, I might sit down? I am not as agile as once I was, and my stomach makes inordinate demands on my ib, demands I own I fail more often than not."

"You will oblige me by stepping into my cabin, where I have a wine I would value your opinion of, Pallan Zavarin."

Again he cocked those poached-egg eyes at me. He nodded. So we went into my cabin and he tasted the wine and pronounced it better than the muck they were forced to drink since all the best had been consumed and that cramph prince Glycas sat down before their walls. He had seen that a period of bargaining lay ahead. As to the idiot Ztrom Nalgre ti Zharan, well, Zavarin said, the king valued him as a fighting-man. That was all.

"And you?"

He smiled and drank, wiping his plump and shining purple mouth most prettily. I had expected to have to browbeat the messenger from the king. That I was not doing so pleased me.

"I served King Zinna long and faithfully. I know Zandikar. The treasury—" Here he shrugged in a way more French than I cared for. "The king holds that with his own key. His paktuns took the important offices after Zinna was murdered—I mean, after King Zenno ascended the Roo[15] Throne. And for me—" Here he turned his lace-ruffled wrist meaningfully. "I know much of Zandikar. I am Battle Pallan, and thankful for it."

I knew what he meant. Battle Pallan is a somewhat lurid way of saying Secretary of War, or War Minister. I imagined Nath Zavarin had not willingly wielded a sword in earnest for many a long season. King Zenno had him under his thumb, and could draw on his knowledge of the city's ways, and, confirming my judgment, Zavarin said he personally enjoyed much popular support.

"The people must be fed," I said. "That is the first concern. The king's men have interfered with that."

"I agree. But the king holds all food under his hand."

"I agree that to be a sound method. We have mergem and to spare. I do not wish the king to charge money for my food."

'The king will do what the king wishes."

"And you remember King Zinna?"

He drank again, and I saw he did so to stop himself from speaking what boiled in his brain. He was very frightened. That was clear, yet he put a bold front on it, this fat ridiculous man.

To divert that line of talk, he swallowed and said, "I am fat. I have always been fat. It is a misfortune. In time of siege it can be fatal."

"Yes. I can see that."

"The king commanded me to bring you to his palace."

"Did he not stop to think why his onker of a Ztrom had not done so?"

This fat Pallan looked at me, searchingly, and made a face, and said, "The king did not expect him to. Ztrom Nalgre was under instructions to slay you and take all the food."

"I am not surprised."

"You are a strange man. There is artillery on the walls. They could sink your ships."

"Seawater and mergem can be mixed. I do not recommend it."

The sweat shone on the immense rounded surfaces of his cheeks. He wiped his brow again, taking the red hat off and laying it upon the table. His fear had ebbed a little and puzzlement was beginning to replace the terror and revive his natural instincts. A political, this man. To my own vast surprise I found I was quite taking to him, fat and all.

"Now that King Zenno rules in Zandikar," I said, "and the people live under his hand, you must be proud that you assisted him to ascend the Roo Throne. I could understand that."

He sucked in his breath, making all his chins wobble and his cheeks abruptly hollow. "I did not strike a blow or instigate one scheme against Zinna!"

"Ah!" I said.

He glared at me. "You are a cunning rogue, Dak of Nowhere. I cannot open my heart to you. Suppose Zenno uses his arts of torment upon you?"

I ignored that unwholesome thought and put questions to him about the siege and the state of the city. The Grodnims had put in three major set-piece assaults and had been beaten off, each time with increasing difficulty. The food we had brought would put heart and strength into the soldiery. Yes, said Zavarin, the soldiers were loyal, for they fought for the city. As for Zenno and his pack of hangers-on, they made hay while the sun shone. Paktuns, employed to fight for hire, they had seized the throne and now lolled about in comfort. It was all one to them. The siege went on apace, for they wished to appear to keep faith with the city. In the paktun philosophy of living in the immediate present, they took what they could and let tomorrow take care of itself. "But—" said Zavarin, and paused, sweating.

I finished it for him. "But this cramph Zenno—or Starkey the Wersting—will strike a bargain. As soon as he feels safe from the anger of the people, or as soon as they are beaten down enough, he will parley with Glycas, and open the gates. Yes, it all fits."

Anyone of the city—citizen, sailor, soldier, refugee farmer—who attempted to object to Zenno was mercilessly put down by the mail-clad riders. A siege existed outside the walls, and a reign of terror swept everyone within.

I felt this conversation had not gone far enough. From my first vague stirrings of schemes I had now reached certain conclusions. They seem obvious enough now. But this was like wading through a marsh by the light of Drig's Lanterns, every step treacherous. This Nath Zavarin caught my drift at once when I said, "How many men has Zenno in his pocket? His paktuns?"

"You must understand, I am no party to anything. My concern is for Zandikar."

"I do not blame you if you do not trust me."

"You are unknown. You arrive with five ships and food, you chain up the king's councillor, you utter threats, you do not treat the King's Pallan with deference—not that I am concerned over that. You act as though you were a king yourself, or a Krozair."

"A Krozair of Zamu commands one of my vessels."

His puffy lips let his little gasp past with a plop.

He recovered himself. "We of Zandikar are famous for our archers, our gregarians, the difficulty of finding the open channels, and for the songs made by King Zonar five hundred seasons ago. Although I daresay it was the king's minstrel, in truth, who composed them. But—we have no Red Brotherhood. I have often desired an Order of Crimson Chivalry. I love Zandikar."

Before I could speak, for I own this fat and no longer ridiculous man's words affected me, Duhrra burst in. I swung about in the chair prepared to be nasty to him; I saw his face and with a flung word to Zavarin walked quickly into the side cabin with Duhrra. He was excited and annoyed, twitching his steel hand.

"Master! Duh—I do not know—"

"Spit it out!"

"It is Vax! The young onker! He dived over the side and has swum to the city. We saw him, running past the ship sheds into Zandikar."

Fourteen
Of a conspiracy and of Queen Miam

The news appalled me.

"The young rip said he wanted to come here because of a girl, master. I did not think— But we are anchored here, doing nothing."

"We do a great deal, Duhrra. But this makes me think I must do a great deal more."

"Aye, master." He did not know Vax was my son, Jaidur of Valka, Prince of Vallia. But I was sure he guessed that there was something more in my feelings for the rascal Vax than he could fathom out.

I went back to Zavarin. He saw instantly my changed demeanor. I did not beat about the bush.

"I do not suppose I could bribe you, Zavarin. I would try if I thought I could. I do not do so. That is not because I do not wish to insult you, but because I recognize your integrity. I tell you, Battle Pallan, the Grodnims will not be cheaply allowed to walk into Zandikar. There is more at stake here than the foul lives of a bunch of miserable foresworn paktuns. If this Zenno has to die, then he will die, and none to mourn him. Go back and tell him what you will. But add that if he makes a pact with Glycas and opens the gates, he will surely be hanged and drawn and quartered. This is not a threat. It is a statement of fact."

He rose, somewhat unsteadily, and groped for his hat.

"I will tell him what I think politic, Dak, as you know. I think I shall embroider a little. By Zair! I think I shall enjoy something for the first time since— Well, he will be working himself into a rage. I must go. I thank you for the wine."

"Take a few bottles with you. See my Palinter. I have work to do—and when I call on you, Nath Zavarin, I shall expect a prompt and purposeful answer."

"Aye, Dak of Nowhere. I think you will."

The crafty old devil went out. He didn't commit himself. In his position, of course, no man would.

The suns beat down on deck with soothing warmth. The day would be fine. Men worked about the ship and some slaves had been released to haul up buckets of seawater and hurl them down over their fellow-sufferers on the oar tiers. Everything appeared normal, for Fazhan ran a taut ship. I looked at the four other vessels and saw nothing that appeared amiss. Well, I was going to alter all that. I shouted at Zavarin as he walked along the gangway bearing two bottles clasped to his pudgy chest.

"Wait a moment, Zavarin." To Duhrra I said, "Bring out that fine golden mixing bowl we took from that Grodnim broad ship—the one with a captain like a vosk."

"He pulls with the thalamites now," said Duhrra, and ran back to the treasure storehouse by my cabin. When he reappeared the golden krater winked and gleamed magnificently under the suns. I held it out to Zavarin.

"Give this to the king with my compliments. Your man will handle it with care, for it is of great value. Tell him we can discuss the disposal of the mergem as soon as he wishes."

Zavarin's jaw did not drop. But he looked at me as though I had been stricken with lunacy before his eyes.

"I do not understand, Dak."

"There are reasons. Three hundred, you said? A fair force to keep order."

He shuffled his feet as his men took the wine and the krater away to his boat. He lifted that bulbous face of his and looked at me straight. In a low voice, he said, "We have had news, secret and sure, that Prince Glycas intends a fresh assault on the day after tomorrow. We have spies. The day will be hard for the soldiers. That might be a time of opportunity."

I said, "I cannot wait all that long."

He looked bewildered.

Then, "The people believe Zenno, for I have told them he is the true king, after Zinna. This I was forced to do. They will fight well against the cramphs of Grodnim."

'They had best do so, for the sake of Zair. Take this fool Ztrom Nalgre with you, him and his men. I do not want them fouling my ship."

By the time the Ztrom and his party were over the side, and Zavarin with much wheezing and puffing had been manipulated down the ladder and into his boat, I had prepared. Dolan the Bow had said, simply, that he would follow me. He knew Zandikar. It was his home. Duhrra and Nath the Slinger would not be dissuaded. So I told Fazhan to take over. He would consult with Pur Naghan and the other skippers. They were to do nothing until they heard from me. With that the four of us went down into a boat with half a dozen sacks of mergem and pulled gently across to an inconspicuous wharf that Dolan said was used to ship in animals' intestines used in tanning.

411

The city appeared to slumber in the warmth. The gray-white stone and the red roofs glittered with a soft brightness, many points of light combining into a brilliant yet gentle haze. Towers and domes floated over the golden mist of colored rooftops. On one of the arms of land embracing the outer harbor the massy pile of the seaward fortress, the Helmet of Buzro, glowered down, and yet for all its vastness and grimness appearing only a fairy-story castle, flaunting its red banners against the blue radiant sky.

"He said she lived in a place called the Ivory Pavilion," said Duhrra. "And her name is Miam."

"The Ivory Pavilion," said Dolan as the boat touched the stones and I leaped out. "Yes, I know it. A palace on a hill, grand and beautiful. Of course, I have never been inside."

"You will today," I said.

I felt the hurt in me. My son could tell these things to Duhrra, who was his oar-comrade, things he had not cared to tell me. Why should he? I was a comrade and his captain. Had he known I was his father he'd no doubt have told me with a sword.

We had been through adventures together and I knew, from what Duhrra told me, that Vax regarded me as a good captain and a good warrior. He had, so Duhrra said, a high regard for me and my prowess. As to affection, that remained an imponderable. Duhrra suggested that Vax went in some awe of me, which thought I heartily disliked. Yet he copied my ways, I knew, and that must mean something.

The look Nath Zavarin had given me as I lifted and handed the golden krater across had apprised me that he recognized my strength. Duhrra had strained a trifle to lift the golden mixing bowl. Perhaps Vax merely envied my strength. Well, if he was his father's son he'd inherit that, particularly after his stint as an oar-slave. I tried not to think of Delia, for I had harsh and unpleasant duties to perform. The little girl we had taken from the sacrifice to the Beast of Time remained fast shut in the ship, a source of temptation to lecherous sailormen. I had barely spoken to her, save to learn her name was Lena, and that she came from a dusty and forgotten little village called Fairmont and that she was truly a virgin and thus fit for the sacrifice. I had told her that so long as she remained in my care she would preserve her virginity. She was illiterate, as so many poor folk are on Kregen, and was dizzied by her experiences, having been snatched away from home and stripped and loaded with gold and gems and lashed to a sacrificial stone block.

I must think only of the fate of my son Vax. The streets and alleys of Zandikar wound and wended in the usual haphazard way of most Zairian cities. Dolan led on, carrying one sack of mergem. Duhrra and I carried two each, and Nath the last. The houses showed evidence of the siege, many having been pulled down to provide stones for the catapults and varters.

A dim murmur like bees in summer rose from the inland walls where the siege went on. Nothing much would happen until the onslaught of the day after tomorrow. The suns burned down and we padded swiftly along the cobbles, mounting between tall gray-white walls to the hill on which stood the Ivory Pavilion.

No one paid us much attention. We looked desperate enough, Zair knows, and the mergem we had earlier landed was now being mixed and cooked and eaten.

Parties of soldiers were rarely to be seen; they would be moving between their billets and the walls. A fire began past the hill and we could see only the ugly waft of black smoke.

Presently, panting, Dolan said, "The gate ahead."

A long gray-white wall flanked the top of the hill. Much vegetation grew beyond, and flowers depended over the walls. The gate was barred by iron, and inside a man carrying a spear stood guard. To him I said: "Llahal, dom. We have food. Let us in."

"Who are you?" He squinted, and turned his head in the bronze helmet from side to side to get us in his sights.

"Friends of the lady Miam."

He sniffed at this; but Duhrra let his two sacks down and extended his left hand with a golden zo-piece glittering on his palm. "We come in friendship with food. Do you think your mistress would be pleased if you sent us away?"

"You are from the king?"

Duhrra opened his mouth and I said, harshly, "No. Open up."

As I had chanced the throw, so that remark reassured him and the iron gate swung open. We were escorted by three guards, men who all looked unfit for fighting on the walls, up to the palace. Whatever happened, I was prepared to wait until I saw Vax. What happened then would depend on how he had fared.

A considerable bustle had just subsided as we entered the porticoed way and marched into the antechamber. The place was a palace right enough, with quantities of marble and statuary, a fine balcony, tall windows, and with intricate mosaic pavements cool beneath the feet. I dumped my mergem down as a tall, elegant middle-aged man stepped toward us. He bore the stamp of authority; but he bore it as though he understood the responsibilities as well as the perquisites of power. His robes were of white, dazzlingly clean, trimmed with red, and at his side he bore a scabbarded, golden-hilted sword of the solaik variety.[16] He looked to be a man I could talk to.

He said, "What do you here? We have naught left—"

I said, "I have brought food for the lady Miam. I would like to see her. I am Dak. There is not much time."

413

He bristled; but he was intrigued. At his side a shadow moved and a man stepped out. He was a dwarf. He had a finely shaped head; his body was stunted but strong. He held a crossbow and the quarrel centered on my heart. His clothes were an incongruous mixture of reds and golds and mail.

I looked at him. I did not smile. He was deadly.

"No one comes here for the lady Miam without a ready explanation."

"Send for her and you will have your explanation."

He hesitated and the dwarf cocked an eye up at him.

"You say you have food for her? You are from the ships in the outer harbor?"

"Yes and yes. Now—whoever you are—send for the lady Miam, or I shall have to penetrate the women's quarters myself."

A nasty scene was spared by the entrance of the lady herself.

I have seen many beautiful women. I have seen many women lovely in the sight of men. There have never been any women to match in beauty my Delia—and, at this time, my dear dead Velia—yet this Miam bore herself with beauty and with demureness, her color high, her long braided brown hair glowing in the lights through the tall windows. Her white dress moved over her bosom with an agitation I did not connect with my arrival. The young devil! Mind you, I was wrong...

"I am here, Uncle—if this fierce warrior is Dak—"

"He is, niece."

"Then all is well. I have had news—such strange news—that Zeg wishes to be remembered to me. That is all."

I gaped. Zeg! Zeg was the Krozair name my son Segnik had taken, and he would fight anyone who added the "nik" to his name. I looked at Miam and I burst out—I, cunning, canny, cynical old Dray Prescot—I burst out like any callow youth, "But I thought it was Vax—"

She laughed. The tinkling, refreshing, superbly rational sound drove all the cobwebs away. Naught of evil could live in the sound of that laugh.

"Vax brings me news of his brother and assures himself I am safe. He does not love me."

"In that, my lady Miam," said Vax's voice as he stepped into the room, "you wound me sore. You do me an injustice."

"Oh, yes, Vax, I know! But you know what I mean."

"I do." He looked at me and had the grace to look suddenly confused and to look away sharply.

I said, "If you do anything stupid like this again, I'll tan your backside myself."

He bridled. His hand whipped to his sword—to that superb Krozair brand I had given him. His lips pouted into a sullen droop, and his head snapped erect, his eyes glaring.

"Do not think I would not, Vax, for all you are a great warrior now. Anyway, you did not think to bring any food for your friends."

"Come, come," said this Miam's uncle, spreading his arms. "It seems we are all friends here. Let us have no more unpleasantness." He turned to me. "Lahal, Dak. I am Janri Zunderhan, Roz of Thoth Zeresh. We have no wine fit to drink to offer; but we have a little tea left."

"Tea is better than wine any day. I will have supplies brought up from my ships. I thank you for your hospitality. Lahal, Roz Janri."

He looked quite pleased, no doubt expecting some uncouth paktunlike remark. We all went into an inner room and soon the confusion was sorted out. This lady Miam was the great-granddaughter of the dead king Zinna. She hadn't even been a gleam in her father's eye when last I'd been in the Eye of the World. She and Zeg, I gathered, had more or less decided to set up house together. He was off corsairing on the inner sea and she was shut up here under siege. I had an idea Zeg didn't know that. And here was I, sitting with one son and talking about another son, and denied all the heartburning words I longed to speak!

I turned the conversation the way I wanted it to go and learned that Nath Zavarin was regarded not as a fat fool, or even a fat hulu, but as a man desirous of serving his city who was being forced into bad company and bad ways. He was regarded as being clever to have avoided being chopped by Starkey the Wersting. They had a finicky disability over calling Starkey King Zenno in this household. Miam could prove an embarrassment to the new king and she was being kept very quiet indeed. All the fit men were off fighting on the walls; but Roz Janri indicated that all here would fight to the death for the lady Miam and himself. Her relations were all dead, as were his. They had found good comradeship in each other's company.

The dwarf, Roko, bustled about bossing the serving wenches, waddling along on his big flat feet, a cheery, cheeky little man, a man to be reckoned with. I thought the back of his neck must ache with the continual looking up he must do. Still, I supposed he was used to it.

It is not necessary for me to go into every tiny detail of my movements over the rest of that day, or of the plans I formulated almost bur by bur. Everything fell into place with an ease I would have regarded with great suspicion had the circumstances been other than they were. I wondered—true—if the veiled hand of Zena Iztar could be found in this. She could well be manipulating events. Zair knew, she, like the Star Lords, had power enough.

The upshot was that, as the Suns of Scorpio sank in floods of fire and the first stars began to shine out, my sea-leems quit the ships in silence, their weapons muffled. The very first star of Kregen was a huge blue fat beauty, shining with a calm refulgence, extraordinarily bright at this time of the approach of orbits. This is the planet Kregans call Soothe. Soothe is one of the more famous Goddesses of Love, and her voluptuous representation is found all over Kregen, in apim or numin, sylvie or Fristle form, in any of the shapes of females most admired by lecherous men. Soothe and Venus—if this was mere coincidence, I did not know.

So, under the fat blue gleam of Soothe, and with the first of the hurtling moons skating low over the city, we rowed ashore. Everything went as Roz Janri and Nath Zavarin had promised.

The paktuns, once they had overcome their initial astonishment, fought well. But there could be no time for finesse. They must be subjugated as fast as possible. In the event as we roared into the Palace of Fragrant Incense— and trust the Zandikarese to call a palace that was a fortress by a pretty name like that!—and drove the paktuns yelling before us, we overcame their last resistance and still over a hundred yet lived.

Starkey the Wersting, who called himself King Zenno, was bundled out of bed and the sylvie with him fled, shrieking in her nakedness. We showed him a bloodstained blade and he was very agreeable to do our bidding. I say *our*, for Vax and Dolan and little Roko were most active in this coup.

Nath Zavarin came a-running and panting in his slippers, pulling on a grave black hat of judgment, gasping with the effort of hauling his bulk into the High Hall of the palace. Torches lit the scene. Roz Janri and his people were there. The paktuns, disarmed, stood under guard along the side to watch. The scene held the starkness of midnight drama, when men are tumbled out of beds, and heads roll, and the fortunes of crowns and cities change hands.

I said to King Zenno, "You may stay as Starkey the Wersting and fight for us for hire. You may take a boat and seek to escape with such of your men as will go with you. You may not communicate with Prince Glycas." He glared at me—this sharp-faced, vicious rast of a fellow—hardly crediting what had hit him. "Or, of course," I said, offhandedly, "if you wish you can be killed, here and now."

"I would dislike that," said Roz Janri. "Yet it might be the most sensible course."

"I am not a man of blood," I said. I saw Vax and the little smile on his face, and through the sudden chill that smote me, I struggled on. Truth to tell, that knowing little smile on my son's face made up my mind for me. "You will sail in a boat. Tonight," I had to add, out of shame or out of a desire to convince Vax I did not know. "I am not a man of blood; but I am not averse to spilling kleesh blood. You have an abundance of that, Starkey."

"May Zagri rot your eyes and liver!" this King Zenno that was burst out, raving. He spit, choking, demented. "May Zagri cave in your chest and soften your sinews, and—" He would have gone on, for Zagri is a most powerful demon and well-called on in times of stress and cursing. Vax stepped up and rapped the fellow on the nose enough to tap his claret, and said words in the ex-king's ear that hauled him up all standing.

"If you say another word, cramph, I shall pull your vile tongue out by the roots."

Everyone there in the High Hall knew that this young tearaway, Vax Neemusbane, meant what he said.

And this was my son.

Just about then strong parties of soldiers from the walls rushed in, demanding to know if the Grodnims had struck here. I realized they had a good reason to suspect the possibility that attack could reach the city-center, and I filed the information away. With a great yell I jumped up—most blasphemously—onto the Roo Throne. The throne is called this because the city is protected by the Ten Dikars, and the throne is the eleventh to guard all. Had Kregen possessed in addition to its seven moons and two suns one more heavenly body, then on the nights of blackness it would not be Notor Zan which rose but Notor Roo.

"Listen to me, soldiers!" I bellowed in my old sailorman's voice. "The usurping dog of a paktun is thrown down! The true lineage is preserved. Queen Miam rules now in Zandikar! She will lead us all to victory against the Zair-forsaken Grodnims!"

The expected outburst of cheering broke against the high ceiling rafters. If it was grossly unfair to saddle a young girl with such onerous responsibility, I can plead only that I was in a hurry and that, anyway, she was the great-granddaughter of a king and must therefore expect to be thrust forward into positions of power and peril.

"Queen Miam, the true daughter of Zandikar, leads us on to victory!" I glared down on them as they waved their swords on high. Zair knows, I have stared down on mighty warriors waving their swords and shouting the "Hai Jikai!" often enough. But, this time, they were not shouting for me. I rather liked that. "Glycas and his Green cramphs will never take the city! We have food! We have strong arms! And we have a queen! Every man will do his duty for her sake." Then I bashed it out just as in the old days, the old vicious intemperate Dray Prescot bawling his head off to a ravening pack of fighting-men. "And if any man seeks to cower away and fail the queen I'll have his entrails out for varter springs!"

They howled at this, indignant at any suggestion impugning their honor. I quieted them down and told them to pass the word to their comrades on the walls. I mentioned that we had brought food into the city more than once, just to keep the notion fresh in their minds.

The scenes of wild enthusiasm persisted as individual warriors, convinced that they were orators, shouted their own promises of valor and what they would do to the Grodnims. Later in a small inner sanctum we conspirators met. The ex-king Zenno and those men of his who wished to go with him had been taken down and stuffed into a small boat, to be dispatched. I did not think he would seek to join Glycas. Glycas, the mean cramph, would probably hand him over to his tormentors for failing his plans.

In the small room with the lamps burning nastily with cheap mineral oil, for all the samphron oil was long since used, Miam said to me, "I do not know if I should thank you or hate you."

"Many people hate me, Miam. And a few thank me. You must make up your own mind."

Vax bristled; but he was really coming to know my ways, and understood I spoke like this to make the girl see reality.

I bore down the other speakers. We had a great deal to do and precious little time in which to do it. I gave orders. Oh, yes, I gave orders. At first there was opposition, then reluctance, finally acceptance, and, at the end, enthusiasm. I felt the trace of tiredness. But tiredness is a sin, especially when there is a queen to make safe on her throne and a city to save—quite apart from all my own concerns, by Vox!

Early the next day I rode one of Roz Janri's sectrixes on a circuit of the walls. They had stood up to the bombardment very well. The besieging army dug their trenches close and closer. Areas of tents covered the ground where the gregarian groves had been ruthlessly cut down. Smoke lifted from many cooking fires. The infantry out there dug and sweated and the cavalry trotted about looking magnificent. There was no chance of the solid phalanx in this siege. Or, so the Grodnims would think, not until the final breach had been made. Then the cavalry on which they doted would charge in and the mercenary warriors earn their hire. I studied everything carefully. I had had a few burs' sleep; tonight I would sleep longer. Now there was work to do.

At a spot in the inland walls where the cracks looked ominously gaping and the wall had been hastily repaired, I stopped.

"Here, Roz Janri," I said. "This is the breach. Here they will break in. This is the spot."

Fifteen
The Siege of Zandikar: I
A Savapim holds the gate

Everyone who could be spared worked. We had the oar-slaves up out of the swifters and set them to hauling stones. I took pains to make sure houses of architectural merit were not knocked down; but we took ruthlessly all the stone we needed. What I proposed was no new thing; but if the Grodnims persisted in their high-handed arrogant ways it was a winner. Or so I hoped. I will not go into every detail of the Siege of Zandikar. A great song was made, later, and in it, among a wealth of stirring anecdote and much Jikai, the part of Dak is mentioned with some frequency. But, so are the names of all my comrades who labored with me.

If the stunning ease with which we had disposed of King Zenno indicated to me that Zena Iztar had taken a hand, I did not think she gave overt assistance during the stages of the siege itself. Sieges are fascinating. They are also quite horrible. The horror detracts, for my part, from the fascination.

On this day, the day before we expected the next grand assault, an event occurred that made me once again revile the ethics of some paktuns, and to realize afresh that other and greater forces invested effort in this siege, despite the aloofness of Zena Iztar.

Some seventy or so paktuns had elected to stay and fight with us, acknowledging the sovereignty of Queen Miam. Her coronation would have to wait, as Queen Thyllis had waited for hers in distant Hamal. I had ridden over to see how the work on the new wall progressed—as I say, the plan was simple—when a rider flogging his sectrix roared up and screamed of an attack on the western wall. We all turned at once and spurred to the point threatened.

When I say all I mean the officers and staff with me and the escort; not the workers. Also, I bellowed at a likely Jiktar who seemed a smart man, to go personally to the eastern wall and check that the attack on the west was no feint.

We arrived at a scene of dust being kicked up as men battled in the open space between the houses and the walls. The Grodnims had scaled the walls and dropped down, howling in triumph, intending to reach the nearest gate and fling it wide to their waiting cavalry. A Hikdar, one ear missing and his helmet a blaze of blood, husked out that some of the paktuns on duty here on the walls had betrayed their post. It had been concerted. The Grodnims would have dropped down and opened the gate. But, said the Hikdar, a warrior appeared and halted them in time for reinforcements to come up and engage them. I looked at the fight, and my anger against the treacherous paktuns was overlaid by conjectures. Surely, I thought, surely I shall see a man who, although I will not recognize him, I will know?

With wild and savage shouts the men with me drove in on the fight. The dust smoked higher. Men on the walls were shooting outward, and I knew they were keeping back the cavalry out there, which were impatient to spur in through the gate they expected to open at any moment. Shrill shrieks rent the air. Dust and blood cloyed on the tongue. Then I was in among the melee and slicing down with my Ghittawrer brand at a red-faced fellow trying to degut my sectrix. With him disposed of, I was faced with others trying to reach the inner gateway. We smashed and bashed around in the dust for a space, working them in to the wall and finally ringing them and so disposing of them. They were of the Green.

When it was all over I mounted to the wall and looked out.

A mass of infantry was drawn up in impeccable formation out of varter shot. Cavalry moved impatiently between, the green pennons flying, the glitter of their war harness brave under the suns. Back and forth they cantered, their swords breaking the light into fragments of radiance, back and forth. But the gate would not open for them this day.

"Bring me the warrior who stemmed the first attack."

"Quidang!"

He was brought. I stood on the ramparts of the wall and looked at him. Yes, I did not know him; but I knew him.

He wore mail, which altered his appearance; but over that he wore russet hunting leathers, and leather harness, and a short red cape descended from his shoulders—just to be on the safe side, I assumed. He wore a helmet over his coif. His face was hard, dedicated, filled with the knowledge that had been denied me.

I did not say, "Happy Swinging, dom." I wished to preserve my anonymity here. I said, instead, "You wear a strange sword, dom." I held out my hand.

He was a proud, fine upstanding young man, as they all are. I heard him say something, half under his breath. He spoke in English. "They warned me," he said, half complaining, half rueful. "They are barbarians. But this fellow—not even a thank you."

I held out my hand and I did not move a muscle of my face.

He let me take the sword. Again I held in my grip a real Savanti sword. Oh, well, it is a long time ago, now, and we were in the middle of a siege and I was in dire trouble with just about everyone except the new comrades with me in the siege. I held the sword and felt that marvelous grip and the subtle cunning of the blade, the balance, the sensuous feel of it, and abruptly I thrust it back at the Savapim.

"You have our deepest thanks for your assistance. The gate would have been lost but for you."

He looked at me oddly.

"You do not ask me where I come from?" He, also, had swallowed one of those magically scientific genetic pills and so could converse in languages. He spoke well and forthrightly.

"No." I eyed him severely. "Do you intend to stay to fight at our side in this siege?"

"Who are you? You speak as though—but, no... Who are you?"

"I am Dak."

420

"And I am Irwin."

I wanted him off-balance. "Irwin what?"

"Irwin W. Emerson, Junior." He shut his mouth, suddenly. Then, slowly, he said, "The name must mean nothing to you, Dak."

"No," I said. "I do not know anyone of that name. But it is a fine name. It has a ring to it. You come from a proud line."

"I like to think so."

Duhrra loomed up then, still cleaning the blood off his blade, to tell me a Deldar was dying and wanted to talk to me before he went. I nodded to Irwin and clattered down off the wall.

Ord-Deldar Nalgre the Twist lay in the dust, his left arm missing, the rags stuffed to his stump stained in a most ugly and dreadful way, his face white and drawn. I knelt at his side.

"Dak—Dak—I'm on the way to the Ice Floes."

"You are a fine helm-Deldar, Nalgre. I trust you. As an ord-Deldar you have standing; but I would like you to go as a Hikdar. Does that please you?"

His face regarded me gravely, white and suffering, yet understanding I did this thing for myself, not for him.

"Thank you, Dak. In the brotherhood I was known… I shall go to Sicce as a Hikdar. It may help me there."

"You will sit on the right hand of Zair in the radiance of Zim. Take the Hikdar and lift up your head."

"Zair—" he said.

He died then, and I hoped being a Hikdar would aid him as he sought his seat among the millions sitting on the right hand of Zair in the radiance of Zim.

When I looked up to the walls again, Irwin had gone.

After that we split the paktuns up, as I should have done in the first instance, and set them with men we knew to be loyal, so that thereafter we had no further trouble from the mercenaries.

The interesting fact was that all the diffs among the paktuns had elected to go with Starkey, the ex-king Zenno. They were as well aware as anyone else of the dislike for diffs of the apims of Zairia. Among the Grodnims who had scaled the wall in treachery there had been a goodly number of diffs. It had been a Chulik who had taken Deldar Nalgre's arm off and broken up his insides as he fell. I saw an omen in this, something very obvious, really. The Savanti, those awesomely mysterious supermen of Aphrasöe, the Swinging City, had sent one of their agents, a Savapim, to assist in the vital moment when the city might have fallen. I knew this Irwin would moments before he landed here in Zandikar have been in Aphrasöe, being briefed for his mission. The Savanti had sent a Savapim to protect apims from diffs in a tavern brawl in Ruathytu. They must be taking like hands

421

in many places of Kregen. I decided then that the Savanti were definitely fighting on the side of Zairia against Grodnim. This cheered me.

Our preparations continued. As I worked and checked and issued orders so I kept a lookout for Irwin, and sent messengers to find him. They returned empty-handed. I fancied he'd been whisked back to Aphrasöe—wherever the Swinging City was—his mission accomplished.

I could have used a regiment of Savapims just then.

Any fighting lord could use Savapims at any time.

That night we had the inner wall, built in a square against the weakened outer main wall, up to head height.

"We must build high enough so the cramphs of sectrixmen cannot jump the wall," I said. "All night we go on. Use wood for the walkways. Tell the archers to get some rest. They will be vital on the morrow." My orders were obeyed.

I made a point of asking Miam, who was now Queen Miam and a trifle dazed by events, to dress in her finest and to ride a milk-white sectrix—an unusual beast, an albino and somewhat weak—around the fortifications with me. She made a superb impression on the minds of all who saw her and the rolling thunders of the acclamations followed wherever she rode.

I told my son Vax to go always with her, as her protector and my liaison with her. He was not loath. I liked, more than I had expected I would, his devotion to his brother Zeg. Most young men in a like situation would have tried a little pelft on their own behalf—or almost most. But Vax, I saw with pleasure, had imbibed notions of honor from somewhere, as well as from his mother Delia. They had not come from me. The Krzy had most probably done a thorough job on him before my Apushniad had driven him away in shame from their august ranks.

When the lambent blue spark of Soothe appeared in the sky and the stars twinkled out to follow, we began to take down the outer wall. The job had to be done with exquisite care, so that nothing showed from the outside. We carried the blocks of stone and raised our new inner wall with them. The inside of the main wall was eaten away, leaving a mere shell. Zandikar, as I have indicated, was just the same luxury-loving, indolent, careless city as most any other of Zairia. Her people had built a good strong wall around the city and then had knocked off to sing and dance and quaff wine. Well, if Zandikar had been my city I'd have had three walls, at the least, knowing the damned Grodnims as I did.

Sanurkazz boasts seven walls in places.

The Twins rose and by their light we labored on.

Vax, rubbing his eyes, found me bellowing in a whisper, a most fearsome way of putting hell into a workman, on the inner wall. "Dak," he said. "The queen would like to talk to you."

"That's the style, Naghan," I said to the naked workman who was guiding a new block into place, whip in hand, directing the line of sweating naked slaves. "You're building well."

Then I went with Vax to the Palace of Fragrant Incense to crave an audience with the new queen. I put it like that, for the whole affair smacked of the grotesque to me, so conscious of the ravening leems of Grodnims beyond the walls. She received me in all dignity, superbly clad, wearing a crown, the torches smoking down, lighting in flickers of orange fire the gems and the gold and silver, the feathers and silks. Yet she looked imposing and grand in an altogether human way. I could not smile at her; but I did not, at the least, frown overmuch.

She did not waste time on preamble.

"On the morrow we beat the accursed Grodnims. I am the queen of Zandikar. I shall stand on the wall so that all my people may see me."

"And get a quarrel through your pretty head."

She flushed. "If Zair so ordains—"

"Zair would ordain nothing so foolish. Anyway, I forbid it."

"You! I am the queen!"

"You are the queen. You have responsibilities. If you are slain, and slain so stupidly, what will happen to the loyalties of your people? Could you care for them then? And what of my—what of this man Zeg you prate of? Is he Vax's brother or not? Would you spite him?"

Her face blazed scarlet in the torchlight. She fumbled with the golden mortil-crowned staff, the emblem of Zandikar.

"You speak boldly, my lord."

"You call me jernu. I am Dak."

Nath Zavarin, sweating and panting as usual, coughed and said, "It would be meet for the queen, whose name be revered, to witness the fight from afar. But in a place where her loyal warriors may easily see her and be heartened thereby."

"Find such a place out of arrow range," I said. "And I agree. But not otherwise."

Vax scowled at me.

I said to him, straight, "If the queen is slain, what do you say to Zeg?"

He did not answer, but the hilt of the Krozair longsword went down under his fist and the scabbarded blade licked up, most evilly.

Then it was the turn of Roz Janri to be dissuaded from putting himself in the forefront of the fight. I had to be brisk; but I think he understood. I gave him the task, which he accepted, of bringing up our cavalry at the decisive moment. I did not tell him I devoutly wanted the thing done before our sectrixmen became involved. The poor beasts were very tottery on their legs, and a lot had been eaten so that our chivalry was weak.

In the crowd waiting in the High Hall it was easy enough to pick out Dolan. I said to him, "Dolan the Bow. Will you pick me out a bow—a good one—and a couple of quivers? I think I will join you at the breastworks tomorrow. I have not shot of late. I need practice."

"Right gladly, Dak."

He was as good as his word and produced a good specimen of a Zandikarese bow. I know Seg Segutorio would have smiled quietly had he seen it, for it was a puny thing compared to the great Lohvian longbow. But to my misfortune we had not a single one of the Kregen-famous Bowmen of Loh in our ranks. There was a small corps of the redheaded archers from Loh with Glycas. I gave orders about them, not caring overmuch for what we would have to do to them. The main missile strength of the Grodnims lay in their sextets of crossbowmen, working to the system I had devised so long ago in the warrens of Magdag for my old vosk-skulls.

Many imponderables must weigh down one side or the other of the balances; success or failure would be a composite of many disparate events. We did all we could to weigh down our balance pan to success and then, after that, it would be up to Oxkalin the Blind Spirit.

The vacuum in the higher commands left by the evanishment of the paktuns meant that my own men could be employed, and there were many good men of Zandikar. Zena Iztar had aided us then; in the siege and more particularly in this coming fight we were on our own. Unless the Savanti decided to send more Savapims, of course.

It seems scarcely necessary to mention that all day the incoming hails of warning went up. The boys on the ramparts would beat their gongs and the yells of "Incoming" would shriek out and we'd all either duck or stand stoically until the spinning chunk of rock had found a billet inside the walls. The Grodnims used catapults for this general mayhem; they had gigantic varters designed as wall-smashers lined up against the point of the breach. The catapult throws with a high trajectory; the varter with its ballista-like action hurls with a low trajectory. Glycas had at least six fine engines, not as sophisticated as the gros-varters of Vallia; but big. They played on the point that both Glycas and I had selected as the point d'appui, and very early in the morning the first stones tumbled free and the evident cracks, visible from outside, widened to let daylight through.

A great cry went up from the assembled Greens.

We let them have an answering cheer.

To an impartial observer the decisive moment would clearly be seen to be at hand. As the suns shone down and the varters clanged, huge chunks of rock smote into the wall. Stones chipped into dust and fractured and fell. The parapet vanished. The wall slumped as rock after rock smashed in. Fountains of rock chips burst upward, the dust made men cough, the noise clanged on and on. During the morning two feint attacks were made and disposed of. By midday Glycas had moved all his wall-smashing artillery to this decisive point. From the vantage point of a tower I could see the solid square of his infantry paraded, ready to deal with any sortie we might make. His cavalry waited in long glittering lines. The mercenaries seethed in clumps of never-ending movement. And still the wall was bitten away.

Our work from the inside brought all down with a run as the suns began their decline. We would have a long afternoon.

So thorough was the work and so sudden the final collapse that the way was just practicable for sectrixes. But, like a sensible commander, Glycas sent in his mercenaries first.

Howling and shrieking, waving their weapons, they poured forward in a living tide of destruction. At least, they no doubt assumed themselves to be a living tide of destruction. We Zandikarese archers looked forward with calm confidence to the ebbing of the tide.

Breaking down the walls of fortresses usually takes time and patience with the battering engines. Glycas had picked this weak spot and now he saw victory opening before his eyes, all in a day. The trumpets of Grodno pealed triumphantly above the charging masses as they clambered the low breach and flung themselves forward into Zandikar.

The lethal horizontal sleeting death awaited them.

They pitched to the dust in droves. The high triumphant yells turned in an instant to shrieks of agony. Remorselessly the shafts drove in. More and more men clambered up only to jump down to death. When they stopped coming we clambered up in our turn, and jeered and taunted the massive ranks of the Magdaggian army poised beyond artillery range, and yet still and not moving. The cavalry made one or two feint advances, and then retired. The varters took up their bashing work and the catapults began to sing.

Within that square of stone the ground ran red. A shambles in very truth we had created. Now was a time for clearing up and rebuilding the wall more strongly. The resistance to the Green attack had been decisive, without the desperate touch-and-go incoherence of the previous assaults, and it marked a new stage in the siege operations.

That was the end of the beginning of the Siege of Zandikar.

Sixteen
The Siege of Zandikar: II
I am short with a Krozair of Zy

I do not wish to dwell overlong on the Siege of Zandikar. From that day of the slaughter of the mercenaries in our trap it was a constant round of repelling assaults, of building walls, of keeping awake, of siting varters and catapults in advantageous positions, of keeping alert, of making the rounds, of maintaining morale, and of building walls and building more walls.

Twice more we caught the damned overlords of Magdag in the same trap. The second occasion was noteworthy, for we used a gateway, the gateway on the east of the city called the Gate of Happy Absolution. Instead of building a square of stone walls within the gate, we built a wedge shape, a triangle of death. One of the paktuns whom I felt I could trust repeated the exploit of his compatriot and betrayed us to Prince Glycas. He must have spoken eloquently for he returned with a bag of golden oars and news that all would go as planned.

So the shooting intensified around the Gate of Happy Absolution, and then as the return shots came in, slackened and died away. We began a great shout within the battlemented towers of the gate, shrieking for: "Shafts! Shafts! In the name of Zair bring up arrows!"

From a rearward tower I watched. This time Queen Miam stood to watch with me, and Vax hovered nearby. We saw the mailed chivalry of Magdag trampling up, proud in their power. They formed before the gate as infantry ran in with hide-covered rams and smashed in the gate. We had removed the good stout bars and replaced them with old beams that were artfully sawed and cut so as to break with a satisfyingly genuine rending of wood. The gates flew open. The siege-batterers leaped clear and, heads down, swords pointed, the overlords of Magdag charged in through the gateway.

We repeated the previous two performances, and this time we drove our shafts with such an unholy joy that the hated overlords themselves felt each biting head.

After the second trap we had discovered the bodies of several Bowmen of Loh scattered on the rubble where they had been shot attempting to shoot in the attack. So I had a great Lohvian longbow to my hand. I could not stop myself from going down among the archers of Zandikar and showing them what a Lohvian longbow might do in the hands of a skilled archer.

The cruel walled funnel is a bitter trick. The riders rode boldly through and charged on, yelling, and so the farther they galloped the more compressed became their ranks. Confusion set in; they recoiled and men toppled from the high saddles; they shrieked now as the arrow storm sleeted upon them. The bow of Zandikar may be only puny compared to a longbow; but it could wreak havoc in these conditions where the shafts sped so thickly that the air appeared filled with their whispering death.

Sectrixes screamed and thrashed their six hooves. Men fell, to be battered to death. The arrows never ceased their spiteful singing. A handful of mail-clad riders reached the far wall and I leaped up, placing the longbow down carefully first, and so went at them on a level with the Ghittawrer blade. It was all pulsing and high excitement for a space; we beat down those who had survived to reach the end of the funnel. They died unable to fall, so great was the crush. Men in the gate towers shot into the riders from above, and great stones fell upon them.

By the time we closed the doors and put the stout beams back and walled up the aperture, my men were stripping off the harnesses and mail, leading away those animals that had not died, carting off the corpses, collecting up the weapons. Details of archers with wicker baskets picked up all the shafts. The broken ones would go back to the factories, where women and girls would reshaft the old heads, fletch them with the feathers of the Zandikarese chiuli bird—a deep plum color, most pleasing.

"How long can they sustain such losses?" demanded Janri.

"As long as this genius king orders them to," I said.

Thereafter we maintained a careful watch upon all the walls and beat back sudden attacks, and prepared for grand assaults, and listened for mining operations, and so caved in two tunnels upon the diggers beneath. The siege went on.

I said to the Queen's Council in the High Hall of the Palace of Fragrant Incense, "I think Glycas will try an assault from the sea."

Pur Naghan ti Perzefn, a Krozair of Zamu, leaped up, declaring, "Let me take the swifters and ram and sink them!"

He was given permission and took as well as our three swifters the four smaller swifters the Zandikarese navy had left of those they had begun the war with. On the day the expected attack developed the land operations demanded my attention. Pur Naghan reported in as the suns sank, smiling, blood-spattered, grim, and triumphant.

"We lost *Zandikar Mortil* and *Pearl*," he said. "But we took four and sank three. It was most satisfactory."

"Hai Jikai, Pur Naghan," I said. "The queen will see you."

Queen Miam, without much prompting from me, expressed her thanks to Naghan, and then said, "We feel it right in the Jikai that you should be known henceforth as Pur Nazhan. Do you agree?"

"I agree, Majestrix. I thank you."

So Pur Naghan became Pur Nazhan. I was happy for him.

The siege went on.

All this time, for all the power I could exercise in the city, I did not forget that, in truth, I was in deep dire trouble in the areas of life that mattered to me. I might bellow orders and send mailed men scampering into action, whip my blade down and so order the release of five hundred deadly shafts from the bows of the Zandikarese archers, I might chivy and cajole and instruct a queen, I might be imperious with Pallans and Chuktars; all the time I remembered I was Apushniad, outlawed from the Krozairs, debarred from returning home to Valka and my Delia.

And, too, I had most certainly not lost sight of my business with King

Genod—the genius at war, who had murdered my daughter Velia—and with Gafard, the King's Striker, the Sea Zhantil, Velia's lawful husband.

We knew these two were not with the army of Prince Glycas, and we surmised they were with the Grodnim army of the west, pressing on along the coast, and no doubt thinking about encircling Zimuzz, if they had not already taken that great city. Genod's plans had worked so far, for he had enclosed various centers of resistance as in a nutcracker. We could afford no assistance to Zimuzz. They could not aid us. Zamu, the next great fortress-city to the east, would be the next to fall, and then it would be Sanurkazz—Holy Sanurkazz.

Pur Naghan—or, as he now was, Pur Nazhan—had scored a notable victory and as a result four of the Ten Dikars were open again. This was small consolation to us, penned in Zandikar, for we knew there were no forces at sea waiting to come to our relief. We were wrong in our suppositions, and the correction of our misapprehension came one dark night before She of the Veils rose to flood down in fuzzy pink moonlight. I had just completed one of my eternal circuits of the walls and had thrown myself down in the small room of the palace I used for sleeping when I could. Duhrra snored noisily in the corner. Roko, Roz Janri's dwarf and chief chamberlain, bustled in flat-footed with a girl bearing a torch. He shook me awake.

"A messenger, Dak—a Krozair of Zy! Just come in." Rubbing the sleep from my eyes and girding on my weapons, I followed Roko to the High Hall. I let Duhrra slumber on. The hall held a narrow cold look and a feeling of meanness in the night as I entered. Numbers of the high officials of Zandikar waited whispering together. The queen arrived shortly afterward and seated herself on the throne, with her handmaidens and guards about her. She had not yet adopted any throne step pets; I'd had experience of neemus and Manhounds and chavonths; I wondered what she might choose when she understood more of her power. Her small elfin face looked sleep-drugged, as did all our faces, for the sake of Zair; but we knew what we were about.

I was prepared for the newly arrived Krozair of Zy to take one look at me and to whip out his sword and bellow, "Pur Dray! The Lord of Strombor! Apushniad!"

But he did not. I did not know him. He looked a proper Krozair, well-built, erect, clear-eyed, with the fierce upthrusting moustaches of a Zairian. We ex-oar-slaves had grown most of our hair back by now, although still somewhat straggly. I looked at the coruscating device on his white surcoat, that hubless spoked wheel within the circle, and I own I felt an ache. He was all business.

"The Grodnims take all along the southern coast to the west. Zy still holds. We have been bypassed. Zimuzz is about to fall. The king is there, may Zair torture him eternally."

I stood half in the shadows at the foot of the throne steps and I did not speak. Roz Janri stood at the side of the throne, a tall and dignified figure, and he it was who said, "You are welcome here, Pur Trazhan. Have you no good news for us in our darkness?"

This Pur Trazhan smiled. "Yes, Roz Janri. I am bid to tell you that the city of Zandikar must not fall. You must hold. An army is on the way. It is a strange army, for it is composed of men who do not swear by Zair, and who fly in the air in metal boats."

There was a quick buzz of surprised comment and conjecture at this startling news. I felt a glow all over my limbs. But—of course!—it was Vax who started forward, eagerly, calling excitedly above the hubbub.

"This army of men who fly in the air, Pur Trazhan! Are they of Vallia?"

"Yes, they are." Trazhan was clearly not quite sure what to call Vax or how to address him.

"Then, by Vox!" exclaimed Vax. "It is Prince Drak and the army of Vallia, with fliers! It must be!"

"That is so," said Trazhan. "It is Pur Drak, a great and renowned Krozair of Zy, who leads them. Long have we awaited their coming, since the Call went out. And now Pur Drak has answered the Azhurad, as he promised he would when he was given permission to go to his home country, wherever that may be."

So that explained what Drak had been up to. My eldest son had answered the Call in a typically Prescot way. He'd sought help from his own. I learned that he had brought vollers by sea from Vallia, vollers loaned by his grandfather, the emperor of Vallia. They had sailed all the way in those marvelous race-built galleons of Vallia. I knew why they'd sailed and not flown. The same reason had prompted Rees and Chido to sail and not fly. And, it also meant that the emperor, the tightfisted old devil, had not spared first-quality vollers. He'd let his grandson have those fliers bought from Hamal and therefore suspect, not safe for long aerial journeys. I did not blame Drak for sailing. This way, he brought all his men and fliers into the Eye of the World instead of leaving them stranded all the way across the Sunset Sea, the Klackadrin, the Hostile Territories and The Stratemsk. Soon, he would be here and we would be relieved!

"I have heard of Pur Drak," said Roz Janri. A frown crossed his face. "He is the son of Pur Dray Prescot, the Lord of Strombor, once the most renowned Krozair upon the Eye of the World. But that was long ago. Now this Pur Dray is Apushniad. It is common knowledge."

Vax did not say a word.

"Certainly Pur Drak is the son of this accursed Dray Prescot," said Trazhan. "But Pur Drak is an honorable man. He is well worthy of the trust of the Krozairs of Zy and the respect of ordinary men."

That was a clear and chilling reminder that Krozairs were not as ordinary men. Nor are they, by Zair!

Vax did not step forward, and his voice was almost steady, as he said, "And his brother, Pur Zeg?"

"At sea, upholding the glory of Zair for the Brotherhood."

"Do these two brothers speak of their father?"

I heard a noise and saw that Duhrra had rolled into the High Hall, yawning. He gazed around sleepily, puffy faced.

"They say of him that what has been ordained is just." Trazhan peered into the shadows at Vax. "Why do you ask?"

Before Vax could answer, I said, "Do these brothers hate their father as much as this young man Vax hates his?"

I own I wanted to stir it a bit, feeling vicious; but at the same time I wanted to know the answer to my question.

Trazhan put his left fist onto his sword-hilt. "Who can say? They do not speak of him to others. He is Apushniad and therefore less than nothing. Now I would like to rest, and—"

"You are, Pur Trazhan," I said, trying not to sound too cold, "I trust, empowered to stay and fight with us?"

"Well—" he began.

I admit, with only a little shame, that I wanted to hit out. I owed the Krozairs nothing at this time. One of their number was fair game. They had done what they had done to me, and I was going to prove them wrong; but right now I would make this high and mighty Krzy wriggle a trifle. "After all, Pur Trazhan, you have admitted that Zy is not attacked, therefore your duty cannot lie there. Zimuzz is about to fall, and so to go there is useless. Here in Zandikar we successfully resist the cramphs of Grodnims and will never surrender. I would have thought a man's duties lay here. Particularly if he happened to be a Krozair of Zy."

He took a half-step, and paused, and peered belligerently into the shadows.

"Who are you, who speaks thus to a Krozair?"

"I am Dak."

"Dak," he said. "I think the name is familiar—"

"Oh, there may not be as many Daks as there are Naths and Naghans and Nalgres; but there are a lot of us." I shot the last words at him like crossbow bolts. "Are you staying or not?"

He swung his head at me, and then looked at Miam.

"Who is this man?"

Before she could speak I took a pace or two forward and planted myself in front of him. I glared at him evilly.

"You may be a Krozair of Zy. But you address the queen of Zandikar in a proper and respectful fashion, or, by Zair, I'll pull your damned tongue out!"

He wanted to start on me, then and there, but I would have none of it, not with poor Miam looking on distressed, and I backed away and bellowed for everyone to calm down. I finished, "And this great and famous Krozair, this Pur Trazhan, will be happy to stay with us and fight for Zandikar. He will honor his oaths. And, anyway," I ended with gruesome levity, "we have ample mergem to feed him and his crew."

After the fuss Trazhan agreed to stay and fight. Of course, poor devil, he could do nothing else.

Mind you, I was not altogether happy about his performance. No Krozair I had known, for all we put no great store by kings and queens, would have flung up so brusque a question to a young queen like that. To some fabled Queen of Pain, perhaps... Maybe standards were lowered in the Krozairs and they were being forced to let in a rabble. I own I can be most arrogant when it comes to those people and institutions in which I put value. But I had, at this time, still to remember I was an outcast, Apushniad.

Just before we all left about our business, Queen Miam lifted her hand and we fell silent. She said something that was unnecessary and yet, at the same time, it made me feel warm to her. I figured Zeg would be a lucky fellow.

"This man Dak," said Queen Miam, "is the heart and soul of the defense of Zandikar."

While it was not true—well, not altogether—it had a pretty ring.

I bowed to her, and from somewhere deep in the bowels of Cottmer's Caverns, I shouldn't wonder, I scraped up a smile for her. She smiled back, so I fancy my face indicated some grotesque caricature of a smile.

"We shall hold Zandikar, Queen Miam," I said.

"I wish to talk to you privately for a crooked mur, Dak."

By "a crooked mur" Kregans mean a minute or two. We went into the small luxurious room behind the throne where she might doff the heavy robes of state and the crown and mortil-headed staff. When she was clad again in her own simple white gown she shooed out her handmaidens and turned to me, one hand to her breast.

"I wanted to ask you, dear Dak, of your goodness, not to mention that you know Prince Zeg, Pur Zeg, to be Vax's brother. It is a thing he would not wish known."

"Why does he not ask me himself?"

"I rather think he does not realize what he has let slip to you as to me. If it is known... Is this Dray Prescot, then, so terrible a beast?"

I looked at her in the lamplight. She was beautiful. I felt for Zeg, not envying him, but feeling happy for him.

"I think most young men take against their fathers at some time in their lives. When they mature they come to a better understanding—if their fathers are worthy, of course."

"You do not answer my question."

"No, Miam, I do not. I do not know. I have heard stories. I think it probable he was unjustly stricken from the Order of Krozairs of Zy. To be made Apushniad is a horrible fate."

"Oh, yes!"

"He will be your father-in-law. I think you would make any man see reason."

We passed a few more words, then she said, "And you will remember about Vax and his father?" and I said, "I will," and we parted.

The name of Dray Prescot, the Lord of Strombor, once Krozair of Zy, could arouse as passionate a response here in Zairia as it inevitably could in Green Grodnim. I had heard more than one old soldier curse and spit and say he wished to Zair that Pur Dray was not Apushniad and could be in the forefront of the battle with his comrades in his accustomed place in the struggle against the rasts of Magdaggians. I was there, although they did not know it. But I wanted the Krozairs to reinstate me, not so that I might fight on for Zair, but so that I might go home to Delia.

A few days after that, as the siege dragged on, Prince Glycas tried a new trick. He must have had the beasts landed from animal-carrying broad ships and driven them up to the walls of the city. The shouts rose as the lookouts bellowed the warning in a misty dawn light. By the time I was up onto my favorite tower, midway along the inland wall, with a fine varter to hand, I could see the mists coiling and rising, emerald and ruby in the mingled streaming light of Antares, see the huge rounded backs of the turiloths as they waddled ponderously on, see the crowding warriors following these mammoth beasts.

"Turiloths! Turiloths!" the cries racketed about.

Archers began to shoot. Their shafts simply bounced off the hard gray upper hide. The turiloth's hide altered in color to a dark bottle-green along the sides and a grayish streak ran along the belly. Sixteen legs has a turiloth, with six tusks and a tendrilous mass of whiplash tails, a veritable forest of Kataki tails at his rear. He has an enormous underslung mouth equipped with suitable fangery, and he is keen scented and he has three hearts. If this description sounds familiar, I assure you it is; the turiloth of Turismond is very similar to the boloth of Chem. I had fought a boloth on a notable occasion in the arena. Now we had twenty of these gigantic beasts plodding along to smash down the gates of Zandikar and let the swarm of warriors in to an orgy of destruction.

A paktun near me screamed, "All is lost! We are doomed! Doomed!" He scrambled madly down the tower, running away. The panic spread.

Seventeen
The Siege of Zandikar: III
The turiloths attack

"We are doomed!"

The cries rang out with chilling panic through the early morning mists.

This was a time for instant action.

There was no time to shaft the running paktun, as he deserved. I grabbed a varterist by the ear and ran him up to his engine. I hurled both of us at the windlass, for the varters were kept unspun to save their springs, and began a frenzied winding. "Orlon!" I bellowed at another varterist, who hung over the battlements, gaping. "Shove a dart in! Hurry, man!"

The dart slapped into the chute as the nut engaged and the windlass clanked full. I swung the varter on its gimbals and sighted on a vast bottle-green hide and pressed the trigger.

Praise Zair—or praise Erthyr the Bow, the guiding spirit of Erthyrdrin bowmen—the dart flew true. Its massive bulk smashed into the tough hide where an arrow would break or spin free. The turiloth squealed at first, and then when he realized how deeply he had been wounded, he began to scream. His six tusks whipped about as he tried to reach back to dislodge the cruel barb in his guts. His tendrilous tails lashed in frenzy. But he was not the monster aimed for the gate beneath our feet. I had had to shoot in enfilade to hit a flank. I glared about for Sniz the Horn, my trumpeter, and yelled, "Load another! Get at it, you onkers! These are only beasts and may be slain, the poor hulus! Sniz! Sound the rally! Blow hard!"

"Quidang, Dak!"

I had spared the time to shoot, myself. Now all who looked over the battlements could see at least one monster screaming in agony, and slowly sinking down onto his sixteen knees. Turiloths are usually ponderous and slow; but with their three hearts they can be whipped up into a short and vicious charge of surprising speed. If that happened before we got them all, any one of them could go straight through the timbers of the gate as a swifter's ram smashes through the scantlings of a broad ship.

The watchfires of the night had not yet been doused.

"Torches!" I roared. "Torches to set their tails alight!"

After that first blind, unthinking panic my men rallied. Varters clanged from the towers along the walls. Torches were catapulted out. We had rocks ready, and vast caldrons of hot water that would come to the boil as the fires were stoked. It was a pretty set-to while it lasted. But with Sniz blowing his lungs out and the drums rolling and the air filled with varters and torches, with the boiling water spilling out and down on the last tur- iloth that lumbered into a charge, we held them. It was a near thing. The last one, bearing two varter darts, four of his six tusks knocked away by a rock, boiling water fuming from his gray back, slumped to his knees before the gate. One of his remaining tusks touched the wood. It made a sound so small it was lost in the uproar of continuing battle.

For the Grodnims charged in, anyway, bearing scaling ladders. Their towers had been set alight many times and still they built more and shielded them with wet hides and sheets of bronze. We smashed them with varter rocks. The scaling ladders were pushed away with forked sticks. Arrows darkened the bright morning as the mists burned away. It was a merry set-to, as I say, and many a good man went down to the Ice Floes of Sicce, or up to sit in glory on the right hand of Zair or Grodno in the radi- ance of Zim or Genodras, according to his color.

Before the Hour of Mid the last few Grodnims were shafted and sent reeling, the main pack retreating sullenly. Among the attackers there had been men who bore pikes, men with shields, men compact in the grouping of six cross-bowmen in sextets. So Glycas was sending in the new army, was he? Actually committing men trained to fight in the open in phalanx into the messy business of assaulting a wall? That was a fine omen for our continued holding.

When the excitement had died down Duhrra found me. He did not look pleased.

"Nath the Slinger has been wounded, a shaft through his arm. Oh, and the Krozair, Pur Trazhan, is dead."

I said, "Fetch me his sword, Duhrra."

Oh, yes, it was callous. But other good men were dead. And I could use the Krozair brand, where probably others could not. If pride had gone to my head, I trust I understood why. I went to see Nath the Slinger and found him cursing away, in good spirits, but very foulmouthed about the Magdaggians.

"My shots were bouncing off their shields, Dak. A coward's trick, the shield."

He but mouthed the usual opinion in Turismond.

"I got one of 'em, though, a beauty right under the helmet rim. And then his mate shot me in the arm."

"Rest and have it seen to and you will be fine."

"Oh, aye, I'll be fine. By Zair! It is not my slinging arm!"

The turiloths were the subject of conversation for the rest of the day. As was my custom I sent strong parties out, well screened, to pick up every weapon they could among the corpses. As for them, we scattered pungent ibroi on them and gradually the smell went away. The boloth of Chem has eight tusks, and is apple-green and yellow; otherwise he is much the same as a turiloth. I thought of Delia, naked, tied with silver chains to the stake, and of the boloth—and of Oby and Tilly and Naghan the Gnat. By Kaidun! If a man could get out of a scrape like that, with good friends like Seg and Inch and Turko the Shield, then surely I could get out of this one with my son Drak flying to our rescue! The problem there was, as Pur Trazhan who was now dead had said, that Drak's army would most likely relieve Zimuzz first. We just had to hold. So I glared upon the gigantic mute corpses of the turiloths as my men picked up weapons, and debated how to dispose of the monstrous things before they choked us out with their stink.

In the end the clouds of warvols attracted to any scene of death floated on their wide black wings from the sky and settled on the corpses and began the long and succulent job of picking the bones clean. The vulture-like warvol has his uses in nature. I had my eye on the bones, for the meat was not pleasant enough for us to eat, rich as we were with mergem. If we starved, we'd eat turiloth meat and gag and chew and choke, but we'd eat it right enough.

This siege would be decided one way or the other before the mergem ran out. A small teaspoonful of mergem in two pints of water, boiled up, produces a rich and nourishing broth, with all the proteins and vitamins and whatnot a man's metabolism requires. For roughage we ate of the chipalines, and almost everywhere possible in Zandikar the flowers had been replaced by vegetables. Only along walls in those days were flowers to be seen in the besieged city.

No, I will not detail all our sufferings and tribulations during the Siege of Zandikar. That siege was not really one of the great and illustrious defenses of Kregen; for one thing we did not starve. But we fought well. We held the Greens off. They vastly outnumbered us, and for all that we kept on killing the rasts, still they seemed never to decrease in number. Glycas had used a part of the famous new army of King Genod in the assault; so we were hurting them. A frenzy grew in the attacks. They became more and more desperate, lacking in finesse, wave after wave of yelling men hurling themselves frantically at the gray-white walls of Zandikar, screaming, "Grodno! Grodno! Magdag!" We heard the shouts for Prince Glycas, and, also, the shouts for King Genod. But for all the shouting and the onslaughts they did not pierce or climb the walls—unless we allowed them.

On one crucial night attack a brave party of Grodnims managed to make a lodgment on the walls. They held a wall and a flanking tower. We came up, realizing we faced a task of gigantic proportions to force them off. But they did not drop down on the inside. They made a deal of noise, banging drums and blowing trumpets; but we released a series of firepots into the darkness beyond the walls and after a time the Grodnims dropped back outside the walls, abandoning what they had achieved.

Roz Janri and Pallan Zavarin and others of the high officers were puzzled.

They had become used to decisiveness in the Magdaggian army. I said, "This is a great and good sign. The rasts believed we prepared a trap for them. They have been caught before. They thought that if they attacked further we were waiting. Well, the mind is often more powerful than the muscle."

The information heartened everyone in Zandikar.

Now we believed we would hold.

Then came the moment that I, alone among all those people with such high hopes in Zandikar, had dreaded.

Yes, I had told the people of the city: yes, we will hold.

But I had not told them that King Genod had formed an alliance with the empress Thyllis in far Hamal. I had not told them that Genod had bought fliers and saddle-birds from Thyllis. I had not told them that as soon as the king arrived he would bring with him vollers and fliers.

We did not know if he had been reducing Zimuzz, or if he had tried a fling at the sacred Isle of Zy. All we knew early one morning was that King Genod, the war genius, had arrived in his camp before besieged Zandikar.

We saw the dots in the high air. People looked up and pointed. Exclamations broke out. They had seen the flier that Duhrra and Vax had brought here with Hikdar Ornol ti Zab. That had long since been smashed and no one knew where Ornol was. So they knew what these fliers were, and they also knew what they portended.

I knew that this day, the very same day he landed here, the genius at war, King Genod, would launch his aerial armada against Zandikar. The walls would avail nothing. Assailed at a hundred points within the city itself, Zandikar must fall.

Eighteen
Pur Zeg, Prince of Vallia, Krzy

Had Miam not been the great-granddaughter of old King Zinna and the rightful heir to the throne, or had Starkey the Wersting realized enough to have had her killed, or had some other reason debarred her from being the pawn in my machinations, I believe Zena Iztar, whose supernatural powers were of an extent I could not comprehend, would have found some other road for me and my comrades to preserve the city of Zandikar. I did not believe she would have plotted as she had only to let all go to waste. No help in the shape of a vast sky army was to be expected from the Savanti. They might transit more Savapims. As for the Star Lords, well, the Everoinye had been very quiet of late and I fancied that was because in this internecine war of the inner sea they backed the Greens.

The damned fliers and flyers of King Genod landed on the flat expanse outside the soldiers' camps. I made myself stand and watch them. I counted. At least a hundred vollers, and perhaps merely twenty fluttrells, turning their headvanes with the wind as they landed with widespread feet and downturned tails, amid much wing-fluttering and dust. Their riders were ill-trained. That made sense in a society like the one of the inner sea where airboats and saddle-birds were exotic phenomena.

There remained to me now one course of action.

As I prepared, hurriedly, bellowing for Duhrra and Sniz and Dolan, sending them scurrying about the things needful, I wondered if I was to be cast in the role of Pakkad. Whether or not he was merely a legendary figure—or if red blood had flowed in his veins, and he had been clothed in flesh, a real man of some distant epoch—neither I nor any other human of Kregen knew. But poor Pakkad had been cruelly treated by Mitronoton, the Reducer of Towers, the Destroyer of Cities, a very devil. Now his story formed part of the mythology of Kregen, and Pakkad himself stood as a symbol for the outcast, the downtrodden, the unwanted, the pariah. Well, I was to meet a latter-day incarnation of Mitronoton, as you shall hear, during the Time of Troubles, and if I do not speak often of that man-god-devil I follow only a general custom. One does not call lightly on Mitronoton, the Leveler of Ways.

Fazhan bustled up, saying, "The swifter is prepared, Dak."

'Then let all repair aboard. We have little time."

We took the swifter brought in by Pur Trazhan, who no longer needed her, being dead. She was single-banked, with two men to an oar and fifteen oars a side, of the style called, in Zairia, chavinter. There are many and many names for the different sizes and styles of swifters of the inner sea, of course; I usually refer to them all indifferently as swifters to save confusion. Every oarsman was a free man, a warrior, and he pulled with his weapons ready to hand. The narrow central gangway extended aft into a quarterdeck by courtesy only, and I stood there ready to command the ship as Dolan the Bow conned her out through the Dikars.

Nath the Slinger, cursing by Zogo the Hyrwhip, and fulminating against the zigging Grodnims, raced along the quayside and fairly leaped aboard, landing in a sprawl and a bellow of pain as he jolted his wounded arm. He staggered up, shouting, "And you would sail without me, Dak the Ingrate!"

"Welcome, Nath—you may observe the fantamyrrh, if you will."

On the quayside Nath Zavarin and Roz Janri watched us leave, puzzled even though I had sworn by Zair I was not deserting them. Queen Miam, attended by her people, came down to see us off. They all knew I was about a desperate enterprise, and they wished me well, casting my fortunes into the hands of Zair.

They would see that the soldiers and warriors fought when the attack came in. I knew that. And, knowing that, I wondered only a little if I did this thing for Zandikar or for the memory of Velia.

Since Trazhan had slipped through the channels in the night after Pur Nazhan had opened up four of the Dikars, we guessed the Grodnims would have reestablished patrols and probably sealed up most, if not all of them again. We had to sail through in daylight. We pulled so as not to lift a sail above the low-lying islands; and past the cliff-sided islands the wind would often fall away to nothing. We glided on and we waited for the attack we all felt certain would come, although I heartily wished to get through the ring without an encounter.

"Mother Zinzu the Blessed!" quoth Nath the Slinger, lowering the goblet and wiping his lips. "I needed that."

"You have a wounded arm," I said, "and therefore cannot pull at the oars. I believe you to be a very cunning man, Nath the Slinger, by the disgusting nostrils of Makki-Grodno!"

"Aye, Dak, that I am." And he belched most comfortably.

I thought of my old oar-comrade, Nath, and I sighed, and watched the openings of the myriad mazy channels as they passed away astern.

The swifter was low and lean, and standing on the deck raised a man little more than four feet above the water. Her name was *Marigold*, and she was a dinky little craft and her ram was short and stubby and sharp, a vicious hacking tooth that would do a ship's business for her. The oars had been muffled and we glided as silently as a vessel ever can glide through chinking water. We crept along stealthily and we watched with alert eyes and even then were nearly caught. No one spoke an unnecessary word and then only in a whisper. Dolan the Bow up with the prijikers signaled with a smashing cut of his hand and we understood. Fazhan gave the signal to the oarsmen—we were not using a drum, of course—and they swung the ship away from the channel on our larboard bow. We glided into a deviating channel to the right and everyone heard the creak of oars and the splashing as a swifter prowled past. We went on, and if a swifter's crew can be said to have bated breath—we did, by Vox!

Very softly, so that only I heard him, Nath the Slinger said, "By Zinter the Afflicted! I would welcome a few handstrokes. My arm pains me."

I did not reply. Dolan came aft, walking along the gangway with the habitual grace of the swifterman. He, too, whispered.

"We approach an area of great danger. An open reach. We will have to pull at top speed to get in among the rushes to seaward. If we're caught in the open—" He had no need to spell it out. Fazhan caught my eye and I nodded and he went along the benches whispering to the oarsmen. Free men. They would pull.

This Fazhan ti Rozilloi had grown in stature since we had labored at the oar benches in *Green Magodont*. He was an oar-comrade. And yet he did not possess the superficial brilliance of character so many men have; he was quiet and contained, with nothing of the coarse virility of Nath the Slinger. He was a gentleman of Zairia. There are not many of them.

So we dug in the oars and *Marigold* leaped forward. We burst from the narrow channel and a wide and open stretch of water showed ahead, reaching for perhaps three ulms. A damned long way to row. The water glimmered silver in the light as clouds passed over the Suns of Scorpio. There were very few wild fowl, for they had been hunted mercilessly during the siege. The water chuckled and ran past and the oars dug and pulled and lifted and so dug and pulled again. The men threw their backs into it. We foamed along.

Just under halfway I heard Nath shout a short, sharp obscenity and so before I turned I knew.

From the starboard side a channel opened and from the channel leaped a Magdaggian swifter. Lean and feral, with a single bank, she pounced down on us. She had twenty-five oars a side and I guessed four men to a loom. She was altogether bigger than *Marigold*. We swerved as the helm-Deldars threw their weight on the steering handles. Our starboard bank would have gone on pulling, blind and determined in their rowing; but I yelled, high and harsh, "Ship oars! Weapons! For Zair!"

So the two vessels closed and the struggle began.

We could not have escaped being touched had we rowed on, and we risked having our wings clipped. Also, although mail-clad men clustered on her forecastle and quarterdeck, she would be pulled by slaves and so we might outnumber her fighting-men. And, too, we might play the old Render trick and get among her oar-slaves and free them to fight on our side.

Dolan the Bow flowered his shafts from the forecastle and I saw them like leaping salmon hurling into the men packed on the Magdaggians forecastle. Nath was cursing and slinging like a madman, screaming to Zinter the Afflicted that his arm felt like a dish of palines. The Magdaggian hauled off and tried to give us the ram; but our swerve eluded him and he fell aboard bow to bow. In moments we were at hand-strokes.

The Grodnims took a nasty shock when the oarsmen rose in fury and snatched weapons and smashed back at them. But we were after all outnumbered. The Green cramphs poured aboard and our prijiker party battling back either went down or hurled themselves along the gangway where the oarsmen formed a solid wall. This was no time for me to skulk on the quarterdeck.

"Zair!" I bellowed. "Zandikar!"

The answering yells spurted up, brief and vicious. "Grodno! Magdag! Magdag!"

The beautifully balanced blade of the Krozair longsword flamed in the cloud-broken suns-light. I whirled and thrust, and we cleared a space and saw the crossbowmen in the Grodnim swifter lining up. We had no shields. I would not have my men stand, however bravely, and be shot down without a chance to fight back. I yelled, coarsely.

"To the quarterdeck! We smash them there!"

My men understood instantly. With sixty oarsmen milling in so narrow and frail a craft, we'd all as likely pitch into the water. In a solid clump we leaped the narrowing gap, clambering up and using oars and wales as toeholds, and ravened up over the bulwarks and the apostis down onto the gangway. The fight spread all along the Grodnims' deck. There was time only to smite and smite again, and not ever think, but go on smiting, over and over.

We reached the Magdaggians quarterdeck in a snarling mass of venom. We were outnumbered, for the Grodnim was packed with soldiers as a gregarian is packed with fruit-juice. I saw our men going down, and I raved on, for all this consumed time I did not have to spare. Nath and Fazhan and, miraculously, Dolan were there with me. Other men formed and fought and now the shafts could get at us. Dolan concentrated on the Green crossbowmen with the few bowmen he had left. We kept smashing forward into the Greens and then skipping back, trying both to use them as a wall of defense and to slay them at the same time.

I fancy we would have come out on top in the end, for they had not completely cleared our men from their decks and we held the quarterdeck and their captain was slain. Occupied in the immediate fighting—and, although believing we would win, becoming concerned over the eventual outcome and the cost of this struggle—I barely noticed the jarring shock and the rocking of the Grodnim swifter. I took a glance at *Marigold;* she still floated and must have swung in to bump the side.

The noise increased.

Back into the fight I went, like a madman. The Krozair brand gleamed redly wet from point to hilt.

The shouts and screams increased, the swifter rocked under the violence of the struggle, and now as the yells of "Magdag! Magdag!" and "Zair! Zandikar!" racketed up, above them all a new and powerful war cry blasted into the overheated air.

"Zair! Krozair! Krozair!"

I had struck down a Grodnim and had just reached out for the next when I saw his face. I saw the tightly clenched jaw, the staring eyes, the black down-drooping Magdaggian moustaches. And I saw the sudden appalled look of horror flash into that face as the fellow heard that deep and menacing war cry. "Krozair!" He never knew what hit him and sent him to Cottmer's Caverns, most likely. "Krozair!"

I swirled my blade around and deflected a Chulik's blade. He pressed on with vehemence, for he, like everyone else, could hear those ferocious war cries blasting up at his rear. I clashed blades again, and looked past the Chulik for an instant, took in what I saw, and then went back to work.

Beyond the bows of this Grodnim swifter a larger swifter had eased up, a double-banked vessel. She lofted over the fighting-men, and warriors poured from her—and, they wore the red, the glorious red, and at their head punched a tight and compact knot of Krozairs, their brands living flames in the speckled light.

I took the Chulik with the old underhand and he toppled back, yelling, for even a Chulik may yell when he has been hurt to death. He fell. Now the decks were clearing. Grodnims were hurling themselves overboard. A few more sought to stem this fresh and sudden onslaught, and then saw that the fight was hopeless. Those who did not jump overboard were cut down. A crossbowman took a last shot at me. The Krozair brand, held in that cunning Krozair grip, flicked the bolt away.

Blood ran across the decks. The slaves were caterwauling like men released from hell. Well, they were, of course.

I stood lightly, holding the sword-point down so that blood spread from that sharp point across the deck. I looked at the men—at the man who led the newcomers.

Yes, I recalled that moment with a mixture of pungent emotions. I remembered it often and I remember it today.

They strode through the shambles toward us survivors. They looked magnificent. Their mail shimmered, their white surcoats blazed with the coruscating device of the hubless spoked wheel within the circle. They were Krozairs. Their hard mahogany faces with the harsh upthrusting moustaches, their helmets crowned with flaunting masses of scarlet feathers, their Krozair longswords held still at the ready, they bore down on us blood-covered men as beings apart, dedicated, relentless in their fanaticism, puritan in their Zairian zeal. And, of them all, the man at their head, their leader, most brilliantly illuminated all the superb qualities of a Krozair. This man was fit to lead.

"Llahal, jernus," he said in a strong, though pleasant voice, giving us the courtesy. "It seems we were just in time."

"Llahal," I said. "We had them on the run." I made my voice flat and hard. I could not afford to waste a mur.

"Indeed?" His voice took on the inflexible tone of harsh authority smelling out rank heresy. "Has the city fallen? Do you with the rough tongue flee from Zandikar, like a rast?"

"The city has not fallen—yet." I bellowed to my men. "All aboard *Marigold!* Schtump! Leave the shambles here." The Krozairs went with us, for they sensed treachery. "No, the city holds. That cramph king Genod has brought up an army and flying boats. Your help will be warmly received."

"So you scuttle from the last fight?"

"Fambly," I said, for I was anxious to press on and there was much to do. "Gerblish fambly! We go to prevent Genod—"

His sword whipped up in a smoky flash of light and the tip hovered at my throat. His handsome face, young, strong, brilliant, glared in fury. His brown eyes bore down on me.

"I am a Krozair and do not relish being called a fambly by scum who desert a despairing city."

The sword could be slipped, Krozair though he was. I know more tricks than even the Krozairs teach. I stood. I said, "Your swifter—the golden chavonth as figurehead. I salute you as a great Krozair captain."

I remembered how this Krozair vessel, *Golden Chavonth,* had so plagued Gafard, the Sea Zhantil, burning his broad ships and fleetly avoiding his war swifters.

This young man looked resplendent in his youthful power. Strength and authority flowed from him. I knew he possessed a goodly share of the yrium. Resplendent... resplendent...

"You address me as Krozair, jernu or sir. I ask you again. Do you flee from Zandikar?"

"No," I said. "And I would like to know your name." I thought I already knew, and the ache bit into me, bit hard and fearsomely, like a cancer in my breast.

He did not move the longsword. He wore a solaik sword scabbarded above the scabbard of the Krozair longsword. He looked at me, and he looked puzzled.

I said, "I am Dak. I would know your name."

He shook his head. The sword did not tremble.

"I am Pur Zeg."

I hardly heard the rest. Pur Zeg, Krzy, Prince of Vallia, whom I had last seen as a shouting, laughing, tumbling three-year-old in far Esser Rarioch! Oh, how I cursed those damnable Star Lords. For I saw through all the splendid shimmer of power and gallantry in this young man the inner core of harsh bitterness. I thought then that his hatred of his father would make the hatred of Vax as the mewling of a kitten.

Someone at my back said, not loudly but loudly enough for us all to hear, "It is the famous Krozair, Pur Zeg. The son of Pur Dray Prescot!"

"Aye!" shouted Zeg. He whirled past me and the blade switched from my throat. I did not think there were many men who would have been allowed to keep a blade at my throat like that. "Aye! I am the son of Pur Dray Prescot. And if any man speaks the name again, I shall—"

With the old venom cutting through my voice so that my son Zeg swung back, shocked, I said as I had said to Vax, "And do you hate your father so?"

442

"If the yetch were here I would strike him down without another thought than that of justice achieved."

I could see Fazhan, who had gone into the knot of Krozairs, talking away and nodding his head and pointing at me. He was a good man. Zeg, who had once been three years old and called Segnik, after my comrade Seg Segutorio, swung back to glare at me in a way I fancied I had seen in my mirror.

"You who call yourself Dak! You do not address a Krozair with fitting respect. Do you not know the Krozairs are the only salvation of Zair? Only we can save you. You have been deserting and have been taken up. You will all hang."

My men started yelling at this, and then a Krozair Brother, an experienced fighter, stepped forward and spoke privately to Zeg. I had searched each Krozair face and knew none of them. Had one been present in the Hall of Judgment in Zy then I would have had a pretty dance before I won free. But none had. They had all been out aroving the inner sea, fighting-Krozairs. This Red Brother spoke to Zeg and Zeg turned to me and had the grace to say, "I understand you command in Zandikar, and that King Zinna is dead." And then—and I swear Zeg was a Krozair first, last, and all the time—I saw the abrupt and brutal horror flower in his face.

Before he could agonize too long, I said, "Miam is safe. She is the queen of Zandikar. I am about her business. Cast off your *Golden Chavonth* and pull up to her. Tell her you saw me and that all goes well—if I can get free of a pack of chattering Krozairs and go fight Magdaggians."

Some of the Krozairs let rip gasps of outraged horror at this. But time *was* running on. If I didn't do what I intended to do pretty quick it would be too late to save Zandikar. Although even if the city went up in flames I would still do as I intended.

"You speak with a big mouth, Dak."

"Pur Zeg." I said the word and savored it. One day he would tell me how he had achieved the coveted "Z." If we both lived, that was. "I must go. For the sweet sake of Zair, clear your ship from my bows. Do you want the city to fall?"

He glared; but already men were pushing the swifters free. I shouted a few short, harsh commands, for the seamen of *Golden Chavonth* handled out little *Marigold* as though she were a mighty three-banked zhantiller instead of a little chavinter.

"I came straight here as soon as I heard the city was besieged. The Dikar was open; but I think you will find it closed by Green swifters by now."

"Thank you for the warning. Now pull into Zandikar and bid them carry out my instructions faithfully. They are to concentrate in the strong places and resist. You know your brother Drak flies here with an aerial armada?"

443

His face lit up. Well, that might be brotherly love. It could merely be a warrior's joy that reinforcements were on the way.

"I will pardon your uncouth manners, fambly, for that great news. But, the next time we meet, I warn you. Keep a civil tongue in your head lest you lose it."

I said, "Do you mean the head or the tongue or both? Did you not receive proper tuition in Kregish?"

Before he could react, for although he was very quick I think his old father still held an edge there, I bellowed off forward and my oarsmen settled at their looms. There were no longer sixty of them, alas, and I turned from the forecastle and roared back, "are you sailing with us or not? Your swifter has her oars out. If you do not use them in a moment or two we'll be on our way."

The Krozairs jumped up onto the bulwarks and ran along the oars and thence along their own oars to their ship. I guessed they were fuming. But Zeg might still suspect our motives and he would wish to be with Miam and where the fighting was to be expected. What he would say when he saw Vax intrigued me.

He shouted a last baleful warning as the ships parted company. "Do not forget what I have promised you, Dak, when you return—if you return." The words spit into the overclouded sky. "You have the word of a Krozair."

He had looked resplendent—superb, brilliant—striding down the blood-soaked deck among the corpses, his weapons agleam, his helmet flaunting the brave scarlet feathers, his white surcoat with the coruscating device of the Krzy. He was my son. And all we could do was shout threats at each other. So, and to the vast surprise of my men, I bellowed back mildly. "I'll be back. And mind you keep Zandikar safe for Queen Miam—Krozair."

All the same, as we glided on and at last and thankfully plunged into the concealment of the rushes, I reflected that he had been overly mild for a Krozair. I know I have a daunting way with me; but Zeg was of that stamp of young men fanatical about their beliefs. That was clear. I had heard it spoken and had joyed in it. He had gone to the sacred Isle of Zy at a very young age, soon after I had disappeared when he'd been three. He had not had the earlier and wider education of Drak. He was obsessed with his Krozair vows, the Disciplines, the mysticism. The Krozairs had molded him completely—or so I had thought. And yet...?

The uproar in that open reach of water might easily bring inquisitive Magdaggian swifters. I fancied Zeg would dispose of them smartly enough, and he had taken the swifter we had captured, manned by her ex-oar-slaves. As for us, we ghosted on and soon were able to turn and so make a landing on the mainland.

Here I had to be extraordinarily nasty to Duhrra and the others.

"No, you pack of famblies! I can get through—I hope. But you would all be taken up. Why, you'd start a-yelling Zair at any moment. This is Green work." And I wrapped about myself the green cloth that I had brought and changed my Red helmet for a captured one sporting green feathers. "See?"

Duhrra said, "I was renegade, also, Gadak."

"Gadak, is it? That proves nothing. I go alone."

"Gadak" was the Grodnim name given to me by Gafard when I'd pretended to become a renegade. Duhrra had never got along with "Guhrra." As for the others— "Take great care on your way back. And tell that fam— tell that Zeg to fight like a Valkan."

Even if they did not fully understand, they would pass the message. Zeg was known to be a prince of Vallia, Zeg of Valka.

I did not wait for them to shove off but sprinted for the nearest cover. I did not even look back. The land here rose from the Dikars, with their ribbons of shining water, and trended upward and then leveled off. I passed through ruined gregarian groves, and through kools of land where the wheat had been cut down and used by damned Grodnims. Soon the camp appeared ahead, rows of tents, with lines of tethered sectrixes, lines of hebras, the artillery park where a few varters were being repaired. One or two fluttrells flew in the sky and so I walked with a brisk military gait, not running and not slouching. If anyone questioned me, I was a scout returning with information.

The park where the vollers had touched down lay over the other side of the camp. This was the main siege camp; there were others on the other flanks of the city walls. It should be mentioned here that I carried an arsenal of weapons, with reason. I had buckled on the Ghittawrer blade, the device removed. I had belted on a Genodder, the Grodnim shortsword, above that, to the right. The great Krozair blade hung down my back, and the green cape hid the hilt. Also I carried the Lohvian longbow and a quiver of arrows. I might not use all of these weapons; I felt it certain I would use some.

When I add that the old seaman's knife snugged over my right hip, those of you who have followed my story so far will know that was a habitual fashion with me.

At the center and in a cleared space lofted the ornate green and white tent of the king. I walked through the alleyways between the surrounding tents. Gafard's tent would be nearby. No airboats lifted into the sky, so I was in time. I let out a long breath and stepped past the last tent. Guards ringed the king's abode and tethered hebras waited patiently. The rast was in conference, then. He had slipped up, the cramph.

I put my foot down to stalk arrogantly on and a voice said, "Why, by Grotal the Reducer! Gadak! Gadak, as I live and breathe!"

I turned. Grogor, Gafard's second in command, stood there, hands on hips, his face astounded, gaping at me.

Nineteen
"Then die, Dray Prescot, die!"

"Grogor!" I said, booming it out in hearty good fellowship. "How grand to see a friendly face again, by the Holy Bones of Genodras!"

"Gadak…" He goggled at me. "But we all thought you gone to the swifters, dead."

"To the swifters but not dead. I have been remitted. How is our master, Gafard, the King's Striker? He is well, I trust?"

"As well as that prince Glycas will let him be. The king is changed—well, it is not for me to prattle on. So you come to serve my lord Gafard again?"

"My lord Gafard," I said, realizing I'd forgotten the "my lord" bit, thinking so often of him as Gafard. "Aye. If you will take me to him."

"He is closeted with the king and Prince Glycas. They plan this afternoon's strike at that accursed city."

"The siege goes well, I trust?"

"If you trusted less, Gadak, and opened your Grodno-forsaken eyes, you would see how we fare here. Our bellies rumble."

I had eaten well of mergem before I'd quit *Marigold*. This news heartened me. Genod had a large army here, and the way across the Eye of the World from Magdag, and from the nearer Green cities, was long and arduous. With bold sea-rovers like my lad Zeg ranging like sea leem, food would be a problem after they'd eaten the district empty. Logistics play havoc with the calculations of kings.

I handed Grogor a handful of palines. His eyes widened.

"How came you by these? They fetch golden oars here."

"I remember you shot an arrow at a certain saddle-bird, Grogor. I remember you rode to save my Lady of the Stars." I could not tell him the Lady of the Stars was my daughter Velia. "I think I misjudged you when first we met."

"Aye. Mayhap I did, also. And I give thanks to Grodno for the palines." He put one in his mouth and the paline-look passed hedonistically across his plug-ugly face.

We walked slowly toward Gafard's tent. I had until this afternoon. Rather, I had until the conference ended. I had a plan. It was feeble and must change as events progressed; but as a scheme it ought to be foolproof, given the technology of the inner sea.

The soldiers busy about the unending duties of swods all carried that pinched look of hunger about them. But, also, they held a new and eager look of conquest. I knew why. Their great king had just arrived, with flying boats. Soon, this very afternoon, they would be wafted over the infernal walls of Zandikar, which had withstood every attempt for so long, and then they could run riot within the city in an orgy of rapine. They were soldiers, simple men, and by the reckoning of men of Zair evil until the Last Day and beyond. But to me, a simple sailorman and an equally simple soldier, they were just swods. I would joy to go into action with them against the hated shanks, those devils from over the curve of the world, demons who would give us much trouble in all the lands of the Outer Oceans in the future.

Wo is Kregish for zero. Swods in their rough, jocular way like to dub themselves wo-Deldars, zero-Deldars. It is an irony.

Because this army of swods fought for the Green and King Genod I would have to go into battle against them.

Always I find this unsettling, that one can sing and roister with common soldiers, and find them human beings, and on the next day encounter them in battle and find them transformed into leems. Of course, this holds true for the men of Zairia, and my warriors of Valka and Strombor. As for my Djangs, well, those four-armed demons are fighting-men first and last, and warriors of the hyr Jikai in between.

A number of the men I had known when I served Gafard came up and we talked and I was seemingly free and open in my conversation, telling them I was glad to be remitted from the galleys—a stupidly obvious statement—and happy to be back with Gafard and my comrades. Presently Grogor said, "The conference is breaking up. The generals and Chuktars ride off. Soon the three leaders will appear. Then we will know."

As though drawn by a magnet, a crowd of men gathered in a vast ring around the king's tent. When, at last, he stepped out, a great cheer went up. "Magdag! Genod! Genod!"

I looked at this yetch, this nulsh, this kleesh whom I had been instrumental in bringing into this marvelous world of Kregen. He looked handsome, puffed up with pride, garish in his green and gold. But he was a fighting-man and could use the Genodder, the shortsword he had invented and named, with a skill no other fighting-man of Grodnim could match.

After him stepped Prince Glycas and Gafard, together, shoulder to shoulder, and it was clear they struggled for precedence. As for this Glycas, I remembered him. He might remember me, for all that it was over fifty years ago I had stayed in his Emerald Eye Palace and avoided his sister, the princess Susheeng. He was unpleasant. I would have short shrift with him.

As for my lord Gafard, Rog of Guamelga, the King's Striker, Prince of the Central Sea, the Reducer of Zair, Sea Zhantil, Ghittawrer of Genod, and many another resounding title, he was the widower of my daughter Velia, my son-in-law, the hulu, and ripe for mischief.

I remembered what Duhrra had said, and I, too, felt I would not willingly slay this man Gafard, for all he was a renegade from Zair, bowing
down to Grodno, a hated enemy. He was a rogue and a rascal, intensely
courageous, a Jikaidast, a man.

The noise subsided and the dust clouds settled and the king spoke. It was
all fustian stuff; but it drove heart into the men and roused them, and gave
them enthusiasm. This cramph Genod, who had murdered my daughter,
was accounted a genius at war. He told the men Zimuzz had fallen, at which
I let rip a few shouts, because that was expected. Now, this very afternoon,
he said, we would fly over the accursed walls of Zandikar. Then it would be
every man for himself. The city would be given over to the sack.

They started in a-yelling, "Zamu! Sanurkazz!" and the rast promised
them those great cities for the sacking, also.

Amid frantic scenes of wild enthusiasm the king passed among his
men. They even began the great shout of "Hai Jikai!" and this I would not
shout. Grogor, too, did not shout. He said, sourly, "Wait until the city is
ours before we shout the Hai Jikai."

"Let us move nearer to my lord Gafard."

So we forced our way through the throng as the dust rose billowing and
the blades flashed in the light of the suns. For the dappled clouds had all
passed away and the gloriously mingled, streaming light of the Suns of Scorpio flooded down over that ecstatic scene as a king moved among his army.

The men were halted at last by a line of blank yellow-faced Chuliks.
Their long pigtails were dyed green. They wore mail and they would cut
down anyone at the order of their Chuktar. Grogor advanced confidently.
The king and his advisers had passed beyond the line of Chulik mercenaries, into a cleared space where a small flier rested. They were talking
gravely together, with much nodding of heads and gesticulations.

Grogor said to the Hikdar in command of the Chulik detail, "Lahal,
Hikdar Gachung. I must speak with my lord Gafard. This man is with
me."

"Lahal, Jiktar Grogor. You may pass."

The Chuliks are usually stiff and formal in military matters.

As we passed their impressive line and walked toward the group of high
dignitaries by the voller, I said to Grogor, "Nothing was said, then, about
your shot at the bird? You escaped?"

"Gafard accepted the loss of his Lady of the Stars. It hurt him. I know
that. But the king has the yrium, and the king may do all. My lord Gafard
interceded for me, and pleaded I did not know it was the king. There were
politics involved." Grogor's face showed what he thought of politics. "My
lord Gafard is sorely tried by Prince Glycas."

"The king plays one off against the other? This I do not like, for I believe
my lord Gafard to be the better man as mergem is better than dilse."

448

"Aye."

"And did my lord Gafard truly reconcile himself to the king, afterward? His lady was dead, and it was the king's doing."

"I did not see. No one knows how she died. They say you were with the body. But you went to the swifters. I think Glycas had misbehaved himself at the time, and the king inclined toward our lord."

The king stood with his back to us, talking and waving his hands about in graphic gestures. His voice was mellow and strong and everyone listened intently. Gafard saw Grogor. Then he saw me. His eyes widened. He switched back at once to listening to the king; but I saw his hand grip the hilt of his Ghittawrer blade.

A fussy aide bustled up and Grogor cut him to size and told him we waited for Gafard with news. The king must be allowed to finish his instructions. We moved off and I heard Genod saying importantly, "I shall fly over the city now and inspect the defenses. The rasts of Zairians will never stand against us, as we descend upon them from the skies. But, by Goyt, I must conserve my army against the assault on Zamu. And there is Sanurkazz after." He swung his arms violently. "You, Gafard, will accompany me."

Glycas, stung, said, "I would fly with you, Majister."

"If you wish, for you may see what has held you up so long."

Glycas, it was clear, was in King Genod's bad books.

During the time we waited and looked like gawping onkers at the voller, the continual hum and buzz of a great military camp rose about us. The sense of impending great deeds filled the air with tension. The suns-light smoked more brilliantly in every bright trapping and gem and sword-blade. We all shared the feeling we were gods, treading no mortal path.

When we heard the sounds indicating that the group was breaking up, Grogor said, "Let us go and see my lord."

"Yes," I said, and stumbled and sprawled in the dust.

Grogor laughed. "Onker." Then, as I lay there, "You are all right, Gadak? Nothing broken?"

"My leg," I said. "By Iangle! It stings like the bite of a lairgodont!"

"Do not move and I will fetch a needleman."

As Grogor ran off I felt again that I would stay my hand in battle against him, even though he was renegade, hulu.

I heard the men on the other side of the voller. The air-boat itself was a roomy craft, with an open central well with seating around the sides. Her hull was wood over wooden formers. She was a simple commercial craft, cheaply produced in Hamal and sold to Genod. The bloods of the sacred quarter of Ruathytu I had known would never give her room in their vollerdromes. Yet her petal shape conveyed enormous powers here in the Eye of the World.

I stood up when Grogor vanished around her prow, and peeked over the coaming. Gafard was assiduously climbing into the airboat and managing to push Glycas out of the way. The king already stood just aft of the pilot, his back to me.

Glycas—and how I remembered his evil rast-face!—said most petulantly, "Let me up, gernu, you rast."

"Up as high as you like, Prince, cramph," said Gafard.

There was no love lost between these two even in semi-privacy. The king did not move. The pilot sat petrified at his controls. He was a Grodnim. I put both my hands on the coaming.

Men have said I am quick. Well, Djan knows, I have need to be, to stay alive on Kregen.

With a single heave I went up over the coaming. I heard a distant yell, "Onker! Stand aside from the king's flying boat," and I knew no guard in the whole army would risk a shot with the king so near. I jumped across the airboat and knocked the king aside. I hit the control levers, hard and full, to send the boat leaping skyward. I heard an abrupt shriek from the side and rear and guessed Glycas had not made it and had fallen back. If he'd broken his neck it would save the hangman a job. King Genod stumbled back, clearly not understanding what was going on. I caught the pilot around the waist and heaved the poor devil over the side. He fell and did not kill himself.

Then the voller sped up into the bright sky and King Genod, Gafard, the King's Striker, and I faced one another.

No one drew a weapon.

The king hauled himself up. He stared at me with the puzzled look of a man finding a cockroach under his salad.

"You realize you are a dead man?"

I ignored him.

"Gafard," I said. "You know me."

"Aye." He half turned to the king. "This is that wild leem Gadak, who was sent to the swifters." He shook his head. "He must have been remitted, although I did not know."

"What do you here, dead man?" said Genod.

I said, "I was not remitted, Gafard. I escaped. Do you remember what passed between us the last time I saw you? In the Zhantil's Lair, when you heard this kleesh had stolen away my Lady of the Stars?"

Gafard sucked in his breath. The king's hand hovered over the hilt of his Genodder. That hilt blazed with gems. The blade would be the finest the smithies of Magdag could produce.

"I—I do not fully remember. But the king has the yrium. Surrender yourself to his mercy. We must return to the ground."

"You poor fool! Know you not this genius king of yours is evil? Evil and vile and ready for the justice of Drig's heavy hand?"

The king had had enough. This Genod Gannius had made himself king of Magdag and led the Grodnim confederation. He had humored me. Now he would slay me. He whipped out the Genodder and threw himself into an attacking crouch. The blade gleamed.

"I shall cut you up myself, rast."

"Surrender, Gadak! The king has no equal with the shortsword. Throw yourself on his mercy," Gafard pleaded.

"He knows nothing of mercy." I drew the Genodder at my right side. "Let me show you what he thinks of mercy."

Genod had not come to power merely because he was a genius at war. Anyway, I suspected shrewdly that his genius was a propaganda fiction; he had been successful because of the new army his father had created on the model of my old vosk-skulls from the warrens of Magdag. With a screech our blades met.

He was very good with the shortsword. As always in a fight I go into the combat with the stark knowledge that this could be the last fight, the final conflict, and that I will be shipped out to the Ice Floes of Sicce at the end. This evil king had risen to power as much through his prowess as a fighting-man as through his war genius.

His skin was extraordinarily smooth. Pale and soft like a woman's skin, it covered muscles whipcord tough. He feinted and lunged and I covered and showed the point. He parried and the blades ground resonantly and parted. He jumped back. "Give yourself up, cramph, to the kingly justice!"

I leaped in and twisted the Genodder about in a way that owed nothing to the skills of Green Magdag but rather to the wild outlandish skirlings of my Clansmen. We used the shortsword out there on the wide Plains of Segesthes. In shortsword work a Clansman would have cut up any Genod-derman of Magdag, aye, and quaffed his wine as he fought. Hap Loder would have.

Genod's face took on a sudden strained look as he feinted and lunged. Gafard cried out, expecting the blow to be mortal, but the king's blade went nowhere near me and I slashed and his bright green cloak fell away, the golden cords cut through. He stumbled back. But he had courage, the rast, and he came in again. And again I parried and foined with him and so cut away the brilliant gold and green tunic to reveal the mail beneath, and went on and so slashed and cut him about until all his gorgeous apparel had been ripped away and he stood in the mail alone. Then, and only then, I used the old but always cunning lever on him and the Genodder spun from his hand and flew up and out to plunge down to the ground beneath.

He panted. His face had turned lemon-green. His eyes were wild upon me as he shrank back.

"If you are the best Genodderman in Magdag, you cramph," I said, "your Zair-forsaken land is doomed, and praise to Zair for that!"

"Who are you?" he croaked.

Gafard did not draw. I flicked the sword about, between them, and I said to Gafard, "Tell him who I am."

"You—" Gafard's hands trembled. He gripped the hilt of his Ghittawrer longsword and the scabbard shook. "You are Gadak, who was Dak, and yet I think—"

"Yes, Gafard. You think?"

"What you said, there in the Zhantil's Lair. I have tried to think. You would not go after my Lady of the Stars, even though I pleaded as best I could—and you knew I loved her—and—"

"Aye, you loved her, Gafard. She told me that. And she loved you. Never was man more blessed than to receive the love of my Lady of the Stars."

"Yes—you would not go—and then—then you did go. Did I say something, anything—I cannot remember—"

I did not know if he was speaking the truth. Yet the horrific scene in the hunting lodge when I had discovered that the Lady of the Stars was my daughter could have been so painful to him that he had shut it out of his mind. It is known. I glared at him.

"You told me, in all truth, who my Lady of the Stars was."

"Ah! And then you went?"

"Yes."

He trembled uncontrollably now. He had doted on his lady, and he had yearned to emulate the exploits of her father, saying there was a matter between him and Pur Dray. Now I had realized he did not mean he wished to fight me, as I had then thought. He had wished to talk to his father-in-law. As was, in very truth, proper. For I would have a hand in the bokkertu.

The king roused himself. He looked ghastly. "What is all this nonsense, Gafard! Kill the cramph, here and now!"

"I do not think I can do that, Majister."

"Then try, you ungrateful cramph!"

"Tell him who I am, Gafard."

Gafard's face had lost all its color. His bronze tan floated on his skin. He looked frenzied. "I—I think—"

"Why should I not slay you now, Gafard—you who bow down to his kleesh of a king? Oh, yes, Gafard, you know who I am. You have dreamed of this meeting. You save relics. You say there is a matter between us. By Zair! There is a matter between us!"

He gasped and tried to speak and his mouth merely opened and closed.

"There is a matter! I want to know why you fawn on this foul object, and let him steal away my daughter, Velia!"

He did not fall. In truth, the shock of the meeting would have felled a lesser man with all the passionate longings he had put into just such a confrontation. He wet his lips. The cords in his neck strained like ropes in a hurricane. He croaked, and tried again, and, at last, he could say the words.

"Pur Dray! Pur Dray Prescot! The Lord of Strombor! Krozair of Zy!"

The king shrieked at this, and cowered away, his hands fumbling at his throat. Like a fool, I ignored him.

"No, Gafard—*son-in-law!* I am no longer a Krozair of Zy, for I am Apushniad. But—yes, I am Dray Prescot!"

For a moment no one spoke. The moment was too heavy for mere words.

The king levered himself up. His anguished face bore the look of a madman. His hand fumbled at his neck.

"Dray Prescot! The Bane of Grodno!" His hand whipped the cunning little throwing knife from the sheath at his back. "Then die, Dray Prescot, die!"

Twenty
The Siege of Zandikar: IV
Of partings and of meetings

"Die, Dray Prescot, die!"

The glittering throwing knife hurtled from the fingers of the king straight at my face.

And, in that selfsame instant, as though time shuttered through a macabre repetition, I caught a single flashing glimpse over the side of the voller of a gorgeous scarlet and golden bird of prey in full diving vicious attack upon a shining white dove.

The two scenes merged and melded in my eyes and became one.

The golden and scarlet raptor of the Star Lords, their spy and messenger, striking with black-taloned claws at the white dove of the Savanti, and the glittering terchick, the Kregan throwing knife, hurled full at my face, were one and the same. I saw the Savanti dove hesitate and swerve and the lancing blow of scarlet and gold shriek past. The Genodder in my fist sprang up and twitched in the old cunning Disciplines and the terchick rang like a gong-note of despair, clanging against the blade and springing in a gleaming curve away into the vast reaches of the sky. The king's mouth slobbered wetly and he began to claw out his Ghittawrer longsword.

"He is a Krozair, Majister," said Gafard, staring at me with hunger and despair.

"You call this object 'Majister,' Gafard. Yet he stole my daughter away from you, and now she is dead. You are a man. I know that. You prated on about the Lord of Strombor, and you emulated my deeds and sought my renown. I would surrender all those deeds and give all that renown if my Velia were back with me, alive!"

He pushed himself up. He had stopped shaking. "I, too, Pur Dray, would give everything I own, everything I am—"

"The girl was a fool, a shishi!" shrieked Genod. "I am the king. It is my right to take—"

"Your rights will be allowed you when you are judged. For I take you back to Zandikar. There you will be judged for murder."

"Murder?" Gafard's jaw muscles ridged. He stared at me. His eyes held a look no man should suffer—a look I had borne as I cradled my Velia in my arms and watched her die.

"Aye, Gafard—murder. This kleesh's fluttrell was wounded by Grogor's shot. The bird was falling. Velia was callously thrown off by this kleesh to save himself."

"It is a lie!" Genod staggered up, distraught, panting, whooping great gulps of air. He had drawn his Ghittawrer blade with the tawdry emblem of his Green Brotherhood upon it. "A lie!"

"I never heard the Lord of Strombor was a Krozair who lied."

"I speak the truth, Gafard. This kleesh whom you worship threw my daughter down to her death—threw down your wife!"

Once the first stone is dislodged in a wall or a dam the final pressure mounts swiftly and more swiftly to the point of breaking and utter collapse. This Gafard—the King's Striker, Sea Zhantil, my *son-in-law*—had revered the genius king Genod, the king with the yrium, had worshiped my daughter Velia, and had envied my reputation upon the Eye of the World and had attempted to emulate me. Zair knows, the poor hulu was a tormented man. Struck and buffeted by passions and beliefs, by desires and duties, he had been caught in a mind-shattering trap. Renegade, loyal Grodnim of Magdag, once a loyal Zairian, he now faced the final collapse of everything in his life. He had been tortured in his ib by beliefs and truths beyond the breaking of a mortal man. Even as King Genod, foaming, berserk, launched himself forward with the Ghittawrer blade lifting, so Gafard bellowed and flung himself at the king.

"King Genod!"

"Stand aside, Gafard, you rast, while I cut down this devil."

"Genod—murderer!" Gafard's howl pricked the nape of the neck. "I have served you faithfully. I revered you past reason. You repay me by murdering my Velia, the only woman in the world—"

"Lies! Lies!"

They stood for perhaps a half dozen heartbeats, their chests laboring to draw breath as they shouted, their faces demoniac with convulsive rage and revelation.

Then Genod lunged viciously forward, shrieking he would slay us both, and Gafard, with a snarl like a wild beast dragged heels first from its lair into the hostile world, leaped on the king, one hand to his throat, the other around his waist. So they struggled, bodies locked, animated with hatred and passion.

The rest of their contorted yells were lost as they struggled. The Ghittawrer blade slashed down and Gafard ignored it and forced the king back. I jumped forward to separate them, for I wanted to take Genod for trial—I truly believe I wished this—and the struggle carried them raving to the coaming of the voller.

Without a pause in their struggle one with the other they toppled over the coaming and pitched out over the side of the voller. I put my hand on the coaming and looked down.

Over and over they toppled, falling through the thin air as my Velia had fallen. They still fought as they fell. I did not turn away with a shudder. I watched them as they dwindled and fell away and so I remained, graven, watching as the king and Gafard, the King's Striker, smashed to red jelly in the central square of Zandikar.

The single thought burning in my brain as I brought the voller to land was that Grogor must not be slain in the coming battle, for Grogor would know where Didi, the daughter of Gafard and Velia, was kept hidden. Somewhere in Magdag or on one of Gafard's estates; yes, Grogor would take me to my granddaughter.

The kyro filled with a rushing clamor as the people and the soldiers ran. Life, which had for a moment turned aside, now resumed the reins. Gafard was dead. There would be a proper time to mourn. I did not forget that apocalyptic vision of the Gdoinye, the spy of the Star Lords, and its deliberate attack on the white dove of the Savanti. I knew, with that special doom I feel is laid upon me, that the toils of supernatural manipulations had been only temporarily evaded.

The consternation and then the bemused wonder and then the joyful acclamations seized all Zandikar. Everyone understood what the death of this vile king Genod would mean. I had to quiet the uproar, raising my hands, bellowing to make them listen.

"Prince Glycas is not dead. That cramph will lead now. We must still fight!"

"Aye!" they bellowed. And then I heard the name the people of Zandikar shouted, the name they screeched in their determination to resist to the end. "Aye, Zadak! We will fight and never surrender! We fight for Zadak and Zandikar!"

In the hullabaloo I found Queen Miam. Zeg stood at her side and they were both removed from common cares, entranced with each other—as was very proper in ordinary times; but of little use to us here in the siege. Others crowded around.

"Who is this Zadak, Miam? I would care to meet him."

She laughed—Miam's laugh was always a wonder. "I think I should like that, also." She clung on to Zeg's arm. He looked down on her with that look—well, we all know about that. She beckoned to me. "I introduce you with the full pappattu to Zadak. For the Dak that was is the Zadak of Zandikar. Do you agree?"

I repeated the formula. "I agree, Queen Miam. I thank you."

Then they all began cheering. Well, the famous old "Z" had been added to my name, and that was all very well and fine; but the battle remained to be won. The feeling was a strange one. As I seldom had used King Zo's gift of the title of Sea Zhantil, so I seldom used Zadray. I would always think of the Sea Zhantil as being Gafard. He had earned the title. I said to Zeg and Vax, harshly, coldly, "Come with me."

Zeg was too mazed with love to bristle, and Vax knew me by now. They followed me, these two hulking sons of mine, and we strode through the people to the cleared area where the king of Magdag and his favorite lay in the dust.

They had fought bitterly until the end. Genod had landed first. Gafard was not, therefore, so badly crushed. The fingers of the King's Striker were still tightly wrapped around the throat of the king. He had choked the kleesh. I just hoped Genod had not been dead before he hit.

I turned them over and freed the gripping fingers. Blood ran everywhere. I pulled Gafard over onto his back. He flopped.

"Look on this man's face, Vax. Look well." I spoke with a savage bitterness that chilled Vax. "Look on this man's face, Zeg. Look well. Remember him. Remember him."

Zeg started to say something, a farrago about my calling him Pur Zeg and being respectful to a Krozair Brother.

"Look, Zeg, on this man's face. Make sure you remember every line of it." I bent down and brushed my fingers and thumb over the black moustaches. I forced them away from their silly downturned Magdaggian shape and brushed them up into the old arrogant Zairian fashion. "Look on this man Gafard. There are those to whom you will be asked to speak of Gafard. Do not forget him."

I stalked away and Zeg caught my shoulder and said, harshly, "You may be called Zadak of Zandikar now, Dak the Insolent. But I shall not tolerate your insolence! Either you—"

I swung about and shook his hand free. I glared at him. He did not flinch back—for which I was pleased—but he stopped talking. "Do not say it, Pur Zeg, Krozair of Zy, jernu, Prince. Do not say what you will regret."

What might have happened then, Zair knows; a shrilling shout racketed from the walls and so we all knew the last fight had begun.

There were things to be done. I said to Vax, "Prince Zeg will take care

456

of the queen now. We have one vol—flying boat. Will you take her, with fighting-men, and do what you can?"

Before Vax could answer and so show me up for the onker I was, Duhrra boomed his idiotic bellow. "Duh—Dak! Vax flew the flying boat when we had to leave you on the beach. I'm going with him. It is all arranged."

I did not smile. "So be it." I glared at my son. "And may Zair and this Opaz you speak of go with you."

Everyone ran to take up their appointed stations. Everyone felt convinced this was the last fight. We watched as the vollers rose from the camp of the Grodnims. They soared up and formed ready to sweep over the walls of Zandikar. We all let out huge shouts of joy when two fliers collided. And we all shouted with joy again when two more suddenly dropped down to crash onto the ground. No one here—apart from myself and my two sons—could understand why the airboats should fall and crash.

"Glycas is out for all the glory himself. Well, we will give him a bellyful before the day is done."

We all knew the city was doomed, for we had nothing with which to counteract the fliers. In that moment as the vollers, all flying their green swifter pennons and standards, soared up to destroy us, a fresh series of shouts broke out from the seaward walls. I looked back—and *up*.

Queen Miam put a hand on Zeg's arm, and swayed. Zeg held her. Roz Janri and Pallan Zavarin exclaimed in joy. Up there, sweeping in over the city, flew vollers. And each flier bore the red flags of Zair.

"It is my brother, Prince Drak!" roared Zeg. "It must be! By Zair! He cuts his time fine!"

I was busily counting the vollers sweeping in so grandly with their red banners flying. Fifty! Fifty against over ninety. The plans must change. I bellowed out the orders. Sniz blew his guts out. Messengers galloped. We would hold the walls as we had done for so long. With vollers to fight vollers we had a chance.

As the main bulk of the Zairian aerial armada sailed on over the city to engage the oncoming Green fleet, the lead ship curved through the sky. We waved a multitude of red flags from our tower atop the Palace of Fragrant Incense, and Drak brought his flagship down in a courtyard below. We all met in the High Hall, halfway between up and down, and the greetings! The roarings! The back-thumpings! I stood in the shadows, and I looked at my eldest son.

Drak had been fourteen when I'd been ejected from Kregen and thrust back to Earth. Now he was a big, tough mature man, grown into Kregan manhood. The marks of power were on him, and yet I judged—I hoped, by Vox!—that he had not forgotten the lessons drummed into him by Delia and me, lessons designed to prevent the disease of uncontrollable power from corrupting him. I had the gloomiest of forebodings that for

Zeg power had already done its not-so-insidious work. The two brothers embraced each other with genuine warmth, and Zeg said, swiftly, that Jaidur was here and aloft, at which Drak said that, by Vox, that was where *he* should be, but he had alighted to learn our plans. So he was not altogether a headlong fool, then.

"And where is Zadak that he may come forward!" said Miam, who was known to Drak and who kissed him with sisterly affection.

It was no use shilly-shallying anymore in the shadows of the High Hall. I stamped a scowl over my ugly old face and stepped forward. If Drak recognized me that would not make any difference to the battle. I planted myself down, and I growled out, "Llahal, Prince Drak, Krozair. If you hold the zigging Grodnim flying boats in check, we will hold the walls."

Drak looked at me, taken aback. Then his eyebrows lifted by a hairbreadth and a shadow passed over his face. I glared at him malignantly.

"The queen has told me of you, Zadak. I give you Lahal. I am outnumbered two to one. But we will hold the Grodnims until not one of us flies."

He spoke up in a grave way, as a man with the cares of high office speaks. I liked the set of his head on his shoulders, the way he held himself. If Vax was still a young tearaway and Zeg a haughty and imperious killer, Drak was a darkly powerful man of affairs, versed in the ways of Kregen; a true prince of Vallia.

What a situation! I stood with my three sons, and could not acknowledge them, could not stride forward and clasp them in my arms. I suppose something more demoniacal than mere malignity showed on my face. I half turned away and shouted, "The prince has spoken! We resist to the end!"

"Hai!" came the answering shouts. "Hai, Jikai!"

"You—" said my son Drak. "We have never met, I know, and yet, something in you—it is odd." On that darkly handsome face of his, in which the beauty of his mother had somehow not been altogether overlaid by my own ugly features, although he was not as handsome as Vax, and not as brilliant in appearance as Zeg, a small, puzzled smile flitted. "It is a long time ago, now, and I grieve for that. But, by Vox, you remind me of my father."

"And do you hate your father, as your brothers do?"

"Of course he does!" Zeg said sharply. "For we have been cruelly treated. Apushniad! Let us get to work."

"Hatred?" said Drak. "Sometimes I think—but, this is a private affair, of the family and of honor. I give you respect for your defense of Zandikar, Zadak. But this is not a matter to discuss in public."

"I agree. Before you go aloft, I beg a favor. Go down with me to the central square. There is a man I would wish you to see before he is dumped in an unmarked grave."

The last was not strictly true. I'd see that a marker was set up—if I lived.

So Drak, too, stared down on the dead face of his brother-in-law. I spoke to him as I had to Zeg and Vax. He understood I wanted to boast of my prowess, and he frowned, and I did not disabuse him. He soared aloft to join his little fleet as the two aerial armadas clashed.

The fight that followed bellowed and clanged away in grisly style. We faced great odds. One enormous advantage we had, for the men of Vallia and Valka flying our vollers were trained men, many of them of the Vallian Air Service, and their experience in the air served them well in the fight against twice their number. Even then I saw a couple of Vallian vollers flutter to the ground, victims of the inferior workmanship with which Hamal cursed all the fliers she sold abroad.

The tactics of Glycas were simple. While some fliers attempted to get through and land parties of men inside the city, others settled just inside the walls and made determined onslaughts on the gates to open them to the waiting army. These we attacked with grim and savage ferocity, knowing that the opening of one gate would finish us. We fought desperately. But I saw, as I was staggering back from a charge that had destroyed the men from four fliers but had withered our own men away, that we were losing. More and more fliers settled inside and the green banners waved thickly in clumps, here and there. At any moment now a gate would go down and the damned Grodnims would be in.

"I think." said Zeg as he wiped his dripping blade, "they have us now."

"Do not speak like that, Zeg!"

He glared at me, his eyes over bright, his mouth ugly.

"You and I will settle this, if we live. You deserve to be jikaidered for your foulmouthed insolence. Ha! My brother Drak was right when he compared you with our father! He must be just such a braggart as you."

If that was not fair I had no time to care as once again we went hammer and tongs into a pack of Fristles running, screeching, from a newly landed flier. Our varters shot-in our attack and we routed them. The Zandikarese archers proved their worth on this day, and my Lohvian longbow sang sweetly whenever a target looked likely. But, all the same, we could last little longer.

A particularly fierce attack developed against that nodal central gate of the landward wall. Outside, waiting, the Magdaggian army stood at ease, drawn up in formation, ready to burst in. Over our heads the vollers circled and clashed and men and fliers fell from the sky. Many a green flag smashed into the dust and many a red flag followed. Our strength was being whittled away, and yet even as our fliers dwindled in numbers so did the Grodnim vollers shrink. There remained the force ready to launch itself at the central gate, and here we positioned ourselves to withstand the assault that might end all.

"If only our mean old devil of a grandfather had spared Drak good vollers!" said Zeg, with a vicious burst of anger. "He has them, for our cramph of a father took them in the Battle of Jholaix."

"We must fight with what we have, lad." I made up my mind. "If the city does fall, you must take a voller and Miam and escape."

He roared at me then, as a Valkan prince might roar. I bellowed over his furious protests. "Do you want to see what will happen to Miam? Are you that callous and hardhearted—and stupid?"

"And the warriors and the people, you rast! Do I leave them?"

"If they cannot escape, at least you and Miam—"

He turned away from me, unable to answer so base a suggestion as it should be answered, with a blow or the sword, for through all his Zairian fervor he recognized this Zadak was useful to Zandikar in a fight. He did say, bitterly, "But *you* will escape?"

I did not answer. Sniz was there, a bloody bandage around his head. "Blow, Sniz! Blow as you have never blown before."

Everything depended on this gate. Glycas had ceased to throw his fliers haphazardly into the city, where we waited for them and shot his soldiers up as they disembarked. Now he put everything into this last attack. The vollers descended and we could see their brave green banners, the fierce glint of weapons, and hear the ferocious shrilling war chants. "Magdag! Grodno!"

"Zair!" we yelled, and our archers shot. "Zair! Zandikar!"

The Green vollers descended in clouds, like flies onto a carcass. The wall, the gate-towers, the courtyards, filled with battling men. We heard the shrill yelping of men and trumpets from outside. With a crash that tore at our heartstrings we saw the gate burst in with a smother of flying chips of wood. The gate burst and went down and hordes of Green mailed warriors broke through, yelling in triumph.

"Now is the end!" bellowed Zeg and he leaped forward, swirling his Krozair longsword above his head, resplendent, shining in mail and blood, smashing a bloody trail through the Greens. I used the Lohvian longbow and preserved his life, as Seg had done for me in the long-ago. Other red banners pressed in from the side and for a space, a tiny space, we held them. But we could not hold the pressure. We sagged back. We sagged and stumbled back, and wounded men fell and dead men were crushed and it seemed that this final moment was the end.

We saw the ranks of Green draw back a space and knew they summoned up their energies for the last smashing attack. Duhrra stood at my side, splashed with blood, fearsome in his might. Vax was with him. Their flier had been smashed and they had lived so that they might die here, at the gate of Zandikar. Drak was there, calm and powerful, darkly dominant, giving orders that tightened up a flank. Our exhausted men ran to do his bidding. So, for that tiny space, we stood there, Drak, Zeg, and Jaidur—for that was Vax's name. We stood there, three sons who did not know their hated father stood with them in the final hour, and I, that same father who had so failed his sons.

I saw the green-clad ranks forming for the next charge, saw them sorting themselves out after the skirling charge that had driven them through the gate. Now they formed the phalanx, that phalanx I had created in the warrens of Magdag. I saw the pikes all slanting forward, the halberdiers and swordsmen in the front ranks. The sextets of crossbowmen took up their positions in flank. This was a mighty force, this killing instrument of war. It would roll over us, as we smashed with our swords, roll over us and obliterate us. Theory might say otherwise; but I had trained well and I knew Genod's father had carried on that training, and King Genod, who was now dead, the rast, had profited by it.

So we braced ourselves for the final charge of that superb machine of war. Then I saw men looking up and a shadow pressed down over the gateway. Like a clump of thistledown in lightness and like a floating solid fortress for power, an enormous skyship landed gently before the gate and stoppered the smashed opening with solid lenken walls bristling with varters and longbowmen.

The sleeting discharge of darts and shafts shattered the phalanx. The smashing force of varter-driven rocks carved bloody pathways through rived mail and tattered flesh. The Archers of Valka drove their shafts pitilessly into the gaps. The shields of the phalanx could not withstand the magnitude of the blows: rocks and darts and shafts. The phalanx was shredded to pulp.

"By Opaz!" said Drak. "By Zair!" said Zeg. "By Vox!" said Vax.

I did not say anything. Excited screams burst out all about us. The men of Zandikar knew when succor had arrived. I saw the huge bulk of the skyship, enormous, deck piled on deck, all sustained and driven through the air by the power of the aerial mechanism, the silver boxes, deep in her hull. I looked. She seemed smothered with flags. There was the red of Zairia. But, over all, dominating and fluttering in the brave Kregen sunshine—Old Superb! My own flag, the yellow cross on the scarlet ground. Old Superb, my battle flag, floating in the streaming rays of the Suns of Scorpio.

At the jackstaff flew the yellow saltire on the red ground, the flag of the Empire of Vallia. Many red and white flags of Valka, famous in song, fluttered from the masts. And there were other flags, also, flags I recognized as the flags of friends.

Another shadow sped across the ground and we all looked up, a flower-bed of faces, and another huge skyship circled up there and rained death and destruction down upon the Grodnim army.

As though casually, a varter-sped rock flew and knocked from the sky the last Grodnim voller. It snapped and fell.

My three sons were gabbling away together, and Miam clasped Zeg, and
I turned away, for even Duhrra stood by Vax, beaming in his cheerful idi-
otic way. Roz Janri and Pallan Zavarin joined them. I heard what was said,
Drak dominating all.

"We have been saved by warriors from my own country. See the flags,
the Vallian, the Valkan. And yet—Old Superb—our father's flag. That has
not been flown for many years."

"It is of no consequence!" shouted Zeg as we waited for the people
from the skyship to join us. "See the Blue Mountain Boys! See the flags
of Falinur and the Black Mountains! That means Seg and Inch! And the
valkavol standards of Valka!"

The skyship was lifting to join her sisters in the sky as they went methodically about exterminating the least sign of Green. Now a fresh wonder
was vouchsafed us. The people from the skyship were approaching us. But
we looked up. A mass of flying specks leaped from the ship, fanning out,
and the wide wings of saddle-birds beat against the sky. Orange streamers identified them, if the flutduins had not—my Djangs! Those ferocious
four-armed warrior Djangs! How the fluttrells wearing the green plunged
and scattered like breeze-driven smoke!

I swallowed down, hard. By God! I am an old cynical case-hardened
warrior. But in that moment—in that glorious moment—I relished as seldom I relished the mingled sunshine of Kregen, the heady intoxicating
air, and the deep sure knowledge of friendship I know I do not deserve but
which has blessed me in my new life on the planet four hundred light-years
from the world of my birth.

They were all there. It seemed to me they were *all* there.

Seg and Inch, striding on, beaming. Turko the Shield, Balass the Hawk,
Naghan the Gnat, Oby, Melow the Supple. Korf Aighos was there, Tilly,
Kytun Kholin Dorn, his four arms windmilling in his excitement, but
Ortyg Fellin Coper was not there, as was proper, for he would hold Djan-
duin when Kytun and I were both away. And—Prince Varden Wanek
strode along brave in the powder blue of the Ewards. And, with him, Gloag!
And Hap Loder! Incredible! I gaped. What had she been up to? Raising
half of Kregen after me?

The Wizard of Loh, Khe-In-Bjanching, strode on busily talking to Evold
Scavander, two wise Sans absorbed in arcane lore despite their surround-
ings. And there were others there I knew, men like Wersting Rogahan, and
Jiktar Orlon Llodar. I guessed Vangar ti Valkanium and Tom Tomor, Elten
of Avanar, were aloft conducting the aerial operations and finishing the
Magdaggians.

Drak and Zeg and Vax took a few paces forward, free of the rest of us, as
the crowd from the skyship approached. It struck none of us to rush forward. We stood. And, among the crowd walking toward us all smiling and

laughing—I might have guessed!—staggered two rascals skylarking and upturning bottles. "Stylor!" they crowed, beaming and drinking by turns. Oh, yes, they were there, my two favorite rascals, my two oar-comrades, Nath and Zolta.

So the crowd around Queen Miam waited, and the three princes of Vallia stepped forth proudly in this moment of victory. I stood a little to one side of them, in the random shadow of a tower, and I, too, savored the moment of victory. But more than that I savored, I luxuriated in, I stared devouringly at she who walked at the head of all my friends. Slender, lissome, superb, clad in russet hunting leathers, with the brave old scarlet sash about her, the rapier and the dagger swinging at her sides, her long brown hair free about her shoulders with the suns casting gorgeous auburn highlights in that lush profusion of beauty, she walked in light, glorious, glorious...

Drak and Zeg and Vax who was Jaidur took another step forward. They held out their arms in welcome. I stood to the side and watched, for I could not see their faces, but I know they were smiling and happy. Her three sons welcomed her, and they called, "Mother!" Drak and Zeg and Jaidur, happy, laughing, calling, "Mother!"

She lifted her own arms. She was smiling and I felt myself trembling, felt the choke, the ache in my throat.

"Mother!" called the three brothers and held out their arms.

She held out her own arms and began to run because she could not hold back in regal dignity any longer. The moment for ritual observances had flown. No longer was she the Princess Majestrix, imperial granddaughter of the emperor of Vallia, she was a woman and her heart, like mine, was bursting. Straight toward her three sons she ran. I stood to the rear of them and to the side, in the shadows, and I felt all the crushing weight of twenty-one years pressing down on me. Directly toward the outstretched arms of those three stalwart young men ran their mother and they broke and ran toward her in filial love.

Straight past them she ran. Past their outstretched arms, past the welcoming smiles upon their faces, past the three of them, and so I stood forward. And she threw herself into my arms and I held her close, close, and I could not see anything in the whole world of Kregen but my Delia.

Twenty-one
Krozair of Zy

"My *father!*"

"That insolent rast my *father!*"

"The hyr Jikai Zadak my *father!*"

Well, poor lads, it was hard for them.

There is little left to tell.

I, Dray Prescot, Prince Majister of Vallia, Strom of Valka, King of Djanduin, Lord of Strombor—and much else besides—held my Delia and I most certainly would not let her go. We gathered in the High Hall and there was the most sumptuous shindig.

I forced away the dark and terrible news I must tell Delia. Her daughter Velia was dead. But she had news for me that set me back, for she had gone home from the inner sea when Seg and Inch had come for her on the island of Zy after I had seen her in a stinking fish cell. Those two had stolen a skyship from the emperor and gone looking for me. Seg had been in Erthyrdrin and Inch in Ng'groga when my letters at last reached them. But they had taken Delia back, for she had seen me and understood that with the help of Nath and Zolta I must work out my own salvation. At home in Esser Rarioch she had given birth to a daughter. We would call this dearly beloved daughter Velia.

"So now you know why I made you look at the dead face of Gafard. He was not an altogether evil man." The three faces of my sons reflected indescribable emotions. "He was your brother-in-law."

Delia insisted on looking, also, and she turned away and held me close, and said, "Dear Velia. Dear Velia."

She would overcome her sorrow in time.

As to Zeg and Jaidur, they were hot for continuing the war against the Grodnims. The situation of the Eye of the World was now back to where it had been before Genod had set out on his road of conquest. With his genius for war removed, the Red southern shore would be cleansed of the Green centers of infection. From Zimuzz west to Shazmoz all would be Red once more. Drak put his chin in his hands and said he had to return to Vallia, for trouble brewed there and the Racters were not the only ones involved.

Just what their attitude to me would be, now that they knew just who I was, remained to be seen. They studiously avoided any mention of the past differences. But I said, "I go to Zy. There is a matter between me and Pur Kazz, the Grand Archbold."

As Krozairs of Zy, Drak and Zeg would attend. Delia said, simply, "I'm not letting you out of my sight again, and you needn't think otherwise."

I gave orders that resulted in a disheveled, bloody, swearing Grogor being brought in and dumped down, all messy and filthy, before me. "Jiktar Grogor!" I said and his head snapped up. "You will do a certain thing for me, or, by Zair, you'll find out where our lord Gafard has gone!"

"Gadak—?"

He shook his head, stunned, when he was told.

So we took our fleet of skyships off to Zy. Seg and Inch had simply stolen the huge vessels. What the emperor would say did not worry them. He had been mean with Drak, saying that what consequence was it to him of a struggle in some distant and forgotten sea around the world? I promised to sort him out when we returned to Vallia. And before I could do that the Apushniad must be removed. I recalled the scarlet and golden Gdoinye, and the white Savanti dove. Vast forces moved behind the scenes here, supernatural powers that sought to control our lives, and I felt a hint of evasiveness, a suggestion of a lack of full control. I wanted to see Zena Iztar again; but she made no occult appearance. And so we flew to Zy.

You may well imagine the carryings-on in the skyships as our old friends rejoiced. It had been a long time. The news! The events that had passed on Kregen—well, all will be told in due time, as they fit into the jigsaw of motives and events of my life on Kregen under the Suns of Scorpio.

The Krozairs of Zy had been apprised of our coming and awaited us in the Outer Hall, for so many with me were not Krozairs. Pur Kazz, the Grand Archbold, sat on the Ombor Throne, for that was proper. The Krozairs sat ranked in their stalls along one side and my people sat on the other. If it came to a fight I would not like to predict the outcome. I most certainly felt torn. But a few four-armed Djangs, and Hap's Clansmen, and the Archers of Valka, and the Blue Mountain Boys, and—well, the Krozairs of Zy are renowned warriors, and I feel that had we come to handstrokes a Kregan Gotterdammerung would have ensued. Pride is a fearful thing. I determined to remain cool. It was a good intention.

Pur Zenkiren, vastly recovered and almost back to his old self, greeted me kindly. "Pur Kazz is sick, Dray. He has ordered certain things that I, for one, cannot approve of. I think you may find support—if your cause is just."

"I did not answer the Call because I was unable to do so. I take my vows as a Krzy far too seriously to lie about them. I was not able to answer the Call, and after I have told Delia, you will be the first to hear what, I fear, you may not believe."

Then he said something that rocked me.

"I have talked with Zena Iztar. She is a remarkable woman. She tells me she works for Zair."

I gaped at him like any onker. He went on quickly to tell me that Zena Iztar confirmed my inability to answer the Azhurad. From what he said I understood he did not know the full extent of Zena Iztar's supernatural powers—that I had not been on Kregen at the time of the Call. But he was fully aware that some of the mysticism of the Krozairs—of which I do not speak—had revealed itself.

The adjudicator sat on his throne. Pur Kazz, on the Ombor Throne— the genuine one moved here, for there is only the one—leaned over and spoke to the adjudicator and the proceedings opened.

'This is a preliminary hearing,' said the adjudicator. Well, of course. The Krzy would not settle so important a matter with so many non-Krozairs present. If I could win here, then the final hearing in the Hall of Judgment should also be won. But not necessarily. The case was put afresh.

"You, Dray Prescot, Apushniad, stand condemned on two counts. It is known that it is impossible for a living Brother not to hear the Call. If you did hear and did not come, you stand condemned. If you did not hear, you were never fully a Krzy, you were never pure enough of spirit, your ib remained befouled, and you stand very properly condemned Apushniad."

"Ib-befoulment cannot be proved against me. I have worked for Zair. There are witnesses." I detested this crawling and pleading; but I wanted to go home. "I pretended to turn renegade and serve the vile Grodnims and their evil Grodno. Thus in the end perished this Zair-forsaken king Genod."

"All that is very well!" screeched down Pur Kazz. I glared at him. I felt very differently from the dazed wretch who had stood under his enmity in the Hall of Judgment. The terrible scar down his face drew his mouth into a cruel grimace. His eyes gleamed in the lamplight like two feral leem's eyes. I felt sorry for him. But if he stopped me, as he apparently still intended, I must deal with him. Once, he had been a fine Krzy. "You are condemned and no man here will alter that. I will not allow it, not allow such blasphemy." His voice rose still higher, screeching like steel across metal, and he lapsed into an unintelligible screech. I believe at that point I realized I would win this just fight.

I will not go into all the tortuous arguments. Casuistry is a high art among the Krozairs. I based my claim on deeds open to all. I offered the instance of the clearing of the Grodnims from the southern shore, a process still proceeding but all too plainly about to finalize successfully for the Zairians.

"Impious braggart!" shouted Kazz. "You claim this great work is your doing, when the thanks go to Zair?"

"I helped," I said. I heard the growls from my people and I hoped they wouldn't break out. At least, not yet.

Pur Zenkiren said, "I speak for the Apushniad. He has accomplished much. I would give him the High Jikai!"

"Aye!" bellowed my people. "Dray Prescot! Hai Jikai!"

"If they do not behave they will be ejected," snarled Kazz.

Of them all it had to be Korf Aighos who laughed. I wondered how much loot he had stuffed into his sacks, the great reiver.

The arguments went on. It was becoming clear to all that Pur Kazz, while still retaining his mystical authority as Grand Archbold, was in very truth a sick man. The wound across his face had driven deep into his mind as well as his body. And yet he was the Grand Archbold, and he owed the allegiance of the Krozairs for his position, and his near-divine ordinances must be obeyed. No one there would cross him.

I detested, as I say, what I was slowly being forced to do. In good times a maniacal Grand Archbold may be tolerated. But in times of war and stress, a man is needed at the helm who may hold total affection from Krozairs as well as total authority. Krozairs may not be driven by the whip, to shouts of "Grak."

So I began a new tack in the arguments. I reiterated that I had been unable to answer the Call, and then went on subtly to gnaw away at the position of Pur Kazz himself. I cited his rages, his incoherences. I said that Pur Zenkiren through his great knowledge of the Mysteries knew I spoke the truth, that all who knew the truth knew I did not lie. The Krozairs remained very quiet. My people, too, remained reasonably quiet.

I said, harshly, "Pur Kazz has been wounded. The sword that struck his face struck through to his ib. He is no longer one of us. He is Makib! Makib! He is unfit to hold the high office! The supreme man who should have held the high office of Grand Archbold was foisted off, was betrayed. Now he should receive the high due he deserves. It is Pur Zenkiren who should be Grand Archbold!"

My people were not slow to take up the call, and the yells of Pur Zenkiren for Grand Archbold racketed out as though we shouted for our favorite riders in the zorca races.

Pur Zenkiren flung me a startled look. He stood up and somehow silence returned.

"It is not fitting that such grave matters be discussed in the Outer Hall. These are weighty things. You speak aright, Dray Prescot, and yet I will not speak for myself."

At this Pur Kazz foamed and raved and tried to speak and only produced an eerie gargling. The poor devil was mad, right enough; Makib; insane through no fault of his. But he was not the man to hold down the supreme post of Grand Archbold. The other Krozairs saw this, and yet could do nothing.

So Pur Kazz and I fronted each other.

I just hoped none of my men would shaft the onker.

The final stroke seized him as the adjudicator, alarmed, rose to suspend the proceedings. Pur Kazz, foam around his mouth like the foam as a chunkrah runs itself to death, flopped over the side of the Ombor Throne. He was dying as his aides reached him. In a last moment of lucidity, he said, "Krozair! I am a Krozair of Zy!" Then he died, and, despite all, I was sorry for the poor devil.

After that we adjourned to the Hall of Judgment, where only Krozair Brothers might venture.

I will not detail the events there, for, although I was in the right, the means I had used to prove my point did not exactly make me feel pride. In the event, Pur Zenkiren was unanimously elected Grand Archbold, and I was purged of the Apushniad. Once again I was a Krozair of Zy. Then I set forth my son Jaidur, Jaidur of Valka, Prince of Vallia, also known as Vax Neemusbane, for election. He had completed his training. Again, unanimously, Jaidur was elected and ordained. The ceremony would take place later. For now, Jaidur was a Krzy.

When I told Delia she was pleased.

"When you went away, Dray, and I will tell you of that later, Drak was mad to join the Krozairs, as you had instructed. So I sent Segnik there very young. And he—"

"He will stay in the Eye of the World and become the king of Zandikar. Later on he will mature. Now he is obsessed."

"Yes, Dray. And Jaidur, too, wanted to go—and—"

"I would have liked him to be named for Inch."

She looked up at me. We stood on the high outer terrace of the sacred Isle of Zy. Our friends laughed and sang and drank within hail. She said, "But he is. Inch is only Inch's use-name. Jaidur is Jaidur's use-name. Their real name is the same and is known only to them."

I nodded. It was right.

"You have done what you said you would do." She leaned close.

"Yes, my heart. And I will tell you what I should have told you seasons and seasons ago. But only when we are safe in Esser Rarioch."

"And what of Nath and Zolta?"

"They seem to get on well with the other rascals. I think they might relish a visit home." I held her to me. "And Lela and Dayra?"

"They are about their business. The Sisters of the Rose make demands very like your famous Krozairs of Zy."

"Hai!" I said, and I laughed. "But although we have won through against great peril, there is a thing we must do yet."

"Yes. You are a Krozair again, and I am happy. This inner sea is a wonderful place; but I yearn for Vallia!"

"Drak is anxious to return to Vallia. He tells me there are forces at work your father would do well to take notice of. And—"

"Hush, dear heart! The stars shine and the breeze is soft and all the problems of Vallia can wait a while."

"Yet will I call Grogor, who is a renegade and should be chopped for it, and yet who tried to help our daughter Velia."

"Yes—you will tell me of this Gafard?"

"I will."

"Did you know that when Seg heard this king Zo in Sanurkazz had you on his list of infamy, Seg said—did you know?"

"No." But I could imagine.

"Seg just stroked one of his terrible steel-tipped arrows and said, 'If this onker, King Zo, does not rub my old dom's name from his damned list we shall have to pay him a visit.' And, dear heart, he meant it!"

"Oh, aye," I said. "That would be like Seg Segutorio."

"And Inch said his great ax was feeling dry again."

"Let us forget everything for tonight," I said, holding my Delia. She lifted her face to me, rosy in the streaming pink moons-light, for the Maiden with the Many Smiles and She of the Veils smiled down on our foolishness.

"Yes, my heart," said my Delia of the Blue Mountains, my Delia of Delphond.

"Although," I told her as, our arms about each other, we went into the chamber prepared for us, "we must take that great rogue Grogor and go to Green Magdag of the Megaliths and there find our granddaughter, Didi, and bring her home with us."

"Yes. Do you think Gafard would have liked that—for I know Velia would have longed for it."

"I think Gafard would," I said, and turned to close the shutters. I thought I caught a hint of lambent blueness beyond the window.

A Glossary to the Krozair Cycle of the Saga of Dray Prescot

References to the three books of the cycle are given as:

TIK: Tides of Kregen
REK: Renegade of Kregen
KRK: Krozair of Kregen

NB: Previous glossaries will be found in Volume 5: Prince of Scorpio; *Volume 7:* Arena of Antares; *Volume 11:* Armada of Antares.

Alley of a Thousand Bangles: jewelry alley in Magdag where Prescot received the poison from the king's conspirators. (rek)
Andapon, Captain: master of the Menaham argenter Chavonth of Mem in which Prescot and Duhrra attempted to leave the inner sea. (rek)
Appar: place in Proconia. The Battle of Appar halted Grodnim aggression at the eastern end of the inner sea.
Apushniad: ejection in disgrace from the Orders of Krozairs.
Arsenal of the Jikgernus: imposing military warehouse for the swifters in Magdag.
Athgar the Neemu: ferocious Kataki fought by Vax in the Hyr Jikordur. (krk)
Azhurad: the Call summoning Krozairs in times of emergency.

Bane of Grodno: term of vituperation given by Grodnims to the Krozairs of Zair.
Battle of Pynzalo: in which King Genod's new army commanded by Gafard defeated a Zairian host.
black lotus flowers of Hodan-Set: legendary flowers of evil.
Black Spider Caves of Gratz: a Kregan hell.
Blood of Dag: a bright green wine of Magdag.
Blue Cloud: a high-quality sectrix given to Prescot by Gafard. (rek)
Bright Brilliance of Genodras, the Palace of: chief palace of King Genod in Magdag
broken from the ib: a ghost.
Buzro's Magic Staff: a Zairian oath.

Chavinter: a small class of swifter.

Chavonth of Mem: a Menaham argenter. (rek)

"Chuktar with the Glass Eye, The": a rollicking Zairian song.

Cottmer's Caverns: a Kregan hell, possibly part of the Ice Floes of Sicce.

Crazmoz: small town on River of Golden Smiles, home of Duhrra.

crickle nut: rich nut with wrinkled brown shell.

crimson faril: beloved of the Red; Zairian term for gentleman.

Crimson Magodont: new name of Green Magodont, a fine swifter.

crooked mur, a: for a few moments.

Dak: an old man, over two hundred years old, who fought gallantly and was slain trying to protect his lord, a Red Brother of the Red Brethren of Jikmarz Prescot took the name Dak in all honor, during his time of Apushniad.

Dag, River: on the delta of the River Dag stands Magdag.

Dayra: daughter of Delia and Prescot; twin to Jaidur.

dernun savvy? Capish? do you understand? Not very polite.

"Destiny of the Fishmonger of Magdag, The": a cheerfully insulting Zairian song

Didi: daughter of Velia and Gafard; granddaughter of Delia and Prescot. Hidden safely in Guamelga by Gafard.

Drig's Lanterns: will-o'-the-wisp.

Dolan the Bow: an archer of Zandikar who joined forces with Prescot.

Duhrra: a massively built wrestler who lost his right hand. Dubbed "Duhrra of the Days" by Prescot. Hails from Crazmos. An oar-comrade to Prescot and to Vax.

dwabur: measurement of length, approximately five miles.

Fazhan ti Rozilloi: ship-Hikdar (first lieutenant) in Crimson Magodont; an oar-comrade to Prescot.

Felteraz: a harbor, town, fortress, and estate a few dwaburs east of Sanurkazz. A spot of exceptional beauty. Home of Mayfwy.

Fenzerdrin: peninsula of the southern shore of the inner sea northwest of Sanurkazz.

flibre: remarkably light and strong wood used in swifters.

Fragrant Incense, Palace of: royal palace of Zandikar.

Gadak: name given to Prescot, as Dak, in Magdag.

Gafard: Rog of Guamelga, the King's Striker, Prince of the Central Sea, the Reducer of Zair, Sea Zhantil, Ghittawrer of Genod, etc. King Genod's favorite. Son-in-law to Prescot; husband of Velia of Vallia. Renegade.

Gashil: Grodnim patron spirit of footpads.

Genod: King Genod Gannius, son of Gahan Gannius and Valima of Malig. Genius at war; made himself king of Magdag. His parents were saved from death by Prescot on his third visit to Kregen, at the command of the Star Lords.

Genodder: shortsword invented by King Genod.

gernu: Grodnim form of jernu—lord.

Ghittawrer: Grodnim approximation to Krozair.

Ghittawrers of Genod: a Green Brotherhood founded by King Genod.

Glycas: a prince of Magdag; vied with Gafard for king's favor.

Golden Chavonth: dekares swifter commanded by Pur Zeg, Krzy.

Golden Smiles, River of: on which stands Sanurkazz.

Goyt: Grodnim spirit much used in oaths.

Green Brotherhood: Orders of Grodnim chivalry in imitation of the Red Brotherhoods of Zair.

Green Magodont: Magdaggian swifter in which Prescot was oar-slave. (krk)

gray ones: eerie spirits who greet the traveler to the Ice Floes of Sicce.

Grodno: the deity of the green sun Genodras.

Grogor: Jiktar; second in command to Gafard.

Grom: Grodnim form of Zairian Ztrom—Strom, count.

Grotal the Reducer: horrific Grodnim spirit of destruction.

Guamelga: city and province north of Magdag on River Dag. Gafard was its Rog.

Hall of Judgment: small chamber in rock of Isle of Zy where trials are held and judgments given.

Hammer of Retribution: used to smash the sword of a Krozair declared Apushniad.

hebra: four-legged saddle-animal of North Turismond.

hlamek: sand scarf and face protector of South Zairia.

Horn of Azhurad: a device deep within the Isle of Zy used to send out the Call to summon the Krozairs.

huliper pie: a sailors' delicacy of Magdag.

Hyr Jikordur: rules and ritual of challenge and combat in duels.

Iangle: Grodnim spirit of sword-fighters.

Ilkenesk, Mountains of: mountain range of South Zairia.

Irwin: Irwin W. Emerson, a Savapim who fought in the Siege of Zandikar. (krk)

Island of Pliks: tiny island of the inner sea where Prescot and his men learned Zandikar lay under siege.

Ivanovna, Madam: name used by Zena Iztar on Earth.

Ivory Pavilion: palace of Roz Janri in Zandikar.

Iztar, Zena: mysterious woman of supernatural power who assisted Prescot without committing herself to either the Star Lords or the Savanti but appears to be in communication with the Krozairs of Zy.

Jaidur: third son of Delia and Prescot; twin to Dayra.
Jade Palace: Gafard's palace in Magdag.
Jikai: a word of complex meaning; used in different forms means: Kill! or Bravo! warrior; a noble feat of arms, and many related concepts to do with honor and pride and warrior-status. A Jikai may be given for a heroic deed; the High Jikai is extraordinarily difficult to win.
Jikaidast: a professional player of Jikaida.
Jikmarz: a Zairian city of the west coast of the Sea of Swords.
jernu: Zairian term for lord.

Kalveng: a seafaring folk with havens along the west coast of Northern Turismond.
Kazz, Pur, of Tremzo: Grand Archbold of the Krozairs of Zy.
krahnik: very small form of chunkrah used as draft animal.
Krozair: member of a mystic and martial Order of Chivalry dedicated to Zair. Membership is attained only after long and arduous training in the Disciplines. Prescot mentions at this time three Orders of Krozairs, those of Zy, Zamu, and Zimuzz. To be a Krz is to stand apart from ordinary men.
Krzi: abbreviation for Krozair of Zimuzz.
Krzm: abbreviation for Krozair of Zamu.
Krzy: abbreviation for Krozair of Zy.

Lady of the Stars: name of concealment used by Velia of Vallia.
Laggig-Laggu: large conurbation of Grodnim up the River Laggu.
Lahal: universal greeting for friend or acquaintance.
lairgodont: a vicious, quick, difficult-to-kill risslaca. Not overlarge, with scaled body, sinuous neck and back, skull-crushing talons, and serrated fangs in gap-jawed mouth, forked tail. Most common in North Turismond.
Llahal: universal greeting for stranger.
longsword, the Krozair: a perfectly balanced two-handed longsword with wide-spaced handgrips; can be used one-handed; subject of rigorous and demanding training and mystical exercises. A terrible weapon of destruction. The Ghittawrer longsword is an attempt to copy the Krozair longsword, but is generally regarded as inferior. The common longsword is usually a one-handed weapon, although hand-and-a-half swords are known.

Magdag: chief city of Grodno on north shore of inner sea.

magodont: resembles the lairgodont of the godont family of risslacas.

Makib: insane.

maktikos: white mice. Informers in a ship's company.

Malig: Grodnim fortress-city east of the Grand Canal.

Masks, Palace of: small palace of Magdag owned by King Genod.

mergem: leguminous plant, dried and reconstituted, gives protein, vitamins, minerals, and the like. A high yield for small weight and bulk.

Miam: niece of Roz Janri; created Queen of Zandikar by Prescot. Betrothed to Pur Zeg.

Mitronoton: the Reducer of Towers, the Destroyer of Cities; a legendary man-god-devil, part of the mythology of Kregen.

mortil: a wild animal almost as large and powerful as a zhantil.

Naghan, Pur, ti Perzefn: Krozair of Zamu. Swifter captain commanding Pearl in Render squadron. Fought under Prescot's orders as Render and in Siege of Zandikar.

Nath the Slinger: oar-comrade with Prescot. Comes from Mountains of Ilkenesk; has decided views on archers.

Nazhan: Queen Miam bestowed the "Z" on Pur Naghan during the Siege of Zandikar for smart work in the Dikars. (krk)

needleman: slang term for doctor.

Net and Trident, The: a tavern on the waterfront in Magdag.

nikobi: Pachaks' code of great integrity to which they adhere when hiring out as mercenaries and paktuns.

nikzo: half a golden zo-piece.

Nodgen the Faithful: chief of King Genod's conspirators attempting to abduct the Lady of the Stars from Gafard. (rek)

Nose of Zogo: promontory between Zandikar and Zamu.

"Obdwa Song": marching song of the swods of Magdag.

Oblifanters: under instructions from the Todalpheme of the Akhram, they give orders to the workers for the opening or closing of the Dam of Days.

Odifor: deity sworn on by Fristles.

Oidrictzhn: ancient and evil god of horror summoned up by superstitious villagers along the Shadow Coast. His legend is Of the Abominations of Oidrictzhn. Known as the Beast out of Time.

Ombor Throne: throne of the Grand Archbold in the Isle of Zy.

Onyx Sea: in the northeast of the Eye of the World, populated mostly by diffs.

Ophig Mountains: mountain range north of Magdag.

Pakkad: legendary figure cast down by Mitronoton, now the symbol for the outcast, the downtrodden, the unwanted, the pariah.

pakmort: symbol of the paktun. A silver mortil-head worn in the same fashion as the pakzhan.

pakzhan: small gold zhantil-head worn on cord looped through a top buttonhole. Symbol of the hyr-paktun. The cord is silk and may be worn over a shoulder knot.

Papachak the All-Powerful: Pachak deity.

Pa-We, Logu: a Pachak hyr-paktun who assisted Prescot and Duhrra to enter Shazmoz. (tik)

Phangursh: Grodnim city sited at junction of River Daphig with River Dag, west of Mountains of Ophig, north of Magdag.

prijiker: stem-fighter. A warrior who fights from the forecastle and beakhead of a swifter. The post of most danger in ramming.

prychan: very much like a neemu, save that its fur is tawny gold.

pungent ibroi: a disinfectant.

Pur: not a rank or a title (although apparently used as such); a badge of chivalry and honor, a pledge that the holder is a true Krozair. Prefixed to the holder's name, as: Pur Dray.

Pynzalo: fortress-city of Zairia.

Quidang!: at once. Equates with, "Aye aye, sir!"

Quinney, Doctor: charlatan who found so-called mediums for Prescot when banished to Earth. He introduced Zena Iztar and so served a purpose and earned his fee. (tik)

Red Brethren: fighting Orders devoted to Zair. Prescot mentions three Red Brotherhoods at this time: those of Lizz and Jikmarz, based on the cities of those names; and the Red Brethren of Zul, based on the city of Zulfiria. The Red Brotherhoods do not possess the same high mysticisms or Disciplines as the Krozairs, and are easier to enter.

Rog: Grodnim term equating with Zairian Roz—Kov, duke.

Roo Throne: throne in the Palace of Fragrant Incense in Zandikar. Roo is Kregish for eleven, and the throne is regarded as the eleventh guardian after the Ten Dikars.

Roz: Zairian term for Kov—duke.

Rukker: a Kataki lord from Urntakkar. Slaved with Prescot on same oar loom. Is haughty and ferocious like all Katakis; but Prescot says he has a touch of humanity. Does not like to discuss things that embarrass him.

Sanurkazz: chief city of Zairia.

Scarf of Our Lady Monafeyom, the: when all the seven moons shine at the full together for that brief period.

Sea Werstings: name given by Grodnims to the Kalveng.

Sea Zhantil: title of honor given by King Zo to Prescot when he was the foremost Krozair upon the inner sea. Gafard given the title by King Genod. Prescot thinks of Gafard as the Sea Zhantil, in remembrance.

sectrix: six-legged saddle-animal; blunt-headed, wicked-eyed, pricked of ear, slate-blue hide covered with scanty coarse hair. One of the trix family of animals.

Seeds of Zantristar: clusters of many small islands off Shazmoz.

Seeds of Ganfowang: Grodnim name for Seeds of Zantristar.

Shadow Coast: short stretch of coast between Zimuzz and Zandikar with an evil reputation.

Shagash: Grodnim patron spirit of banquets.

Shazash: Zairian patron spirit of banquets.

Shazmoz: fortress-city of Zairia of the west.

Shorush-Tish: blue-maned sea-god whose temples are found in all the seaports of the Eye of the World.

Sisters of the Rose: seminary of virtue at which Delia and her daughters received much of their education.

Sniz the Horn: Prescot's trumpeter at the Siege of Zandikar. (krk)

solaik: three-quarter.

Soothe: planet of Antares appearing in the sky of Kregen as a large blue star at approach of orbits. Is a famous Goddess of Love, represented all over Kregen. Prescot says he wonders if the coincidence of Soothe and Venus is a coincidence.

Souk of Silks: in Magdag, where a man was killed in mistake for Prescot. (rek)

Souk of Trophies: in Magdag, where the loot of Zairia is sold.

Stones of Repudiation: twin basaltic blocks across which the sword of a Krozair declared Apushniad is broken.

"Swifter with the Kink, The": a rollicking song of Zairia in which the swifter with the kink appears to ram herself up her own stern.

Takroti: minor deity of the Katakis.

Three Mirrors of the Ib: positioned so that a Krozair in the Hall of Judgment may see himself and understand his own dishonor.

Todalpheme: astronomers and mathematicians dedicated to serving all in forecasting the Tides. Immune from slavery.

Tower of True Contentment: tower of the Jade Palace. Here Velia lived when in Magdag with Gafard.

turiloth: a large animal of Turismond, similar to the boloth of Chem, with six tusks, sixteen legs, a tendrilous mass of whiplash tails. The hide is hard and gray along the back, bottle-green along the sides and gray beneath. Normally slow, but fast in a short dash. Has an enormous underslung fanged mouth; is keen scented and has three hearts.

Tyvold ti Vruerdensmot: a Kalveng helped by Prescot to escape from slavery under the Grodnims. (rek)

Ugas: diffs of many tribes and nations of Northern Turismond; nomads and city dwellers, not barbarians.

ulm: unit of measurement, approximately 1,500 yards.

Uncle Zobab: patron spirit of Fenzerdrin.

Urntakkar: area north of the Onyx Sea. Home of Rukker the Kataki.

Vax: name assumed by Jaidur of Vallia in the Eye of the World. (krk)

Velia: second daughter of Delia and Prescot; twin to Zeg. Married to Gafard; mother of Didi. Murdered by King Genod. (rek)

Velia: fourth daughter of Delia and Prescot. No twin.

Veng: deity of the Kalveng.

volgodont: flying form of godont. A powerful aerial killer.

Volgodont's Fang: swifter commanded by Gafard. (rek)

Volgodonts' Aerie: hunting lodge near Guamelga.

Wabinosk: island of western inner sea used as base by Renders.

warvol: vulturelike carrion-eating bird.

"Weng da!": "Who goes there!"

wo-Deldar: wo is Kregish for zero. Ironical appellation to themselves by swods of most Kregan armies.

Yoggur: area to the northeast of inner sea.

"Your orders, my commands!": Grodnim equivalent to "Quidang!"— "Aye aye, sir."

Zadak: name won by Prescot, as Dak, from Queen Miam. (krk)

Zagri: a powerful demon spirit of the inner sea.

Zandikar: fortress-city of Zairia, scene of the famous siege.

Zavarin, Nath: Pallan of Zandikar. Very fat; but loyal to his city.

Zenno, King: name assumed by Starkey the Wersting in Zandikar. (krk)

Zeg: Pur Zeg Prescot, Krzy, Prince of Vallia. Second son of Delia and Prescot; twin to Velia. Grew out of name Segnik.

zhantiller: type of the large swifter of inner sea.

Zhantil's Lair: hunting lodge near Guamelga.

Zhuannar of the Storm: spirit of the sea who raises rashoons.

Zimuzz: fortress-city of Zairia, home of the Krozairs of Zimuzz.

Zinkara, River: runs north from the Mountains of Ilkenesk.

Zinna: deposed king of Zandikar; grandfather of Miam.

zinzer: sixty silver Zairian zinzers make one gold zo-piece.

Zogo the Hyrwhip: name used in a Zairian oath

zo-piece: gold coin of Sanurkazz.

Ztrom: Zairian form of Strom—count.

Zunderhan, Janri, Roz of Thoth Zeresh: noble of Zandikar; uncle of Queen Miam.

Endnotes

1: *Dbs:* dwaburs per bur. A dwabur is five miles and a bur is forty minutes. Dbs is the usual measurement for fliers. Land or sea transport speed is more often given in ubs, ulms per bur. An ulm is about 1,500 yards. [A.B.A.]

2: See *Warrior of Scorpio,* Dray Prescot #3. Prescot's account of how he escaped the Phokaym and crossed the Klackadrin on foot is, unfortunately, lost. [A.B.A.]

3: *Jernu:* This word for *lord* belongs to the Zairians and is not often used by Prescot. It equates with the Vallian *Jen* and the Hamalian *Notor.* Its correct use is clear in this context. *A.B.A.*

4: *Weng da:* Who goes there?

5: *Roz:* title of nobility similar to outer oceans' *Kov, Duke.*

6: This refers to the map Prescot drew that is appended to Volume 5 of his saga, *Prince of Scorpio.* It is quite clear that this map was a mere sketch to indicate the main landmasses and seas. No doubt more detailed maps will eventually appear. Prescot has provided a map of the inner sea and this will be appended to Volume 3 of the Krozair Cycle. A.B.A.

7: Yrium: a word of profound and complex meaning, more than charisma—force, power conveyed by office or strength of character, or given to a person in a way that curses or blesses him with undisputed power over his fellows. A.B.A.

8: Wenda: Let's go.

9: Ley: four

10: See *The Suns of Scorpio, Dray Prescot #2.*

11: *Dernun: "Savvy; capiche; do you understand?" Not a particularly polite way of making the inquiry. A.B.A.*

12: *Prescot spells this name out carefully. He pronounces it Oy-drick-t-shin. However he may recount his experiences here, there is no doubt they made a profound and uneasy impression on him. A.B.A.*

13: *Quidang: At once. Equates with "Aye aye, sir!"*

14: *Ztrom: Zairian equivalent to Strom—count. The Grodnim title is Grom.*

15: *Roo: Eleven.*

16: *Solaik: threequarter.*

About the author

Alan Burt Akers was a pen name of the prolific British author Kenneth Bulmer, who died in December 2005 aged eighty-four.

Bulmer wrote over 160 novels and countless short stories, predominantly science fiction, both under his real name and numerous pseudonyms, including Alan Burt Akers, Frank Brandon, Rupert Clinton, Ernest Corley, Peter Green, Adam Hardy, Philip Kent, Bruno Krauss, Karl Maras, Manning Norvil, Chesman Scot, Nelson Sherwood, Richard Silver, H. Philip Stratford, and Tully Zetford. Kenneth Johns was a collective pseudonym used for a collaboration with author John Newman. Some of Bulmer's works were published along with the works of other authors under "house names" (collective pseudonyms) such as Ken Blake (for a series of tie-ins with the 1970s television programme The Professionals), Arthur Frazier, Neil Langholm, Charles R. Pike, and Andrew Quiller.

Bulmer was also active in science fiction fandom, and in the 1970s he edited nine issues of the New Writings in Science Fiction anthology series in succession to John Carnell, who originated the series.